I0645245

Books Four Through Six of the West Baden Murders Series

SNOWBOUND

GHOSTS OF WEST BADEN

THE DOOMSDAY CLOCK

Patrick J. O'Brian

PUBLISHED BY FIDELI PUBLISHING INC.

ISBN: 978-1-60414-977-7

Acknowledgements

This is for all of the volunteers who have kept the West Baden Springs Hotel looking beautiful all these years. I appreciate you all putting up with me, and want you all to know we don't take the hard work you do in the garden, giving tours, and behind the scenes for granted. Thank you all very much!

Thanks to Brad Wiemer, Carol Pyle, Mark Adams, Nannette Bell, Joy Winslow, Shane Buis, Jeff Lane, and Sandi Woodward, for their insight and contributions.

Thanks to Dave Blackford, Chi Baldwin, Bob Fergison, Bruce Steward, Mike Ritchie, John Craiger, Melissa Epping, and Rob Fedorchak for assistance of a different kind.

Special thanks to Kendrick Shadoan at KLS Digital for creating the cover, handling photography, and doing a great job as always.

Visit www.klsdigital.com

Another special thanks to Amy Drake for the cover's background photo and for the author photo.

Visit www.smalltownphotographs.com

Other novels by
Patrick J. O'Brian include:

The Fallen

The Brotherhood

Reaper: Book One of the West Baden Murders Series

Retribution: Book Two of the West Baden Murders Series

Sins of the Father: Book Three of the West Baden Murders Series

Stolen Time

Six Days

Dysfunction

The Sleeping Phoenix

Sawmill Road

Red Rain

Sin Killer

Hallowed Grounds

Non-fiction projects by Patrick J. O'Brian include:

Risen from the Ashes: The History of the West Baden Springs Hotel

Pluto in the Valley: The History of the French Lick Springs Hotel

www.pjobooks.com

SNOWBOUND

Book Four of the West Baden Murders Series

This manuscript is dedicated to firefighters,
police officers, emergency medical technicians and paramedics
everywhere who put their lives on the line every day.

Forward

Factual History of West Baden Springs

1855 —   Dr. John A. Lane builds and opens the Mile Lick Inn a mile from French Lick, Indiana. He renames the inn to West Baden after Weisbaden, Germany and renames the hotel the West Baden Hotel.

1888 —   Indiana banker Lee Wiley Sinclair gains controlling interest in the hotel, changing its name to the West Baden Springs Hotel. The hotel is transformed into a world-class resort, adding an opera house, bicycle and pony track, casino, and a regulation-size baseball diamond. Local mineral water is touted as a cure for many ailments.

1901 —   On June 14 a fire breaks out at the hotel, consuming the entire wood-frame building. Sinclair vows to rebuild a better hotel that is fireproof within the year. West Virginia architect Harrison Albright designs and builds a freestanding 200-foot dome at a cost of $414,000. Construction begins on October 15.

1902 —   Sinclair moves into his apartment at the hotel on the one-year anniversary of the fire. The hotel receives its first guests on September 15.

1916 —   Sinclair passes away on September 7, then lay in state in the Grand Atrium before his burial in Salem, Indiana. His daughter Lillian and son-in-law Charles Rexford inherit the hotel.

1917 —   The couple makes significant changes to the hotel including: Repainting the fireplace in the atrium. Adding a sunken garden with a fountain centerpiece. The Seal Fountain is moved from the atrium to the driveway in front of the hotel. A veranda is constructed that wraps around one-quarter of the building. Brick spring houses replace the old wooden structures. Over 12-million small tiles are placed as the new atrium flooring. Benches, statues, trees, and urns are placed throughout the atrium for decoration.

1918 — The hotel is leased by the government, serving as a military hospital during World War I.

1919 — The hospital is closed, allowing the hotel to reopen for regular business once more.

1923 — After her divorce from Rexford is final, Lillian sells the hotel to Ed Ballard for $1 million. Ballard is an entrepreneur known for his ties with circuses and gambling. Half the money repays the debt the Rexfords owed Ballard for hotel renovations, while the other half allows Lillian and her new husband to live out their dreams.

1929 — The stock market crashes on October 29, leaving the hotel virtually empty within four days as the country entered the Great Depression.

1932 — Poor economy forces Ballard to close the hotel for good on June 30.

1934 — Ballard sells the hotel to the Jesuits for one dollar. The Catholic sect uses the hotel as a seminary called West Baden College. They remove many of the hotel's elaborate decorations, opting for plain adornments.

1964 — Sometime in June the Jesuits closed the campus, moving to Chicago, Illinois.

1966 — On November 2, the hotel is purchased at auction by the Whitings from Midland, Michigan.

1967 — The Whitings donate the grounds to Northwood Institute for use as an Indiana campus.

1974 — The building is listed on the National Register of Historic Places.

1983 — Rising maintenance costs and several other factors force Northwood Institute to close their Indiana campus. The hotel has remained vacant since that time.

1987 — The hotel is named a National Historic Landmark.

1991 — An ice buildup and construction flaws cause a portion of the exterior wall to collapse.

1992 — The Historic Landmarks Foundation of Indiana spends $200,000 for emergency repairs to repair and structurally stabilize the building.

1996 — Historic Landmarks purchases the grounds for $250,000, which came from an anonymous donor.

Forward II

Where the Trilogy Picked Up

In 1998, I took my first tour of the grounds on a weekend when I had nothing else better to do. Though my parents had visited the grounds when they were in disrepair, I passed on the opportunity.

Regrettably.

My first look at the hotel's atrium awed me, and I still had the rest of the tour to finish. With the flash from my camera popping every several seconds, likely annoying those around me, I grew fascinated with the building in a heartbeat.

Immediately wheels spun inside my mind, telling me I had to write a novel centered around the West Baden Springs Hotel. Being a horror movie buff, this was my first attempt at a mystery novel with horror elements.

The story follows a professional firefighter who works part-time helping to restore WBS, when he discovers the gruesome murder of his wife may be pinned on him by local detectives. Making matters worse, more murders happen around the hotel, which makes him the prime suspect in everyone's eyes.

The primary mystery behind the murders stems from the hotel's factual past, which helped me create several colorful characters. Toward the end of *Reaper*, my first hotel novel, I decided to follow it up with a tale of revenge, keeping the same core characters.

While in the early stages of writing *Retribution* it became painfully clear the characters needed even more development, so the trilogy was born with a major plot twist at the end of the second installment.

Everything ended on a happy note, closing the chapter of the hotel's restoration era...at least fictionally.

In the real world, Bill and Gayle Cook have done an exceptional job stabilizing and renovating the grounds. I commend them on the beautiful work they and their teams have done restoring the building and garden to their previous splendor.

Orange County residents voted, though not overwhelmingly, to allow gambling in their county, which allowed the Cook Group to take bids from other companies. What looked like a sure thing with the corporation voted to lead the project ended in disaster when that group filed for bankruptcy.

Luckily, Bill Cook chose to finish the renovation himself, creating another chapter in the legacy of WBS. Now, with the atrium, the ground floor, and the grounds completely finished, work has begun on model rooms. Next, the remaining five floors will see finished rooms, allowing the building to function as a hotel for the first time in decades.

Perhaps even by the time this book is complete and printed, which brings me to the reason for a fourth book.

While the trilogy focused on the restoration era, the new book, and any following it, will deal with current events in Orange County. They will allude to the events in the trilogy, but more importantly, the hotel's true past will be involved in solving any mysteries divulged by the characters.

Please keep in mind the events mentioned in this book from the restoration era through the present refer to my original trilogy, which is why the aforementioned time line stops abruptly in 1996. This is by no means an effort to diminish the rest of the hotel's history, or the hard work of the Historic Landmarks employees, but rather my way of keeping the continuity from the trilogy carrying into this new project.

Hopefully you've enjoyed the trilogy because this new chapter in the West Baden saga will revisit the past while bringing up new questions. It is meant to be a great read for newcomers to the series, yet highly rewarding for those who have experienced the trilogy.

Chapter 1

Jana Privett's life read like a harlequin novel with bittersweet twists and turns, but no happy romantic ending.

Over the course of the past year, she had ended a sham of a marriage, lost her job at a tax firm, and redefined herself as an independent woman.

Despite losing custody of her only child to her unfaithful husband before he moved to Georgia, Jana refused to lie down and die. She found new work with an understanding boss soon after the settlement. She literally had to blow the dust off her real estate license after being hired by a firm that dealt almost exclusively with upscale properties.

Working in a more private sector, Jana loved the absence of squabbling over commission, and the competition conventional real estate sales brought. She had quickly gained confidence about selling upscale property, including the grounds she currently stood upon.

Jana felt more than a little strange standing in the parking lot outside the West Baden Springs Hotel grounds in Southern Indiana. After all, the hotel a short walk up a red brick drive had a sordid past. Though rich in history, its floors had seen their share of spilled blood.

By all rights, she had permission to enter the grounds at her leisure from the man who owned them, but it seemed prudent to learn something about the hotel's history.

When Paul Clouse asked her firm to sell the grounds she jumped at the chance to make a big sale for a major client. Of course, the hotel had a checkered history, but mostly from rumors that circulated after Clouse survived several attempts on his life.

She recalled his trouble occurring around the Halloween season several years in a row. Ironically, today was October 30th, but she felt safe considering the hotel and Clouse had led quiet lives the past several years.

Around her, people either sat on several benches, or paced along the brick lot beside the ticket booth. After buying a ticket, Jana was given a white bordered sticker with a "12" printed on it in black marker. The numeral indicated she was part of the noon tour, meant to keep her from trying to take the tour twice.

Taking a moment to observe the dozen or so people taking the tour with her, Jana noticed most of them appeared to be older couples. A glance at their license plates indicated most of them visited from other parts of Indiana. One Illinois plate caught her eye, but she focused more on the tour, wondering how her new boss convinced Clouse to let their firm find the hotel new ownership.

Jana's position didn't allow her to ask too many questions of her boss because she was still his newest hire. Being a former resident of Orange County gave her an edge over her colleagues when Bryan Bell made his decision about who would show the property.

Some of the agents wanted no part of the assignment, considering the hotel's reported history.

Especially the murders.

She had one month to prepare herself for the first investment firms and casino companies wanting to make their bids on the property, so Jana simply focused on the task at hand.

Working with Bell, she formulated several ideas how to do more than simply show the hotel like a realtor might run prospective buyers through a regular home.

"We're ready to go," she heard a man's voice say, causing everyone to look up like dogs being called inside for dinner.

Following her fellow tourists toward a man wearing a green shirt and tan baseball cap with West Baden Springs emblems on them, Jana stole a look at his nametag. She learned her tour guide's name was Max as the older man motioned to the group to walk behind him.

Most of the tour guides at the hotel were retired, or worked jobs allowing them to dedicate time to giving tours. Jana guessed Max to be a retired man from the gray hair protruding from the ball cap. His skin looked somewhat weathered from years of outdoor activity, but Jana figured him to be in his mid-sixties.

He carried a large binder of some sort, which appeared to contain photos and documents in protective plastic sleeves.

Thunder rolled in the distance as gray clouds overtook the sunny sky several miles away, ominously rolling in their direction. Jana couldn't recall the last time Southern Indiana had a rainy Halloween, but the forecast called for wet weather into early November.

"We should probably get started," Max said in his deep voice. "We should be inside by the time the rain hits."

Everyone huddled close together as they passed under the arch at the front of the grand hotel. Once through the opening they spread out along one of the brick paths leading up to the building. The two paths once served as drives up to the hotel, their red coloration unblemished by years of sunlight.

"Today we're going to take a trip back in time. Imagine if you will that visitors a hundred years ago visited these grounds for simple pleasures. The West Baden Springs Hotel was a pleasure resort known as far away as Europe. As many as fourteen trains per day might have stopped in the valley, bringing visitors to any number of pleasure resorts in the area."

Between the two drives a thick column containing a variety of garden plants and Victorian-style lamps led up to the hotel. Jana noticed the lamps all had small dedication plaques attached about eye-level on their green posts.

Keeping his back to the hotel and his eyes on the tourists, Max began speaking about halfway up the path, continuing to walk backwards as he did so.

"Back in 1887, when the railroad came to West Baden and French Lick, Lee Wiley Sinclair, a textile mill owner and banker, stepped off the train finding opportunity abound. He saw the future of big business, and knew there was money to be made through tourism. He wanted to make significant changes to the hotel as a new shareholder, but the other investors bucked the idea."

Max drew a crooked smile, pausing for effect. His eyes grazed over each member of the tour, drawing each of them into his story.

"He showed them by buying enough stocks to gain controlling interest of the hotel, and eventually changed the name to the West Baden Springs Hotel."

Stopping just short of the hotel itself, Max pointed to his left, still facing the guests on his tour.

"On your right is the old golf course," he began, prompting everyone to look to a mammoth yard beside them. "Guests could tee off from the hotel's veranda if they so chose."

A few trees and some sort of small gazebo were the only objects blocking their view to the highway in the distance.

"Boxer Joe Lewis often came to the valley to train for his fights," Max commented, leading them a bit further down the path, glancing toward the ominous sky in the distance before continuing. "To your left, we have the footbridge that led to the Number 7 Spring, also known as Sprudel."

Max paused for everyone to look as he pointed toward the bridge before leading them down some brick steps into the sunken garden.

Jana looked around the garden, still colorful from the summer season, undisturbed by any fall frosts. A sudden breeze beat down some of the taller plants, bringing a cool chill along with it. She folded her arms, returning her attention to Max's presentation.

"Across the garden we have Hygeia, otherwise known as the Number 1 Spring in the day," Max said, pointing across the grounds to a beige structure about the size of a residential garage.

"Why did they have names *and* numbers?" one of the tourists inquired.

"It's believed the springs were all given odd numbers here because the French Lick Springs Hotel had springs with even numbers. The two hotels were rivals in the early 1900's with businessman Thomas Taggart owning the resort down the road. They were originally numbered, but with the 1917 renovation, Lillian Sinclair wanted a more personal touch, so she named each of the springs instead. The original wooden structures were replaced with new brick exteriors, only two of which remain today."

Max took them over to Apollo, another of the named springs, leading them to the edge of the intricate concrete monument that once served as a source of mineral water.

"All of the springs were capped when the Jesuits took over the grounds," Max explained, "but when renovation began in 1996 the springs were permanently sealed with concrete to keep them from bubbling up and disrupting the foundation of any buildings."

Thunder grumbled and clapped in the distance, growing closer.

And louder.

"Let's head across the garden," Max suggested.

He stopped at the fountain centered in the sunken garden, talking about the original fountain being removed from the grounds years prior. Likely destroyed in the process, the fountain needed replacing because the garden appeared empty without it to the renovation crews.

Jana noticed concrete turtles and frogs spitting water streams at one another from rings inside the design element. Water continued to spurt upward from the centerpiece, surprising her that they left the fountain running so late in the season.

Max explained a bit more about the fountain to them, then led the group toward the small building he had identified as Hygeia. He led the way through the spring building's two doors, pausing until everyone squeezed inside behind him. Jana discovered relatively new concrete flooring where the spring had been capped, with stained glass windows and a single light fixture above.

Outside, the spring building had acquired foliage in the form of vines and plants along either of its lengthy sides, but inside Jana heard an echo from Max when he next spoke within the confined space.

"This is one of two remaining springs on the grounds. You've seen the walkway and bridge that led to the Sprudel Spring. That spring was capped with rocks and concrete blocks during the Jesuit era, and subsequently torn down sometime during Northwood Institute's tenure."

Max went on to explain some of the eras of the hotel, including its service as a hospital, the Jesuit era after the stock market crash, and the Northwood Institute days when it served as a college. He spoke briefly about dollar amounts and the parties involved with each transaction.

"If we time this right, we can be inside the hotel by the time the thunderstorm reaches us," Max commented. "You're on your own after the tours ends."

Everyone chuckled, including Jana, who suppressed urges to use her authorization to walk the grounds at her leisure.

She knew the tours were restricted, failing to cover every area of the grounds. If she planned to sell the hotel, she needed to know the building and the grounds like her own house. Grand ideas raced through her mind about how to present the property as the perfect business opportunity when the time came.

Bell actively sought investors who might want the property, thinking he already had five potential buyers, so Jana needed to formulate a plan somewhat quickly.

"I'd be remiss if I didn't give you a look at the old bowling alley and the cemetery," Max noted aloud, leading them toward a building with a front that looked like an old city hall.

Colored the same yellow as a freshly baked cake, the building had writing inscribed within several bricks used to construct the facility that identified it.

"This is the old bowling and billiards pavilion," Max said, allowing people to peek through the front windows as they passed by. "Used for storage during the renovation, this building now sits empty until new ownership decides what to use it for. You can see the discoloration on the bricks from the flood waters that come once or twice a year."

Jana noticed a slightly darker tone along the paint where stagnant water had left its dirty fingerprints from waist-level to the ground.

He led the way toward a cemetery visible across the brick road that served as an employee and volunteer entrance. It too was brick like the main walk from the highway to the hotel's front entrance. No traffic passed by, but Max kept them at the edge of the garden, allowing only a distant view.

Jana took in the battered white crosses behind a series of winding brick steps with trimmed shrubs acting as borders. Perfectly mowed, the area sat partway up a hill with a full grove of trees behind it. She seemed to recall that the virtual forest behind the hotel grounds once served as a golf course for entertaining guests.

Some of the graves stood to the right side of the shrubs leading the way up, but Jana noticed something strange about one of the plots, finding Max staring at it as well. He quickly regained his composure, turning to usher the group toward the hotel.

"What is it?" she decided to ask him before he said a word.

"Nothing that concerns you, dear," he commented, forcing a thin smile.

Jana turned to look once again as he rounded the group up, saying something about them needing to beat the rain inside.

To the side of one tombstone a bit lighter in color than the others sat a mound of dirt. She immediately recalled something about Clouse's trouble beginning when a Jesuit body was found inside the hotel basement after being dug up. This mound looked far too large to be the work of an animal.

It appeared deliberately dug, since part of the grave looked disturbed, but Jana had little time to take in the view as Max called for the rest of the group to join him.

She initially decided to exercise her right to roam the grounds, but when she saw Max lag behind the group to call in something on the portable radio he plucked from his belt, Jana changed her mind.

As she rejoined the group, her mind wandered to Paul Clouse and the rumors about his troubles with the property. Perhaps the stories were more than just urban legends after all.

Chapter 2

Two Weeks Later

Jana still couldn't believe she was invited to dinner with Paul Clouse to discuss her plans about how to present the hotel to potential buyers.

Her concerns about the disturbed grave reached his ears, through security at the hotel, giving her an opening to address security at the grounds when she invited out-of-state groups. Bell had already extended invitations to four groups, promising them details by the end of the week, which brought Jana face to face with the hotel's owner.

Seated at a corner booth in the back of the restaurant, Jana had a view of the entire place, including the maître d' near the front door. A look at her watch indicated Clouse was fashionably late, causing her to wonder if he might cancel. The few wealthy clients she met through Bell seemed extremely full of themselves, caring little about anyone's time except their own.

Pleasant smells of grilled beef and some sort of garlic seasoning entered her nostrils, making her wish she were ready to order. She occasionally looked to the door, having expectations of how Clouse might look after seeing only newspaper clippings of the man from years past.

When a tall, slender man approached her in blue jeans, a tan flannel shirt, and a cautious grin, she thought for certain a lumberjack was about to ask her out.

"Jana?" he asked, surprising her enough that she had to quickly withdraw the stunned look crossing her face.

"Mr. Clouse?" she stammered, half expecting the man to show up in a tuxedo or suit of some sort, especially since the restaurant came just short of requiring ties and sport coats.

Apparently inheriting riches did little to change Clouse's lifestyle.

"I apologize," he said, taking a seat across from her. "I've been running errands all day, and there was no time to change."

He didn't even give her time to stand or shake hands. She was about to offer a handshake when their waitress approached, then the notion completely left her mind.

"I'm *so* sorry I didn't realize it was you."

"Don't worry about it," he said, waving off the mistake airily.

A few minutes later, the two had placed their drink and dinner orders. Jana felt guilty about ordering a seafood platter, but he insisted she order whatever she wanted. She ordered a glass of domestic red wine while Clouse ordered an import beer with a name that escaped her.

She studied the man now named one of the wealthiest men in America by several magazines. Perhaps he chose to lay low, or maybe his fortune failed to change Clouse, but Jana noticed he probably hadn't shaved in a day or two. His brown hair appeared well-kept, combed to one side, and the thick mustache he always sported in photos remained present.

His blue eyes occasionally met hers, but Jana fought to remind herself this was a business dinner. Flirting with a handsome billionaire served her in no way, except to put her career in harm's way.

Besides, he was happily married with a son and a stepdaughter.

"I looked over your proposal to woo prospective buyers and it looks good," Clouse said before sipping from his complimentary glass of ice water.

"Thank you."

"Using the old mansion for lodging is a very nice touch."

Jana nodded again, feeling her cheeks warm as she blushed. Being complimented by the owner came completely unexpected to her, but she quickly disguised her girlish feelings, deciding she needed answers to a few questions.

Their waitress returned, setting their drinks down before whisking herself away like the wind. Jana wondered how the woman learned the art of virtually being a ghost when passing by, ensuring she didn't interrupt conversations.

"I know Bryan doesn't want me prying, but I have to ask why you would want to sell the property."

Clouse nodded, taking a swig from his beer this time.

"If you don't want to answer, I understand," she added quickly.

"No, no," he insisted. "It's fine. There are no taboo questions with me, Jana. I'm an old farm boy at heart and nothing is ever going to change that."

He paused, thinking of how to formulate his answer.

"As much as I love the hotel, it just holds a lot of bad memories for me," he answered finally. "I'm sure you heard about the murders there."

She nodded, putting forth a compassionate appearance.

"I lost a lot of friends," he continued. "Two of my best friends in fact. I just don't have the ambition to carry out the casino plans, but the county desperately needs the revenue. *Someone* should take advantage of the opportunity, but it won't be me."

Jana could hardly blame him. He already had money, so he planned to do the right thing by letting others profit by allowing the hotel to become what it was meant to be.

And once had been.

"I absolutely love the place, but as long as I'm affiliated with it I think it'll be cursed," he confessed.

Clearing her throat, Jana let him know she had a question based on part of his statement.

"Is something wrong?" he asked.

"The grave disturbance last month. Is that something we need to be worried about?"

Clouse sat silently a moment, cupping his chin with his hands.

"I don't think so. Nothing was removed, so I think it was some sort of prank."

"It was Martin Smith's grave."

Clouse smirked uneasily, obviously already knowing that information.

"I'm aware of what it was, Miss Privett. The fact that Martin Smith's body was exhumed and moved to that hill was a travesty."

"Wasn't that a legal battle of some sort?"

"Yes. And one I lost at that."

Jana seemed to recall some strange circumstances about Smith's death, or his two deaths that the newspapers hinted about. She decided not to press the issue, considering Clouse seemed somewhat testy about her probing into the sore parts of his past. Despite his earlier statement, perhaps there were some forbidden questions.

"To answer your concern, I don't anticipate any trouble with security on the grounds. We still have off-duty state police working there around the clock, so one of them will be there whenever you have guests."

"So you approve of my ideas as a whole?"

"I think they're fine. Having the guests stay at the mansion is a good idea because it would save me selling it separately if they liked the idea of a package deal."

"Bryan thought the same thing. He went to college at the hotel when it was Northwood, but he lives just north of Bloomington now."

Clouse nodded as she spoke, indicating he actually listened to what she had to say. She really expected a man in his position to be more callous and unconcerned with the lives of other people. Perhaps money didn't change people after all.

"Is there anything I should know about the mansion?" Jana asked, receiving a curious look. "I mean does the building have any history behind it?"

"Smith built it shortly before renovation started," Clouse answered. "He wanted to live near the grounds to monitor the construction himself. I found out later why he was so consumed with seeing daily progress. He kept to himself, but he observed what Dave Landamere and I dug up when we searched, because the items were important to him."

"Have you ever stayed there before?"

"At the mansion? No. My wife said it gave her the creeps the one time she went through it to inventory Smith's belongings."

A road ran along the far side of the hotel grounds, giving access to another road for employees and volunteers on the grounds. An access code moved a gate aside for people to drive through, but the road also ran further up a hill. The second golf course and a Catholic church once comprised much of the hill directly behind the domed hotel, but they were long since gone.

Jana recalled her one visit to the mansion just one week prior. Every piece of furniture had some form of plastic or cloth covering it. Though the mansion remained in perfect condition because of climate control, it reminded her of old monster movies where white cloth and cobwebs overwhelmed the central settings.

"I'll have a crew go through and clean the place before we entertain overnight guests," Jana informed him.

Their waitress stopped by, informing them their meals would soon be ready. Clouse thanked her, immediately returning his attention to Jana.

"I think Bryan knows my terms better than anyone. When the hotel finds a new owner, I don't want to be a deal stopper. My family doesn't need VIP treatment, we don't need our own personal room, and *if* I ever make my way to West Baden, it will be as a regular person. I relinquish all rights and privileges to the hotel when I sign on the dotted line."

"It shouldn't take long with the number of investment firms Bryan has invited."

"I'm hoping to have it out of the way pretty soon. The courts have tied my hands long enough over Smith's estate. With everything legally in my possession, I'm ready to move on with my life and cut some loose ends."

"I see. Anything special you want me to know about before people begin arriving?"

Clouse sat back, thinking a moment.

"Whatever the public thinks happened a few years back, and whatever *you* think happened, is irrelevant. We need to put a positive spin on the grounds. Stick to the facts you know about. The history, the good times, and the future are what people want to hear about."

He paused again, a hurt look crossing his face, then vanishing when she blinked. Whatever memories haunted the man, he kept them to himself, refusing to burden those around him.

"Think you can put a positive spin on all of this?" he asked, looking her in the eyes.

"Probably," Jana said, putting forth her best business face. "It's been a few years, so public fears should be subsided. I won't lie to people, but I will skirt around the facts. People want a casino in this county. They want revenue. I'm not going to let them down, and I'm not going to let you down either."

Raising his beer glass, Clouse waited until Jana tapped it with her wine glass.

"I'd say we'll both be happy if this goes off without a hitch," he said before taking a drink.

Jana put forth a smile, secretly wondering if selling the hotel was an opportunity for advancement or a death sentence.

Chapter 3

Two Months Later

Cloudy skies hovered over the West Baden Springs Hotel as Dan Duncan walked along the brick path between the front gate and the hotel itself. A special pass got him past the volunteers at the front gate after tours concluded for the day.

He prayed he wasn't too late for an opportunity to purchase the hotel with his investment group. More than anyone else in the group, Duncan's bloodline connected him with the grounds, making their two-day tour of the hotel personal to say the least.

Now splitting his time between Nashville, Tennessee and a residence just outside Salem, Indiana, Duncan owned riches passed down from three generations. His great-grandfather helped bring the railroad to West Baden, investing heavily in the market, and in local construction at the time.

Andrew Duncan made his millions, invested it wisely, and died before his fiftieth birthday. His son escaped the Great Depression with minimal financial casualties, leaving the family inheritance intact for future generations.

Duncan picked up his walk, heading toward the hotel. So far as he knew no one else from his group had arrived, leaving him some private time with the old grounds. After all, their official tour was the next day, but he wanted to arrive a day early to reminisce.

It took a great deal of figurative arm-twisting to convince his investment partners to simply *look* at the grounds. Getting a majority vote to buy the hotel and the grounds was the next battle, but he planned to win on both fronts.

Approaching the sunken garden, Duncan looked over the flower tops, observing the two remaining springs, along with the old bowling pavilion behind them. Where others saw history and local ties, he found possibility. He knew the current owner of the French Lick Springs Hotel down the road wanted to sell, despite the possibility of a casino drawing unlimited cash.

In need of upgrades and repairs, the resort needed several million dollars to make it a realistic luxury hotel. The owner seemed content to leave it running for convention business and tourism, but Duncan's insider sources told him the man wanted to sell if the right offer came along.

Buying both hotels assured the group control of the grounds on which a casino could be built and run efficiently. Duncan worked during his teenage years for his father, eventually taking over several family businesses. No stranger to management, he knew casino ownership was significantly different from his own experience, but figured the group members had solid contacts that ran hotels and casinos.

Ordinarily Duncan rode his motorcycle everywhere until roads became slick or icy. Because of impending snowy weather, he brought his truck with a trailer attached to the hitch. He hauled his new Harley-Davidson Road King, which he rode from the resort down the road, leaving his truck behind.

Because of the cold conditions, Duncan wore full leather chaps and a thick black leather riding jacket. He left his skullcap and gloves with his bike at the entrance, not planning to stay long. His stomach grumbled because he had only eaten once since leaving Tennessee shortly after dawn.

Duncan had celebrated New Year's Eve in Tennessee the previous week, drinking far more than usual. It took him several days to recover, but what he recalled of the lavish party he attended made his misery somewhat worth the sickness and suffering.

He strolled into the garden, thinking back to the photos of his great-grandfather around the hotel. Most of them showed Andrew Duncan posed with friends or clients atop what was known as the Water Wagon in the day.

In the early days, the hotel had numerous forms of entertainment aside from the bowling and billiards hall. An opera house stood near the pavilion, a bicycle and pony track was located a short walk from there, and an indoor pool was erected beside the grand building. Usually some sort of show or convention kept guests busy, and some came to West Baden simply to partake in the mineral water, which they believed had healing powers.

From what Duncan knew, the Water Wagon was built and owned by a man hired by the hotel to take water from one station to another along the hotel grounds. Constructed entirely of wood, the wagon looked like a giant keg lying horizontally along an axle, which served as the wagon, drawn by a single horse.

Many a photo opportunity occurred on or beside the wagon. Everything from couples to groups of a dozen men had been captured on film during the hotel's heyday with the wagon. Duncan suspected photographs served as a form of entertainment on the hotel grounds, if not just another way for the ownership to line their pockets with extra funds.

Just a month over fifty-years-old, Duncan definitely felt his age, especially when he rode his motorcycle on long trips. He had never been married, had no children, and no significant other at the moment. His longest relationship went sour the year prior, after his girlfriend decided she wanted to see other people, officially breaking up after eight years.

They were off and on, living together sometimes, though usually just getting together for trips or events like normal couples. Duncan kept expecting her to call during the first few months, but when she didn't, he gave up completely, throwing himself into his work.

Around that time, he heard rumors about the West Baden hotels possibly coming up for sale after the casino bill passed. Something sounded right about leaving Tennessee for a fresh start, so he convinced Red Sanders to look at the hotel with the group.

He knew some of the investment group members remained skeptical about the building's potential versus the investment, but Red and his brother, Keith, created the Lone Star Investment Corporation. Their mission was simply to make sound investments, and though Duncan was biased in this particular scenario, he felt the hotel was a sound buy.

Split between Tennessee and Texas, the group typically worked as two separate teams, but this time they came together for an out-of-state venture. Red lived in Tennessee, making his millions from a prospering trucking business. Keith owned a dozen ranches in Texas, gaining his initial wealth from oil and cattle.

While Red had an interest in the hotel, several other group members remained skeptical about Duncan's idea. Some didn't trust Duncan, while a few thought the hotel needed too much work before becoming operational.

Putting any negative thoughts aside, Duncan moved toward the hotel, looking up to the top level.

"Needs work my ass," he commented.

After taking several extended tours, he knew Clouse had fully finished the hotel, but tragic events prevented it from opening several years prior. The atrium, the basement, and each room were fully restored, but Duncan wondered if his fellow investors would approve of the changes Clouse made.

Deciding the chilly weather made it too miserable to stand still he walked toward the hotel itself, wanting a look inside before anyone else from his group arrived. He doubted many of them wanted to spend a night inside anything except the mansion, meaning he might be the only one in town at the moment. Some of them were pampered, not accustomed to working with anything except their minds.

Duncan looked at his hands, noticing calloused and rough skin. He worked, but he also found time to play around. Taking his time as he walked up the steps to the secondary entrance, he looked behind him, watching the garden fade as twilight engulfed it.

Turning around, he bumped into someone who had silently made his way behind the millionaire.

"Sorry about that," the man immediately stated as Duncan noticed the gun at his hip. "I'm Brent Guthrie, one of the state police who'll be watching over your group this weekend."

Duncan let a quirky grin escape his lips.

"So, you know who I am?"

Guthrie appeared at least as old as Duncan, so the investor wondered if he might be a retired state trooper.

"They radio everything back to me, so I heard a member of the latest group to tour the grounds was on his way in."

"Latest?"

"Two other groups have already done overnight stays."

Duncan supposed the idea was competitive bids, which meant he had two hurdles to clear. Not only did he have to convince his group to seek the property, but he had to make certain they presented the nicest package to Clouse for his approval.

"You might find some of the locals unfriendly, since some of them didn't like the casino bill passing," Guthrie noted.

Duncan grunted to himself, knowing how religious the county remained. Despite having some of the worst employment figures in the entire state, Orange County seemed to put religious teachings above financial improvement.

"Some of them will tell you stories about screams and moans up the hill there," the trooper said, nodding toward the wooded area behind the hotel. "They say late at night you sometimes hear things going on up there."

Duncan grinned, though uncomfortably. Guthrie didn't seem entirely convinced something *wasn't* happening in the hills.

"Were you here when all of that stuff happened a few years ago?" he asked.

"Yeah. For all of it."

Since the trooper wasn't forthcoming, Duncan didn't push the issue.

"I doubt you'll have to worry much about the locals with this wintery front coming through tomorrow. You may want to get your tour in early."

"I can't believe we're getting snow here at all," Duncan commented. "I grew up around here, and it seemed every year we got an inch of snow maybe once or twice a year. And never at Christmas."

"I'd say you're going to more than make up for it this time around. Every so often we get a front that dumps a load on us, and this is one of those rare times."

Duncan thought Guthrie seemed a bit too cheerful about a snowstorm heading their way. He couldn't imagine worse possible circumstances for an overnight stay on the grounds. If his group had a bad experience, they might never vote to purchase the property. Bad weather would prohibit viewing some of the hotel's greatest assets, which placed a sour feeling in the pit of Duncan's stomach.

"Where you staying tonight?" Guthrie inquired.

"Down the road at the resort."

Giving a nod, the trooper seemed ready to lock up for the night as he began looking around. Most of the tourists had departed, leaving only volunteers and staff inside the building.

"Can I get a quick look around before you lock up?"

"Sure. We have someone here around the clock, so take your time."

Duncan followed him inside, immediately seeing the grand atrium beyond the hallway. It teased him because the entrance obscured its full beauty, which he was unable to see until he stepped into the opening, seeing six stories of rooms looming above him. Literally a round atrium, it held several balconies from particular rooms, topped off by a drum and chandelier in the center of the roof.

From one end to the other was practically the length of a football field, and everything seemed to echo when less than a handful of people made any kind of noise within its confines.

He said nothing, but Duncan remained awed, as always, by the spectacle before him. He wondered how his great-grandfather felt about the grounds, considering the man visited the hotel almost daily to chat with friends and business partners.

Just looking at the atrium brought a tingle to Duncan's spine because he knew of the hotel's good history. He wanted to usher in a new, better era for the hotel to erase any ill-will toward the place from local residents. A sense of family pride urged him to purchase the grounds, no matter the cost in money or time.

If meeting Clouse in person became necessary to secure his wish, Duncan planned to make it so. Looking to his left, he thought he saw a shadow inside the old barbershop across the floor from the corner of his eye. By the time his blue eyes focused on the barber shop the shadow was gone.

Or never existed.

He stared harder, seeing no movement over the next few seconds.

Grunting to himself, he decided to get back to the resort. He planned to monitor the weather through the Weather Channel by the hour, praying against the impending snow.

Chapter 4

The front door made an eerie creaking sound when Maria Richards entered the mansion up the road from the hotel grounds.

Contracted to clean the house the day before the next batch of tourists visited, she still wondered why they chose her, a relative newcomer to the cleaning business, over more popular, professional cleaners. One of her competitors had cleaned the house the previous two times, which she heard about through local gossip.

Tired from a full day of work, she hated cleaning the mansion after dark, but she wasn't about to disappoint her regular clients for a one-time job. Besides, there was no one around to criticize her, and no one staying in the large building until the next day.

Most of her equipment remained inside her van because Maria wanted to analyze exactly what needed cleaning the most. Since people had stayed there as recently as two weeks prior, she doubted the dust buildup was extensive.

Unfamiliar with the building, Maria stepped inside before closing the creaky metal door. Surprised that none of the three sets of deadbolt locks were in use, she looked around the mansion's main lobby. Two sets of rooms on her left appeared to be living and entertaining space while two rooms on her right were possibly bedrooms or kitchens. The lobby ahead of her appeared more like a mammoth foyer the size of a sports field.

Before her, the main staircase, which was constructed completely from hardwood and stained to a shimmering caramel finish, stood as wide as most cars were long. It led to a second floor with a wraparound balcony and at least eight more rooms she readily counted.

"Wow," she muttered, wondering where to begin.

During her conversation with Jana Privett she learned about a full restaurant-style cooking area in the basement, complete with dumbwaiter, industrial stoves and refrigerators, a large aluminum preparation table, and at least three sets of cooking wares and utensils.

Maria's instructions made it clear that the bedrooms and living areas needed her full attention. Vacuuming, dusting, and if necessary, carpet shampooing were among the chores she needed to have completed by the next morning.

From outside, the mansion appeared to have three stories, but the stairs stopped at the second landing. She wondered what the third level held, or if it might simply be an aesthetic feature built to enhance the building's luxurious appearance.

Starting her own business less than a year after her divorce took courage, but there were times she doubted it would work out. Her ex-husband's money and the business knowledge he instilled upon her before sleeping around, allowed her enough success to keep the business open.

Only now were larger clients beginning to seek her services, apparently sensing she was a mainstay in the West Baden area.

Knowing she had a long night ahead of her, Maria took a peek in each of the downstairs rooms, finding them loaded with expensive furniture and decorations. Why no one resided in such a house escaped her, but her jaw remained agape throughout most of the personal tour.

Upstairs provided even more surprises because she found twelve separate bedrooms, each with its own full bathroom and walk-in closet. They looked practically immaculate already, so Maria wondered exactly why she was hired to clean the place. Shrugging as she left the last bedroom, she supposed rich people had outlandish standards so one hair out of place might throw them into a tizzy.

What impressed her most was how each bedroom contained a different theme, complete with various colors and accent pieces. The place seemed meant for entertaining and lavish parties, yet it remained vacant. Evidence of covered furniture and cobwebs disappeared with the previous cleaning jobs, leaving Maria the much simpler task of dusting.

Prepared to fetch her cleaning tools from the van, she started down the elegant stairway, watching the carpet that ran from top to bottom. Containing a red, black, and charcoal dotted pattern that virtually entranced her, Maria only looked up as she neared the bottom stair.

Her eyes widened at the sight of a man clad in a black robe blocking the front door. No face emerged from beneath the shrouded hood because some sort of dark mask covered it. Slowly, the face lifted from some deep stare at the floor, but what chilled Maria to the bone was the gleam from a sharpened knife in his right hand.

Shrieking, she turned to dash up the stairs, knowing the entire second floor wrapped around the staircase railings, meaning she couldn't be cornered.

In an instant, the man clad in black gave pursuit, grabbing her ankle halfway up the stairs. She fell forward, instinctively kicking him in the face before he had a chance to use the knife on her. He fell back several steps, allowing her to reach the top of the stairs without injury.

Maria stared down, seeing him dart up the stairs with barely a moment's hesitation. She had no doubt a man was chasing her, because he was tall, with a grip like that of a gorilla. Making her way around the banister atop the stairs, Maria watched him join her on the second floor, deciding that entering any of the rooms meant certain death.

She had to lure him away from the stairs before attempting any kind of escape, but any rational thoughts were drowned out by the thumping of her heart. She was absolutely terrified by the urban legends concerning the hotel; she suspected they held some merit because no one she knew would play such a sick joke on her.

"What do you want?" she demanded loudly, trying to stall for time as she carefully walked, touching the railing with shaky fingers.

In response, he slowly rotated the knife with his right hand, indicating he wanted to twist it once it plunged through her soft skin.

She waited until he began making his way around the railing before dashing in the opposite direction. Like a cheetah, he gained ground on his prey with amazing speed and skill. Knowing there was no way to outrun him, she turned to backhand his face, which felt soft beneath the mask. The move registered no pain or sound from her attacker, so she launched a foot into his groin.

He doubled over, giving her time to dash down the stairs toward freedom.

Reaching the bottom stair, Maria stumbled, but kept her balance long enough to use the door as a backstop. She twisted and yanked the doorknob to no avail because the deadbolts were all locked.

"Damn it," she muttered, ducking just quickly enough to avoid the blade that clanked harmlessly against the door.

Her informal tour of the mansion had informed Maria of several other exits and the location of the catering area in the basement. Though she hadn't visited the industrial kitchen, she decided it might be the safest area for her because it would likely offer some cover.

She dashed toward the kitchen, finding nothing in her path to throw down as a form of hindrance for her pursuer, and no time to lock the door at the kitchen entrance. Once inside, however, Maria discovered the basement door. She yanked it open, expecting to be knifed from behind at any moment, but managed to close it behind her. Her assailant entered the main doorway too late to attack her as she shut him out.

A stairway led down to the basement with occasional bulbs to light the way. Maria didn't question why the bulbs were on, simply thankful not to be in complete darkness. She reached the bottom step, desperately looking around for cover, despite hearing no one behind her.

It appeared very much like she envisioned it based on Jana Privett's description and the floor plans Maria had viewed before taking the job. Along one of the other walls, she heard a strange clunking noise, like something being dragged by a chain.

She cursed under her breath, suspecting the dumbwaiter was being lowered toward her.

But why?

Hesitantly drawing closer to the contraption, Maria found a small elevator that had an up button only fixed upon the wall. She never saw an elevator on the second floor, meaning it likely went exclusively to the third floor.

Was there some sort of grand dining room or ballroom up there? She couldn't picture guests being ushered through the basement toward the dining area. No, she thought, something far more sinister or dark waited for her on the other end of that elevator shaft.

Slowly backing away from the single elevator door, Maria chose to risk confronting the killer instead of trapping herself on the third floor. As she made her way around the stainless steel worktable, she heard footsteps hurriedly marching down the main stairs, instantly changing her mind for her.

"Shit."

Returning to the elevator in a run just short of a sprint, she pushed the elevator button several times in desperation. As she waited, listening to her nervous breathing, Maria looked around her, finding several covered tables nearby. An idea came to her, so she peeked around the corner, but no one was visible.

Her plans changed in a blink.

Swallowing hard, she decided to approach the main stairwell, wanting nothing to do with the elevator. Suddenly it felt as though the entire mansion was possessed entirely by some form of evil. The person chasing her was somehow a minion of the building, tied in with whatever secret it harbored.

Listening intently, Maria drew closer to the stairs, hearing a creak from the end of the table that reached her ears too late for an appropriate reaction.

As she turned to run for the elevator, her attacker sprung from behind the table's end, dashing after her with ill intent. Knowing she couldn't outrun him, Maria snatched a wooden rolling pin from the table, swinging it at his head while she spun around.

Instead of connecting, however, the makeshift weapon missed completely as the cloaked attacker ducked, scooping Maria into his arms as the rolling pin fell from her hand.

"No!" she screamed, resisting with kicks and flailing arms. "No!"

Suspecting her life was about to end, she continued to fight as he carried her in a modified bear hug toward the elevator. Now her suspicions of the third floor felt verified, but she wanted nothing to do with its mystery.

As the elevator door opened with a ding, Maria fought against her attacker's grip in futility. He carried her inside the elevator car as she let out a bloodcurdling scream that ceased when the door sealed behind them, swallowing them whole.

Chapter 5

J ana woke up early the next morning, making the trip to French Lick hours before the arranged time of noon when she planned to meet the investment group.

With the impending snow, her plans had changed slightly. Putting off the tour of the West Baden Springs Hotel grounds could no longer wait until after lunch and an initial meeting. She felt as though she might be cheating the group of the tour's full effect by altering the itinerary given to the other groups.

Carrying a personal planner with her, Jana entered the French Lick Springs Hotel expecting to meet at least a few of the investment group members. She stepped inside the main lobby, finding very few guests up and about.

A look at her watch revealed it was barely past eight o'clock, but even if she failed to locate anyone from the group, Jana had plenty of things to accomplish by noon.

Including a rewrite of her planned tour and lodging schedule.

A look at the group's website gave her short biographies and photos of each member, since it felt somewhat inappropriate asking Red Sanders for additional information. His secretary had already forwarded paperwork about the group's mission and formal accomplishments. The additional materials simply gave her an opportunity to familiarize herself with the members before they arrived.

In business, nothing felt more embarrassing than not knowing the people one met by name. Clients tended to want special treatment, and in her business, bad first impressions usually meant a failed property closing.

Walking through the lobby, Jana made her way to the restaurant housed within the resort where a buffet breakfast was being served. Doing her best not to appear snoopy, Jana's gaze panned from one end of the seating area to the other.

Despite a packed dining area, she found two of her guests seated in the far corner. They sat across from one another, speaking casually with their plates in front of them. Thinking she might be interrupting as she drew closer, Jana noticed napkins and silverware atop their plates, indicating they were finished eating.

"Excuse me," she said as she approached, drawing their attention immediately.

Both were easily recognizable from her dossiers. Dan Duncan was the only man in the group with blond hair, though it had grayed around his temples. He obviously ate well, because he sported a small potbelly. Based on the black leather jacket behind him and the sunglasses perched atop his head, he rode motorcycles. The weathered skin on his face acted as evidence that the man worked and played hard, despite having money.

Dennis "Red" Sanders sat to Jana's right side. With a full head of rustic hair and blue eyes, he failed to challenge her memory because he too was unique within the arriving group. She assumed his nickname came from his hair color, but knew very little about the man. His funds came from owning a trucking company, which she heard his older brother helped him start.

She recalled his listed age being forty-nine, a few years younger than his brother, but he looked years younger to her.

"I'm hoping you're Jana," Red stated. "We're not used to having stalkers."

They all chuckled a moment, lightening the mood.

She shook hands with both of them quickly before Duncan motioned to her to sit down.

"I hope I'm not imposing," she said. "I just wanted to see if any of you had arrived before we started the tour this afternoon."

"We're looking forward to it," Duncan said, though a look at Red's face didn't reveal quite the same enthusiasm.

"Dan here prodded us into coming down here," he admitted. "The rest of us are reserving judgment until we see the place, and the possibilities."

Jana grinned, understanding their hesitation.

"The property *will* sell," she assured them. "It's just a matter of who wants it most, and their ability to maintain the historic integrity."

"I'm very much for that," Duncan said sincerely. "My great-grandfather frequented the hotel during its prime, so I guess you could say I have a link to it."

"So I've heard," Jana said, much more knowledgeable about the hotel's history than before she took the assignment to sell the property.

Red continued to look doubtful about something, despite his friend's eagerness.

"I've done some research," he said. "This is the second poorest county in Indiana as far as tax base and average wages. How do you expect a casino to draw in enough cash flow to stay afloat?"

A strange look crossed his face.

"No pun intended," he added, since the casino design would have to be a large riverboat.

Indiana legislature made certain any gambling facilities never touched base on Indiana soil. What started as a riverboat concept along the state's rivers and lakes was adapted for Orange County and a few other needy areas.

"There are no guarantees," Jana stated, "but if you look at Corydon and New Albany, their tax bases more than doubled the first year their casinos opened. If you open the casino, you bring new jobs and hope to this area."

"There is such a thing as flooding the market," Red argued. "There isn't much else around here besides the historical value. I just can't see why people would come here over the established places near bigger cities."

Duncan stepped in, seeing Jana wasn't getting through to his friend.

"There is a lot of convention business in the area, Red. You more or less said it yourself, there's nothing else to do around here."

"But we don't have a *major* highway anywhere close, and there's a lot of negative publicity from the Bible beaters around here. There could be a lot of heat over this project."

"Are you even giving this a realistic chance?" Duncan asked a loaded question.

"I'm here for *you*, Dan. This is your thing, and I'm going to give it a thorough look, but above all else, I'm a businessman. If I'm asking this many questions, just imagine what Keith is going to say when he gets here."

"Why don't you ask him yourself?" Jana heard someone ask in a Southern drawl just over her shoulder.

Everyone turned to see a man in his early fifties standing behind her. Dressed in slacks, cowboy boots, and a bolo tie, Keith Sanders looked very much like Jana expected a successful Texas rancher to look. The little bit of his dark hair Jana noticed beneath his black Stetson had grayed, including the mustache he sported. She continued to study the man as Red stood to give his older brother a hug.

She doubted they saw one another much, living in different states, so this trip was probably an excuse for them to get together.

Keith appeared even more rugged than Duncan, likely spending afternoons and weekends on horseback, or working his ranch. His face had a few wrinkles, but he remained slender, showing no signs of his age slowing him down.

"About time you got here, you old coot," Red told his brother.

"Goddamn airport security and their *random* searches got me this time."

He looked down as though seeing Jana for the first time.

"Oh, sorry about my language," he quickly apologized, taking Jana's hand before gently planting a kiss on it.

He put forth a crooked grin that seemed boyish for such a distinguished man.

Jana thought true gentlemen were extinct, but Keith's charms caused her to rethink her preconceived notions. He seemed genuine, like a cowboy hero out of the old westerns her father watched on weekends when she was growing up.

"Thank you, Mr. Sanders," she said, standing up because everyone else already had.

Keith looked surprised she knew his name until Jana introduced herself with a formal handshake.

"Pleasure, Miss Privett," he said after discovering her identity. "It is 'Miss' isn't it?"

She nodded, feeling her face blush.

"Ignore my brother's Southern charm," Red spoke up. "He's on his way to a blissful union this spring."

"Not *that* blissful," his older brother noted gruffly, almost under his breath.

"And to a bride barely old enough to be his daughter," Red added, aside to Jana, drawing a scornful stare from his brother.

Neither of the previous visiting groups proved so informal or friendly. Comparatively speaking, they were bland and extremely rigid. Jana had yet to meet half of the Star Investments group, yet she felt at home with them already. She especially liked Duncan's personal interest in the property, but wondered if he fought an uphill battle, convincing his group the hotel was a profitable purchase.

She decided to check on the grounds, and the mansion, before meeting the entire group at noon. Staffing on the grounds was minimal, with only a state trooper providing security and two people from a catering service providing dinner for the group in the hotel's sixth floor suite.

While Red and Duncan remained behind to leave a tip, Jana and Keith walked toward the lobby.

"My brother likes to speak out of turn," Keith assured her as they left the dining area.

"It's okay," she replied. "Really."

"I just don't want you to get the wrong idea. I'm not some pervert who hits on every woman I meet."

Jana smiled, though more uneasily than she intended.

"I wasn't worried about it."

Keith didn't look reassured, but put forth a strong front as his brother and Duncan caught up with them.

"I've got a few things to prepare," Jana informed the trio. "I'll see you all at noon?"

All three nodded.

Jana approached the front entrance to walk outside, seeing an unusual sight through the glass doors before she even touched them. What looked like sheets of snow fell from the sky, limiting her line of sight to about twenty yards outside. So far, the moist ground refused to accept a white lining, but as the temperature dropped, and far more precipitation fell, it would yield to a snowy blanket.

Her hesitation allowed Duncan to approach her without the brothers.

"I stayed up half the night watching the weather reports," he confessed. "I was afraid of this."

"So was I, but the grounds still look beautiful with snow. And the inside doesn't look any different."

Duncan's concern showed.

"This is my one shot at convincing my group this is a good idea. It's the first time I've ever asked them to invest in one of *my* ideas, so it's a big deal."

Jana couldn't find the words to comfort him. It seemed as though he might be hinting around for some help, but Jana had no tips to offer. She knew competition for the hotel was destined to be fierce, and his group already sounded skeptical about viewing the grounds, much less buying them.

"I know you're just selling the place, and you probably think we're all rich snobs, but I actually live around here most of the year. There's nothing that would make me happier than running this place."

Grinning to himself, Duncan seemed to recollect something as he stared outside almost blankly.

"When I was a kid, I used to visit the hotel with my father. He told me about our family's link to West Baden, so when the grounds closed for good, I sometimes snuck in for a look. Every time I saw that atrium it just took my breath away, and I dreamed of owning the building one day."

Jana looked at him, wondering how many people daydreamed about the near impossible notion of owning the property.

"See, I understand the old days," Duncan continued. "I don't want to own it for selfish reasons, like making more money, or being a big shot. I watched the building decay, then start falling to the ground. It upset me to see it fall from grace like that, so my dream has been to restore it and see it reopened like it used to be."

Now she understood his plight, feeling his pain through what sorrowful expressions he let slip past his macho biker facade.

Jana knew the West Baden Springs Hotel hadn't functioned as a hotel in decades. The Great Depression decimated its appeal to the wealthy, taking with it the county's ability to expand.

"There aren't many hints I can give you," Jana admitted after some silent reflection. "Paul Clouse makes the final decision about who gets the place. No one else has shown as much devotion as you have to this project, and I think he'll really appreciate that."

Duncan's face began glowing as she spoke the words. He seemed relieved, if not holding back refrained ecstasy, that Clouse shared his values for the hotel.

"I really have to get some things prepared," Jana said, inching toward the grand entrance. "I'll see you at noon."

Duncan nodded, still walking on air after her encouraging words.

"Drive safely out there," he said.

"I will."

Jana stepped outside, immediately finding her overcoat covered by fluffy snowflakes. If the forecast proved accurate, she would have to leave early, or risk being stuck on the grounds overnight. She owed it to the group to give them the full tour, even if that meant spending the night away from her cat.

One thing seemed certain.

The day ahead would certainly be etched in her memory for years to come.

Chapter 6

A warm, sunny atmosphere surrounded the grounds as Dave McCully walked in front of a large domed building. He walked in what he considered the front yard, but as he looked to his left, he noticed several men standing behind a man about to tee off during a round of golf.

Curious, he wondered why anyone chose to place a golf course in front of a building, in plain view from the road. Continuing to stroll, he rounded the front of the building, finding a set of stairs that led to a veranda where women in what he termed Victorian dresses drank tea.

They sat on wooden chairs, rocking easily as they enjoyed the beautiful weather. To his left, he spied a footbridge and a sunken garden, solving the mystery of where he was standing.

But not when.

McCully had seen brochures and photos of the West Baden Springs Hotel, but why he stood in the middle of a working hotel, obviously decades before he was born, eluded him. Having out-of-body experiences was nothing new, but traveling through space and time without provocation felt odd.

And a bit scary.

While most people only encounter strange new experiences through dreams, McCully had experienced visions since a very young age. They didn't come often, but usually delivered some sort of purpose or meaning to him.

Sometimes his visions came through dreams, but most of the time contact with people or objects provoked his mind to jump into another time and place. McCully had seen the past, present, and future with his visions, realizing the public viewed his psychic powers or "ability" as abnormal and strange. He remained very self-conscious and secretive about the visions, aand frustrated because he had no one to confide in when it grew too weird for him.

Twice in his life, he had tried explaining the sensation to a close friend, and both times he lost a friendship. Those around him always seemed to know something wasn't quite right, but they said very little. He heard rumors about his sexual preference being questioned, or about him being a recluse, which commonly irritated him.

While some people considered them a gift, he regarded his visions as a curse.

Walking along, he went unnoticed by the guests patronizing the hotel. The visions never allowed him to interact with others. Like a ghost, he typically made his way around to whatever intrigued him most about the scene. No one ever saw him, so he tended to overhear strange conversations, or observe private rituals without interruption.

"Why am I here?" he asked himself, since no one else would hear.

Everything around him looked lush and green, but the air felt comfortable, leading him to believe the season was late spring. Visions allowed him to actively partake in the environment, as though his senses received stimuli from whatever setting he visualized. McCully suspected his mind just simulated the sensations, but he had no proof either way.

The grounds appeared busy compared to the photos he had viewed on the internet and the package the sellers sent his group. He noticed three springs right away, a bicycle and horse track, a mowed baseball diamond, and as he walked toward the building's rear, a large church with stained-glass windows.

"Wow," he murmured, his eyes following the winding steps up the hill until they finally landed at the front door.

He knew the church had been torn down at some point, but one gaze upon the beautiful structure had him questioning the logic of whoever made that decision. An extension of the golf course, or a completely different course, remained hidden from him over the hill's crest, but he heard chatter, and the occasional "Fore!" being yelled.

When he looked to his right, he spied three men standing beside a backdoor that apparently led to the dining room inside. He drew closer, unable to hear their conversation. It appeared as though two of them were trying to convince the third man of something.

McCully instantly felt connected somehow to the third man, who spoke to the two men with animated hands, one of which clasped a cigar between two fingers.

Sensing this particular man was the reason for his vision, McCully slowly approached the trio, as though expecting to be seen any moment.

He observed the man, noticing he wore a felt fedora hat, rather than a derby or cap. Dressed in a full suit with a tie, the man had shined two-tone shoes, giving the impression he wasn't just a regular guest at the hotel. If memory served McCully correctly, his attire seemed indicative of the 1920s.

Regardless of how he looked, he seemed important.

"I can't go through with it," McCully heard the man say before a hand smacked his arm, bringing him back to the real world.

With sleepy eyes, McCully regained his senses slowly as greenish colors blurred past the window beside him. He quickly remembered letting his agent take over the driving duty after they passed Louisville.

A country singer and songwriter from Nashville, Tennessee, McCully had enjoyed moderate success, mostly through his songs being picked up by major recording artists. In turn, he joined Lone Star Investments after Frank Oswalt, his agent, talked him into making the 'smartest decision of his life' a few years prior.

"We there yet?" McCully asked between yawns.

"About ten minutes out."

A closer examination of his surroundings revealed more white than green along the state highway. As Oswalt rolled up his window, a pungent sweet odor crossed McCully's nose, which he readily recognized as pipe tobacco.

"You been smoking in my car?"

"Why, no," Oswalt answered with feigned hurt since he knew he was caught.

"I'm going to write a song about a close friend dying of cancer."

His agent hesitated a moment, clearing his throat, before replying.

"And I'll probably go buy a new car with my cut after it goes to number one."

McCully chuckled to himself.

"You're too much."

Studying his surroundings, McCully looked from the road to Oswalt, who appeared a bit fatigued. Though he complained about making trips, Oswalt needed a few days away from work every so often. He led a frantic life dealing with music superstars and blossoming rookies. McCully hoped the man made enough money to retire early, though he would miss having Oswalt's representation.

And having to find a new agent.

A few years over fifty, Oswalt moved a little bit slower, but he appeared healthy most of the time. He had rough nights with little sleep so dark bags under his eyes weren't uncommon. His dark hair remained parted to one side, and he had grown in a full peppered goatee the past few weeks.

A moment of silence passed before the agent spoke again.

"Is Dan off his noggin by dragging us up here?"

"Hard telling. He's pretty passionate about the area, but I don't think he's the type to jump into a bad investment."

"There's already too many casinos sprouting up in the area," Oswalt complained. "We may be the ones to flood the market to the point of extinction."

McCully wondered if there *was* such a thing as a flooded market so far as casinos were concerned.

He stared at the pasty snowflakes attaching themselves to his side window. Most were large enough that he could see their distinct patterns before they melted or floated away.

"You're not fixin' to fall asleep on me again, are you?" Oswalt asked in his raspy voice.

"Nope. I'm ready to see this place for myself."

Their relationship had grown beyond a simple agent and songwriter capacity. If not for some key choices on McCully's part, the two might never have enjoyed a working relationship.

McCully found himself in the music business at an early age, working local gigs with his father, brother, and two other band members. George McCully redefined bluegrass music the way a select few brokers altered the course of the stock market. Among true bluegrass followers, George McCully was a household name.

Following in his father's footsteps, and learning from the man directly most of the time, young David learned to play a banjo because the instrument's sound fascinated him from an early age. When he turned fourteen, he played several local shows with his father when the Midnight Run's banjo player fell ill.

Midnight Run was one of many bands George McCully played in, or founded, during his years of bluegrass music. Dave lost track of how many bands his father played with until George found some commercial success in 1989 with Union Crossing, the last band he joined before forming a new band that brought along both of his sons.

While Dave enjoyed the success of being in a mainstream bluegrass band, he devoted much of his spare time to writing songs. Some were perfect for the bluegrass genre, while others seemed too deep in country roots for George to use on his albums.

"Try selling them in Nashville," his father told him one time at a family picnic. "That's just the kind of thing those kids are playing these days."

His father never criticized his playing, or his song writing. It seemed to sadden him when things blossomed for his son, not because he envied Dave, but because he knew their time together was growing shorter.

The elder McCully had recently parted ways with his last agent when he suggested Dave take his songs to Nashville. It just so happened Frank Oswalt was an agent with connections in Music City, and the George McCully Band's emergence as a bluegrass mainstay brought them into his stable.

Dave's hidden talent for writing songs didn't remain secret for long.

Within two years, recording artists landed three of his songs in the Billboard charts, two of which cracked the Top Twenty. Suddenly his writing became a focus for him because he was very much in demand.

While he never officially left his father's band, he took time off to write more music and eventually record a solo album that followed a mainstream country sound, rather than bluegrass.

He played guitar, rather than the banjo, on the album, showing another dimension to his talent base. The album enjoyed moderate success, mostly from his father's faithful followers, and a few people who saw the one music video he made that ended up on CMT for several weeks.

Oswalt regularly found buyers for his songs, from rookie singers making their first album to veteran performers wanting something different to resurrect their careers. McCully wrote about life experiences, things he knew about from Tennessee, and the wonders of his country that caught his eye while on various tours.

He seldom wrote love songs, because he had never experienced marriage, or a relationship that lasted beyond eight months. Being on the road made relationships nearly impossible unless a performer found just the right partner.

McCully envied his father for finding such a woman as his mother so easily.

Now in their sixties, the couple had recently celebrated their 41st wedding anniversary.

"Quit daydreaming," Oswalt said, drawing his attention once again. "There it is."

Following the pointed finger of his agent, McCully saw a mammoth dome in the distance, partially obscured by tall trees and the translucent curtain of falling snow.

"Wow," McCully couldn't help but mutter.

"We're a little bit early, Dave. Want a bite to eat before we meet up with the others?"

"Sure."

Oswalt continued past the hotel on the highway, slowing slightly as they passed upon McCully's request, so he could see the grand hotel a little better. Even the second look failed to satiate his desire to see the building up close and inside. His tours had landed him in all kinds of historic and interesting locations, but this building intrigued him.

Able to place some of the now missing buildings from his vision, McCully felt like a kid being promised a trip to the toy store. He could barely contain himself as they passed the grounds, because he wanted to know more about what awaited him inside.

And why he had a vision about the place that occurred almost a hundred years ago.

While most people harkened back to their childhood with fond memories, his mind clung to images of the unknown. Most of his visions foretold of terrible occurrences, sometimes even violent encounters he found himself unable to forget.

He reflected often in the family scrapbook his mother made him for happier times. One picture of him sitting on his father's lap as a toddler, holding a banjo, often brought a grin to his face. It was black and white, and they looked like poor cabin folks with his father in bib overalls and him wearing blue jeans with two distinct patches in plaid patterns.

McCully grinned with delight in the photo as his tiny fingers strummed the banjo. His hair looked like it had been combed with salad tongs pulling up, down, and to the sides in random order.

Memories like that never stayed in his mind. He needed photographs and family videos to remember such things. He blamed it on all of the visions running through his mind, filling his head like a computer hard drive. Apparently, his brain deleted the oldest files first, because he never remembered much about his childhood until he viewed his personal collection.

To some, his life would seem lavish and virtually perfect, but McCully felt a void that came from being alone. He found it impossible to talk about his *abilities* to other people, and functioning in society felt awkward, because he never knew when a vision might strike.

People might misinterpret him as having a seizure, doing more harm than good for him. At the very least, medical personnel might come to persuade him to ride with them to the hospital for a checkup.

"I didn't have a seizure, I had a psychic vision that transported my mind to another time and place," never seemed the logical or sane thing to tell them. The few times it had occurred in public, he simply signed the release form and answered their competency questions.

Luckily, the media never ran any stories about the incidents, but McCully supposed they had far more high profile celebrities to bash in the tabloids.

Sitting back, he enjoyed the rest of the ride, hoping his mind stayed at rest during the overnight stay.

Chapter 7

Glenn Turner had found most of his visit to West Baden uninviting so far. Choosing to avoid flying to Indiana from Tennessee was the one choice he made that seemed wise. He made good time, reaching the hotel's front gate in six hours, finding no one awaiting his arrival, including his fellow group members.

Cursing under his breath, he parked his Mercedes in the front lot long enough to pull out a map. He quickly realized he was less than half a mile from a nearby access road that passed the hotel's southwest corner on the way up a hill toward the mansion.

Somewhat tired from the drive, he decided to see if anyone might have dropped by the mansion ahead of schedule. Putting the map down, he turned his car around toward Highway 56 once again.

Because of a business meeting the night before, Turner chose to turn in early, waking at three in the morning. He left after a quick shower, bringing only a light suitcase with him. After hearing a weather report that predicted heavy snow in Southern Indiana and parts of Kentucky, he decided to stop only once for gas and a meal.

Now twisting his neck in an attempt to stretch it before it grew any stiffer, Turner followed the road up to the mansion. He drove slowly, taking in the view of the grounds. The hotel appeared miles away, with several buildings and the large garden between the road and the dome.

He drew closer to the mansion, spying the large gate to his right. Fortunately the wrought iron partitions were open, but he saw no vehicles parked near the mansion.

"Just my luck," he commented sourly as he pulled his car into the crescent-shaped driveway, caddy corner to the building.

A larger paved area remained further to the side for multiple vehicle parking. He stood from the car, finding his legs behaving like stiff rubber. They ached, feeling somewhat numb from being cramped inside a car for hours on end.

A few years away from middle-age, Turner knew what to expect from his body as he grew older. The past several years had provided hints about the progression of his body's slow deterioration as it aged.

He knew tired legs would eventually be the least of his worries.

While blood pulsated inside his legs, Turner simply stood by his car, momentarily taking in the view.

Though built in modern times, the mansion had a gothic feel about it. Most of the exterior was gray stone, giving it the feel of several French cathedrals Turner had seen in books. Somewhat of a classic building buff, he admired any building with good craftsmanship and attention to details.

He drew closer to the mansion, eyeing the intricate details carved into the stone facade of the mansion, as though it was indeed a church, rather than a residence. One look at the robed figures carved into the building gave Turner the impression they were biblical figures of some sort. His knowledge of the Bible was limited to church sermons from his childhood, and what tidbits he learned from game shows.

Spaced evenly across the front of the building, almost discreetly, the carvings reminded Turner of the Stations of the Cross found in Catholic churches. He wondered if the Jesuits, who inhabited the hotel for the better part of three decades, somehow served as inspiration for the artwork.

Deciding he had all evening to ponder the custom artwork, Turner stepped to the front door, expecting the knob to resist as he turned it.

It didn't.

Stepping inside, Turner looked around, seeing no luggage, and no indication anyone from his group had stopped by the mansion. He felt utterly surprised no one guarded the property or met him at the door.

"Hello?" he called, expecting to be caught inside the place ahead of the scheduled time.

No one answered.

A quick look around indicated four rooms on the lower level and sleeping quarters on the second floor. He ascended the stairs, finding each room with the intended occupant's name on the door in an etched copper nameplate.

Turner grunted to himself, uncertain of how to take assigned rooms, or the fact the mansion appeared abandoned. He found his room, slowly opening the door as though expecting to find a housekeeper desperately doing last minute tidying.

As the door swung open, he stared inside, finding a king-size bed complete with satin sheets and what appeared to be a custom comforter. Several hardwood dressers with articulate engravings led Turner to believe they were antiques, sitting on either side of the bed. An end table with a Victorian-style lamp also rested beside the bed.

Much like a hotel suite, the room also contained a small desk with small amenities such as a calculator, laptop computer, desk lamp, and a printer/fax/copier combination. He suspected the mansion often served as an overnight residence for important people.

A sofa, television, and complete stereo system completed the room, leaving any guest little else to long for, short of food.

By no means a celebrity, Turner retained a profile slightly more public than those of his investment colleagues. Almost ten years working as a model for a western wear distributer from the Nashville area left Turner wealthy enough to buy into the company when the time came for a 'fresh face' to model their clothing lines.

Shortly after a few gray hairs replaced their black counterparts, and his face showed the first signs of aging, the company wanted younger talent. The trend in western wear had gone from realistic, rugged, and handsome to sexy and cute. Turner had never considered himself a male model in the traditional sense anyhow. He wasn't the type an underwear manufacturer might contact to stand half-naked in their ads.

Based on discussions over the years with the company's owners, he knew the day would come, but the Ranchero Company continually showed a profit, even after the line dancing craze faded just before the new millennium.

They tapped into the internet market immediately, rather than waiting like some now defunct companies. Their return policies remained liberal throughout the years, satisfying many customers across the country. Ranchero also carried many of the top brands in cowboy boots, vests, blazers, and hats, rather than marketing cheap imitations.

His financial status never allowed him to gain controlling interest of the company, but Turner had some influence over their decisions. He made millions through his shares, helping promote the company personally, while using his experience to assist in marketing and product selection.

In turn, his newfound funds provided him ample opportunity to make more money when he joined Red Sanders and Lone Star Investments. They were introduced through a mutual friend at a charity dinner, but their conversation eventually gave way to their careers and a discussion about their retirement plans.

After doing some research and discussing the idea of joining Lone Star with his lawyer, Turner decided to branch out his earnings, seeing no way of losing money because he had a vote in where the group spent it.

Giving the room one last look from wall to wall, he decided to search for his investment partners elsewhere when a noise came from the next room, or perhaps the closet.

Sounding like a young child, a voice called out, somewhat muffled by walls or the closet door. Turner couldn't decipher exactly what the voice said, but it sounded as though it might be calling for a mother or father.

Then it came again.

"Mommy?" he heard more clearly this time as he stepped toward the closet.

He opened the door slowly, looking inside the darkened walk-in closet. Unable to see, he flipped the light switch, illuminating the area to reveal another door within the closet at the far end.

"What the hell?" he muttered, wondering if a child might be trapped within the closet.

Or worse, intentionally placed there.

Having two children of his own, Turner knew his ability to think and act rationally might literally fall apart if anything happened to them. Like most parents, he dreaded the thought of them being abducted or accidentally killed. He watched them like a hawk when he was home, which made him wonder if someone had done harm to a child literally this close to him.

Edging toward the door, he placed his hand on the knob, refusing to turn it. He wondered if he should get the police, or find someone else, before looking inside. If indeed someone had abducted a child, they might know he found the hiding place and take the kid somewhere else.

He had to act now.

Turning the knob, Turner found the room ahead entirely dark, and small. He found no light switch beside the door, meaning he needed to step inside a pitch-black room or find a flashlight first.

"Hello?" he asked cautiously, taking his first step forward.

Sticking his left arm forward, he felt ahead of him for any objects, or perhaps a human being.

Feeling and hearing nothing, he stepped inside a bit further. Keeping his foot against the door, Turner felt nothing except bare walls all around him. It felt as though he might be inside a one-person elevator car.

He began feeling upward, wondering if there might be something on the walls that led somewhere else. Very little light followed him inside, so his search was blind. His hand patted the wall until one of his fingers touched something sharp — like a thorn — that pricked his finger.

Fighting the urge to withdraw his hand, he continued to probe the object more carefully, keeping his foot propped against the door. Some part of him feared being trapped inside the dark room, especially since no one seemed to be inside.

He wondered if the voice came from another room, or perhaps a partition above or below him. His fingers began to feel around the thorny area, discovering a leather strap of some sort amongst several thorns, as though they were one intertwined unit.

About to explore the device further through the sense of touch, Turner never received the opportunity as a metal brace wrapped around his hand, pulling him into the wall. He hit with a thud, seeing the light and any opportunity to escape the small room dissipate within a second.

He felt several metal thorns dig into his wrist as the brace clamped around it, keeping him trapped against the wall. Turner panicked, imprisoned within a tiny dark room, as his heart pounded within his chest. He tugged at the shackle, which only served to injure his wrist more as skin tore against the thorns and blood drizzled down his arm.

Making matters worse, he felt the entire room begin to move, exactly like an elevator, terrorizing the former model even worse. He was ascending into a world of darkness, unaware of what awaited him at the next stop.

This was no time to be proud.

"Help!" he screamed, feeling rather certain no one heard his pleas for assistance during the darkest hour of his life. "Help!"

Chapter 8

Following the schedule Jana provided ahead of time, the investment team members met at the mansion up the hill from the hotel grounds, bringing their individual vehicles with them. Some had stayed at the French Lick Springs Hotel overnight, while others had just arrived.

Duncan brought his suitcase through the front door with him, leaving his motorcycle secured and covered in the trailer behind his truck. A lone servant waited outside to bring in belongings and take their coats, but Duncan preferred to keep his suitcase with him. Only a few group members required pampering, while most of them had worked for a living at some time in their lives.

Water dripped onto his hands as though it was raining, but one look down told him that snowflakes had settled onto his clothing, then melted when he stepped inside.

"Pretty thick out there," Red noted as he walked through the door. "We don't get much of this in Tennessee, do we?"

Duncan smirked.

"We're lucky to survive springtime tornados down there though."

Looking upward, Duncan noticed how open the mansion looked, even from the front door. Like the hotel, it drew attention to itself the moment a person entered its threshold. He saw no access to a floor above the second level, considering the possibility another set of stairs remained hidden from view.

He glanced at his watch, wondering how much time remained to explore the place before the tour.

11:45 a.m.

Setting down his suitcase, Duncan wandered to his left. Two rooms took up vast amounts of space along the left side, but the first room grabbed his attention.

Like something out of the movies, the room held everything a person might want for entertaining himself on any given evening at home.

A customized red carpet ran the length of the room with gold trim around its outskirts and a center that looked like something out of a classic cathedral. Golden leaves and tails ran in and out of one another as far as the eye could see along the trim.

The entire back wall consisted of bookshelves twice as tall as any normal man, with a rolling ladder to access the upper levels. Not one inch of the custom stained oak shelving remained empty.

Several decorative lamps rested atop end tables or by themselves with tall, elaborate stands, but the chandelier centered in the room drew Duncan's attention upward. Thousands of crystals shimmered from over a dozen bulbs in the fixture's center.

Along the outside wall, a fireplace contained a large fire while a small stack of evenly cut logs waited their turn to keep the fire going. Comprised of old stone, the fireplace looked like something from colonial days gone by, but Duncan suspected its aesthetic appearance gave way to contemporary housing codes.

Furniture appeared strategically placed throughout the room, giving it enough space for a person to walk around comfortably, but enough seating to entertain a moderate gathering.

Opposite the fireplace, a mounted stereo system played the soft jazz music Duncan heard from speakers all around him. He looked around, seeing no speakers readily visible, guessing they were hidden behind the love seats and chairs. Much like a bank or restaurant might have, the mansion likely had speakers built into the ceiling, with virtually invisible holes allowing sound to filter downward.

"What do you think?" Jana asked, taking his side.

"It's impressive. I guess I don't put much thought into decorating my houses."

Technically a bachelor, Duncan had no reason to spend money on home decor. Owning two houses dipped into his funds enough that he needed to watch how he spent his inheritance and earnings. If his company won the right to open a casino and own the hotel, he planned to sell his place in Tennessee and personally oversee local operations.

Much like his great-grandfather had.

"I moved the dinner from the sixth floor suite to the dining room here," Jana informed him. "With the snow piling up, I didn't want us to get stuck over there without supplies or any communication."

"You think it's going to get that bad?"

"The weather reports say we may get a foot or two dumped on us overnight. We're a day or two away from a significant warming trend, so it could get bad."

Duncan had no previous engagements, but most of his colleagues had to work on Monday. He knew Keith and a few others had flights scheduled to depart Sunday evening for the return trip to Texas.

Ending the tour on a sour note was the last thing Duncan wanted. Southern Indiana seldom saw six inches of snow an entire winter, much less two feet in a day's time. He looked outside the window, seeing little more than a white blur.

"You okay?" Jana asked him, breaking his train of thought from the depressing path that lay before him.

"Yeah. I guess I'm thinking too much about everything that could go wrong to focus on getting the group to buy the place. There's no way I can afford the grounds by myself, so I'm relying on them for help."

Jana smiled easily.

"There *are* other investment groups."

"Yeah, but there's no time left. By March, Mr. Clouse is going to make a decision. Isn't he?"

"His decision could be not to accept any of the applicants. He's picky about who takes over the hotel."

Duncan looked to his watch again, seeing it was nearly time to begin the tour.

"Hopefully my fellow investors can overlook the problems and see what a worthwhile place the hotel can be."

Jana nodded as they returned to the foyer, finding the rest of the group awaiting instructions.

Quickly counting heads, Duncan realized someone wasn't present.

"You seen Glenn Turner?" he asked Red.

"No. I think he was driving up, but I haven't seen his car anywhere."

"Maybe he stopped at the hotel," someone suggested.

Duncan wondered if the man might have encountered some bad weather during his trip. He watched Red pull out a cell phone to search his contact list before hitting a button. Nearly half a minute passed before he folded the phone shut.

"I got his voice mail," Red reported.

From what little bit he knew of Turner, the man didn't seem like one to leave his phone too far behind. Turner wasn't absolutely needed, because a majority vote within the group determined if they were pursuing the hotel officially.

Or not.

Growing concerned, Duncan knew the group couldn't afford to wait long for Turner. It made no sense that he would still be in transit if he wasn't answering his cell phone.

"How long do we wait for him?" Jana asked, her tone indicating that waiting might prove troublesome.

"It's your gig, but I say we don't," Duncan answered just above a whisper.

He looked at his fellow investors, who appeared ready to take the tour, noticing a strange, almost quizzical stare from Dave McCully.

***

McCully couldn't help but look at Duncan, realizing the man looked very much like the man who spoke at the end of his vision.

Though he tried being coy about his observation, Duncan caught him.

McCully quickly diverted his eyes, taking notice of the two women in the group.

Laura Compton was close to his own age, finding success through wealthy parents and a strong education in business. He knew of rumors that she had some sort of relationship with Keith, despite him being old enough to be her father.

Beside her stood Judith Parks, a lovely brunette who kept her personal life a closed book to the others. She had briefly dated Red Sanders, but their day and night personalities kept it from working. They both had money, so McCully imagined their brief relationship blossomed from their business ties. She dressed fashionably, always in the latest styles, despite Red seldom changing a thing about his attire or his outlook on life.

He seldom saw them speak to one another unless they had business to discuss.

Of anyone in the group, Judith was the least likely to be sold on the idea of buying the hotel. She seldom liked anyone else's ideas, which tended to dissuade them from voting for her projects. McCully had been personally burned on an idea to buy land just outside of Knoxville for development.

He found a perfect lot for condos or a small hotel near a new housing development. New businesses had flocked to the area, so he wanted to buy the land for resale, if nothing else. Judith shot down his idea, saying their profit would have been minimal at best. Red stuck by her decision, despite knowing better, and swayed the group's vote.

McCully checked on the land a few months later, discovering it was bought by a Tampa company that had already begun construction on a Holiday Inn Express. Though not one to hold a grudge, McCully had voted against several of their ideas that seemed far less stable than his own potential venture. He didn't always win, but his point was taken by nearly everyone in the group.

Jana called for everyone's attention, which they readily gave.

"Due to the weather, we're not going to wait for Mr. Turner to arrive," she announced. "I have a shuttle van outside if you would all be so kind as to make your way out there."

She led the way toward the front door, already beginning part of the tour by taking them through the motions.

"We'll begin by touring the sunken garden outside the hotel itself. From there, we will quickly observe some of the out buildings before making our way inside."

A moment later, everyone was seated comfortably inside the already heated van, which had its own driver from the rental service. McCully sat beside Oswalt, who had been engaged in conversation with Red Sanders while they waited inside the mansion.

"Nice of you to join me," McCully commented with a verbal jab.

"It's not every day I get to see Red," Oswalt said in his defense. "I'm stuck with *you* all the time."

Grinning to himself, McCully realized how often he saw his agent, whether it was conducting music business, or their investment meetings.

Soon enough the group members found themselves at the hotel's front gate huddled in a group like penguins to avoid the falling snow. McCully noticed the climate didn't feel too bad, considering the temperature remained near the freezing point. The wind chilled him a bit, but he hadn't expected a mild blizzard while he packed for his trip.

"I'll try to make this brief," Jana virtually yelled through the elements so the group could hear.

She led them down the path, explaining some of the hotel's history to them, until they walked into the garden. After a quick look around the snow-covered flowers and shrubs, which had already met their seasonal demise around the holidays, she took them inside one of the two remaining springs.

"This is Hygeia," Jana noted, waving one arm slowly around the open area like a game show hostess.

McCully noticed sound resonated nicely inside the glazed brick structure. The acoustics might provide a nice staging area for a small band, he decided.

Roomy enough to accommodate a small party, the spring had a nice walkway on two of its sides. McCully noticed withered vines still wrapped around the support columns and trellises along both ends. He suspected they created a form of privacy for anyone visiting the spring during the summer because the leafy vines became a wall of their own.

"The spring's name originates from the Greek goddess of health, and is where we get our modern day word 'hygiene' from. The Jesuits capped the spring when they took over the hotel because it was prone to flooding. At one time, guests walked fifteen feet down for a drink of the mineral water."

Subtle stained glass in some of the windows gave McCully the impression the Jesuits had left their mark when they owned the hotel. The interior was completely white, appearing more so with the falling snow outside the abundance of windows that allowed natural light to flood the spring building.

By no means heated, the building only offered partial shelter from the elements. McCully exhaled through his mouth, seeing his breath in the air. A peek outside one of the smaller windows indicated the snow was already several inches deep on the ground.

Chancing a glimpse toward Duncan, he noticed the normally rugged biker looked concerned, yet attentive. He knew this project meant everything to the man, because he failed to contain his enthusiasm on more than one occasion after their meetings.

McCully couldn't shake the feeling the man looked very much like the last person he saw in his vision. It seemed impossible because the scene he witnessed was nearly a hundred-years-old. To him, things weren't adding up.

Never had his visions taken him so far back in time, and lately he required little or no physical contact to initiate them. Something about the grounds he stood upon heightened the abilities he often wished he'd never possessed.

Even the foreshadowing of coming to West Baden triggered something inside his mind.

Whatever Jana said went unheard as he lost himself in thought, staring at the snowflakes floating downward outside.

"Let's head inside the main building and get warm," he finally heard her say.

Like everyone around him, McCully was awestruck at the sight of the atrium a few minutes later. Six levels of hotel rooms were in complete view from one spot, some with balconies, all of them surrounded by intricate paint and Victorian artwork. Above it all, they spotted the chandelier below a round metal drum.

The roof consisted of glass and metal panels, aligned beside one another around the dome. It looked somewhat like a flying saucer with large windows from below. The huge windows allowed light to freely illuminate the entire atrium.

Instead of acting as an eyesore, the metal framework that supported the dome from the ground up was lost in the hand-painted artwork just above the rooms. The metal arms spanned from large pillars to the center drum above the chandelier, directly beneath the metal panels of the same sandy color, allowing them to virtually go unnoticed.

"The atrium has seen everything from dinners, to car shows, to circuses," Jana stated. "As you can see, it has space enough for virtually anything you might wish to hold in the hotel. The Jesuits found it too large for their needs, so they converted the lobby into their chapel."

Jana led them across the atrium, showing them the old office, what was a smoking room in its day, the dining room, the kitchen, and the old barber shop along the first floor. They stopped at the emporium, which appeared closed.

"This is where regular tourists purchase gifts after their tours," Jana explained. "Occasionally the gift shop management hosts book signings for authors who write about the area. We'll stop by here after we get done upstairs, because I think you'll like the museum in the back."

Jana took them to the second floor, showing them the ballroom, now finished by Clouse's development team. She explained the metal beams used to solidify the upper floors created a problem with the ballroom because the floor was raised almost two feet.

"You can imagine how it looked having windows that reached down to your feet," she said. "But Mr. Clouse came up with a solution that left the windows outside intact for historical purposes, but also made them pleasing in here."

McCully noticed small crescent tables placed before the windows with open bases that matched the room's decor. They each had a glass top, allowing light to shine upward through them, or stream outside their bases. He knelt beside one, noticing the rustic red color of the metal bars holding up the table. Inside he spied some sort of light orb, not much different from a rotating disco ball atop a base.

"Functional *and* pretty," McCully uttered barely above a whisper.

"Isn't it?" Oswalt asked in a somewhat huffed tone, as though the tour bored him.

"What crawled up your ass and died?"

His agent shrugged.

"I came here for the food and the company, not the grand tour."

"Ever the consummate respect for history and lore, I see."

Oswalt sighed, returning to the rest of the group.

Jana led them to several other areas, including a balcony overlooking the lobby where she said women once wrote letters home while the men enjoyed the outdoors. Able to see the intricate artwork up close, McCully virtually felt the place come alive inside his mind, and through his veins.

He was a complete stranger from another state, yet he shared an unfamiliar kinship with the hotel.

They visited another balcony that overlooked the atrium. It gave visitors a sense of anonymity when they viewed the atrium, because anyone below couldn't see them unless they stepped forward to the railing.

Most of the remaining floors looked the same, with finished rooms that Clouse and his team had completed several years prior. They were fully furnished with beds, desks, lamps, and beautiful bathrooms, topped off with fantastic views of either the atrium or the grounds. The view depended upon whether a person had a room on the inside ring, or the outside.

When they reached the sixth floor after a ride on one of the two elevators, the group followed Jana into a small lobby that led to a suite. At long last, the investors found themselves in familiar territory because the suite came equipped with a conference table, big screen television, kitchenette, and two bedrooms. Each of the bedrooms came equipped with a full bath, their walls covered from floor to ceiling in tiles with a marble finish.

McCully found himself impressed by the hotel's design, particularly since it was built over a century prior. He liked the idea of the hotel coming to life again, but he felt biased after seeing how it looked when it was open for business.

Hesitantly, he touched the conference table, wondering if it might set off a vision in front of his colleagues.

Nothing happened.

Since the table was evidently new from the renovation, it held no memories to trigger his ability.

"You gonna propose to it or what?" Keith Sanders asked as he took McCully's side.

He felt somewhat taken aback that Keith spoke to him outside of a business meeting, because he sometimes wondered if the man knew anything outside of ranching and investing.

Slowly chuckling to himself, McCully figured he probably looked a bit strange running his fingers along a tabletop.

"Maybe I was admiring the finish."

"Uh huh," Keith said with a skeptical raise of one eyebrow.

Both stood there awkwardly a moment, unsure of what to say next. Jana led the rest of the group through the suite, then out to the lobby for a bird's-eye view of the atrium.

"What do you think of it?" he dared ask the unofficial leader of their firm.

"I like the place, but I'm still not sold on the casino notion."

"Ever known a casino to lose money? Or go bankrupt?"

Now it was Keith's turn to laugh.

"I guess not. It'll just take some time for our lawyers to go through the Indiana laws before we commit all the way."

"It's a bit different, isn't it?"

"How so?"

"Usually we're the middleman; buying then selling. This project requires some hands on operation."

Keith nodded in agreement.

"This place sat vacant for almost twenty years with a selling price a fraction of the price *we're* looking at paying. I guess it would be a sink or swim venture, wouldn't it?"

"I think Dan has enough inspiration for all of us."

"The lad certainly does. At first, I wondered why he had such a hard-on for this place, but I'm beginning to understand. I just wish it wasn't in the middle of nowhere."

McCully followed Keith toward the group, catching part of Jana's latest speech about the only confirmed death at the hotel while it was operating. It seemed a professional baseball manager took his own life while the team was at the hotel for spring training.

A few minutes later, the group members found themselves downstairs, wandering around the gift shop. McCully saw gift shops all around the nation whenever he toured, so he immediately looked for anything unique to the area. He seldom bought anything, because his house was already full of memorabilia from his father, and from the recording industry. His life had little room for hobbies and collectibles.

Finding little of interest, McCully milled toward the museum. Merely an extension of the larger gift shop, the museum was separated in principle only by an arched doorway. When McCully passed through the doorway, he felt strange, as though the room held something for him, bursting to reveal its secret.

Only Judith Parks stood inside the room with him, studying some before and after composites placed on the walls. The photos depicted the hotel when weeds overtook the lawn and garden areas, the fallen wall portion, and the decay inside the atrium. Beside them, other photos displayed what the group had just seen.

A fully restored hotel.

Deciding to look at something other than the photos, McCully turned to his right, seeing old artifacts from the hotel's heyday, such as a dipping glass from the springs, and an old room key. He glided to his right, observing another glass case with different donations inside. Mostly old postcards and souvenirs such as plates and engraved spoons, the items took him back to the vision.

He had crouched for a better look at some of the items, but as he slowly stood, McCully's eyes fixed themselves on a photograph set atop the display case. Enlarged, the photograph displayed a dozen men seated upon a dark buggy named the 'Water Wagon' in bright paint along its side. Another man stood at the back of the wagon with his hands upon the wooden frame.

Impressive as the photo may have been on its own, giving visitors a glimpse of life around 1900, McCully focused on one man in particular. Wearing a dark suit and a tan cap, the man held a walking stick in his left hand, while his right thumbed a cigar.

"Dear God," McCully muttered as someone brushed his side.

As though in a dream, or some slow-motion movie sequence, he looked to his left, seeing Dan Duncan look at the photograph, then to him. If Duncan noticed the bewildered look scrawled across his face, it didn't register on his.

"That why you've been giving me funny stares all morning?" Duncan inquired, though not rudely.

McCully couldn't readily answer.

Of course, the reason was the man in the photo, but he couldn't begin to conjure up a story to explain how he had virtually traveled back in time to see the man.

He looked from the man in the photo to Duncan once more, seeing only subtle differences between the two men. Duncan had a lighter-colored mustache, being blond instead of dark brown, and his face appeared a bit more weathered.

"Who is he?" McCully asked his investment partner, sensing Duncan knew the answer.

Duncan looked at him suspiciously a moment before answering.

"My grandfather."

Chapter 9

"Did you ever meet him?" McCully asked as they both looked to the photograph.

"No. He died pretty young."

Judith passed them as she left the room, giving them more privacy.

"What do you know about my grandfather?" Duncan virtually demanded in a hushed tone.

"I've seen him before. These images are for sale on eBay all the time."

He hated telling a white lie, but had little choice.

Saying "I had a flashback to a time when your grandfather was a regular at this place" didn't sound very appropriate.

Or sane.

McCully had indeed searched online auctions for the hotel's memorabilia, which provided him the excuse. It seemed the old Water Wagon was somewhat of a photo backdrop, in addition to traveling around the grounds to provide mineral water. Many images were converted into postcards sold at the hotel, now stuffed in shoeboxes and old scrapbooks inside closets or garages.

Many were probably lost forever.

"What was his name?" McCully asked Duncan, though unsure why he pressed the issue, or even wanted to know.

"Andrew. He was actually my great-grandfather."

Duncan still appeared somewhat concerned that McCully had any kind of connection to his family, legitimate or not.

"I see the connection," McCully said, staring intently at the photograph.

He wanted to touch it, but not in front of anyone. If it were indeed an original, it would probably send him into a vision. Though his visions sometimes unfolded over minutes inside his mind, only a second or two passed in real life.

People had reported how his body stiffened or he appeared clinically insane for those few seconds, as though possessed. McCully had no desire to carry out any theatrics, intentional or not, before his fellow investors.

Only Oswalt had ever seen him in the strange condition, and he never pretended to understand in any capacity.

Oswalt was very much old-fashioned, explaining why George McCully chose him as his agent. He didn't believe in aliens, government conspiracies, or using the stock market, much less psychic powers.

"I realize we don't know one another much beyond our business," Duncan said, "but I get the impression you know something you're not telling me."

McCully ignored the statement, seeing no positives about telling the truth.

"Your grandfather dressed fairly plain, didn't he?"

"That wasn't plain back then," Duncan noted. "How often do you wear a carnation pinned on your sport coat these days?"

McCully nodded, getting the point.

Each of the men in the photograph had a flower pinned to their jacket. They wore vests, and while some of them wore ties, others had on shirts with turtlenecks. Their headdress was a potpourri of derby hats and cloth caps.

"Is he the reason you're so interested in this place?"

Duncan seemed to light up at the idea of talking about his interest in West Baden. He obviously knew bidding on the place was a hard sell to his colleagues.

"He helped bring the railroad here in 1887. It shaped the course of history as far as this area is concerned, and he made his fortune."

"When was this photo taken?"

"Probably sometime between 1899 and 1917, before they renovated the grounds," Duncan surmised. "A lot of these photos are taken near the old opera house and the early wooden springs."

"When did he die, if you don't mind my asking?"

"There was an accident in 1923. They found him one morning along the railroad tracks."

McCully simply nodded, not wishing to press the issue. The year sounded very much like the era during his vision.

"We're not so different," he said instead. "My family had success before I was born."

Duncan didn't appear sold, but he wasn't about to lose an ally in the battle to own the property.

"I've worked for a living," he said.

"You may not consider learning to play three instruments and touring the country on weekends and holidays work, but it isn't particularly easy."

Duncan looked to the photo once more, letting a strange, almost remorseful grin cross his face.

"We should probably get back," he said uneasily.

"Yeah," McCully said under his breath as the grandson of a railroad tycoon left the room.

Looking to the photograph, McCully caught himself reaching for it as his fingers neared the frame. He hesitated, seeing no one looking his way. Wondering if anything would even happen, he let his fingertips draw near the wooden frame's finish.

Somehow doubting the picture could trigger an event, he let one finger graze the frame, instantly transplanting his mind and body to another time.

Outside once more, McCully took a quick look around, seeing wooden structures everywhere on what seemed to be otherwise familiar ground. Everything appeared lush and green around him, unlike the sepia images representing the only captured moments of the hotel's better days.

Nearby he spied the Water Wagon parked within the area he now knew as the sunken garden. Very little about the grounds appeared the same, aside from the general shape. None of the buildings had brick exteriors, the bicycle track loomed in the background, and the church stood atop the hill, overlooking the original hotel.

"Come on, Andy," a man said beside the wagon.

McCully noticed a group of men nearby, some appearing agitated as this man tried convincing Andrew Duncan of something.

"One picture isn't going to kill you," the man continued.

McCully seemed to recognize him as one of the men beside Duncan in his earlier vision. Apparently, they shared some sort of friendship, or at least a partnership.

Shaking his head negatively, Duncan seemed to give in, stepping toward the wagon. A photographer lined them up on the wagon, putting Duncan near the center. He asked for a show of hands about how many of the men wanted copies.

McCully realized he was witnessing the creation of the modern day postcards he occasionally saw online. The photographer took orders, because he needed to shoot a photograph for each individual who wanted a personalized postcard made. To his surprise, Duncan raised his hand with several others.

Duncan's friend stood proudly behind him, wearing a light derby. Duncan himself looked away on most of the shots, appearing timid about looking directly at the camera. Perhaps the flash bothered him, but McCully sensed something deeper about his reluctance.

As the flash went off the third or fourth time, McCully's eyes diverted to the grounds, finding several people walking around while others milled near the springs. Compared to modern life, everything looked and felt tranquil. The highway was nothing more than a dirt path, people rode horses or took buggies for transportation, and nature looked unblemished everywhere around him.

Watching the people walk around the grounds felt something like viewing a slow-motion movie scene. In the distance, some of them looked like ants because the vast grounds appeared to have no end.

"You okay, Andy?" the friend asked once they were done, stepping off the wagon.

"I'm fine. Just a busy day ahead of me is all."

Duncan seemed like a local learning the walk and talk of the ritzy people who visited the grounds.

"Surely the wealthiest man in the valley doesn't have worries," his friend said playfully.

Giving an uneasy smile, Duncan led the way toward the hotel, noticing several people looking his way when his friend said the words. McCully observed this carefully, noting that Andrew Duncan was a private individual. For a railroad baron, he didn't fit the typical mold.

"I'm having lunch with the wealthiest man in the valley, Ben. Or high tea, or whatever the hell it is they call it. I can't get used to all these rituals."

"Then why participate?"

"It's expected," Duncan answered as though God Himself might strike him down if he failed to attend functions in the valley.

"You wanted money and power when you bought up railroad shares, Andy. You can't deny it. What you do with your life is your business, but you shouldn't be living to satisfy other people."

Shrugging uneasily, Duncan took a book of matches from inside his sport coat, lighting the cigar he had been toying with since the Water Wagon photo. He drew on it for several seconds before watching a smoke ring dissipate into the air when he exhaled.

"When you have lunch with Sinclair, just remember he wouldn't have found this hotel if you hadn't put the wheels in motion for the railroad that brought him."

Duncan didn't appear convinced.

"The hotel was up and running before he ever traveled this way. He just took advantage of a situation like I did."

"We're getting off the topic. We were talking about your goals now that you've accomplished riches and a title. If you were in England you might be knighted, you know."

Chuckling, Duncan appeared far more at ease around his friend than he had moments prior.

"So, we were talking about my goals, were we?"

"Good man, certainly you have ambitions to marry and spread your seed across the valley, don't you?"

Duncan appeared amused at the statement.

"Mr. Williams, I believe what you are suggesting would make me the father of many a bastard child."

"I suggest no such thing."

Puffing on his cigar to keep it from dying off, Duncan kept one eye fixed on his friend, waiting for an elaboration.

"It just so happens there is a beautiful young lady a few miles away who has asked yours truly about any single friends he might know."

Williams held out an open palm toward his friend, indicating Duncan needed to indicate interest, or manufacture an excellent excuse if he wasn't interested.

"I suppose we *could* go for a horseback ride this afternoon," he said after a few seconds. "There are always a few detours along the way, aren't there?"

"That's the spirit, Andy."

McCully felt a presence beside him that brought him back to his current snowy world.

He looked to his left, seeing Jana staring at him with a concerned, curious look.

"You okay?" she asked. "You've been staring at the photo for a few minutes now."

"I guess you could say I was somewhere else."

"Well, everyone else is getting into the van. I was going to lock up the emporium if you were ready to go."

Feeling as though he had been disturbed during a deep sleep, McCully wanted to see the vision through, suspecting it might lead him down a disturbing path. He typically disliked his abilities, but something about the hotel grounds intensified them, teasing him with bygone images.

As he followed Jana to the door, he wondered if they might be warning him about impending danger. Trying to shake the feeling from his mind, he walked toward the glass entrance doors, seeing snow piling up outside. The sunken garden and buildings beyond the van barely remained visible through the falling flakes.

While Tennessee felt some cold temperatures during the winter months, the state seldom saw any snow accumulation.

Something about the weather worried him, though he lacked any evidence why it might prove harmful. He opened the door for Jana, following her into the cold, wondering what events the evening held for his group.

Chapter 10

When the group returned to the mansion Duncan noticed it was almost two in the afternoon. A few inches of snow now rested atop his truck and the trailer hauling his motorcycle. He groaned inwardly at the thought of lost enjoyment during his weekend homecoming.

Stepping from the van, he stood outside as everyone else went inside. Thoughts of the hotel ran through his mind, along with a burning desire to own or run the building.

His conversation with McCully plagued him, but he didn't suspect the man harbored any dark secrets. If anything, his interest in Andrew Duncan seemed genuine, though awkward in its timing.

Once everyone exited the van, it departed through the front gate, leaving the guests by themselves at the mansion.

Another tour was planned for the next morning in case the group had any concerns or questions about the hotel. Jana had taken them through the entire hotel, though somewhat quickly. Duncan felt bad that the garden and some of the outlying buildings were skimmed over during the walk because of the weather.

Though the highway was plowed, the road from the hotel to the mansion remained very much snow covered. If the front gate was capable of being closed, it might remain stuck if the snow froze it to the ground.

Duncan doubted any looters or thieves dared brave the elements to visit the seldom inhabited mansion. Turning around, he noticed everyone else had retreated to warmer shelter, so he decided to do the same. As he sauntered toward the front door, the images carved along the front of the building caught his attention.

He took a moment to study the carving nearest the door, finding its craftsmanship impeccable. In great detail, it showed an image of a young man tied down atop a stone tablet with an older man ready to plunge a dagger into his heart. Behind them, tangled in the brush, stood a ram, bringing to mind an old biblical story about Abraham being tested by God. Prepared to sacrifice his son to honor the Lord's wishes, God then spoke to him and told him it was simply a test. Abraham then found a nearby ram to offer as a sacrifice instead.

Beneath the image, also carved into the mansion's stone foundation, Duncan found a set of numbers.

6:14.

Far removed from his church school days, Duncan believed most or all passages from the Bible had some sort of notation preceding their numbered paragraphs. He wondered if his guess about Abraham was accurate, deciding to check his room for a Bible later.

He stepped inside, wondering what the group was supposed to do for entertainment the rest of the evening. Most of his colleagues were already out of sight, likely unpacking inside their private rooms.

No one really gave him much indication about their impressions of the hotel. He caught several looks of astonishment when they entered the hotel's atrium, thinking perhaps they felt some of the nostalgia that ran through his veins.

"What happened to the servant?" he asked Jana as she passed him.

"He was just here for the morning," she explained. "I have the caterer here now. Was there something you needed?"

"No. Not at all."

Duncan put forth a cheerful look, though his insides felt like a dishrag being wrung out.

Picking up his suitcase, he started toward the stairway, hesitating on the second step as an uncomfortable feeling overtook his mind. He realized the probability of being snowed in for a day or two worried some of his partners, but something felt dangerous about his surroundings.

Glancing around, he saw no one wandering through the mansion, but several pleasant aromas rose from the kitchen. Letting his mind return to unpacking and relaxing, Duncan entertained notions of driving to the hotel later. His truck possessed off-road capabilities, so wintery weather typically did little to slow it down.

Supper was the only scheduled event left for the evening, then the guests were free to discuss the hotel or do as they pleased. Though the van driver had left, Jana remained behind, likely spending the evening with them. Radio reports indicated most of the highways were treacherous, with a dozen accidents already preoccupying police and county road crews.

Duncan trudged upstairs, his mind never venturing far from thoughts of the nearby hotel grounds until he noticed McCully emerge from his room.

Both men exchanged uncomfortable looks, inevitably avoiding one another as they passed in the second floor hallway.

Reading the placards along each door until he found his room, he turned the knob, stepping inside. Though he liked the room, he set down his suitcase, opting to return downstairs to get a feel for the opinions of his fellow investors.

He removed his heavy jacket, tossing it to the bed as his mind reflected on the day's events.

Glenn Turner had yet to show up or call. Red had tried phoning him several times, to no avail.

At first Duncan felt angry, thinking Turner shrugged off the tour, or simply chickened out. Now he worried the weather might have incapacitated Turner, or left him stranded somewhere. The man was professional enough to answer his phone, or at least return a call the moment he found himself free to do so.

Sighing outwardly, he sauntered down the stairs, prepared to see if there were any new developments.

Chapter 11

In downtown French Lick, the sheriff of Orange County sat inside a local bar he had frequented for years, sipping a beer from his chilled mug.

The bar had gone through several name changes over the years, the latest coming when a retired couple bought the place and named it Berkie's. The atmosphere changed little, as did the clientele, but Sheriff Roland Brown made certain the riffraff stayed clear of the place.

With the prospect of a casino coming to town, his job was suddenly watched more closely by the local media. The following year was an election year, and with one more term available to him, Brown wanted to make certain West Baden and French Lick remained free of problems.

Sitting across from his son at a table, he looked to the clock since none of the windows allowed a clear view of the snow falling outside.

"Almost four," he said in his son's general direction.

"In a hurry?" Arlan Brown asked.

"It's just this shitty weather. You know how things get when it snows just a few inches. People drive worse than usual around here."

Arlan took a swig from his beer bottle. This was his first of two days off.

Roland kept a tighter leash on his son than any of his other deputies. They seldom worked together, but away from work, they were virtually inseparable. Between fishing, horseback riding, and traveling to watch sporting events, few days passed when they didn't see or talk to one another.

"You got plans tonight?" Roland asked his son.

"Not really. I might stop by the video store on the way home."

His son had been dating the young woman who owned the local video store in West Baden. Until the casino was built, bringing all kinds of national chains to their little towns, she provided the only means of DVD and video rentals.

For the longest time his son hadn't dated after coming off a bad relationship. He was in his early thirties, thinking he was on the road to marriage when his world came crashing down.

Roland hadn't been the best role model, divorcing twice before he turned fifty. After retiring from a local police chief's position, he ran for county sheriff and won, to his own surprise. Luckily, Arlan already had a job with the county force, sparing them from nepotism claims.

"What are you doing?" Arlan inquired.

The sheriff thought a moment before answering, staring at the nearly empty mug on the table. One beer was his limit on any given night, because his job required him to remain on-call all day and night.

"I'll probably take a few runs through town before heading home. The locals like seeing us out there doing our job."

Arlan flashed a crooked grin.

"Shaking hands and kissing babies *will* get you further."

Shoving his mug away from him, Roland groaned to himself. He believed the public liked seeing the sheriff in person, instead of viewing him as a photo in the paper after a big arrest or publicity function. He attended the largest church in the area simply to make himself known. Major crimes seldom occurred within the county, forcing Roland to draw attention to public relations. Because of limited crime, his force remained relatively small.

Nine officers served under him, which would likely increase after the casino issue was settled. Part of his structured redevelopment was to have his intern write grants for new officer positions to the government. Though the intern received no pay for such tedious work, he had the opportunity to create himself a position within the department if the federal government deemed the department worthy of funding.

Roland knew how to use incentives to his advantage.

His mind wandered to the fact that another group was touring the hotel, then staying overnight in the mansion. Thankfully, things had gone smoothly with the first two tours.

Roland came into his position toward the end of the West Baden fiasco revolving around Paul Clouse. Very little about the hotel's history or Martin Smith made sense to him. Conflicting stories made it difficult to ascertain exactly what the hell happened on those grounds over a period of three years.

"You ever wonder how much things are going to change around here once the casino moves in?" he asked his son.

"Probably for the better. I keep hearing all about how New Albany and Corydon have better tax bases because of their casinos. I remember how rundown Corydon used to look when I was in school. They've changed that place for the better."

"Hopefully we can do the same here, son."

Arlan looked at him curiously.

"You okay? You seem on edge tonight."

"I don't know what it is. This snow, the hotel being looked at...something feels real strange."

Finishing his beer, Arlan set the bottle down hard enough that it thumped against the table.

"You grew up around here. I don't imagine you've seen much of this stuff over the years."

Roland forced a chuckle.

"No, I don't suppose I have."

He paused momentarily, placing both hands before him on the table.

"I can remember a time when that hotel was nothing more than overgrown weeds and crumbling walls. Now they're talking about making it a Five Star affair. We've never had anything like that before, and I'm afraid it's going to get fucked up like it did the last time they tried opening it."

"You worry too much," his son noted, stretching his arms as he stood. "I'm getting home so I can shovel my drive."

"I'll see you in the morning."

Arlan nodded, giving an informal salute before he headed for the door.

With his son gone, only Roland and two other patrons remained inside the bar. Tom Watkins, the man who owned the establishment, remained behind the bar as he cleaned glasses, preparing for his nightly sweep of the floor shortly.

Suspecting the man wanted to close up and get home, Roland decided to leave for the night when his cellular phone rang. Plucking it from his belt, he noticed the number coming from the West Baden Springs Hotel where a few of his state police buddies sometimes worked security.

"Hello?" he answered simply.

"Roland, this is Brent Guthrie. I'm working at the hotel tonight, and I have a little situation I want you to look at."

"Something bad?"

"I hate to drag you out in the weather, but it's something I really can't discuss on the phone."

Exhaling through his nose in thought, the sheriff wondered why in the world Guthrie wanted him specifically at the hotel. He also questioned why the retired state trooper phoned him directly when there were obviously county units on patrol.

"I'm just down the road," he finally answered. "Give me ten minutes."

"Okay. Be careful."

A click reached the sheriff's ears, but something about the way Guthrie ended the call worried him. The way he said 'be careful' sounded deeper than obvious concern over the weather. It occurred to him that Guthrie seldom spoke vaguely about any topic. They both knew cellular phone calls weren't traceable, short of high tech equipment.

Keeping his calm demeanor, Roland stood from the wooden chair. On his way out he gave Tom Watkins a quick wave, then decided to speak with the man as a precaution. Why he felt a need to let someone know his intentions eluded him, but something instinctively told him this was no ordinary night.

Perhaps the freak storm put him on edge, or the fact he was traveling to the hotel gave him goose bumps, but he needed to leave some kind of breadcrumb trail.

"If Arlan calls, I'm heading to the West Baden hotel," he told the establishment's owner. "I'll be heading home after I'm done there."

"Okay, Sheriff," Watkins said with an acknowledging nod.

"Take care, Tom."

Stepping outside, the sheriff encountered snow halfway to his knees. He looked up, pasted immediately in the face by giant white flakes. Walking toward the four-wheel-drive Ford Explorer he purchased almost immediately after taking office, he realized he now had justification for such a purchase.

Painted in the dull brown and tan colors of most all Indiana county police vehicles, it had a third color of snowy white atop the roof and hood. From the door, the Orange County seal shimmered against the exterior lights from the tavern. He opened the door, climbed in, and started the vehicle to let it warm up a few minutes.

When he stepped out of the Explorer, he fished a cigarette from his breast pocket, lighting it quickly before staring upward at the thousands of snowflakes dropping gracefully from the sky. Though most restaurants and bars still allowed smoking within their facilities, he chose to keep his habit from public view. Feeling as though he spent his career under a microscope, the sheriff attempted to be his own public relations specialist.

Elections brought out mudslinging, so he tried his best to maintain a flawless image and record while he held office.

A few minutes later, his vehicle's heater produced adequate heat, so he took a final drag, flicked the cigarette away and climbed inside. He flipped on the windshield wipers, ready to see what Guthrie needed at the dome.

Something told him he wasn't going to like what he found.

***

The drive to the hotel did little to knock the mounds of snow from Roland's vehicle. Unable to drive the speed limit because of the slick roads, it took longer than ten minutes to arrive.

Using the back entrance, which required a code to open the security gate, the sheriff typed in the code given to any police officers who patrolled the area. The gate slowly moved aside, revealing an unplowed road ahead.

"Shit," he muttered to himself, wishing the eventual change in ownership didn't create such piss poor conditions during the transition.

By no means a long driveway, Roland discovered it took several minutes to navigate because of snowdrifts. Able to observe the grounds from the garden lighting, he saw nothing disturbed, and no vehicles other than Guthrie's sedan.

Considering at least one person remained on hotel security detail at any given time, county and local officers had no keys to the dome. The sheriff, on the other hand, had a master key for the hotel and several other significant buildings within his vehicle. Many local businesses allowed police and fire departments to keep copied keys on their vehicles to avoid forced doors or broken windows on emergency runs.

Stepping from his vehicle, Roland snatched the keys from behind his seat since Guthrie didn't step out the backdoor, or either of the main entrances, to meet him.

Instead of simply using the backdoor, the sheriff made his way along the veranda, which had only a dusting of snow the winds had deposited onto its concrete surface. The front steps, however, appeared engulfed by white mounds.

Like the rest of the grounds, they were left unattended during the brief snowstorm.

Roland preferred the days when volunteers participated on a daily basis. The hotel and grounds were always spotless back then, but since Clouse had decided to sell the place, their role diminished. No longer was the hotel a historic landmark in desperate need of funding to save its future. It now had a business face that indicated volunteers were being phased out in lieu of design teams stepping onto the grounds.

He reached the first set of glass doors, tugging lightly on one of them. Much to his surprise, it opened. The security personnel and volunteers typically kept it locked at all times after tours ended.

Hesitantly stepping inside, he pulled the next set of doors open. Once inside, he stood perfectly still a moment as his eyes adjusted to the low lighting inside the hotel. Even the atrium ahead seemed dim because snow covered the dome, and the dusk was readily approaching outside.

When he finally took a step, the noise echoed throughout the hotel, giving him the creeps. Roland immediately headed for the security office, prepared to demand some answers from Guthrie once he found him. Nothing seemed out of place *except* for the retired trooper's call.

The observation room where the security personnel monitored the hotel grounds was literally several feet down the hall. He walked the distance to the door, finding it slightly ajar, which seemed unusual. The troopers typically sat inside, keeping the door locked behind them, or locked whenever they walked their rounds.

While the hotel had no security cameras, the room itself provided a great vantage point because it allowed the troopers to observe the garden, the road leading to the front gate, and some of the back parking lot.

Pushing the door in slowly, he listened to it creak as he cautiously slid past the door itself. He focused on the far room where the troopers typically sat. The sheriff's trained eyes immediately spied a small crimson stream atop the floor, setting off alarms within his mind.

Instinctively, he reached for his firearm, but he had gone home to change before heading to the bar. Frequenting taverns in his official uniform made for bad public opinion during an election year.

As he moved closer to the room, a black shoe came into view. Knowing Guthrie often wore casual dress attire, he swallowed hard, beginning to wonder if all the gruesome murder scenes he missed before taking office looked like this.

Guthrie was sprawled face-down on the floor, his eyes still open with a pool of blood beneath his body. Roland felt horrified as he knelt beside the fresh corpse, seeing a stab wound in the man's back, but no knife. Looking to the man's clip-on holster, he also found no gun.

From habit alone, he touched the neck to feel for a pulse, finding none. No rise of the chest, or the back in this case, indicated Guthrie certainly wasn't breathing. Even if Roland attempted CPR, the lack of blood inside the retired trooper's body would make the effort futile.

He had just confirmed Guthrie was forced to call him, but by whom?

Before assessing the murder further, he looked around to ensure his own safety. Seeing no one, he wondered where the knife and the murderer had gone.

Carefully stepping around the body, he reached for the phone atop the desk. Plucking it from the receiver, he placed it near his ear, hearing no dial tone. Either the weather had somehow taken out the phone lines, or someone cut the hotel's phone line intentionally.

Roland suspected the latter.

"Shit."

He reached for his cellular phone, but a noise outside the main door drew his attention before he freed it from his belt.

Exercising extreme caution because he was unarmed, Roland walked toward the door, seeing nothing around him that appeared useful as a weapon. Why someone would kill Guthrie escaped him, but what concerned him more at the moment was why that person lured him to the hotel.

Nearing the door, he peered from side to side without framing himself directly inside the doorway. The last thing he wanted to do was make himself an easy target, so he looked across the room, seeing a second door within the same room. A bookshelf blocked it to prevent people from using it as an entrance to the security room.

He walked to it hurriedly, trying the knob without moving the shelving unit.

The knob refused to turn.

Deciding against smashing down the door and creating a ruckus, Roland moved toward the other door, giving a quick peek outside before stepping outside the door. He scooted to the area he knew was safe, giving a look the other way from the corner of his eye. Seeing he was safe, the sheriff breathed a sigh of relief, catching his breath a moment.

Able to see a little over twenty feet in either direction, the sheriff wondered if either of the bending hallways was safe to travel. The circular shape of the entire hotel made walking around the floors a mystery every time. Only the lights and doors seemed to remain in place, because the floor and ceiling were simply one continuous pattern if they were the only thing a walker looked at.

Picking a direction, Roland walked along the dim hallway. The only lighting came from small light bulbs shaped like candles in sets of three. They were spaced far enough apart that they lit the hallway, but didn't put out much overall light.

As he neared an entrance to the atrium, Roland pulled out his cell phone, using the contact function to call his department. Putting the phone up to his ear, he heard nothing but a strange airy silence.

One look at his phone indicated he had no signal. The severe weather likely blocked incoming and outgoing cell phone signals, as well as any satellite dish reception.

Alone and weaponless, Roland decided to go for help, rather than search for the killer himself. He crossed the atrium to the back exit where his Explorer was parked.

Pushing the white exit door open, he stood in shock a moment at the scene laid before him.

The hood of his vehicle looked like an open mouth, except its tongue had been ripped out. Strands of wires and spare parts were scattered randomly across the engine block. He didn't have to move from the doorway to know his Explorer wasn't starting anytime soon.

His mind raced for a solution to the dangerous dilemma he found himself trapped within. Walking seemed foolish because he wasn't dressed for long-term exposure to the cold, and he could envision a driver turning him into road kill after recklessly driving too fast in the snow and ice.

Besides, the closest business had to be almost a mile down the road. Many businesses closed early because of the storm, so finding one open might prove a craps shoot.

An idea suddenly struck him that the sixth floor suite had a phone, even if none of the other rooms did. Determined to exhaust every other possibility before walking, he turned around to find the nearest stairwell or elevator inside the hotel.

As he spun around a dark blur caught his eye before something heavy hit the side of his head, sending him spiraling down into an unconscious heap.

Chapter 12

Throughout the afternoon, the caterer provided snacks for the group until dinner was served in the late afternoon. Most of the guests, McCully included, spent the day milling around the mansion, thinking about the hotel.

Toward the end of their dinner, Laura stood up suddenly, stating she wasn't feeling very well. After barely eating, she excused herself from the table, informing Jana she planned to rest upstairs for an hour or two.

McCully had overheard part of the conversation, so he talked to Jana a moment after everyone had finished dinner. She walked with him into the living room, while most of the guests went upstairs or talked in the entertainment room.

"Was Laura okay?" he inquired.

"I think so. She said she had a headache and a little dizziness."

"So how does working for one of the richest men in the country suit you?"

Jana returned a cautious smile.

"I don't actually work for him. He's a client."

McCully shrugged.

"You know what I mean."

"I suppose I do. And to answer your question, it can be a little intimidating."

Both of them walked toward the fireplace, which radiated heat throughout the room while providing most of the light, since the overhead chandelier was dimmed.

"What about *you*?" Jana asked. "You must have stories from life on the road."

"You know, it looks the same everywhere we go. There isn't much to tell, because we're always crammed in some hotel room, or riding in the back of a tour bus. I don't get a whole lot of time for sightseeing."

"Still, it must be somewhat adventurous. I've only left Indiana a couple times my whole life."

"And I've only *been* to Indiana a few times. My father likes performing at the Little Nashville Opry."

"Maybe I'll come see you perform, since I have more time on my hands."

McCully turned to see her expression, finding her a bit glum.

"Been too busy living the American dream?" McCully asked as they stood before the roaring fire, sticking their hands out to absorb the heat.

Jana let a disgruntled sigh answer his question in part.

"I thought I was happily married, beginning the perfect family, but I guess we drifted apart without me knowing it."

"What happened?" McCully asked before realizing it sounded like he was prying. "If you don't mind my asking."

"I started hearing things at my old job about him. People raised questions. They asked me how life at home was going. That sort of thing. Then one day he served me with divorce papers at the worst possible time in my life."

McCully said nothing, simply trying to be a good listener. He could tell it pained Jana to speak about the divorce, yet it appeared therapeutic for her.

"He timed it perfectly so that he could get custody of our daughter, then he ran off to Georgia with his new fling. Now I only get to see Miranda once a month on weekends, and some holidays. I've been saving back for a good lawyer, so I can take him to court for full custody."

"How old is your daughter?"

"Four. She's been confused by all of this."

"I'd imagine so. Sounds like your ex wanted his cake and ate it, too."

Jana wiped her eye, though she hadn't cried. McCully felt bad for her, coming from a very close family himself. If his father had ever been unfaithful, he did an incredible job of covering his tracks.

"I'm sorry," Jana apologized. "I didn't mean to bring this down on you."

"It's okay. Really."

"No it's not. I'm supposed to be the professional salesperson and here I am babbling on about my personal woes."

McCully understood exactly what it was like having no one to talk to. It felt good to release pent up frustration every so often.

"It's not that I really minded him wanting out of the marriage," Jana said almost as a way of closing their conversation. "It's just the way he went about it, waiting until I was making less money at work so he could take me to the cleaners in court."

"Some people think the world revolves around them," McCully offered. "I still tend to think people who fight the good fight find true happiness in the end."

Jana looked at him, almost amused by the words.

"True words from a songwriter?"

"I like to think so."

Jana looked toward the foyer.

"I guess I'd better get back to some hostess duties before they have to come find me."

McCully nodded, thinking he had a few things to discuss with Oswalt when he found his agent. But first, he wanted a few minutes of quiet time.

He discovered some of the group members talking within their cliques when he passed the living room area. Not much for conversation about stocks, economic development, or war stories, he walked upstairs, finding a set of double doors along the mansion's rear.

He opened them, stepping onto a second story deck that provided a beautiful view of the woods behind the mansion.

Though cool outside, it felt nice to be in the elements a moment. He felt a need to clear his head, because the visions had left him worried about the overnight stay. Granted, nothing within them indicated danger, but his visions typically ended badly. They were appearing inside his mind for a reason.

"You okay, kid?" Oswalt asked, stepping onto the deck with him a moment later, packing his pipe with tobacco.

"I'm not sure. This whole trip seems warped."

Giving a suspicious smirk, his agent seemed to sense he wasn't getting the full story.

"I'm sure the fact that you're keeping your distance as though the rest of us were lepers isn't helping much."

"Sorry about that. I just have a lot on my mind."

"You were a chatterbox until we got here, Dave. If you don't tell me what's the matter, I'll have to tell your daddy you were misbehaving under my care."

McCully chuckled. His father tended to have a mother hen nature concerning his band members, but it stopped short of having Oswalt report to him.

He hoped.

"Something about this whole trip is giving me the willies, Frank. Duncan thinks I'm nuts, but there was a photo of his grandfather in the museum, and I think I've seen the guy before."

McCully knew he was telling a half-truth to his agent, but he needed to say something about what he'd seen before he went crazy.

Oswalt lit his pipe before exhaling bluish-gray smoke as he stared at the snow, evidently digesting what McCully told him.

"You having one of those, uh, episodes again?"

"You might say that."

An uncomfortable silence fell between them for several seconds.

"We're in the middle of some highly unusual weather for this area, I've got what I can only imagine might be ghosts inside my mind, and this mansion doesn't do much to reassure me that we're in safe seclusion."

"You're paranoid, Dave. I think your schedule is getting to you."

"Maybe I am a little worried, but my schedule has nothing to do with it. I heard through the grapevine Martin Smith built this mansion before his death."

Oswalt puffed on his pipe, the name obviously not registering in his mind.

"Dr. Smith," McCully repeated again. "The guy they think was responsible for close to two dozen deaths around the hotel grounds."

"I thought he died in some accident outside the hotel."

"I don't think so."

Oswalt appeared openly skeptical.

"You think he's back from the dead to come after us?"

"No, but this mansion is extremely weird the way it's laid out. The stone carvings, the open second floor, the fact that we can't access the third level."

"You're being paranoid. That's all there is to it."

McCully nearly missed the last statement because his eyes fell to the ground below them, spying a set of footprints in otherwise undisturbed snow. He followed them to the mansion, needing to lean over the top of the railing to see that they ended to his right.

He felt reasonably certain they stopped near the kitchen area.

Some sort of steel access door had created a snow angel wing of sorts across the ground when it opened. McCully gauged that it was recently used, having no idea where it led. If the caterer had used it to discard something, no evidence remained atop the snowy accumulation.

"You even listening to me?" Oswalt asked testily, catching his attention, though he had missed the past few statements his agent issued.

"Something about me being paranoid and a disgrace to my family?"

"Right on one count. You might be the other if you keep acting so odd."

McCully decided against pointing out the footsteps to Oswalt, suspecting his agent might get the others to lock him inside a closet.

"Let's talk about something else," he suggested instead.

"Good idea."

Oswalt sounded concerned, yet somewhat irritated. He hated hearing anything about the visions, probably because he knew they typically led to disaster somewhere for someone.

Visions about the hotel had to make him uneasy, much like they kept McCully on edge.

Knocking his pipe against the balcony railing, Oswalt let the spent tobacco fall to the ground below, obviously perturbed from their discussion. His shoulders openly shivered, indicating his indoor attire no longer protected him from the elements.

"You know, I think I'll join the others downstairs," he said suddenly. "I need to clear my mind."

"I'll catch up," McCully said, wanting some more time to himself.

Perhaps enough time to investigate the tracks below him.

He was about to head inside when Duncan appeared, blocking his egress from the balcony.

"What brings you up here?"

Duncan produced a humidor from inside his leather jacket, pulling a cigar from it, saying nothing. McCully suddenly felt uncomfortable around the man, as though they were both on the verge of spilling secrets, but neither wanted to speak first.

"I always enjoy an after-dinner cigar," Duncan confessed as he sliced one end evenly with a guillotine cigar cutter, sauntering past McCully on the balcony.

"Can't say I've ever taken up the habit."

"Not really a habit," Duncan corrected him. "These are all natural, so they don't have the addictive chemicals like cigarettes. Some people like wine, just like some of us like cigars. It's not a fix, but rather a satisfaction."

McCully wasn't sure what brought about the sermon, but as Duncan used a butane lighter to light the cigar in front of him, rather than traditionally, he felt compelled to ask.

"Why do you light it down there?"

"Butane gives it better flavor than a regular lighter. You don't taste any of the gas this way. And it makes for a more even burn."

McCully nodded, though still uneducated on the finer points of cigar etiquette. He had enough pointers for one night, so he decided to leave, or steer the conversation elsewhere.

The one thing he clearly understood was the bond, perhaps more than simple lineage that Duncan shared with his great-grandfather. Their bond transcended time. Both enjoyed cigars and vast wealth, but their traits and appearance seemed remarkably similar to the casual observer lucky enough to know both of them in a limited way.

Andrew rode horses, while his grandson preferred the newer, steel version of riding adventure.

"You going to shave that rug of yours anytime soon?" Duncan inquired momentarily, making conversation since they both skirted the real issue between them.

McCully rubbed his new beard almost absently. He had grown it during the holidays, since his father's band didn't have another gig until February. George McCully believed in family time around the holidays, and despite pleas from his fans, took nearly a month off from touring every year around the holiday season.

"I kind of like it, but my father will say it's not very traditional bluegrass."

"You're lucky. I can't even grow a good one."

"It'll be gone by the time we hit the road again," McCully stated, always the dutiful son. "West Coast in February, the central states in March, and back home for spring. Not much ever changes with our schedule."

"Weekends only," Duncan commented thoughtfully. "Must be a bummer sometimes."

"It's not so bad. We practice during the week, but I have a lot of time to write songs and get things done."

"I don't see a wedding band on that strumming hand of yours."

McCully realized this was probably the deepest conversation he and Duncan had ever engaged in. Still, it seemed to be leading back to the topic he wanted to avoid.

"Seems to me you don't have one either, Dan. Or was that a common-law marriage you ended last year?"

Duncan cleared his throat, indicating McCully had gone a bit far with his retaliation.

"I'd really appreciate it if you came clean with me about my grandfather," Duncan finally said after a few puffs on the cigar.

"I really don't know much," McCully replied. "You're not going to believe me, but I saw your great-grandfather in a dream of sorts. Except it was real."

Standing with his hands placed carefully atop the railing, Duncan stared at the nearby barren trees. His eyes wandered to the ground, evidently noticing the footprints in the snow by the way his eyes widened momentarily. Even so, he said nothing for a moment.

"Andrew died under strange circumstances," he finally said. "I thought maybe you knew something about his death that you weren't telling me."

"I only know what I've seen," McCully said. "Did he have a friend named Ben Williams?"

Duncan shrugged.

"I heard a lot of the stories about him when I was a kid. I've slept since then."

"I'll take that as a 'no'?"

It took a moment for Duncan to answer. He appeared discontent with their direction of their conversation.

"I'm not sure where you're going with this dream thing, but I wish you'd be straight with me about what you know."

"I don't know the whole story, and you're not telling me how your grandfather died."

McCully hesitated before making his next statement.

"I understand you're very much for buying the hotel, but something isn't right about those grounds. How much do you know about what happened there a few years ago?"

Duncan stood a moment, fingering his cigar before taking a thoughtful drag.

"Enough to know it's over and Mr. Clouse is moving on. You've got to understand this is my one shot to live out my life's dream. There are people in the valley counting on me to pull this off."

"I'm not against you. In fact, I might be the only one guaranteed to vote your way when the time comes. That's assuming nothing comes up that changes my mind."

"Such as?"

"Like finding out what happened here a few years ago isn't going to happen all over again. You live around here half the year. What happened?"

Duncan grunted to himself.

"I was in Tennessee when most of it unfolded. The locals say there was a cover-up of sorts, but they aren't sure what happened."

"What kind of cover up?"

"They think Clouse paid off police, and possibly the newspaper, to keep things under wraps, because the cops were very tight-lipped about the findings on the hotel grounds."

"What do *you* think?"

"I'm a businessman. What I think is irrelevant to what the future holds. What *our* future holds if we buy the place."

McCully preferred Oswalt's cold shoulder to his present company. The idea of Duncan neglecting the hotel's sordid past worried him.

"It's getting cold out here," he said, trying to brush past Duncan to the warm interior inviting him back.

"Wait," Duncan said, clasping his hand.

McCully felt as though static electricity passed through his body, but in reality his mind traveled to a different time and place once again.

***

"You can't possibly pass up an opportunity like this," the man McCully now knew as Ben Williams told Andrew Duncan.

McCully recognized the area as the rear of the hotel, probably in the early 1920s, picking up where his first hotel vision left off. Apparently, several years later than the vision where Williams and Duncan planned to ride horseback, things seemed rather tense between them.

The third man appeared stoic, almost unmoving and uncaring. Oswalt was the most driven man McCully knew personally, but this man seemed set on one goal, his green eyes burning into Andrew Duncan.

"What you're proposing isn't right," Duncan argued. "On so many levels it's just not right."

"There's going to come a day when you and the millions you've amassed are going to retire and live it up," Williams stated. "But one day you're going to grow old and all the money in the world isn't going to change the fact that you're a mortal man. What I'm proposing isn't something we don't do anyway, in some shape or form."

"What you're proposing is *murder*, plain and simple," Duncan virtually spat back.

He nervously puffed on his cigar a moment more, refusing to look the third man in the eye. He barely glanced at the man, and never more than a split-second at a time. It appeared Williams was the one vote he needed to swing his way, because he wanted no part of whatever conspiracy had been forged without his full consent.

Though he respected Duncan's moral stand, McCully felt appalled such a conversation ever took place on the hotel grounds. He might have expected mob hits ordered by Al Capone or other notorious gangsters who stayed in the valley, but this was something completely out of the blue.

What on earth did these two men want done?

"Think of it as an insurance policy," Williams said, unwavering against his friend's argument.

"I can't believe we're even having this conversation, Ben. First of all, we're talking a lot of money, second of all, you don't know if these cubes do anything or not, and thirdly, you're talking about taking human lives to find out if they work."

"They work. I've seen it."

Drawing on his cigar, Duncan appeared unconvinced and as visibly hostile to the idea as ever.

"Seen it, huh?"

Williams nodded, not revealing any details. The look on his friend's face soured completely, knowing Williams had crossed the line of no return in both their friendship and moral corruption.

"If they work, who would be willing to sell off such a device?"

Duncan was obviously covering every angle to distance himself from whatever proposition Williams and the mystery man brought to him.

"We've found a man whose father used the cubes before his murder. I told him we'd bury the things where no one would ever find them and he believed me. The fool doesn't see what a complete waste that would be."

"I think the man knows what happened to his father was a result of using those cubes. Whether they work or not, they have a power over people, Ben. Now you're falling prey to it."

"You're not looking at this the right way, Andy. This is an opportunity — a dream come true."

The look on Duncan's face indicated he had heard enough, and there was no changing his mind. He gave an unsettled look to his friend, then a downright hateful stare toward the other man.

"You can both go to hell," he said before storming off toward the main entrance. "And you probably will."

Both men looked after him a moment, then turned grim as they continued their conversation.

"I thought you said he'd back us on this," the mysterious man said.

"Give me another day or two. I can bring Andy around to our way of thinking."

"No," the other said sternly. "He's a liability. We can't afford the risk of him telling anyone else our plans."

Williams apparently understood exactly what the man meant. He appeared unhappy about the idea of killing his friend, but a realization crossed his face that indicated the plan came before all else.

"What do you have in mind?" he asked.

Another jolt took hold of McCully's body and mind, returning him to the present.

He felt unnerved a moment, looking at Duncan, but he reassured himself it was the great-grandson standing before him, and not the man who refused unethical advances.

"What the hell was that?" Duncan asked, a perplexed, worrisome look scrawled across his face.

"Your grandfather was murdered," McCully stated as no other words came to mind.

Taking a step back, Duncan dropped his cigar, which the snowy balcony instantly swallowed whole. He didn't bother to pick it up because his eyes locked on McCully without blinking.

"Murdered how?"

"I'm not sure the 'how' is as important as the 'why' in this case."

Duncan shook his head in disbelief.

"You're telling me you just saw in a split-second's time why my great-grandfather died?"

"It was only a second?" McCully questioned, wondering how his mind processed the visions so quickly.

"You jumped like your ass had just been bit, kid."

McCully decided not to pursue any more answers because he felt it was more important to focus on solving the mystery that revealed itself in pieces.

"Your grandfather was involved with some shady individuals," he stated. "They wanted his money to fund some kind of buy, but he refused to give his support. He knew they were going to murder someone, so he refused to help. After he left, they decided to kill him so he wouldn't foil their plans."

Duncan appeared skeptical, but in some small way, accepting. He walked around a moment, occasionally scratching his head. McCully knew people liked to test psychic powers, to see if the bearers were legitimate, and he sensed Duncan wanted proof of his abilities. The great-grandson seemed to sense McCully's ability, though unable to verbalize his accusation.

Unlike regular psychic powers, visions chose to appear when they wanted to. McCully couldn't simply touch objects and pick up mental images of the owner's life. He could only report the facts.

"It's been said Andrew's son thought he was killed to cover something up," Duncan finally revealed. "My family thought it was something more than an accident, but they could never prove anything."

"How did he die?"

"That's what seemed really odd, almost symbolic if you think about it. He was found with severe head injuries beside the Monon Route railroad tracks. The authorities said they thought he got drunk and walked into a moving locomotive. There were two problems with that. One, he seldom drank heavily, and two, he knew the railroad exceptionally well after helping bring it to the valley."

"Whatever he got involved in is still a danger today, or I wouldn't have seen it."

Duncan's face corkscrewed.

"Are you a psychic or something?"

"I have...abilities. And until now, I've been able to suppress them. Something about this place is bringing them back with a vengeance."

Duncan appeared openly perplexed. Not only was he digesting information from the vision, but his dreams of owning the hotel were teetering atop a dangerous slope.

"Unless you come up with some proof that we're in danger, I don't want to tell the others anything about this."

"Me neither. I'm not going to endanger your pet project unless I know what's wrong around here."

"How can you be sure something *is* wrong?"

"These visions don't come to me unless something bad is coming. I've never had a vision go back in time before, so there must be something important I need to know."

Duncan turned, opening the door with a purpose to return inside. He stopped in the threshold, facing McCully once again.

"If you find anything else out, I'd like a heads up."

"So you believe me?"

"I don't think you're completely crazy. Right now, that's the best I can give you."

He stepped inside, shutting the door behind him.

"I guess that'll have to do," McCully muttered to himself.

Chapter 13

Jana watched as the caterer pulled out of the driveway, chancing the trip home through the snowstorm.

She felt somewhat depressed because she hadn't planned on staying overnight at the mansion. With no change of clothes, and no room to speak of, she would stay in the servants' quarters, or one of the empty rooms upstairs.

When she last listened to the radio, the news sounded bleak. Traffic jams lined the roads between West Baden and Bloomington because over a foot of snow had already fallen. Southern Indiana townships typically remain unprepared for anything more than a dusting of snow. Most small towns purchase only one snowplow, putting tax dollars toward more practical equipment.

Most everything else had gone according to plan. The tour went well, the dinner was excellent, and plenty of snacks and leftovers remained. One thing the guests didn't have to fear was starvation.

"You look bummed," Keith Sanders said as he approached her, putting forth an understanding grin.

"It could be worse," Jana thought aloud. "Better to stay here than ruin tomorrow for all of you."

Keith stared outside a moment, virtually mesmerized by the white flakes drifting toward the ground.

"We don't see that down in Texas."

"I suspect you don't," Jana said, giggling conservatively.

She hated appearing the least bit unprofessional around the group. Judith Parks in particular seemed to eye her every move like a madam grooming a pageant candidate.

Accustomed to the pressure of being perfect around investment groups, Jana presented the hotel tour equally well to all three groups. Being around this set of investors felt good, especially because Keith and Red were such characters.

Every so often during the tour they made quirky remarks or played tricks on one another. Their brotherhood was evident, despite the fact they lived hundreds of miles apart.

"Can I ask you something?" Jana asked, noticing Keith hadn't once removed his hat all day long.

Even at dinner, he kept it on after Red removed his.

"You've had that on all day," she said, nodding toward his Stetson. "Is that customary for ranchers?"

"Ah," Keith said thoughtfully. "A true cowboy doesn't take off his hat," he admitted, "but *my* reason for leaving it on is the diminishing hairline underneath it."

"Someone in your position shouldn't have to worry about his image," Jana said, trying to avoid saying something inappropriate.

"Maybe I just don't have enough other things to worry about," he said casually with a genuine smile.

Jana looked out the window, wondering how any of them would escape the confines of the mansion's grounds if no one plowed or shoveled the driveway. She doubted the small county road beside the West Baden Springs Hotel would receive professional plowing anytime soon.

Keith spoke a moment later, breaking her concentration.

"You mentioned during dinner there was a DVD presentation about the hotel we could watch if we wanted to. Duncan's been pestering us to watch the dang thing, so I thought we could gather the troops and get it over with."

Jana glanced into the living room space, seeing several of the Star Investments members killing time.

"We'll have to get everyone into the entertainment room," Jana informed him. "I'll look upstairs if you want to rally everyone down here."

Most everyone had to be in one of two rooms downstairs, if they hadn't retreated to private quarters on the second floor.

"Sure," Keith said before walking into the mammoth living room.

Jana heard him yell something playfully at his brother while she ascended the stairs.

Within a few minutes, she found McCully returning from the outside balcony, Duncan unpacking a few things, and Judith exiting her room after a change of clothes. Even in casual dress, she appeared somewhat regal. Jana thought she conducted herself very well now that she had met the woman. Everything she had heard suggested Judith Parks was a battleaxe in the business world, but she said nothing unkind about the hotel or anyone around her.

Skipping Laura Compton's room because of her early departure from dinner, Jana walked downstairs. When she entered the entertainment room Jana did a quick headcount, finding everyone present except for Laura.

"I decided not to knock on her door," Jana said.

Red looked to Keith, who returned a sour stare, as though they were airing dirty laundry.

"I'll go check on her and see if she's feeling better," Keith finally said, heading out of the room.

Oswalt leaned in toward Jana.

"Keith and Laura had something going a couple years back," he said just above a whisper.

Jana realized the rancher certainly did have a thing for younger women, wondering how innocent their first encounter had really been.

A few minutes later, Keith returned to the room, calling for Red to join him. Everyone sensed something odd had Keith worried.

The brothers walked upstairs together, returning a few minutes later with worried expressions.

"She wasn't up there," Keith finally announced. "We gave every room a quick search and didn't find her."

Everyone suddenly appeared a bit more concerned.

Jana suspected Laura wasn't one to go exploring the mansion alone, probably having little need to see either kitchen area, or the dining room they used just over an hour ago.

Going outside seemed completely insane, while the idea of her exploring other guest rooms upstairs was unlikely. Somehow, without explanation, Laura had vanished from the mansion. Jana wondered if her early departure from dinner might have been an excuse for something else altogether.

"We saw footsteps out back," McCully said, thumbing toward Oswalt.

Everyone looked their way with mixed reactions.

"We didn't think anything of it," Oswalt spoke up. "There was one set of tracks that looked like they came from the woods toward the hotel."

"Let's take a look then," Keith ordered more than suggested.

Jana had an idea he was the group leader in more than one capacity.

Everyone moved toward the double French doors beside the entertainment room. Jana followed Keith outside, noticing the footsteps indeed pointed toward the hotel, namely a steel door with a pushbutton code box above the handle.

"What's the combination?" Keith asked her.

"I don't know."

"Where does it lead?"

"I'm not sure. Probably the basement, because there's no door in the upper kitchen area."

Keith's expression crossed between exasperation and dread as Jana suspected he somehow blamed her for Laura's disappearance.

While the group stood awkwardly at the doorway, Jana stole a glance their way, noticing more carvings along the mansion's foundation. Subconsciously she wondered if the six out front were equaled by six more along the back.

Everyone made room for Keith as he returned inside, his cowboy boots covered with snow. He quickly stomped the white powder off, then looked to Jana.

"Let's have a look downstairs," he stated. "I'll let you lead the way."

No one else moved from the lobby area, worrying Jana because Keith was acting erratically compared to his normal composure.

Jana led him through the kitchen, then into the cooking and storage area downstairs. They reached the bottom step rather quickly, allowing Keith to search around the walls for a doorway.

She hesitantly followed his lead, wondering where the steel door went, if not the basement. Agreeing with Oswalt's assessment that the footsteps aimed toward the building instead of the woods, she wondered if the group had two mysteries to solve.

"This is all concrete down here," Keith noted, staring at the walls.

A large storage shelf covered the back wall of a portion that jutted back from the main wall. Keith walked up to the shelf, examining it carefully. From what Jana could see behind the shelving unit, everything appeared concrete.

Just like every other inch of the walls.

"Damn it," he said through clenched teeth.

"We still haven't checked the rest of the mansion," Jana said calmly. "There are a lot of rooms including closets, pantries, and bathrooms we can check."

"She's not a kid," Keith said a bit more harshly than he likely planned to. "She's not going to hide somewhere."

Unsure of what else to say, Jana turned to head upstairs. Keith lingered a moment, looking around to ensure he didn't miss any possible clue, then followed Jana.

When they reached the main floor, half the group was missing. Jana felt as though she was losing control of the situation, but after dinner the guests were on their own whether she stayed overnight or not.

Regardless of her liability, Jana wanted the guests to remain comfortable. What seemed like a flawless tour and layover, except for the snowstorm, seemed to be spiraling out of control.

"They went looking upstairs for Laura," Judith announced, calming Keith somewhat.

"We haven't checked out front," Jana suggested, never once imagining Laura had any reason to walk around outside.

Deciding to take initiative, mostly to keep Keith from suspecting her of wrongdoing, Jana took long strides toward the front door, unlocking three locks before pulling it open.

She gasped at the sight of a bearded man in camouflage, holding a hunting rifle, looking equally wide-eyed as though he were caught breaking the law.

Chapter 14

Jana thought momentarily about slamming the door and locking it, but the man pulled his free arm back from where the doorbell was located. His look went from surprised to somewhat needful. Reading his chocolate-colored eyes, Jana sensed he was no threat, but rather in danger of succumbing to the elements if he remained outside.

"Are you okay?" she asked, noticing he was shaking visibly, barely able to keep hold of the rifle through his gloves.

He stammered as he spoke.

"I can't find my dog," he stated as his teeth chattered.

Jana knew it wasn't extremely cold outside, but he wasn't dressed for a prolonged stay outside, wearing only one layer of clothing beneath his camouflage bib overalls. Much of his clothing appeared soaked, as though he had taken several tumbles in the snow, perhaps into some puddles.

"Who's this?" Keith questioned, approaching her from behind.

"I'm not sure. I think he's lost."

Giving what Jana termed a low growl, Keith stood there momentarily as though debating whether to continue searching for Laura or interrogate the lost hunter standing on their doorstep.

"Come in," Jana said, taking the man's hand to lead him inside.

Keith snatched the rifle away from the hunter as though he might be a terrorist luring everyone into a false sense of security before striking.

A fleeting glance was all the hunter gave his rifle, apparently thrilled to be indoors. He didn't show much emotion because he appeared to be in some form of mild shock.

Leading him toward a chair in the living room area, Jana helped him remove his jacket before sitting him down. His teeth continued to chatter, despite being in warmer quarters.

Duncan and Red entered the room, standing behind Jana like watchdogs.

"He's completely drenched," Jana said as she began removing his overalls. "We need to get him a change of clothes."

"I think the bedrooms have spare clothes in the closets," Red stated. "I'll see what I can find."

He looked to Duncan before walking away, indicating he shouldn't leave Jana alone with the stranger.

"What's your name, buddy?" Duncan asked, kneeling beside the stranger.

"Craig," the hunter answered with slow deliberation, as though he needed a moment to think about it. "Craig Jennings."

Duncan helped Jana pull down the overalls, revealing soaked blue jeans and a tattered flannel shirt. They were cold to the touch.

"Craig, I'm suspecting you weren't making snow angels out there. So how about you tell us what happened?"

"I decided I wanted to go rabbit hunting in the snow," he said slowly, though a bit more evenly with his drenched clothes being removed. "We just don't get snow down here very often, and they *are* in season."

He made the last statement defensively, as though someone might question his legal right to hunt.

"My dog went running into the woods and I couldn't find him. Before I knew it, I got lost because my tracks kept disappearing. Then I came across this place."

"Do you know where you are?" Jana asked.

"The mansion. No one's ever here, but I saw the cars outside, so I thought I'd try the buzzer."

Without Jennings noticing, Duncan made a strange face at Jana, as though he didn't believe the story, or thought it seemed suspicious.

"Do you work around here?" Jana asked him, deciding she wanted more information.

"I'm a shop teacher at the high school," he readily answered.

She didn't notice a wedding band on his left hand, so she decided to probe a bit further.

"Married?"

"Yeah," he answered, his head drooping a bit from embarrassment. "The whole reason I left the house was because me and the wife had a fight. I took the dog and went out to cool off."

He chuckled only a second or two.

"No pun intended."

Jana felt reasonably convinced the man spoke the truth, but Duncan proved to be a harder sell.

"We'll be right back, buddy," he said to Jennings before subtly leading Jana out of the room.

"What's the matter?" she asked once they were a distance away.

"Laura comes up missing and this guy shows up? It's gotta be more than coincidence."

"Have you seen what it's like out there?" she countered. "I'm surprised we haven't had stranded motorists asking for our help."

Duncan remained unwavering.

"It might be about time we call the police," he said.

"You're jumping to conclusions. Laura might still turn up, and this poor guy may simply be lost in the woods like he says."

"It's not likely she's going to turn up," McCully said as he approached them. "We've been everywhere in this place and there's no sign of her."

"What about outside?" Duncan asked, glancing toward Jennings, who shivered slightly as he sat in the cozy chair a room away.

McCully looked skeptical.

"Why the hell would she go outside?"

"I don't know," Duncan said, "but Keith is going to fly off the handle if we don't find her soon."

"Guilty conscience?" McCully asked with a sharp tone.

The exact meaning of the words eluded Jana, but she deeply suspected Laura and Keith had a relationship that somehow ended badly.

"Just get someone to go with you and check outside so he doesn't freak out," Duncan insisted.

McCully nodded before leaving to continue the search.

"We're treating this as though Laura was a defenseless creature left in the woods," Jana told Duncan. "You're all very quick to assume she hasn't wandered off somewhere on her own."

"Call me paranoid, but I'm beginning to wonder why Glenn Turner never showed up. All day we haven't been able to reach him, and now Laura disappears. I know there's a blizzard outside, but I'm starting to think Dave was right. Whatever bad karma the hotel has might be rubbing off on this place."

"We don't know that for certain, Mr. Duncan."

He shook his head negatively. Secretly, Jana couldn't help but share his concerns. Absolutely nothing had gone wrong with the first two visiting groups, but it seemed like nothing could go right for these people.

"Someone doesn't want this place to be bought," Duncan said. "It's just like before. Someone is going to do whatever it takes to scare people away from the hotel, even if it means taking innocent lives."

Jana felt as though her whole world was collapsing around her. Within ten minutes, the investment group's male members were reverting back to some primitive state of mind, prepared to suspect everyone around them with little or no proof of wrongdoing.

Even Duncan, whose dream since childhood was to own the hotel, seemed susceptible to the curse.

The lights flickered twice within an instant, bringing them back to the reality that there was indeed a snowstorm outside, and one of their companions was missing. Jana began to realize a walk outside was pure madness, drawing near the closest window to see the flakes falling faster, and more abundantly, than before.

"Does this place have a generator?" Keith asked, returning to her side.

"Yes," Jana answered from memory alone. "I believe it's outside."

A thought suddenly came to her.

"I think there are some cottages out back as well."

"Why didn't you mention that sooner?"

"My boss mentioned it in passing one time. They're down near the tree line, so you wouldn't see them unless you went looking for them."

Now dressed for the outdoors, as much as one could expect, Keith stood beside McCully, who had donned a coat to brave the cold weather. The pair reminded Jana of witch hunters, ready to go outside and cleanse the mansion of whatever evil was abducting its membership.

McCully looked less than thrilled about venturing outside, but the way his eyes kept shifting toward Keith indicated his faith in the man's leadership might be faltering.

Jana doubted some homicidal maniac was waiting to pick them off one by one, but she shared some of their concern over Laura's disappearance. All of the trouble at the hotel during Clouse's employment there, and his ownership later, supposedly concluded two years prior.

"Let's go," Keith told McCully, who followed him outside to brave the elements.

A moment later, Red returned from his upstairs search carrying a small pile of clothes with him.

"I found some shirts and pants that look to be in his size," he said. "And a blanket to help warm him up."

Jana followed him into the room where Jennings warmed his bones, beginning to remove more of his wet clothing by himself. Duncan tagged along because there was nothing else for him to do. Since their new guest had started to move, perhaps he could talk and reveal more of his story to them.

If he didn't, she feared the group might torture him until they heard something they wanted to hear, even if it wasn't true.

***

"It's freezing out here," McCully commented as he followed Keith down the length of the mansion's facade.

The reply came in the form of another grunt from Keith, likely suggesting he thought his colleague was spoiled. He often talked about the tough times in his life, and how he'd worked since his teenage years, breaking horses and mending fences to make ends meet.

To him, everyone else had life so much easier because they never worked nearly as hard for anything.

Every several yards McCully noticed a stone carving along the wall. They looked impressive, but he had little time to study them because keeping up with Keith's brisk pace required his full attention.

Snow came up to his knees, letting him know how Jennings got so wet during his trek. If not for the good lighting inside the mansion gleaming through the windows, their journey would be pitch black. The pair quickly made it to the far corner, peeking around to discover the cottages were little more than silhouettes half a football field's length away from them.

McCully wished he had found a flashlight somewhere within the mansion before stepping outside, but his day was comprised of one misfortune after another.

By no means a tracker or even a weekend camper, McCully had enough sense to realize there was no evidence of footprints outside the mansion's front door, except for the hunter's.

Jennings' footprints came directly from the road, without any sign of outgoing tracks.

When they reached the back corner of the grand building, he saw no tracks leading toward the cottages. Despite the snowfall, some evidence of tracks would have survived during the short time between Laura's disappearance and the present.

"No one's been there," he told Keith, who simply looked back at him with a look of disdain.

McCully wondered why exactly Keith's problem was, because he wasn't very forthcoming. It seemed as though he had some duty to find Laura at any cost.

Perhaps Keith figured the others would hold him responsible, or think *he* personally had something to do with her disappearance. McCully recalled him being around his brother most of the time, and close to several others, so Keith was undoubtedly innocent of any wrongdoing.

"Stay there, in case anything happens," Keith ordered.

McCully sighed audibly, but Keith never heard him because he was already halfway across the lawn toward the cottages. Staying at the corner, McCully split his attention between Keith and the engraving near the end of the mansion.

He hadn't really seen any of the carved messages along the back wall yet, but this one appeared far different than any of the six along the front. An unusual piece of artwork, the carving displayed a man smearing the blood of a human and a sacrificial lamb, both of which lay to either side of him. A pool of blood drained from each corpse as the man swiped them both with his hands, creating a mixture.

"Weird," McCully commented, seeing a number below the sculpted piece.

9:7.

He looked up again, finding Keith peering through the cottage windows like a child at a candy store, with both hands against the glass.

"Find anything?" he called.

Keith shook his head negatively.

"The rooms look empty. I need a flashlight."

"Good luck with that," McCully muttered to himself.

As though Keith understood what he said, McCully received a long, hard stare. It took a moment, but he then realized his colleague wanted him to find a flashlight inside the mansion. So far he hadn't seen any, but Jana probably knew where most things were located.

"I'll see what I can find," he said before turning toward the front.

Somewhat thankful to see the warm indoors, if only for a moment, he trudged through the snow until he reached the front door. As he turned the doorknob, he realized how cold his feet were from standing in snow for several minutes.

Jana stood outside the living room area as Red and Duncan helped Jennings change clothes, as though making certain they didn't mishandle him.

"Are there any flashlights around here?" he asked without hesitation.

"The kitchen," she answered, leading him that way.

"Is the hunter talking?" McCully asked as they crossed the foyer.

"He says he was hunting rabbits with his dog and got lost in the snow. He lives a few miles away, outside of town."

McCully realized little else aside from fields and a few swampy areas surrounded the mansion as far as the eye could see, making the story plausible. The man's timing, however, seemed absolutely terrible considering the events after dinner.

"Have we called the police, or let him phone his relatives?"

"We called 911, but they told us it might be hours before they can send someone out. Their cars can barely get through the snow, and they've been swamped with wrecks and people stuck in snowdrifts."

"So we're on our own," McCully muttered, beginning to believe Laura's only hope of being found was a larger search party.

Jana led him into the kitchen, finding several rechargeable flashlights alongside cupboards. She opened a few of the cupboard doors, showing him they had candles in case the power failed completely.

He picked out one of the flashlights with an orange exterior and large square ends like fire departments often use. He suspected it put out sufficient light for any situation, deciding to wait until he stepped outside before he tried it out.

"I'd better go check on his highness before he comes looking for me."

Jana's expression showed she agreed, but a guilty wave came over her, wiping it from her face immediately.

As McCully turned to leave, Jana called after him.

"Good luck."

He turned just long enough to give a reassuring grin, opening the front door to find Keith before the older man did something to get himself into trouble.

When he returned to the rear corner, McCully switched on the light, seeing no one in sight. Two trails of tracks seemed to lead everywhere around the cottages, then along the back of the mansion. His heart skipped a beat, immediately fearing the worst, but McCully calmed himself enough to begin looking.

For some reason the present situation reminded him a little bit of playing hide and seek with his cousins during childhood. He always remembered following their tracks through mud or snow, finding them quicker than they ever found him.

"Keith?" he called out.

No answer returned.

He yelled a bit louder several times over, receiving no reply.

Taking a quick look around the cottages and the nearby generator, McCully found no sign of Keith. He then followed the tracks behind the mansion, realizing halfway along the building's rear side they veered into the woods.

"Damn it," he said under his breath, quickly following them.

The tracks appeared to be made by one person, so if Keith was in any way abducted, he was slung over someone's shoulder. Since there was no sign of his Stetson anywhere, McCully felt somewhat relieved, knowing it would have toppled to the ground during a struggle.

"Keith?" he called out once more, praying for some kind of response.

A few seconds later, it came.

"Get over here, kid," he heard the man's soft drawl call through the woods.

Glancing to his left, he found the cattle rancher centered in a small clearing, staring at the mansion from a distance.

"What the hell are you doing?" McCully asked pointedly, since he feared the worst when he couldn't find the man.

"Look how tall that place is," Keith noted. "We only get to go up two floors."

"So?"

"So there's at least one more floor up there."

"You trying to say this place has secret passageways and tunnels?"

"It has *something*. It's just stone and plasterboard, kid. We can bust through it if we have to."

McCully felt his feet begin to tingle again from the cold.

"Let's make our way inside, unless you've got something else you want to search for out here."

Keith's head dejectedly bowed toward the ground, his thoughts likely consumed with finding Laura and shame for not having done so yet.

"Let's check these cabins real quick. Then we can get warm."

Chapter 15

"**C**an I call my wife?" Jennings asked Red once he was changed into warmer clothing.

"Sure," Red answered, trying to think of where the closest phone might be.

For some reason the living room and entertainment room didn't have phones, but the dining area and kitchen both did.

Thankfully, the hunter had recovered enough to undress himself and put new clothes on without assistance. Red and Duncan simply watched over him to make sure he remained in good health, and didn't mean harm to the guests.

When they removed his camouflage cap, they realized why Jennings needed headgear in the cold climate. His dark brown hair had receded to little more than a fringe, despite being somewhere in his forties. Red guessed the man to be close to ten years younger than himself.

Once he warmed up, the hunter spoke a little more often, giving Red hope that he was exactly who he said he was. Jennings appeared thankful for the hospitality, cautiously flashing a smile every so often.

"Come with me," Red instructed Jennings, who seemed somewhat stiff as he rose from the chair.

His new clothes weren't a perfect fit, but he seemed much more comfortable, and warm, inside them.

Duncan and Jana remained behind as Red took Jennings to the phone inside the dining room. They observed the new guest carefully, but remained in the foyer.

"Everyone's acting a little tense around here," Jennings noted. "Any particular reason why?"

"Let's just say you picked a bad time to arrive. Things have kind of fallen apart around here in the last hour."

Jennings gave him a quizzical look, but didn't press the issue.

Red handed him the receiver, watching as the hunter dialed a number, hating to deny the man privacy, but feeling little other choice.

Jennings seemed to sense mild trepidation, even hostility toward his arrival, but said very little about the subject. No one had taken the time to thoroughly explain Laura's disappearance to him, hoping perhaps he might say something out of place to reveal his true nature.

If he was hiding something.

"The line's dead," the hunter announced after a few seconds, when he finally placed the receiver to his ear.

Red hung up the phone, picked it up, then placed it to his own ear.

Dead silence.

"Shit," he grumbled.

Plucking the cellular phone from his side, he saw absolutely no signal bars visible, indicating the precipitation, and the clouds that brought it, blocked his phone's signal.

Inhaling deeply through his nose, Red tried to think of any reasonable means of communication, but none came to mind. Either local phone lines were down, or someone had cut the line leading into the mansion.

Neither prospect sounded good, but he dreaded the latter, wondering if someone had diabolical plans for the groups.

His mind wandered further, wondering if that particular someone might be part of his group.

"What's the matter?" Jennings asked while Red continued to stare at his cell phone.

"I guess we're cut off from the real world, my friend."

Red realized if someone had intentionally cut the phone line, which was still only a possibility, the hunter had to be innocent.

Unless he had a partner.

After all, he was already inside when the group dialed 911 for help.

Driving himself crazy over conspiracy theories wasn't productive, so Red shook his head, trying to free his mind of all negative thoughts. The possibility remained that a series of strange coincidences, beginning with Laura's disappearance, put the group on edge.

Red debated his next move when his brother walked through the door with McCully.

"Find anything?" he asked Keith.

"Not yet. The cottages were empty, but the generator looks good if we have any power problems."

Though not fantastic news, Red felt comforted that his brother returned so quickly with assurances that not every comfort inside the mansion was jeopardized. Without power, the group would be hard-pressed to stay warm, particularly over a two or three day span.

Keith shot Jennings a hard stare without provocation, so Red drew close to his brother.

"Take it easy," he said in a hushed voice. "I don't think he had anything to do with Laura disappearing."

"He better not have," Keith growled, "or he'll be getting the pointy end of my boot up his ass."

Red patted his brother on the shoulder gently.

"Take it easy, big brother. We'll find her."

"But in what condition?" Keith questioned, his blue eyes a bit misty from either concern over his former girlfriend, or the harsh weather.

Red knew better than anyone else in the group what Keith and Laura shared. His older brother had a reputation for dating younger women after his divorce almost ten years prior. The divorce stemmed from his wife wanting half of his money and a new life, but she made the mistake of waiting until their three children were legally adults, receiving far less in the settlement than she wanted.

Not until the divorce was final did Keith officially lay the groundwork for Lone Star Investments. He met Laura several years later, dating her a few years after that. Their relationship lasted just over a year, but it ended well, leaving their friendship and partnership through the firm intact.

So far as Red knew, the two never took their relationship to a sexual level again, though they remained close.

Now engaged to be married, Keith had dated the young lady for nearly two years, earning him a reputation as sugar daddy among some of his peers. Red knew they shared the same interests, originally set up on a blind date by a common friend. Keith didn't worry much about what other people thought, so Red turned the other cheek when he heard derogatory remarks about his brother's social life.

"What do we do now?" he asked of Keith.

"We search this place from head to tail until we figure out how to get to the third floor."

"Third floor?"

"You didn't notice how tall this place is?" Keith questioned.

"I guess I didn't think much about it."

Keith stood a moment, stealing a glance at Jennings, who had engaged McCully in conversation. Just when Red figured he was lost in thought, he spoke again.

"There aren't any doors or stairways leading up there, so I'm wondering if we can find an access hatchway to the attic, or whatever's up there."

"Shouldn't be hard to find."

"If we don't find anything, I want to tear through the ceiling until we find our way up there."

Red couldn't help chuckling despite the irritated expression his brother gave him.

"In case you didn't notice, we don't exactly have heavy tools around here."

"I'll use a screwdriver and pry away the ceiling tile if I have to."

Realizing his brother was serious, Red decided to suggest more logical alternatives.

"We'll help you look for a way up there. Maybe there's some tools and ladders in the garage."

Located on the other side of the mansion from the cottages and generator, the spacious garage had yet to be accessed by anyone from the group. Red had just remembered its existence himself.

"I can't believe I forgot all about checking back there," Keith said, ready to begin his search anew.

He started toward the door until Red caught him by the shoulder, lightly pulling him back.

"You're not going out there alone."

Keith's eyes immediately went toward McCully, but Red intervened, knowing the songwriter wasn't anxious to step outside again.

"I'll go with you."

Red thought a fresh pair of eyes might be useful if anyone was going outside again.

"Why don't you let me take someone else with me? You can start your search in here and save some time."

Keith looked hesitant about turning over control of the exterior search.

"You trust me, don't you?" Red prodded.

Continuing to balk, Keith's chest rose and fell as he took several deep, thoughtful breaths.

"Okay. But don't leave one stone unturned, little brother."

"I promise."

***

When searching for a companion to search the garage with, Red found himself limited on choices.

Oswalt was grumpy, not wishing to venture outside, Jennings was out of the question, McCully had just returned from the chilly weather, Jana and Judith couldn't help very well with moving heavy objects, and Duncan seemed preoccupied with his thoughts.

Red couldn't imagine Judith doing any kind of intensive labor to help him. By no means a lifetime prima donna, she had stated on more than one occasion her working days were well behind her because her money afforded her workers for her every need. He had little to say to her after their brief relationship, and faking any sort of friendship made it worse. What drew them together was their opposite nature.

Later, it served to drive them apart.

After weighing his options, he selected Duncan by default.

"You want me to go out to the garage with you?" were the first words Duncan uttered after Red explained the situation to him.

"It'll just take a minute," Red replied without trying to sound desperate. "We go out there, check for Laura, and come right back in. Keith is happy, every square inch of the grounds is checked, and we can sit back and wait for the police."

Duncan didn't appear impressed by the plan, but quickly resolved to get their task out of the way.

"I have to get my jacket and gloves," he said. "I'll be right back."

Red watched Duncan trudge upstairs to fetch his gear from his quarters. He couldn't understand how a simple overnight stay now bordered on complete disaster.

A few minutes later, Duncan returned with his motorcycle jacket and thick gloves. He even put on a cloth skullcap to keep his head warm. Anxious to get the task over with, he opened the front door for Red, who gladly led the way toward the garage.

With the snow falling indiscriminately, the driveway and yard appeared the same. Both had over a foot of white precipitation covering them, so Red simply walked behind the main building, looking for the garage near the woods.

Luckily he had snagged the flashlight from McCully before venturing outside, but it did little to penetrate the swirling mist of snow still coming down.

"Is that it?" Duncan asked, squinting to see through the white flakes.

"I think so," Red answered, discovering the outline of what appeared to be a large building a short distance from the mansion.

Set back from the main building, the garage was found down a small hill, which obscured it from view unless someone walked toward it.

"You can keep your shitty weather," Red commented as they drew near the building.

"This is new to me," Duncan replied. "It takes us years to accumulate this many inches of snow."

When the two finally reached the side door that accessed the garage, they looked to the door with a padlock in addition to a deadbolt and a conventional lock, exchanging weary glances.

"Figures," Red stated sourly. "I don't suppose you saw any remotes for the overhead doors around."

"Can't say I did."

Red looked around for any other way into the garage, finding several windows too far off the ground, the sealed overhead doors, and nothing else.

Since Duncan was wearing his heavy biker boots, Red decided to ask him the obvious question.

"Can you kick that door in?"

The reply came in the form of a strange expression and raised eyebrows.

"Please tell me you're kidding."

"I wish I were. If you can't, we're going to have to find some kind of battering ram."

Quickly sighing, Duncan turned his back to the door, kicking forcefully backward like a mule three times before the door began awkwardly falling inward along the hinged side. Strangely, the three locks continued to hold the secured side until Duncan gave the door one more swift kick, groaning painfully as he did so.

"You okay?" Red asked.

"Yeah," Duncan answered slowly. "My knees just aren't what they used to be." He held his right knee gingerly a moment before taking a few hesitant steps. "I'll be fine," he finally said.

Red stepped inside first, feeling for a light switch until he remembered to turn on the flashlight in his other hand.

After switching on the light, he found a panel nearby, bringing the entire garage's interior into plain view. One switch brought every fluorescent light overhead to life, while the second switch Red flipped turned on four powerful bulb lights that slowly gained strength over several seconds, much like gymnasium lighting.

Impressively large as the garage might have been, it held no vehicles, displaying everything openly to its two visitors. A smooth concrete floor awaited new vehicles, while the white aluminum walls looked brand new, with no discoloration, and no visible wear.

Able to hold four vehicles behind its overhead doors, the building contained additional square footage on a second level, only partially visible to the two men because stairs in the opposite corner invited them up to a wooden loft. They could see along the closest edge of the loft, but the rest was lost in the vast square footage.

"Take a look at that," Duncan said.

Red followed the man's stare to a smudged footprint near one of the overhead doors. What looked like a greasy outline from a distance horrified Red as he drew closer, kneeling down to examine it.

"Blood," he said, swiping a wet trace of the substance with two fingers. "And it's fresh."

Considering it wasn't dried or frozen, it had to be quite fresh.

"But there weren't any footprints outside," Duncan pointed out.

"No, but the way this snow is falling, it doesn't take long for tracks to get buried."

"But why just one print?"

Red shrugged before looking toward the loft area.

Duncan appeared very uncertain about checking the upstairs.

"I promised Keith I'd check every square inch of the place," Red told his colleague.

"I'm right behind you," Duncan reluctantly replied.

The entire climb up the stairs was well lit, removing any apprehension Red might have otherwise felt. Because they were constructed of wood they creaked, but neither man showed any outward fear as they neared the top.

Red felt certain he was going to find some bloody corpse atop the stairs, or a severed limb. Instead of finding the stuff of nightmares, he only noticed two small crates the size of footlockers in the far corner.

"You know, maybe I'm getting too caught up in this area's past," he confessed to Duncan. "I keep expecting all of these bad things, and none of them have turned up."

"I know what you mean."

While he popped the top off one crate, Duncan worked on the other. A few seconds later, both were open, revealing their contents.

"Now I kinda feel bad for kicking in the door," Duncan stated as he lifted several photographs and postcards out of the crate.

Red's box contained more of the same. Dozens of photographs, postcards, and souvenirs lined the crates from top to bottom, most of which appeared to capture the West Baden Springs Hotel during its heyday.

While Red contemplated his next move, Duncan continued to paw through the items until he stopped at one particular scrapbook, staring at a particular newspaper clipping inside it.

"What's wrong?" Red questioned.

"This is the newspaper article about my great-grandfather's death," he answered. "I haven't seen one like it for years."

"Did he die *here*?" Red felt compelled to ask.

"In the valley, near the railroad tracks," Duncan answered almost blankly before his eyes showed signs of life. "Can you help me carry one of these inside? I'd like to have a look through both boxes."

Not in the mood to argue, Red nodded affirmatively. He decided it wasn't much work carrying a little crate inside the mansion, though he questioned Duncan's thought process, considering they had more pressing issues to confront.

He continued to hold out hope that Laura's disappearance was her own doing, but as he descended the stairs, he knew Keith wasn't going to be pleased about their lack of findings.

Somehow, he suspected his older brother had occupied his time with a new search and rescue tactic.

Chapter 16

"I'm starting to think he's gone insane," McCully confessed to Jana as he watched Keith go from room to room, checking every ceiling, wall, and door he encountered.

No visible proof that a third floor even existed presented itself, but Keith seemed certain there was some kind of anomaly in the mansion that accessed such a place. McCully had seen movies with secret rooms and false bookcases that granted access to other areas of the house, but they typically had farfetched monsters and schemes he didn't see here.

"I'm starting to think Laura found a place to hide out for a while," Jana replied. "She hasn't even been gone that long."

Strangely enough, Judith and Oswalt kept the hunter company while McCully and Jana monitored Keith. Had Keith approached him with a sound, saner plan, McCully might have been inclined to offer help, but Keith wanted to check the entire second floor himself. The way things stood, McCully felt certain Oswalt and Judith had outsmarted him by rushing downstairs.

"I was never told of a third floor," Jana informed him, "and my job was to sell the place with the hotel if possible."

"You say 'was' like your career is over."

"I dare say it's not looking very promising at the moment."

"This isn't your fault," McCully said in his best assuring tone. "You weren't our babysitter."

Both of them paused to observe Keith leaving one room, entering the next in line just as quickly.

"I can't help but wonder what happened to Mr. Turner," Jana wondered aloud.

"He probably stopped off somewhere to get a motel with some bimbo."

McCully realized he had probably revealed too much about a fellow business partner.

"Strike that from the record," he added.

Jana laughed just a bit at the remark, despite the dire circumstances surrounding them.

"Glenn tends to get distracted easily," McCully said in place of his initial comment. "He probably meant to come up here and had something come up at the last minute."

"But why wouldn't he answer his phone?"

"He probably thinks we're pissed at him and doesn't want to hear about it."

Hearing a noise downstairs, McCully walked to the railing to find Red and Duncan returning from their outdoor expedition. Duncan's eyes immediately locked on him, but his look appeared almost excitable, far different from the skeptical terms they last parted on.

"Got a minute?" he called from below.

"Sure," McCully answered, seeing each man carrying a small crate.

He turned to Jana.

"Can you keep an eye on Keith in case he goes completely batty?"

"I could call the men in white coats, but they'd probably take longer than the police."

Now McCully chuckled.

"That's probably true."

McCully headed downstairs, wondering what brought about Duncan's change of attitude toward him.

"Please tell me you found something good out there," he commented when he reached the bottom step.

"Just heavy as a stack of Bibles," Red mumbled as he set down his crate, looking to the second floor. "Is my brother on a mission?"

"Quite," McCully answered.

Red gave little more than a sigh before ascending the stairs to take McCully's place at Jana's side.

"What's going on?" McCully asked Duncan once they were fairly isolated from the others.

"This," Duncan answered, virtually thrusting a scrapbook toward McCully, which he reluctantly accepted.

As McCully began flipping through the pages, he noticed Duncan studying him, as though expecting him to stiffen any moment when a new vision hit him.

"Can I ask what you're expecting from this?" McCully finally asked as he turned to the fifth page.

"There's an article in there about my grandfather's death. I thought it might complete the mystery for you."

McCully intentionally gave him a discouraging stare.

"For *me*, huh?" He paused. "It doesn't work like that. Just because I touch something doesn't mean I'm guaranteed to have a vision about it."

"But you said the grounds were bringing out the best of your, uh, abilities," Duncan said with unwavering optimism.

"I can't believe you're asking me to do this while everyone else is still looking for Laura," he said quietly enough that no one within earshot could hear.

Duncan appeared unaffected by the words.

"You said yourself we were possibly in danger. Maybe if you figure out what happened to my great-grandfather, you'll know what's wrong with this place."

"I feel used," McCully said evenly as he turned to the article.

"Well, don't. I'll be the first to admit I want to know what happened to my grandfather, but I'd also like to see this meeting have a happy ending."

Giving a tired sigh, McCully placed his palm on top of the article.

Nothing happened.

His eyes met Duncan's, seeing all hope drain from the man's face.

"Like I said, it doesn't usually work like that."

"Then try this," Duncan said, thrusting his hand forward, clasping McCully's right hand.

Before McCully could even think to pull his appendage away, he was transported to another time and place, much different than the warm confines of the mansion.

He saw Ben Williams standing with two men in the dark of night beside a train depot. Though he had no proof, McCully suspected it was the route that brought thousands to West Baden over the span of five decades.

At the moment, no train was stationed at the depot, leaving empty tracks and what appeared to be an empty building where tickets were bought. A clock inside revealed it was well past the witching hour, so the depot was abandoned of all life, aside from Williams and the two men.

In the chilly night, he saw the breath of all three men in the air when they exhaled. While Williams stood in the open, beside the station, the other two men remained beside the wall, concealed from anyone walking toward the depot from the staging area.

Williams' companions looked like well-dressed bouncers from a nightclub, but he noticed a scar across the larger man's chin. These men were hardened, probably the type who worked for money without a care for the poor sap they injured. Their fists looked hardened with what McCully thought might be blood streaks, but a closer examination revealed detailed scars.

A light, misty fog lingered near the ground, but the eerie silence caught McCully's attention more than anything. The occasional cricket chirped, but the sounds of traffic and city life were something unknown to the valley in those days. Even the train yard appeared devoid of activity in the early morning hours.

Something felt very wrong, because they seemed to be waiting for something to happen.

Or someone to venture their way.

Suddenly wishing he weren't there to witness what he suspected was Andrew Duncan's demise, he wanted to turn around and run. Unfortunately, he was a captive within his own visions, forced to witness whatever event he was meant to see.

A moment later, Duncan approached his longtime friend with an unhappy look. Despite the late hour, Duncan was dressed as nicely as ever, sporting a full suit and shined shoes. A fedora hat covered his head, but beneath the brim, his eyes appeared troubled and sleepless.

McCully wondered why the man even bothered to show up, suspecting Williams used some ploy to lure him there.

"You have some nerve threatening my family," Duncan said with controlled rage, his right hand already curled into a fist. "My wife almost saw that little memo you sent to my house this morning."

"I'm just glad you got the message," Williams said somewhat coldly. "This is the last time we'll be seeing one another."

"It had better be. You got what you wanted, so there's no need for you to play me like a fiddle anymore."

At this point the two men stepped forward, openly concerning Duncan as his eyes shifted between them and Williams. To McCully, they looked like mafia types from the big city, hired for one single purpose.

Duncan looked as though he wanted to run, but the thought was fleeting. Whatever fate Williams planned for him ended here or it would spill over to his family. He seemed resolved in accepting whatever evil plan his former friend had in store for him, but he wasn't about to lie down like a dog waiting to be shot.

When Williams turned his back, as though unable to stomach the impending sight of his friend being tortured, Duncan jabbed the first large thug in the jaw, flooring him against the wooden platform.

He ducked a punch from the second man, swiftly launching his own fist into the man's chin, fazing him temporarily. McCully was impressed the doomed man put up such a fight. By this time, he had to be in his late forties at best, but his riches hadn't softened him.

The advantage was temporary, however, because both men regrouped before attacking a second time. While one held Duncan from behind the other launched fists across his face and into his stomach, quickly subduing him. His fedora hat fell to the ground with several speckles of blood covering its otherwise brown felt.

"Here," Williams said, thrusting some sort of alcoholic bottle into one of the thug's hands. "Take him down the tracks and finish it."

Cramming Duncan's hat onto his head, the two men began dragging him down the tracks, occasionally having to strike him because he resisted their efforts.

Williams looked around, seeing no witnesses, then walked the stretch of the platform to return to wherever he was staying. McCully, on the other hand, followed the action down the tracks. Compelled to see the end result, he found the men nearly a hundred yards down the track, forcing Duncan to drink heavily from the bottle. They tipped the bottle upward, forcing him to drink down whatever he could until he needed to breathe.

Whenever he put up resistance, they struck him with fists or feet until he cooperated. McCully hardly called it cooperation, because the man continued to spit up what little bit of the alcohol he could.

By this time, his nose was obviously broken. Blood leaked from several opened gashes along his face and forehead. McCully couldn't believe a friendship was torn apart over money so easily. Whatever Williams purchased was apparently worth killing his good friend over, to keep it secret for all time.

McCully shuddered, turning away momentarily as the thrashing continued.

When he finally dared look again, he heard Duncan moaning in agony, barely conscious, as the two large thugs each held one of his arms. Basically, the only thing keeping him from collapsing entirely, the men paused momentarily to assess the damage. One finally displayed the bottle to the other, indicating some unsaid signal between them.

The second man placed Duncan on his knees and elbows, barely keeping him off the ground as the man with the bottle swung it downward across the helpless man's head.

Duncan collapsed in a heap with a final moan as the shattered bottle landed beside him.

"He's still breathing," one of the men said after momentarily observing their prey.

"Grab a rock. The boss said to finish it."

"He also said to make it look like an accident," the other argued.

"It will. Just grab the goddamn rock, will ya?"

McCully watched the man wander just a few feet away, picking up a stone slightly larger than his fist, holding it with a solid grip. He desperately wanted to interfere, but he was no time traveler. In fact, he was a specter, unable to touch anything, and completely undetectable to everyone around him because he didn't exist when such events transpired.

His heart went out to Duncan, because the man obviously had a family at this point in life. Why he chose this path, rather than contacting police, or hiring his own help, was beyond McCully's comprehension. Perhaps he clung to hope that Williams might change, or had no idea what evil things his friend was capable of doing.

Barely able to watch, McCully witnessed the man with the rock clubbing Duncan in the back of the skull twice. While the first blow seemed like a warm-up swing, the second cracked Duncan's skull, drawing both blood and tissue. McCully wasn't sure there weren't some bone fragments mixed in the fleshy gash.

He felt sick, wanting to vomit, but ghosts and holographs did no such thing, so he simply continued letting the events lead him.

Both men waited a moment to see if their victim had expired, which he apparently had, because they each took one end of Duncan's body, moving it near the tracks.

"Let's go celebrate," one said as though they had just won a company softball game, rather than murdered a human being. "I've got another bottle where that came from."

How heartless, McCully thought, taking a step toward the body, wishing he knew more about Andrew Duncan and the man's life. Somehow seeing random highlights didn't feel satisfactory to him, particularly since most of them related to his demise.

He still had no idea why Williams needed him dead. It had something to do with the purchase Williams made, but the story about cubes made little sense. McCully wished he knew more about the man's evil motivations, but his time viewing the past had come to an end.

Chapter 17

"Dear Jesus," McCully muttered when his eyes found the contemporary Duncan standing in front of him.

"What happened?" Duncan asked with concern.

Taking a moment to collect his thoughts, McCully pushed both Duncan and the scrapbook away from him to ensure no other gruesome scenes overtook his conscious mind.

Duncan stayed a few steps away. The look on his face indicated he understood his investment partner had seen something few human beings ever witnessed.

"Was he murdered?" he finally asked.

"Yes."

An uncomfortable silence surrounded both men momentarily as everyone else was preoccupied elsewhere in the mansion.

"What does it have to do with us?" Duncan questioned once enough time passed.

"Nothing," McCully answered. "At least not that I saw."

"Can you talk about it?"

Nervously rubbing his jawbone, McCully had no idea where to begin such a woeful tale.

"Your great-grandfather's best friend had him killed by two thugs," he said a moment later. "It was staged to look like a railroad accident, but they beat him up, forced him to down a bottle of whiskey, then knocked him over the head with a large rock."

There, that's it, McCully thought, hoping Duncan didn't press with more questions.

"But why?"

"He refused to help his friend buy some objects because it meant killing people, and his friend couldn't afford the risk of your grandfather telling anyone about it."

"What the hell was it?"

"Some sort of cubes."

"Cubes?" Duncan asked skeptically.

"That's what I thought, but there's something more to it that I never got to see."

Duncan stood silently a moment, pondering something, but Keith came down the stairs before their discussion concluded. His face bore a disgusted look, which McCully couldn't decipher. Keith was either irritated because they weren't helping in the search for Laura, or because he hadn't found her.

"This is bullshit," Keith stammered angrily. "We're stuck here, we can't call for help, and two of our people are missing."

"Two?" McCully asked.

"Well, Glenn never made it. How do we know something didn't happen to him?"

"We don't," Duncan answered. "But that doesn't mean someone has it in for us. Two other groups walked away from this place without any issues, so we're just having some bad luck."

"Bad luck?" Keith fired back. "The *Titanic* sinking was bad luck. People disappearing for no reason has nothing to do with luck, or karma, or any of that shit."

McCully continued questioning whether Laura's disappearance might be her own doing. They had no evidence of any abduction and so far as he knew, no one could enter the mansion unless they used the front door.

"Laura isn't in this building," he dared say, contradicting Keith's opinion. "Maybe we should get everyone together so we can figure this out."

Keith considered the idea, momentarily looking up to the second floor as though not convinced he was wrong about a third floor.

"We need to contact someone right away," he finally said. "I don't care what it's doing outside."

"That means one or more of us trying to get somewhere else, because none of the phones work in this building," McCully stated. "Can you get everyone to meet down here?"

Keith looked around, noticing most everyone nearby as McCully already had. He stared a bit longer at Jennings, but returned his attention to McCully a moment later.

"I can get everyone down here, but what do you have in mind?"

"The hotel isn't that far from here. If I can't find a vehicle able to cut through the snow, I can probably walk there. I can take someone with me and leave the bulk of you here, so no one else gets lost or hurt."

"What if *you* get lost or hurt?" Keith countered.

"You aren't the only one who grew up in a tough environment, Keith. I can take care of myself, and like I said, I'll have someone with me."

Duncan looked toward him, but McCully didn't feel the man was very excited about the notion of hiking to the hotel.

"Take Red with you," Keith said, leading McCully to wonder if Keith wanted him monitored by someone he trusted implicitly.

"Fine," McCully agreed. "Let's get everyone in the living room and explain what's going on."

***

Five minutes later, everyone took a seat or looked out a window into the darkness as McCully stood by Red, who had been informed of their impending journey.

One look outside informed McCully he had signed up for a perilous trek, even by modern standards, because he didn't pack for a hike through miles of snowdrifts. At least visibility seemed incredibly good for nighttime. Across the grounds and vehicles parked out front, pure white snow blanketed everything, helping illuminate the area as though experiencing a long dusk.

Not once had a plow, or any vehicle, passed by the mansion that anyone reported seeing. Of course, the building was set back from the road, but McCully felt certain any of them would notice headlights, or hear the sound of a vehicle powerful enough to tame the drifting snow.

Looking around, he noticed Oswalt, Duncan, Jennings, Jana, Keith, and Judith all present. No one appeared thrilled about being summoned together, as though they held out hope for Laura to walk through the door any moment. McCully couldn't imagine what kind of explanation she would offer for being gone so long, so he didn't share their optimism.

"Dave and Red are going to the hotel to see if they can phone for help," Keith began rather bluntly, never one to mince words. "None of our cell phones are working in this storm, and all land lines to the mansion are dead."

"Wouldn't it be safer to stick together?" Judith asked.

Unlike everyone else in the group, she never lacked courage to question Keith's leadership and decisions when necessary.

"We *will* stick together," Keith insisted. "Red and Dave will be gone just long enough to phone for help, then they'll be back."

Jennings stepped forward, turning heads.

"I can help them get to the hotel quicker if they have to walk."

"We were hoping to drive there," McCully said. "Dan has a four-wheel-drive truck."

A skeptical look crossed the hunter's face. As someone who lived in the area, and experienced the storm's vicious nature firsthand, he would know whether or not a truck could navigate the roads.

"If those plows haven't come through, you're going to get stuck."

"And what exactly are you proposing?" Keith asked the hunter sharply.

"I know the area pretty well. We could cut across a few fields and be there in no time."

Keith gave a chuckle, but it was laced with ill intentions.

"This coming from a guy who got lost after taking a walk out of his own yard?"

"I didn't get lost," Jennings said, losing patience with the cattle rancher. "I wouldn't have inconvenienced your dysfunctional meeting if I hadn't almost froze to death."

"You watch your tone, mister," Keith said, taking a step forward before Oswalt intercepted him. "One of our people is missing, and I'm not convinced you're not responsible."

Jennings shook his head with a frustrated look. For some reason he couldn't explain, McCully tended to believe the hunter was entirely innocent. If he had anything to do with Laura's disappearance, Jennings had no reason to return to the mansion.

Unless, of course, he got stuck down the road while attempting his escape.

"Can I have a second?" he asked, directing his question toward Keith.

Both men left the room before McCully offered a modified proposal toward the investment group's leader.

"I want him with us," he stated.

"Why? He's nothing but trouble."

"Maybe. Maybe not. You aren't going to have the resources to monitor him and see if Laura comes back. And *if* he had anything to do with her disappearance, this is my one chance to see if he slips up and lets us know something. Red and I can handle ourselves."

Keith seemed convinced, but concerned.

"There's something you're not telling me, kid."

"If anyone took Laura anywhere, they didn't get far. This is hypothetical of course, but if he, or anyone, drove away with her, there's a good chance their vehicle is stuck along the side of the road."

"But if you take him, you're not going to use the road, are you?"

"I need a look at the roads first. Maybe Dan's truck can make it if the drifts aren't too bad. I'll just tell him I want him along as backup."

An uneasy moment passed between them. Keith made no secret of the fact he had trust issues with the hunter. Now McCully was asking him to send the man with his brother to an isolated location.

"What if you can't even get inside the hotel?" he questioned.

"We'll find a way inside. There's supposed to be security there around the clock."

"Okay," Keith said with as much resolve as he could muster. "But watch your back."

He motioned to his brother to join them. A few minutes later, Red understood what Keith expected, then the three returned to the room, finding curious stares directed their way.

"Your clothes dry?" Red asked Jennings, keeping his brother from speaking with the man.

Jennings nodded, gathering them from one of the nearby fireplaces. He left the room to change, likely glad he was leaving the turmoil of the mansion behind.

"Dan, can we borrow your truck?" McCully asked Duncan officially.

"I'll have to take the trailer off the ball hitch," came the answer with an affirmative nod.

McCully threw a coat on, following Duncan outside. A moment later, the two began undoing the restraint that kept the trailer attached to the truck's hitch.

"I hope you guys are careful," Duncan commented.

"I'll try not to wreck it."

"I wasn't talking about the truck. It's insured."

McCully caught his drift.

"Just make sure you lock up behind us. We don't want anyone getting into the mansion who shouldn't be there."

"That shouldn't be a problem. Keith will probably shoot anyone who doesn't know the secret knock."

"Please tell me he doesn't have a gun."

Duncan smirked.

"Well, he took the hunter's rifle."

"Great."

Carefully removing the trailer's connection from his truck, Duncan shoved it back. He handed McCully the keys to his truck rather slowly, as though expecting to shock the country songwriter into another vision.

Taking the keys, McCully half expected the same result, but it never happened. He pocketed the keys, allowing Duncan to lead him toward the front door.

Stopping just short of the threshold, Duncan turned to him.

"Did you really mean everything you said about my grandfather dying over some cubes?"

"They were something special, maybe valuable. And I'm not sure they were worth dollars so much as holding a different importance to Andrew's buddy."

"I can't honestly say I understand what you're telling me."

"It doesn't make much sense to me either, but maybe this little trip to the hotel will help me figure things out."

Duncan nodded, opening the door for them to step inside.

Keith greeted them immediately, with Jennings remaining a few steps behind the figurative leader. The hunter had changed to his warmer gear once more, appearing anxious to leave the premises.

Technically, the hunter had the option of leaving at any given time, so McCully wondered why he continued to stay with the group. Perhaps a sense of obligation, returning the favor for their help, kept him around. The way Keith had badgered the man with his rants and raves, they were lucky Jennings hadn't abandoned him the second his clothes dried.

"Good luck," Keith said, giving his younger brother a quick embrace.

McCully saw him whisper something to Red, but couldn't decipher the words. Jennings didn't appear very comfortable around Keith, so McCully wondered if the two men had heated words while he helped Duncan outside.

Having someone around whom the group couldn't trust made McCully uneasy, but he wondered if his mistrust was simply an extension of Keith's worries. He opened the door for Red and Jennings, deciding to focus on the task ahead of them, rather than his faith in the two men accompanying him.

As he stepped outside, snowflakes immediately smacked him in the face as though to say they weren't letting up anytime soon. He pulled the truck's keys from his pocket, giving one last look back toward the window where Duncan and the others looked out toward the departing group.

A strange feeling came over him, as though he might be doing the wrong thing by leaving for help. He wondered if the others were somehow vulnerable since they were less in number, but shrugged the feeling out of his mind.

The three men spent a few minutes dusting snow off the truck's hood and windshield by hand so they could see.

One look toward the road revealed a treacherous course ahead because snow had drifted, creating pockets between six inches and two feet deep in random fashion.

"Ready for this?" he asked Red as they opened opposite doors.

"As I'll ever be."

McCully assumed the driver's seat, Red rode shotgun, and Jennings squeezed into the back through the truck's third door.

The hunter remained silent, which didn't alarm McCully. After all, the man was near Red, the brother of his one outspoken adversary since his arrival to the mansion.

After placing the key inside the ignition, McCully brought the truck to life with a roar from the engine. He hoped the truck's power on the road matched its bark, throwing the shifter into drive.

Chapter 18

"I said this was a bad idea," were the first words Jennings muttered when McCully encountered their first large snowdrift halfway down the hill.

Unfortunately, the snow accumulation was only half the problem. McCully quickly discovered brakes provided very little stopping power on the icy sheets beneath a deceptively fluffy covering.

Despite Duncan's truck having anti-lock brakes, McCully carefully tapped the brake pedal as the truck swerved violently like a hooked trout, fighting for its existence. Strangely, his surroundings remained highly visible, and for a fleeting moment he contemplated which tree might provide a less dangerous crash if no other way of stopping presented itself.

From memory he recalled that the hill didn't even out the least little bit until it reached the highway, meaning he had seconds to bring the truck under control or risk being smashed like a bug against a snowplow or building.

"What's wrong?" Red asked from the passenger's seat.

"It's sheer ice under us," McCully answered quickly, still tapping the brakes as the truck began to respond.

Apparently, the road wasn't completely ice, because the truck skidded to a stop within twenty feet, allowing McCully to observe his surroundings as he caught his breath.

"This is going to be problematic," he noted aloud. "Even if we make it down the hill in one piece, we may never make it uphill to the mansion."

He turned to Jennings.

"Which way is it to the hotel from here on foot, and how far are we talking?"

Jennings pointed out the direction, taking a moment to decide the distance.

"It's almost a straight line there," he finally answered. "Maybe a mile or so if we cut through the woods and a couple fields."

Red looked dissatisfied when McCully turned his way.

"If we make it to the bottom of the hill, we can pull up to the hotel," he said with confidence. "That way we don't have to walk through all of this shit both ways."

Realistically, they didn't need to make it all the way to the bottom, McCully deduced. The side entrance to the hotel had an electronic gate where he could park the truck, leaving them only a few hundred yards to walk. Of course, that particular location would leave them virtually the hill to climb with the truck before reaching the mansion as well.

"If I start this thing and don't get control of it within a few seconds, we're basically going to be riding a roller coaster with no safety features," he informed Red.

"I'm willing to take that chance."

Jennings shook his head negatively, openly against the idea of driving any further. Considering he was dressed for the elements, a hike probably didn't sound quite so hazardous to him.

"Screw it," McCully said, easing off the brake, wondering if he was going to maintain control of the truck, or send it spiraling toward a dangerous collision course.

His answer seemed the latter momentarily as the truck refused to brake when he touched the pedal again, but after a few seconds the tires touched paved road once more, allowing McCully to steer toward the side. Though the shoulder of the road was barely a foot in width before extending to a large ditch, it provided a hard dirt surface for the right tire to grip.

Answering his silent prayer, the truck stayed a straight course because very little snow accumulated on the shoulder. Near the edge, the drifts leveled out as the snow toppled into the ditch.

"I hate to think what'll happen if we come across another vehicle," he said, talking to calm himself more than make conversation.

"I'd say our chances are slim," Red answered grimly.

It took several minutes, but McCully navigated the truck down the slope until their salvation came into view. Through the falling snow, he spied the side gate that led into the hotel grounds. Considering it was on the opposite side of the road, he needed to steer the truck perfectly into the small drive beside the gate while maintaining an ideal speed.

"Heads up," Jennings said, taking notice of the gate coming quicker than any of them wanted it to.

Once more McCully carefully tapped the brakes, finding more success as he brought the truck gently over to the opposite shoulder. The gravel beneath the snow kept the truck under control while he steered it into the short driveway until it came within inches of the gate.

"I don't suppose you know the combination to get in," Red inquired.

"There's no need. It's a short walk to the hotel."

"And a long hike back to the mansion," Jennings said.

All three men exited the truck rather quickly, finding the wind circling and howling around them. McCully and Red bundled up the best they could, pulling their jackets up to their cheeks while Jennings stood calmly near the truck's front end.

"Let's go," Red stated, taking charge much like his brother often did.

McCully walked around the gate's side, quickly returning to the red brick path, now covered in layers of snow, because he had no idea how the grounds were laid out. He knew a stream ran through part of the sunken garden, but he didn't know if other watery areas existed around the satellite buildings. Falling into a sinkhole was about the last thing he wanted to do after seeing the hunter's fate earlier.

Trudging through the snow proved more difficult than McCully envisioned, particularly without good boots on his feet. Snow immediately found its way into the exposed areas of his clothing, instantly melting into frigid sprinkles of displeasure. The thick socks he had found at the mansion did little except hold the miserable reminders of winter against his skin longer.

The three men drew near the cemetery where several dozen Jesuit priests were buried. A concrete walkway jaggedly led the way to the tombstones placed further up the hill. Surrounded by shrubs that acted as a railing of sorts, the steps were now entirely covered in snow, while the grave markers barely peeked above the accumulation.

Without realizing it, McCully stopped momentarily. He stared at the graveyard as the vision of a disturbed grave during the fall flashed through his mind in an instant. Unblinking, his eyes remained fixed on the wintery scene as another vision raced across his mind.

This one seemed far more disturbing because it also looked like the fall season based on the foliage coloration. A number of specters dressed like robed priests stared back at him from various positions behind tombstones. Some of them appeared injured, almost like zombies, because of head wounds or blood smeared across their faces. Several had agape mouths, but they all maintained blank stares, as though waiting in some sort of purgatory for the appropriate action to free them.

One in particular seemed to stare directly at him. His flesh appeared burned in some areas, very much charred in others. Fleshy tissue hung from his face along the cheeks and forehead, but his eyes caught McCully's attention the most.

Unlike the others, this man didn't appear very much like a priest at all, mainly because his stare felt as heated as his burned flesh looked. Tattered clothes hung from his body, also damaged from fire, which led McCully to suspect he died a horrible, fiery death.

To McCully, the priest's stare felt scolding, like his life as a specter had been disrupted by the man's visions. He suddenly realized the hotel's past contained other mysteries his powers had yet to reveal.

Like snapshots, the visions were gone, leaving McCully in the cold with fewer answers than questions. He quickly took up walking again before his two companions noticed his awkward stare.

Most of the buildings, and even the sunken garden itself, seemed indiscernible under sheets of white. Only the hotel was mammoth enough to resist being covered in any sense. The yellow globes atop lampposts, combined with the bright ground, illuminated the large building like a ship appearing from out of a foggy bank. Very few lights were visible inside the structure, even as they drew near, because only a few lights were necessary to run the building.

Only light enough to run tours and guide security through the building seemed necessary, but several lights on the upper floors caught McCully's attention. He witnessed one bulb go out, then another turn on just a few rooms down, along the third floor.

"Did you guys see that?" he asked, wondering if ghosts were indeed toying with him.

Both turned around to look at him before staring upward where his eyes remained locked.

"No," Red answered. "What was it?"

"A light just switched off up there."

"So the security guard is probably doing rounds. No big deal."

McCully thought differently, but said nothing as he followed Red's lead toward the front door. Two sets of double glass doors prevented their entry as Red tried every single door without success.

"I'll try the back," McCully suggested, starting to walk that way.

He stepped over a few large piles of snow, making his way toward the rear entrance, when he spied what looked like an unmarked police car, and beside it, a Ford Explorer with police decals. The second vehicle worried McCully a bit, because several wires dangled along the side from beneath the hood. Either someone had serious engine trouble, or the vehicle was sabotaged in a major way.

Trying to subdue the worries that crept through his mind, McCully reached the white door in the back, finding it opened without hesitation. He slipped inside, making his way around the first floor hallway toward the lobby doors. After passing the restrooms and the gift shop, he unlocked the first set of double glass doors by turning a lock at their base, then stepped into a short lobby. Undoing the lock to the outside glass doors, he let Red and Jennings inside.

Both men visibly shrugged off the cold as they stared into the darkened atrium, then the hallway to either side.

"The security office was to the right, wasn't it?" Red asked, the exterior doors now behind him.

Every sound they made echoed throughout the vacant building, including speech.

"This way," McCully said, leading the way toward the office Jana pointed out during their tour.

Mere paces down the curved hallway, he found the security office door slightly ajar with a single light source barely visible from around a doorway partly obscured by a hanging cloth.

Not quite finished, the office had bare floors and walls desperately in need of paint or wallpaper. McCully found a light switch to one side, flipped it, and a single, dim overhead light came to life.

The room the three men stood within was devoid of furniture and accessories, as though a front for something else. Beyond the room, divided by the cloth, the security room awaited the visitors. McCully now saw the single light source was a television playing some sort of movie from a DVD player beside it.

Since the hotel had no cable or satellite dish connections, he suspected watching movies was how the state troopers entertained themselves when not on rounds.

Brushing the curtain aside, he also questioned why the hotel had absolutely no cameras or monitors.

A quick examination of the room revealed no clues about Brent Guthrie's whereabouts. McCully found no personal belongings, except for a paperback novel set atop the table, and a lunch box. The single rolling desk chair sat in the far corner, which seemed odd.

"He must be walking upstairs like I said," Red stated in a partially reassured voice.

"I'm not so sure about that," McCully answered, kneeling down to swipe up a shimmering liquid with his two forefingers.

"What is it?" Jennings asked.

"Blood. And there's a lot of it."

Someone had done a sloppy job of cleaning up a fairly large pool of blood. Despite the obvious smears and smudges along the floor's concrete surface, enough remained that McCully doubted it found its way to the floor by accident.

Red searched the desk, finding a phone on the opposite side of the television. He scooped up the receiver, placed it to his ear, and displayed a discouraged frown almost immediately.

"Dead."

"What a wasted trip," McCully muttered, turning to see Jennings shifting uneasily as his eyes panned the small room.

Looking up to Red, McCully waited a moment until his stare was returned.

"What now?" he asked once he had the man's attention.

"There has to be another phone in this place, or some way to get help."

"Either the phones are dead throughout the town, or someone cut the lines at the mansion and this place."

Silence filled the room momentarily.

"I don't like this," Jennings complained just above a whisper.

"And we didn't ask you to stumble into our lives," Red responded in an unfriendly tone, not much different than his brother's.

"I'll gladly hike back to my house if you prefer."

"You're not leaving my sight until I know you aren't responsible for Laura's disappearance."

Now Red sounded *exactly* like his brother. Just when McCully thought the number of sane people in his group outnumbered the psychological breakdowns, Red made him rethink his situation.

"Maybe we should have a look around the place before we take off," McCully suggested. "I'll take Craig with me and we can explore the first three floors. You can get the top three, and we'll meet back here."

Red didn't seem fond of the idea, perhaps because it wasn't his own, but he slowly nodded in agreement.

"Be careful," the older man warned, though McCully wasn't sure if he meant to be cautious around the darkened hotel floors, or Jennings.

***

Jana had the feeling everything had spiraled out of her control.

Keith had more or less ordered her, and everyone else, to remain downstairs while he continued his search for Laura. She understood how dogs felt when their owners left them chained up while they left to do errands.

"This is bullshit," Duncan stated to no one in particular. "He tells us to stick together while he runs off to find his ex. That's a bit hypocritical."

"More than a bit," Judith said, not hiding her irritation.

She was the only one seated within the room.

"I'm a bit confused," Jana admitted. "He's acting like she's the love of his life the way he's gone looking for her."

"You've got to understand Keith," Oswalt said. "He has a one-track mind once he decides on something."

What she truly couldn't grasp was why he wanted to continue the search by himself when he apparently thought some form of danger existed toward the group. His logic made sense, because the mansion appeared far more vast from the outside than the two finished levels.

"You're the authority on this area," Oswalt noted. "What happened here a few years ago?"

"That's a good question," she replied. "The newspapers and authorities kept everything very much under wraps to protect the hotel and Paul Clouse. There's no denying there *were* murders at the hotel. Of that, I can assure you."

Duncan appeared openly unhappy about her statement.

"We all thought it was behind us," Jana said for his benefit. "I believe Mr. Clouse understands there are families out there who will never get over what happened, which is part of the reason he decided to sell."

"Sounds like the place is cursed," Oswalt stated.

"I don't know about that," Jana said in the hotel's defense. "The legend of a Jesuit priest named Ernest has passed down through the decades, but what happened a few years ago was the result of one man."

"Who?"

"Martin Smith, the hotel's previous owner. Again, much of it was covered up, but it seems he was the puppeteer behind most, or all, of the murders."

Everyone digested her words a moment.

"What about this place?" Oswalt inquired. "What's the story behind it?"

"Smith built this after his acquisition of the hotel so he had someplace to stay nearby. There's a mansion between French Lick and here, but it was turned into a museum, so he had to compromise."

Silence filled the room as everyone looked away from Jana. She felt as though she had said something terrible and didn't realize it.

"What's wrong?"

A few more seconds passed until Duncan spoke.

"You just said Smith caused several murders just a few years ago, and he owned this place."

"I made no secret about that information earlier today."

"True, but you didn't connect all the dots, either. Is it possible the man brought harm to Glenn and Laura?"

"He's dead," Jana said assuredly.

Then a memory struck her like a knife through the heart.

The image of a disturbed grave during the fall entered her mind, as well as a newspaper article from several years prior. A catalyst, or at least the first chapter, of the tragic events while Clouse worked at the hotel began with an illegally exhumed body.

She shook off the idea that someone returned from the grave to commit murder, but wondered if someone might be using the past to carry out a new agenda.

Only one person came to mind who might know the two properties well enough to devise such an evil plan, but Paul Clouse had no motive.

Unless he had slowly gone insane.

"You know, I'm going to buck the system and step outside a moment," Oswalt said, plucking his pipe and tobacco pouch from inside his sport coat.

"You probably shouldn't go alone," Duncan teased, though he showed no inclination to join the talent agent.

Jana wanted to look outside, mainly to see if there was any hope of assistance coming their way anytime soon.

"I'll keep you safe," she kidded, grabbing her coat from a nearby chair.

"Well, there you go," Oswalt said to Duncan.

Judith stood from her chair, openly unhappy.

"I don't care what Mr. Sanders thinks we are, but I'm not sitting around like a grounded child. I'll be in my room if any of you need me."

Everyone simply exchanged stunned glances as she left the room, too stupefied to say a word.

Oswalt simply grunted to himself, walking toward the front door. Jana followed him, but looked back to see Judith ascending the stairs without an ounce of fear, considering she directly disobeyed Keith's orders.

"Shouldn't one of us go after her?" Jana asked as she stepped into the winter wonderland beyond the front door.

"Won't do any good," Oswalt answered, lighting his pipe. "She's too stubborn to listen to *any* of us, much less Keith."

"I'm sorry things have gone so wrong," she apologized, though entirely unsure why she said the words at that particular moment.

"It's not your fault. There's probably a logical explanation to all of this. Glenn probably got stuck somewhere between Tennessee and here, and Laura might have wandered off."

Jana looked out to their vehicles, now looking more like snow forts than machines. She felt unprofessional, perhaps even stupid, for not making better preparations. Everything she planned turned out perfectly until two feet of snow landed in the valley. Very few professional snow removers lived in the West Baden area, but she could have found one, had any of the phones worked.

Now they were stranded without police assistance, and no chance of reaching main roads, even if the roads were plowed by morning, because the driveway was littered with white powder.

"It figures the weekend we come up here, the whole place falls apart," Oswalt said with a light chuckle. "We hardly ever see snow around Nashville."

"Southern Indiana isn't much different. If we get an inch or two, it's usually enough to cancel school and every public meeting in the area."

Jana turned around, seeing one of the stone carvings near her with the strange number beneath it. A few exterior Victorian-style lamps illuminated the front yard, allowing her to see most of the mansion's lower front wall.

She sauntered toward the second engraved image without much thought. The snow easily reached her knees, but she didn't care. A plethora of blankets and a hearty fire awaited her inside. Without much to do, she could wait inside until help arrived, or McCully and the others returned from the hotel.

Ignoring the image a moment, she looked to the number scrawled beneath it. 11:2.

"Hey, that's my birthday," Oswalt stated offhandedly, startling her a bit as his approach had gone unheard.

"Birthday?" she asked before she even realized it.

The numbers all seemed the same. One number, a colon, then another number.

Jana instinctively thought they were biblically tied, never considering the notion of them standing for something else.

Of course, biblical numbers by themselves were worthless without a testament name to accompany them.

She wanted to walk to the end of the mansion to examine the rest of the numbers, but Oswalt stared inside one of the windows, looking her way uneasily.

"There's no one in there."

"Where did Duncan go?"

"I don't know, but we'd better find out."

Oswalt knocked out his pipe against one of the pillars near the front door before opening the door for Jana. She stepped inside first, looking around to find no one nearby. An eerie silence overtook the mansion, and as she moved forward, the sound of her own steps was the only noise entering her ears.

"Dan?" Oswalt called out.

Jana suspected Judith had retired for the evening, or simply didn't want company. No one knew where Keith had gone, or what his agenda might be. She only knew it didn't include room for anyone else.

A moment later, Duncan appeared at the balcony atop the stairs with a worrisome look.

"I heard a scream, but when I got up here to check, Judith was gone."

Oswalt shot Jana the briefest of skeptical looks, as though suddenly not trusting Duncan, and bolted up the stairway for a firsthand look.

Quickly following, Jana began fearing the plan to split the group might be the worst possible idea. Now two groups remained isolated, and ripe for the pickings, if someone had evil intentions in mind.

Chapter 19

"This isn't how I planned on spending my night," McCully confessed as he and Jennings walked along the second floor.

"Me neither."

The pair had quickly checked the third floor, finding nothing out of place. Every room was unlocked, allowing them a brief search inside, but nothing turned up. A descent of the nearest stairwell brought them to the second floor where they immediately began opening doors to opposite rooms across the hallway.

McCully didn't dare fully trust Jennings, but to state his mistrust meant alienating the hunter. He tried to tell himself he was falling into Keith's cynical trap, but the fact that the hunter showed up right after their problems began did seem suspicious.

For the moment, he continued to check the rooms on the inner hallway that faced the grand atrium. He consciously scanned the floor for any further bloodstains or other evidence, but found nothing along the dark carpeting.

Saying nothing, he ducked inside several more rooms, meeting Jennings in the hallway as they exited their rooms simultaneously.

"Nothing," the hunter said.

"Same here."

A thought occurred to McCully that they hadn't checked the vehicles parked beside the building before walking inside. At the time, they had no reason to think the security guard would be missing, much less wounded or dead.

Dead.

Missing.

He pondered the two thoughts for a moment, then looked to Jennings, wondering exactly what the hunter had done before reaching the mansion.

"What's that look for?" Jennings inquired somewhat defensively.

McCully realized he had left his emotions on his sleeve. Anything he said now would sound like backpedaling, so he decided not to make excuses.

"Nothing. I just wish we could find the security guard and get out of here."

He began doubting their chances of locating the guard alive. It felt as though their entire trip, even the weather, had been custom ordered by someone with an agenda.

They checked several more rooms until McCully stared out a window toward the atrium. Lit only by the atrium's overhead windows and a few dim bulbs scattered along the various floors, he found himself able to see much of the building's interior. Movement along the first floor caught his attention, but someone crossed one of the four atrium thresholds before he noticed any details.

Unless Red opened no doors whatsoever, then dashed downstairs, there was absolutely no way he cast the shadow McCully saw near the entrance. He continued to stare downward until a hand touched his lower back, startling him enough that he jumped an inch off the ground.

"Christ," he muttered, regaining his composure after the unusual outburst, considering he worked on several gospel albums with his father.

Jennings had a worried look, glancing from McCully to the first floor through the window. He appeared on edge, almost as though he sensed something evil stalked them through the hotel's hallways.

"What's wrong?" he asked.

"Someone was walking through the downstairs."

Jennings stood there a moment, just gawking at him as though wrestling with his thoughts.

"We're almost done on this floor. You wanna head down there?"

"We probably should," McCully decided aloud.

His trust in the hunter reached a new high after seeing an unidentified stranger along the first floor. He doubted the security guard had any reason to be sneaking around, and based on the bloody streaks in the office, he doubted the man was in any condition to walk.

Leading Jennings to the next set of stairs, he put his hand on the guide rail, wondering how many times Andrew Duncan had descended the same set of stairs before his untimely death. In a sense, the hotel shared his fate. Though rich with history, hosting thousands of guests during its first century, the building virtually died the day of the stock market crash.

Yes, it functioned in some capacity during the following decades, but lost its title and purpose as a hotel. The grandest, most expensive resort of its day no longer catered to the rich and famous, hosted professional baseball teams, or bottled mineral water in its garden.

Like most things in the world, it changed and adapted through its ownership, lucky to have survived so many threats over the years.

McCully admired the building, both architecturally and historically, wishing for some way to avoid the deadly collision course it seemed he and his group were destined to find.

"You visited this place much?" he asked Jennings just above a whisper as they followed the turns of the staircase.

"As a kid, I used to sneak in here for looks at the atrium. It wasn't much to look at back then, but it was still awesome. It was overgrown outside, and the atrium was in disrepair, but you could still see the craftsmanship through the mold and faded paint."

"I'll bet."

McCully recalled viewing some photos of the hotel during its gravest era. How the building remained standing before the historical preservation groups stepped in was beyond his comprehension.

He reached the bottom step, looking around cautiously before walking onto the floor. They were now in the main lobby, an area with tiled floor, which muffled little or no sound when walked upon.

When empty, much of the hotel echoed and reverberated any speech or footsteps. He didn't like the idea of separating from Jennings, but decided quickly their search would produce better results if they split up.

"Check that way and I'll meet you in the middle," he said softly enough to the hunter that it didn't sound like an order.

Jennings nodded, walking in the opposite direction.

Able to hear his own steps, McCully thankfully exited the lobby quickly, knowing only a handful of small rooms stood between him and Jennings around the circular hallway.

After taking a look through an open lounge, McCully walked until he came across a storage room on his right, which had been carpeted during renovation, but left bare otherwise. He slowly opened the door, peeked inside, and closed the door, wondering if the person he saw wished to remain inconspicuous.

As he closed the door, the answer came to his left.

Holding a revolver pointed directly at McCully's face, a younger man wearing a thick duster gave him a dead-serious look with unblinking blue eyes. His right hand brushed back the duster, as though in an old western, to reveal a silver star along his torso that revealed he was a deputy for the county police.

"This isn't how it looks," McCully quickly stated.

"You have about thirty seconds to explain exactly how it *does* look, or I put a bullet between your eyes."

Chapter 20

In absolute frustration, Keith tore through the basement inside the mansion, tossing pots and pans as he searched for some way to reach the third level he felt positive existed.

Oblivious to his colleagues' whereabouts during his search, he suspected they would do as they were told. He led the group in virtually every way, and they typically obeyed him. Red certainly listened to him, providing him some assistance by leaving the mansion with McCully and the troublesome hunter.

He patted his hands along every wall, looking for some secret passage, or perhaps some shaft that led upward. The dumbwaiter had definite ends in the basement kitchen and the first floor.

Finding Laura became his number one priority the second he discovered she went missing.

No harm came to anyone in his group while he was in charge, and a quick survey of the grounds outside revealed it highly unlikely she had strolled out either doorway. Turner not showing up for the tour could be dismissed several ways, but Laura was not one to simply disappear.

By no means needy or starved for attention, she had intelligence and an enduring will to get her by. Keith enjoyed the brief time they dated, but both realized business came first, and their relationship hurt the firm.

To him, leadership meant more than just guiding his people. He needed to take care of them as well, which meant discovering why Laura had disappeared.

Technically, taking care of his remaining people was important as well, but his standing order should have kept them safe, if they listened. They were responsible adults, capable of reason. Knowing there might be danger from outside forces, or Keith himself if they disobeyed, they would stay put.

He ran his hand along the inside wall, finding nothing unusual. Metal work tables stood in the room's center, and along several walls, creating a protective blanket around the room that Keith decided might harbor the mansion's darker secrets.

Quickly checking several cabinets along a different wall, he found more utensils, but no secrets. He removed his leather sport coat and black Stetson, which was far less common for him to do, but sweat continued to pour down his face and forehead. Setting the two items atop the center counter, he began his search anew.

Wiping his forehead with his shirt's long sleeve, Keith looked around the room, spying a shelving unit sitting in front of what he considered an unusual section of the wall. About four square feet of indentation broke up what was otherwise a solid wall the length of the room. Though an industrial woven metal shelf currently sat there, he suspected the area served a dual purpose.

A small table sat directly in front of the shelving unit, which made it appear even odder, as though someone had deliberately cluttered the area to keep anyone from snooping.

Keith easily moved the table aside, examining the twisted metal fibers that comprised the unit as he ran his hands along their polished grooves. He noticed only a few large cans of food occupied the shelves, so he shoved them aside, reaching to the back end of the unit to touch the wall.

His fingertips and palm pressed to the wall like a child might absently touch the glass display of a candy store. What he felt, however, came nowhere close to what he expected.

Aside from being raised around horses, Keith learned quite a bit about construction from his father. His hands found the surface of the wall to be some kind of wallpaper that had yet to finish drying. Several air pockets refused to dissipate, meaning someone had hurriedly put the wallpaper up very recently.

His knuckles tapped against the surface, allowing him to discover the paper covered a thin particleboard. Yanking the shelving toward him, Keith tossed it behind him, having no concern about who heard the noise, or found the damage. He suspected the fledgling wall was placed there to hide something, so he looked for the quickest means with which to tear it down.

He never expected to find tools within a restaurant-style kitchen, but one of the drawers contained several screwdrivers, wrenches, and a hammer. Grabbing the hammer from the drawer, Keith began smashing into the thin covering, revealing something that widened his blue eyes momentarily.

Shimmering elevator doors gave him the assurance he needed, informing him that his hunch was accurate. Without taking a moment to assess the situation, he pressed the button with the up arrow, immediately regretting the decision.

"Damn," he muttered, wondering if he might have tipped off someone lying in wait upstairs.

Strength in numbers sounded much more reasonable, but the elevator was already coming down. Frantically looking around, he spied a knife rack nearby, snatching a sharpened blade from the wooden rack in case he needed to defend himself.

The option of retreat remained, but he doubted anyone upstairs might provide him much support in any kind of skirmish.

He also doubted anyone was riding the elevator down.

Except for the button, the elevator displayed no other features. There was no floor indicator, because the device only linked two distinct areas. Considering no evidence of an elevator existed on the second floor, Keith knew he had guessed correctly.

Some form of a third floor awaited him.

A ding alerted him that the doors were about to draw open, but as they did so, a darkly clad figure immediately burst forth, catching him by surprise before he could raise the knife to defend himself.

Armed with a knife himself, the figure simply raised the blade upward, catching the underside of Keith's left arm with the sharpened end, creating a red slit. Yelping in pain, Keith punched the man in the side of the head, refusing to be a victim. He stunned the man momentarily, but as he went to use the blade, his wrist was struck.

His knife dropped uselessly to the ground, so Keith wrapped his hands around the assailant's neck as the two bounded from wall to wall, struggling and grappling. It took most of his effort to keep the attacker's knife from plunging into his chest, assuming that's where it was aimed.

Keith maneuvered the arm away from his body, pointing the blade toward the attacker as he kneed the man in the groin, doubling him over.

He immediately had the choice of fleeing, or taking the elevator upstairs. A glance revealed that the mobile box continued to wait for him, doors ajar, as though inviting him to see the secret it helped hide.

Lingering a moment too long, Keith allowed the dark figure to grasp his leg, but a swift kick from his boot to the head gave him time enough to stumble toward the open elevator.

As though desperate to keep some dark secret, the assailant grabbed Keith by the ankle, nearly pulling off his boot. Keith punched him in the head, near the temple, before he was tackled to the ground by the recovering figure.

Another skirmish ensued, but this time Keith threw several hard punches against the side of the man's head. The hood had some rubberized mask beneath it, absorbing some of his fury. He felt a powerful hand wrap itself around his throat, immediately cutting off the oxygen to his lungs.

Keith found a discarded frying pan nearby, using his fingers like feelers to find the handle before grasping it. When his knuckles finally locked around the wooden handle, he prepared to swing it, but found a knife swiftly swinging toward his chest. He went to block the blow, deflecting the blade enough that it lodged in his shoulder, dropping the frying utensil in the process.

As he yelled in pain, his left arm instinctively moved toward the wound to assess the damage or remove the knife. It bled, but the blade prevented the blood from gushing. Rolling over, he crawled and clawed his way toward the elevator, trying to distance himself from the dark figure.

Within a few seconds, he neared the elevator, propped on his elbows to keep the knife's butt from touching the ground and sinking the blade further into his flesh. A strong hand grasped his foot as Keith drew near his discarded knife, with thoughts of certain escape crossing his mind.

His hand clasped the weapon's handle as he dared look behind him, his eyes adjusting too late to the dark shape now looming above him.

The delay cost him dearly as the frying pan, now wielded by the assailant, struck him upside the head, sending his consciousness spinning into a black void.

Leaving him at the mercy of a vicious stranger.

Chapter 21

"Exactly who are you, and why did you break into the hotel?" the deputy asked McCully, who felt positive for the first time in his life he was about to die.

"My name is Dave McCully, and I didn't break in here. I'm with the investment group who toured the place earlier today."

"I didn't hear of any special tours."

A perplexed look crossed the deputy's face, indicating he really knew nothing about the group, making McCully's battle very much uphill.

"We got here and the security guard was missing," McCully explained. "We found blood near his post, so we went looking around."

The deputy didn't seem to buy his story, his hold on the gun unflinching.

McCully tried to think of some presentable proof, but nothing immediately came to mind. He wasn't issued a receipt or ticket, he had no letter from Jana Privett, and every form of communication appeared lost or broken.

His only hope was to explain his way out of this frightening situation.

"We're a group of perspective buyers for the property. We took a tour of the place this afternoon, and most of the group is up the hill at the old mansion."

"Who's here with you?"

"A few of us came down here to see if the phones were working. Our cell phones couldn't get a signal in the storm."

Lowering the weapon just slightly, the man seemed to find some credibility in McCully's story.

"You didn't exactly answer my question," he stated just the same.

"I'm here with another member of my group," McCully told a partial truth, hoping if Jennings showed up, he might know the deputy.

Or bail him out of trouble, even if he didn't.

Now the deputy pulled back on the revolver's hammer, aiming it straight at McCully's forehead. Appearing dead serious, he left the bluegrass singer wondering exactly why he was at the hotel in such ferocious weather, and why he acted so cross.

"I suspect you have better things to do than check on the hotel in this weather," he said, trying to get some answers. "And you're not in uniform, so this must be a personal matter."

"I'll ask the questions, mister, starting with the what you know about the vehicles parked out back."

"Absolutely nothing. They were here when we got here. The truck we brought down from the mansion is parked near the employee gate."

Taking a moment to digest the information, the deputy refused to lower his weapon. Their conversation came to a screeching halt when footsteps echoed down the hallway. The county officer motioned to McCully to quietly move to a nearby wall where they were out of sight from whoever approached the area.

If he were held at gunpoint by a kidnapper or known felon, McCully might have dared attack the man at a convenient moment, but this was an officer of the law. To this point, he had every reason to believe the man had only good intentions for stopping at the hotel, so he complied.

When Red stepped into view, it surprised McCully, but surprised the older man even more. Upon seeing the deputy's firearm, Red immediately held his hands halfway up in a defensive posture.

"I very much want to hear your version of things," the deputy said, waving the gun for Red to move beside McCully, which he did.

"My side?" Red questioned, giving McCully a questioning glance.

"Tell me what the fuck you're doing here."

The man flashed his badge toward Red, authenticating himself once more.

"Well, we were stuck at the mansion and one of our people went missing, so we thought we'd see if the phones down here worked," Red replied far more calmly than McCully had.

Everyone stood silently a moment.

"Can I ask what you're doing here in this weather, officer?" Red dared inquire. "We called 911 over an hour ago and they said the police were too busy at traffic wrecks to come help us."

Looking between McCully and Red, the deputy seemed to question why both of them had asked the same question. He appeared suspicious of them, as though they were the reason he felt compelled to brave the weather and check on the hotel.

"Someone important to me is missing," the deputy answered gruffly. "I tracked his movements to this location."

McCully recalled seeing the damaged county police vehicle outside.

"We saw the Ford outside," he said. "That wasn't yours, was it?"

"No. I got here the only way I could. Horseback."

McCully looked outside, though the dim lighting only provided a limited view of the grounds. Everything looked a hazy yellow from the limited bulb lighting and heavy snow.

"He's inside the old pavilion," the man answered, guessing his thoughts correctly.

"We might be able to help you find him or her," Red suggested in a neutral tone, still acting the calmest of the group.

"I don't think so. In fact, I have to decide what I'm going to do with you two while I search for him."

McCully looked from the corner of his eye toward Red, who didn't appear thrilled about their predicament. They had little time to waste, and a group of people at the mansion to rendezvous with before conditions grew any worse.

"You don't have to *do* anything," Red stated. "We're who we say we are, and we're here to get help. If you're really a deputy, we could use some assistance finding our missing person."

Now the man gave an uneasy chuckle.

"*If* I'm a deputy? I'm holding a gun, and I think that's about all the authority I need at the moment."

A thud surprised both McCully and Red as the deputy lurched forward, then collapsed to the ground, falling forward to reveal Jennings holding the culprit.

In his hands, he clasped a short spade shovel.

"I found it in the basement after I saw you were in trouble," he informed McCully.

"You know who he is?" Red asked.

"He's the sheriff's son."

McCully and Red exchanged confused looks.

"And you still slugged him?"

"He gave me a speeding ticket last year I didn't deserve."

All three suppressed laughs, looking down at the unconscious deputy.

"What do we do with him now?" McCully asked once their chuckles subsided.

"We get that gun away from him and do what we came here to do," Red answered. "I couldn't find a phone on the sixth floor, but that doesn't mean we've struck out completely."

Unsure that he felt equally confident, McCully kicked the gun away from the deputy's limp hand, hoping things at the mansion were going smoother.

***

"I can't believe this," Oswalt commented, standing at the doorway of Judith's room.

Jana looked from him to Duncan, beginning to wonder who within the group could be trusted. Considering they hadn't heard one word from the three men who left for the hotel, it wasn't beyond the realm of possibility one of them incapacitated the other two and returned.

She tried to shake the feeling someone in the group came to Indiana with ill intent, because there seemed no other way anyone might enter the mansion.

Unless they had hidden away the entire time.

"I searched the whole room," Duncan said immediately, as though noticing their suspicions. "No sign of any foul play. She's just gone."

Everything inside the room appeared orderly to Jana. She checked the closet, under the bed, and inside the bathroom to confirm Duncan's report.

Oswalt shook his head, wearing a frustrated look. He left the doorway, calling back as he went down the stairway.

"I'm going to find Keith. You two can search the other rooms."

It sounded more like an order than a suggestion.

"Patsy," Duncan commented. "I think he's more devoted to Keith than he is his own clients."

Jana said nothing, contemplating their situation in her mind instead. A sinking feeling overtook her rational thoughts because Judith simply disappeared, just like Laura.

This wasn't a practical joke, she had decided. Obviously, leaving the mansion wasn't a realistic option. No help could be reached, and even if they talked to a dispatcher or police officer, the chances of them coming to the mansion remained slim. The only thing Jana thought might make the situation worse was a power outage.

Or being left completely alone.

She put aside any mistrust of Duncan, sensing he might be the one genuine person in the entire group. His love for the hotel, and its history, eliminated him as a suspect because he had no ulterior motive for harming his group members.

"Want to check the rest of these rooms real quick?" he asked her.

"You haven't already?"

"I called her name, but I didn't poke around a whole lot," he confessed.

Jana nodded easily, almost in defeat before they even began searching.

"Let's go check."

A little over ten minutes later, the pair finished checking the upstairs with negative results. Oswalt had yet to return, so they walked down the main stairwell, utilizing the bird's-eye view to observe the area below.

Nothing stood out, so they made their way downstairs, finding the place extremely desolate without the sounds or sights of other people.

"Where the hell could he be?" Duncan questioned.

"Hopefully with Judith and Keith."

"Something tells me we're not that lucky."

As they reached the bottom stair, Duncan looked around the area with a concerned expression.

"Can you check those two rooms real quick?" he asked, nodding toward the living and entertainment rooms.

Alone? Jana thought, unsure of how the disappearances were occurring, but positive about one thing.

Everyone who came up missing had left the company of others.

"Okay," she answered anyway, deciding not to enter either room.

A quick glance inside each one would suffice.

And it did.

Jana saw nothing unusual in either room, beginning to wonder if aliens were transporting her guests into their flying saucers, completely undetected.

To her, Keith's third floor theory seemed unfounded, if not unsound, but unless the entire group was playing some sort of practical joke on her, she had no other realistic explanation.

She walked toward the middle of the room, expecting to find Duncan nearby. When Jana reached the stairway, she peered cautiously around, hoping to see someone familiar standing there.

"Dan?" she called, stepping toward the kitchen area on the other side of the stairs.

"I'm here," he said, suddenly emerging from the doorway, startling her.

He looked more concerned than ever.

"I didn't see anyone downstairs, but I found Keith's hat and coat. He was down there at some point."

Jana felt true panic for the first time, struggling to keep her composure. She knew Duncan was genuinely worried about his colleagues, but he said very little, keeping his thoughts to himself.

She wanted to check downstairs for herself, simply to eliminate him as a suspect from her mind more than anything else. Daring to request such a search provided no other positive aspects for her, so she said nothing.

Perhaps an opportunity to search downstairs might present itself later, so Jana decided to stay by Duncan's side, hoping any fears she harbored were unfounded.

"What are we going to do?" she asked him, wondering if any new ideas had come to the man who knew the area better than anyone in his group.

"We're screwed until the others get back," he answered. "They took my truck, which is the only good vehicle in this weather we have. If they get stuck down there, we may be on our own the rest of the night."

Jana didn't recall weather reports mentioning anything about a quick warm-up after the initial snowfall hit. Sleeping at the mansion overnight might prove just the beginning of their stay if road conditions didn't improve.

"We should have left when we had the chance," Jana said with a sigh.

A loud series of knocks at the front door startled them both as their feet left the ground. After a moment of regaining their composure, Duncan and Jana looked to one another, then directed their attention toward the front door.

Jana wondered what other surprises awaited them, hoping one or all of the men who went to the hotel might be returning. She started toward the door to answer it, but Duncan caught her arm.

"Shouldn't we have a weapon or something?" he asked.

"Like what? A spatula from the kitchen?"

"That hunter's gun is somewhere around here."

Jana decided opening the door was a safe option if they ascertained the identity of the person on the other side.

"We don't have time for this," she stated more boldly than she intended. "Let's find out who's out there."

Chapter 22

McCully waited by himself for the deputy to awaken within the security office. He should have felt comforted by the fact that the man, now identified as Arlan Brown, was bound to a chair.

But he didn't.

Before leaving to explore more of the hotel, Red and Jennings had pulled the deputy's license from his wallet. They now knew exactly who the man was, confirming the hunter's initial identification, but McCully wanted to know his motivation for holding them at gunpoint.

Jennings apparently had extensive knowledge in knots, because he tied the deputy to the chair quicker, and with better quality, than McCully recalled ever seeing any object bound. Almost twenty minutes had passed since Jennings struck the man, leaving Brown slumped in a chair with his chin buried in his chest.

McCully half expected to see him drooling on himself in his limp state, but it didn't happen. He wanted to converse with the man, if only to know what brought him to the hotel. Expecting assistance from Brown seemed farfetched, but beggars can't be choosers, he decided.

Despite the major storm gripping the valley, two group member disappearances seemed highly unlikely without some outside meddling. He considered Turner a missing person, since the man never called or showed up. Until the security guard came up missing, he felt most every odd occurrence could be explained.

Something felt wrong about separating the group at the hotel, as though they might be following an intended harmful path. McCully couldn't place the feeling, but his heightened awareness usually provided him better intuition.

To put his suspicions aside, more so than anything else, McCully reached over to touch the man's arm. His fingertips grazed the man's shirtsleeve, which typically provided a vision if one was to be found.

But nothing happened.

He would have breathed a sigh of relief if not for the man stiffening to a full upright position immediately. His eyes appeared wide with confusion, and possibly some anger, but they came to rest on McCully after surveying his surroundings.

"The last thing you want to do is keep me tied up," he said momentarily, after regaining his composure.

"Seems during our last encounter you had a gun pointed at my face," McCully answered, refusing to back down.

"Assaulting me is a criminal offense."

"Assaulting *anyone* is a criminal offense. And I believe battery is putting your hands on someone, isn't it?"

Brown didn't appear the least bit amused.

"Maybe if you had been more forthcoming, instead of accusing my friends and me of breaking and entering, we wouldn't be in this position," McCully offered.

"And you weren't breaking and entering?" Brown said, openly amused at such a statement.

"I suppose technically we were, but we were looking for help. One of our party is missing from the mansion up the hill. Care to tell me who you were looking for?"

"It would be a lot easier if you untied me."

McCully flashed a suspicious smile, but didn't budge from his position.

"I'd like to hear your story first."

Brown sighed, relegating himself to his current situation.

"My father came over here after a phone call, and I haven't seen or heard from him since."

"And you came out in this shitty weather to find him?"

"My dad was supposed to contact me, and never did. I couldn't get him by home phone, cell phone, or radio, so I knew something was wrong. He's always out working during storms and major events."

"Working?" McCully asked, trying to pry additional information from Brown to make their conversation a bit smoother.

"He's the sheriff."

McCully got what he wanted. Though he already knew that piece of information, he wanted Brown to say it. He could now take a different direction with his questions without implicating Jennings as the person who struck Brown in the head with the shovel.

"So that's his Ford out back?"

"Yes. And the sooner you get me out of here, the sooner I can get looking for him."

McCully recalled the engine compartment of the sheriff's vehicle openly displaying its damage.

"We've been through the whole place and found nothing," he revealed. "The security guard was missing, and we found a pool of blood near his desk."

"I know," Brown said impatiently. "That's why I figured you and your buddies took him out. I'm still not convinced otherwise."

"If I were murderous enough to kill a retired state trooper, do you really think I would have simply tied you up?"

Brown shrugged what little he could.

At the same time, McCully began wondering how interconnected the strange occurrences around them might tie into one another. The only logical explanation seemed to be an elaborate scheme to slowly break up the investment group, while taking out the sheriff to ensure the plan reached its conclusion.

Shaking his head, McCully felt certain his mind was wandering too far, because the weather could easily be the cause of Turner's disappearance, the sheriff's mishap, and possibly Laura wandering off and getting lost in the snow. It didn't feel right, but McCully had no explanation why someone might bring harm to anyone in the group.

"So you're really staying at the old mansion?" Brown asked, suddenly showing modest interest in McCully's story.

"Yes. I think we've covered this ground already. And, no, I haven't seen your father. In fact, you're the first stranger I've seen since we saw the security guy this afternoon."

McCully thought a moment.

"Well, I guess the catering crew was hired by our tour guide."

"Tour guide?"

"The woman who showed us the grounds this afternoon. We're the third group to come through here. Surely you've heard something about it."

Brown nodded.

"Sure. But I didn't hear much, because apparently the first two groups didn't cause much of a stir."

"Funny," McCully commented. "This place must be some bread and butter for you locals."

Now the deputy shot him an irritated stare.

"Is that how you think of us? As piss ant local hicks?"

"Not at all. Maybe I don't have the local connection to this place that my colleague Duncan does, but I understand the history of the place."

McCully dropped Duncan's name, hoping for a positive connection from the deputy, but it didn't come.

"You're wasting time I could be spending by searching for my father," he said instead.

McCully realized the man was right. He traveled to the hotel with Red and Jennings to find help, or Laura, so their situation had an eerie similarity.

"I'll get you out of here, but first I have to see what my two colleagues have found."

He hoped more than anything they hadn't found any corpses, but the grim reality that the storm brought more than just piles of snow settled in his mind.

"I'll be waiting," Brown said in a displeased tone.

McCully stepped into the hallway, instinctively looking both ways. He worked one summer in a factory, where he learned to always look both ways. Failure to do so got several workers struck by forklifts and machines carrying hot liquid metal. McCully listened during orientation to the horror stories, making certain he paid attention at all times.

After that summer, the habit stuck, no matter where he went.

Working in the factory was his father's idea, to teach him what real work was like. It was that summer McCully decided he wanted to follow in George McCully's footsteps. Not that he minded hard work, but the entertainment business provided many more luxuries and fringe benefits.

He didn't dare call out for Jennings or Red, so he stepped as quietly as possible down the hallway, listening for their voices or footsteps.

No sound entered his eardrums, but he wondered if they might take the elevator instead of the stairs. Noise only carried so far throughout the hotel, despite the echoing effect when it was vacant.

McCully expected to hear conversation or doors closing at the very least. He reached a window in one of the first floor lounge rooms, staring outside momentarily.

Snow finally began tapering off, but the damage appeared to be done. Strong winds continued to create new drifts, and any lights normally seen beyond the end of the hotel's long driveway were hidden or nonexistent. For all he knew, West Baden might be a ghost town, partly or completely deprived of power.

The Victorian-style lanterns along the main drive remained lit, but the bulbs looked like hazy globes painted on canvas in the wintry night. At least the hotel had power, which meant the mansion probably continued to provide warmth for the people left behind.

McCully whirled around upon hearing conversation in the distance.

He walked briskly to the door, stepping into the hallway. Stopping just long enough to detect the area where Red and Jennings were walking, he heard a slight echo, guessing they might be crossing the grand atrium.

It took little time to reach the nearest of the four open entrances to the atrium. He found the two men near the center of the large open area, talking quietly as they walked. McCully felt better that the two were speaking at last, but noticed something in Red's right hand that looked like a sheet of paper.

Instead of calling to them, in case someone watched their activities from above, McCully stepped into the atrium, the echoes of his movements immediately alerting his colleagues to his presence.

"What are you doing out here?" Red asked once he intercepted them.

"I decided to check on you two. You were gone quite a while."

"How's our deputy?" Jennings inquired, looking sheepishly guilty after his actions.

"Grumpy. He's still tied up, but I found out a few things once I got him talking."

"Such as?" Red inquired, leading the way toward the security office.

McCully and Jennings quickly followed, not wishing to be left in the unnerving darkness of the atrium.

"His father is indeed the sheriff, and he came here looking for the man."

"So?"

"So, his father is missing, the security guy is missing, and Laura is missing. This place is a stone's throw from the mansion, so don't you think something weird is going on?"

Red stopped mid-stride to ponder the evidence presented to him. His upper body shivered as a cold draft passed through the group, and he said nothing for a moment.

"That police vehicle outside looked trashed," he finally stated. "We found this on the dashboard inside."

Red handed him a sheet of paper with some scribbled writing on it.

He read the note to himself.

Trouble at the old Smith mansion.
Two missing.

"Two missing?" McCully questioned. "What the hell?"

"That's what we were wondering," Jennings said.

McCully deduced the original message might have been inaccurate, the writer got the information wrong, or he and his two colleagues were a step behind someone's fiendish plan.

"We need to talk to our deputy," he said. "Maybe he has a clue about what's going on."

All three quickly made their way to the security room, but when they arrived it was vacant. The ropes formerly binding the deputy lay uselessly on the floor.

"Shit," McCully said under his breath.

Red had the man's gun, but there was no telling if the deputy planned to enlist help, track them down, or escape with his newfound freedom to search for his father.

"Well this isn't good," Jennings said, swallowing hard.

Chapter 23

A pounding came to the front door several more times before Jana unlocked it, yanking it open to find Oswalt standing in the cold, his hands held in front of his chest as though he were in prayer.

They were a faded pink color, indicating the pose was meant to simply keep them warm.

"About time," he said gruffly as he stepped inside, immediately shivering.

"What happened to you?" Duncan questioned, thinking much like Jana that Oswalt had no reason to step outside without proper clothing.

"I thought I saw a streak of light outside, so I ran out there hoping to flag someone down."

"And?" Jana inquired.

"It was a snowplow, but they were too far gone to see me."

"Did you find Keith?"

"No. I found his stuff in the basement, but no sign of him."

Oswalt's voice trembled when he spoke, because the cold had numbed his body. Jana hadn't thought it was exceptionally cold outside, but she noticed the man wore nothing more than thin socks and some kind of sport sandals on his feet. Some of the guests had dressed down after dinner.

Everyone stood silently a moment. Oswalt continued to shiver, so Jana grabbed one of the blankets Jennings had used from a nearby chair.

"Thanks," he said, wrapping himself inside it like a cocooned worm.

He waited a few seconds to regain his composure before speaking again.

"We have other problems."

Duncan looked at him as though wondering how their situation could really get any worse.

"Every tire was slashed on every single vehicle."

Jana glanced at Duncan, who appeared to instantaneously be caught between rage and utter desperation. He darted to the window, looking outside for confirmation of Oswalt's news, but shook his head.

"I can't see anything out there," he reported, apparently having no desire to step outside by himself.

"Trust me," Oswalt said. "We aren't getting out of here tonight."

Duncan looked hard to Oswalt momentarily, his expression barely softening when he looked to Jana. She read it plainly, fighting not to give away Duncan's secret message.

I'm not sure I trust him anymore.

The thought of Oswalt slashing every tire seemed preposterous to her, despite the length of time he was away from them. She knew something wasn't right about their stay at the mansion, but trusting absolutely no one seemed counterproductive.

She saw no motive in Oswalt harming Keith, or stranding them at the hotel, but she wasn't going to simply sit around and wait to disappear next.

"We have to do something to get out of here, or get help," she said.

"Like what?" Duncan asked. "You're the local person. If there was something we could do, wouldn't you have thought of it already?"

His argument was sound, but Jana had no friends or contacts as far south as West Baden. At this point, braving the elements to walk to the nearest police station or open business sounded better than waiting inside the mysterious building.

Jana decided if they couldn't leave the grounds, perhaps their time might be better spent solving the mystery at hand. Anything sounded better than waiting for McCully and the others to return, or searching the mansion for Laura and Keith.

She wanted them back safely, but they were simply nowhere to be found, and risking three more lives to find them sounded illogical.

"We have to find out what happened to Keith," she finally said, deciding it was time to check downstairs for her own piece of mind.

Oswalt and Duncan had likely done hurried searches for their group's leader. Keith certainly hadn't vanished into thin air, and no signs of anyone exiting the building presented themselves.

Both men appeared reluctant to conduct another search, as though they might be next on someone's hit list.

"Fine," Jana said more sternly than she felt. "I'll go check by myself."

She knew, or at least hoped, they wouldn't *really* let her stray from them. Duncan stepped forward first, giving her an internal sigh of relief.

"I'll go. I didn't get to look around very much the first time, so maybe we'll find some clues."

Oswalt continued to shiver, pulling the blanket tighter around his entire body.

"You'll forgive me if I don't join you? I promise I won't go anywhere."

Jana nodded before stepping toward the kitchen area with Duncan in tow. They quickly passed through the kitchen area, noticing that the pleasant lingering odors of their evening meal remained. Jana opened the door to the downstairs, turned on the light, and took the lead.

"I think he's hiding something from us," Duncan commented on the way down.

"Something tells me if he was behind any of this, he would have been much smarter about it."

"What do you mean?"

"If Oswalt wanted the tires slashed, he could have done it hours ago. And why would he turn around and tell us about it?"

Duncan had no reply.

They reached the bottom step, but Jana turned to speak with Duncan, rather than immediately begin their search.

"Maybe he wanted half of the group gone so he could toy with us," Duncan said before she could offer a suggestion.

"I doubt it. Someone who knows this area and this mansion very well is behind the strange goings on."

Duncan reluctantly nodded in agreement.

Turning around, Jana wondered where to begin their search for Keith, because he certainly hadn't left them any clues.

***

"How do we know he's not still lurking around here?" Jennings questioned as the three men refused to leave the sanctity of the security office.

"And how do we know he isn't responsible for any of this?" Red questioned McCully, who still felt positive the deputy was truthful during their conversation, albeit while he was in captivity.

Jennings shook his head, disagreeing.

"He's kind of a jerk, but I don't think he's the homicidal type. If he was looking for his dad, he probably took off to the bar down the road. That's where the two of them hang out all the time."

"I doubt it," McCully muttered barely above a whisper.

Red clearly looked disturbed by the turn of events. He exhaled audibly through his nostrils before speaking.

"There's nothing in this place that's going to get us any help any sooner, and if he goes and finds his dad first, our situation might get worse."

"Are you suggesting we find him and toss him in the brig?" Jennings asked.

"No. I'm suggesting we find him and work this out before it gets messy. We don't have time to waste with all the weird stuff going on around here."

McCully had an idea where to find the deputy before the storm engulfed him.

"I'll check outside and see if there's any tracks."

Red nodded his approval, and said something that sounded like orders to Jennings as McCully wasted little time exiting through the building's front entrance. He supposed building security was hardly a worry when no one could feasibly step onto the grounds without adapted travel methods.

Despite the snow tapering off, he found himself unable to see past the brick driveway, now layered in pure white. McCully stepped forward, making his way toward the sunken garden through the impeding snow.

Feeling somewhat disadvantaged tracking an officer of the law, he wondered if Brown had really planned to retreat, or if the deputy planned on enacting some revenge. Standing completely still on the stairs, McCully looked cautiously around before continuing his descent. He then looked upward, studying the windows that loomed over six stories above.

No shadows broke any of the light patterns, and no lights switched on or off. Returning his attention to the garden, he stepped forward, finding a dark figure moving along the garden beside the closest spring.

Too large to be a person, McCully figured he had just found Bigfoot, or the deputy was on horseback.

"Shit," he muttered, wondering what Brown had in mind.

While the snowdrifts reached his knees and beyond, McCully noticed the horse having little trouble navigating the garden as Brown directed him toward the side gate. A terrible thought crossed his mind as he contemplated the deputy taking the time to disable Duncan's truck.

If he even had the means to do so.

Most saddles can carry multiple objects, including shotguns, food, bedding, and possibly even a knife of some sort.

Another glance toward the garden revealed the shape nearing the gate. A mad dash through the snow might allow McCully to catch Brown in the act of slashing tires, if that was indeed his desire, but not in time to prevent the act entirely.

He quickly returned inside to inform Jennings and Red of their new problem. Even if Brown didn't slash their tires, he would certainly reach the mansion before any of them could. At this point, McCully had no idea what the man's frame of mind might be.

Yanking open one door, then the next, he reached the inside, hearing no sign of his two colleagues. Since they were the only people in the hotel, so far as he knew, he decided to call out this time.

"Red! Jennings!"

No answer.

"Red? Craig?"

A few seconds passed before a response came.

"Over here," Jennings called, entering the atrium from the other side.

Both men walked halfway across, meeting in the center beneath the overhead chandelier.

"Where's Red?"

"He said he wanted to check on something in the basement," Jennings answered.

"Our deputy is mobile, and he just took his horse out the side gate."

Jennings stood a moment, trying to reason what McCully's point was exactly. A strange look crossed his face when the answer came to him.

"He's heading for the mansion?"

"I sort of let him know there was a group of us staying up there."

"Yeah, but why would he care?"

"Maybe he thinks we did something with his dad."

Jennings soured a bit, openly trying to guess the deputy's typical movements.

"His dad and him are close. There's a chance he might have gone off the deep end if he thinks we did something to him."

McCully realized he had no time to waste.

"I'm heading for the mansion. He might have slashed the tires on the truck, but if he didn't, I'll be back for you."

"You can't just leave-"

"I don't have a choice. Hell, I'm not even sure the truck will make that hill. In the meantime, you two can look for a way to contact the police, or maybe some blueprints from the mansion."

"That's a longshot," Jennings scoffed. "But I *can* take the shortcut back to the mansion if Red and I need to get back there."

McCully turned to leave, only taking a step before turning around in mid-stride.

"And maybe our cell phones will start working with this storm front deteriorating."

Jennings nodded, allowing McCully to continue on his way, wondering exactly what had transpired at the mansion in his absence.

Chapter 24

Oswalt felt warmer within a few minutes of being inside, but his extremities still tingled with numbness as they gradually regained their circulation. He flexed them in and out, trying to get them warm but they simply responded with shooting pain, as though he were trying to push a Ping-Pong ball through a straw.

His veins were no bigger than straws, meaning they could only withstand so much regained blood flow at once.

Standing from the chair, he decided to walk around, hoping he might feel better. At the very least, he wanted to think about something other than the frigid weather.

A noise caught his attention from across the main entrance that sounded like a door latching.

Or locking.

He quickly dismissed it as Duncan and Jana conducting their search. Oswalt sensed they didn't fully trust him, but no definitive sign of Keith showed up during his personal search, and he had legitimately run outside to flag down some help. He suspected the plows were owned by the county, meaning the drivers likely had radio contact with a home base, or perhaps the police.

Feeling certain he had left the door unlocked when he stepped out, Oswalt dismissed his memory as fleeting because of the excitement. He wasn't ready to call himself absentminded just yet, because Keith was still missing, and either foul play was involved, or he and Laura had set them up for a well-planned prank.

But Turner had never shown up, either. The more he thought about it, the more Oswalt began to suspect someone had plans for his group.

And he suddenly didn't like being alone in the mammoth structure by himself.

Walking as far as the stairs, Oswalt stopped, peering toward the kitchen area, not daring to go any further. Jana and Duncan were together, so he dismissed the noise as them aggressively searching every inch of the basement. He immediately doubted his analysis, wondering if the mansion would actually allow noise of any kind to transcend its floors or walls.

He doubted it.

A different sound caught his attention, but this one came from above. More like a moan or cry, it sounded feminine, drawing him toward the staircase. Before he consciously realized it, his hand glided along the finished wooden railing as he dared take a step or two upward.

For some reason, his mind began contemplating how a devious mind might lure him upstairs under false pretenses. If not for people disappearing without reason, Oswalt would ordinarily rush upstairs to render help to whoever needed it. The investment group was a fairly close bunch, despite enjoying successes early in their lives.

He took a few steps upward, hearing a different sort of moan from above, more painful and drawn out.

"No way," he muttered, refusing to take another step forward.

Sensing something almost prodding him from behind, he slowly turned his head, then his upper torso, to look at the stairwell's base.

Standing there, as though on cue, a darkly cloaked figure held a knife in one hand, rubbing his thumb and forefinger along the blade's sides ominously. Oswalt fought the instinct to simply run upstairs, thinking he might have a chance to overpower the man, knowing this was no joke.

It took mere seconds for his mind to realize this man had likely murdered Jana and Duncan downstairs, which explained the closing door he heard. He knew just enough about the problems surrounding the hotel a few years prior to understand the dangerous situation he now found himself entangled within.

Deciding to save face while saving his own life, Oswalt slowly ascended the stairs, walking backwards to keep the figure in his view. For a moment, the man stood there, looking upward through a dark mask that revealed no features. It wasn't until he charged upward that Oswalt felt enough urgency to do the same.

If nothing else, he at least wanted even ground on which to defend himself.

He reached the top step first, but the assailant tripped him by clasping his foot. Oswalt stumbled before rolling several times over along the carpeted floor.

His attacker definitely seemed younger and stronger, but Oswalt punched him defensively when he drew closer with the knife.

Looking desperately around for any kind of household item he might use to defend himself, the music agent saw nothing except a vase in one of the corners. He felt somewhat unmanly searching for a weapon, but the attacker did have a knife.

Oswalt reached the vase while the figure was stunned, striking him over the head with it, shattering the possibly rare antique into thousands of shards. The attack failed to do more than momentarily stun the man, leaving Oswalt at a loss for what to do. He had no phone, no one around, and very few places to hide.

Deciding his room might be as safe as any, he darted for it, slamming the door in the attacker's face before locking it. He knew the door provided a temporary safe haven at best, because its flimsy frame could easily be knocked down by an average man.

Knowing this, Oswalt rummaged through his belongings, hoping he brought something useful. He owned several firearms, but left them in Tennessee because they were unnecessary on what he considered a hospitable business trip.

He found nothing useful, but not one sound barged through the door from the other side. Leaving his baggage momentarily, Oswalt stood erect, listening for any sounds. Frozen to the spot, he didn't dare move forward in case the door burst toward him.

The last thing he wanted was a swinging door incapacitating him.

A few minutes passed, feeling more like an hour, as he remained perfectly still, breathing slowly and quietly enough that he barely heard his own exhales.

Oswalt had nearly decided to test the door when a moan originated from the closet within his room. His attention immediately focused on the closed door, wondering what awaited him on the other side.

He snagged a plastic letter opener from the desktop, thinking it was better than no defense whatsoever. Clutching it in his left hand, he slowly reached for the closet door with his right.

"Laura?" he asked cautiously toward the door.

No answer returned.

His hand had nearly reached the knob when the door to his room smashed open with wooden splinters hurling toward him, revealing his assailant once more. This time the man charged him immediately, blocking his attempt to use the letter opener, creating a bloody slit along Oswalt's arm as the knife traveled along his forearm in a flash. Though not deep, the injury proved painful, forcing a cry from the agent.

Without hesitation, the figure slugged him across the face, stunning him enough that the room began spinning. Oswalt could still see well enough to know the man was opening the closet door. Before he was able to put up any resistance, he felt himself being shoved into the room, the door slamming behind him.

Now locked in complete darkness, he tried to regain his senses, but the floor began moving upward, like an elevator. He felt his weight shift until he slammed into a wall, realizing too late the combination of being punched and losing some blood had taken a toll on his ability to function normally.

A sensation of complete helplessness overtook him as the ride turned bumpy, giving him an idea of what miners felt like when they rode rickety winch-driven elevators from the underground to the surface.

Except they had flashlights.

Seconds later, the ride abruptly stopped with a thud that sounded like metal against metal, leaving him to wonder exactly what his fate might be.

***

McCully didn't particularly like the idea of leaving Jennings and Red behind, but his primary concern steadfastly remained with the people at the mansion.

He trudged through the snow as quickly as his inappropriate winter gear and the elements allowed, finding the journey to the edge of the property difficult. His body tired quickly after repeatedly lifting his knees high enough to cross the snowdrifts, and McCully prayed Brown had passed the truck without disabling it.

Reasonably certain he locked it, McCully figured the only thing Brown might realistically do without breaking a window would be slashing the tires.

A few minutes later, he neared the truck, finding his fears unwarranted.

Everything about the truck appeared fine, so he unlocked it, climbed inside, and found the cab equally cold to the outside. As he started the vehicle, he wondered if it possessed the ability to climb the hill. Duncan had done nothing to weight down the back for snowy conditions, because he obviously never expected to be driving in snow.

In his haste, McCully made the mistake of living for the moment, failing to weight down the back as well. He knew the truck could make the trip down the hill, but completely forgot about the notion of a return trip.

"Too late now," he muttered, putting the truck in reverse.

Much to his surprise, a snowplow had passed through, shoving the snow to one side of the road while dropping sand atop the slick surface.

He suddenly felt better about returning to the mansion in one piece as he aligned the truck with the plowed path. It immediately informed him a clear trail wasn't a perfect one as the tires struggled to grip the angled surface, spinning as the truck began traveling sideways toward the hotel's security gate.

"Fuck," he said in a raspy whisper to himself, struggling with the steering wheel and brake pedal to keep from wrecking his colleague's vehicle.

When the tires reached solid snow, they finally gripped, allowing him to begin his ascent toward the hotel, slow as it was destined to be.

He doubted the truck could catch Brown and his horse for two reasons. One, a horse could navigate the easiest path on or off the road. Two, the truck was already several minutes behind, and unable to reach what McCully considered a decent speed.

Looking at the dashboard to ensure the truck was in four-wheel-drive, McCully listened to the vehicle struggling to maintain its uphill course. His mind raced to decide an appropriate action when he arrived at the mansion. With so many unknown factors, he knew the first thing he wanted to do was survey the property to see if Brown indeed beat him there.

It took several more minutes of navigating slick roads in virtually complete darkness. Even with snowfall tapering off, the headlights barely penetrated the strange foggy mist that seemed to come from changing air temperatures. McCully knew he would be giving away his destination to Brown if the deputy had chosen a path beside the road.

Cat and mouse games didn't suit him, but he wasn't about to let Brown torment anyone at the mansion in the search for his father.

Another concern passing through his mind was whether or not the deputy might be armed. McCully had no defense against a shotgun, and without warning, his colleagues at the hotel would have no time to find any of the weapons left at the mansion.

"Maybe I'm just blowing this out of proportion," he told himself when the mansion's iron gates finally came into view.

He stopped at the edge of the driveway, immediately noticing something wrong with the vehicles parked near the mansion. It took a moment before he registered that they sat a bit lower than usual, some extremely close to the ground.

Every tire on every vehicle had been slashed. Though he initially figured the deputy had gone insane and disabled the vehicles, he dismissed the notion just as quickly. If Brown had beaten him to the property, there wasn't time enough to do so much damage.

Which meant someone else meant to keep the group members exactly where they were.

McCully parked the truck at an awkward angle, quickly jumping out to discover the whereabouts and conditions of everyone left behind. He suddenly regretted leaving Red and Jennings behind, because both were obviously innocent of any wrongdoing.

Despite the cool breeze swirling inside his eardrums, McCully heard a snort that sounded distinctively like that of a horse. Unable to immediately determine the direction, he ducked behind the truck, hoping Brown hadn't spotted him. He suspected the deputy was just reaching the property, but whether or not Brown would recognize the truck had yet to be determined.

He heard another snort, followed by heavy footsteps, meaning the horse drew closer, rather than simply standing in one spot.

McCully waited and listened for the moment when he could jump the deputy, not wanting to complicate whatever problems might be happening inside. Feeling his muscles tense, he waited for the moment when the deputy crossed his path, ready to strike like a cobra.

Chapter 25

"I can't believe he left us here for dead."

Red virtually spat the words after Jennings explained their current situation to him.

"I didn't exactly say he abandoned us," Jennings corrected him. "The deputy took off, so he went after him to protect the others at the mansion. He didn't feel there was time to find both of us before he left."

Taking a moment to think things over, and pace the tiled floor of the lobby, Red didn't like being left behind, especially since there was nothing left to accomplish at the hotel.

"We can get back there through the fields," Jennings offered.

"How long would it take?"

"Maybe fifteen minutes."

Red contemplated the urgency of the situation, trying to think of any stone left unturned before they left the grounds.

"We really didn't turn over those two cars out back, did we?" he thought aloud.

Jennings nodded. They had found the strange note and abandoned their search of the vehicles rather quickly.

"What are you hoping to find?" Jennings inquired.

"Maybe a cell phone with better tower coverage, or another gun. I want to find something useful before we go hiking."

He walked toward the backdoor with the hunter close behind, thinking something was deeply wrong with their situation. Someone had devised a plan long before his group ever arrived, which targeted them and anyone who made contact with them. Divide and conquer came to mind, but he hoped to turn the tables by making haste in returning to the mansion.

Red shoved the backdoor open, immediately spotting the two disabled vehicles nearby. Jennings pulled out a flashlight they had found in the security office, turning it on before shining its beam into the sheriff's vehicle.

"What if the deputy killed his father and made up a story about it?" Jennings asked.

"You know him better than we do," Red answered. "What do you think?"

The hunter shrugged.

"Stranger things have happened."

Red examined the back of the Ford, finding several locked strong boxes he assumed contained guns and other police items the common public shouldn't have access to. The locks were embedded within the cases, meaning he needed the keys to open either one.

"Seen any keys for this thing?" he asked Jennings.

"Sure haven't."

Jennings immediately checked the overhead visor, and under the seat, just in case. He then checked the drink holder in the middle just to be certain.

"Nothing."

Red rummaged through the remaining items in the back, discovering the truck had already been ransacked by someone else, based on the loose papers and debris scattered everywhere. He wished time permitted to force the containers open, but getting back to the mansion was his number one priority.

"Anything in the car?" he asked Jennings as the hunter accessed the interior of the car with his flashlight beam.

"No keys in there; and it's locked," he replied.

"Par for the course," Red muttered disgustedly.

Jennings walked around the car to try every door of the four-door sedan, finding them all locked. Because the car had been parked right beside the building the snow drifts around it were considerably lower due to the hotel blocking much of the wind and snow. Jennings dropped to his knees, shining the flashlight underneath and around the vehicle.

"We don't have time for this," Red stated, assuming the man was looking for discarded keys.

His words apparently went unheard as Jennings fished through the snow, bobbing his beam in front of him as he went. While he continued to search,

Red opened his cell phone, seeing no signal bars in the top left corner. He dialed 911, but a scolding series of beeps reached his ear, indicating his call was going nowhere.

Jennings made a strange gleeful sound, smiling cautiously as he returned into view, jingling a set of car keys in one hand.

"Where were those?"

"In a little snow bank a few feet from the car. I saw a hole, so I dug around a little bit."

Jennings removed a glove to gain a better grip on the keys, unlocking the driver's side door momentarily. Red watched as he poked around inside, finding nothing useful.

"What about the glove compartment?" Red asked, wondering if all cops kept spare firearms nearby in case of emergency.

Even if they didn't all carry spare guns, he was glad the retired state trooper did, because Jennings came up with a small revolver.

"Keep it," Red stated, already armed with the deputy's confiscated handgun.

Jennings pocketed the gun, finding a red button inside the glove compartment. He pushed it, allowing a cuh-chunk noise to enter their ears when the trunk popped open.

Both men briskly walked to the back of the car, where the trunk lid sat just above its seam, waiting to be lifted fully open.

Red wasn't sure why he felt hesitant about opening it until he saw a few speckles of blood beneath one of the taillights. He groaned inwardly, lifting the trunk to find what he least wanted, but half expected to find.

"Shit," Jennings muttered nervously, initially turning away from the sight.

Despite killing and gutting deer, he seemed squeamish about seeing a deceased human being.

Placed awkwardly on his side, with appendages lying in various directions, the retired state trooper he remembered seeing during their tour had a large bloody wound in his back. His eyes remained open, his mouth partly agape, as though forever frozen in the moment where he was surprised from behind by an attacker.

Jennings recovered, reaching inside the trunk, which prompted Red to grasp his hand.

"You probably don't want to touch the body," he advised.

"I was just going to see if his gun was still there."

"How many do you think we need?"

Jennings shrugged defensively.

Preserving the body seemed trivial compared to the other concerns weighing on Red's mind. He now had confirmation the retired trooper was murdered, meaning Laura's disappearance, and Turner never showing up, were probably planned events.

"We have to get back there," he said without even realizing it.

In response, Jennings gave him a gravely concerned look.

"What's wrong?"

"You're talking about walking into the lion's den," he replied. "What if it's a trap, and every one of you ends up springing it?"

Red considered the man was trying to back out of assisting him, but realized the hunter had no vested interest in their dilemma, and probably had a family awaiting his return. And, if he was right, both of them walking into a trap left no one to seek help if their situation became otherwise hopeless.

"Despite what happened earlier, I don't want to see anything happen to any of you," Jennings said. "We have local authorities in West Baden, and maybe I can find someone at the police station if I walk there."

"How far is it?"

"Farther than the mansion, but I can make it."

Red looked to the wooded area behind him, then to the road leading toward the side gate where McCully had gone to retrieve the truck. God only knew what had become of McCully and the deputy, since someone had likely done harm to the sheriff. If it *was* his son, then every single one of them was in danger.

"How do I get back?"

"I'd suggest you take the road in case your buddy's truck had problems."

Red had new respect for the hunter, because the man seemed wise and level-headed, even in the face of danger.

Extending his hand, Red waited until Jennings reluctantly shook it like a dead fish. Neither wanted to admit it, but they knew this might be the last time they saw one another, at least under decent circumstances.

"If I get help, I'll be up there lickety-split," Jennings promised.

"Hopefully there won't be a need for the police, other than this poor fellow in the trunk, but I'm not holding my breath."

"Just be careful."

Jennings looked to the gate on the far end of the driveway.

"I can at least walk with you that far."

Red nodded, feeling as though they were two friends destined to part ways for the summer, not knowing if they would meet again. Their dire surroundings quickly brought his mind back to the reality that he might not survive to see Jennings again if he wasn't careful.

Walking to the mansion was half the battle, but getting inside safely might prove far more difficult. In the back of his mind, he hoped everyone would be at the front door awaiting his safe return, but a pang in his stomach suggested he expect otherwise.

A few minutes later, the two men reached the edge of the brick drive, looking at one another momentarily without words.

"Good luck," Jennings said, offering his hand this time.

"Thanks," Red replied as they shook. "I know you have nothing in this, so I appreciate your help that much more. And I'm sorry we doubted you in the beginning."

Jennings let a smirk slip.

"Well, it's understandable."

A moment of silence passed between them, neither knowing the appropriate words to say before parting.

"I'll see you in a little bit," Jennings finally said. "I know the way there."

"Glad *you* do," Red replied, implying he wasn't so certain about his own sense of direction. "Take care of yourself."

Jennings gave a nod, and the two men walked in opposite directions, each hoping to complete a small objective that might ultimately save lives. Red had no idea why anyone wanted to harm his group, much less murder a retired state trooper, but he intended to find out why. His right hand patted the gun tucked inside his coat as he trudged up the snowy hill.

Taking notice of the plowed road, Red tested the ground, finding it reasonably tolerant of human footprints. The sand kept him from slipping, but the surface felt like sheer ice in some areas. Red chose to maintain his present course, rather than wear himself out by stepping over and around snow mounds beside the road.

He quickly realized the trek would take far longer than a few minutes, but he pressed onward, hoping to find his brother alive and well. He wanted answers, and was beginning to understand why some locals claimed the hotel was cursed.

If only he would have paid more attention to the hotel's history, he might have gained an understanding of the plot unfolding around him.

Realizing it was too late to change the past, he trudged forward, determined to reach the mansion before anyone else came up missing, or got hurt.

Chapter 26

McCully waited patiently, unable to see anything from his vantage point. If he dared peek over the top of the truck, Brown would spot him. He tried peering under the truck, but snow mounds everywhere prevented him from seeing anything except the color white.

While his position felt uncomfortable, he deemed it necessary. Cold from the snow began soaking his pants, but he remained still, listening for the deputy's movements. Another snort from the horse reached his ears, as well as the clop from its hooves as it stepped onto the concrete driveway.

McCully had been in one fistfight in his life, and it was broken up by a teacher. By nature, he was a pacifist, not because of his religion or family beliefs, but mostly because of his public image. After releasing a solo album, and being part of a group effort with his family, he refused to do anything that might embarrass them.

His stand on violence caused him to rethink his strategy. If the deputy was a reasonable man, telling him the truth at the hotel, then he might work with McCully, saving them both painful swelling and bruises.

What seemed a noble thought cost him the advantage in what he termed the worst scenario possible. Before dismounting, Brown surveyed the area, spotting McCully after his horse passed the truck. His eyes widened as he reached for something on the opposite side, forcing McCully into action as he sprang to his feet, grabbing the deputy by his free left foot, flipping him completely over the horse.

Brown landed hard, never grabbing whatever object he reached for, with a bewildered look that McCully had beaten him to the mansion. McCully refused to waste one second against a seasoned peace officer, scurrying around the horse to confront the grounded deputy. He slipped along the ice, but regained his footing as Brown managed to get to one knee before being tackled into a snow pile.

Using McCully's momentum against him, the deputy threw the potential investor over him, but McCully scrambled back quickly to grasp the deputy's arm. He now saw that Brown was reaching for a shotgun, which caused him to wonder why the man needed any weaponry to search for his father.

As he grabbed Brown's arm, the man threw up an elbow, hitting McCully squarely enough in the nose that he saw a white flash as though someone had taken his picture from a foot away. The sharp pain in his nose told him it might be broken, or at least cut open, but he kicked toward Brown, catching the shotgun as the deputy went to raise it.

Without giving his next move much thought, he charged Brown, sending them both falling into a snowdrift. Buried in snow, and unable to see through the millions of flakes around and on top of him, McCully grasped in desperation until his hands wrapped themselves around Brown's throat.

He noticed his self-preservation instincts taking over his rational thought, perhaps because his nose hurt so badly. A few seconds later, he realized the shotgun was far enough away that neither man could readily grab it, and Brown was beginning to resist less and less.

McCully released the stranglehold before he killed the man, falling back to a seated position in the snow. As much as his breathing seemed to come in heaves from the excitement, and his injury, Brown's sounded worse as the man coughed to regain normal breaths.

"You're the killer, aren't you?" McCully accused the man between chilled inhales that felt like nitrogen gas entering his lungs.

"You're insane," Brown spat in reply. "I don't know what you're hiding, but I'm going to find out."

"I'm not hiding anything. I came up here to keep you from harming my friends."

McCully rubbed the side of his nose, feeling blood where the skin had split open. It continued to throb, and if it wasn't broken, he would be surprised.

"I'm looking for my father," Brown insisted.

"And we're looking for our missing friend. We can either duke it out, or we can walk in there together like civilized human beings."

The look on Brown's face indicated he did not trust McCully, so it was no surprise when he lurched for the gun once again. McCully tried to block this attempt, but slipped momentarily in the snow, allowing the deputy to slug him with the shotgun's stock. Though a glancing blow, it knocked McCully to the ground, allowing Brown to hammer him in the head with the gun's butt, bringing about a calming darkness.

***

Jana looked at Keith's discarded belongings lying on one of the industrial metal cooking tables. She sensed their search, or at least Keith's trail, grew cold in the very spot where she stood, but saw no sign of any other exits.

"What is this place?" Duncan asked. "The Clue Mansion?"

"I'm waiting to find the secret passageway that takes us to the entertainment room," she replied, playing along.

"And I'm waiting to find out if it was Colonel Mustard with the candlestick that dragged Keith away."

Jana remained silent a moment, touching one of the nearby walls as she examined a small indented area that looked wallpapered. A shelving unit sat almost perfectly inside, holding an array of canned goods. She looked on top of one can, noticing a thin dusty coating that indicated the can had been there for some time.

She wondered if the cleaning lady missed certain areas during her rounds, doubting the cooking area was a high priority because guests wouldn't normally travel to the cellar. Strangely, Jana never met the woman in person. Their phone conversation led to Jana faxing over a list of instructions, along with the contact information to send an invoice for payment.

They had not spoken since their initial conversation, but Jana hadn't seen any issues with the housekeeping upstairs.

"Penny for your thoughts," Duncan said, bringing her back to their plight.

"I'm beginning to think there's something secret about this room that we're not seeing, all joking aside. Maybe Keith was right about the third floor we saw from outside."

"You're the hostess. Do you want to tear this place apart and see what we find?"

Jana wasn't worried about damages, thinking the consequences of losing several important clients would be much more detrimental than replacing walls and fixtures. Her concern stemmed from the time, or lack thereof, left to find the missing guests.

"I don't know," she replied. "Keith went through the second floor and didn't find anything helpful."

"But now he's gone," Duncan retorted. "And we were near the only real door in this place the entire time. That doesn't leave a whole lot of places to hide."

It suddenly occurred to her that leaving Oswalt alone probably wasn't the wisest move on their part. Granted, he said he wasn't going anywhere, but Keith, Judith, and Laura all vanished without a trace.

Or one uttered word.

"We need to check on Oswalt," she said with more urgency than she intended.

Duncan read her meaning, leading the way toward the stairs. He took hold of her hand, more as a protective measure, rather than a display of affection. Jana felt reassured because of his protectiveness, but even more so that he understood the danger she sensed around them.

He let go of her hand after his body crumpled against the door atop the stairs. His attempt to open it failed, so Duncan crashed against the door, discovering it was stuck in place.

"Ouch," he said, rubbing his left shoulder.

"What's the matter?"

"I think someone locked us in here."

They exchanged concerned looks, knowing Oswalt was responsible for some dastardly acts, or became another missing person during their absence.

Duncan turned the knob more carefully this time, pushing against the door with his shoulder, yielding no success. He looked to Jana with a distraught look.

"Oh, well," he said before thrusting his shoulder against the door once, then twice, before it finally burst outward.

Jana noticed a thin cutting board splintered along the floor, indicating someone had rigged it to block the door. It seemed a weak attempt at keeping them downstairs, so she wondered if it was a stall tactic.

Duncan walked with a purpose through the kitchen area, reaching the doorway as Jana shuffled her feet to keep pace. They both found no people, and no sound, when they reached the open downstairs area. Jana stole a glance toward the chair where Oswalt last sat, seeing only the blanket draped over the arms as though thrown there hastily.

"Maybe he stepped outside," Duncan suggested, stepping toward the door.

He hesitated when his hand touched the knob, deciding to look out a nearby window before stepping outside. Jana noticed the deadbolt and lock were both secured, so it seemed unlikely, if not impossible, that Oswalt had locked them unless he had a set of keys.

The deadbolt turned internally by hand, meaning only a key could access it from outside, or it needed to be locked from the inside. Duncan had exhibited good judgment thus far, so Jana joined him at the window to peer outside, rather than stepping outside.

"My truck," Duncan said on the verge of exclamation.

As quickly as relief crossed his face, it passed. Jana wondered why his truck would be back without any of its last three occupants knocking on the door. Apparently, similar thoughts ran through Duncan's mind.

"We're getting out of here," Duncan said, his voice barely hiding the trepidation they both felt.

"How?" Jana felt compelled to ask, knowing the only reason they remained behind was a lack of reliable transportation.

Duncan reached inside each of his pockets, looking more desperate by the second.

"I have a second set of keys," he told her after coming up empty. "They're upstairs with my stuff. I'm getting them, and we're using my truck to go get help."

Jana wanted to argue, but decided she wanted to leave. His truck had apparently made the trip down the hill and back, but she hated the idea of them being separated, even momentarily.

"Be careful," she said quickly, returning her gaze to the window as he headed for the stairs, walking briskly, barely able to maintain his composure.

Thinking she saw a shadow outside, Jana started to follow Duncan's path upstairs, but decided to wait for him instead. Until someone knocked on the door, or attempted to break their way inside, she could simply hope for the best.

A minute or so passed with no activity, and not even the slightest of noises, worrying her. She looked to the door, staring intently at the knob a moment, then hesitantly began ascending the stairway to find Duncan. Every breath came with a sense of dread attached to it, but Jana fought to maintain her composure, wondering deep down if she was the sole survivor of someone's murderous plan.

She recalled how vague Clouse had been concerning the hotel's past, but she knew enough, even though the television news and newspapers provided stories with sketchy details. Murders had occurred at the hotel, and not the poisoned sipping tea kind, either. Bloodshed and gore were symbolic of the grisly murders at the West Baden Springs Hotel several years prior, and only now did she begin to wonder who might have enough inside information to orchestrate such a fiendish scheme.

"Dan?" she called, waiting several seconds for an answer that never came.

A shiver ran from head to toe as she grasped the railing for support, her hand trembling from fear of the unknown. Taking a deep breath she took another step forward, beginning to wonder what sights awaited her on the second level.

Chapter 27

cCully somehow knew he had sunken into a strange level of unconsciousness that transported him once again to a different time, but not a different place.

He couldn't tell the year, because the mansion appeared very much the same. Now able to stand up, he found no snow around him. In fact, the climate looked like an early morning in the spring or fall because fog banks lingered in the nearby hilly fields. Several partly turned leaves were scattered across the yard, indicating it was probably late fall.

Most of the grass appeared a healthy green, covered lightly in moisture as though a giant wet hand grazed the tops of the stout blades. No cars cluttered the driveway to his right, and for a moment, it seemed he stood completely alone. The crunch of leaves closer to the mansion drew his attention to two men standing beside one of the twelve stone carvings.

One of the men had his back completely turned to McCully, but the other gentleman seemed older, almost decrepit, the native Tennessean thought. Based on their attire, he guessed this conversation somewhat recent, certainly within the past decade.

Clothing from his childhood certainly had a different look, and he readily recognized such outfits as those he hated from his school photographs. Their clothes looked nowhere near that dated, and McCully thought they looked fairly expensive, like designer brands.

"I take it you've called me here for a reason," the man with his back to McCully stated.

"I've called you here because I'm dying, and I have a need for a man of your talents before my time comes."

"You know I don't come cheap, but I suppose that doesn't much matter to you."

The older man let a grin emerge from behind the wrinkles in his face. McCully felt certain this was a sinister grin, which seemed out of place based on the conversation so far.

"I've saved enough back that I can still adequately cover your fee."

Who was this old man? He spoke softly, eloquently, like a scholar.

A thought suddenly occurred to McCully about who owned the mansion, and the hotel, at one time. He felt reasonably certain he was staring at Doctor Martin Smith, but he couldn't guarantee it unless they spoke one another's names.

"I've taken measures to *prolong* my life, if you will. But I'm not certain how my master plan will unfold."

"Considering the nosedive you almost took off your hotel, I'd say you're lucky to be having this conversation."

Nosedive? McCully wondered. He remembered something about Smith allegedly being murdered when he was thrown from the hotel's roof. It also seemed his death was later disputed by several news agencies. Some of the news made national headlines, and McCully had made a point to do some online research before leaving Tennessee.

"Again, that was part of my plan," the old man said easily. "I'm now able to move about undetected without fear of interference from Clouse or his friends."

McCully didn't recognize the voice of the man conspiring with the older man, but he had some notions about where the conversation was headed. If this man was the one behind all of the disappearances and murders, it made sense, but he couldn't see the man's face or recognize the voice. His vision had taken the liberty of planting him in one spot for the duration once he drew this close to the men.

"Move about?" the man questioned. "You're the richest man in the state. No one's going to touch you unless you allow them to."

Again, the old man let a thin smile slip, but this time it bore a look of understanding toward the man's ignorance.

"If my plan works as I hope, I will have no need for your services, but if I should fail, and Clouse or his comrades kill me, I will need you to bring me back."

The man shook his head from one side to the other several times, not comprehending what the doctor had told him. McCully wondered if the mystery man was also a doctor, or possibly a paramedic, based on the older man's words.

"You see, my good man, what I plan on doing is not moral, nor is it legal. And I have it on good authority that you are a man who gets things done for people, no matter what."

"Obviously you know who I am, and what I do, so I wonder if I'm allowed to ask a few questions before you get to the meat of the conversation."

"Feel free."

"Why would you go after Clouse? I thought he was like a son to you."

"Let's just say he took something very precious from me. What he took left a terrible void in my heart that can never be replaced. I had intended to leave him out of my terrible future doings, but what he did cannot be forgiven."

The man nodded in understanding, though McCully still felt confused about what Clouse had done to the man. From what Jana and the media told, he was a pretty upstanding guy.

"Very well then, doc. I'm not a medical expert, but I have a suspicion you're going to have a hard time enacting revenge against Clouse in your condition. Is that part of why I'm here?"

"Not at all. The next time you see me, my good man, I'll appear younger by twenty years or more, and be completely healthy."

McCully couldn't see the man's expression, but his body language told enough, because he stiffened in surprise.

"You're shittin' me, right?"

"Not at all. The one thing money can't buy is life, but I've found a way to cheat death for as long as I choose. And when I'm finished with Mr. Clouse, I'll have everything I want."

"So if I'm not here to help you against *him*, what exactly am I here for?"

Now the man sounded a bit uncertain, as though he thought the elderly man might make him the next victim in some kind of bizarre plot.

"As I've stated, you are here in case I fail. In case I need to be resurrected to finish my work."

An uncomfortable silence filled the air momentarily. McCully understood the mystery man's position, because he felt utterly confused as well.

"You see, with the same forces that will make me younger the next time I see you, I can be brought back from the dead."

The man remained silent a few more seconds before speaking again.

"I take it you aren't talking about Catholic sanctioned practices here."

"Not quite," the older man answered, holding up his forefinger. "But I think you have an idea about what I speak of."

"I do, but I'm not sure I buy into black magic or witchcraft."

"You needn't buy into it. When we meet again, you'll have your proof."

"And if you're right, what's to keep me from using this miracle cure for myself?"

"A general lack of knowledge on the subject, and the vast amount of money I plan to pay for your services."

Now the man crossed his arms, intently listening. McCully sensed the man was certainly no fool, and his elder had obviously planned this meeting quite thoroughly. The man he believed was Smith seemed to have the answer for any and every question.

"In the unfortunate event of my death, I need you to carry out a certain ritual that will, in theory, bring me back to this world."

McCully realized if this was true, money and the right thugs certainly could buy eternal life. But at what price? In lore, vampires murdered others to maintain their livelihood, so he wondered if sacrifices were necessary to keep Smith young, healthy, and alive.

"See these carvings?" the old man asked, pointing to one of the biblical tales carved in the mansion's stone. "There are twelve in all, and they weren't put here for their symbolism or beauty. They are part of a ritual that must be carried out."

"What ritual?"

"First, should I die, my body must be buried at the hotel grounds for no less than twenty-four hours. Then, it should be transported to this very building with some of the soil from the hotel accompanying it. You see, these twelve pieces of art have numbers, which are significant dates in the history of my hotel down the road."

"You're going a little fast, doc. Isn't there some elder scroll or something I'm supposed to follow?"

"You would be wise to hold your tongue, young man. Mocking me is not something I pay good money to hear."

The mystery man cleared his throat uncomfortably.

"No disrespect, doc, but this doesn't sound like my kind of work."

"Your 'kind of work'?" the reply came with a raised eyebrow. "I think theft, deceit, and murder are right up your alley. Beyond that, the ritual is putting everything into place and pushing a button. I've arranged absolutely everything to keep this simple and foolproof."

A few seconds of silence passed.

"You see," the older man said, "if I die, I don't want to leave my *Easter Sunday* to chance. There is half a million dollars for you right now, to keep you interested in my affairs, and another five-million, if and when the time comes for you to do the deed. You collect a dozen specific people, you hook them up to the contraption I have inside this building, and you walk away. It's not even murder, really. It's more of an assisted suicide, if that eases your conscience. Of course, you'd have to stay in the area and create a cover identity for yourself. Think of it as being the spider spinning the perfect web with which to lure your prey."

The man simply rubbed the back of his neck in thought momentarily.

"Five-million is enough for most men to retire on for the rest of their lives," the old man prodded. "Even a man of your talent and tastes could surely make that last several years."

"I don't suppose it would count if I killed you and brought you back?" the man said, making bad humor that his companion simply scoffed at.

"Your pay would be substantially less, my boy. Now, would you care to have a look inside at the device, or is this where we part ways and never speak of this conversation to anyone again?"

McCully already knew the forthcoming answer, wishing he were back in real time to do something about the tragic events he now understood something about.

"After you," the man said, outstretching his arm toward the front door.

***

Jana debated whether or not she really wanted to search for Duncan alone on the second floor. Something told her she was already too late if he had been abducted, or worse, so she stood midway up the stairwell for a moment.

"Dan?" she called again, trying not to sound meek or mild in case she found him safe and sound.

She hated appearing weak in front of men, but this time Jana had legitimate reasons to be worried. Her entire life, beginning with her father, she had been subliminally taught that women were inferior. It wasn't until her parents divorced that her mother finally had some talks with her. Going to college for several years put

Jana in touch with roommates who were anything but shy, helping her blossom into the independent woman she always wanted to be.

The same drive that brought her success in business now prodded her to take another step upward, then another. She reached the top step a moment later, seeing no evidence of Duncan, or anyone else.

Six rooms to either side of her all had their doors closed. One looked damaged around one side of its frame, indicating it had been kicked inward. What, if anything, lurked behind each of them required her to open them. It occurred to her that Duncan had no reason to shut his door if he simply planned on grabbing keys and a warm coat. She examined the tags on each door, frantically trying to recall which room she assigned him to.

When she found it, Jana walked briskly to the door, then listened, trying to decipher if there was any activity inside. She heard nothing, so she slowly opened the door, hoping perhaps to find Duncan packing a suitcase, or desperately searching for his keys.

It emitted a long, almost painful creak as it swung inward, revealing a strange sight to Jana, barely visible in the low lighting. She stepped inside, putting a hand to her mouth, suppressing a gasp.

Only the desk lamp illuminated the room, throwing strange shadows everywhere. What appeared to be a long, shiny serpent taking up half of the room began to take shape when she dared draw closer.

A crinkling noise entered her ears as the serpentine form jiggled back and forth, sounding somewhat like a cat playing inside a plastic bag. She then heard grunting, like someone struggling to finish a task.

Or break free.

"Oh my God," she said under her breath, seeing the true form before her for the first time.

A person she assumed had to be Duncan appeared trapped inside some sort of long, clear plastic trap that not only ensnared him, but seemed to be dragging him toward the opposite side of the room. The only details she found were the shimmering black from beneath the clear coating that could only be Duncan's motorcycle jacket. She stepped closer, finding his blond hair at the end of the trap, though he seemed completely unaware of her presence.

"Dan!" she shouted to gain his attention. "I'm here."

Only muffled cries returned, so she knew the trap had fiercely taken hold of him.

She reached forward, touching the plastic like someone might test a hot stove, fearing it might have some sort of stickiness or other device to pull her in as well. Getting herself trapped did neither of them any good.

On the surface, the plastic felt somewhat like a thick painter's tarp, but some sort of substance lurked just beneath the surface, likely acting as some sort of fly-trap to keep Duncan from breaking free. It felt about as thick as bubble wrap used to package shipping items, but legitimately solid all the way through.

Duncan grunted and groaned a few more times, then sort of whimpered, as though giving up hope.

When the device moved several feet away from her, toward the closet, she pounced on the end just below Duncan's feet, preventing it from moving further. Peering around the room, Jana's eyes came to rest at the desk, spying some scissors, pens, and a letter opener jutting from a desk organizer.

She leapt from atop the trap to snatch the scissors, allowing the mysterious force from within the closet to reel in the plastic like a fish. Duncan thumped along the floor several times, beginning to fight once more to free himself.

Having no idea whether the man consciously knew she was helping him or not, she patted the plastic until she found his feet, immediately diving into the plastic with the scissors. The edges seemed too worn to have much effect on the trap, but some of it split open, revealing a sticky inner liner.

Jana shrieked inadvertently when her fingers rubbed against the substance, immediately believing she was another fly stuck in the web. She pulled free, but decided the scissors put her in harm's way. Something larger, like a garden tool, felt more appropriate for such a task. Time, however, didn't allow for any trips outside to explore the garage.

"Damn it!" she said to herself, searching for a way to stop the trap from completely drawing Duncan into its clutches.

She knew if he disappeared into the closet, he would certainly be lost to the inner sanctum of the house none of the guests had found. Keith had been right, and if someone had believed in him sooner, none of them would be in such grave danger.

Duncan struggled against the covering as she sat atop a non-sticky portion of the snare, trying to slow it down. Jana wondered how the man could breathe at all, because the plastic seemed to wrap itself tightly against his body, like a latex glove over a hand.

Though she felt a tug from beneath her, the tarp failed to move any closer to the closet. Now engaged in a losing battle, Jana needed to decide whether to seek a way to cut Duncan free, or simply keep him from being swallowed by the closet, and ultimately, the mansion itself.

Another problem presented itself when the room's main door creaked once again, revealing a shadowy figure standing in the threshold. The low lighting prevented Jana from identifying the person, but the way in which he stood silently made her suspect he wasn't someone friendly.

Making the situation more ominous, it appeared his right hand clutched a shotgun.

After giving him a few seconds to speak, Jana wondered if he was stunned, taking in this strange sight rather than admiring an evil plan coming together.

"Either tell me who you are, and what you want, or get over here and help me," she demanded, wanting answers.

A few silent seconds passed.

"What the fuck is that?" a male voice with just a hint of a drawl asked.

"I don't know, but it's trying to drag my friend into the closet."

Since the man inquired about the device restraining Duncan, Jana assumed he was friendly, or at least not the cause of her problems.

"I need something to cut him out of this. Can you get a kitchen knife, or something larger, if you can find it?"

Instead of complying or answering, the man stepped forward, finally kneeling down beside the synthetic material. He touched it, giving Jana an opportunity to examine him a bit more closely. He set the gun to his side, which set some of her fears at ease.

In essence, he didn't look much different than the guests from the investment group, wearing cowboy boots and a thick duster. He appeared rugged, but not unkempt or unclean. She guessed he might be a local to the West Baden area, but didn't recognize him. A strange smell she couldn't place crossed her nostrils, finally coming to her a few seconds later.

He smelled a little bit like the inside of a barn, which she recalled from visits to her uncle's farm as a child.

His curious blue eyes surveyed the trap before looking to Jana with a degree of uncertainty, as though wondering how far his trust extended.

Looking to his right, the stranger seemed to examine the device restraining the great-grandson of a prominent businessman.

"Where does it lead?" he asked with a bit more emotion than before.

"I don't know," Jana said. "Into that closet, and probably into some secret room. We don't have time to wait, or it'll take him."

Duncan grunted once more, disrupting the break in their conversation. They both had unanswered questions lingering between them, but Jana felt certain Duncan couldn't last much longer in a suffocating elongated bag.

However the device was constructed, it was meant to conduct its business quickly, and without interruption. Perhaps the house itself was haunted, or evil, but she couldn't let it obtain Duncan without a fight. She took the scissors up, carefully feeling for his face through the plastic, slitting holes in the substance so he could breathe.

An immediate sigh of relief came from Duncan's mouth as he took in fresh air. Though he seemed unable to formulate words, the entire ordeal appeared to convince the new stranger that something unusual had taken hold of the guests.

"I'll see what I can find downstairs," the stranger finally said of Jana's request for a larger tool with which to cut the plastic, taking up the shotgun. "I've only got two shells for this, and they probably wouldn't want me tearing holes in their new floor."

"At this point, I don't care," Jana replied.

"Give me a minute. I'll find you a big knife, or we'll use this if we have to," he said, holding up the shotgun.

"There are two kitchen areas," she informed him. "The bigger one is actually in the cellar."

"Okay," he said with a nod.

With that, he headed out the door, his footsteps growing less audible as he headed for the stairs.

Jana returned to a seated position on the plastic, feeling it strain as it was tugged with their combined weight upon it. She worried about someone else coming up the stairs, still not completely convinced the new stranger was a friend, rather than a foe.

Chapter 28

Red continued to walk along the road toward the hotel, wondering how much further he had left to travel. Going downhill in the truck seemed so much faster, especially when he wondered if his life might be taken at any moment.

He worried about Keith and the others, wishing there were some way to simply call and talk to them. The freakish storm had knocked out their cellular phones, and without the benefit of landlines at the mansion or hotel, they were basically stranded. Sheer luck had left power intact at both places, and with the snowfall decreasing, he hoped help might arrive sooner than the next morning.

Looking at his watch, he found it was just past ten o'clock. Though a few hours removed from the witching hour, but he felt exhausted enough to crawl into bed and sleep until noon the next day.

If only the strange events wouldn't plague his mind while he rested.

Red trudged uphill, hoping Jennings had better luck in town. He didn't recall where the town or county police stations were located, but he knew they had to be in the heart of the town, likely in French Lick. If that was so, Jennings had nearly a mile to walk, even after he reached the highway.

Enough snow covered the ground that it looked like early dawn all around him. Even with the cloud cover, the night revealed most everything to him, like a movie shot with a bad filter that didn't quite give it a nighttime effect. He saw bare trees, open fields, and the remains of broken fences on both sides of the road.

Now that he trusted Jennings, Red needed to reevaluate his trust within the investment group. He began wondering if someone had brought them to Indiana for malicious reasons as a whole, or if they had fallen prey to a local maniac.

Duncan was the person bent on bringing them to see the hotel, but Red saw no reason how the man would benefit from injuring or killing others.

Duncan needed funding from the group if he wanted the hotel. Of course, being a sole survivor and suing the hotel's current owner might bring about wealth enough to attain the property in a settlement.

Red shook off the negative notion, dismissing Duncan as a real suspect. Snow began chilling the lower parts of his legs, where he had no protection from the elements. Years of working ranches with Keith, and driving big rigs, had taken a toll on his knees. They felt more brittle and achy than usual, reminding him why he enjoyed living south of Kentucky.

He distracted himself again by thinking of the people in his group, and his opinions of them.

There was McCully, the young singer who had come from an already famous family. Despite moderate success, the man remained modest, even introverted some of the time. Red recalled seeing a documentary covering the history of bluegrass music where one already successful female singer made a bold statement.

Red grumbled the words, or at least a close rendition, to himself in recollection. "Everyone who knew anything about bluegrass wanted to be a McCully."

Why Dave McCully had avoided settling down like everyone else in his family eluded Red, but he supposed the man had his reasons. He wasn't one to sleep around with groupies, or throw his money around in public, but something about him wasn't completely normal either.

His thoughts took a right turn, thinking about Oswalt. The music agent wasn't at all shy, and he had been married and divorced several times, as though he just wanted the title of husband for conversation's sake. When there was business to be conducted, he was one of the shrewdest men Red had ever met, but he changed faster than Superman when the time to celebrate arrived.

Oswalt occasionally got slobbering drunk, but always found his way home, or to some woman's apartment for the night. It amazed Red the man's wallet had never been stolen during one of his rendezvous.

Of course, he trusted Keith. Not only was the man his older brother, and the one who helped raise him more than his parents at times, but he had no incentive to plan murder or abduction. Above all else, Keith possessed morals and a fear of God that kept him in place before he ever let his emotions lead him into trouble.

Realizing his legs were drenched below the knees, Red began to slow from the uphill journey, feeling sluggish and cold. He needed warmth, and soon, or the snow might swallow him whole. Though it wasn't extremely cold or windy at the moment, the combination of the long hike and the cold wetness creeping up his body gave him concern.

Think of the names, he chastised himself, trying to keep his mind off his troubles. Laura and Turner were missing, which gave them opportunity without being suspected or seen. No, no, he thought.

Jana? He hardly pictured her able to subdue Turner, and she hadn't left the mansion, meaning she could not have killed the retired trooper.

Judith's alibi seemed very similar. Though sometimes a cold fish, Judith was above any illegal activity. She came from nothing, earning everything she had in life on her own terms, none of which meant stepping on other people or taking shortcuts.

Red's thoughts came screeching to a halt when headlights appeared ahead of him, over the hill. They came his way, bobbing up and down, and at a greater speed than he suspected any sane person might drive.

He wondered if joyriding teenagers might be sloshing through the snow and ice recklessly, not daring to stand in the road to flag the driver down. Standing at the side instead, he waited until the car, a little Buick of some sort, came into view before throwing his hands into the air. He crossed his arms back and forth like a plane handler with glow sticks along an airport runway, signaling for help, hoping the driver might be sympathetic.

As though the driver never saw him, the car continued to speed ahead, flying over one short bump, changing its direction just enough that Red felt certain it was going to clip him. He dove to the side of the road as the car continued onward without as much as a tap on the brakes.

Red landed in the ditch, soaking himself to the core as he looked back. He wondered if the driver even noticed that he almost struck a man, not daring to stop for fear of Red's wrath. Perhaps the driver was drunk, never even seeing the pedestrian at the road's edge.

At this point Red didn't care. He felt certain if the driver had stopped, he still might have been inclined to plant a kiss on him or her for helping him. Any anger would have been tossed aside like dirty water out the backdoor on a farm.

For a moment, Red remained on all fours, water dripping from his chin, and off his jacket. Every inch of both legs now felt cold and wet as a shiver shot through the length of his body.

He propped himself up to a kneeling position, realizing he now had little time to reach the mansion, or find shelter, before his body completely failed him. Regaining his feet, he plodded up the hill, wishing McCully would return for him, or Jennings might find him any moment with help from the town. He felt both scenarios were unrealistic, which drove him forward, desperate to check on his brother with the deadly new circumstances surrounding the group.

***

Arlan Brown couldn't believe the events unfolding before his eyes. Had he been drunk beyond belief, or under the influence of some illegal substance, everything might have looked more plausible.

He found himself in the mansion's kitchen, looking for a long knife of some sort, when he really just wanted answers about his father. Pulling out several drawers, he found nothing useful, wondering if the men he found at the hotel were being truthful.

Seeing someone trapped in what he considered an industrial, lengthy garbage bag upstairs unnerved him, but he now believed something very wrong had occurred at the hotel, and this property. And his father was somehow trapped by it as well.

Finding a knife set at the counter's far end, Brown discovered only the smaller knives remained fastened to their holder. He wondered if some conspiracy had enveloped within the mansion, and if his father had found himself in the wrong place at the wrong time.

He took the largest knife possible from the set, thinking scissors were probably a better alternative. Refusing to give up, he opened several more drawers, pawing through them for anything useful. He discovered everything from cheese graters to rolling pins, but nothing with a better, sharper blade.

"Shit," he mumbled as a slight creaking noise entered his ears from behind him.

His shotgun was a few feet from him, but within reach, as he spun around, finding the cellar door Jana had mentioned slightly ajar. He debated how much time he realistically had to save the man wrapped inside the plastic before he was pulled inside the closet, or suffocated from the sticky inner liner.

He decided a trip downstairs couldn't take long, so he scooped up the gun, using it to prop open the door long enough for him to slide past. A quick descent of the stairs led him directly to the very industrial kitchen, which obviously served as the heart and soul of any cooking activities.

Brown recognized the room as a kitchen, but barely. It appeared as though a tornado had swept through the room, recklessly reorganizing everything in its path. Pots, pans, and utensils were strewn across the counter tops and floors, immediately causing him to regret the trek downstairs.

When he turned to leave, the ding of an elevator door stopped him cold. Brown slowly turned, wondering where in the room an elevator might be. He dared not waste valuable time, but he wanted to see if the elevator doors were readily visible before heading back.

He cautiously moved from his safe spot toward the area where the ding originated, cranking his neck forward to see around a small corner to his left. After seeing the bizarre scene upstairs, Brown had no desire to be wrapped in plastic or abducted in some other way. Of course, he had his trusty shotgun with him, so he felt a bit more at ease.

A shotgun shell possessed the ability to shred almost any object into Swiss cheese at close range. Brown held it in a ready position, hearing a ding, followed by the sound of an elevator door opening.

Unfortunately, Brown had no visual to go with the sound because a strange pantry filled with canned goods stood before a papered wall. Standing momentarily in confusion, he allowed the gun to complacently fall limp in his right hand. He looked at the covering behind the woven metal rack, observing too late that the covering was little more than cardboard doctored up with wallpaper to hide the truth.

Before Brown could contemplate his next move, the false partition and everything in front of it tumbled toward him, knocking him to the ground. He found himself sprawled out and pinned beneath the metal rack with heavy cans of food falling across his body. Several cans injured him, but one in particular struck the side of his head with more than a glancing blow.

The deputy had no time to nurse his wounds because a dark figure gracefully climbed through the tangled mess with dexterity, carrying a large knife. Brown understood now why there had been no large knives around, scanning the area with his eyes for his shotgun while his right hand reached out like an antenna.

He felt only debris with his hand, quickly diverting his attention to the man who seemed intent on attacking him. Both of the deputy's hands thrust upward to stop the knife from plunging into his heart. Still pinned by the shelving, which had become awkwardly propped into the elevator area, Brown had only his arms with which to defend himself.

His assailant rammed the back of his skull into the concrete floor, stunning him momentarily, but not enough to disable him. Brown launched a fist into the figure's face, kicking fiercely with his legs to free himself from the entanglement of shelving and cans.

Again the assailant thrust downward with the knife, but Brown brushed the attack aside with a sweep of his arms. He glanced once more, unable to see his shotgun, which had slid somewhere under the preparation tables. Ensured he had a few seconds without the threat of more assaults, he threw the shelving unit up enough to slide his legs free.

He stood up, finding himself staring into the vacant hood of who he assumed was the newest killer in a line of people obsessed with the West Baden Springs Hotel. Though Brown didn't know all of the facts about the earlier murders, he knew the motivation stemmed as far back as the 1934 when the Jesuits took possession of the place.

Police detectives from Bloomington, along with the state police, headed the earlier investigations, virtually shutting his father's county police force out entirely. He recalled his father griping about how uncooperative the other agencies were in teaming with him, since he was a new sheriff.

Like his fellow county officers, Brown was shut out of the investigation as well, particularly after one of their own officers was butchered.

Considering he didn't have a weapon in-hand, Brown found himself at a slight disadvantage, but at least he had a vertical base, and an ample opportunity to defend himself. He plucked a rolling pin from the table beside him, somewhat surprised it didn't roll off to strike him in the head like everything else.

Boring a stare into the masked assailant, he flinched forward, faking an attack.

Falling for it, the figure took a half step back, allowing Brown to charge him and swing the rolling pin toward his head. The figure ducked, taking the blow in the shoulder blade instead, but Brown swung again, finding his arm slashed by the knife before the rolling pin left a mark. Instead, it dropped to the ground, rolling away from both combatants.

The wound stung, dripping blood immediately, but Brown clasped the man's knife hand with both of his, swinging the assailant into the wall. He felt relatively certain the cut hit a blood vessel of some sort, but he had no time to assess the wound.

Brown kneed the figure in the groin, trying to gain advantage any way he could. The attack proved effective, hunching the man forward with an audible groan. Brown picked up the rolling pin once more, striking the man in the side of the head with a weakened blow. His injured arm writhed with pain, as though a thousand wasps had stung him at once. His grip on the pin had been weak, indicating his muscles were also injured during the attack.

Basically, his right arm had become useless to him. He crossed the figure's face with a left hook, trying to buy some time. Though he shot a gun right-handed, Brown was in fact a southpaw. As the figure slumped against the wall, apparently nearing unconsciousness, Brown scurried toward the elevator in search of his shotgun.

He reached the debris field in front of the elevator, dropping to his knees to look for his shotgun, which he discovered closer to the other side of the table. With his injured hand, the weapon was certainly out of reach, because he now had trouble grasping objects. The knife had apparently done nerve or tendon damage as well.

Hearing a noise behind him, Brown kicked outward like a mule with one leg, catching the assailant squarely in the abdomen. He then made his way around the table, since it was too low for him to roll beneath. Quickly locating the shotgun, Brown reached with his good hand to pluck it from the cold ground when the figure leapt onto the narrow side of the table, sliding along it like some barroom brawl scene from a movie.

It all happened so fast that Brown couldn't avoid being tackled to the ground. He never grasped his weapon, so the deputy was again forced to use only his hands, one of which was virtually disabled.

He immediately went for the figure's throat, trying to find it beneath the folds of black cloth. His plan immediately went south as the figure produced his knife once again, aiming it toward Brown's chest. Blocking the attempt with both hands, Brown left himself exposed in other areas, and this time it was the attacker who kneed him in the groin.

Pain shot through his crotch, but he continued to block the other attack until he thrust himself away from the figure.

Brown dashed toward his shotgun before standing up completely, looking like a monkey on all fours as he struggled to maintain his balance. He reached the gun, clasped it with both hands, and turned to confront the figure before accomplishing a ready position.

When he turned, he found his assailant already beside him, clasping the shotgun with both hands as well. Brown's injured arm provided about as much strength as a small child might muster, so when the figure thrust the cold metal into his nose, there was virtually no resistance. It busted his nose open, at the bridge, allowing blood to readily cascade down his face.

Several droplets landed in his eyes, blinding him long enough for the figure to ram the shotgun into his nose again, doubling the pain as his eyesight went from a blinding white to strange black circles like solar eclipses. His fingers lost their grip on the weapon, allowing the figure to steal it away. When Brown recovered enough to look up again, the shotgun's stock had already taken a path leading directly toward the back of his head.

Unimaginable pain shot through his skull within a fraction of a second before everything went black.

Chapter 29

McCully found himself napping in a snow bank near the mansion's front wall where Brown had apparently left him. His head ached, but he managed to regain his footing, bracing an arm against the stone wall for support.

He had yet to digest the wealth of information presented to him in the vision, but now understood why his colleagues were so important. They were the fuel for some sort of machine meant to bring a now dead man back to life.

Based on his interpretation of the vision, McCully assumed his hypothesis was correct, and that was why he saw *that* particular set of events during his unconscious state.

Stumbling along toward the front door, he felt certain any passersby would deem him drunk off his ass as he stiff-armed the wall. He felt cold all over, but considered himself lucky Brown didn't bind him, or bury him in the snow. Perhaps the deputy wasn't blinded by rage or a deranged killer, but McCully now wondered if the man might be a victim.

His feet felt numb, likely a combination of awkward positioning and snow packed around them like ice packs. They began painfully tingling, causing McCully to wish for all of the feeling back, sooner than later.

Shaking each leg as he supported himself against the front door's threshold, he hesitated a moment before touching the doorknob. Entering through the front door might be obvious and just plain stupid if things weren't safe inside.

He had no idea what had transpired in his absence, so he decided to look around the building before walking inside. His hand wrapped around the doorknob, though only to test it, finding it locked. Grunting to himself, he cautiously walked around the corner, finding much more feeling returning to his extremities.

Though the mansion's side had only a few windows, McCully found enough light outside emanating from the snow to guide him. As he rounded the corner, he spied a glass shard of some sort in the snow, immediately wondering how it sat atop a foot of the fluffy substance. He crouched down, plucking it carefully between his thumb and forefinger, examining it closely without cutting himself.

Green in color, it appeared to be about an inch long, and straight, letting him know it wasn't from a discarded bottle. It felt smooth, not like the ruffled glass used in making stained glass. McCully stared at it momentarily, then ran his thumb across the surface, planning to toss it aside afterward.

He missed the opportunity to interact further with the shard when his mind was transported to another time and place once again.

This time he found himself centered in the sunken garden of the West Baden Springs Hotel. It occurred to him that many of the images associated with negativity stemmed from the grounds, but he supposed the place did have a vast amount of history to it.

Looking around, he saw nothing of interest, and only a few people milling through the summertime blossoms surrounding the hotel. He saw a robed figure near the hotel, immediately indicating the time frame. Several feet to one side, a priest worked at planting several colorful plants within the garden, surprising him a bit, since the Jesuits upheld a life of poverty.

Perhaps everyone was entitled to add some beauty to his life, McCully decided, taking a few steps forward.

On the hill, the cemetery was immediately visible, but far fewer tombstones lined the lush, green grass surrounding them.

He saw a boy playing on the hill, near the edge of the tree line. Sensing the boy was the reason for him being there, McCully walked toward the hill as the boy began walking further from the garden, toward the edge of the grounds. Apparently back in the day, the hotel had no fences or enforced boundaries to speak of. Still, the boy didn't seem like a townie just there to play.

Something told McCully he was a permanent fixture around the hotel grounds, though he had no idea why a boy might live within a seminary filled with priests and brothers in training. The boy appeared carefree, jumping, skipping, and picking flowers near the road. The road McCully had nearly killed himself on just an hour or so prior looked like little more than a worn horse trail.

Blacktop and pavement were a distant wave of future during the early years of the Jesuit stay at West Baden. Strangely, McCully noticed sounds were scarce everywhere around him. Even the boy didn't make a single utterance. No singing, no talking to himself, and certainly no talking to an imaginary friend.

He didn't even whistle.

A car crept up the road from what he knew as Highway 56, likely a brand new car in the day, adorned with polished chrome, shined black tires, and a beautiful black paint job. By no means a car expert, McCully knew the car was a Cadillac, though he questioned the year. He thought 1937 sounded like a fair guess, partly because he knew the Jesuits inhabited the hotel during that decade.

He noticed a single person in the driver's seat without companionship.

McCully never quite got over seeing historical events in real time. It felt like standing on the set of a Hollywood film, but he knew better.

As the car drew to little more than a crawl, he began wondering if the man driving the car wanted directions. Back then, kids were regarded as adults somewhat early in life, but this boy was still very young. It occurred to him that perhaps the man had more evil intentions for the boy, so he strolled their way.

He hated being a passive participant in the visions, especially when things went wrong, but as the man drew his car to a stop, McCully felt dread fill his veins when the man stepped out.

"Williams," he said to himself as the man stiffly straightened his suit jacket with a tug on the front flaps.

From what little bit McCully had seen of the man, loathing didn't quite cover the span of emotions he felt toward the murderous son-of-a-bitch. He had witnessed the man's power and influence when Andrew Duncan last met him at the train station. Now he was by himself, apparently showing off his riches in the valley.

McCully felt somewhat surprised the man remained in the area, but perhaps he felt safer there, and maybe people didn't know about his fiendish ways.

Or perhaps they did, and they simply lived in fear of him.

Either way, the boy didn't seem fazed by his arrival. An odd moment of silence passed before Williams addressed the boy, apparently recognizing him from somewhere.

"Do you live here, boy?" he inquired.

The boy nodded, saying nothing aloud.

"Aren't you the boy the papers talked about? The one the brothers adopted from the streets?"

Again the boy nodded, but this time his discomfort began to show. McCully assumed the boy was homeless by Williams' meaning, taken in by the priests.

He stepped forward defensively, remembering he couldn't do a thing, even if he wanted to.

"I need someone to show me a couple places around town," Williams said. "There's an ice-cream cone in it for you if you want to be my guide. Double scoop."

"Liar," McCully said the unheard words in a growl.

As though sensing the same thing, the boy slowly shook his head, beginning to back away.

McCully wondered if Williams was some sort of deranged child molester. Such things were unheard of in the day, not because they didn't happen, but because they weren't publicized. Fetishes were bizarre occurrences swept under the carpet by families and the media.

A light bulb switched on in the recesses of his mind, reminding him that Williams had discovered some sort of fountain of youth. The very reason he murdered his best friend now, more than likely, had him targeting a young boy he figured no one would miss. Although the boy might not know any of Williams' secrets, he might be a useful sacrifice because he wouldn't be missed.

Even the brotherhood might simply suspect he went back to the streets to live, or found a better deal somewhere else.

"What do you say, kid?" Williams prompted for an answer, fighting back his impatience.

"Tell him to fuck off," McCully said to himself, finding no reason to state his answer any louder.

No one would hear anyway.

Looking behind him, perhaps for assistance that was too far away, the boy had already made up his mind. He didn't want to go with Williams, but the man wasn't going to simply let him go after this encounter.

A silent, awkward moment passed between them as neither moved or said a word. The boy looked from the man to the grounds, then to the grass at his feet, as though about to give in.

"Don't do it," McCully pleaded to the boy who couldn't hear him.

Left with little other option, the boy broke into a sprint along the edge of the property, heading up the hill as he followed the road.

Unlike modern times, the hill behind the hotel had a golf course during its heyday, rather than a dense woods. McCully watched Williams jump into his car, starting it with the strange winding noise vehicles in the day always made, taking chase. He wasn't about to let the boy get away from him to ruin his reputation and expose his secrets.

While the boy darted up the hill, full of youthful energy, Williams struggled to get his car motivated. McCully followed the action, wondering which direction the boy might take. If he stayed by the roadside, he would be easy prey for Williams, and if he broke to the right, he might find help on the old golf course.

Reaching the area first before the child, McCully saw no one near the course. In fact, it displayed the first offspring of what would become the dense woods behind the hotel. The priests had intentionally neglected the area, letting the vegetation, trees, and shrubs overtake the old course. No longer did lawn mowers trim the grass, or players chase little white balls toward flag markers.

And this is precisely why the boy chose to cut across the field, rather than stay near the road. McCully suspected he wanted to double back to the hotel to find help.

By now, Williams had left his vehicle by the road to pursue the boy on foot. Strategically, this made sense because it was quieter, created less distraction, and Williams could navigate the terrain. Though obviously a bit older than when McCully last saw him, Williams remained in excellent physical condition, quickly catching up to the boy.

A trail of rocks and larger smooth stones slowed the boy's run, but Williams moved over them as easily as he might a sidewalk. The boy remained silent, never calling for help, grunting, panting, or emitting any other sort of noise. Williams closed in dangerously upon the boy, causing McCully to lurch forward with a natural reaction that amounted to nothing.

McCully had no physical impact on the world around him, particularly since the events transpired decades before he was conceived.

He stopped short of trying to touch either person before him, partly because he knew his involvement was a moot point, but more importantly because someone else had seen the same events unfolding.

Just as Williams came upon the boy, grabbing him harshly with both hands, McCully noticed one of the priests dashing up the path from the hotel toward the edge of the property. At first he appeared to be searching for the boy, but quickly zeroed in upon the attempted abduction. Now a race ensued with the priest attempting to catch Williams before the man reached his car with the boy.

By no means a passive victim, the boy bit and clawed at his abductor's arms, trying to free himself as he kicked wildly.

His actions allowed the priest to catch up with them quickly, so McCully stood in place, watching the action unfold before him.

"Stop, you!" the priest shouted, apparently realizing there was no sense reasoning with the man.

Or perhaps he knew Williams by reputation.

McCully always pictured priests and pastors as passive, peaceful people, but what happened next changed his perception. Perhaps the priest had a particular attachment to the boy, or simply saw no other way to deal with the situation, but he turned Williams toward him, striking the man across the jaw with a closed fist.

Williams released the boy from his grasp to deal with the interference. The boy fell hard, but quickly regained enough composure to dart several feet away for a safe vantage point.

"Run, Henry!" the priest ordered, but the boy remained frozen with terror.

Not for himself, but for the man defending him, putting his life on the line.

McCully immediately sensed a deep connection between the two. If Williams had known, he might never have targeted young Henry as a sacrifice to benefit himself. Why a man in such good physical condition needed a sacrifice for any reason eluded McCully, because he recalled Williams telling his best friend something about an object that cured or healed with an appropriate sacrifice.

While his experience with the paranormal centered mainly around his own abilities, McCully knew a little something about cursed objects from documentaries and movies. They offered a benefit to an owner, but at the expense of human suffering or death.

He watched as the priest and the wealthy kingpin struggled over the path of rocks, which were now seated about five feet below them as Williams had run slightly uphill in his escape attempt. They grappled like professional wrestlers a moment, each trying to cast the other into the dangerous rock pile below.

Williams broke free, swinging wildly at the priest, but the man ducked, thrusting a fist into the wealthy man's gut. Williams doubled over, receiving a brutal knee to his face. McCully stood in shock, though not because of the violence. Modern television and film had long since conditioned him to brutal, bloody battles. He never envisioned a man of the cloth directing such anger toward another human being.

He supposed even priests had normal lives at one time, and it was human nature to revert to what one knew.

"Don't you know who I am?" Williams spat the words from his knees.

"Yes, and I don't care," the priest answered somewhat coldly. "You don't lay your hands on any child, especially not one in my care."

Williams growled, announcing his next attack before he dove for the priest. The older man dodged the attack, plucking Williams from the ground by the shirt. McCully sensed the man hesitated, unsure of what to do with his attacker because Williams certainly had opportunity to break off the skirmish several times.

McCully doubted anyone would pursue him if Williams chose to retreat to his car, but the priest showed little fear. A call to the authorities would certainly be the next scene in this drama if that were to happen.

"Leave now, or I won't be responsible for what happens next," the priest informed Williams. "Your tyranny has gone far enough."

Williams definitely had a reputation that preceded him.

"I've donated to you people, and this is how you repay me?" Williams stammered with a sneer.

"You think you can simply buy people? You can pay your thugs to protect you and bully the people in this valley, but you aren't taking this boy."

McCully saw Williams reach behind him, thinking he might have a revolver tucked into his belt, but he produced a knife instead.

His hand immediately thrust toward the robed priest, but the man already knew, perhaps even sensing the attack. Simply stepping aside, he twisted Williams' arm in one motion, thrusting the man's own arm toward his abdomen with the sharp end of the knife. Perhaps he expected Williams to drop the knife, or simply didn't care either way, but the attacker stuck the knife deep into his own guts with guidance from the brother.

For some reason McCully wondered if God Himself had intervened when he saw the shocked look on Williams' face before the priest tossed him to the rocks below. Williams landed face down, already dead upon impact. It appeared purely accidental, perhaps even suicidal by some standards back then. McCully suspected no one would give much of a fuss about Williams dying, wondering if the authorities might quickly dismiss the death as a suicide and lose no sleep over it.

Henry, who had remained nearby the entire time, appeared quite shaken until the priest called him over. Kneeling down, the man embraced him so closely that it appeared his robe devoured the boy. For the first time the boy made noise, softly crying against the man's chest, showing he wasn't completely incapable of sound.

After a few minutes, the man held Henry at an arm's length to gain the boy's attention, though he did so softly and with genuine concern.

"What happened here wasn't your fault," the man stated. "This man was an evil predator who made his fortune by hurting others. I don't know what he wanted from you, but I know it wasn't anything good. And you knew that too, didn't you?"

Henry nodded affirmatively, and adamantly, the way kids often do. Reddish pools formed around his eyes from all of the crying. The whites of his eyes, still misty, began looking pink from so many tears, and from rubbing them away.

"I know it isn't right, but I'm going to tell the authorities, and the brothers, that we found this man dead out here. If I tell them the truth, they might take you away. We don't want that, do we?"

Henry shook his head negatively this time.

"Good."

When the priest stood up, something near or on the body caught his attention, because he climbed down the rocks for a closer look, risking his own cover story by lingering at the scene.

He picked up a wooden crucifix that had fallen from Williams' sport coat. It looked somewhat plain to McCully, but a strange red cube toward the bottom of the main stake caught his attention as well. He wondered if this might be what Williams was obsessed over, and how such a curious object might be of any use to him.

The priest tucked it under his robe, placed his arm around Henry, and began walking toward the converted hotel to report the story to the others. McCully realized the close bond between the priest and the boy was strictly plutonic, like brothers, or perhaps an uncle to a close nephew. This was going to be a secret both of them took to the grave, because neither wished to risk their bond being destroyed needlessly.

When he finally emerged from the vision, McCully dropped the glass shard into the snow, wondering if it might be some of the old stained glass from the hotel after all. The Jesuits had added it during their tenure.

He stood up, looked around, and began wondering what the appropriate next move might be.

Chapter 30

Jana remained perfectly still on the trap holding Duncan on the floor, hoping the stranger might return with something useful. Minutes passed while her hopes fleeted from the lack of sound or the sight of a saving grace.

Duncan continued to struggle against the plastic restraints to no avail. He made sounds that barely escaped the trap, but seemed able to breathe just fine. Whatever pulled at the other end of the trap didn't cease tugging for one second. It wanted Duncan the way a fisherman might battle a tuna for an hour or more to claim his prize.

She had gotten to know the device a little better, realizing even a sharp knife might not easily cut the thick substance. Though it felt like plastic, it had a virtually unending thickness to it. And now it began to pull closer to the closet, ignoring the additional weight she added to its body.

"No," she said under her breath, frantically looking around for any way to slow it, or find a cutting device she might have missed earlier.

When she moved slightly off the plastic, it moved much more quickly than the slow, inching process of before. Shrieking lightly to herself, Jana grabbed onto the snare, pulling for Duncan's life with no success. It began dragging her along as Duncan's muffled cries for help reached her ears.

"I'm trying," she said, doubting it comforted him one bit.

Duncan was the last confirmed person remaining in the mansion. To lose him meant losing any security Jana felt around her, even if he was in a helpless position. Being alone, knowing the events surrounding the valley the past five years, would make even the most courageous person wonder what to do.

At the moment, Jana felt anything but courageous. She fought to keep her attention on saving Duncan, rather than worrying about how to save herself if everyone around her went missing.

Picking up the letter opener with newfound determination, she began tearing and cutting into the plastic the best she could, injuring her hand in the process. Though the task seemed pointless because the snare refused to be defeated, she continued, even as Duncan neared the closet door.

If he disappeared into the closet, all hope was lost.

Jana continued slashing at the plastic, seeing it shred in several areas, but even her added weight made little difference to whatever device pulled the plastic from the other end.

A single glance toward the main door changed everything when Jana noticed a cloaked figure standing there ominously, staring at her through a blank, black mask recessed beneath a hood. She gasped, absently removing herself from the trap as she backed away from the figure when she noticed a knife in his right hand.

She suppressed a concerned moan when Duncan disappeared into the closet, lost to her like everyone else who came to the mansion under her supervision. Now in fear for her own life beyond everything else, Jana backed toward a wall, debating how to elude the person behind all of her troubles.

If elusion was even possible.

"Who are you?" she asked when the figure took a step forward.

He stopped as though ready to answer, then raised the knife and began a slow, purposeful walk directly toward her.

Now completely alone, and realizing that simple fact, Jana didn't want to be cornered, so she kept hold of the letter opener, picking up a nearby lamp before tossing it against the figure's head when he drew close enough. He made a pained noise, putting his hands up to block the lamp's shattering pieces. Jana used the opportunity to stab him in the shoulder with the letter opener, drawing another pained cry as the opener's plastic handle cut another slit along her palm.

She ignored the pain as best she could, dashing for the door.

A sense of reserved relief came to her with the safety the open upstairs provided. She quickly weighed the options of hiding in another room, or running downstairs. All of the doors were closed, meaning she might waste too much time checking to see if they were unlocked. Already the figure was recovering, now stiffly walking toward her.

Jana took to the stairs, quickly descending them until she reached the front door. She quickly undid the lock on the knob, tugging on the door to no avail. Someone had snapped off the deadbolt lock above it, meaning it was stuck in a locked position. Short of finding a pair of pliers, she had no way of opening it.

"Shit," she muttered, glancing back to see him descending the stairs one step at a time, apparently in no hurry to apprehend or kill his quarry.

Purely cat and mouse, just like the slasher movies.

She started toward the entertainment room before remembering it led to a dead end. Deciding to look for a weapon, despite the risk, she ran into the room, finding little else aside from hulking furniture and electronics.

"Knife," she murmured, deciding to make her way to the kitchen if possible.

It made sense to her that this man might be the stranger she met upstairs, but why would he bother to leave the room, just to put on a disguise? Her thoughts quickly turned to self-preservation again as she picked up a walking stick from beside the door, hiding behind the doorway until the dark figure passed by.

With a solid swing using both hands, she struck the figure across the head with the walking stick, flooring him. She had never been so glad her parents encouraged her to participate in high school softball.

Jana whacked the figure in the head several more times like a child attempting to bust open a piñata, despite him lying motionless on the floor. Each time his body convulsed a bit, indicating he remained alive, and able to feel pain on some level.

Standing over him for just a few seconds gave her the idea of pulling off his mask, but she decided to find a way out instead. Knowing his identity did little good if she was stuck inside the mansion with him, unable to summon help from the police.

Quickly crossing the lower level, Jana made her way into the dining room where a terrible surprise awaited her. Clasping both of her hands over her mouth, she suppressed a gasp at the sight set across the table before her. One of her arms swung out to catch herself from falling as her hand clutched the doorway, allowing her to steady herself.

Atop the table, Judith Parks was laid out like some sort of strange Roman sacrifice, streaks of blood trailing down her throat from where it had been slit. Her eyes remained open, glazed in a death trance that eerily stared Jana's way. Both of her arms were laid out to either side, palms facing upward, while her legs were crossed atop one another, the knees slightly buckled. To Jana it appeared almost like the way Christ was often portrayed on the crucifix.

Though she kept herself from screaming, Jana held back several muffled sobs, realizing she was certainly not in the middle of some joke. For some reason, the West Baden Springs Murders had begun once again.

Regaining her wits, Jana darted toward the upper kitchen area, hoping to find a knife or better means of defending herself. She saw a mess atop the counter and preparation areas, spotting only a few tiny knives. Seeing the door to the down-stairs, she decided not to access it because the last thing she wanted was to enter an enclosed room.

Instead, she hurried to the pantry door, jiggling the handle a few times to swing it outward. The open door produced another body that spilled outward, forcing a shriek from Jana that she quickly regretted. Laura Compton fell face-down on the floor, obviously dead from the amount of blood soaked into her clothes. Jana reeled, taking a step back to regain her senses. She stared at the corpse, wondering if everyone around her was dead, and how in the world she could escape this mansion of death.

She wanted to touch the body, to see how Laura had died, but she knew it didn't matter. If Jana wasted too much time, she would be the next body someone stumbled upon unwittingly. Instinct told her to check the room's main door, to ensure she was safe another minute or so. She stumbled toward the door, feeling numbed by the death surrounding her, wondering how she ever let herself get talked into taking on such a controversial project. Because the first two visiting investment groups didn't have an ounce of trouble, she allowed herself to be lulled into a false sense of security.

A quick check at the doorway revealed the figure was up and moving, but he was searching an area across the hall, knife in hand. Since he failed to see her, Jana quietly moved to the door for the lower kitchen level where knives would surely be in abundance.

As the door swung open, another body revealed itself, but this one remained in the doorway, blocking her egress. She stifled any cries with her hands, taking an absent step back.

Hands strung above his head, a man she thought she recognized from some-where simply twirled a few inches in each direction. His head slumped downward with no blood, causing Jana to wonder if he was even dead. She carefully reached forward, touching his face.

No reaction.

His skin felt warm, rather than cold and clammy, but she had no time to further evaluate his status as a fresh corpse or unconscious victim.

She checked the door again, but this time the figure spotted her, immediately charging toward the kitchen. Slamming the door just short of his face, Jana used a sliding lock, doubting it would hold. She grabbed a nearby wooden chair, jamming it under the doorknob to buy some time.

Keeping close watch on the door, Jana saw the knob jiggle as someone tried to open it from the other side. It made a clacking noise, adding to the intensity of the situation. Jana backed away, trying to remain silent while keeping her composure. Banging, then slamming sounds boomed throughout the room as one side of the door threatened to give way.

Jana backed away from the door, debating her next move, overwhelmed by the thought of dying in such a horrific way.

A rapping sound from behind her startled her, because her mind immediately thought someone else might be coming through the window for her.

Whirling around, she found McCully tapping the exterior window with his knuckles. He looked concerned, but not nearly to the extent she felt. Jana knew he wasn't the figure chasing her around the mansion, so she tossed aside her trust issues, hurrying toward the window.

She went to throw it upward, realizing the locks kept it in place. The two latches faced opposite directions, so she twisted one to its other side as the thumping behind her at the door grew louder.

The figure was about to break through the lock, and the chair began twisting awkwardly, indicating it might break any second. Jana desperately tried to lift the window once more, finding she had turned the lock the wrong way. She fumbled with the locks once more as McCully watched helplessly from the other side. If the killer got inside, Jana would have no defense, and no one else to help her fend off his attack.

Her fingers felt as stiff and immobile as tree limbs when they tried to switch the locks to the opposite position.

"Other way," McCully encouraged from the outside, his eyes dancing between her dilemma and the door, which now had a knife plunging through its wooden frame.

Jana finally threw both locks into the other direction, lifting the window hard enough that it shuddered within its frame. McCully had already removed the screen, now putting up his arms to help her down as the door burst open behind her.

Letting out a brief shriek as she dived through the window into McCully's arms, Jana landed atop her new hero as the figure emerged at the window, staring down ominously before dashing toward the mansion's front.

"What the hell?" McCully asked of the situation in general.

"Everyone's dead," Jana managed to state as they both stood from the cold ground. "We've got to get out of here and get help."

McCully stared at her a moment, as though unable to comprehend everyone in his group might actually be dead, then fished inside his front pocket for keys.

"Dan's truck is out front. We can get into town with it."

Taking her by the hand, McCully led the way toward the front of the house, around the front corner. From nowhere, the figure tackled McCully to the ground as the two began battling for position. The truck keys flew clear of their skirmish, landing in a pile of snow. Though concerned for McCully's safety, she immediately began searching for the keys, hoping to retrieve them for a speedy exit if necessary.

"Get out of here!" McCully managed to bark between punches from the killer to his face.

"But-" Jana began to argue.

"Go!"

She ran toward the truck, turning only once to see the killer getting the best of the bluegrass musician. The keyless remote gained her quick access to the truck, and once inside, Jana immediately started the engine. It purred to life instantly as she switched on the headlights, looking back to find the distance between her and the mansion too great to witness the battle between McCully and the figure.

Everything between her and the mansion had been engulfed by shadows.

She sat a moment inside the truck, waiting to see if McCully might appear. As a precaution, Jana locked the doors and put the truck into reverse for a quick escape.

Taking her by surprise, the killer popped both of his hands against her side window, knife grasped in one of them. He pulled that particular hand back, as though he planned to smash the window with it, but Jana stomped on the accelerator, throwing the truck back hard enough that it smashed one of the other vehicles. She quickly shifted into forward, starting toward the road as the truck began to fishtail in the snow.

A look in the rearview mirror revealed the figure stalking the truck as far as the road, then standing in the center of the street with knife in hand, simply staring forward. Jana quickly diverted her attention to her driving, mainly because the truck's grip on the pavement quickly diminished.

"Whoa," Jana said to herself, trying to keep the truck from sliding into either ditch.

Despite slightly warmer air temperatures, the roads seemed extremely slick because of thawing and secondary freezing. Jana nearly had the truck under control when someone jumped out from the side of the road, frantically waving his arms.

Without much thought, Jana stepped on the brakes, quickly finding the truck violently swerving back and forth once again. The back end clipped whoever had stepped onto the road, thumping him haplessly into the ditch as Jana fought the steering wheel for control. Her mind barely comprehended the fact that she likely struck Red Sanders, because he seemed to recognize the truck, as she veered dangerously toward the opposite ditch.

Accidentally correcting the truck too much, she sent it into a skid that dumped it front-first into the ditch, thrusting her against the wheel as the airbag deployed. She felt as though her face had just been struck by a boxing glove the size of a beach ball, but Jana rubbed her forehead, moaning to herself.

Thankfully, she hadn't lost consciousness, but a wave of terrible thoughts ran through her mind. McCully had likely given his life to protect her, she may have just killed Red in a hit-and-run type accident, and the police were nowhere to be found.

Realizing she might be the only person left to find help and bring the killer to justice, she tried the door, finding it stuck against the side of the ditch. In the distance, she heard a motor start, sounding slightly like a chainsaw, then spied a single headlight peering over the hill from above.

A snowmobile?

"Damn it," she cursed, feeling unwavering resolve to survive this terrible ordeal around her.

Since the passenger side appeared wedged against the opposite side of the ditch, Jana looked behind her, realizing the rear window had shifted position during the crash. The truck's frame and upper molding had been compromised, leaving the rear window on the verge of falling out.

Undoing her seatbelt, Jana turned around, kicking at the window twice before it fell into the truck's bed. She climbed out through the back, using every ounce of strength and willpower within her to clear the cab. She might as well have been a contortionist the way she maneuvered her arms and legs like a spider to drag herself out.

As she reached fresh air and a stiff breeze once more, she saw the headlight of the snowmobile or a four-wheeler bob over the hilltop, realizing she had mere seconds to move before the figure found her once again.

Chapter 31

cCully found himself embedded in the cold ground once more, wondering if the same man had bested him twice in the same evening. He sometimes wished he had grown up scrappier like his father, but extended hard labor and fistfights were among the list of things he never experienced growing up.

He rubbed the side of his head, wondering where everyone had gone, and why he was still alive. The last thing he remembered was the cloaked figure ramming his head against a nearby rock.

Apparently, the man decided to chase Jana, rather than finish the job at hand.

Seeing the truck now gone, he hoped she had made it to safety. Plucking his cellular phone from his side, he checked for a signal. One bar of signal strength presented itself, but as soon as he dialed 911 for assistance, the signal cut out, leaving him alone in the world.

McCully decided to go inside for warmth, and perhaps some answers about the strange events surrounding him. The front door, now slightly ajar, allowed him to easily slide by, revealing an eerie scene of a well-lit mansion with no sounds, and no one else nearby.

Curious, he immediately turned his attention to the upper kitchen area, where he had rescued Jana through the window. Though difficult to see from outside, McCully felt reasonably certain he saw the lifeless bodies of several investment group members.

Drifting carefully to the right of the main entrance, McCully spied the body of Judith Parks lying across a table. He stopped short of the doorway, having no reason to doubt she was dead, and not wanting to disturb evidence for the police. Refusing to envision himself as a corpse, McCully tried to remain calm and focused, but his mind refused to process the horrific events around him very easily.

"Dear Christ," he said to himself, leaning an arm against the doorway for support.

He suddenly felt wary of his surroundings, wondering if the killer had definitely left the premises. It made sense for him to chase Jana before she found help, but it would take mere seconds to kill McCully himself if he wasn't suspecting an attack.

Turning to look around, he heard no footsteps, and saw no one else inside the mansion.

Proceeding to the next doorway, he stopped short once again, seeing Laura Compton slumped awkwardly along the floor. He told himself she had to be dead, even though he didn't want to believe it. It humbled him to think he had narrowly survived an encounter with the person who murdered part of his group.

Not knowing who the man swaying in the doorway might be he cautiously stepped over, using a nearby paper towel to first turn the man away from him, and then to pluck his wallet from his pants. He didn't want to leave any fingerprints or contaminate any evidence if possible. McCully flipped it open, instantly seeing a golden badge inside with five tips. A certain portion of the wallet was dedicated to carrying business cards, which informed him the dangling man was indeed the local sheriff.

"Holy shit," he muttered, taking another look at the body, which seemed full of color for a corpse.

McCully began studying the man, who hung from a doorway via tied hands. He swung slightly to and fro, especially after being turned to retrieve the wallet. The examination came to a screeching halt when a drawn out creaking noise came from behind McCully.

Someone had opened the front door.

He quickly rushed out of the room, half expecting to confront the killer right there in the foyer. With no one in sight, he quickly panned the large room, seeing no one once again. He returned his attention to the door, seeing it had swung open, despite McCully believing he closed it tightly.

A stiff breeze broke up the otherwise warm confines of the mansion, chilling McCully enough to send shivers through his muscles. He convulsed slightly before heading toward the door to shut it, stopped in his tracks when someone passed the door opening along the outside, stumbling in McCully's opinion, until he or she fell out of sight.

As though someone stole his ability to breathe, McCully froze like a statue, unblinking as he waited to see another glimpse of whoever had staggered across the doorway. He remained near the bottom of the stairs, providing himself another avenue of escape since he possessed no weapons for defensive purposes.

After several tense seconds passed, he slowly made his way toward the front door, leery of the person just outside. Fearing a knife or some other weapon might lunge at him from the outdoors, McCully cautiously placed his back along the wall beside the open door. He chose the opposite side of the opening from where the person had possibly fallen, worried about peering outside.

For all he knew this was the killer trying to lure him in for the kill. Perhaps the figure had an accomplice, allowing them to double their efforts in abducting and murdering the investment group. The possibility also existed that someone might need his help, which reminded him of what happened when he assisted Jana.

He felt nervous, though in control of his emotions as he began peering around the door's frame. His peek around the side revealed nothing at first, but McCully recoiled when someone fell through the open doorway, landing hard on the foyer floor.

"Red?" he questioned, kneeling down to examine his colleague as the man clutched his leg around the knee. "What the hell happened?"

"I got clipped by a truck. I think the son-of-a-bitch was trying to finish me off, but I hobbled and crawled here along the side of the road."

"Is it broken?" McCully inquired, noticing he clutched the leg right beneath the knee.

From high school biology, McCully recalled two separate bones comprising the human leg below the knee. Both were fairly thin, and easily broken by a hard collision.

"I heard a snap," Red reported. "I can't put any weight on it."

He wondered if the killer had somehow commandeered a vehicle to pursue Jana, and if so, McCully hoped against all odds she was alive and well.

Carefully helping Red to his feet, he heard a noise in the distance that sounded like a small, motorized vehicle revving up to full speed.

"Let's get you warm," McCully said, putting forth a braver front than he felt.

The night's events had taken a toll on him, and until help arrived, relief would be a distant hope.

***

Jana jumped clear of the truck as a four-wheeler came over the hill with a cloaked figure steering it directly toward the wreck. Looking like some kind of hokey horror movie spoof toy, the sight of the figure mounting an off-road vehicle might have seemed humorous if not for the dire circumstances.

She darted behind several nearby shrubs as he jumped off the four-wheeler, desperately, even angrily searching the area. He ran to the window, fighting off the snow at his feet, still holding a knife in his right hand. Seeing nothing there, he began circling the truck.

Jana looked from the truck to her trail, realizing her footprints led to the exact spot where she crouched behind the bushes. A mere second after her realization, he discovered the flawless footprint trail left in the snow.

The chase was on.

Jana took off further into the wooded area behind the wreck, hoping the four-wheeler couldn't cross the large ditch and navigate the terrain. Barely audible over the sounds of her own heavy breathing, Jana heard the four-wheeler start, move forward over the course of a few seconds, then stop again.

She suspected he had quickly abandoned his mode of transportation, but wasn't about to stop for verification. Branches smacked her in the head as she passed, realizing she was actually heading toward the mansion, deviating from her original plan to find help.

At this point, preserving her own life became Jana's number one priority.

Weaponless, and not exactly what she considered dressed for winter, Jana stumbled through the snow as best she could. Though she had dressed warm when Duncan originally wanted to leave the mansion, her attire still lacked appropriate layers for snow and windy conditions.

Bad planning?

No. She fully expected to return home after the tour and dinner, never anticipating the sky would dump two feet of snow on the valley.

Bad luck?

Perhaps. The snow, combined with an individual, or two, sabotaging any means of communication and travel had allowed the entire investment group to be systematically picked off.

Jana tripped over a branch, barely keeping her feet under her to avoid the cliché helpless female in the horror movie routine where she would fall on her face.

The group members were unsuspecting victims, while Jana planned to outlast and outwit the man pursuing her.

But how?

Surely, the killer knew the area, and the mansion, very well. She had grown up in the area, but that meant nothing in the middle of the night surrounded by trees and shrubs. She might as well have been wearing a black light to lure the killer closer.

That's it, she thought, beginning to realize she made herself easier to track if she remained mobile.

Now far enough ahead of him, she doubled back along her own tracks nearly a bus length. Jana created a new path that led into a small tree grove where the leaves, water droplets, and fallen branches from above broke up the snow-covered ground. Without wasting much time, she stomped around the area a little bit to add to the mess, then took a large leap out of the grove, taking a completely different direction than before.

While her direction loosely aimed her toward the mansion, her route now became more roundabout, taking her further into the woods. Though dangerous territory for a stranger to the land, she figured the killer would believe she took the route easiest to navigate, and return to the road.

Realizing the noise from her running and heavy breathing might be enough to draw the killer her way, Jana stopped momentarily behind a tree. There, she rested as she caught her breath, listening for approaching footsteps. Hearing none, she took off once more, beginning to veer her course toward the road after another hundred yards.

While the road afforded her less cover, its snowy covering wasn't deep enough to leave footprints as traceable evidence. She jumped over the ditch when she reached it, landing on the road with enough balance that she quickly crouched down, judging her distance from the totaled truck down the hill.

Feeling relatively safe, she began running up the hill toward the mansion, hoping the eerie nighttime light cast by the snow didn't make her an easy target.

She stayed on the opposite edge of the road from the wreck, wondering how long it would take the killer to discover her ruse. When he did, even the mansion wouldn't provide a safe haven from his wrath.

Though it wasn't yet in sight, the mansion materialized in her mind, perhaps because she so desperately wanted to be out of the elements and harm's way. As the hill's angle grew steeper Jana struggled to keep her footing. She nearly tripped and fell, but caught herself once again.

A moment later, the mansion's gate came into view as the sound of a motor echoed behind her, driving her forward. One glance behind her showed a headlight gleaming like the Northern Star in the distance, fragmented by the misty air. He was already heading her way, either giving up on finding her, or realizing the truth about her deception.

Jana jumped into the ditch, figuring he hadn't seen her. She waited until the headlight drew near, feeling as though someone was standing on her insides. Sucking in her last breath, Jana expected the four-wheeler to stop, the man to jump off, and the chase to begin all over again. At this point, she felt she had little resistance left. Her mind and body felt numb, as though conspiring against her.

Apparently, they had decided death sounded better than the strenuous effort of running for dear life.

Jana hadn't.

Her concerns drifted away with the passing of the off-road vehicle, leaving her several alternatives, none of which felt too safe. Venturing through the woods could get her lost, while staying near the road might get her killed.

She stood up, seeing a pair of tracks along the road, pointed toward the mansion. They looked like cowboy boot tracks, and they seemed awkwardly staggered, like someone had walked with a limp.

"Red."

Even if she didn't rush inside to his aid, Jana decided she wanted to assess the situation and help him if she found the injured man. Drawing closer to the front gate, Jana realized she didn't hear the sound of the four-wheeler, as though it had stopped short of the mansion. Sensing grave danger, she remained at the edge of the gate, waiting to see someone, anyone, before making her next move.

Chapter 32

Inside the mansion, McCully had also heard the sound of a motor outside. With Red now inside, and the both of them toward the back of the mansion, he suppressed his curiosity. For all he knew, Jennings might have returned with help, or the killer was now mobile.

"This is ridiculous," Red complained as McCully adjusted his position inside a fairly spacious utility closet within the entertainment room.

"You're going to be safer in here with that leg than you will running around with me."

"Was that supposed to be funny? Running?"

"No. Any sense of humor I might have had abandoned me when Laura disappeared."

McCully set Red with his back against the closet's far wall, enabling him to fire upon any unwanted visitors with the weapon he took from the deputy at the hotel.

"Don't you be getting antsy and trying to get out of here," McCully warned. "I'll be back for you as soon as I can."

"I hate being cooped up. It's bad enough your new girlfriend tried to run me down."

McCully had accidentally spilled the beans about Jana driving Duncan's truck.

"I only said I thought she got into it. Hell, the killer might have chased her away and stole it for all I know."

"The only thing I know is that it crashed after clipping me, so I suspect she was driving."

McCully wondered if that might be a disparaging remark about female drivers, opting not to press the issue. He handed Red a flashlight he found after a brief trip to the first floor kitchen, thinking the man might need extra light while cooped up in such a tiny space.

"Where are you going?" Red asked, since they hadn't discussed much of a game plan.

"To town if I have to, but I'm going to find some help."

"The hunter already went that way, and he's not back yet."

Shaking his head, McCully decided he wasn't leaving anything to chance.

"For all we know, the man went home, or the killer got to him. There's still an outside chance he's not on our side, too."

"Who the fuck can we trust?"

It took a moment for McCully to answer, because he really didn't trust anyone at the moment, although he felt compelled to believe Red and Jana were certainly innocent.

"I don't know. But I'm not waiting around here to become another victim. I'll get some help, then I'll come back for you."

He started to back out of the closet door when Red motioned to him to wait.

"What?"

"I want a code."

"A *what?*"

"Some kind of signal or knock so I don't blow you away when you come back. You know, like they do on commercial flights for cockpit access."

Sighing aloud, McCully knocked on the door three times, then once more after a brief pause.

"Three, then one. Okay?"

Red readily nodded in agreement. It seemed as though he really didn't like the idea of being left alone, and McCully couldn't blame him. If the roles were reversed, he would probably take a chance and hobble as far as he could from the mansion.

"I'll be back," he promised, shutting the door behind him before Red could protest.

He decided to check on the noise he heard earlier from the front yard before going anywhere. Instinct told him to be cautious, but he felt an obligation to assist anyone else who had eluded capture or a worse fate.

Peering out the large living room's first window, he saw nothing aside from the disabled vehicles. Beside him, a pair of pliers sat atop a small table, which had likely turned the broken deadbolt lock.

He dared open the front door, finding nothing noteworthy except for a pair of tracks that looked like they were made from a four-wheeler. He saw no middle track, and the treads were too large to be that of a snowmobile.

He remembered seeing snowmobile tracks on a vacation trip to Wyoming with his family. The treads on the side made a small indentation in snow, while the snowmobile's rear typically made a solid streak, as though someone had dragged a lunch box across the snow's surface.

The realization he had no reliable or quick method of transportation dawned on him, so he decided to check out one last area before making his departure. He felt guilty for stuffing Red into a closet without carrying through on his promise immediately, but knew they were both safer without the threat of his limp making them easy targets.

Leaving the security of the open foyer, McCully moved toward the upper kitchen, ignoring the ghastly scene in the dining area when he passed by. He found it difficult to believe dinner was the last time anyone in his group felt remotely comfortable and safe. Putting the memory to rest, he cautiously moved toward the kitchen, finding it strewn with litter, but something missing.

While Laura's body remained on the opposite end of the room, the man bound at the doorway was now gone. McCully froze in his tracks, slowly turning to look behind him. He almost expected someone to be standing there with a knife, or a corpse he somehow missed lying near the stairs.

Neither of his dreaded thoughts proved real, so he returned his attention to the room, stepping inside as he peered behind the door to ensure no one was lying in wait. Finding himself safe once more, he let his blue eyes wander to the door that led downstairs.

Taking a moment to consider the possibilities, he wondered if the bound man might have somehow escaped the mansion, or possibly been the killer using a clever ruse. After all, who would suspect a sheriff, or someone *posing* as a lawman?

He also considered the possibility that the killer simply moved the body elsewhere.

Feeling both tense and more than a little frightened, McCully stepped with trepidation toward the door. Already open enough for him to see down the stairwell and behind the door, he took a deep breath to calm himself as he peered downstairs. Flipping the light switch just beyond the doorway, McCully watched the fluorescent lights below slowly flicker to life as he took the first step down.

He stepped slowly, careful to prevent his feet from making noise enough to alert anyone to his current position. Able to see the entire length of the stairwell, McCully found visibility equally good across the length of the downstairs kitchen.

Much like the upstairs kitchen, this one looked as though someone had ransacked it. One of the tables and some shelving were lying across the floor as though knocked down during a skirmish. Adding proof to his fresh theory, McCully found speckles of blood along the floor beside the shelving, and even more near the discarded table.

He scooped up a large droplet, rubbing it between his fingers and thumb before wiping it on a nearby towel.

Now he felt even less optimistic about the survival of his fellow group members. He saw Keith's hat and sport coat nearby, then he spied something that changed everything about his search.

An elevator.

"What the hell?" he asked, standing to investigate this strange new development, wondering what awaited him at the elevator's upmost stop.

***

Jana decided she had waited long enough for events to unfold at the mansion. She stood outside, looking up at the strange third level that couldn't be explained. Red's tracks led to the mansion, so Jana figured he had returned, wondering exactly where he might have gone.

She approached the front door, turning the knob slowly. With the foyer completely in view, Jana stepped inside, quietly closing the door behind her. Feeling as though she had somehow betrayed Duncan by letting him get swallowed by the trap upstairs, she wanted to see if he was indeed gone.

If so, she wanted to know how the device worked, and if any chance to save him remained.

With a clear path ahead of her, Jana made her way up the stairs sensing no one around. To call out would obviously be foolhardy, so she walked silently, finding the door to Duncan's room still slightly ajar.

Her memory flashed back to what seemed like moments prior, when the killer chased her out of the house. Only McCully's intervention saved her, and now he couldn't be found.

Having absolutely no desire to search the mansion for Red and McCully, she worried about finding the one person she didn't care to see. As she drew near Duncan's room, she felt somewhat apprehensive until she peered inside, discovering an empty room with no visible threats.

She stepped inside, flipped on the lights, and began examining the strange closet, which showed absolutely no signs it had swallowed a human being whole, less than an hour prior. In fact, it looked solid, indicating no sliding doors, trick walls, or imprisoning devices of any sort. It simply looked like any normal closet.

Frustrated, Jana felt around the walls, careful not to trigger anything too suddenly, which might deliver her to wherever Duncan had been dragged. It dawned on her, as she searched, that each of the guests had a specified room. *She* had not picked the room, which also got her thinking the entire mansion stay was an orchestrated event, used to fulfill someone's devious plan.

It suddenly dawned on her as she exited the closet, unable to believe her own misguided analysis of who had coldly murdered at least two people. The very man who hired her.

As the door slowly swung open, she saw the dark figure once more, but there was no visible knife this time, and she felt far less fear confronting him.

"Why?" she demanded in an exasperated tone. "Why would you do any of this?"

"I'm simply following orders," the figure replied, pulling the hood back from his head, revealing his face for the first time.

Indeed Bryan Bell, the man who hired her to sell investment property, stood before her, now producing a knife from a sheath located at his side.

Several years older than Jana, Bell always had a professional air about him. He never hit on her, or made any kind of sexual jokes or comments around her. He maintained a steady flow of business throughout his agency, and drew the attention of young ladies everywhere in Bloomington.

Jana supposed his picture perfect lifestyle provided the ideal cover for his evil deeds, though his motive continued to elude her.

"You don't seem surprised," he commented, giving her an eerie grin.

"No, because I finally realized who created this environment, who wanted this group here, and who ordered me to change things at the last minute. The only thing I don't know is why, but I'm sure you'll tell me."

"It's quite a long story. Where would you like me to begin?"

Jana's eyes searched the room for something to use against him if he drew closer, but she needed to stall if she hoped to find any useful tools or weapons.

"From the beginning."

***

McCully discovered the elevator serviced only two floors, namely the basement level, and an upper level he assumed was hidden away from anyone inside the conventional portions of the mansion.

Already inside the car, he pushed the up button, watched the doors close, and felt a steady pressure as the elevator moved upward. It lacked a floor indicator, but he tried to reason the number of floors it passed during its ascent, figuring he was on the third level when the car gently stopped.

Strangely absent were the dings that accompanied most commercial elevators when the door opened. He found that odd, considering it made a noise on the basement level, almost like a Venus flytrap luring its prey.

When the door finally opened, McCully found a dark horror before him like nothing he had ever imagined, or visualized subconsciously. Nearly the size of a basketball court, he found the room encompassed by darkness with only small, subtle lights lined up in rows along the floor. It took his eyes a moment to adjust to the dimly lit areas, but when they did, he found something that looked like a scene from some alien abduction movie.

Two sounds reached his ears as he remained perfectly still.

A constant low hum overtook the entire room, likely from some machine performing a task associated with the light at each of the twelve stations he found on the third floor. Each light was placed at the base of a slab just larger than the human being each one held. Barely enough light to see by, McCully thought the devices looked like a museum after hours, allowing someone to navigate the room.

The other rhythmic noise came from in and out breathing of the people attached to some form of restraining devices beside each light. He took a step forward, finding his footstep echo throughout the room over the ambient sounds.

When he approached the first victim, he discovered the deputy from the hotel strapped to some sort of flat, black board. The device stood almost vertically, inclined ever so slightly so its captive's feet barely left the ground. McCully doubted the tilting was for added comfort because it seemed painfully obvious the man was in some sort of unconscious or semi-conscious state.

He breathed in and out, but two tubes ran from his left arm, disappearing into the machine that kept him in place. McCully saw liquids flow through each of the tubes, having no idea what purpose they served. With his eyes now growing accustomed to the darkness, he found most of the devices held someone in their clutches, each alive and in some comatose state.

"No wonder he killed only two of them," he muttered, reflecting upon the vision where Smith talked of extended life.

Someone had plans to use the people strapped to the tables as sacrifices to carry out some sort of ritual.

McCully moved to the closest wall, finding unusual inventions along each block where a person was stationed, beginning to piece together a likely scenario. Though each device appeared different in make and design, they served a common purpose. Each sat atop a mobile pedestal that traveled downward into each guest's room with the intent of luring and ensnaring.

Had McCully not left the hotel with Red and Jennings, he too might have suffered a fate like those of Laura and Judith. It seemed they were expendable in the plan, but why? One table remained open on the opposite side of the room.

"Birthdays," he recalled one of the guests saying about the stone carvings outside.

Stone carvings that almost certainly aligned perfectly with the traps he now looked upon.

While the mansion served as Smith's home for years, it harbored a deeper, darker purpose. McCully realized the building was constructed for the sole purpose of this particular day.

"A three-story human sacrifice," he said to himself, returning to the deputy's side.

He looked at the tubes entering his arm before his eyes wandered to a strange needle looming above the man's chest. Attached to a spring, it looked much like it was designed to plunge downward. Based on the tube attached to its hind end, he believed it would stab into the heart, drawing vast amounts of blood to a centralized location.

His eyes followed the tube in question to the floor, tracing it along several beams to the centerpiece he had missed earlier, because it had no illumination surrounding it. Though the size of a coffin, it lacked the intricate design and carved patterns one might find when attending calling hours at a funeral home.

In fact, it looked homemade, like something placed in a yard around Halloween. Painted completely black, some of the brush strokes remained visible, even in the dim lighting.

McCully didn't suppose it needed to look fancy. This was hardly Frankenstein's castle or a movie set, so details mattered very little. What concerned McCully were the twelve tubes running into the box, and even more so, the bizarre green cube set in its own specially carved area atop the box so it didn't come loose.

Since the box's cover seemed loose, he dared move it aside, wondering if he was the bumbling idiot who unknowingly opened Dracula's coffin, receiving certain death as a reward.

Made of lightweight wood, the cover slid easily to one side, revealing a sight McCully truly didn't expect. All twelve tubes ran through the sides of the box, then inside where they ended at a needle. This didn't surprise or shock him, but what the needles were lodged into gave McCully the creeps.

He sucked in a breath and held it, anticipating a terrible odor that never wafted his way.

Somewhere between mummified and petrified, an unrecognizable corpse had been placed into the makeshift casket. Each of the twelve needles found a home, embedded within the dried skin, causing McCully to wonder how long the body had been removed from its earthy covering. Looking far from restful, the corpse seemed quite worn for someone allegedly dead for only two years.

Rotting teeth showed past the decaying skin, which looked flaky on the surface. McCully reached toward the body to see how the skin felt, then thought better of it. Even the suit looked tattered, as though worms had been eating through it. A man of Smith's position surely had a huge funeral, complete with the best of caskets and burial plots. Something about McCully's original theory didn't feel right after seeing the recipient of the potential human sacrifice.

He replaced the casket's top to keep from giving away his activities before backing away from the coffin, feeling extremely uneasy. Whether or not the human sacrifice would work was irrelevant in his eyes. The fact that someone would even attempt to take a dozen lives to resurrect one disturbed him greatly.

Relief came in the fact that the eleven people surrounding him were still alive, but he suspected their condition was temporary if the twelfth person was caught. He didn't know where to begin if he wanted to release them from the snares. There could be booby-traps on each one, or he might kill one of the victims by pulling out the wrong needle. The situation unfolding before him was best left to the police and medical personnel.

Making rounds, he began to see familiar faces, careful not to touch any of the devices keeping them in place. In addition to the deputy, he found Keith, Oswalt, Turner, and Duncan among the ensnared people, raising his desire to find help.

And quickly.

Each of them appeared in good health, still breathing, though none of them noticed his presence. They remained in an unconscious state, whether drug induced or by some other means, closer to death than any of them possibly knew.

Many of the people were strangers to him, some looking very thin and pale, like comatose patients lying around in a hospital without the benefit of movement or company. Thinking a bit deeper on the subject, McCully realized several had disheveled hair and untrimmed fingernails, the way nursing home patients were sometimes neglected when they had no real motor functions, or little brain activity.

These people were kept alive, but at minimum expense and effort. McCully's group had provided the last of the crop for the killer, but he wondered who the twelfth victim might be. Only a few of them remained, including himself, which caused him to wonder if the killer had left him alive for a reason.

"Jana," he said to himself, remembering how the killer desperately chased after her.

At first, McCully had reasoned she was a dangerous witness, capable of getting police and foiling the killer's plan. Now, he believed she might have been the final intended target. Either way, he needed her in place before he carried out whatever the now dead doctor's final instructions might have been.

Knowing he could simply lie in wait for the killer to arrive with Jana, McCully decided passiveness served little purpose. Red was trapped inside a closet with no physical means of escape, while Jennings or other visitors might stumble into the mansion, unaware of the danger.

No, he decided, walking toward the elevator. Waiting around for the killer to arrive might cause more spilled blood, and he wanted no part of anyone else dying.

McCully pushed the button, ready to find the killer and confront him before anyone else was hurt. He now knew the truth, and this began and ended with one person's evil dream. If he had his way, the dream would be buried forever inside the mansion.

Chapter 33

Jana couldn't shake the feeling she was dreaming, about to wake up when daylight streamed through her window. She felt exhausted, her mind wandering to all sorts of bizarre scenarios, even as her boss stood before her with a knife. Ex-boss, she decided immediately.

"I'm in no hurry to drag you downstairs," Bell confessed, "so I'm going to tell you everything before the longest day of my life comes to an end."

Jana waved her hand across her front like a game show hostess, indicating he could begin any time.

"You're just hoping the extra few minutes you get while I tell this tale will bring some savior through the front door, don't you?" he teased, running his fingers across the knife's flat side. "But I want you to know exactly what your sacrifice will mean to its recipient, and to me."

"Then just get on with it," Jana stated, knowing Bell had a surprise coming if he thought she was just going to cordially walk downstairs with him in a few minutes.

"As you wish," Bell replied, a strange, sinister grin crossing his face.

Jana began to realize he wasn't going to kill her outright with the knife. She had only seen two bodies, while everyone else had disappeared. Her mind scrambled to decipher what he meant by sacrifice, suspecting he needed her alive and intact long enough to carry out some kind of ritual in the basement, or the secret third level.

"I wasn't always a real estate baron," Bell confessed. "In fact, until two years ago, I never thought of it as any kind of career option for me. In some circuits, I was known as a mercenary, an enforcer perhaps. Some called me a con artist, but they didn't realize my talents for what they were. Well, one dying man recognized my talents, and he asked me to do something for him I'd never done before."

Bell paused.

"Kill."

He loosely waved the knife with one hand as he began entering a comfort zone while his tale unfolded.

"It took me awhile, weighing the whole heaven and hell, does God really exist thing, but in the end I thought 'fuck it' because we're only on this planet once, and we might as well live a good life while we're here. And don't get me wrong; I don't like having to kill people, which is why I'm so glad the whole sacrifice process is self-inclusive. Getting messy isn't my thing, either, so I'll just wait to see what happens, then take my cut."

"You're not making any sense," Jana told him. "There are a few gaping holes in your story."

"Such as?"

"Such as who hired you, and how this process of yours works without you."

"I was getting there," Bell replied with a snappy tone. "It'll be better for me to *show* you how the process works, but as for who hired me, let's just say Dr. Martin Smith didn't want to rest in peace after all."

Jana felt floored. Utter insanity entered her ears, but her brain wasn't able to process it correctly. Her mind recalled the ambiguity with which the media covered his "second" death a few years earlier, partially because they lacked evidence of his involvement. The word was that the man faked his death the first time, tried to kill Clouse and the man's family, then died for real. The story had more holes than Swiss cheese, but the public seemed to buy it without very much hoopla.

Perhaps because Smith had no family to speak of, no one really cared if his name was slandered, or maybe it wasn't slandered at all.

Only one person probably knew the whole truth, and Clouse wasn't around to explain anything to her. Damn him for getting her into this whole mess, she thought. Clouse hired Bell, who in turn hired her, creating this catastrophic chain of events she found herself centered within.

"How did you get Clouse to hire you, being so new to property sales?" she asked her former boss.

"He trusts people far too easily. For someone with lots of money, he doesn't have the brains or experience to go along with it. I knew he was going to unload the property eventually, so I dropped a bug in his ear with an e-mail about a year ago. I simply gave my name and contact information, then let him know we would find the property some ownership with integrity, that would keep the hotel historically accurate, and keep his name out of the press."

"Everything he wanted to hear," Jana said, thinking of Clouse as less of a guilty party.

He simply wanted things right for everyone, and now he was partly responsible for another string of abductions and murders, as well as all of the negative repercussions sure to follow. Lawsuits and negative press were on the coattails of this evening, Jana thought, still trying to find a monkey wrench that could stop Bell's plan.

"There are a lot of other things you need to know," Bell admitted, continuing to block the room's only realistic escape route. "Like why this group, why not the first two?"

"Sure. Why?"

"Because their birthdays are important to making the process work."

"Process? You make this sound like slaughtering mindless cattle, not taking human lives."

Bell feigned a hurt expression.

"Funny you should make that analogy, considering half these people are country folk. But what's most important about them is their birthdays. Well, a few of them anyway."

"Why their birthdays? Does it tie into the carvings outside?"

"Oh, it does *much* more than that," Bell said, a nearly orgasmic look crossing his face, proving he believed in what he was doing. "See, the birthdays are intricately tied into the grounds Dr. Smith fought to keep. The same grounds his son was murdered on, in fact. Where he witnessed murders as a child, and where the deep secret of several very special cubes was revealed to him one fine day."

Little of this explanation made sense to Jana, but she believed Bell was telling the truth, at least as Smith had told it to him. Perhaps Smith had taken Bell under his wing, as only a father could, to replace the loss of his own son. Convincing Bell his experiment was ill-conceived seemed unlikely, leading her to wonder if Smith grasped at straws near the end of his life, or he believed in dark magic himself.

"How do you have any idea if this works or not?" Jana asked, trying to interject some reason into his inconceivable plan.

"Because I met a man near death, and the next time I saw him, he was my age. He had reversed his age and the condition killing him from the inside."

"But at what cost?" Jana asked, infuriated that anyone could be so selfish.

She had been raised around the church all her life with her mother and grandmother, understanding the careful balance between life and death, right and wrong. She believed in a spiritual world, doing right in her one earthly life to attain the right to enter the gates of heaven. To take human life for one's own benefit was worse than personal conquest in her eyes.

"Obviously at the cost of human life, my dear," Bell scoffed as though she had asked him a rhetorical question. "And to think I had such high hopes for you when I brought you into the firm."

"And why did you set me up for this? Why me?"

"Isn't it obvious? You're the last person I need before this little experiment goes live."

Jana wanted the complete answer, and Bell seemed to detect this by the way she stared a hole through him.

"In the year 1966, Mr. and Mrs. Whiting from Michigan bought the hotel at auction for less than half its original value. This particular purchase changed history and saved what would have been a doomed West Baden Springs Hotel. Therefore, it is one of the most important dates in the hotel's storied past. And like the eleven other people awaiting your presence, who share important dates from the hotel's past, you fit into the puzzle because of the day you were born."

"November 2," she murmured.

"Bingo. It takes extremely powerful spiritual presences to make this shit work," Bell stated. "Dates, times, people," he said with an airy wave, "all make the magic work. You can think I'm disillusioned or just after the money, and you'd be partly right. Smith offered me a lot of cash to finish the job I started."

"And how do you know he won't just murder you to cover his tracks, even if this insane plan of yours actually works?"

"I've taken all kinds of precautionary measures. The old man might have had this mansion built to suit his own purposes, but I made a few modifications in his absence in case he tries anything crazy."

Bell held the knife up, forcing a complimentary smile.

"Now I think I've told you everything you needed to hear. I'm sorry you won't be around to see the end result, but you'll go out knowing you served a greater purpose."

"Your bank account?"

"Oh, you're taking this so badly, Jana," he said, feigning emotional hurt once again. "I realize you thought I hired you for your brains, or your good looks, so this must be quite a letdown for you. But you'll have to forgive me. I've had a very rough day after several of your clients and a certain deputy sheriff roughed me up, so I'm going to ask you to just make this easy and walk downstairs with me."

Jana needed a few more minutes, hoping someone remained to help her. If not, she felt mentally prepared to engineer her own escape.

"Why kill Laura and Judith if you can't stand taking lives, as you say?"

"They both caught me preparing the traps for the other guests. You see, each of these closets has a device used to lure and ensnare unsuspecting guests into them. It's ingenious really. I can't *wait* to show you when we get to the main room. I'm sure you noticed I kept the sheriff alive, Jana. I needed him until his lackey son came after him, but I didn't have the heart to kill him. Doc can decide what to do with him when he comes back to the land of the living. I've never had much use for peace officers myself, but killing a sheriff does draw a lot of unwanted attention I'm sure Dr. Smith won't want."

"You'll send the good doctor my condolences?" Jana remarked sarcastically.

Bell seemed to enjoy the comment, his expression lightening considerably.

"Now that's what I'm going to miss about you. Your wit and charm."

"And I'm going to miss my paycheck," she said, walking toward him since she had yet to find a suitable weapon. "But we all have to move on, don't we?"

Bell openly didn't like her walking toward him, but his threat with the knife seemed halfhearted, giving her an opening to launch her right foot toward his groin. Bell tried to block it with one hand, allowing Jana time to grab a lamp off a nearby end table, which she smashed over his head.

And the chase was on once again.

Chapter 34

Jana thought she had safely cleared the room's main door when Bell's hand grasped her ankle, tripping her enough that she toppled to the ground. She saw another pair of feet appear before her, thinking Bell had a partner and her life was at a certain end. She looked up to see McCully deck Bell before the man could launch another attack.

"Come on," McCully said, hurriedly helping her up by one arm.

He took her hand, leading her toward the stairs, as she looked back to see an infuriated Bell pursuing them, knife in hand.

"Who is he?" McCully asked when they reached the bottom step, rushing directly toward the front door.

"My boss," Jana answered, drawing a perplexed look from McCully as he tried opening the front door, only to find it locked and jammed once more.

"Fuck."

Taking Jana by the hand, he led her toward the kitchen area, narrowly missing having a knife stuck in the side of his head when Bell lodged it into the front door instead. Unlike Jana, McCully served no useful purpose to Bell if he remained alive.

"You're both dead," Bell called behind them angrily. "You're going to die slow and painful-like, country boy."

McCully took Jana as far as the upper kitchen area before he blocked the doorway.

"Get out of here," he told her.

"No!" Jana yelled her reply, partly because she didn't want McCully getting killed, and partly because Bell was drawing near.

Jana felt cold air rushing inside from the open window she had used before. Escape was so close, and so easy, but where would she go? Where would she find help? The sheriff and one of his deputies were already prisoners inside the mansion.

She snatched a glass pitcher from the kitchen counter, and as McCully engaged Bell, he immediately fought to keep the knife from plunging into his side. Jana seized the opportunity, smashing the pitcher over Bell's head, buying them a few moments of time to rethink their strategy. Bell fell to the ground, by no means unconscious, but in no condition to pursue them immediately.

"Come on," McCully said, leading her toward the stairwell once again.

"There's no way out that way," Jana said, looking back to see Bell remaining stunned on the ground.

"Yes, there is," McCully countered. "Come on."

Refusing to release her hand, even for a second, McCully charged up the stairway. When they reached the top step, he let go of her hand to dash into the closest bedroom. He returned with a bed sheet in hand, then repeated his efforts in the next room. When he emerged from the room, he glanced downstairs to check on Bell as he began tying the sheets together.

"You're not serious," Jana said, beginning to comprehend the plan inside his mind.

"Unfortunately, I am."

"He'll just follow us," Jana insisted.

"Maybe. But you still have the truck keys, right?"

She nodded, feeling comforted by his confidence, but lacking time enough to reveal the truck's condition to him.

"Open up the balcony doors," he requested as he finished tying the sheets together, now spiraling them so they formed a shape that resembled a thick rope.

Jana did so, finding herself constantly looking behind her toward the stairway. A burst of cold air rushed inside the warm confines of the mansion as McCully finished a makeshift braiding of the sheets. He took one end of the sheets, tying it tightly around the balcony railing as Jana dared to look down at the snow-covered ground. It almost looked safe enough to jump upon, but she knew better.

"Get ready," McCully said, cinching the knot as tight as the cloth allowed.

Jana wondered if he had Boy Scouts or military training, because he seemed much calmer than she felt.

She wanted to ask if he expected her to climb down bed sheets to safety, but decided she already knew the answer. Watching him test the knot with a solid tug, Jana forgot all about Bell until the man surprised them both by rushing through the open balcony doors, knife held high by both hands.

McCully whirled too late to save himself from injury, though he deflected the knife upward. It sunk into his right shoulder, forcing a pained cry, as his other elbow clipped Bell in the chin. Jana stepped back, preparing for the worst-case scenario, which came almost immediately.

Bell recovered quickly, clasping McCully's foot, then throwing him over the balcony in one motion because the man only had one useful arm. She saw his hand flail, grasping for dear life at the balcony railing, then fall out of sight after the rest of him.

Jana now found herself completely on her own.

"No!" she shrieked, looking over the railing to see her one remaining source of help lying awkwardly on the ground, either dead or unconscious.

A small blood pool formed in the snow beside him from the shoulder wound, continuing to grow until Jana felt two strong arms wrap themselves around her. Though she kicked, fought, and screamed bloody murder into the surrounding woods, Bell inevitably dragged her into the mansion.

Her head struck the doorway, probably from Bell's intentional doing, and the world around her whirled like a typhoon before going black.

Chapter 35

When Jana next awoke, she found herself inside a large dark room that felt strangely cold to her.

In more ways than one.

Though the temperature felt somewhat chilly, the room contained devices with various people strapped into them. They breathed systematically, like coma patients, unaware of their surroundings, or their impending fate.

Lying on the ground, Jana tried to stand, but quickly realized her hands were bound behind her. Her head ached, but not too badly. Obviously, she hadn't been out very long, indicating the bump that knocked her out was minimal.

"Don't struggle," Bell said from behind her. "It'll be easier in the end."

She managed to swing her body around, finding him readying a device for use.

"There's still time to stop this," Jana insisted, trying to reason with him. "These people are alive. You can still save them."

"Save them?" Bell scoffed. "I'm the one who put them here."

"But you don't have to do this. You don't know for certain it'll work. And if it doesn't, you've just wasted twelve lives, and ruined all of their families."

"You don't think I've reasoned this out?" Bell said, adjusting a leather strap meant to restrain a victim into place. "You can give me all the spiritual mumbo jumbo you want, but you're not going to sway me. I've come too far to just give up."

Realizing her bonds were braided rope, Jana twisted her hands, rubbing them up and down against one another as she tried loosening the bonds. She needed to keep Bell talking, but he seemed content to work on the device.

"How exactly does that work?" she asked, hoping to find a way to counter it if she failed to undo her restraints.

"Yours will work a little bit differently," Bell confessed. "Some of these people have been here for weeks, so they have nutrient tubes to keep their bodies satiated. *You* won't have to worry about any of that. The other tube you see is to keep them sedated. If it makes you feel better, I can put you out before the process begins. It's really the least I can do."

"How kind of you," Jana said, her words dripping with sarcasm.

Bell chuckled as she checked over the needles and tubes surrounding the restraining device.

"I suppose I should have done this sooner," he commented, "but it's just been such a busy night. You wouldn't believe the planning and timing that goes into pulling something like this off."

Jana wanted to stand up and smack him, but she continued working on the ropes. Not only did he lack a conscience, but his sense of humor stunk.

"Oh, the cleaning lady you hired is over there," he said, pointing across the room to an unconscious woman tied down to a tilted slab. "She probably regrets ever taking this job."

"You were the one who recommended her," Jana said, feeling defeat within her voice. "I should have figured it out sooner that you were behind this."

"Don't be so hard on yourself, dear. Your blind devotion to your job made this far too easy for me. Most employers love your qualities in their workers, whereas I just cared about the date of your birth. After tonight, I'm retiring, but I'll take time before my trip to the Bahamas to place some nice flowers on your grave."

Jana seethed with anger toward him, wishing she could break free just to give him a few swift kicks, if nothing else. Then she felt a small strand of the rope break apart. Feeling it with her fingers, she discovered it had all kinds of loose strands on the outside, meaning the rope was an old utility rope, disintegrating from years of being used in the elements.

"This last needle, though, is the one you've gotta watch out for," Bell continued, oblivious to Jana's progress.

He held up the last tube and needle contraption so she could see it, but to her it looked exactly the same.

"All twelve of you will have this plunged directly into your hearts simultaneously, killing each of you instantly, and bringing the life juices to the good doctor over there."

Jana noticed a box centered in the room for the first time where twelve tubes fed directly into the sides. She dreaded the thought of dying, but detested the idea of helping bring back someone who obviously held very little regard for human life even more.

Some doctor, she thought.

"Doc was kind enough to teach me everything I needed to know before his tragic passing a few years ago," Bell continued. "There wasn't very much fanfare surrounding his second funeral, but I guess the cops thought silence was the best thing for everyone involved. It just made my job that much easier."

Bell continued to double-check every last connection on the leather straps, the needles, and the tubes while Jana broke several more strands on the rope. She refused to simply lie back and be a victim. Not only could she save her own life, but eleven others who didn't deserve any of the torture Bell had put them through.

"Everything will change tonight with the simple flip of a switch," Bell added with an air of vanity that his entire plan came together so nicely.

"Where?"

"'Where' what?"

"Where is the switch you're talking about?"

Bell nodded toward the large box centered in the room.

"Beside it. Once all of you are sedated and I'm certain the needles are in their correct positions, it'll be a matter of seconds before Dr. Smith is awakened and I get paid my stipend."

Jana thought back to her October tour. She wondered if the grave disturbance had been related to Bell digging up the body. Considering Smith had two funerals, it sounded reasonable, but burying such a man with the Jesuit priests sounded entirely blasphemous. She recalled Clouse stating something about losing a court case, forced to bury Smith within the property he loved.

After two years, the man's body had to be deteriorated in some regards. If he was embalmed, there would be no blood within him, so how could he function? The entire plan sounded incredibly farfetched to Jana as she snapped another two outer strands away from the rope.

"Well, it looks as though we're ready," Bell said, turning from the device to confront Jana, who had yet to free her hands.

He started reaching toward her when the elevator doors opened from across the room, drawing their attention.

Chapter 36

When the elevator door slid open, no one emerged from inside, causing Jana to wonder if some glitch had caused the movement. Several of the devices blocked the view of the elevator's lower half for both her and Bell, so her captor cautiously moved toward the only entrance in the third level.

"Your boyfriend isn't going to like finding me here," Bell said, giving a hardened stare at Jana before taking another step toward the elevator.

He searched the area momentarily, discovering no one around or inside the car, so he returned, determined to end his task without delay.

"I'm going to get you strapped in, *then* I'm going to throw that switch," he proclaimed. "After that, I'll deal with any stragglers left around this place, including your new boyfriend."

Jana resented the remark, partly because his accusation was simply false, and because Bell talked about McCully as though he were a slab of ground chuck.

From the looks of the device, Bell needed to untie her before restraining her with the leather straps, both around her wrists, and around her body. He reached down, plucking her off the floor with a hard jerk that allowed her to break the last few remaining strands around her wrist. She launched a knee into his groin, connecting entirely this time, before using the length of rope that once bound her wrists, to slash him across the face.

Bell yelled in agony as he fell to the floor, allowing Jana time to run for the elevator. She hated to leave the others behind, but without her, Bell couldn't throw the switch, meaning they were in no real danger.

Jana hit a slick spot along the floor that tripped her up. She hit the floor hard, sliding against the side of the elevator as Bell regained his footing. Jana scrambled to her feet, virtually launching herself into the elevator as she fumbled for the down button. Bell reached the elevator as the door began closing, causing her to kick toward him, which immediately reversed the door's movement.

Thinking she had attempted her last escape, Jana prepared to fend off Bell's next attack when someone streaked across the open door, tackling Bell to the ground. Jana stepped forward to observe her latest savior when a noise from above captured her attention.

She looked up, spinning defensively to find Craig Jennings climbing down from the elevator's emergency hatch. Fearing the worst, she wondered if Jennings had teamed with Bell long before the visitors ever reached the mansion, but he jumped down, gave her a reassuring nod, and stepped forward. She realized he was looking for the skirmish at hand, so Jana also left the elevator car, finding Bell getting the best of McCully until Jennings grabbed him from behind.

For his trouble, the hunter received a knife to the side of his right calve muscle, flooring him as he hollered in pain. Jana realized the two men had formulated a quick plan to ride the elevator up. One of them had apparently observed the third level earlier, knowing Bell would instantly be aware of their presence when the elevator opened.

Fighting like a cornered badger, Bell seemed to handle both of his injured attackers with ferocity and intensity unlike anything Jana had ever witnessed. He threw McCully against a nearby wall, where the bluegrass singer hit back first, then slumped to the ground in a heap. Bell then turned on Jennings, who had been distracted by his new injury.

The hunter looked up when Bell closed in, unable to prevent the killer from stomping on the injured leg. Jennings screamed again, but Bell's close proximity allowed the hunter to buck with his good leg, kicking Bell in the kneecap. Though Jana didn't hear a crack to indicate any broken bones, the blow crumpled Bell to the floor, temporarily giving the three men even footing.

Jana decided to cripple Bell the best way possible as her eyes surveyed the room.

She ran over to the closest victim, who happened to be Oswalt, and began pulling the needles from where they entered his skin. Held in place by bandage tabs, the needles easily slid outward, then dropped to the floor when Jana let go. Knowing what purpose the tubes served, she let go of any fear that she might hurt the victims. She assumed Bell had told her the truth, because he seemed so confident his plan was about to end perfectly.

Fighting activity resumed nearby, but Jana paid minimal attention to it as she went cot to cot, freeing each of the victims from their feeding tubes and whatever form of anesthesia kept them sedated. Hearing a yelp of pain, she looked up to find Bell hurling Jennings into the elevator car, pushing a button inside before the doors closed.

For the moment, Jennings was removed from the battle against Bell, who now turned his attention toward Jana.

Infuriated by her actions, he clenched his fists before stomping toward her. With six of the victims now freed from their tubes and bonds, Jana stared directly at Bell while she undid the restraints on Keith's cot. The needles dropped to the floor as Bell reached the cot, but she had already sought shelter behind the next slab.

"You bitch," Bell stammered, his fury quite obvious.

If he were a cartoon character, steam would blow out the sides of his ears. And in a cartoon, the knife clutched in his right hand probably wouldn't seem nearly as ominous.

She didn't consider herself untouchable, but felt it necessary to make a statement that she wasn't going to cower before him. Undoing Keith's restraints while looking at him got her point across, but now Jana found herself without assistance, and few places to run.

"This time I'm going to choke you out before I put you on that slab," Bell sneered. "Then I'm going to gut every one of your little helpers."

"Thought you didn't like getting your hands dirty," Jana retorted, trying to stall once again.

"I'll make an exception for you, sweetie."

Bell waited behind one of the filled slabs, trying to time when Jana would run. She tested the waters by pretending to dart one way, then pulling herself back to the safety of the slab. Bell didn't fall for it, poising himself for whichever way she chose to run. When she finally left her cover, like a rabbit cornered by a coyote, he dove and missed her feet by inches.

Making her way to the next restraining cot, Jana released a stranger from the confines of the straps and the tubes. She had only three people left to free, but Bell was already on his feet, pursuing her once again.

Despite his injuries, McCully made another valiant effort to stop Bell. From out of nowhere, he rammed Bell from the side, knocking them both to the floor. This time Jana got a closer look at his shoulder wound, which continued to bleed, based on the shiny liquid pooling atop his clothes. She suspected he was in great pain, and likely on the verge of losing consciousness after losing so much blood.

The elevator door opened, panning more light into the room once more. Jennings stepped out, looked around hurriedly, and found Bell beginning to get the better of McCully. He tried intervening once, found himself thrown back for his efforts, and scrambled to pull Bell away from McCully a second time without hesitation.

Jana took advantage of the distraction, quickly undoing the tubing and bonds from another captive. She looked over, finding McCully receiving a vicious punch from Bell before Jennings struck him from behind. Barely fazed, Bell turned on the hunter, kicking his wounded leg again. Jennings reached for the injured appendage, allowing Bell to shove him away.

Hearing a thunderous crash from Jennings falling over a pile of discarded clothing, Jana returned to the task of freeing the two remaining prisoners. She heard several painful grunts, looking up to see Bell repeated kicking and stomping Jennings in the area of his stomach and ribs.

Refusing to be distracted, she continued her work, hoping their efforts to distract Bell weren't in vain.

While undoing the leather straps holding the final stranger, she heard a clanking noise across the room, thinking perhaps a knife had hit the wall, or perhaps been dropped to the floor.

She dropped the final set of tubes to the floor with a wave of relief crossing her mind.

With all of the captives out of immediate danger, she looked for something to use against Bell, who had once again gotten the better of his two assailants. McCully and Jennings had bravely confronted him, but he had a size and strength advantage, as well as bladed weapons.

In the center of the room, she spied the switch Bell had referred to at the base of the large makeshift coffin. Though she didn't have time to study it further, Jana decided it looked very simplistic. One simple push forward likely activated the spring loaded joints meant to plunge the last needle into every prisoner's heart.

Jana had removed all of the tubes, and in most cases, snapped the killing needles from their deadly mechanisms. If Bell wanted to kill them all tonight, he would be spending countless hours putting the contraptions back together.

After a quick but fruitless search, Jana looked up, seeing Bell standing over both McCully and Jennings with no weapon in hand. She immediately looked for it, thinking it might be lodged somewhere in one of the men, but saw no knife handle. Hearing a groan from along the floor, she saw both of them move slightly, indicating they were alive, but in bad condition.

"I never would have hired you, had I thought you were so disobedient," Bell said, taking an ominous step toward her.

"You must have missed the part where I turned in my two weeks' notice," Jana countered, bringing a sinister grin to his face.

"That's okay. I'm going to give you a severance package you won't soon forget."

Jana began backing away from him, knowing she was truly on her own this time. Weaponless, she ducked behind one of the slabs for cover, simply prolonging the inevitable. In nearly complete darkness she managed to elude the shrewd eyes of a predator she once called her boss.

"You can't get away," Bell chided as she crawled from one device to another, hoping the low lighting didn't give her away. "Even if you make it to the elevator, you won't get the doors closed."

He continued to search for her, apparently unable to see her, or any shadows she made while crawling. Grasping around one of the cots, he missed her, because she was now three slabs away from him, looking up at Dan Duncan's unconscious form, thinking back to the last time she saw him wrapped in plastic.

His jacket and jeans contained sticky residue, as did his face. The plastic wrap had acted as a thick spider web of sorts, containing him until Bell subdued and unwrapped him. He looked peaceful, breathing in and out, but Jana refused to be mesmerized by the sight. She also refused to give up hope on Duncan and the other captives.

She needed a way out of this situation, away from Bell to buy some time.

The closet traps, she thought suddenly. A fleeting and hopeless thought, she decided quickly was using a trap from one of the twelve rooms to assist her. She had no idea how they worked, or how to open them, so Jana quickly moved on to simple preservation.

She made her way over to her injured protectors, finding McCully first. He didn't seem aware of her presence, but she couldn't do much for him without being noticed.

"Dave?" she whispered to him. "Dave, it's Jana. Can you hear me?"

His eyes remained closed, so she ran her hand up his back to detect his condition, and whether or not he was breathing. From beside her, Jennings groaned lightly, distracting her before she could analyze McCully.

She saw the hunter's eyes flutter open, regain a little focus, and look beyond her. At first, she thought he might be looking toward the pearly white gates in a death trance, then his lips moved.

"Behind you."

Jana whirled around, catching Bell by the right arm, but he forced her to the floor without hesitation or the least bit of trouble. Hitting hard, Jana injured her left wrist, but backpedaled away from Bell until she struck the narrow side of the coffin.

She hit headfirst, nearly knocking her senseless.

Bell took advantage of the opportunity, wrapping his hands around her throat, immediately cutting off the air to her lungs. Gasping for air, Jana heard a strange croak emit from her throat she'd never heard before. Before she was too far gone, she dug her nails into his forearms, scratching a trail from his hands to his elbows before he released his grip.

"That does it," he spat angrily, reaching again for her throat.

Jana had spotted a set of fully intact needles and tubes on the ground beside her, so instead of defending herself, she plucked them from the ground. As Bell lurched forward to strangle her, Jana plunged the needles with all her might into what she believed was his heart, using both hands.

A stunned look crossed Bell's face, almost paralyzing Jana with fear because he didn't fall over dead. Instead, he looked from the needles to her in obvious pain and utter shock. She recovered her senses enough to reach behind her, flipping the switch beside the coffin. Hoping the needles and tubes had enough kick to finish the job, she wriggled her way free from under him, then used both hands to give the needles one last shove into his chest.

The tube meant to plunge into the heart of its intended victims had already begun drawing fluids, and she now knew Bell had been mortally wounded. His eyelids fluttered momentarily, ceasing all of the sudden. A death trance crossed his face as he crashed to the floor. His eyes remained open, despite his head landing hard against the bare floor, his mouth partly agape.

Bell's death stare looked anything but peaceful.

Jana thought once of verifying his death, but decided to check on McCully and Jennings first.

Standing up, she heard only the sound of her footsteps as she crossed the room. When she reached the two injured men, she found Jennings attempting to sit up, clutching his ribs as he did so.

"You okay?" she inquired.

"I think so," he said, beginning to test his ribs by rubbing them. "I don't think any of them are broke."

Jana gently rolled McCully onto his back, trying to assess what Bell had done to him. He seemed to be breathing, but his chest rose and receded in a very shallow pattern. She detected no other open wounds aside from the shoulder, so she decided to test his consciousness.

"Just nod if you can hear me," she said in a soft voice, her face mere inches from his.

"I'm not deaf," he murmured in reply. "And I must say you still smell really nice for what you've been through."

He opened his eyes painfully, wincing when he tried sitting up.

"I hope you two didn't fake unconsciousness so I'd save you," Jana said, trying to break any remaining tension.

"There was no faking," Jennings said, still rubbing his side. "He put an ass-whoopin' on us."

Jana heard the suction of the tubes from behind her, so she stood to turn off the device, realizing quite a bit of Bell's bodily fluids had already been drained. She found a rag draped over one of the slabs, so she snagged it to apply pressure on McCully's wound. He didn't make a sound when she covered his wound, indicating some form of shock had overtaken part of his mind.

"We have to get Red," he stated, though not moving.

"Where is he?" Jana asked, thankful to hear he was alive.

"I left him in a closet downstairs with a gun."

Jana wondered why Red wouldn't have helped overpower Bell.

"Why didn't he come up with you?"

"His leg is broken. I put him in there for his own safety, thinking the killer might come after him."

Realizing she had most certainly struck Red with the truck, Jana felt bad, wondering if perhaps she had saved him in a roundabout way.

"How did you get back here?" she asked Jennings.

"I got to town and couldn't find any help, so I doubled back through the woods and found Dave downstairs. He told me what this place looked like, so we used the elevator and hid out to fool the bad guy."

"My boss," Jana revealed, drawing stares somewhere between mystified and deeply concerned from both men. "Well, ex-boss."

All three chuckled, momentarily too tired to find help, leave the room, or even get up from the floor.

Chapter 37

By early morning, everyone inside the third level had recovered to the point they were awake and able to be moved downstairs. Like refugees, they sat or stood throughout the downstairs. Most were covered with blankets, refusing to stray very far from the safety of other people.

Jana noticed a variety of emotions and expressions from the survivors. Some appeared shocked, while others cried. Some simply sat quietly, while others found comfort in conversation.

McCully and Jennings found the sheriff in the basement kitchen area lying against the far wall. He seemed quite irritated, but in excellent health. Bell had indeed left him alive, though sedated and bound. The two men freed him, explaining the situation as best they could.

Brown listened, only after verifying his son was among the living, though he seemed dismayed about Bell's crazy plan. Jana felt better knowing the best local legal authority knew the real story before anyone else, so they didn't all sound crazy when the time for questions came later.

As the storm front passed through Southern Indiana, Red finally got a signal from his cellular phone, allowing him to call the authorities. Jana tried keeping everyone away from the grizzly death scene in the dining area and upper kitchen, but Keith refused to be denied. He grieved Laura in his own way, though he didn't actually touch the body thanks to advice from his brother.

"He's taking it hard," she commented to Red.

He simply nodded, supporting himself on a doorframe as they waited for the police and ambulances to arrive.

"You really should sit down," Jana told him.

"It's okay. I guess tonight made me realize how important friends and family are. I'm just really glad I didn't lose *him*."

His blue eyes continued to stare at Keith, although his older brother seemed frustrated, angry, and saddened all at the same time. Perhaps he held himself partly responsible, but Bryan Bell wouldn't want to share his credit, or the money he might have received for his services.

Keith seemed to be holding back his emotions, and possibly some tears, but he paced the foyer, occasionally punching a wall as his head drooped toward the floor. For the first time Jana had seen the man without his hat and sport coat. He didn't appear nearly as distinguished, looking disheveled after losing his temper, and some self-control.

"I'm not sure I understand all of this," Red told Jana.

"Me neither," she answered. "I keep thinking this is some weird dream and I'm going to wake up from it any minute."

She looked around, finding the mansion far more peaceful, like the aftermath of a weathered hurricane. A few of the long-term prisoners appeared weak, pale, and dreadfully thin. Jana wished she could cook them up a quick meal, or at least serve them a hot drink, but going into the kitchen wasn't an option.

McCully had said a few things to her that indicated he knew quite a bit about how the device upstairs worked, and how Bell and Smith knew one another. She didn't press for information, because she still felt thoroughly confused about the situation. What the hell was she going to tell the police?

Placing the blame on Bell's insanity, or at least the insanity of his plan, seemed appropriate, but no one could verify her story. Jana only knew she wanted to speak with the police, because it would surely be mandatory. After that, she could go home to a hot bath.

She found McCully waiting by the front door, so she walked over to him, gently putting a hand across his back. Staring out the same glass trim, she noticed the snow had begun melting outside as a warm front moved into the area.

Despite his injuries, McCully refused to rest until the others were freed. Jana nursed his wounds the best she could, applying fresh towels to the stab wound in his shoulder. She also found bandages for his busted nose, knowing it would require stitches to heal correctly.

Staring at the snow banks, she knew it might take a few days for the snow to completely disappear, but depressions along the tops of the snow piles indicated warmer air was already moving through. A dark purple horizon appeared over the tree line, indicating dawn was inevitable.

"Easy come, easy go," McCully said, his eyes still fixed beyond the window. "I can't believe we were trapped here all night, and now the weather clears up. It's almost like your boss had custom ordered it."

"No," Jana replied evenly. "The blizzard splitting us up might have been the only thing that saved us."

"Tell that to Laura and Judith."

Having no reply to such a comment, Jana simply took hold of his nearest arm, trying to pat it reassuringly. McCully didn't resist, so she assumed he still wanted company.

"This house might have been built for the wrong reasons, but the weather was a saving grace," she added a moment later. "Things could have been a lot worse."

Blue and red lights appeared like beacons in the distance, looking something like blinking Christmas lights against the snow outside. At last, the authorities had made their way up the hill, now nearing the mansion.

"The cavalry," McCully said with absolutely no enthusiasm.

A moment passed as they waited for the police cars to make their way up the treacherous road, then park as close as they could to the mansion.

"Where do you go from here?" McCully asked Jana, as though realizing he had been absorbed in his own thoughts all evening.

"I guess I'll be searching for a new job," Jana said in a lighthearted voice, though knowing she spoke the truth. "Maybe Mr. Clouse needs an executive assistant."

"He'll be needing something, alright. After tonight, I doubt his empire will be the same."

McCully paused, momentarily thinking about something.

"Smith really hated him."

"How do you *know* that?" Jana inquired, suspecting McCully told the truth, though unsure where he attained such information.

"I just do. He thought Clouse caused his son's death, and I guess I can relate to a father and son bond. Just makes me wonder what the truth really is."

Jana counted three police cars in the driveway, hearing more sirens in the distance. Two county officers and one town marshal from West Baden made their way toward the mansion as she and McCully stepped aside to let them through.

All three men stepped inside, saying nothing momentarily as they surveyed the walking wounded with confused stares.

"Who called this in?" one the county officers finally asked, despite Roland and Arlan Brown sitting near everyone else.

"I did," Red claimed, hobbling on his good leg toward the officers. "You're going to need a few ambulances and a couple of thick notepads, boys."

***

It felt like forever as the group waited for medical attention while the officers took their statements. Everyone wanted to go home, or at least escape the confines of the mansion.

McCully had already given his statement to an officer, or at least the parts of it he felt comfortable speaking about. One word about psychic visions would instantly discredit him as a viable witness, so he kept quiet about the insider details.

One officer taped off the area surrounding the two bodies downstairs, leaving the lower level entry door free for travel. The officers seemed hesitant about going near the bodies, mainly because the coroner had informed them he was en route.

McCully currently sat by himself in the large living room, looking at the survivors around him. Most of them he didn't know, but Oswalt and Duncan made their way toward him once the police finished with them.

It seemed the authorities deemed it necessary to interview everyone right away to preserve evidence, as though some of them might change their stories or forget details.

"How are you two?" McCully asked, truly wondering what each of them had experienced.

Jana had informed him about Duncan's struggle with a certain plastic trap.

"Better," Duncan admitted, still trying to peel some of the sticky substance from his clothing.

The residue spots along his jacket and jeans looked as though someone had taken a paintbrush and dotted him intermittently with rubber cement.

Jana had given him a wet cloth to wipe the residue from his hands and face. She had no idea what the substance might have been, but it held a stout man in check without fail. Smith had planned the sacrifice perfectly, using his medical expertise and some creative inventions.

"I'll never get this shit off my jacket," Duncan complained, trying to wash it off with the wet rag.

"And I thought my last divorce settlement was the worst day of my life," Oswalt said, indicating his wry sense of humor had already returned.

"Jana isn't saying much," Duncan stated, "so can you tell me what the hell just happened up there, and why?"

McCully sat a moment, thinking of exactly how he wanted to craft his words.

"Seems to me someone wanted to bring a warped, rich, old man back to life. You guys were the sacrificial lambs."

"I gathered that," Duncan said stiffly. "I guess my real question is, would the thing have worked?"

McCully believed with all of his heart the device actually would have succeeded. He doubted Dr. Smith was a fool, or a man who wasted valuable time and energy on anything lacking merit.

"You know, I've experienced some weird things in my life," McCully admitted, "so I wouldn't doubt the thing might have worked. I guess it's a good thing we didn't find out."

Oswalt sat pensively a moment, probably reflecting on the night, and how close to death he truly came. He sniffled as he breathed in, though McCully couldn't tell if he had a cold, or emotions had overwhelmed him. The agent rubbed his cheeks momentarily before burying his entire face within his palms.

A moment later, he looked up with a more resolved appearance.

"For what it's worth, thanks for everything you did up there," he finally said to McCully.

"Jana did most of it, but you're welcome."

Both men seemed reluctant to give Jana any credit, despite her efforts to save Duncan from his earlier predicament.

"If it wasn't for her, we wouldn't have been here," Oswalt commented.

"No," Duncan stated very sternly. "If not for *me*, you wouldn't have been here. I was the one who got us into this mess. I let my devotion toward this place and my grandfather blind me."

McCully didn't feel like placing blame. Simply happy to be alive, he didn't want to think about touring with his father, or investing in property. He wanted to lay his head on a pillow inside some well-secured hotel room and forget about the past twenty-four hours.

"Don't blame yourself," he told Duncan. "There's no way we could've known this was all a trap."

He then turned to his agent.

"And don't blame Jana. She was duped like the rest of us, and if Bell had gotten her strapped in that thing upstairs, you all would have been dead."

Oswalt gave a genuine nod that he understood. Everyone had survived a major ordeal, so emotions ran unchecked as they recalled the experience. McCully stood, placing an understanding hand on Oswalt's shoulder.

"You going to be okay?"

"I'll be fine."

"Good. It's all over, so don't sweat it, Frank."

Oswalt nodded once more, though his eyes seemed to drift to a faraway place.

When the coroner arrived a few minutes later, more questions ensued. He spoke mainly with the police officers, eventually turning his attention to Red, who simply shrugged at most of the questions. McCully imagined he was inquiring about any witnesses to the deaths of Laura and Judith, but of course, no one had seen either incident.

The mansion had a way of hiding its events.

The coroner retreated to the outdoors, returning with his camera momentarily. With a police officer keeping close watch on the door, he began snapping photographs of the death scenes. McCully thought it somewhat odd the coroner worried about interference from people who had no desire to see their dead colleague a second time.

McCully found himself watching the business of the coroner and the police, to satisfy personal curiosity more than anything, from the foyer. He left Oswalt and Duncan to talk amongst themselves, but no words seemed to express their true feelings after surviving such an ordeal.

The town marshal returned from the lower kitchen with an exasperated look on his face. Though no lip reader, McCully thought he recognized the word "body" from the man's lips. He subconsciously began stepping closer, wondering what the fuss was about, because the officer's expression seemed unusually concerned.

All morning the officers had secretly exchanged smirks and jokes when they thought none of the guests were looking, but McCully noticed. He drew as close as he could to the door without looking like he was eavesdropping, then remained perfectly still.

"They said there were two bodies on the third level," the officer reported to the county officer in charge, and the coroner. "I only found one."

All three exchanged worried looks.

"Talk to some of the guests again," the county officer said, wanting verification. "I'm sure they said there were two."

McCully watched him ask a few of the guests who had been ushered from the third level hurriedly to keep them from seeing the bodies. They simply shrugged, saying they had no idea how many bodies were upstairs.

For a moment, he wondered if they didn't count the shriveled corpse as a body, thinking there were supposed to be two fresh corpses. He doubted the marshal would be so naïve, nor would he return without checking the entire upstairs thoroughly.

McCully motioned for Jana and Jennings to join him as the marshal made his way toward them. He wanted the two people who could confirm what he knew to be the truth with him when the question was asked. Both had snuck a peek at Smith's corpse while they waited for the other prisoners to revive.

"What's wrong?" Jennings questioned.

"You're about to find out."

Holding his hat in his hands, the marshal made his way over to them, looking uneasy. McCully sensed the man hated to bother them, especially since everyone else had said they knew nothing about bodies upstairs.

"Folks, I hate to bother you, but I have to ask a question."

He hesitated until he received the full attention of all three people. Jana had continued looking to McCully for answers, but he simply nodded toward the marshal, hoping she would do the same.

"How many bodies were there upstairs?"

"Two," Jennings answered immediately, his answer confirmed by nods from Jana and McCully.

Now he appeared even more discontent about their conversation.

"You're positive?"

"Absolutely," McCully said. "One was the killer who masterminded the whole thing, and there was another one inside that coffin thing in the middle of the room."

Simply nodding, the marshal turned to report to the county officer.

In his heart, McCully already knew the answer to the new mystery, but Jana took a step forward, grasping the marshal's arm.

"What's wrong?" she virtually demanded. "Bryan was dead. I'm sure of it."

Now caught by his own actions, the marshal swallowed hard, forced to reveal something about the new development.

"Ma'am, he was up there. It was the *other* body we couldn't find."

Jana's grasp released the officer's arm, her hands falling away like wilting vines from a fence post. She turned to McCully with a look of disbelief and horror, asking what in the hell happened upstairs without uttering one word.

Jennings appeared equally stunned, but he immediately shook his head in disbelief aimed at the cops, rather than the impossible possibility all three initially questioned.

"They're covering it up again," he stammered angrily. "I can see the writing on the wall."

Jana looked confused, then bought into his theory because it seemed so much more realistic, and easier for the mind to digest. McCully pulled her into an embrace as her world crumbled around her, believing differently than his two companions. He had seen the look on the marshal's face when he emerged from the kitchen stairway.

Like Jennings and Jana at first, his face displayed total disbelief. Though McCully thought it impossible through conventional wisdom and simple logic, he wondered if Bryan Bell had indeed given life to the dead through his *own* sacrifice.

Counting himself lucky to be alive, McCully didn't dare pose questions he couldn't answer. Something told him if this mystery wasn't finished, his mind would let him know it in due time.

He watched the exasperated marshal explaining the situation to the county officer and the coroner, his arms doing some of the talking for him. McCully kept his arms wrapped around Jana while Jennings continued to fume over what he considered a police scandal. Local people had been given a raw deal by the press and police before, so his thought process seemed logical.

Taking in a deep breath, McCully created his own vision, placing himself sleeping the rest of the day before heading home to Tennessee. Perhaps one day he would write a song based on his tragic experience in Orange County, but right now, he felt content just being alive.

GHOSTS
OF WEST BADEN:

Book Five of the West Baden Murders Series

This is for Joy Winslow, my agent, my friend, and the one person who understands the quirky little issues I have in this thing called life.

Thanks to Brad Wiemer, Carol Pyle, Mark Adams, Nannette Bell, Joy Winslow, Dave Blackford, Mike Ritchie, Kevin Brown, Jennifer Stapleton, Korby Sommers, Todd Lee, Andy Shellabarger, Mike Chambers, and Rick Shellabarger for their contributions.

Special thanks to Kendrick Shadoan at KLS Digital for creating the cover, handling photography, and doing a great job as always. Visit www.klsdigital.com

Another special thanks to Amy Drake because I messed up her thank you in the last West Baden novel. Sorry, Amy! Amy does professional photos of West Baden and is a major part of the local historical society there. Visit www.smalltownphotographs.com

Patrick J. O'Brian

Chapter 1

Paul Clouse felt certain his life had reached a miserable low.

At least he knew the answer to whether money made people happier or not.

It didn't.

Standing beside a good friend, he watched heavy construction equipment tear into, then haul away, the remains of a relatively new mansion seated atop the crest of a steep road. Cool air from the Southern Indiana February forced them both to wear jackets, but at least the sun peeked through the nearby trees.

An industrial smell filled the air, the kind created when metal and heavy rock butted heads.

Both men knew why the mansion had to go, despite being younger in age than either of them. What Clouse told the public provided a necessary smoke-screen to put a positive spin on recent events.

Numerous conversations with his lawyer had engraved the phrase "positive spin" in the recesses of Clouse's mind.

While his press agent told the media the mansion had foundation and erosion issues, Clouse knew the mansion served a far more sinister purpose than to provide lavish shelter.

It was designed to take lives efficiently, supplying adequate cover from the outside world.

"Kind of a shame," Mark Daniels said at his side.

"How's that?"

"All that labor and material going to waste."

Clouse had donated every brick, window, and piece of furniture to needy organizations, but his friend didn't mean *that* kind of waste.

He meant the waste of a man who built it on false pretenses, tricking an entire community, including countless families, politicians, and law enforcers who unknowingly backed his evil plans.

Clouse himself had fallen victim to the old man's charms. Even in death Martin Smith gave him grief, because he left Clouse the billions he had amassed over the years from his legitimate empire. It was the other side of Smith that Clouse feared when he discovered the man's evil intentions after he turned up alive after faking his own death. Smith finally died for real at the hands of Clouse, purely out of self-defense.

To think of such things disturbed Clouse, mainly because Smith continued to reach out to him from the grave. An event less than two months old left him cleaning up more messes in and out of the courtroom. He had three pending lawsuits, and possibly more on the way.

All of the cases were linked to events that happened in the partial mansion before him.

"What now?" Daniels asked him. "You can't keep running from a ghost."

Daniels, a police detective in nearby Bloomington, befriended Clouse shortly after Clouse's first wife was brutally murdered. The two got to know one another during the investigation, and despite the officer's own marriage apparently coming to an end, they kept in touch.

"I can't run from a ghost who has real life goons fucking up my life, Mark."

Smith had used his wealth and connections prior to his death to set certain events in motion, which included the unfounded notion he could be brought back to life using a certain ritual along with a cursed object. While the attempt failed miserably, three people died, and Smith's body disappeared along with a curious green cube that witnesses felt certain was the cursed object in question.

Some believed his plan worked, and he simply walked out of the mansion to enact revenge on Clouse at a time and place of his choosing. Others, including Clouse, thought the conspiracy ran deeper, and someone removed the body from the mansion to attempt even more ludicrous resurrections.

Watching a dump truck leave with heavy stone destined to help build a church, Clouse wondered exactly where his life was going. After the last incident, he hired a private investigator to flush out any of Smith's remaining connections and dig into the dead man's past. Thus far, the search provided him with very few answers.

Constantly surrounded by bodyguards, which led to more arguments with his wife, Clouse wished things were normal again. He wanted his two best friends back, both of whom died at murderous hands, and he missed his job as a full-time firefighter. Things were simpler back then, and while bills weren't always as easy to pay, he enjoyed life.

He traced his misery back to the day he met with Martin Smith for the first time, wishing he could have seen through the man.

"What if I go into the casino business, Mark?" he finally asked, drawing a raised eyebrow from his friend.

"Well, you own the French Lick and West Baden hotels, so there's nothing stopping you there."

"And Orange County voted to let gambling into the Valley," Clouse added. "I've always loved the dome, Mark. Maybe it's just meant to be that I keep the thing."

"Sounds to me like you've already made up your mind."

Clouse looked to the ground, kicking a few loose pebbles with the tan lizard skin cowboy boots he often wore. Riches were never going to change some things about him.

He had purchased the French Lick grounds down the road about a month prior, deciding it was the icing on the cake for a casino package. Whether he completed a casino project himself, or sold all of the property, it made good business sense.

Considering himself a businessman in no sense of the word, Clouse felt awed to possess properties that industrialists like Lee Wiley Sinclair and Thomas Taggart once owned.

"I guess I've been tossing around the idea of keeping the place for a while now, Mark. I know things haven't been going so great for you lately, but I was wondering if you might want to come work for me."

Daniels now shot him a skeptical look, as though Clouse was offering him a sympathy position because of the divorce.

"I need a head of security when the casino opens up. It'll pay more than double what you make at the police department and-"

"Whoa, Paul," Daniels said, holding his hand up like a stop sign. "You're about three steps ahead of me right now. You've been doing more than tossing around ideas."

Unable to look at his friend a moment, Clouse knew he had already made up his mind. Part of him wanted to own the West Baden Springs Hotel, but from a business standpoint, the move allowed him to escape a few potential lawsuits by bringing certain individuals under his wing.

"There are classes in Las Vegas, Mark. The thing wouldn't be built for another year or two, and I'd pay you to learn everything you need to know in the meantime."

"And throw away my government pension?"

Clouse scoffed.

"You don't think I'm going to take care of you on your retirement and benefits? Jane would kill me if I didn't treat my employees like gold."

Daniels rubbed his neck, openly uncomfortable with his good friend becoming his employer.

"I didn't mean it like that," Clouse said, on the verge of inserting his foot where it belonged. "With the divorce, you could probably use some extra funds."

Rubbing his jawbone thoughtfully, Daniels said nothing as an excavator made a grinding noise, trying to unearth part of the mansion's partially loose foundation.

"How long have you been thinking about this?"

"A few months now."

"And what does Jane think?"

Clouse shrugged.

"She's like me. Whatever's going to come, it'll come for us anywhere."

"*If* anything comes."

Instead of arguing, Clouse shot him a look that spoke volumes.

"You can't live your life in paranoia, Paul. Bodyguards, private schools, whatever helps you sleep at night. It has to end somewhere, so why can't it be over with?"

"I thought it was done two years ago with Smith's death, but his scheming went deeper than I ever imagined."

"Look, if your private investigator isn't finding anything, maybe it's really over this time."

Clouse looked skyward, where no answers were forthcoming.

"If you're so confident it's over then come work for me, Mark. Clean slate for both of us."

Daniels grinned, still not looking at him.

"I'll give it some thought. That's all I can promise right now."

Refusing to take "no" for an answer, Clouse decided to have his lawyer draw up an employment contract immediately for his friend to review. He wanted to keep his friends close, all the while hoping it didn't draw his enemies closer.

Chapter 2

Two years, three months later

Clouse spent two years completing three objectives, which included a remodel of the French Lick Springs Hotel, updating the West Baden Springs Hotel, and building a casino from scratch.

Unconventional gambling laws in Indiana required casinos to technically be afloat, so a riverboat casino was constructed before a small pond was added beneath it. Though it looked functional, the casino was not a working boat. A hallway and a parking lot attached it to the French Lick hotel, leaving it nearly a mile from the love of his life.

Architecturally speaking.

On a mid-May afternoon, Clouse found himself standing on the West Baden Spring Hotel's veranda, looking out toward the sunken garden. Completed in 1902, the hotel had a storied history with numerous changes throughout its various ownership periods. Two of the old brick spring houses in the garden before him were evidence of early 20th Century design. The hotel itself was the largest freestanding dome in the United States until the Coliseum was completed in 1955 in Charlotte, North Carolina.

Spring water initially drew guests to the hotel, but gambling eventually became the prime attraction, luring the rich and famous to the area, even when the courts closed down casinos for a brief period. Now, more than a century later, gambling was going to keep both of the area's major hotels functional, while providing much needed jobs within the county.

Clouse still marveled at the building's architecture, though he had seen every square inch of it during good times and bad. Indescribably beautiful on the inside and exterior, the hotel had survived a partial collapse in 1991 to receive funding from supportive groups. His university graduate work brought Clouse aboard on the project, which seemed like a dream come true at the time.

Now he had mixed feelings, knowing he would never have met Jane, if not for his work at the hotel, but many of his friends might still be alive if things had turned out differently.

His son and stepdaughter were still in school, and his mind weighed heavily with the grand reopening affairs fast approaching.

Five days until Saturday, he thought.

His worries stemmed from far greater concerns than guest lists and festivities.

The last time someone tried to open the hotel, a man was murdered when someone set him on fire. While Clouse wasn't present, he heard it made quite a spectacle on the evening news.

Somehow no one particular murder had worried or hardened him. It took the culmination of everything he'd seen over the past five years to accomplish that, all because Martin Smith wanted the one thing everyone wanted, but no one could attain.

Eternal life.

"You okay?" Jane inquired as she took his side, wrapping her hands around his arm.

"I'm coping. And you?"

"Could be worse, I suppose."

Jane had been a trooper, not complaining much about the bodyguards following her or the children the past few weeks. Clouse had cut his security for a time, but with major events on the horizon, he upgraded the force once more. He told the men, mostly ex-military or former cops, to watch like hawks, but give his family some space.

Her flowing brown locks touched her shoulders, as gorgeous as any model's hair in television commercials. Jane's blue eyes had a way of reading people while comforting them at the same time. She easily could have abandoned the medical practice completely, when money came their way, but she worked several days a week at a nearby clinic in Paoli.

Giving Clouse some additional support, Daniels had signed a contract, spending time between Las Vegas and Miami at several important schools, relieving the couple somewhat. Clouse needed someone who knew the business aspect of overseeing casino operations, and he didn't want to import someone. Daniels would focus on cheating, general complaints, chip distribution, and funds, regardless of where money traveled in the casino.

Of course he had people under him who carried out most of the duties.

"You worried about this weekend?" Jane inquired.

"I'm worried about life in general. That dinner we had with Jana Privett didn't do much to ease my mind."

While the couple had spoken personally with several survivors after the mansion incident, her testimony struck them as the most brutally honest and sincere. She had a grasp about what drastic measures Martin Smith had taken before his death to ensure he didn't stay that way. Of sound state of mind, she also believed his corpse hadn't been whisked away, but rather walked out of the mansion's secret third level that fateful night.

She moved south, though Clouse couldn't recall the area, never once threatening legal action. Of all people, she had a right, because Clouse accidentally placed her in harm's way by asking her to sell the West Baden Springs Hotel for him.

"We can't hole up the rest of our lives," Jane told him earnestly. "Money hasn't changed who we are, Paul, even if you think ghosts are waiting around every corner."

The "ghosts" that disturbed him most were the haunting memories of the friends and colleagues he lost during Smith's reckless searches. Their only crime was befriending him, and Smith used them to his advantage, ruining Clouse's life.

"I don't want Zach growing up to think life is always going to be this way," he admitted.

His son, now ten-years-old, had spent half of his life living with Katie, Jane's daughter from a previous marriage the same age as Zach.

Clouse and Jane had discussed moving to another state, but most of his family wouldn't follow, and he didn't want to leave his parents behind. Deep down, he hoped drawing his friends closer might keep them all safe, if indeed danger lurked in unseen places.

On the bright side, he had lots of new friends and acquaintances that came with acquiring the French Lick property, and opening the hotel he currently stood within.

The brick driveway between Clouse and the garden area had several cars parked on it as guests loaded and unloaded their belongings. In the second week of a soft opening, the hotel had entertained friends, family members, and some people Clouse had never met before, simply to work out any issues with the staff. So far, not an ounce of trouble was reported, which eased his mind a bit.

He tried to keep himself from thinking it was the calm before the storm because his life had returned to normal too many times before.

Behind him, a few construction workers walked across the veranda, picking up a roll of carpeting as efficiently as worker ants before retreating indoors. Only a few minor adjustments remained before the hotel was a 5-Star wonder, welcoming the general public for the first time since 1932 as a functioning hotel.

Complete with every amenity available to guests, the six-story building included wireless Internet, dozens of lounging chairs and sofas in the grand atrium, a brand new pool, and a beautified property unrivaled by any building within a hundred miles.

"Does it ever feel like a dream to you?" he asked his wife.

"Sometimes. The whole ordeal, all of this, seems weird with everything we've been through."

"We should be happier, shouldn't we?"

Jane gave an understanding gaze.

"I know what the papers say about you gets you down sometimes, but the public can't really understand, because we can't tell them *everything*."

By "everything" Jane meant the details science failed to explain.

Coverage of him wasn't as kind as it once had been, particularly after the mansion incident. People loved that he was opening up the hotel and bringing jobs and revenue to the county, but somewhere along the way general trust was tossed aside like common trash.

"Want to go for a walk my dear?" Clouse asked his wife, nodding toward the garden.

"Certainly," she answered, purposely formal. "If only I had my parasol with me."

Clouse hooked his arm through hers before walking her toward the garden, hoping the rest of their days might be as pleasant.

"If I bought you one of those old-fashioned girdles would you wear that, too?"

"Not likely, dear."

Chapter 3

Two days later Clouse didn't feel much better about the opening of *his* hotel. It almost didn't feel right having his name on any deed after self-made millionaires owned the property during its early years.

He wondered how history would remember him in years to come, when scores of tourists walked through the front arched gates. Previous owners hid some of their secrets within the property, which only true enthusiasts knew anything about. Clouse led his life as an open book, whether he chose to or not.

On the sixth floor of his hotel, he sat across from Raymond Bloom, a retired FBI agent who took on private investigator jobs for the right people, at the right price.

In his mid-fifties, Bloom maintained a tan throughout the year, wore custom-tailored suits, sported a Rolex, and kept just a few strands of gray in his otherwise sandy-colored hair for realism. Thus far, Clouse felt shorted by the funding to results ratio.

Their conversation drew near a close, Bloom providing few answers to Clouse's questions about Smith and the man's activities before his death.

"The book may really be closed on him, Mr. Clouse," Bloom suggested.

"I've fallen for that one before, Ray. He had a backup plan in place two years ago, and I have to think he had contingencies elsewhere."

"I can't exactly go door to door and ask people if they've been recruited by the Coven, now can I?"

Bloom sounded a bit testy, and Clouse couldn't entirely blame him. He was being asked to search out a group loyal to Smith, and very secretive at that. At the risk of sounding insane, Clouse failed to divulge certain pieces of information when he brought the former agent into his fold.

Bloom knew the players and the score, which needed to be enough at this point.

"Someone took Smith's body from the upstairs of that mansion," Clouse reiterated. "That means there's still someone out there who poses a threat to me and my family."

"You said it yourself. There was secret passage after secret passage in that place. Anyone could have snuck in there and stole that body."

"What about the police?" Clouse persisted. "They were the first ones to enter that room once the guests were safe."

Bloom looked at him with mild disbelief.

"Even *if* a cop took that body out of there, how could he have done it without his buddies noticing? And I can't go checking every local cop's background. My Bureau contacts can only take me so far before things blow back in my face."

"I need some answers, Ray. If I don't think my family is safe, I might start looking in your direction as being part of my problem. There are other private investigators."

Bloom looked entirely displeased, but he liked his paycheck too much to retort heavily. Clouse had already considered the idea of hiring a second investigator, considering loyalty often took a backseat to greed when it concerned the hotel property.

"I'll keep digging," Bloom answered. "We're walking a fine line with the locals by prodding around."

"I can't afford to take chances, Ray. Not with the grand opening just days away. If you have to ruffle a few feathers, then do it."

Bloom nodded before showing himself to the door.

Clouse stood from the conference table centered in the sixth floor suite. Complete with a kitchenette, two bedrooms, a conference area, and a few other perks, it was originally designed to house the hotel owners whenever they wanted to stay the night, or conduct business.

Smith had taken that measure before his death, but Clouse chose to occupy the entire sixth floor because he and Jane decided to live at the hotel full-time. There, security could keep a close watch on the children, guests made good witnesses and watchdogs, and simple measures kept anyone unwanted off the floor.

Elevators didn't reach it without a special key card, and staircases met with locked doors on the top level, accessed only by card readers and fingerprint scanners. The deeper into the floor someone went, the more security they found in place.

Two dozen windows overlooked the atrium, but access to them from the outside required excellent stealth, and skills possessed by those experienced in rappelling from buildings.

A knock came to the suite's entrance, pulling Clouse away from a window view of the grounds below.

"Come in."

Todd Parish, one of his husky bodyguards, stepped in halfway. Once a college football player while in the United States Army, Parish wore a black suit that looked strained to maintain his upper body.

A thick, dark goatee encircled his lips, though his hair appeared a little thinner every time Clouse saw him. Parish had been recruited after college to guard celebrities by a California firm. His size made it easy for him to keep Paparazzi away from clients, but a costly lawsuit halted his career, bringing him home to the Bloomington area in despair.

Clouse heard of Parish, deciding to send someone to bring him by for an informal interview. Parish was working as a meat packer at his father's business when Clouse discovered him two years prior, saving the man in more ways than one while protecting his loved ones when he hired him.

Indescribably loyal, Parish had almost become a part of the family, constantly with Zach and Katie. In a few hours he would pick them up from school, treating them like he did his own two children.

"Sir," Parish began, "there's a Randy Niemeyer downstairs. He says it's urgent and he knows you."

Clouse stiffened.

He hadn't spoken to the younger brother of his deceased high school friend in a few years. News through the grapevine revealed that Niemeyer finished college, eventually testing for the state police twice. He completed the academy, found a position in Bloomington near his family, and never once spoke to Clouse about any of his accomplishments.

Deep down, Clouse suspected the young man always wanted to know the truth about Smith and the Coven members who killed his brother. If the state police didn't gain him enough access, the FBI might offer a higher power to satisfy his curiosity.

"Do you want me to tell him you're busy, sir?" Parish asked in a softer tone.

"No, Todd. Please send him up."

Parish nodded, then disappeared from the doorway, silently closing the door behind him.

When Niemeyer walked in a few minutes later, Clouse immediately recognized him, especially since he wasn't in uniform. One look at the man's sea-blue eyes reminded Clouse of Tim. Their eyes, and their faces, always looked eerily similar despite two years difference between them. More than ever Randy looked very much like his older brother, except he shaved his head, and not his face, for drug task force work. He had also put on some weight for his specialized assignment, which also made him look more like Tim.

His look displayed a mix of contained excitement and determination. In his left hand Niemeyer carried a thin plastic case containing a compact disc.

"Good to see you," Clouse said as they quickly shook hands, judging Niemeyer's reaction to him as friendly.

"Paul, I may have unbelievably great news," Niemeyer said, waving the disc. "Got a player?"

"What's this about, Randy?"

"Just watch the disc and judge for yourself."

Clouse led him to a state-of-the-art entertainment center beyond the conference table. Complete with surround sound, a stereo, and every kind of media player available surrounding it, the appropriate player swallowed the disc and began playing immediately until Clouse paused it with the remote control.

He looked to Niemeyer, who had the expression of a kid about to unwrap the biggest present under the Christmas tree, a contrast to his usually stoic disposition.

Pressing the play button, Clouse watched a view from what appeared to be a security camera aimed overhead at a jail cell of some sort. A wide angle provided the viewer with a look at a single cell along a hallway, zooming in toward a lone figure seated in the cell a few seconds later.

Wearing tattered clothes like war prisoners in the *Rambo* movies, the man sat on a bench, head in hands a moment until he stood up and paced the small cell.

Clouse thought he recognized the man, which explained Niemeyer's odd behavior. He reserved judgment, because the camera, like most of its kind, provided lukewarm details.

He observed the prisoner, seeing the man had grown a thick beard from a complete absence of shaving, appearing a bit thinner than the person he originally suspected. Before his death, Tim Niemeyer had been arrested one time over a misunderstanding, but he certainly didn't have a grizzled beard or clothes unfit for waxing cars.

When the man looked up to the camera, the lens zoomed closer, revealing the face of a high school friend who should have been in a coffin nearly five years now.

The screen went black less than a second after the man he believed to be Tim Niemeyer looked into his eyes from beyond the screen.

And possibly beyond the grave.

"Impossible," Clouse muttered, his mind immediately running conspiracy theories in sprints.

"Not impossible," Randy Niemeyer said, standing himself directly in front of Clouse. "My brother is alive. Somewhere, he's alive."

"It can't *be*, Randy," Clouse explained the only rational belief swirling in his head. "You were *there*. You saw Tim die right before your eyes, and you told the police that."

"I knew you'd say it was some kind of trick, or a trap, but after what Martin Smith did to resurrect himself, don't tell me anything is impossible."

What Smith had done went beyond biblical miracles, though he used the darker end of the religious spectrum to accomplish his goals.

"Why would someone keep Tim alive all this time? And why the hell would they let you get your hands on that disc?"

Niemeyer looked stupefied.

"You act like you don't *want* Tim to be alive."

Placing his hands squarely on Niemeyer's shoulders, Clouse looked him in the eyes without so much as a blink.

"Aside from you and your family, there is no one on this planet who would love to have Tim back with us besides me. You're a cop now, Randy. Look at the bigger picture."

Pulling away from Clouse, the younger man wandered in thought momentarily.

"How did you get the disc?"

"It showed up in my mailbox at work one day."

"Mailbox?"

"We each have slots at the post where they leave us notes and stuff. I've already tried to trace it back, but no one will own up to putting it in there, and the guys don't know where it came from."

Untraceable.

Clouse didn't like the sound of the mysterious disc already, especially if someone wanted Niemeyer to see it. When it came to Smith or the mystery surrounding his former hotel, no one simply gave away information.

Any chance of his friend being alive thrilled Clouse, but he kept his emotions in check. With Niemeyer already prepared to start a witch-hunt, someone needed to provide the voice of reason.

"Where do you want to take this?" Clouse asked, ejecting the disc and holding it up.

He didn't speak of the disc, but rather Niemeyer's intentions.

"You have people who can analyze that scene, maybe tell us where they're keeping Tim."

If this isn't a hoax, Clouse thought.

"What about your labs?" Clouse countered, knowing the state police possessed adequate technological capabilities.

"I don't have seniority or pull enough to ask for this kind of favor, and you know that. Besides, this needs to be kept quiet."

Clouse paced the floor a moment, unable to decide exactly which course of action sounded best.

"If there was *any* chance to save Tim, you'd do anything," Niemeyer coaxed. "Wouldn't you?"

Already knowing the answer, Clouse slid the disc into its case, then closed it.

"I'll have my people look at it, Randy. Just promise you won't badger me about it."

Niemeyer failed to contain his enthusiasm, smiling from ear to ear. He truly believed his brother was imprisoned and alive, though Clouse still wasn't sold.

Personal experience kept him from raising his hopes.

"You're not to mention this to anyone," he told Niemeyer. "The only person I'm going to talk to is the man I'll ask to investigate it. So don't be talking to Jane or my staff about this disc, or my help ceases immediately."

Niemeyer nodded. He knew the score if he wanted cooperation in finding the truth.

"Don't get me wrong, Randy. I hope to God this is true, I really do."

Chapter 4

In a manner of speaking, Sheriff Roland Brown had received his wish. The new casino brought in additional revenue, allowing him to expand his staff through tax and federal grant money. He planned to finish his second term as sheriff, hoping to fall into a good casino job if retirement didn't suit him.

He had worked hand-in-hand with Craig Jennings, the man hired by Clouse to head up security at the two hotels. Making friends with Mark Daniels proved a bit more difficult, since the man seemed guarded against everyone except Clouse. As a fellow survivor of horrifying incidents, the sheriff understood, so he didn't push the issue.

Besides, he was the only person outside the casino triangle who had full access to the buildings, schedules, and operating systems. The volunteer fire department shared some of the same privileges, but even they didn't have access to the secretive sixth floor at the West Baden Springs Hotel.

Clouse assured them staff would always be present to give them access to the floor.

Brown had no intention of invading the family's privacy or abusing their trust, though it felt nice that Clouse put faith in him.

Only a day away from the grand opening at the domed hotel, Brown walked through his house, getting things ready for his appearance at the event. His formal uniform hung nearby in a closet, freshly returned from the cleaners. He needed to shine his shoes and get a haircut when he went to town, but otherwise felt ready.

His special invitation rested atop his kitchen counter where he often set reminders and time sensitive documents such as bills. Living between the hotels and the town of Paoli, the sheriff had no neighbors nearby. He enjoyed living in a remote part of Orange County with his son living a few miles away. Arlan, also one of his deputies, though not through nepotism, visited him more often at home than work.

Today his son patrolled their county roads, keeping the locals safe, while he wandered through his house in sweat pants and a stained T-shirt trying to organize his short-term future.

He had just opened his closet to dig out his dress shoes when the phone rang down the hall. Rushing to the living room to answer it, he snatched it from the charger on the third ring.

"Hello?"

No answer came back, which caused him to think he had missed the call.

Holding the phone to his ear momentarily, he thought he heard breathing from the other end.

"Hello?" he asked again.

This time a click reached his ears.

Stunned a moment, he slowly put the phone into its cradle.

"Wrong number," he muttered.

A few minutes later, as he rummaged through long since worn clothes in his closet, Brown thought he heard a thumping noise. He stood perfectly still a moment, listening intently for a repeat performance. In his neck of the woods he seldom heard anything except animal noises or the occasional bump atop his roof from falling woodland debris.

When another thump reached his ears, they located the origin point like a sonar device tracks submarines. The back of his house had twice been violated by something or someone.

He threw on a pair of work boots, giving him the appearance of a man with stunted fashion sense. Stepping outside, he expected to find a raccoon causing mischief near one of his trash cans, but no obvious signs of trouble confronted him when he rounded the corner.

A thick wooded area ran behind his house, and to the sides, as far as the eye could see. He turned to look, spying someone running away from the house, swallowed almost immediately by the shrubs and trees.

"Shit!" he said, taking chase.

He immediately regretted not having a weapon, though he figured the fleeing figure was a teenager having a good time throwing rocks at his house.

Once he reached the woods, Brown navigated the trail of broken stems and saplings in pursuit, realizing his trespasser had already vanished from sight.

He spent the next ten minutes forging further into the woods until he realized the trail lacked a complete sense of direction. In fact, it had started back toward his house several times over, as though serving simply as a decoy.

Remembering his front door was unlocked, and everything he owned completely in the open, he started in the direction of his house, or at least what he believed to be the right direction. It took almost another ten minutes to locate any kind of familiar landmark, which ended up being the county road about a quarter mile from his residence.

Brown found himself completely winded when he reached his house. Eerie silence and absolutely nothing disturbed inside the house provided signs that his original assessment was in error, but he remained uneasy.

His back woods led to nowhere special, where a getaway vehicle might be waiting, and he seriously doubted his house was the random target of unruly teenagers. Opening a nearby closet, Brown slid his sidearm from its holster, fully sweeping the entire house for an intruder.

Finding none, he returned to the kitchen where his keys and paperwork appeared undisturbed. After surviving the mansion scare two years prior, when a mysterious figure abducted and bound him, the sheriff took nothing lightly. He closed his front door, locking it as he did so before hurriedly checking every other door and window in the house.

Only after completing the task did he breathe a sigh of relief, beginning to wonder if his mind was playing tricks on him. He slumped into his favorite chair, taking a break before tackling more preparations for the grand opening.

Chapter 5

On the afternoon of the grand opening, Clouse walked the five flights of stairs down to the lobby where his hotel staff busily checked people in for the festivities. Some were invited only for the evening event, but those currently checking in were staying the night.

For the first time in decades the hotel was completely redone, scheduled to be filled to capacity by nightfall. Where tile pieces didn't cover the floors, carpeting of intricate designs, some created by Jane, led the way around the atrium floor.

While Jane frantically ran around the hotel, carrying out her civic duty as the fretting hostess, Clouse decided to converse with Craig Jennings, his head of security at both hotels. Jennings held an administrative position, dealing primarily with the hiring, firing, and scheduling of security personnel, along with the overall safety of guests and owners.

At first, Clouse offered him a job to stave off a potential lawsuit from the mansion incident, then discovered the local shop teacher worked for the Military Police in the United States Army when conflicts arose in Iraq the first time.

As he crossed the lobby, one of the receptionists behind the lobby desk called to him.

"Mr. Clouse? This came for you just now."

Clouse looked over, finding a young woman in business attire waving a UPS envelope carefully over her head to avoid damaging the contents.

"Thank you," he said, taking it from her.

He hated the idea of putting himself on a pedestal, thinking the idea of someone sampling his food or opening his mail felt excessive. More so, he hated living life having to look over his shoulder on a daily basis.

No news came his way about Smith's affairs, or the video showing what appeared to be Tim Niemeyer in captivity. Clouse hadn't dwelled on the situation, waiting to hear something more before he formed false hopes. He understood Bloom needed to check countless avenues concerning Smith's contacts, but he expected the investigator to find *something* before the grand opening.

Left with little peace of mind, Clouse waited in the lobby, staring at the stained glass windows left from the hotel's Jesuit era. Jennings emerged from the rounded hallway before Clouse thought to open the sturdy envelope.

"Good morning, sir," Jennings said, not missing a step.

"Morning, Craig."

They shook hands on the fly, making their way into the grand atrium, temporarily filled with covered tables, padded black chairs, and a stage near the old fireplace for keynote speakers and the band.

Dressed in a full suit with a formal red nametag, Jennings looked the part. Though he didn't usually carry a gun, he kept one locked away in his office with Clouse's blessing. Most of his brown hair had receded to a fringe which he kept trimmed. With the warmer summer months beginning, he had recently reduced his beard to a full goatee with some gray hairs emerging along his chin.

"Everything ready for tonight?" Clouse asked his head of security.

"The entire staff will be here, sir. Mark is sending a few of his people over to help with coverage."

The casino and the French Lick Springs Hotel had already been open a few weeks, providing the staff enough time to master their jobs. The security people under Daniels might have been unhappy about the grand opening detail if not for the good overtime pay.

While the two men conversed, the catering staff continued to place silverware, cloth napkins, candles, and floral centerpieces on the dozens of tables. Clouse watched some of the guests saunter around the atrium floor, looking up toward the skylights installed in the dome's center. Natural light illuminated the entire atrium, but that night only candles and overhead lighting would keep the area from being engulfed by darkness.

The atrium's diameter nearly matched the length of a football field, along with a height that drew the eye upward like a grand cathedral. The hotel consisted of two rings of rooms outside of the atrium, one facing into the center, while the other faced the garden and grounds outdoors. Each room on the inner ring contained windows overlooking the festivities below, some with small balconies for guests to step upon while enjoying the view.

"Are you expecting trouble?" Jennings seemed obligated to ask.

He possessed more than a notion about the past troubles on the grounds.

"I don't know what to expect. Considering what happened the last time someone tried a grand opening here, I'm surprised anyone made reservations."

Jennings gave a nervous grin, remembering the incident.

"People have a way of forgetting the things they want to."

Clouse understood his meaning, wishing he could forget the painful memories of his own past.

"Your wife gave me an itinerary this morning. I'll have a meeting with my people an hour before tonight's guests start arriving."

"Safe, but friendly," Clouse stated for what seemed like the fifteenth time that day to any number of employees. "I want our guests to feel safe, but I also want them to have a good time. Everything hinges on this hotel opening smoothly."

"Understood."

Jennings had learned his job rather quickly, attending classes and seminars, because leading a security squad wasn't quite the same as military policing many years prior. Clouse appreciated his dedication, because he suspected deep down Jennings knew his job offer wasn't unlike an insurance company bribing accident victims with a quick buck.

Only once had they spoken of the mansion incident in any detail, now avoiding the subject as though it had been a common friend convicted of murder. Clouse tearing down the mansion healed wounds for a great many people.

One of the healed souls now approached the two men from the lobby area. Dan Duncan's heritage tied him to the property in a major way, though the January tour of the mansion two years earlier nearly buried him there.

"Paul," he said, shaking hands with the hotel owner, then the security director. "Craig."

"Dan," they both replied.

Duncan's great-grandfather helped bring the first railroad to the Springs Valley, getting rich in the process. Over the next three generations, the money trail diminished little, which put Duncan in a position to buy the hotel with an investment group two years earlier. Unspeakable things happened to some of his partners, and he nearly died, gaining him leverage with Clouse.

Because things fell apart so badly after the murders, Clouse decided to continue the casino project personally, though Duncan stated a desire to run the hotel's everyday affairs. Duncan needed no money, but his ties to the area pulsed the desire to remain there through his veins.

Clouse reluctantly handed over the reins once he decided Duncan's intentions were indeed pure. The man still had his own mystery to solve, which included discovering exactly what happened after his great-grandfather's apparent suicide. Duncan now believed Andrew Duncan had been murdered, and Andrew's son sought revenge, but he wanted to learn his true genealogy before the information disappeared forever.

Living the best of both worlds, Duncan managed the hotel and received a healthy salary for doing so. A pleasant surprise to Clouse came when he realized Duncan had a natural talent for business, and for running a 5-Star hotel.

Wearing a black suit, and looking almost unnatural in doing so, Duncan filled it out around his waistline. A diehard motorcycle rider, he typically sauntered into the hotel wearing a leather jacket, chaps, and gloves after riding from his home in nearby Salem. His blond hair was graying along the temples, giving him a fairly distinguished look, along with the mustache he often trimmed before coming to work. During the past few months he had reluctantly started wearing glasses on a regular basis when the license branch required corrective lenses for him to drive.

Unlike Jennings and other hired help, he immediately took to calling Clouse by his first name.

"Things going smoothly?" Clouse inquired.

"So far," Duncan replied. "You shouldn't be so paranoid. French Lick opened without a hitch."

"Yeah, but French Lick doesn't have quite the sordid past this place does."

"I'll see you guys later," Jennings said, excusing himself from the conversation before heading toward his office.

Clouse wondered if the man thought the impending conversation was over his head. Indeed it wasn't, so perhaps Jennings just wanted time to think and prepare.

"You're looking dapper," Clouse commented, eyeing Duncan's suit.

Duncan groaned, much happier during the hotel's occasional casual days when he could get by with slacks and a golf shirt containing the hotel's logo.

"I even drove my truck so it didn't get messed up."

"Feel ready for all this?"

Giving a sly grin, Duncan looked upward where several guests were trying out the balconies attached to their rooms for bird's-eye views of the atrium.

"Are you?"

"I think so. Have you seen my wife? She's the one running around like a chicken with its head cut off."

"Last I saw, she had the catering staff begging for mercy."

"That's Jane."

Duncan placed a sympathetic hand on Clouse's shoulder.

"Don't worry so much. You've got all of us around you now. Sink or swim, we're all in this together."

In the few years since they first met, Clouse felt a kinship with Duncan. Both were considered wealthy men in the public eye, but they both endured hardships to reach their current positions.

Duncan kept him stable often times by providing guidance, like a close uncle. In the business world and life itself, it seemed he had seen most everything. He told some interesting stories about how his father groomed him for the family business by starting him at the bottom.

Now set for life, with no children of his own, Duncan immersed himself in the hotel's resurrection, partly to bring his family legacy full-circle.

"Don't you worry about tonight," Duncan said confidently. "Things'll go better than planned."

Chapter 6

"I'm nowhere near ready for this," Clouse confessed, sitting across from Daniels at the sixth floor conference table.

In less than an hour the atrium below would be packed. He needed to give a flawless speech, and his wife continued to frantically check on every last-minute detail.

After quitting his city job, Daniels grew a beard that seemed to have no seasonal limitations. Since the divorce, the former detective had undergone changes equivalent to a mid-life crisis for many men. He bought a new car, dressed a bit flashier, and for some reason his hair looked a bit thicker, and darker, than its former dirty blond color.

Clouse might have suspected his friend of using coloring products, but the beard was roughly the same shade.

Daniels never said much about the divorce, though Clouse suspected Cindy felt he was too distant after nearly losing his life several times. Somewhat introverted anyway, Daniels drifted from his family and colleagues at the police department after the near death experiences. Some called him a jinx after his partner was killed during an investigation involving the hotel.

As a father he appeared unparalleled, taking his kids somewhere different every weekend he had custody.

"How was the meeting with Craig?" Clouse asked.

"Brief. I should probably be scouring the halls with him and his crew."

Clouse nodded.

"How is Craig doing?"

"He's still a little green, but he's catching on. I think he'll work out."

"Good. I want your crews to get along."

"We're both professionals."

Daniels looked to his watch.

"Time for me to check in with the guys."

"I'd love to tag along, but I have less pleasant tasks to attend to."

"Good luck with that. I'll watch from one of the upper floors."

Daniels turned to leave the room.

"Mark," Clouse called, causing him to turn around.

"Yeah?"

"You have any regrets coming to work here?"

The answer came in the form of an easy shrug with a smirk, meaning he was happy, but wasn't going to make such a statement for fear of their bad luck returning.

"Sometimes I miss my old job," Clouse confessed. "I got to help people, and the guys I worked with were the best."

"You trying to make me feel bad about leaving my career behind?"

"No. I'm glad you're here."

"Quit it. You're making me blush."

With that, Daniels stepped out of the conference room, leaving Clouse with his thoughts, and an unopened UPS envelope. He had set it atop the table earlier in the day, forgetting completely about opening it because every other step he took led to an encounter with a thankful guest, or an employee asking him a question.

He expected an invoice from Jane's expenditures, or an invitation to some gathering where people would undoubtedly attempt to pry his money from his bank account. Only the most lavish junk mail came through the good carriers.

When he tore the envelope open at one end, a simple piece of neatly folded paper slid out. He opened it, finding a typed note that looked like a business letter, and colder in tone than any formal letter Clouse recalled ever receiving.

> *Mr. Clouse,*
>
> *By now you have seen the video I sent Trooper Randy Niemeyer.*
>
> *I have your friend Tim Niemeyer. He's been under my care for the better part of five years.*

> *If you wish to see him again, you will bring one-million cash to the location described in my next note immediately after receiving it.*
>
> *Should you choose not to accept my terms, I will leave Mr. Niemeyer to starve a slow death in darkness.*
>
> *You would be wise to tell <u>no one</u> of this business venture I propose, because I may be much closer to you than you think.*
>
> *I expect payment with unmarked twenties and fifties inside a waterproof bag. No tricks, or your friend will die, and this time it will stick.*

Spellbound for a moment, Clouse stared at the note like an elementary school student stares at his first difficult math exam. He felt trapped, because his misplaced trust in people had bitten him in the ass several times over. By not confiding in anyone, he doomed himself to paying the ransom for a friend he wasn't even certain might be alive.

The last line of the letter bothered him.

"It will stick," he said, wondering exactly what that meant.

Had Tim died and been brought back?

Was the writer being metaphorical?

According to Randy Niemeyer, his brother had died right before his very eyes, but Randy also took time to chase off Tim's six assailants, shooting one of them. Could he have missed something important?

Standing from the table, Clouse walked to the nearest window overlooking the atrium. He looked down at the people filing into his hotel, wondering if he dared trust the note. Worse yet, he questioned the boundaries set for himself when it came to trusting those around him.

Money was no issue. Losing a million dollars to a stranger was worth any chance of having Niemeyer back. Not one day had passed that Clouse didn't blame himself for his two best friends dying. Ken Kaiser wasn't coming back, at least not from any proof Clouse had viewed. Niemeyer, on the other hand, might somehow be among the land of the living.

Clouse folded the note before stuffing it into the pocket of his shirt. Sighing to himself, he snatched his tuxedo jacket from a nearby chair. Though he hated formal wear, he resigned himself to buying a tux because he donned one so often.

Throwing the jacket over his shoulders, he slid one arm into a sleeve, then the other, trying to calm his nerves. Appearances meant everything if he wanted to keep the note a secret, especially from Jane, who read him the way literary scholars mull over the classics.

In a matter of minutes he needed to kick off the gala with a speech, introducing some keynote speakers he hoped wouldn't lull the crowd to sleep. After that, dinner, the band, dancing, and probably some regrettable encounters with alcohol awaited his guests.

He checked to make certain his wallet and key card were in his pockets, then left the suite to join the outside world.

***

Jon Lopez felt reasonably good about his choice to join the hotel security staff, though he had some questions about why the men in charge weren't very experienced.

As a former military man, Lopez felt more qualified than Daniels or Jennings to supervise security personnel. Still, his position paid decently, and he aspired to move up if either of them left for greener pastures.

Currently walking the halls on the prowl for any unsavory characters, he roamed the fourth floor, following his assignment. The hallway rounded, technically never ending as it followed a circular pattern. A few stairwells and the elevator broke the monotony of the doors on either side of him, but he wasn't fond of the Big Band music playing throughout the hallway speakers.

He understood the band hired by the Clouses was going to play similar music that night, making him wonder why everyone didn't have to wear fedoras and cloches. He wasn't paid to think, but rather to protect the grounds, guests, and owners from some unseen force.

The hotel, and Paul Clouse for that matter, were subjects of urban legends. Lopez had no idea how much, if any of them, held true. A friend recommended he apply for the security jobs at the hotel and casino. Two interviews later, Lopez found himself working at the hotel, but he wasn't completely satisfied.

While he saved back money from his new job, he planned to apply for the state police and several local police departments. A year of college and the military had paved the way for his true career ambitions.

Stopping momentarily at a set of windows overlooking the atrium, Lopez saw the tables filling up with well-dressed guests. Some of his colleagues worked the floor below, standing at the four atrium entrances. They all wore dark suits with red ties and name tags of the same color, their positions readily apparent to guests.

"Taking a break?" a familiar voice asked behind him.

He whirled around, wondering if he needed an excuse for his boss, or Jennings really didn't mind.

"Just observing the other areas, sir."

Jennings didn't appear angry, though his appearance on the floor was unexpected.

Everyone at the meeting figured he would schmooze around the rich and famous instead of carrying out his duties. Perhaps he and Daniels provided some checks and balances for one another.

"Seen anything unusual?" Jennings inquired.

"No, sir. Things have been quiet."

Jennings glanced out the window briefly before returning his attention to Lopez.

"I need you to check over the third floor while Harris helps the caterers with their stuff."

What the head of security actually meant was Harris would be checking their supplies and wares against any threats, as a precaution.

"He'll be back in fifteen minutes, so I need you to cover that floor until he gets back."

"Will do."

Lopez had already been assigned the top three floors, so another mattered little to him. Though he didn't understand exactly what the guests needed protecting from, he knew enough to remain wary of anything out of place.

After giving the festivities below another glance, Jennings grunted to himself, then walked briskly down the hallway. Though every one of the security personnel had radios, the units had remained fairly quiet throughout the night. Jennings wasn't a boss who liked the sound of his own voice, and preferred keeping radio chatter to a minimum.

Once Jennings walked away, Lopez checked over the rest of the floor before taking one of the stairways down to the third floor. He found no one walking the hallways of this floor either, leaving him alone with his thoughts.

A few minutes later he had checked over most of the floor. Every door was closed, and not a soul appeared to be straying from the festivities. On the outer portion of the ring he finally saw a light, indicating one of the custodial storage closets was left open.

Thinking little of it, he walked over, closing the door after finding the closet undisturbed inside. Cleaning supplies lined the upper shelves, while a large cleaning cart appeared fully stocked with towels, spray cleaners, and an open trash sack.

He checked the door to make certain it was locked, knowing the custodians all had key sets. Their keys didn't cover as much ground as those carried by security, but they opened most doors. In certain areas the custodians required a security member present to clean or change bedding.

With the Clouse family living in the hotel, security was tighter than ever, though officers were told to maintain low profiles.

Lopez had just rounded the corner, putting the closet out of mind, when he heard something crash behind him. Freezing in his tracks, he slowly turned around to see the closet door slightly ajar.

Feeling certain no one could have dashed down the hallway quickly enough to open the door, he wondered if it had a hinge or lock problem.

Sauntering back to the door, he swung it open, prepared to beckon the maintenance men once he discovered the problem. Instead, a quick, powerful hand pulled him into the closet before a sharp pain thrust into his abdomen. Looking downward, he saw a curved blade retract from his stomach, coated in blood that dripped onto a plastic tarp laid on the closet floor.

Lopez already knew his life was over as his killer thrust him atop the tarp, keeping the carpets nice and clean, thus erasing any evidence this event ever happened.

Groping for his radio as a final effort to contact someone for help, or at least to alert them of impending danger, Lopez felt a heavy foot step on his hand. He felt cold as the blood rushed the wrong way, making it hard to move, or even think.

The killer emptied the lower part of the custodial cart, apparently preparing to wheel him from the premises undetected. With everyone focused on the events downstairs, it seemed unlikely anyone would notice.

As consciousness faded, Lopez knew the next step was death as the dark figure dragged him into the cart's bottom. No one came down the hall, much less to his rescue, leaving him to wonder where and when his body might be discovered. He wanted closure for his parents instead of being the next Jimmy Hoffa.

His head grew heavy, so he relaxed his body, prepared for whatever came after death, hoping his killer was stopped before he harmed anyone else.

Chapter 7

Mark Daniels watched his friend give a fairly brief, though solid opening speech to kick off the event. The keynote speakers weren't so merciful, nearly putting the scores of guests to sleep, though they spoke some inspirational lines.

While the guests ate, the band played soft background music, but after dinner there was no holding back the band. Playing louder, and with a faster tempo, the musicians drew people onto the dance floor with the kind of classic music Daniels figured his grandparents might remember.

Much like a wedding reception, the event lost momentum after the food and entertainment, giving Daniels enough time to step out back. He fished inside his sport coat for a cigarette, lighting up as a few people walked through the sliding glass doors, leaving for the night. A few members of Jennings' crew eyed him carefully, snuffing out their cigarettes before returning to their posts.

Daniels casually observed people coming and going over the next few minutes until Jennings walked through the sliding doors with a worrisome look.

"What's wrong?" Daniels asked.

"Lopez disappeared on me."

"Disappeared?"

"I asked him to cover the third floor a while back, and haven't seen him since."

Taking a final drag from his cigarette, Daniels placed the butt into the extinguishing pole before walking inside with Jennings.

"How's the casino business?" Jennings asked a bit more casually as band music reached their ears.

"Profitable."

Not much for conversation, Daniels said very little when he spoke to Clouse, and even less to other people. He gave orders when necessary, running a tight ship with a veteran crew from police, military, and casino backgrounds. Jennings didn't fare as well, mainly because hotel security wasn't paid as much, leaving the hiring pool a bit shallow.

Both men followed the curved hallway until they reached the main lobby. Jennings approached the receptionists, asking if either had seen Lopez. They shook their heads negatively in response.

"What now?" Jennings asked, seeking an experienced answer.

"If he doesn't show up, he's done. They might bitch about what they're paid, but they can't slack off. Not under these circumstances."

Jennings nodded in agreement. He and Daniels both knew the history of the hotel firsthand.

"Have you been through all of the floors?" Daniels decided to ask.

"I've checked them three times over. No sign of him."

"What about the time clock?"

Jennings stepped behind the reception area, accessing one of the computers. He called up the management area of the employee time records, finding that Lopez had indeed signed out just moments prior.

"That's weird. Why would he just quit like that?"

"Maybe he didn't like what he was getting into."

Jennings didn't look so certain.

"Damn. I hate the thought of having to change the codes and locks."

Daniels shrugged.

"Give him a call in the morning, or see if he turned in his stuff. No need to go bats over it just yet."

"Who says 'bats' anymore? I think this place is brainwashing you."

"Try and help a guy, and he turns on you."

"Sorry," Jennings said with a grin. "I do appreciate the help. Maybe this is all a big misunderstanding."

"Hopefully."

Daniels was about to excuse himself when Clouse stepped through the nearby entrance, looking uncomfortable in his tuxedo, as though his entire body itched from an allergic reaction to the cloth.

"You two look guilty of something," he said.

"Of not rescuing you from your keynote speakers," Daniels commented.

Clouse tried holding back a snicker, but failed.

"I'm so ready for this night to be over," he said with an exasperated look.

"Us, too."

Turning a bit more serious, Clouse addressed them both.

"Anything I need to know?"

Daniels didn't give so much as a glance toward Jennings before answering. All evening Clouse had seemed on edge about something.

"No. Pretty quiet."

If Jennings looked his way, he didn't notice, keeping his eyes trained on Clouse. The last thing he wanted was his friend worried on his big night.

Taking a half step back as though to leave, Clouse gave them both suspicious looks before allowing the crowd inside the atrium to swallow him whole.

"What was that?" Jennings asked Daniels once the coast was clear.

"No sense ruining his night until we know something more."

"He seems nervous about something."

"You would be too if you owned this place."

***

Clouse returned to his table, trying to keep his mind off the note demanding one-million dollars for a friend he believed was lying in a coffin he saw lowered almost five years prior.

Instead of engaging his guests in mindless conversation, he approached his seated wife, offering his hand.

"Care to dance?" he asked her, trying to fake some measure of happiness.

"Certainly," she said, putting her hand in his as she rose elegantly from her chair.

Very few couples took time to step onto the dance floor, despite the band playing several consecutive slow songs. Following Clouse's lead, or subtly attempting to suck up to him, nearly two-dozen people stood to partake in the dancing.

Ignoring everything around him for the moment, he pulled Jane close to him as they swayed rhythmically with the music.

"What's wrong with you tonight?" she asked, a concerned look crossing her face.

He trusted his wife, knowing she had enough worries without him revealing the ransom note. Perhaps when the promised second note arrived, he might spill the beans, though he knew Jane would tell him it was merely a hoax.

"Everything's fine," he lied. "I've just been uptight about the opening."

Saying nothing, she rested her head against his chest, though she didn't feel tense to him. For her, everything probably seemed fine. Once again, Clouse shouldered the burden for those around him, letting potential harm gravitate his way.

As the host, he couldn't exactly leave the party, or leave Jane to fend for herself, but he definitely wanted his privacy back soon.

"Did you ever think we'd see this day?" Jane asked when she looked into his eyes.

"I had my doubts."

"After the deaths at the mansion I worried, but we weathered that storm."

Clouse looked up to the sixth floor, seeing the suite's lights diminished by curtains and window treatments. He pictured Parish monitoring the kids while they played video games, possibly sneaking in a session with them if no one looked. Zach accidentally spoke of his bodyguard playing a racing game with them. Clouse didn't mind, so long as Parish never lost track of his main objective.

Keeping Zach and Katie safe.

Considering the man worked long hours voluntarily, though with extra pay, Clouse felt secure letting the kids out of his sight. Unless Parish grossly neglected his duties, he had a job for as long as he wanted it.

Several times Clouse admired his wife while they danced. Despite their good fortune financially, and bad luck otherwise, she simply wanted to help others. Rumors spread throughout the Valley that she only continued working in the medical field to promote Clouse's impending political career.

Considering he never *once* gave serious thought to running for any office, Clouse wondered how such damning tales were ever started.

Within the hour, the festivities began grinding to a halt as Clouse and Jane shook hands, said good nights to their guests, and watched overnight guests file into the elevator or take the stairs. Clouse discovered Daniels had left when the band played their last few songs. He spied Duncan dancing with a widow from the special guest list, who probably enjoyed the company of a local wealthy man, if only for a few minutes.

As the manager of a luxury hotel, Duncan would have to perform lots of interesting functions over the years. Endearing himself to strangers probably wasn't his forte, but Clouse imagined the man was highly adaptable.

When the final meet and greet ended, Clouse gave Jennings a quick wave before climbing into the elevator with Jane.

His head of security gave a nod and wave, ensuring everything was in good order.

Once they passed the security devices and entered the main portion of the suite, Clouse found the lights turned down in the family room. Jane stepped in ahead of him as he found the kids sleeping on the sofa, game controllers nearby, while Parish sat in a wooden chair, positioned to effectively survey the area.

Standing, he grabbed his sport coat from the chair, saying nothing as he glanced from the kids to his employer.

"Thanks, Todd."

"No problem, boss," Parish mouthed his reply silently, not wanting to wake the kids as he headed for the door. He had the next two days off to spend with his own children.

Clouse and Jane gathered the children in their arms, carrying them to the bedroom. Zach awoke groggily, insisting on walking after his father had carried him halfway. Clouse tucked him in without the benefit of anything more than a quick kiss on the forehead. Zach had entered the age where being carried and bedtime stories were uncool, but Clouse didn't want to deprive him of a regular childhood. Zach had grown up far too fast, seeing the horrors Smith exposed him to.

Jane met him in the hallway, looking a bit fatigued herself. Wrapping her arms around his neck, she let Clouse guide her into their bedroom.

A few minutes later they found themselves beneath the covers, almost too exhausted to fall asleep.

"It went off without a hitch," Jane whispered into his ear. "I told you it would."

"And I'm glad it did."

"Sure something isn't bothering you?"

Clouse gave no immediate reply, not wanting Jane's rational opinions to sway the decision to recover his friend, if Niemeyer was indeed alive.

"I'm fine. Just had a lot on my mind until tonight."

Jane rolled over, giving a barely audible goodnight reply, leaving Clouse to his troubled thoughts before he drifted off to sleep.

Chapter 8

When Clouse ventured downstairs the next morning, he found another envelope waiting for him at the main desk. Separating himself from everyone else, he stepped into the nearby library lounge, reading it to himself.

Typed much like the first letter, it instructed him to gather one-million dollars by the next morning because a final note would be forthcoming.

Stuffing it into the envelope, he pulled out his cell phone. He wanted to call Randy Niemeyer to see what, if anything, the trooper had discovered.

He briefly considered the fact that Niemeyer brought him the video, and that the note's sender cautioned him to remain quiet about the entire ordeal. While he didn't know the younger brother of his friend that well, he doubted Randy had any reason to extort money from him.

Clouse stepped into the atrium for a morning view of guests testing out some of the sofas and chairs in the hotel's grand centerpiece. Couples sat together on oversized chairs, several people stepped out of their rooms onto the balconies above, and some passed through to meet their breakfast reservations.

Beams of sunlight fell from the skylights above, striking the ground in brilliant prisms, rivaling the natural lighting found only in big city architecture. Clouse looked to his cell phone once more, hitting the button to call Niemeyer.

"Hello," the trooper answered two rings later, sounding groggy.

"Randy, this is Paul Clouse."

"Paul?" Niemeyer asked, his voice perking up. "Any news?"

Clouse explained the two notes, listening for any hint that Niemeyer might somehow be the mastermind behind the video and the notes.

"That's incredible," Niemeyer said after the recap. "That means the video is real."

"Not necessarily, Randy. What if someone is taking advantage of us for financial gain?"

"That's my brother in the video, Paul. You know it's true. He looks like Tim, he moves like Tim."

Clouse couldn't disagree, but larger hoaxes had been pulled on far more intelligent people than him.

"You can't tell me you're worried about the money," Niemeyer prodded.

"It's not the money, it's the principle, Randy. I don't like being taken, or this kind of shit will never stop."

An uncomfortable silence separated them momentarily.

"There's something else to consider," Clouse mentioned as he strolled toward the atrium's center, waving to an older couple who recognized him.

"What's that?"

"Was there any doubt in your mind that Tim was dead in that parking lot?"

Another brief pause.

"Of course I thought he was dead. The medics got a pulse after they pumped him full of drugs, but he never breathed on his own."

"Exactly. If that is indeed Tim on that video, he was brought back by unnatural means from the dead."

"Unnatural," Niemeyer repeated with a heavy thought.

"You know what I mean. You saw Smith shave years off his life."

Clouse waved to a woman who virtually swooned as though she had just seen one of the Beatles in their heyday. He gave a friendly wave, still waiting for Niemeyer to reply.

"How do you know that was Smith we did battle with?"

"Because he died, they did DNA testing, and now he's buried."

"You sound as though you don't want Tim back."

"I just don't want to jump into a pool headfirst if there's no water, Randy. Whoever the prick is, he waited five years to contact me, and he's pretty insistent upon payment without giving me solid proof."

"If my brother has been locked in that tiny room for five years, we have to do something."

"You mean *I* have to do something. He's not exactly asking you for a wad of cash."

"I think we clarified that already. Whatever you need, I'm here for you, Paul."

"What I want is a backdoor, Randy. We have time to find this guy before he demands payment. How many places around here can house a jail cell?"

"Who knows? I thought you were going to have your people work that angle."

"I've got someone on it."

"If you're worried about your personal safety, I can-"

"I've got that covered, too. Let's just wait and see what happens."

Niemeyer didn't immediately reply, though Clouse knew he was chomping at the bit to receive more news.

"I'll call you when I have something more," he said.

"Okay. Thanks."

Clouse replaced the phone to his side, heading toward the entrance closest to the restaurant. All of the staff knew him, and his family, not because he demanded it, but because they enjoyed working for him.

He walked inside, sitting down for a morning breakfast before seeing what Jane and the kids had planned.

After placing an order with a regular waitress who readily recognized him, Clouse spotted Daniels wandering into the dining room. His friend looked around, finally spotting him before making his way over.

"To what do I owe the pleasure so early in the morning, Mark?"

"One of Craig's guys quit last night in the middle of his shift."

"Oh?" Clouse asked with raised eyebrows.

He immediately wondered about a security breach.

"Not to worry," Daniels said. "His ID and keys were left at the front desk sometime overnight."

"Why would he quit?"

Daniels shrugged.

"Craig says some of his staff haven't been happy. A few are probably using their positions here to get real police jobs somewhere else."

"Real?"

"You know, a township or city job. Like I used to have. Like *you* used to have."

Clouse recalled the days when he held a city job until his mind drifted, wondering why Jennings hadn't contacted him personally. After dwelling on the bizarre ransom notes lately, he hadn't contemplated much of anything else.

"You okay?" Daniels asked.

"Why do you ask?"

"You just seem a little out there this week. I know you're not stressed about the hotel opening."

"And how do you know that?" Clouse asked with a wry grin.

"Because you've been through all of this stuff before. Nothing's going to happen."

When the waitress returned with his drink, Clouse told Daniels to order whatever he wanted, but the head of casino security waved off the offer.

Daniels was partially right in his statement.

Clouse had been through such things before, and the circumstances surrounding the hotel were much different. He didn't own the building in those days, and it was under construction by limited personnel when the original murders occurred.

Now the building was filled to capacity, and would be throughout the foreseeable future.

"You sure nothing's wrong?" Daniels hounded him, his old detective instincts kicking in.

"Nothing to worry about, old friend."

"Alright then, I've got work to do. My boss is a slave driver."

Clouse caught the joke, pretending to bat him away.

"Shoo! Go get something done."

Daniels chuckled as he left the same way he entered. Alone with his thoughts, Clouse began formulating a plan to gather one-million dollars without Jane knowing about it. She did most of their bookkeeping, despite him wanting to hire an accountant, leaving him in a pinch. Selling off assets or stocks took too long for him to see the cash, meaning he probably needed to dig into their savings and feel the wrath of his wife later.

He contemplated asking Duncan for the cash until he snuck a way around Jane, but the hotel manager probably had his finances tied up in the stock market and retirement funds.

Besides, he didn't want to look desperate in front of a man he hired to avoid a potential lawsuit, especially after their working relationship started better than expected.

As his breakfast was carried through the swinging double doors from the kitchen, Clouse wondered how he was going to get away from the hotel without Jane being suspicious of something. She wanted him to spend more time around the kids, with the opening festivities over, which made the task even more difficult.

Sighing to himself, Clouse knew an idea would come to him.

Chapter 9

Working late into the evening, Ray Bloom received a fax from one of his old FBI partners out of Indianapolis. He began reviewing the information, based on some facts provided to him by Clouse.

Seated behind his desk within a two-room office, Bloom worked beneath a desk lamp that cast shadows across the desk and behind him. The window to his back overlooked the street, remaining open tonight so the sound of an occasional passing car reached the private investigator's ears.

Housed in a building with several other businesses, including insurance salesmen, Bloom liked his location on the outskirts of town. Taxes were lower, and Bloomington residents easily found him when they needed to.

The other office space was reserved for his sister, who worked part-time as his secretary, mainly as a favor to his brother-in-law to keep her occupied. With the advent of computers and voice mail, he didn't desperately need someone to greet clients and organize, but she did a good job and her paychecks didn't break him.

Clouse had asked him to check on some quirky facts regarding missing persons and deaths across several states, though he never gave a specific reason why. Comparing the new data from the missing persons in the tri-state area to what Clouse termed significant dates, Bloom finally struck gold.

He plucked the phone from his receiver, deciding Clouse would want to hear the news, even at the late hour. Looking at the clock, he decided it wasn't late enough to keep him from dialing the man's cell phone.

Clouse picked up in the middle of the second ring.

"Good news?"

"Possibly, Mr. Clouse. I've been comparing your dates to the list of missing persons my contacts sent me. It seems a number of their birthdays match the dates in question."

Clouse said nothing for a moment, possibly stunned by the information.

"How many people?" he finally asked.

"Looks like eleven of them match the dates. They've all gone missing the last year or so."

"And none of them have been found?"

"Not alive or dead, like they fell off the face of the earth."

"Then it's already too late," Clouse muttered across the line.

"Too late for what, Paul? I can't help you if I don't know what you're looking for."

While the line remained silent a moment, Bloom thought he heard the main entrance door in the other room close with its usual clack, since the door didn't fit the frame perfectly.

"Hello?" Bloom called, cupping the phone with his right hand, thinking a client might have dropped by after seeing the lights on.

No answer, though Clouse was asking something over the line.

"What was that, Paul?"

"You got someone there?"

"I might have. Let me check real quick."

"Be careful," Clouse called over the line.

Bloom opened a desk drawer, pulling out a snub-nosed revolver.

He stepped forward, carefully making his way toward the open door between the two offices.

"Anyone there?" he asked, giving any potential intruders one last chance to confront him or flee.

He heard Clouse virtually screaming for him to get out of there from the phone's mouthpiece. Bloom felt reasonably confident he could handle any hooligans invading his office, armed or not.

Bloom approached the door, seeing no one inside the other room. The only objects obscuring his view were the secretary's desk and the large filing cabinet a few feet away from the corner. He carefully checked both areas, finding no one lurking in either place. For a moment he considered locking the main door until his client's voice reached him from the phone in the other room.

Breathing a sigh of relief, he returned to his own office, swiping the earpiece from the desk.

"False alarm," he told Clouse.

"Good. You can't be too careful, Ray. If those eleven people have been abducted, and possibly a twelfth we don't know about, things are about to get *very* dangerous."

"No disrespect, but you're talking like a crazy person. I'm not stupid, Mr. Clouse. I read some of the police statements from the mansion incident, and if you believe that the ghost of Martin Smith is somehow coming back to haunt you, then you're as loony as those people."

"You haven't seen what I've seen, Ray. And if you think I'm too loose a screw to work for, we can settle up when you bring me what you have tomorrow."

Bloom considered his position, which didn't involve very many clients at the moment.

"I don't have a problem working for you, as long as you don't drag me along on ghost-hunts or otherwise endanger my well-being."

"Fine. I'll call you tomorrow morning with a time and place to meet."

Bloom wondered why the place might change. They always met at the hotel, though usually without any family members or employees around to bother them.

"I'll bring anything I come up with between now and tomorrow," Bloom assured his client.

"Good. I'll talk to you in the morning."

Bloom hung up the phone, prepared to call it a night. When a strange creak reached his ears from the window, he turned to see what was wrong with the old building's architecture this time.

Instead, a sharp pain pierced his abdomen as a shadowy figure just outside the window swung a small scythe hard enough that it shredded the flimsy protective screen before injuring him.

Reeling backward, Bloom stumbled as he clipped the corner of his desk, swiping up his revolver in the process. With his free hand, he reached down to his stomach, finding bloody streaks that matched the source of his pain. He held the same hand in front of him, finding it covered in his own blood. Deciding within a second or two that he wasn't mortally wounded, he deliberately held his gun up to the window, prepared to end the life of his attacker.

Except the dark figure wasn't there.

In his place, a rope swung lazily to and fro outside the window, while flaps from the damaged screen flapped in the breeze. Possibly afraid of being caught, the man might have climbed down and fled.

Putting pressure on his wound, Bloom picked up his phone, finding the line completely dead.

"Shit."

Setting his gun down in one corner, he fumbled across his desktop, desperate to find his cell phone while he kept pressure on his wound. Several papers went flying, along with a paperweight and his clock. In the process he knocked his cell phone to the floor as well.

Groaning from the painful wound, he dropped to his knees to pick up the phone, trying to maintain his composure.

Scooping the phone from the floor, he steadily held it in his hands, dialing 911, hoping the county's new dispatch system triangulated his position quickly. He had just hit the send button when the main door flew open, revealing the dark figure once more, holding the small scythe in his right hand.

As a dispatcher answered on the other end of his call, Bloom dropped his phone to the floor, freeing both hands for a grip on his revolver. His assailant closed the gap quickly between the rooms, like a hovering ghost with his black cloak touching the ground only when it chose to. Bloom managed to fire a single shot into the figure's chest, which appeared to have no effect, before the bladed weapon swung upward.

Bloom looked down to his new source of intense pain, finding the weapon's curved blade lodged just beneath his rib cage, penetrating deeply enough that it exited along his backside. His remaining few breaths came in heaves as the dispatcher on the other end said she was sending the authorities.

When the private investigator slumped to the floor, the killer quickly retrieved his weapon, looking over the papers now scattered across the desk and floor. He had only minutes before county and city police swarmed the scene. Finding what he needed in less than thirty seconds, he quickly left the room for the wide-open safety of the outdoors.

***

Not a complete stranger to assaults and murders, Detective Sergeant Troy Tackett stepped into the crime scene half an hour after the 911 call reached dispatchers. A Monroe County patrolman arrived first, giving the county police jurisdiction since Bloom's office was bordering on city limits.

A veteran investigator with the Monroe County Sheriff's Department, Tackett lived outside the city limits on his farm. He had just finished brushing his teeth in anticipation of a good night's sleep when one of his dispatcher's called with the news. As the investigator on-call, he threw on some clothes and drove his county vehicle to the scene.

Approaching the building, he noticed the evidence technician's vehicle parked to the side, then looked up to see a rope dangling from the roof, swaying freely in front of a lit office above.

Carefully stepping inside, Tackett found both an elevator and staircase leading upstairs. Nothing on the ground floor appeared disturbed, which led him up the open stairwell, where he found evidence technician Rob Lowrey studying the private investigator's office. An array of Lowrey's tools of the trade sat neatly inside a tray outside of the murder site.

"What have you found?" Tackett inquired.

"I just got here. The body's over there."

Lowrey pointed, indicating he didn't want either of them stepping into the room until he finished his preliminary investigation. Bloom's corpse was lying close to the desk, partially curled into a fetal position as his right hand clutched the lower abdomen wound.

"He put up a fight," Lowrey observed.

Married, with only two golden retrievers as his children, the evidence technician attended several large seminars annually, teaching classes across the state when time permitted. Though considered a bit strange by some of his colleagues, Lowrey worked effectively and efficiently. He had pet peeves, but typically worked well with investigators if they followed his guidelines.

"How long do you need?" Tackett asked, knowing the technician preferred alone time with corpses and the surrounding area.

"I'll give you a shout in about half an hour."

Tackett nodded, then returned downstairs to seek out witnesses and neighbors. He wasn't sure anyone in either category could be found, but protocol required him to search.

While Lowrey tinkered with bloody streaks and scattered debris, Tackett interviewed everyone outside the building, finding no one with information. Only two other businesses were within sight of the private investigator's office, and both were completely dark. Again, the detective found himself staring up toward the rope dangling in front of Bloom's window.

Taking a used plastic film canister from his pocket, Tackett carefully pulled a pair of latex gloves out before sliding them over his fingers. Now safe from contaminating the crime scene, he gently tugged the rope, finding it securely anchored above.

He wanted to venture up there to see if it was thrown for an ascent, or locked into place before a silent descent. Knowing Lowrey wouldn't be happy if he did so, Tackett spoke with the building's owner instead.

The owner provided little information, stating that Bloom often worked late, especially when business was slow, or he had a client who paid well. The private investigator typically paid rent on schedule, catching up quickly when he missed a due date.

After exhausting his options near the building, Tackett finally joined Lowrey on the roof to examine the climbing mechanism. Kneeling beside the technician, Tackett found a simple three-pronged hook had dug itself into the grooves of a wooden platform that served as a small deck.

"I don't see any indication that our perp ever stepped foot up here," Lowrey stated thoughtfully. "He probably tossed the hook up here, but if it were me, I'd want to know my hook was secure before I went climbing two stories up."

"You think he knew this building?"

"He probably scouted it. This wasn't some robbery gone bad."

"From the sound of it, Bloom wasn't exactly wealthy."

"No, but some of his clients are definitely doing well."

Tackett raised an eyebrow as he turned to his colleague.

"Come on," Lowrey said with a wave toward the roof hatch.

A moment later Tackett officially stepped into the crime scene, kneeling down for a closer look at Bloom's body. No murder weapon had been left at the scene, though two penetrating wounds in his torso were readily visible.

"Have a look up here," Lowrey said, hovering over the desk like a beacon.

Tackett stood, having a look at the sheets of paper Lowrey spread atop the desk.

"Seems one of his clients was Paul Clouse. The billionaire."

Tackett perked up at the sound of the name, though he tried to subdue his surprise.

"Yeah, I know him. He was my neighbor."

Lowrey chuckled, believing the investigator was trying to pull a fast one.

When he saw Tackett wasn't kidding, the smirk disappeared from his face like someone running an eraser across a chalkboard.

"You serious?"

"Yeah. You don't remember my near death experience a few years back?"

Lowrey looked perplexed.

"I was stabbed in Ohio. Ring a bell?"

"No."

"Were you on leave the whole year or something? It was in the papers and on every news station for two nights."

Now the technician gave a helpless shrug.

"Never mind," Tackett scowled, wanting to move on with the investigation.

He sometimes forgot that Lowrey spent most of his time pent up inside an evidence room alone. Seldom did the man make contact, much less small talk, with his fellow officers or supervisors unless they shared a crime scene. Sometimes he went for weeks without talking to anyone except in passing, which might explain how he didn't know about Tackett's horrific incident.

Tackett certainly hadn't forgotten.

His small part in an investigation three years prior led to someone ambushing him in an Ohio gas station restroom.

Answers never really materialized within case files, though Tackett knew the problems stemmed from someone wanting to get at Paul Clouse. A cover-up in "everyone's best interest" satisfied some, but not the detective. He didn't hold Clouse responsible, but he didn't like how the man used his newfound fortune to sweep the truth under a rug of convenience.

Still, he owed it to his former neighbor to make a call once the investigation was complete. He wanted to examine the rest of the paperwork with Lowrey, and if answers weren't forthcoming, possibly ask Clouse why his private investigator might have been murdered.

"We've got a long night ahead of us," Lowrey commented, beginning to open desk drawers in search of clues.

"You ready to call the coroner?" Tackett asked, wanting the body out of the way if Lowrey had finished with that aspect of his crime scene.

"Already have. You want anyone else up here with us once they're done?"

"No. I'll have some of the uniform guys talk with the family. You and I can handle this."

Tackett didn't plan on getting rest anytime soon, though he hoped to find some leads by morning.

Chapter 10

Clouse woke up beside Jane the next morning, thinking of how he had secretly scraped together the requested ransom. His wife's room-darkening drapes showed just a hint of light around the edges.

Swinging his legs from the bed, Clouse quietly stood up, putting on a pair of sweat pants before checking on the kids in their bedrooms. Finding them safely nestled beneath their blankets he took a quick shower, dressed, then walked the full five flights of stairs to the ground level.

Though it was too early in the morning to expect any packages, he checked with the hostess at the front desk. Nothing had come for him, so he walked into the atrium, finding very few people admiring the view at such an early hour.

A light breakfast sounded good, but his cell phone rang before he took any steps in the appropriate direction. He glanced at the number of the incoming call, not recognizing it, but taking a chance as he answered it.

"Clouse."

"Paul, this is Troy Tackett."

Clouse immediately wondered why his former neighbor had let two years slip by since they last conversed. He knew the detective wasn't able to forgive or forget the attack that nearly ended his life, though they spoke several times after Tackett left the hospital.

"What can I do for you, Troy?"

"Hopefully answer a few questions. I just finished investigating a murder scene at the office of your private investigator."

"Bloom?"

Tackett waited a few seconds to speak, leaving Clouse to wonder if he was analyzing his words. Clouse couldn't imagine anyone except Bloom being murdered in his office building, but he needed to know for certain.

"Was Ray the victim?"

"Yeah. Bladed weapon used twice in the abdomen. Sound familiar?"

Clouse stood in shock, unable to answer immediately.

"I...I just talked to him last night, Troy. He had important information about the case I hired him for. I can't believe this."

Really, he could believe it, though he didn't want to.

"We're checking phone records and examining his paperwork right now. Any idea who might want to kill him? Not to sound harsh, but trouble seems to follow you around."

Clouse stiffened.

"Are you implying something, Troy?"

"I'm not saying you had anything to do with it, but based on your past dealings with killer types, you might be the key to me solving this."

What lousy timing, Clouse thought, hoping against all odds Ray Bloom's death wasn't in any way associated with him hiring the man. Of course it was, he deduced just as quickly. His worst fears bared their teeth from the shadows, biting him in the ass for daring let his guard down.

"I want to meet with you, Paul," Tackett finally said what he had been leading to the entire conversation.

"And I really need to know if you find any information from Bloom's paperwork, Troy. If he was right, a lot more people may be in trouble."

"We're going to dig into it this afternoon after I make a trip down there for an interview with you."

Clouse exhaled noisily through his nostrils, not wanting to set a definite time with a package coming for him by late morning. He also didn't want his friends and family alarmed by Tackett visiting the hotel. He supposed the newspapers were bound to make the connection and hound him anyway, so he decided to save face and cooperate.

"Can you call me before you come?"

"I will."

"How did you get my number anyway?"

Clouse made certain to keep his cell phone number very private, with good reason.

"Your buddy Daniels gave it to me. I didn't leave him much of a choice if you're thinking about bitching at him."

"I'm sure he put up a fight."

"I'll call you later."

"Okay. Thanks, Troy."

Replacing the phone at his side, Clouse no longer felt interested in breakfast. Hiring Bloom was Clouse's plan to keep everyone around him safe. Now Bloom had died for no good reason, though his death ensured Clouse all was not right around him, or the hotel.

He couldn't help but wonder if the ransom notes were tied into the murder. Without Bloom, any chances of finding potential links between the two issues were slim. Private investigators with a financial need might take over the case, but most rational people would turn him down.

Clouse couldn't blame them. He certainly didn't want his problems and the threats that came with his past.

Money certainly didn't solve all of his problems. In fact, it added to them.

His stomach felt very uneasy as he dwelled on the murder, coupled with the fact he needed to play a waiting game on a special delivery. He decided to put aside his trust issues, because he didn't want to face both new dilemmas alone. Keeping everything from Jane was going to give him a guilty ulcer, but she was the *last* person he wanted to confide in at the moment.

Most everyone else he knew now worked for him. He typically tried to keep work and personal issues separate so he wasn't constantly taking his friends from their necessary posts.

If he called Daniels over every little problem he *thought* might arise, the man couldn't function as the head of casino security. He had spent time and money to train his friend adequately for the job because the position required a great deal of focus and attention.

No, he decided, he needed to call someone who only worked for him, with no attachments or baggage outside of the employment relationship.

He knew the person he wanted to call, but before he could search for the number, a delivery man entered the lobby through one of the glass doors, carrying a single envelope.

"Shit," Clouse muttered, realizing his day wasn't going to get any better.

***

In the privacy of a nearby lounge, Clouse opened the package left for him at the front desk. In the same font as the previous typed notes, this one read:

> *Mr. Clouse,*
>
> *I see you've been a busy man, scurrying to collect the one-million dollars. Since you've kept your end of the bargain, I'll keep mine.*
>
> *Drop the one-million dollars off in the lobby of the old Hilton property on Highway 37 by noon today.*
>
> *No police, no tricks, and you have your high school pal back by this evening. He's alive and well, and he still talks with that accent of his. There's your proof.*
>
> *Goodbye*

Clouse read the note a second time to make certain he didn't miss any facts. He felt a tingle of restrained delight run through him that he might actually see Tim once more. When he lost his two best friends, he prayed for a way to communicate with them, to talk to them one last time. No one ever expected to lose close friends at such a young age, or so unexpectedly.

He remembered the old Hilton property as land that Tim Niemeyer desperately wanted to purchase. Beverly Hilton, an old widow who stubbornly remained attached to the ruins within the grounds, wouldn't sell it to him. Tim tended to the land, basically watching over it for her, hoping she might someday decide to sell, or will it to him for his kindness.

She passed away nearly four years after Clouse watched his friend's casket lower into the ground. So far as Clouse knew, the land remained in litigation while family members squabbled about who received what portion of her estate.

Still, it provided another attachment to his childhood friend that very few people knew about. He wondered if there might be merit in the alleged abductor's claim.

"I want him back," Clouse muttered to himself, wondering if the glimmer of hope in the recesses of his mind was due to fade like a melting candle.

"What's that?" a familiar voice asked from behind him.

He turned to face his wife, trying to put forth a reassuring smile for her.

"Good morning, dear."

"Good morning. What's that you've got?"

Jane nodded toward the envelope in his hand.

"More inventories I need to give Craig," he lied, trying to avoid thrusting it behind him, though he shifted the paperwork to the other hand.

"They came this early in the morning?"

"Hard to believe," Clouse said, forcing a chuckle while feeling very transparent.

Jane didn't seem to believe him, mainly because he wasn't accustomed to keeping anything from her. She knew of the dangers potentially surrounding him, after surviving several attempts on her own life.

"Are you okay?" she asked, not directly pressing the issue.

"I'm fine. Are the kids up?"

"Not yet. I just took a quick shower and dressed after you came down."

"You look lovely," he said, planting a kiss on her lips.

She returned the favor, giving a little moan, though they seldom showed affection for one another in public. Part of their reason for doing so was because they lived within their business, but occasionally cameras were pointed their way, and the media loved posting any images of them acting out of the norm.

"You are such a liar," Jane said when their lips parted.

Clouse tensed, thinking she was on to his secretive activities.

"I haven't even done my hair and makeup," she added, letting him off the hook before he said something regrettable.

"Got plans today?" he asked, trying to measure his position before he decided his next move.

"I'm going into the clinic for a few hours."

"With the kids?" he inquired as casually as possible.

"No."

The answer came as though the question had been preposterous. Jane never took the kids to the clinic unless she was only passing through.

"I thought you were keeping the kids today, Paul."

"I can."

His mind immediately raced for someone to leave them with who wouldn't rat him out. Considering the circumstances around him, he didn't want the kids left alone for a second, but he needed freedom enough to drop off the ransom money.

"Did you forget today was your day with the kids and make other plans?"

"I said today was my day with the kids, and that's that," Clouse said with resolve.

"Good," Jane said, pecking his cheek before she turned for the door. "I'm grabbing breakfast before I go. Care to join me?"

"I'll catch you later. The kids will be up soon."

He watched his wife head through the lobby, then the atrium, while his mind raced for a solution. Leaving them with someone would certainly get him in trouble with Jane when she found out, but taking them to an unsecured money drop wasn't safe.

An idea that solved his problem of watching the kids and taking someone he trusted with him crept into his mind, but it wasn't readily feasible.

Taking one more look into the atrium to verify Jane crossed the floor to the restaurant, he plucked his cell phone from his belt as he stepped onto the veranda. Guaranteed privacy from his employees and guests, he hit the button for Todd Parish, hating to bother the man on his second of two days off.

He trusted Parish implicitly for two reasons. One, he had sought out the man during the interview process for family protection. Anyone who applied for security positions might have done so with evil intentions. Clouse heard about Parish through local conversations and a Sunday feature newspaper article, so no one he knew personally had recommended the man's services.

The second reason he liked the protector of his children was that Parish couldn't have been involved with Smith, because he spent so much time on the West Coast and in the military during the times in question.

Money didn't seem to be an overwhelming motivator for him, because he chose to return home and work for his father, rather than search for higher paying jobs outside of Indiana. Most people who sided with Martin Smith only did so to line their pockets.

It took only one ring before the cell phone was answered.

"Sir?" Parish answered with his usual polite nature, sounding wide awake for the early hour.

Some people thought Parish simply sucked up to Clouse and other authority figures, but the man's father had once been a minister. Parish was raised to be very respectful of others, his elders in particular.

"Todd, I hate to bug you on your day off, but do you have any major plans?"

Clouse felt a bit sheepish asking his own employee such a thing. He knew many people with riches bullied their employees, but like Parish, Clouse was raised the right way.

"I have baseball with the kids this afternoon, but that's about it. You need me to come in?"

An immediate feeling of regret swept over Clouse. Asking Parish for help endangered a good man with a family, though anyone on Clouse's payroll shared some aspect of risk.

Most of them knew of the danger, which didn't make it acceptable, though it allowed Clouse to sleep at night. He couldn't live with himself if he willingly put people in harm's way without their consent.

"I have a special assignment of sorts for you, Todd," he finally decided to say. "There's a healthy bonus in it for you, and I promise you'll be back in time for your baseball games."

"Mr. Clouse, you already take good care of me. I'm not worried about-"

"No, Todd. I insist. As a father, I understand what I'm doing to you and your marriage by asking you for your time today, so a bonus is the least I can do."

Parish absorbed the words momentarily before speaking again.

"Very well, sir. When and where do you need me?"

Chapter 11

To further keep Jane from suspecting anything, Clouse drove their green Chevy Tahoe into West Baden, meeting Parish in the local grocery store's parking lot.

Seeing Parish standing beside his Honda Shadow, which he had rode in from Bedford, the kids lit up immediately.

"Todd!" Katie exclaimed, nearly leaping out of her seatbelt.

Only a day removed from their protector, the kids had already begun to miss him.

"Stay here, guys," Clouse instructed the kids. "I'll be right back."

As he stepped from the SUV, Clouse was reminded of how Parish slightly resembled his old police buddy Ken Kaiser, who rode a Harley-Davidson motorcycle. Parish had bought his bike used from a family friend who kept it looking brand new for nearly five years. Wearing a black leather jacket to protect him from wind and bugs, the bodyguard appeared a bit different in jeans and a golf shirt as he peeled the jacket from his torso.

One stable element remained at his side in the form of his loaded firearm. He sometimes wore it along his back or in a shoulder holster beneath his sport coat, but the gun always accompanied him per Clouse's orders.

Clouse stepped forward, wanting a word with his employee before they joined the kids, as the two men shook hands.

"My wife can never hear one word about today, Todd."

"Understood, sir."

Parish seldom spoke with either of them, until they addressed him first, so unless Jane decided to push the issue for some reason, Parish would never bring up the topic. In the process of covering his tracks, Clouse figured she wasn't going to know unless the kids said something.

He still had time to think of a way to bribe the kids or construct a reasonable excuse why he called Parish to join them. The latter seemed safer and more practical, because the kids tended to speak before they thought sometimes.

"If Jane asks you anything, just defer her to me."

Parish nodded.

"Can I ask what it is we're doing?"

"I have to drop off an item to a slightly remote location. Thanks to my big mouth I can't leave the kids behind, and this could get a little hairy, so I wanted you along to watch them."

"Hairy?" Parish asked with a raised eyebrow.

Clouse waved off his earlier statement as though he had exaggerated the facts.

"Should be a quick thing. Basically a drive through some back roads with a stop or two, and I want you to stay with the kids while I do my thing."

Parish bobbed his head, though he looked far from thrilled about the vague assignment.

He followed Clouse to the Tahoe, barely seating himself inside before the kids lurched forward and threw their arms around him.

Clouse smirked, wondering why he seldom received such magnetic attraction from them.

"Hey, guys," Parish said, turning to engage them in conversation as Clouse started the engine.

Deciding he needed to make a few stops to distract the kids from his real intentions, Clouse bought them ice-cream just outside of Paoli. Several times Parish had eyed him, as though wanting to ask about the secretive nature of their trip, ultimately not daring to do so.

Clouse also stopped at a playground behind a school, allowing the kids to play kickball with some neighborhood locals while he and Parish watched vigilantly from the sideline.

"It's not right to ask you to keep a secret from my wife unless I tell you a little bit about what's going on, Todd."

"Sir, you don't have to tell me a thing."

"I'm delivering a ransom," Clouse said bluntly, unable to sugarcoat the words.

"Sir?"

Parish went from skeptical to genuinely concerned in a heartbeat.

"What about the police?"

"No. No police, no Jane, no outside help. It's layer upon layer of complication I can't begin to explain."

"You can't just give in to their demands, Mr. Clouse. It'll create trouble for you later."

"That's what I have you and my staff for, Todd. This is something completely different. Something I thought was beyond my control five years ago has come back to haunt me."

Parish's face twisted into a perplexed contortion.

"Sir, can I ask you something personal?"

Clouse nodded.

"I know a little bit about what happened to you and your friends. If this place is such a cesspool of bad memories for you, why the hell do you stay? Especially at the hotel?"

"There are still people I have to protect, Todd," Clouse answered softly, looking out to the children. "I'm not going to deny their grandparents time with them, and I'm not going to run from my problems. This area is the only home I've ever known. There's nowhere else I really want to be."

"I can't begin to tell you what kind of a difference you've made in the Valley. The jobs and the tax dollars the casino provides are just the beginning."

"I know, but it doesn't ease the hurt for some people. Martin Smith built his legacy on lies and deception. Some people think I'm just another version of him, which they consider big trouble."

A few minutes later the kids rushed over, asking if they had time to play another game. Clouse looked to his watch, not wanting to interfere with Parish's afternoon plans.

"Sorry, guys. We've got a few more stops to make. Maybe we can start a kickball game in the old ball diamond tonight."

Both lit up like fireflies at the thought of hosting their own game near the hotel.

Clouse had spent a little extra money to restore the old baseball diamond beyond the sunken garden on the hotel grounds. He had considered rebuilding an exact replica of the old church behind the hotel, but Jane warned him of crossing beyond the limits of practicality by doing so.

A stickler for tradition, Clouse wanted everything restored as it was in the hotel's heyday whenever possible. Because of the one-hundred year flood line, the old bowling and billiards building at the garden's far edge couldn't be restored to its previous grandeur. No one wanted to bowl in water up to their waistline.

It didn't take much longer to reach Beverly Hilton's historic resort, now lying in ruins just off Highway 37. Clouse shot a quick glance toward Parish to make certain the man knew this was the dangerous part of their day trip, receiving a brief nod in return.

"Where are we, Dad?" Zach asked, inquisitive as ever.

"There used to be a hotel here, son. It burned down years ago."

"Why are we here then?"

"I guess you could say I promised an old friend I'd check on something."

Clouse drove about a hundred yards in before spying the stone and brick ruins that remained. The surrounding grass had only begun to turn green, now entering its growth spurt. Weeds sprouted from the hulls of the large resort and its outbuildings, seeping through empty window panes and twisting around partial bricks like spying woodland creatures.

As Parish stepped from the vehicle, taking the kids aside with him, Clouse popped the rear hatch, pulling out the briefcase full of cash before taking his first steps toward the ruins.

Easily navigating his way through the mix of masonry and foliage, he stepped over the old hotel's threshold, finding something unexpected where he planned to set the briefcase.

Centered in the skeletal remains of the hotel, he found a body lying face down in the center of the old wooden floor that once held a grand lobby. Exposed to the elements for decades, and more recently to fire, the buildings were reduced to splintered wood amongst the grassy patches. The body, however, showed no signs of decomposition, looking extremely fresh to a man who once took medical calls for a living.

Clouse had seen his share of bodies during his tenure with the fire department, some in worse condition than others. Though far from being an expert on the subject his experience allowed him to make an educated guess about this particular body.

He looked behind him, finding the kids preoccupied with Parish, before cautiously approaching the body. In the back of his mind he wondered if it might be a trick to lure him close for an assault. Setting the briefcase beside him, Clouse stood over the body, finding an exit wound near the left shoulder blade, indicating the man had been stabbed from behind, or the wound went clear through his heart.

"Holy."

Beside his hand a note rested between some sturdy weeds. Clouse carefully reached for it, finding some writing on one side of the crumpled scrap paper. He recognized the combination of numbers and wording as a county address not far from French Lick.

Feeling along the neck for a pulse, Clouse verified the man was indeed deceased. He thought briefly about calling Parish over, but decided not to involve the bodyguard, or risk horrifying the kids. If he lingered too long, his worst fears would be realized, so he carefully searched the man for identification, touching a wallet through the back pocket.

He decided to leave it alone, fearing he might leave fingerprints on the wallet if he touched it. Pocketing the sheet of paper with the address, he took up the briefcase before heading toward the SUV. Finding a dead body wasn't something he bargained for, and instinct told him this was the man demanding his money, or perhaps an unlucky partner.

Calling Randy Niemeyer sounded like his best option, so he stopped some distance from his vehicle to make the call. If he dared wait, the body might mysteriously disappear before the young trooper could begin an investigation.

Parish eyed him from a distance, glancing to the briefcase Clouse had set down almost suspiciously. With a simple nod, Clouse assured him everything was fine, allowing the bodyguard to chase the kids around a nearby tree, keeping them entertained.

Niemeyer picked up after one ring.

"What do you have, Paul?"

"Problems."

Clouse caught him up to speed on the day's events, along with the last ransom note. Strangely, Niemeyer didn't seem shocked or the least bit distraught about the find. His focus remained on getting his brother back at virtually any cost.

"That note was probably sent yesterday," the trooper guessed aloud. "A lot could have happened."

"I need to know something about this dead guy, Randy. Can you come out here and have a look?"

"It's in Lawrence County, so I can certainly check out an *anonymous* tip."

"Great. I'd be much obliged to know anything you find."

Clouse had intentionally left out any mention of the newest note on purpose, deciding to check out the address himself.

"I can be there in five minutes."

"We'll be long gone, so you can check out your tip in peace."

"I'll call when I get his name. This won't stay quiet for long, so be ready."

"I will be. Just be careful, Trooper Niemeyer."

"Always."

Clouse severed the call, returning to his vehicle with the briefcase in hand. Placing it in the rear hatch, he called for the kids to come back. Parish trailed behind, surveying the area, despite his ignorance of a potentially greater danger.

"Things go badly?" he questioned as the kids climbed into the back seat from opposite doors.

"Not quite as I expected. I'll explain later."

Though he wanted to investigate the mysterious address, he wasn't bringing the kids along, which meant he could let Parish return home for the day. There were other security personnel who could watch over the kids if Jane wasn't home yet.

He also had the meeting with Tackett to consider. Wondering how he could think so rationally after seeing a corpse at the ransom drop spot, he decided experience had simply hardened him.

Clouse's only companion on the return trip to the hotel was the sound of his thoughts. Parish joked and played with the kids to keep them preoccupied from Clouse's distant behavior until Clouse pulled the SUV into the hotel's long brick driveway.

When one of the hotel security members came to fetch the kids, it gave Clouse and Parish an opportunity to talk.

"It's not any of my business, but you didn't leave the briefcase, sir."

"No, I didn't. I went back there, and found a dead body where I was supposed to make the drop."

Parish hesitated, as though expecting a punch line that Clouse wasn't able to provide.

"Sir?"

Clouse rubbed his hands over his eyes, truly taking in the situation for the first time. He didn't want to believe death was forming like a noxious cloud around him once again, but self-preservation forced him to.

"I've already called the police," Clouse said to reassure Parish that he wasn't any part of illicit activities.

"Who was it?"

"I didn't look. The body was fresh, so I think it might very well have been the person demanding the ransom."

Parish looked gravely concerned.

"I take it he didn't kill himself?"

"No, he certainly didn't."

Clouse looked out to the garden, noticing guests and tourists enjoying the tranquil feeling the open space provided. He wished he could know the feeling of carefree living, if only for a moment.

"I'm sorry I dragged you into this, Todd. I had no idea this was going to happen."

"Sir, is there something you're *not* telling me?"

"You've got to be careful, Todd. There are forces out there that wish to bring harm to me or my family. Now that you're a part of all of this, you've got to watch yourself."

"I can take care of myself."

Ken Kaiser often said the same thing after being trained at the state police academy and remaining armed at all times. Clouse knew several well-trained police officers had fallen victim to Smith and his minions.

"I've got to get you back to your bike," Clouse thought aloud. "On the way, I'm going to fill you in about a couple things. If you don't want to work for me after that, I'll understand."

Once again Parish accepted the words, though the vague nature in which they were relayed to him left him looking a bit perplexed. Clouse decided he was going to tell the tale like a politician might, leaving out the entirely unbelievable parts, while getting the important parts across.

He wanted to know Parish understood *exactly* what might be coming for them in case the dead body wasn't an isolated incident of vigilante justice. Something told him their talk wasn't going to end when they reached the grocery store in West Baden.

***

Parish took the tale better than Clouse expected, though the teller left out certain possible supernatural elements of the story. Much to his surprise, Parish seemed adamant about staying on as an employee. Perhaps he liked the dangerous elements associated with the job, or the lack of local stable employment forced Parish's hand, but Clouse was thrilled to keep the man on his payroll.

During the return trip to the hotel, Clouse continued to glance at the scrap paper in his hand with an address on it. He figured he had enough time to visit the address before Tackett called, wondering if he dared travel alone.

After all, he had just found a dead body at the drop point, and a briefcase full of cash sat mere feet behind him.

Assured the kids were in good hands, he stopped by the casino, opting to park his vehicle in the parking garage himself, rather than let the valet service park it for him. He didn't keep a personalized parking spot on the premises, partly for personal security, but also because he didn't mind a little exercise. Clouse was able to see things from the perspective of his clientele, which allowed him to make subtle improvements to the French Lick Springs Hotel and the casino.

Within minutes he parked the SUV on the second level, then took the elevator down to the ground level. Crossing the one-way road to the casino itself, Clouse received nods from employees who may or may not have recognized him. When he stepped inside, two armed security guards stood beside a set of metal detectors. Though the woman to his left didn't recognize him, the gray-haired retired cop did, waving him through.

"Good day, Mr. Clouse."

Clouse gave a brief, but courteous nod as he passed through the metal detector, heading straight for the offices. Because of the casino's design, it provided no other access points, coming or going, except for mandatory fire exits. One way in and out was how the place was designed with good reason.

Normally Clouse might have paid more attention to the blinking lights and arcade-like sounds around him, but today the slot machines and paying customers couldn't distract him. He marched straight into the corporate offices, swiping his access card through the reader to bypass the highest levels of security until he reached Daniels' office.

Stepping in without so much as a knock, he found his friend casually viewing monitors from a room directly adjacent to his main office. Daniels had come to understand the intricacies of cheating at cards, though the casino typically ran very few tables. Other dangers lurked, keeping Daniels alert at all times, including thieves and scam artists. Some thieves believed the crew didn't keep vigil in such a small casino, occasionally attempting to steal chips and wallets from unsuspecting players.

Still, his job hardly provided the intrigue and thrill of the hunt shown on television. Turning around in his swivel chair, Daniels appeared surprised to see Clouse standing there.

"Social visit?"

"Not exactly. Can I borrow you for a little trip down the road?"

"You're the boss," Daniels answered with a quirky grin.

"This isn't exactly company business, Mark. I'll explain on the way."

Nearly ten minutes later, Clouse had relayed details of the ransom notes, the trip to the old resort, and the discovery of the body.

"That's quite a week," Daniels admitted as Clouse drove them out of the casino parking lot.

"Tell me about it. I gave Randy Niemeyer a heads-up on the mystery corpse. Hopefully he finds something useful."

"Then exactly what are we doing?"

"We're going to check out this address I found in the dead guy's hand."

Clouse looked over, catching a concerned look on his friend's face.

"What?" he asked.

"It just sounds weird that the note would be *right* there. Like it was planted or something."

"Maybe the guy was reaching for it when he was killed. I'm not happy about it either, but I want to know what's there."

"You mean you want to know if Tim's there."

Pulling onto the highway that led to the county road he needed, Clouse looked from the note to his friend. Though doused with nervous sweat from his palm, the paper refused to yield the clarity of its message.

"We're not going to do anything illegal, are we?" Daniels inquired.

"Hell, I don't know what we're going to find there, Mark. It could be a fake address for all I know."

The sounds and sights of activity surrounding the casino were soon replaced by trees, the occasional house, and too much silence for Clouse's taste. Even Daniels had little to say at this point, accepting his role in their inquiry. As a former detective, he probably shared some curiosity about what the address held, though he never fancied putting himself at risk.

As they neared the address, Clouse's eyes drifted between the piece of paper and roadside mailboxes. Daniels stole a glance at the paper, deciding to assist him.

"Getting close," he said, which Clouse already knew as a tingle ran through his body.

Strangely, everything passing by the duo came in the form of rural housing. Many of the residences were at least a quarter mile apart, which seemed to make sense for keeping secrets. Clouse couldn't imagine how anyone could keep a prisoner inside a farmhouse, particularly for years on end.

When Clouse finally found what he guessed was the correct house, he noticed the faded black plastic mailbox had no numbers on it. A large two-story blue house looked uninviting, set back from the road. Like the mailbox, its color appeared a bit drained from neglect. The windows and doors looked intact, though the yard was in desperate need of mowing.

"It's beautiful," Daniels commented sarcastically. "I'll take it."

Seeing no realty signs in the yard, or any signs of habitation, Clouse began wondering exactly what purpose the house served.

"You haven't even seen the inside yet, my friend. I'm sure its best features still await us."

Daniels grunted as Clouse pulled into the gravel driveway, which showed signs of succumbing to overgrown weeds. Every shred of evidence around them pointed to the property being completely abandoned.

A crumbling barn some distance back from the house was missing part of its roof, while its weathered exterior appeared near collapse. Based on the rusty tractor beside the structure, Clouse guessed the barn hadn't been utilized in years.

"What do you think?" Clouse asked as they stepped from his vehicle.

"I think we're wasting our time. This has to be a wild goose chase."

Daniels stepped onto the front porch first, narrowly avoiding a large hole between two broken boards. He peered through one of the front windows devoid of coverings as Clouse looked through the other.

A dusty couch and some kind of broken dresser were the only visible pieces of furniture. Daniels tried the doorknob, finding it locked, though without a deadbolt.

"Let's see around back," Clouse suggested.

"Swell."

Finding the view much the same from the backdoor's window, Clouse saw a few cans of food atop a kitchen counter that appeared to have modern labels from local grocery stores.

"See that?"

"So someone eats here while they restore the place," Daniels suggested.

"I don't see much progress with the restoration."

"So they do a few square inches a week. It's not unheard of."

Clouse tried the locked door, testing its sturdiness. It held, though he was able to move it nearly half an inch upward.

"Got any tricks for getting the latch to open?" he asked Daniels.

"How did I know you were going to ask that?"

Opening his wallet, Daniels pulled out a ragged-looking credit card.

"This normally wouldn't work, but this door's seen better days," the former cop said, giving a play-by-play as he wiggled the card between the door jam and the locking mechanism.

It took mere seconds for the old wooden door to give way, allowing them access to the house.

"Sure you've never done that professionally?" Clouse asked with a smirk.

"Police work isn't always on the straight and narrow. Hey, did we ever bother knocking?"

"No, so let's look this place over and get out of here."

While Daniels took the stairwell to the second floor, Clouse checked over the rooms on the lower level, finding them devoid of furnishings and clues. Footsteps boomed above him as though Daniels might come crashing down any moment. Deciding he didn't like the idea of trespassing inside the house nearly as well as walking around outside, Clouse searched for any other rooms.

Inside the kitchen, he found a locked door he guessed might lead down to a basement.

Hesitating momentarily, Clouse decided to brave opening the door rather than waiting for his friend. A padlock hung from a very thin hasp, impeding his search, but a nearby hammer, lying amongst several rusting hand tools, offered some assistance.

Two strikes with the hammer forced the hasp to yield, giving up its secrets as Clouse opened the door to a darkened stairway leading downward. He patted the wall, looking for a light switch before noticing a pull cord overhead. When the light came on, several insects scurried along the walls, giving way to a sight of unfinished panel walls and wooden stairs that looked on the verge of collapse.

Before he dared test the stairs, the door beside him moved, startling him momentarily until Daniels emerged from around the other side.

"What's this?"

"It was locked, but it doesn't look very promising."

Clouse cautiously stepped on the first stair, finding it more solid than expected. He made his way down, finding a drastic change from a deteriorating farmhouse to a recently renovated area just right of the stairs.

Stepping into a much better lit hallway, Clouse found a jail cell and a vacated area that held only a large desk, a tripod, and some open cabinets with boxed and canned foods inside.

"This is just like the video," Clouse muttered, still visually soaking in the area.

He stared into the cell, unwilling to step inside despite the door beside him remaining wide-open. No one sat inside, leaving him to wonder if he was the victim of a cruel hoax, or circumstances beyond his control left him one step behind.

"Look up there," Daniels said, pointing to a steel bracket mounted in the opposite corner from them.

"Perfect spot for a video camera."

Clouse finally stepped into the cell, motioning for his friend to stay back.

"I need a container, or a sandwich bag, Mark."

Daniels gave a hapless shrug before heading upstairs to try and fill the request.

Within the cell Clouse found a toilet, but no sink. A bed with used, dingy sheets took up part of the space, but no other furniture sat inside. A few magazines and books were strewn across the floor, as though disheveled when someone left in a hurry. A closer look at the pillow and a small ledge in the wall behind it provided the evidence he wanted.

"Here," Daniels said, holding an empty pill bottle when he returned.

Clouse placed it beside the smooth surface of the tiny ledge, sweeping hairs and possible skin samples into the pill bottle.

"What's that for?" Daniels asked.

"I have a friend on campus who owes me a favor. I want to know if this DNA matches Tim's."

"You saying you have a sample of Tim's DNA? That's a little creepy, you know."

"I have Tim's brother, which is just as good."

Daniels was about to poke fun at him some more when a noise from the first floor drew their combined attention upward.

"What the hell?" Daniels murmured under his breath as he drew the firearm holstered at his side.

Both quietly moved toward the stairs as a walking noise startled them once more. Daniels led the way up, cautious when he stepped through the door as he glanced both ways. While he took off to search the ground floor, Clouse stepped through the open backdoor, finding no one outside, nor any getaway vehicles.

He knew his mind wasn't playing tricks on him, and the house was far too old to be settling with creaks and groans.

When he returned inside, Daniels greeted him, shaking his head.

"Nothing."

Clouse looked at the pill bottle, which he had capped before dashing upstairs. A strange feeling someone was still lurking inside the house bothered him since a house containing a prison cell might harbor other secrets.

"We should probably get out of here."

"I'm not going to argue with that logic."

As they walked across the abandoned property, Clouse couldn't help but feel slighted. Not only had the ransom drop gone bad, but his best new lead flopped miserably. He definitely wondered if someone had gone through extensive trouble to trick him, using Randy Niemeyer as a pawn. The dark, suspicious side of him thought momentarily that Niemeyer might harbor resentment toward him, possibly conjuring up the ransom plan himself.

Clouse shook off the paranoid thoughts, knowing the trooper was incapable of cold-blooded murder. He wondered if Niemeyer had found the body yet, and if so, what clues he might have unraveled.

He wouldn't find out until late afternoon, because he had an appointment with his former neighbor that didn't look very promising. Raymond Bloom's death brought unfortunate circumstances to him in a number of ways, and a burden that came with knowing someone died because a malicious human being wanted at Clouse.

It constantly felt like he was living a bad dream from which he simply couldn't awaken. Daniels opened the passenger side door, but Clouse hesitated, giving the property one last stare before sliding into the driver's seat.

Chapter 12

Craig Jennings left work around lunchtime, though not to grab a bite to eat. He had concerns about the sudden departure of Jon Lopez from his staff. Though the keycard and keys had shown up the next day, no one ever reported seeing Lopez after the gala that evening.

He showed up at the Paoli apartment complex Lopez listed in his application as a residence, finding a relatively new building appearing almost fully occupied. Three stories in height, the building provided security for its residents in the form of individual buzzers with each room's number beside a gray button.

Because his staff often second-guessed his abilities as a leader, and his experience relating to his position, Jennings sometimes questioned himself.

Not in this instance.

While some accused him of taking an easy way out by working for Paul Clouse, Jennings considered his new job a fresh start from instructing in a dingy industrial shop every day.

And to think, if his dog hadn't run off during a snowy hunting trip, his life would still be an endless cycle of following school calendars.

Jennings pushed the button labeled for the building manager, then waited a few seconds before an answer came.

"Yeah?"

"I'm here to check on Jon Lopez."

A pause.

"You family?"

"I'm his boss. He hasn't been to work in two days."

Another pause, then a click let Jennings know the door was unlocked magnetically.

He stepped inside, finding the building manager dressed in clothes suited for working on plumbing, or perhaps light construction.

Jennings introduced himself, stating where he worked, and for whom.

"George Shoults," the man said, refraining from shaking hands because his own were filthy with grease and residue. "You say Jon hasn't been to work for a few days?"

Jennings nodded.

"That's unusual. He's a pretty responsible guy. Always pays rent on time, don't cause a fuss. The type you'd like to have more of."

Shoults wiped his hands with a clean rag, barely able to remove any blackness from his weathered skin. He looked to be in his early fifties, probably a lifer in the Paoli area who fell into a decent situation with free rent if he took care of building maintenance.

Jennings followed the superintendent up a flight of stairs to the second story. He noticed smells of new carpeting, paint, and glue lingering throughout the air. The building was even newer than he originally speculated.

When Shoults stopped at apartment 218, Jennings smelled something a bit different. Appearing a bit concerned, his face wincing a bit, Shoults shoved the key into the lock, hurriedly letting them inside.

The buzzing sound of numerous flies immediately filled their ears, unlike anything Jennings had ever encountered except in the movies. Jennings immediately suspected the worst, but spied the insects swarming around leftover food on the kitchen table. Minimal remains of fried chicken and mashed potatoes had attracted the flies, leaving Jennings to wonder if Lopez had been home at all the past few days.

He and Shoults quickly checked the rest of the apartment, finding no one home, and nothing disturbed. Strangely, they found no wallet, no car keys, unwashed work clothes, or any signs Lopez had made it home the past few days. Shoults disposed of the troublesome meal, taking out the trash bag as they exited the apartment.

"That was most unusual," Shoults noted without provocation. "Other than the food, it looked like he might be home any minute."

"Yeah," Jennings replied. "That's what worries me."

His concern grew for the hotel employee, because he hadn't spotted Lopez's car in the hotel's parking lot, and as his eyes panned the apartment complex's lot, he found an identical result. Part of the application and screening process for employment at the hotel was proof of vehicle ownership and legal Bureau of Motor Vehicles paperwork, so he knew what Lopez drove.

Disappointed by the lack of forthcoming information, Jennings decided to leave. He reached for the man's hand to shake it, refraining suddenly because of the black grime.

"It's okay," Shoults assured him.

"Thanks for your time, Mr. Shoults."

"No problem."

"Please give me a call if Jon shows up, just so we know he's alright," Jennings added, handing him a business card.

"Will do. Best of luck to you people at the casino. I know some people don't like the idea of that place being down there."

"Honestly, that's the least of my worries lately," Jennings said before heading toward his car.

***

At the moment, Clouse felt like he was standing on a highway with a tractor-trailer coming one way, and a school bus the other, with nowhere to run.

Seated within his own hotel restaurant, he sat across from Tackett and an investigator from the state police. Diane Larson was a beautiful brunette, though her methods were calculating. Wearing her long hair up, and a neatly pressed business suit that accented her curves accurately, her stare bore through Clouse, giving him the impression she had already pegged him as guilty of something.

He felt the need for a lawyer, despite the fact they weren't charging him with anything, because their questions were so pointed. They were treating him like a suspect rather than a cooperative ally.

Over the years Tackett had grown a bit colder toward him for no good reason. Strangely, they had been extremely amicable neighbors until Tackett was attacked and another neighbor's daughter was murdered on Clouse's property.

Since the Ohio stabbing, a few things had changed about the detective. Aside from his less friendly attitude, he had gained some weight, which he attributed to lingering pain when he rode horseback or tried rigorous exercise. He still lived on the same ranch, acquiring new neighbors when the Clouse family moved away.

Tackett's blue eyes remained stern, though he seemed to lack the ability to gaze at Clouse for more than a second at a time. The lack of words exchanged over the past four years created a rift neither of them wanted to deal with because it meant digging up the painful past. Wearing a slightly wrinkled shirt and tie, Tackett looked more like a standard detective than Clouse recalled, with the exception of shined, brown cowboy boots on his feet. His thick Fu Manchu mustache had been replaced with a full goatee of creamed coffee brown and his once parted hair was shaved just millimeters above his scalp.

"You've been tap dancing around my questions," Tackett said, sitting across from Clouse with Diane at his side. "I need some truth here."

Clouse had answered any and all questions about hiring Raymond Bloom with honesty, since he hadn't divulged the strange parts of the past to the private investigator. Questions about Martin Smith and the mansion weren't so easy to answer, because of the unbelievable circumstances surrounding each subject.

"I need the truth and the whole truth from you," Tackett pressed before taking a sip from the iced-tea he had ordered.

Diane had refused to order anything, despite Clouse offering.

Before Clouse could craft his next answer, the cell phone at his side buzzed and vibrated for the third time since the informal interrogation began. Randy Niemeyer wasn't giving up easily, but Clouse could not afford to distract himself from this meeting.

"You're not going to believe me if I tell you absolutely everything," Clouse warned the detective.

"Try me."

"You and me, alone, Troy. I'll tell you absolutely everything and you decide what you want to do with it."

"Fine," Tackett said, openly surprising Diane. "Let's take a walk."

A few minutes later they stepped outside to the rear of the hotel where parking and the old Jesuit observatory were located. Clouse led the way to the end of a small footbridge where he stepped onto asphalt.

"Any reason why the state police are so interested in this?"

"I called them in," Tackett revealed. "Nearly dying once is enough for me, so I wanted some backup."

"Why do you hold such a grudge against me, Troy? I never did one thing to you."

"Nothing wrong ever happened here until you stepped foot on this property."

"Right there is where you're wrong. Martin Smith was ultimately the cause of everything that went wrong around here. You've always acted like I put out some kind of hit on you, but it was *him* who assaulted you in Ohio."

Tackett turned away, gazing toward the new parking lot built for the hotel's full capacity of tours and guests. He appeared torn between his beliefs and the man he once appreciated as a neighbor.

"For years I've been hearing rumors and speculation because even the local cops couldn't figure out what the hell happened down here. Paul, tell me the truth and I'll believe you, because it beats the hell out of me what's real and what's bullshit at this point."

"Where do you want me to start?"

"Dr. Smith's alleged death, the one where he fell from the hotel. It gets a little hazy for me after that point."

Clouse started strolling toward the garden, passing the valet parking attendants who gave courteous nods and waves.

"Smith faked his own death, which allowed him the ability to covertly recover a certain artifact and seek revenge against me."

"For what?"

"Killing his son whom he'd sent to kill me the year prior. It seems the good doctor willed me almost everything except money enough to keep himself hidden a year while he plotted against me."

Clouse stopped at the brick driveway between the hotel and the sunken garden to let a few cars pass before leading Tackett to the more private and inviting garden and spring buildings.

"What's this I hear about him appearing years younger when you killed him?"

"He used what's called a cursed object to literally shed years off his life."

He stopped to look at the detective, expecting to find an incredulous look, but Tackett didn't look dumbfounded, or disbelieving.

"I've heard of them, but always thought they were some sort of urban legend."

"Well they aren't."

"How did this cursed object work?"

"Smith knew about it because he lived with the Jesuits as a child. One of the priests owned a strange crucifix with a red stone embedded in the middle. Apparently when the user killed another person, the cube took the deceased person's life force, then transferred it to the user, making him or her younger and healthier."

Tackett struggled to make sense of Clouse's words.

"So what happened to the cursed object?"

"It's buried in a safe place. I recovered it after Smith died for real."

"Why bury it? Couldn't you cast it into the ocean or destroy it?"

"Cursed objects can't be destroyed. They have to be hidden or locked away."

"Okay, so that explains *that* part of this puzzle. What the hell happened at the mansion a few years back?"

Clouse walked in front of the Apollo spring, with its many faces etched across the rounded top, like some kind of theatrical merry-go-round trim.

"Smith had at least one backup plan to bring him back, just in case his revenge didn't go as planned. Some mercenary named Bell gathered a group of investors there, planning to bring Smith back using some weird ritual and another cursed cube."

"And that failed as well?"

The question alone raised fears within the hotel's owner, but he remained composed beside Tackett.

"We're not sure what happened, Troy. Smith's body disappeared, and the green cube with it. The county mounties never figured out where either got to."

"Hey, hey," Tackett said, taking exception to the county police comment. "In your heart, do you believe Smith walked out of that mansion?"

Clouse shook his head.

"I don't know what to believe. Some research told me there are a dozen or so of those cubes, each with a different, evil ability. The fact that Smith landed at least two of them tells me he's capable of just about anything."

"What about his coffin?"

"What about it?" Clouse asked, looking toward the hill where Smith had requested to be buried, with some disdain. "His body disappeared two years ago."

"Reportedly his body, Paul. Is his casket actually empty?"

"I haven't dug it up, Sergeant Tackett. Are you suggesting I do?"

"I'm suggesting you be a bit more proactive if you believe what you're telling me."

"Me being proactive got Ray Bloom killed. I don't like turning people into sacrificial lambs just to save my own skin."

Tackett tightened his lips, turning his attention to the garden as he cleared his throat. At first Clouse thought the detective was openly doubting him, then he caught the reason for Tackett's discomfort from the corner of his eye.

"What in the hell is going on, Troy?" Jane demanded of Tackett, storming past her husband. "I just got home and my welcome wagon is a state trooper asking me loaded questions? And she's with you?"

Tackett immediately put up his hands defensively.

"Sorry, Jane. She can be a little overzealous."

"A little? And what is all of this about?"

Tackett didn't immediately answer, so she turned to Clouse.

"Ray Bloom's murder, dear."

"And they think *we* had something to do with it?"

"No," Tackett insisted, putting forth calming hand gestures that weren't about to settle her.

"All of the *shit* we've been through, Troy, and you have the audacity to sic your detective friend on me?"

"Jane, I didn't have anything to-"

"I'm so sick of everyone judging us like we're convicted criminals."

Clouse put his arm around Jane, trying to keep her from doing something regrettable. She had bottled up her feelings for so long that her temper finally got the better of her.

"Miss Larson can be a bit abrasive, dear. I think Troy just brought her along for protection."

Tackett cracked a grin, but Jane's penetrating stare quickly sent it into hiding. Clouse began thinking if one of his pets had acted this aggressively toward a guest he would have caged it by now.

He leaned over so only his wife could hear his words.

"Jane, can I have just a moment more with Troy? We were just about finished."

"Fine," she answered in a far calmer voice than he anticipated before walking somewhat stiffly toward the hotel.

When she was out of earshot, the two men exchanged uneasy glances.

"So where do we stand?" Clouse finally asked.

"I tend to believe what you said, but that's not anything I can write down in a report."

"And that's why Ray was investigating half-truths for me. I couldn't tell him all that stuff. He never would have believed me."

"Then why would someone kill him?" Tackett asked, stepping over to the large fountain to dip his hands in the cool water before rubbing them together.

"As a message to me, maybe. Or maybe he found something during his investigation that pissed off the wrong people. Did you find the information about the out-of-state people with the birthdays?"

Tackett simply shot him a perplexed stare.

"Bloom called me the night of his death to tell me there were eleven confirmed missing persons from surrounding states, Troy. Each of them had birth dates matching the potential victims from the mansion scare."

"So what does that mean exactly?"

"It means someone is probably trying to bring Smith back to life again. If that's the case, there's a mole in the local police who worked for Smith without us knowing it."

Tackett rubbed the back of his head in frustration.

"I said I believed you, but this is getting deep, Paul. You're going on theories and conjectures here. There's no hard evidence."

"The Coven isn't exactly a public enterprise. They make things happen by lurking in the shadows and carrying out Smith's wishes because he pays well."

Tackett looked beyond Clouse's shoulder, seeing Diane walk their way.

"Keep her off me," Clouse said.

"I will. It was a mistake bringing her along. Sorry I didn't trust you more in the first place."

"If I think of anything else to do with Ray, I'll call."

"And I'll keep you informed," Tackett said with a handshake in passing.

Clouse watched as he convinced Diane their business at the hotel was finished. Tackett seemed apologetic, as though he had broken a promise that she would get to sink her teeth into some suspects. Both investigators walked along the hotel's rear side toward whatever vehicle they had driven from Bloomington.

Sighing to himself, Clouse finally looked at his cell phone, seeing Randy Niemeyer had called eight times within the past thirty minutes.

Chapter 13

"Please tell me you have good news," Clouse said the next time Niemeyer called him.

"You want me to tell you this guy isn't dead or something?" the trooper's voice replied over the phone testily. "Well, he *is* dead, and even better, he worked for my department."

"Shit," Clouse thought aloud, pacing along the veranda where no hotel guests wandered at the moment.

"I said 'worked' as in past tense. He quit about two years ago abruptly."

"As in quit, or had to resign?"

"Quit. Said he had some other offers to consider."

"I'll say. This really makes things complicated, Randy."

Clouse heard some sounds over the phone, like twigs snapping and bird calls.

"Where are you?"

"I'm still in the woods."

"You've got to get out of there or call it in. Or both."

"I'm going to handle it legally, even though it'll handcuff me with investigating this further."

"What's his name? Maybe I can get some leads through unconventional means."

"Nathan Runnels. He worked on the force about two or three years before he quit."

"Not exactly retirement age, is it?"

Niemeyer said nothing momentarily as Clouse heard a car door open.

"Sounds like he had a plan in motion, Paul. Did you see anything or anyone else around the body before you left?"

"No, but it's funny you should mention plans. I need a sample of your DNA."

"What?"

Clouse took a few minutes to explain the note and the findings, or lack thereof, at the old farmhouse. Though the young trooper said very little during the narration, he breathed heavily and gave an occasional irritated sigh.

"I can't believe you did all that without me," Niemeyer finally stammered with controlled anger. "I want to see this place."

Pulling the piece of paper from his pocket, Clouse read him the address.

"You're not going with me?"

"Why should I? I've seen it."

"I don't want to go barging in there alone. You took Daniels with you."

"You scared?" Clouse asked, feeling as though he were conversing with his son rather than a grown man in law enforcement.

"No," came the defensive answer, "but I thought you'd at least have the common courtesy to tag along."

Clouse exhaled through his nostrils loud enough to make certain the sound crossed the miles between himself and Niemeyer.

"I'd love to tag along, but I've got investigators hounding me about why my private investigator is dead, I've got ransom notes floating in here from your dead buddy, and I'm not sure if Martin Smith is alive or dead. That, coupled with the fact you won't cooperate with me by giving me a DNA sample, means I can't determine if your brother was ever a hostage in the first place."

"Meet me at the house and I'll give you a sample. Hair, urine, semen, whatever you want. I've just got to see that place for myself, and I've got to see it now."

"Fine. Head this way and I'll convince the wife I need to go somewhere. And hair will suffice, thank you."

***

Clouse pulled up to the house a second time, half expecting someone other than Niemeyer awaiting him in the driveway. He spotted a state police cruiser centered in the gravel path, but no occupant.

Stepping from his own vehicle, Clouse walked along the driveway, peering inside the cruiser as he passed it, finding no signs of trouble. His boots crunched along the jagged stones as he approached the house.

"Randy?"

No answer.

"Randy?" he asked, raising his voice.

Hearing no reply, he stepped onto the back porch, slowly opening the door which still showed no signs of forced entry due to Daniels' resourceful nature.

Apparently Niemeyer shared similar skills when it came to breaking and entering.

Clouse found the basement entrance door open, deciding to peek inside the living room area first, just to ensure Niemeyer hadn't decided to explore. Finding no one else inside the ground level, Clouse descended the stairs, finding the trooper staring at the cell.

"This is just like the video," he said upon seeing Clouse.

"I know."

Clouse pulled out a small, new vial he found in one of the hotel gift shops. It contained a lucky penny from the casino, which he discarded before leaving.

"Hair sample, please."

"So you can find out if Tim was really here?"

"No. I can find out if Tim's hair and skin tissue were really here."

"That's a glass half empty view of things."

"Label me a pessimist, I don't care."

Considering Niemeyer kept his head shaved, he plucked a few forearm hairs, carefully handing them over to Clouse.

"How soon will you know?"

"Possibly tomorrow. I'll take a run to Bloomington in the morning."

Carefully touching the bars of the unusual cell, Niemeyer began studying where some of the iron was welded together. Clouse guessed the sections of iron bars were several merged smaller pieces, though he thought little of it.

"The old Bedford jail had bars like these. It closed years ago."

"You think someone bought pieces of it?"

"They might have. It changed hands several times. It was used as a haunted house for a few years."

"And a state trooper certainly would have known who to contact about purchasing some souvenirs."

"That's what I'm thinking. We're awfully resourceful like that."

Clouse held up the vial.

"Maybe tomorrow we'll get some answers on the DNA front."

"And I can check on previous owners of the Bedford jail. These are authentic sections from a jailhouse. You don't buy this kind of thing at a garage sale."

A strange, exaggerated creak sounded from one of the floorboards above them. Clouse listened intently until Niemeyer streaked past him to investigate upstairs.

Clouse followed, but a quick search of the house revealed no other intruders.

"The same thing happened when I was here with Mark."

"Creepy."

As he headed for the door, Clouse turned to see his friend's younger brother looking around the house longingly, as though some sign of Tim Niemeyer might reveal itself.

"You okay?"

"I'm fine."

Clouse led the way through the overgrown yard, keeping track of Niemeyer and the younger man's mental state. While Clouse remained skeptical of the video, the ransom, and even the makeshift cell in the house behind him, the young trooper grew more convinced his brother was alive.

A moment later, Niemeyer leaned against his patrol car, settling in for at least a brief conversation.

"Is there anything you haven't told me about this?"

"No," Clouse answered. "This whole thing is a mystery to me, and it's got me more than a little unraveled."

"I'm not waiting around for DNA results. I'll start looking into Nathan's recent dealings, starting with his home."

"I thought you were letting your people investigate his death."

"They are, but they don't know everything we do. It'll take weeks to untangle that mess, so I'll do a little private investigation."

"Just be careful."

"I will, but something tells me he didn't leave notes lying around about his personal dealings."

"Probably not," Clouse answered, turning to watch a car slowly pass the house along the road. "Maybe it's time we got out of the vicinity."

Niemeyer reached for his car door.

"I'll be in touch."

Chapter 14

Todd Parish went into work the next morning, finding most of the employees carrying out their duties as normal when he passed the front desk and filled his coffee thermos in the restaurant. He could make coffee in the sixth floor suite, but his favorite brand awaited him hot and fresh every morning downstairs, and it was free of charge.

Before heading upstairs, he decided to touch base with Craig Jennings. While Jennings was technically his boss as far as scheduling and pay grade, Parish only answered to Clouse and the man's immediate family.

Parish gave a quick knock, finding Jennings behind his desk as he stepped inside the small office. Only then did he see a frustrated look on the supervisor's face.

"Something wrong?"

"Lopez went AWOL the night of the gala, and I figured he just skipped out for a better job, but now his parents and his sister have left messages because they haven't heard from him."

"Should we be worried?" Parish asked, settling into the seat across from Jennings.

"That's the part I'm not sure about. It's like he just vanished from this place that night."

Jennings folded his hands atop his desk, breathing a heavy sigh.

Unlike some of the security staff, Parish respected the man. Jennings didn't have a cop background like many of his employees, but he once served in the military and dealt with dozens of teenagers daily when he taught at a high school. That alone garnered respect from some of the hotel employees.

"Is it time to call the police?" Parish suggested.

"His parents already filed a police report with the state police. They said it was very uncharacteristic of him not to return calls. Since he's been missing a few days now, I expect a call from the state police later."

Parish recalled the tale Clouse unraveled for him the day before. It almost sounded like fantasy, but the facts meshed with some of the urban legends told locally. Parish recalled his family, mainly his parents and siblings, begging him not to work for Clouse. An attachment to Zach and Katie, along with personal loyalty to his employer, kept him from searching for other employment.

Besides, he felt fully capable of taking care of himself by hand or firearm.

"When you hire these guys, you ever notice they're *former* cops?" Parish goaded. "There's probably a good reason for that."

"You talking about the same way we hire former bodyguards?"

Parish shrugged easily.

"What happened to me was under the bright lights of Hollywood, not some backwoods town."

"Aren't you from a backwoods town?"

Parish grinned, providing an unspoken answer.

"Look, we do a thorough background check on everyone we hire, Todd. A number of these guys actually quit their jobs to work here. You may think we have to go door to door and recruit people, but the fact is I get half a dozen inquiries per day. If one of these guys had a terminable incident in the past, I probably wouldn't touch him."

Jennings gave a crooked grin.

"You know you're an exception since Clouse picked you directly."

"Nice to know I'm so special."

"You're his golden boy."

The statement made Parish a bit uncomfortable, but he refused to show it.

"Good luck with the police interrogation later," Parish said as he stood, prepared to begin his workday. "The first person police suspect with missing persons is always the boss."

Jennings caught the joke, pointing a finger at him.

"You'll be my one phone call if they haul me in."

Parish smiled as he left the office, coffee in hand.

"Hi, Donna," he said to one of the familiar head servers from the restaurant as he strolled along the hallway.

She gave a courteous nod as Parish found himself at the elevator. He pushed the button for the sixth floor, entered an access code, and slid his key card into the security slot. Barely finding enough time to sip his coffee during the ride up, Parish stepped off the elevator as the dinging sound alerted the other guard of his arrival.

Sometimes other security personnel were stationed outside the main portion of the suite, but today only John Schaaf was on duty inside, closing the suite's door behind him as he stepped out.

A slender man in remarkable condition, Schaaf kept his hair trimmed near the scalp to keep his badly receding hairline from showing.

"Todd," he said, greeting Parish.

"John. What's the word?"

"Mrs. Clouse went to the clinic, and Mr. Clouse didn't say much about where he was headed, so it's just you and the kids."

"Quiet night?"

Schaaf gave a quirky grin.

"Aren't they all? Nothing ever happens around here. After they go to bed I watch that door and the television most of the night."

"Feeling guilty about collecting a paycheck?"

"I never said that, big guy. The kids are all yours. I gotta get some sleep before my big date."

Schaaf headed for the elevator, pushing the down button.

"Still seeing that Trisha girl?"

"Nah. That was last week."

"Ever the rolling stone," Parish sighed before putting his keycard into the suite door and letting the computer scan and verify his fingerprints.

While some security members considered the security measures excessive and difficult to learn, Parish had long since mastered every door and mechanism throughout the hotel.

Despite half of his job title being a babysitter, Parish enjoyed watching the kids. Far from typical "rich kids" they weren't snobby or expecting everything to be handed to them. Parish figured good upbringing played a major role in their behavior, but thoughts of danger likely resided in the recesses of their minds. Living with persistent fear kept one humble, he supposed.

Parish stepped inside, made certain to shut the door behind him before walking over to the open concept counter to set his coffee down. Basically a penthouse suite, the main living area was extremely open with the three main bedrooms toward the back and a guest bedroom closer to the entrance.

When Clouse redesigned the suite, he definitely had security in mind, keeping their bedrooms between the guards and the main door. He also expanded the living space with his entire family taking up residence on the sixth floor. Entertaining areas, a large play area, and several other miscellaneous rooms encompassed the floor. Clouse also made certain the kids had to pass at least one guard or take a parent with them to access the other areas of the level.

Sometimes Parish escorted the kids to the restaurant for breakfast, but they always hated the funny stares directed their way. He equated it to being the President's son or daughter the way everyone turned to them at once when they entered a room. Though his cooking didn't quite rival the restaurant, they liked it when he fixed pancakes for them, the aroma often drawing them from the bedrooms.

Parish took a quick swig of coffee before he quietly pulled out the pancake mix, syrup, and a bowl from various cupboards. As he began mixing the ingredients, careful not to dirty his suit, he wondered why both parents had taken off for the morning, only because it seemed unusual.

After the strangely botched ransom the day before, he wondered if Clouse had possibly followed through on steps to unearth more information.

***

"I can't believe I'm actually clearing my schedule just to help you match DNA," Heather Shaw said as she placed the second sample, a gelled solution of Randy Nieymeyer's DNA onto a reasonably small machine.

"You know you wanted to skip class today," Clouse said with a chuckle, not mentioning how he had funded several of her important research projects the past few years.

Heather truly owed him.

Dr. Heather Shaw had attained her doctorate in biology several years prior, but she and Clouse had known one another since their college days of playing intramural softball together. Though they dated several times during their college days, they ultimately kept their relationship at a friendly level, playing sports and working out together.

Their paths took them down separate roads. While Clouse pursued architectural design, Heather traveled abroad to examine dinosaur fossils in several countries. Her experiences broadened her knowledge and enabled her to carbon test fossils of any kind to determine the age. She also learned to compare DNA samples of all kinds, and for numerous reasons.

Clouse grew reacquainted with Heather when Daniels asked him for a DNA favor several years back. She agreed, then asked for some help in convincing certain businessmen to help fund her research projects. Agreeing with her work, and not much for approaching strangers, Clouse funded the projects himself.

Now he had spent the morning with terms figuratively flying over his head such as RFLP and PCR, which he understood to be the current DNA testing method used by police labs.

He chose to visit Heather for privacy reasons as well. Some private labs that tested DNA regularly weren't necessarily as secure as he wanted them to be. Secrets leaked out sometimes, and he didn't want the general public knowing anything about his impromptu research.

Seated in a small, dimly-lit room set adjacent to Heather's much larger, primary lab, Clouse looked at the two computer screens as the second sample began materializing next to the unknown sample.

To him they might as well have been drawings composed by Zach during his kindergarten year. Heather stared at the two images, then pressed a button to capture each of them to a digital image, freezing them on the screen.

She studied the still images a bit more closely, making some intrigued noises as she did so.

"Well?" Clouse asked a moment later.

"Based on what I'm seeing, the two samples share remarkable similarities."

She clicked a button, transforming the raw data into what looked like a lie-detector test printout, one line in black, the other in red.

"They both have Y chromosomes," Heather reported. "That means they're both from male subjects."

"I know," Clouse said testily, now that she was treating him like a mentally-stunted child. "Do you have any useful information?"

"These two samples are so similar I'm going on record and saying they're blood relatives. They aren't identical, but they're too similar not to be related."

Clouse looked at the chart, trusting her judgment. Another question crept into his mind.

"Can you tell how old the DNA is?"

Heather looked from him to the samples.

"Particularly the unknown sample," Clouse urged.

"Well, it appears to be in remarkable condition with none of the strands breaking down. To preserve any hair or skin sample that well is practically unheard of, so my guess is the sample is very fresh."

"Thanks," Clouse said, far from emphatically.

"I figured you'd be happy, Paul. Weren't you looking for a match?"

"To be honest, I'm not sure what I was looking for. But thanks just the same."

"Need a printout for your records?"

"Nah. Thanks again, Heather."

"Anytime."

Clouse walked through the open lab, his mind traveling in a dozen directions. He needed to contact Randy Niemeyer, but he had no real answers for the man. Even if Tim Niemeyer were somehow alive, he was now a missing person.

What felt worse was keeping all of his findings from Jane. He wasn't lying to her, but he might as well have been. While she continued to fight the good fight at the clinic, he snuck around like a thief in the night. Granted, he was helping friends, but he hated keeping anything from Jane.

Even after money came into their marriage, they always promised one another to keep the better aspects of their relationship alive and well.

He wanted to tell her everything, only after he knew the absolute truth. If Tim Niemeyer wasn't dead, she would be thrilled for her husband to have one of his best friends back.

Picking up his cell phone to update Randy Niemeyer, Clouse decided it was time to discover who owned the old farmhouse they had trespassed upon.

Chapter 15

Parish accomplished his goal of waking the kids with aromas of fresh pancakes and warmed genuine maple syrup. He even mixed blueberries into the batter without getting any ingredients on his suit.

Wiping their eyes, both Zach and Katie emerged from their separate bedrooms just minutes apart. After washing his hands, Zach jumped into the seat closest to his favorite bodyguard.

"Good morning, sunshine," Parish kidded.

"Hi, Todd."

"Up for some cakes?"

Zach lit up like a bulb, refreshed as though someone had splashed him with cold water.

"Sure."

Parish set down a plate for him as Katie skipped out of her bedroom. She dashed over, giving Parish a hug before seating herself across from Zach.

"Sleep well?" he asked her.

A vigorous nod was her reply.

While they ate breakfast, he turned the television to their favorite morning channel, then placed the dirty dishes into the dishwasher. The family had servants come in once a day to clean, do dishes, and change the linen, but Parish didn't mind passing time by cleaning up after his own messes.

At home he seldom cooked or cleaned, so he dreaded the day when Zach or Katie told his wife about all the wonderful things he did for them.

Parish walked into the main room, turning off a lamp since daylight now streamed in through the outer windows. He walked over to the closest window, peering outside out of curiosity and to randomly scan for danger. The view of the yard provided no action whatsoever.

As he turned around, the sound of the security system being engaged, then the front door swinging open, caught his attention. Figuring Paul or Jane Clouse had returned, he thought little of it until the door smacked audibly against the wall and a darkly-clad figure stood in the threshold just long enough to survey the interior.

Parish instinctively went for his gun, undoing the holster's latch. Based on everything he knew, his heart began racing because the black cloak revealed no form beneath it.

Not even a face.

"Stop right there!" he ordered, which seemed to prompt the opposite response as the figure charged toward him, raising a gleaming dagger in the process.

He barely heard the shrieks of the kids behind him as his fingers wrapped around his Glock 23, pulling it to a ready position, then at chest level for firing. His fingers felt like chewed gum, his body feeling a subdued tingling sensation that came from knowing he might die any second.

Still, Parish remained in control of his actions as the figure crossed the room with such swiftness that he found no time to yell further commands.

He waited until the figure was within five feet of him, the blade raised for a killing blow, before he fired four shots into the stranger's torso. Each shot staggered the would-be assailant, but failed to floor him, much less finish the job.

Parish fired four more shots into the torso, finding a similar result as the figure charged again, then put two into the center of the hood where a face should have been. A strange brown dust spurted from beneath the hood instead of blood. He now had only three bullets left, and no time to reload.

"Get back!" he yelled to the kids as the figure drew close enough to plunge the knife down upon him.

Hoping someone in the hotel had heard the gunshots, he blocked the attack by thrusting both of his arms upward, knocking his attacker and the blade to one side with a swiping motion.

He found just enough time to fire into the hood one more time at close range, watching more brown dust spew toward him while the figure wasn't deterred one second by his retaliation. Parish took hold of the black robe with one hand, grasping the bony hand clasping the knife with the other. He tugged the figure toward him, but a knee rammed into his sternum, knocking the wind from him.

Falling to one knee against an end table, Parish tried to steady himself as he watched Katie shriek in complete fear for his life.

"Todd!"

Based on the desperation in her face, he knew the knife was already coming down with a precisely placed killing blow.

He lurched upward and to one side as the blade plunged down, aimed between his shoulder blades. Knocking the knife aside, he tried to tug the disguise from his assailant, hearing something drop to the floor before the dark figure decided retreat was the better part of valor.

Parish started to give chase before a glance behind him revealed the two children trembling inside the kitchen, more fearful for him than themselves. Both stared with terrified looks between him and the open door as Parish assessed the damage to himself, finding scrapes and a few minor bloody cuts along his wrists. His primary assignment was to protect them at all costs, meaning he couldn't pursue the cloaked figure because it left them at risk.

It took only seconds for footsteps to thump outside the still open door. As his curious colleagues dashed to investigate, Parish knelt beside the fallen object. He found a small, capped bottle with a handkerchief wrapped around its exterior. If not for the thick carpeting, it might have shattered upon impact.

Parish suspected the attacker wanted to subdue the children and abduct them, but he wasn't about to sniff the contents of the bottle. He set it on the nearby end table, careful not to leave too many fingerprints.

"What happened?" Craig Jennings asked from the doorway, two other security members surveying the damage behind him.

"Someone wearing a black costume came in through the door armed with a knife."

"Kicked in the door?" Jennings asked, looking for damage around the frame.

"No. He somehow bypassed the system. I heard it disengage just before the door opened."

"Where'd he go?"

"I don't know. He took off just a few seconds before you guys got here."

Jennings stepped outside, typing a few commands into the terminal. Turning around, he ordered one of his personnel to go through the stairway to begin a search of the grounds for the intruder.

"Call every available security member from French Lick, too," he ordered before the stairwell door closed behind the security guard.

Jennings tapped his foot as he waited, finally staring with disbelief at whatever answer crossed the screen.

"It says Lopez accessed it, Todd. Was it him?"

"I don't know. The guy was wearing a mask and a black costume. But I do know this, Jon Lopez isn't bulletproof."

Parish had no desire to speak with Jennings or anyone else at the moment. His fellow security members had just let a criminal escape so far as he was concerned. No one else showed even remote concern for the kids, but Parish suddenly felt a wave of guilt for neglecting them long enough to acknowledge Jennings' questions.

"You two okay?" he asked, embracing them both.

"Yeah," Zach answered, no stranger to mysterious masked men.

Katie nodded, still sobbing and sniffling.

Behind him, Jennings eyed the bullet casings on the floor.

"How many times did you fire?"

"Eleven. He barely flinched."

"You hit him all eleven times?"

"Yes," Parish answered wearily. "Can we discuss this later, and not in front of the kids?"

Jennings soured as Dan Duncan approached the scene with disbelief. Figuring he was close to trampling a crime scene, the hotel manager stayed in the hallway, peering inside.

"You want to take them downstairs so we can have a look around?" Jennings asked Parish.

"Sure."

Parish stopped briefly to swipe up some of the brown dust from the floor. It wasn't dirt, looking and feeling similar to tropical fish flakes. He grunted to himself then made his way to the door with the kids in tow as one of the other security personnel knelt beside an object several feet outside the door.

"Maybe this explains how he got in," he said, pointing to a severed hand on the ground, a disgusted look crossing his face.

"Jesus," Jennings said, staring at the hand. "None of this makes any sense."

"How's that?" Parish asked, shielding the kids from the reasonably preserved appendage.

"I took Lopez out of the system the morning after he quit."

Parish could tell Jennings was shaken, not just by the hand, but the fact that the hotel he was placed in charge of securing was now compromised.

Worse yet, he had no idea what evil had eluded his staff upon entry and exit.

"We'll talk after I get them to safety," Parish assured the security director.

As he walked the kids to the closest elevator, Parish heard police sirens in the distance. The hotel allowed sound to reverberate throughout its walls, even from outside sources. For the first time he realized just how close to death he had come. Never before had he needed to draw a firearm, much less fire at someone. While that alone bothered him, he wondered why his bullets hadn't done any noteworthy damage to his assailant.

The first bullet alone would have floored any normal human being.

As they stepped into the elevators, Parish put a hand on each of the children's shoulders.

He looked upward for an access hatch, but this elevator lacked one. Perhaps for security reasons, or because repairs were done from a different access point, the elevator was never provided with a secondary egress.

"You two okay?" he asked the kids again.

Both nodded.

"You're sure?"

He knelt down, allowing them both to embrace him, feeling guilty for not stopping the one threat to their well-being.

"Thanks, Todd," Katie said. "I was so worried he was going to get you."

"I'm fine," he answered. "I'm just worried about you guys."

Suspecting he was about to be the man of the hour that everyone wanted answers from, he decided to find the best place and person to watch over the kids. They weren't going to like the idea of leaving him, but part of his duty was to help find the man who broke into the suite.

Chapter 16

The first thing Paul Clouse told Parish when he returned from his trip was that he didn't want the bodyguard to feel like he was being interrogated. Several local cops and deputies, including the sheriff himself, continued to scour the grounds and the hotel for clues related to the attacker.

As Parish sat inside the library on the ground floor, in one of the leather chairs, he couldn't get comfortable. He watched Clouse talk to Daniels, Duncan, and Jennings before entering the room with a local state trooper. Sensing they each wanted to hear what he had to say, perhaps out of suspicion, Parish felt a bit uneasy. He wondered if the hotel's security cameras had caught a glimpse of the mysterious figure, or if the person knew the hotel well enough to entirely avoid detection.

"Can you make sure no one interrupts us?" Clouse asked of Jennings, who immediately put one of his men beside the entrance.

Less than thirty minutes had passed since the shooting, though Jane now remained with the kids after hearing an abbreviated version of the assault. Parish still felt a strange tingling sensation through his veins that came from adrenaline and coming so close to death. He found himself wanting to be home with his family, or anywhere for that matter, except where he worked.

Just time enough to cool off and collect his bearings.

"I only want to hear this once, Todd, and that will suffice for me," Clouse said with compassion, apparently understanding how Parish felt. "I can't thank you enough for protecting the kids the way you did."

"I only wish I could have caught the man, sir."

"You did fine. This is Trooper Collins from the state police."

Parish guessed Collins to be about ten years his senior from his peppered black and gray hair, and a few wrinkles creeping along his forehead. He appeared to be a no-nonsense officer, but lightened up slightly as he opened his notebook.

"I take it you have a permit for the gun," Collins began.

Parish nodded, which sufficed as an answer and proof for the time being.

His permit remained tucked inside his wallet at all times if he needed it.

"Just tell me what happened," Collins said, taking down notes the next ten minutes as Parish recalled the entire morning to the best of his knowledge.

"You're sure all eleven bullets hit the guy? There isn't any blood up there."

"It was point-blank, sir. Whenever I hit him, this weird brown dust spat out from under his cloak."

Parish caught a strange look cross Clouse's face. Though fleeting, it revealed that his boss knew some inside information that worried him.

Since no murder had officially occurred, Parish doubted a forensics unit would be called to the hotel, but he felt a need to mention every last detail. He suspected Clouse might know more about the situation than anyone, but asking his employer for information wasn't wise.

"One of the security cameras had to have picked up something," Parish suggested.

"Mr. Jennings is checking on that," Collins replied.

Parish had to consciously avoid rolling his eyes. He wasn't sure how far he trusted the security director after the way Jennings treated him upstairs.

So far as he knew, Jennings had no children, which explained why he wasn't overly compassionate about the kids, though he seemed almost hostile about Parish's methods. Clouse had a way of keeping things under wraps, so perhaps he wanted Jennings to act dismissing about certain events.

"Is anyone going to notify Jon Lopez's family?"

The trooper shook his head.

"Not yet. We have an arm, and that's all. Even if we verify it's his, we still don't have proof of a murder. I'll update the family when we get more answers."

"This is the opposite of before," Clouse muttered. "Whoever's doing this is trying to keep it under wraps."

"Sir?"

"When I was here working on the hotel, the killer wanted the murders to be public spectacle."

"Because you were being framed, sir," Parish assured him.

"That's true, but I can't figure out what the angle is this time."

Collins asked Parish some additional questions the next ten minutes or so, then left the room to speak with Jennings.

"I can't thank you enough," Clouse said.

"Sir, it's what you hired me for."

"I know, but I was hoping you'd never have to use deadly force."

Clouse tried to force a grin and failed.

"Wishful thinking, I suppose."

"I hit him *eleven* times, sir. Do you know what that thing was up there?"

"Yeah, I think so."

"Was it Dr. Smith? 'Cause I don't believe in the boogeyman."

"As a matter of fact, I think it was."

Clouse didn't get to elaborate as Jennings returned with grim news.

"We caught glimpses of him on the video, but he's wearing the costume every time we see him."

"So there's no way of identifying him," Parish thought aloud.

"We may have some holes in our security," Jennings added. "I deleted Jon Lopez from our system after the gala, but his fingerprints bypassed the door upstairs. Or rather what's left of his hand did."

"Based on what I'm hearing, someone tried to make an attempt to abduct the kids," Clouse stated. "There's only one person who has the motive to carry out such a sneaky plan. You both know who I'm talking about."

Jennings nodded, but Parish had a bit more trouble with such an alien concept as resurrection via cursed object. Hearing the story from Clouse was one thing, like a bedtime fable of sorts, but seeing it for real took some time to digest.

Feeling a bit shaky from the entire experience finally settling into his mind, Parish excused himself before stepping outside to the veranda. He really didn't want to tell his wife the entire story because she worried about him already.

It also validated his family's worries about him taking the job.

Dan Duncan stepped outside behind him, taking his side as they looked into the vast acreage beside the hotel. Parish worried that the man was going to badger him for details, but Duncan had a different agenda.

"I saw that dust up there," he said, though Parish didn't give a response. "It looked very familiar to me."

"Oh?"

"It looked a lot like the scraps of Martin Smith's body we saw a few years back."

"So you're saying we have a living corpse running around here?"

"They never found his body. He either walked out of that mansion or someone carried the body away."

Parish sighed.

"You're not helping me sleep better at night by saying that."

"No one could sleep well after seeing what happened in that mansion. Your buddy Jennings was there."

"Yeah, my buddy."

Duncan gave him a cagy look before looking to the police car parked along the brick driveway. The two men seldom made conversation other than greetings in passing, mainly because hotel employees tended to stick with people from their areas.

"Jennings knows where he's seen that dust before. That's why he's so spooked."

"He seems more irritated than scared. I had coffee with him this morning, and now it's like he blames me for what happened up there."

"Wouldn't you be worried if you were the head of security and something that evil slipped by your defenses?"

Parish shrugged.

"I suppose."

He looked behind him to make certain no one was eavesdropping.

"Why take this job, Dan? After everything that happened, why not distance yourself from it?"

"There comes a time when we all have to come home. I think you can relate to that."

Parish nodded.

"There's an attraction to this place," Duncan continued. "Maybe that's why our boss can't get away from it. He's tried, but in the end, you get drawn back to it. For us, it took getting away for a few years, but for him it's an albatross that he just can't drop."

"Why would Smith want to come back from the dead if he was going to look like a corpse?"

"The act of living is more important to some people than how we live. Maybe his plan got screwed up along the way. The point is the man may very well be back, and that means we're all in real danger."

Parish looked down to the Glock holstered at his side, not feeling nearly as secure as he had that morning. Despite the fact he had his own family to worry about, he wasn't going to sacrifice Katie or Zach to a madman, whether it be Smith or some other schemer.

"What about you?" Parish asked Duncan. "You don't need the money, do you? And yet you're here."

"Like I said, we all come home eventually. I'll stick it out since all of you burly guys are here to protect me."

Parish chuckled.

"Yeah. As soon as we figure out how to defend ourselves."

***

Clouse viewed the video recordings with Jennings by his side. One of the other security force members punched buttons on the main console to provide them with every view, every glimpse of the cloaked figure as he moved through the halls.

Much of the security hub was adjacent to Jennings' office, including the small, dark room in which they now stood.

"How could no one see him?" Clouse wondered aloud. "How could no one report him?"

"Most of the guests were checking out, or in the atrium," Jennings answered. "People never take the stairs anymore, so the chances of anyone seeing him were slim."

Over the next few minutes Clouse watched the figure glide through the hall at a quick, determined pace. Not once did any flesh, or any clues, show from beneath the black disguise. Black gloves covered the hands, a mask hid the face, and even the attacker's footwear remained beneath the cloth at all times.

Jennings had his employee slow down the video, to a crawl at some points, to no avail. No distinguishing clues surfaced regarding the figure's identity.

"He knew not only the layout, but how to bypass two different security checkpoints," Clouse surmised. "There's a good chance he works somewhere in this building."

"Or knows someone who feeds him the information," Jennings suggested.

"I need you to check and recheck every application and interview, Craig, even outside of your department."

"What about department heads?"

"I'll go through those with you. It may get to the point where we have to start interviewing staff."

Jennings turned to the man stationed at the console.

"Keep your eyes peeled, and let me know if you turn up anything else."

"Yes, sir."

Clouse walked with his security director to a nearby unoccupied lounge.

"How could someone alter your computer system, Craig?"

"It's possible they didn't alter it so much as dig Lopez's deleted file from the computer trash bin."

"Wouldn't that require someone getting into your computer?"

"More than likely, yes. It would also require the perpetrator to have extensive knowledge about computer hard drives."

Jennings realized Clouse was shooting him a questioning stare.

"My office isn't impossible for other people to get into, Mr. Clouse."

"I know. Sorry."

An uncomfortable moment of silence passed.

"I'll, uh, start searching through those applications."

"Thanks, Craig. I've got to see the kids and make sure they're holding up."

Clouse headed toward the elevator, ready to give Jane a break. His head spun with the day's events overwhelming his senses. Jane suspected he was hiding information from her, but there hadn't been time to confide in her. Clouse was done avoiding the horrible truths surfacing around him, but he still had no definite answers for anyone.

Chapter 17

Gina Terrell whistled to herself as she worked in the hotel's basement, which now consisted of three conference rooms, a common hallway, and a kitchenette. Filled out by a few storage areas and a custodial closet, the basement no longer possessed the industrialized look it had before Paul Clouse's complete restoration.

During the warm season the veranda could easily be transformed into an outdoor eating venue suitable for business or pleasure, but the conference rooms provided year-round service. Not only did businesses convene at the hotel, but wedding receptions, retirement celebrations, and birthday parties easily fit into the rooms.

Today Gina had to set up one of the rooms for a convention coming into town the next morning. While she didn't prepare any of the meals, she needed to make certain the room held enough tables and chairs for people and props. Reading over the submitted needs list, she started moving electronics and a laptop computer from the normally locked supply room onto carts, then wheeled them into the conference room.

After attaining a two-year degree in hosting and catering, she worked a number of odd jobs before landing her current position at the hotel. Despite having to work under someone who held the position she truly wanted, Gina plugged away at her duties, hoping to advance at one of Clouse's hotels.

Jobs in Orange County remained scarce, despite the casino's arrival. It turned out people didn't flock to the area to gamble so much as they wanted to see the historic hotels. The luster faded rather quickly once people stayed at the hotel or toured the grounds.

One of the wheels on her small cart squeaked as she pushed the cart into the conference room. The past hour she had been below ground level, working and planning. Fueled by an energy drink purchased at one of the upstairs shops hours prior, Gina planned to head upstairs for a snack and some daylight shortly.

Parking the cart just inside the door, she unloaded the equipment, setting it in specified designated places before plugging in and testing each component. Within minutes she had the room looking perfect for the next morning.

As Gina wheeled the cart toward the storage closet, she heard something aside from its squeaking wheel.

"Hello?" she called. "Who's there?"

The noise sounded like a thump, perhaps a door closing or someone taking a heavy step down the hall.

Gina slowly peered around the closet door, looking for the noise's source.

Her heart nearly stopped when a uniformed man easily old enough to be her father surprised her simply by standing there. He hadn't attempted to frighten her, but he hadn't announced his presence, either.

"Sorry, young lady," he said with a courteous nod. "I'm Sheriff Brown. You seen anything unusual down here?"

"No. It's just been me down here the past hour or so."

She sensed he wasn't paying a casual visit.

"Something wrong?"

Brown seemed to craft his words before answering.

"Nothing for you to worry about. We had an intruder in the hotel earlier and I was just checking that everyone was okay."

"Everything's good down here," Gina answered with more of a giggle than she intended to give.

She attributed her behavior to the unexpected police presence in the basement of all places.

"Mind if I have a look around?" Brown asked.

Gina shrugged.

"Be my guest. I just work here."

Chuckling lightly, the sheriff began going through the rooms, looking up and down, under tables, and inside all of the storage closets. Gina followed him closely, worried that he found it necessary to conduct such a thorough scouring of the premises.

She knew a simple intruder wouldn't warrant the sheriff's personal appearance.

A few minutes later he had checked every inch of the downstairs area, though Gina remained somewhat concerned.

"Looks clear," Brown said, starting for the stairwell.

"Are you sure?"

"Yeah," the sheriff said with a forced smile. "Sorry to have disturbed you."

Brown gave an informal wave then returned upstairs.

Breathing a sigh of relief, Gina returned to the room she had been preparing, noticing a second, larger cart inside the room wasn't parallel to the wall as it had been. Brown's investigation of the room was quick, and she didn't recall him checking the cart at all.

A bit shook up by the search and the likelihood a dangerous trespasser might still be on the grounds, she cautiously took a step toward the cart. She noticed brown speckles lining the light carpeting at the cart's base. An alarm sounded in the back of her mind that something wasn't right. Still at the threshold of the room, Gina raced toward the stairwell, then upstairs to find Brown or another officer.

When the sheriff returned with her, he took her threat seriously enough to rush directly to the cart and check the dust. A concerned look crossed his face as he studied the mysterious substance.

"What is it?" Gina asked.

"We need to get upstairs," Brown said as he stood, right hand placed atop his holstered firearm to undo the latch.

It seemed Gina's fears were justified as the sheriff escorted her upstairs, radioing for backup.

It took another five minutes for several officers to search the downstairs once again as Gina waited with fellow employees who hounded her with questions. She basically shrugged off their inquiries, uncertain of what exactly happened earlier in the suite.

When she finally asked someone, the answers were varied and vague, but she knew one of Clouse's bodyguards had fought off an attacker using his firearm.

Finally the officers returned, shaking their heads with exasperated expressions. Hearing some of their mumbles, Gina got the impression the dangerous person had indeed been downstairs, but disappeared at some point.

"Wow," one of her coworkers said. "You could've died."

***

Though Clouse offered Parish the remainder of the day off, the bodyguard vehemently refused, wanting to stay near the kids until his shift ended. While Parish took the kids to the indoor swimming pool, Clouse found himself at the mercy of his wife, who wasn't happy about being shielded from the truth.

He wished Parish could have whisked him away to the safe haven downstairs, because he knew he was about to feel his wife's wrath.

"I want you to tell me what's been going on right now," Jane demanded as they stood inside their suite on the sixth floor.

She didn't know every secret he'd kept during the past week, but the security members blabbed enough to give her a good idea about the localized problems.

"We think someone killed Jon Lopez and used his credentials to bypass the security system. That same person tried to take the kids."

"Who? Who would want the kids?"

Clouse paced between the large family room and the kitchen, praying it wasn't the obvious choice. He knew Jane suspected the same answer, though she waited for confirmation from him before stating her opinion.

"They never found Smith's body last year, Jane. We both know that."

She shook her head, trying to buck the notion that their nemesis reared his ugly head once more.

"He has a knack for returning from the dead, doesn't he?" Jane questioned, turning from her husband to look at the door the attacker came through.

"Yes, he does."

Clouse looked guiltily toward the floor, which his wife caught when she turned around.

"That's not everything, though, is it?"

"No, it's not."

Jane waited patiently, because he couldn't bring himself to begin such an unbelievable tale easily. He revealed the entire saga concerning Tim Niemeyer, the million dollars, and the farmhouse, to his wife over the course of the next ten minutes.

"And it never occurred to you that this might be something important enough to tell me so I could help you?" she asked when he finally finished.

"Of course it occurred to me. I just didn't want to worry you about something that may or may not have been an issue."

"And Ray's death? Is that tied into all of this?"

"I'm sure it is, but I can't figure out why someone killed him. Maybe Tackett will."

"Maybe it's time we reconsidered the way we live."

"We've been through this before," Clouse said, exasperated. "Running from our problems isn't going to help."

"I'm actually talking about doing the opposite. Maybe Ray got too close to the truth so someone wanted him silenced. If he can find the truth, so can we."

Clouse took his wife's hand. He loved and admired her fighting spirit, but worried about the kids constantly when danger surrounded them.

"We can't let this go further than it has today," Jane insisted. "We're not going to attract guests with gunshots echoing in the hotel on a regular basis."

"You want to move out?"

"No. The kids are happy. We're not moving them again."

"I can increase security up here. Maybe Troy will let us peek at the files in Ray's office so we can get to the bottom of all of this."

Jane's look soured.

"I don't think Troy is your biggest fan right now. We're going to have to do this ourselves."

"I'm no investigator, dear."

"Neither am I, but we have some good contacts and we know how to do research."

"Thank God for college, I guess."

Jane slid her fingers under his shirt collar, pulling him close.

"Am I forgiven?" he asked.

"Maybe. I just don't want you thinking I'm a fragile flower needing to be locked in a case."

"Never," he said, gently kissing her lips. "I just don't want anything happening to you and the kids."

"Then keep me informed."

"Yes, dear. I'll do better."

Chapter 18

Daniels left work earlier than usual, despite the day's events at the hotel. It was his night to pick up the kids, whom he planned to keep during his two scheduled off days from work.

He met Cindy, his ex-wife, at a community soccer field just outside of Bloomington to watch their daughter play against kids from another school. While Renee warmed up for the game, Daniels sat at a picnic table with Cindy, monitoring their nearly five-year-old son as he played in a nearby sandbox with other children.

Now in his early forties, Daniels had no regrets about waiting as long as he had for marriage and children, though the divorce hit him hard. Financially, he felt secure, but emotionally he missed coming home from work and seeing his entire family waiting for him. Blaming no one except himself, he knew his emotional distance throughout some of the rougher times of his police career forced Cindy's hand.

They remained amicable after the separation and even the court proceedings went reasonably well. Thanks to Paul Clouse buying them a waterfront property some years prior for summer retreats, they each had a place to stay that remained familiar to both children.

Still able to talk about many of the things they discussed in marriage, they sometimes seemed on the verge of old times.

"So how are things at work?" Cindy asked after a few minutes of occasional waves to Renee.

At age eight she wanted the attention of both parents, and wanted them back together.

"Not so good lately."

"Oh?"

"The problems around Paul just never seem to go away."

Daniels hated speaking more than necessary, which possibly expedited the communication rifts between them in marriage. While a detective, he carried a heavy burden alone, refusing to talk about the cases that plagued his mind. He thought working in the casino would provide him a different way of seeking justice, but it didn't provide the same rush.

While he went home every night without seeing dead bodies or the worst society had to offer, the thrill of the hunt was gone.

Along with his wife.

"What's wrong this time?"

"I'm not quite sure. His private investigator was killed and today we had a shooting at West Baden."

"A shooting?"

"One of Paul's bodyguards fired at an intruder, but it gets worse. We think the intruder killed someone on the hotel security force."

A look of concern crossed Cindy's face, but she turned away before he could read very deeply into her thoughts. Her blond hair, nearly a cream color in the afternoon sunlight, danced across her shoulders as she turned to watch Renee a moment.

"Are you in danger?" she asked without looking at him.

"No more than I've ever been," he answered with an intentionally vague air. "Paul's trying to keep things under wraps, but we're all afraid it has something to do with Smith."

"You won't quit the casino, will you?"

"Where would I go? I quit my city job, remember? Besides, I'm sticking with Paul. He's the one who got me through some tough times."

Cindy appeared genuinely concerned.

"He's also the one who brought a lot of problems into your life. *Our* lives. You spent a year in a wheelchair for him, Mark."

"I think he's made restitutions enough for my losses. It's the reason we each have a house right now."

Silence filled the air between them momentarily. They watched Renee in a sea of uniforms volleying for control of the soccer ball before Cindy finally spoke.

"I just can't help but think things would have been different between us if..."

"If what?"

"If you had never investigated Angie Clouse's murder."

"It's a little late for all of that now. Back then I was a rookie detective looking to make some points with my supervisors."

He recalled Paul Clouse's first wife being butchered in her own kitchen on Halloween night, six years prior. A grisly scene with lots of blood, deep penetrating wounds, and no sign of forced entry led detectives to believe they were witnessing a crime of passion.

The type of crime only an estranged husband might commit.

Daniels waited a moment, letting the feeling of uneasiness between them remain somewhat unsettled.

"What about us, Cindy? Where exactly do we stand?"

During the past two years neither of them had dated steadily, both too busy with work and raising the kids. Daniels had never fully gotten over his ex-wife, and suspected her feelings might be similar.

She looked at him questioningly. He seldom spoke from the heart, and hardly ever about them as a couple. On the outside, he remained a rock the past two years, but his mental state resembled the durability of an egg yolk inside a thin shell.

"Is this really the place you want to talk about this?"

A defensive move on her part, he figured, to avoid speaking her true feelings.

"When else do we get to talk?"

She turned from him, only slowly returning her attention to him.

"You said I was too distant when you left me," Daniels said, deciding to admit entire truths he hadn't even allowed himself to contemplate since Cindy left him. "I know I wasn't always there for you, and you put a lot of effort into getting me healed after I was shot, and maybe I never thanked you properly."

"You thanked me, but I wasn't sure you really meant it."

"Of course I meant it," Daniels said, insulted by Cindy's words.

"That came out wrong. You meant it, but you never fully appreciated my efforts. Night after night I spent hours with you trying to get you better and you kept to yourself."

"I'm sorry. That was a low point for me, not being able to work or provide for all of you."

"So you kept to yourself more than ever, isolating me and the kids. Not exactly one of your shining moments as a husband or father."

"I can only say I'm sorry so many times, Cindy."

"But you should have said it before."

Daniels sighed, looking out to the field momentarily.

"So where does that leave us now? Do we stay in relationship limbo forever, or do we move forward?"

"Move forward?" Cindy asked somewhat sternly. "I thought the divorce papers said we were moving forward."

Daniels chuckled, though he didn't feel very comical at the moment.

"You're the one going through a mid-life crisis, Mark," Cindy continued like a mother lion going in for the kill. "Sports cars, new clothes, you've even changed your look. It seems you've moved on just fine."

"No," he freely admitted. "Not really. All those years I ate bag lunches and drove the worst personal vehicle of anyone on the department, so we could have a nice house for us and the kids. I just wanted to live a little, to see how it felt. And now that I know, I miss the way things were between us."

"You're not the same person I married, Mark. This thing with Paul, it's...darkened you."

Daniels started to reply, then caught the meaning of what Cindy said. Until he broke away from Clouse, or made certain his friend's problems were forever gone, he would never truly live a normal life.

Taking a deep breath, he watched his son throw sand around the sandbox, wondering how much more of his own life he dared sacrifice before he felt his friend had been repaid for his kindness.

***

Once things settled down for the evening, Clouse entered the hotel's garden for some fresh air. He had long since grown accustomed to the old buildings around him. Flowers and shrubs came and went every year, but the buildings remained a testament to the hotel's origins and durability.

A quiet night at the hotel, the only activity around him came from the veranda where a local company held an employee banquet beneath the awning. Several mosquitos buzzed throughout the area, but even they weren't intrusive enough to prevent the laughter and open conversation on the veranda.

Clouse wondered how much longer business would flock to his hotels if word spread about Jon Lopez's possible death and the other strange events. Lots of positive public relations gave the area a friendly face once again, so the last thing he needed was for his efforts to go bottom up like fish in polluted water.

Something felt different about this wave of terror. Before, the murders were all about creating panic and tragic news to scare away hotel ownership. This time someone was being sneaky, which meant the actions so far were likely part of a larger plan. Clouse didn't take well to someone attempting to abduct his son and stepdaughter.

He had already ordered Jennings to tighten security on the sixth floor, especially around the children.

In the morning he planned to call for a management meeting, hoping to keep Jennings, Duncan, and their crews upbeat. Luckily, most guests were in the atrium, or outside, when the gunfire erupted that morning. Most of them either didn't hear the shots, or mistook them for something else, since the sixth floor was redone with practically soundproof materials.

He also planned on talking or meeting with Randy Niemeyer for an update on the trooper's end.

Clouse looked up at the hotel, knowing two security members stood outside his door to keep Jane and the kids safe. He hated living like a celebrity because everyone viewed him as vain and shallow with security everywhere. Perhaps living in the hotel wasn't the most sensible thing to do, but he still felt safer being constantly surrounded by people.

As the lobby door closest to the road opened, Clouse noticed one of his security people stepping outside, holding his radio near his mouth. Though he couldn't make out what the man said into the mouthpiece, he decided it looked important. The security member never took his eyes off the brick path leading to the highway.

"Something wrong?" Clouse asked, approaching the man.

"Nothing to worry about," the guard answered hastily before recognizing the man who signed his checks. "Oh, sorry, Mr. Clouse. We have report of a disruption near the road. Someone found a man lying face down beside the highway."

"I'll walk with you," Clouse said, all the while thinking he didn't need any more bodies popping up like weeds to strangle his chances of running a successful hotel.

Neither exactly walked, taking up a steady jog toward the road where a small band of people gathered around a prone body. In the darkness Clouse struggled to make out any details as the person came to, quelling some of his worst fears. He and the security guard knelt down beside the man dressed in tattered clothes.

Only a nearby street lamp provided lighting, leaving more shadows than details.

Someone had cradled the fallen man enough to keep his back off the hard concrete and gravel in the vacated parking lot. When the man slowly turned his head toward Clouse, he posed a dazed look while Clouse stared in complete shock. A few seconds later, the man seemed to recognize him as well, though he still appeared dazed.

A babe in the woods after five years of being absent from the real world.

Clouse knew that despite a much different outward appearance, this was one of his best friends.

"Tim?"

Chapter 19

Clouse immediately had his friend brought upstairs to the sixth floor. Several guest rooms were readily available, so he ordered soup and snacks from the kitchen, extra blankets, and bathroom items. While security and housekeeping helped get his friend into bed, Clouse personally called Randy Niemeyer to tell him the news.

It took only two rings for Niemeyer to answer.

"We still on for tomorrow morning?"

"I think you might want to push our meeting up a little."

The few seconds of silence probably left Niemeyer wondering why or how they could meet any sooner than the next morning.

"You're not going to believe who showed up on the hotel doorstep," Clouse said.

"Please tell me you're not fucking with me."

Clouse had never heard the man more excited than at this moment.

"I'm not messing with you. You probably want to get down here, Randy."

"Lights and siren, Paul."

"Don't get yourself killed. I've got Tim upstairs, surrounded by the girls from housekeeping and some burly fellows who won't let any harm come to him."

Clouse heard some shuffling, then something break, as Niemeyer hurriedly got his belongings together for the trip to West Baden.

"I can't believe this. I absolutely can't, Paul."

"You were the one who believed harder than any of us."

"I know, I know. Has he said anything?"

Clouse looked across the hallway where Tim was being fully attended to in bed.

"No. He's been in and out of consciousness the whole time. He either walked here, or someone gave him the boot at the hotel entrance. Jane's going to evaluate him to see if he needs hospitalization or not."

"Sounds good. Thanks for everything, Paul. I'm on my way."

Niemeyer indeed sounded rushed, and thrilled.

As Clouse handed the phone to one of the security members standing outside his own doorway, he walked down the hall to check on his friend.

Much like the video, Niemeyer had a full beard, though he didn't appear starved by any means. His captors apparently hadn't been too abusive, though only Niemeyer could judge the treatment he received.

Clouse shook his head, still thinking it impossible for Niemeyer to be alive. The man's own brother had watched him receive countless, vicious stab wounds from six assailants. The coroner said twenty-two stab wounds to be exact, but one coroner had been on Martin Smith's payroll during that period.

"There has to be an explanation," Clouse muttered to himself, doubting the Lawrence County coroner had also been purchased by Smith's millions.

Within a few minutes everyone left the room, returning to their normal duties, once Niemeyer had everything an ill guest might need. Jane checked his temperature, looked him over, took some vitals with her medical equipment, then looked to her husband.

"He seems to be in reasonably good health," she reported. "Maybe a bit dehydrated and in major need of a bath, but he should be fine."

Clouse said nothing, simply staring at his old friend.

"You look like you want to ask how he can possibly be alive," Jane noted.

"I want to ask just that," he answered numbly. "Has he woke up at all?"

"No, but his pupils look fine, so there's no obvious head trauma or drugging that I can tell."

"Can I have a few minutes with him?"

"Sure."

Clouse felt as though he were asking to see a dying relative for the last time, rather than welcoming a friend back to the world of the living.

Sitting beside the bed, he looked Niemeyer over, seeing his friend had lost minimal weight, and quite a bit of his hair. Other than the full beard, only a very thick fringe of hair remained on his head. He smelled terrible, which could be attributed to limited or no showers the past five years. Clouse's years on the fire department brought him into close contact with plenty of body odor, among other things, so everything about his friend's condition appeared genuine.

Clouse had little doubt his friend had indeed lived and grown older the past five years, but where, and why?

Questions flooded his mind, but the one man who could answer them lie asleep only a few feet away.

"I wish you could tell me what happened to you, my friend."

Niemeyer began to stir, pulling a blanket up to him before rolling to one side. Clouse took this as a good sign that his friend was indeed resting comfortably. No one saw how he ended up beside the highway, but one of the security men surmised that he wasn't there long.

He half expected his friend to wake up and converse with him as though everything was normal, but light snoring sounds echoed throughout the room instead. Clouse stood, walking out of the room where his wife stood waiting for him.

"That's a good sign, isn't it?" he asked, referring to Niemeyer's restful slumber. Jane nodded.

"God, where has he been?"

"I don't know," Jane said, taking his hand, "but I can tell you're glad he's back."

"It's like getting a chance at redemption."

"What happened to him wasn't your fault. You've got to let that go."

"I know," he said, still trying to convince himself of that fact. "I'm just glad for Randy."

A short time later, Niemeyer's younger brother arrived at the hotel, immediately brought to the top floor by security as Clouse instructed. Clouse gave him a brief narrative about how Tim was found near the road, and what they had done for him.

"Thanks for taking such good care of him," Randy said with a grateful look as his eyes misted slightly.

"No problem. It's probably best to leave him here for the night. You're more than welcome to stay with him, if you like."

After a moment of thought, Randy nodded in agreement.

"I can call into work tomorrow and stay with him. I've got some vacation time banked."

"I didn't think you new guys got vacations."

Randy grinned.

"Comp time, actually. The state doesn't like paying out actual cash to its employees for overtime."

"I can put a bed or sofa in there if you want," Clouse suggested.

"That would be great."

Randy looked at his brother momentarily, then to Clouse.

"I told you he was alive," he said, beaming like a kid on Christmas morning. "This is an absolute miracle."

Clouse didn't necessarily agree. Nothing about Tim's death seemed farfetched or potentially false. So if his friend truly died, only one thing, an evil object at that, could have brought him back.

"I know this is a terrible time to ask this, but that Halloween night when you and Tim went out…"

"He was stabbed," Randy said, painfully closing his eyes, "*so* many times. I saw the look on his face when he slumped against the trunk."

"Back then you had no doubt, right?"

"None. I saw my brother die that night, but I've heard things, rumors, about Smith and the things he did."

Clouse shook his head.

"Yeah. He was a piece of work."

Noticing Jane waiting behind him, he decided to leave the brothers together, though he desperately wanted to be there when Tim awoke to ask what felt like a thousand questions.

"I'll have the staff move a bed in here for you, Randy."

"Thanks. Thanks for everything."

"You're welcome. I can't wait to talk to him again."

"Me too. It's just going to be weird for him since the rest of the world's moved on."

Rumors occasionally reached Clouse's little world, including the one about Niemeyer's widow remarrying a few years prior. No one blamed her. She moved on, finding someone new who apparently treated the two kids like his own.

"Well, good night, Randy."

"See you both in the morning. And thanks again."

Clouse nodded, taking his wife's hand as they returned to their own suite to retire for the evening.

Chapter 20

Distant sounds of rolling thunder woke Clouse early the next morning. A subdued purple glow crept around the window blinds, barely illuminating his bedroom. Yawning to himself, he carefully left Jane sleeping as he walked into the marble-tiled bathroom, closing the door for a quick shower.

He quietly dressed, then walked through the living area of the suite to check on the Niemeyer brothers. As he stepped out of the main door, however, he found Todd Parish carrying a coffee mug, about to start his workday. Another security member stood silently near the elevator, down the hall.

An awkward few seconds passed between them.

"Good morning, Todd."

"Morning, sir. One of the guys told me we have additional guests up here."

"The situation has grown a bit more...complicated."

Parish nodded.

"Let me know if you need anything, sir."

"Thanks, Todd. I think the kids will be plenty happy to see you when they get up."

Parish started to step inside, hesitating momentarily instead.

"I heard there was a staff meeting this morning."

"Mostly management stuff. No need for you to worry about it. We're going to discuss what happened yesterday, and how to keep it under wraps. And how to prevent it from happening again."

Raising an eyebrow, the bodyguard seemed to have his own theory.

"Have you looked within our extended family here?"

Clouse dreaded the idea of someone on his payroll plotting against him, but that possibility was precisely why he ordered Jennings to redo background checks on everyone.

"I'm examining every angle, believe me."

"Very well, sir."

Parish accessed the security panel, letting himself into the suite while Clouse peered into the other room. Randy Niemeyer kept watch over his brother, beginning to look exhausted from the past week's toll on his sleep time.

"You been up all night?" Clouse asked.

"I drifted off a few times. Tim hasn't woken up yet."

"He's been through a lot. You want some breakfast?"

Randy appeared torn, half-starved, but not wanting to leave his brother's side.

"I can have the staff bring it up."

"I hate to be any trouble."

"You're not. I feel a lot better with Tim staying here until we know something more about what's going on. That means you're welcome to whatever you need as well."

Clouse walked into the room, looking down at Tim momentarily. He appeared to have better color than the night before, still sleeping peacefully in the bed.

"I think he'll be fine, Randy. God only knows what happened to him before he ended up here."

"I've had a lot of time to think about that. He wasn't at that house when we looked, but he probably wasn't wandering the streets, either."

"Maybe he was dropped off somewhere."

Dropped off, perhaps, but before or after Nathan Runnels died was the question in his mind.

"What did you find out about your old buddy from the state police?"

"Glad you asked. Not my buddy, by the way. It seems he owned the property in question that we visited. He was probably holding Tim all this time, but I can't understand why he waited so long to blackmail you."

"People don't quit their jobs unless there's better money somewhere else, Randy. My guess is Tim was someone's insurance policy, but maybe that deal went south, or Runnels free-lanced to build his own stash."

"Then why fake Tim's death?"

Clouse cleared his throat, indicating he didn't find accuracy in Randy's last statement.

"What? He *was* killed?"

"You tell me. You were there when it happened."

"And it was very convincing. Blood everywhere, Tim's expression when he slumped against the truck, six knives with his blood on them."

It pained Randy to relive the tale, so he squeezed his brother's hand lightly.

"Smith had ways of making things happen," Clouse explained. "Things you couldn't imagine."

"Like killing people and bringing them back?"

"Easier than faking it, I suppose, but I'm not going to dwell on it. We have Tim back, and that's what counts."

Clouse stepped out of the room, calling downstairs for a breakfast delivery to the sixth floor. He then informed the security guard near the elevator about the impending delivery.

"You need a phone to call your bosses?" he asked Randy when he returned.

"I took care of it already."

Oblivious to the world around him, Tim continued to snore lightly, then adjusted his position under the covers.

"I feel like a peeping tom," Clouse said.

"So do I, but I'm just so worried, like I might lose him again."

Clouse chuckled, recalling days gone by.

"He always snored during our sleep overs and kept me and Ken awake."

"Yeah, I remember those weekends when you guys were out having fun and I was stuck at home."

"Ken was always the troublemaker. The ones who become cops are always the wild ones."

Randy shot him a quizzical look.

"Was I that wild?"

"Nah. You were a farm kid. You guys got your asses beat if you got too far out of line."

"Tim was always the industrious one, but he was a straight arrow."

"Except when Ken got him drinking."

"Tim drank?" Randy asked with genuine surprise.

"Only when Ken badgered him for hours on end. He was funny when we got a couple beers in him, but he got mean, too."

"Really?"

"Not toward us, but other people. It was no big deal. You know Tim was always a big teddy bear."

"It's why I missed him so much. These last five years have been unbearable."

"Yeah. I can relate."

Clouse heard the elevator ding behind him, deciding to call his meeting a bit early. If he managed to get Duncan and Jennings on the same page, their staffs would follow suit. He wanted heightened alertness without complete panic.

"Your breakfast is here," he said, thumbing behind him. "I'll see you in a bit. Jane will probably want to check on Tim when she wakes up."

"Okay. Thanks again for everything."

"You don't have to thank me. I owe Tim more than you'll ever know."

***

"Where are we with the background checks?" Clouse asked Jennings once Duncan joined them in a basement meeting room.

"I'm not seeing any red flags, at least not with my people."

"Dan?"

Duncan shrugged helplessly.

"I haven't had time to look through all of mine with getting your suite repaired and talking to the cops. I'll get on it today."

"Please do. I want things to look business as usual around here, but security has to be stepped up. As you both might have heard, I have an important guest staying on the sixth floor."

They swapped questioning looks as though they had no previous knowledge of Tim Niemeyer's stay.

"Craig, you're authorized to use whatever overtime and extra personnel you need until further notice," Clouse said, wasting little time so he could check on his friend sooner.

"We have three casino tour groups here tonight, and four down the road," Duncan stated. "Anything special you want done?"

"No. Just take care of our guests as usual and keep them safe. I want someone attentive monitoring those cameras at all times."

Police unofficially matched the dusty particles in the basement to those found in the suite. While they were being sent to the state police lab for analysis, the sheriff felt that they looked and felt like dead skin.

A strange, deathly odor accompanied the particles as well.

Unfortunately, authorities never figured out where the intruder went, or anything about his identity.

"Based on items left at the scene yesterday, the police believe the intruder meant to abduct my children," Clouse said, confirming what his two employees already knew.

They, too, had spoken with the authorities.

Duncan cleared his throat uncomfortably, causing Jennings to peer his way before looking to their employer.

"We had a little talk after the shooting yesterday," Jennings revealed. "Those particles looked an awful lot like Smith's corpse in that mansion a few years back."

"But that's preposterous," Clouse uttered before realizing he didn't mean the words he said.

Not after what he'd experienced.

"I've heard the accounts," he said after collecting his thoughts. "I'm not ruling out that Smith could actually be among us, but if Bell brought him back to life two years ago, why is he still a dusty bag of bones?"

"Maybe it's a message," Duncan suggested.

"Could you have them check it against Smith's DNA?" Jennings asked.

"If I want to get thrown into a padded room."

Jennings tapped his pen against the table momentarily.

"Everyone knows about the killer garb, but only a handful of us know about what happened at that mansion two years ago."

"Some of us were indisposed," Duncan grumbled.

"The intruder wore gloves, so there weren't fingerprints," Clouse said, steering their conversation toward a conclusion. "I'm not going to assume anything about my new enemy, but I do know vigilant eyes will be a better deterrent than crowding every hallway with our people."

"The news people have been calling," Duncan said. "I've been stalling, but I need to tell them something official about yesterday before the police reports become public."

"Keep it simple, Dan. Tell them we had an intruder and shots were fired, but the man got away. If they want to pursue it, have them talk to the sheriff. Brown doesn't give out information easily."

Jennings held up a newspaper from Louisville, which contained nothing about the incident on the front page.

"We're lucky this isn't exactly the news capital of Southern Indiana."

Some towns had their own newspapers, but a lot of people received printed and television news from Kentucky, which occasionally helped mask some of the unfavorable events at the hotel.

Clouse had trained Duncan and his other manager to seek out the media for any newsworthy public relations events on either property. He continually fought to erase the negative events from public memory since taking over operations at West Baden.

He figured the rumors and memories compounded one another, making both nearly impossible to forget.

"I've got to assume the person who murdered my private investigator in Bloomington is the same person who lopped off Jon Lopez's hand and tried to take my kids, guys. He doesn't want attention, which means we really have to look for any indications he's here. Dan, that starts with you reviewing your personnel, and Craig, with you making your men aware of the situation. I'll talk with Mark about his people, but my focus is here. Remember, no panic."

Both men nodded.

"Good. Then I'll let you get to work."

Clouse stood from the table, staring to the area where the dusty specks were found. He sensed the strange events were quickly culminating toward an unfavorable ending. Despite overcoming the odds in the past, Clouse knew his luck couldn't last forever.

He exited the room, ready to see if his friend was awake and talking.

Chapter 21

Troy Tackett had spent much of his morning sifting through the paperwork removed from Raymond Bloom's office. The person who ransacked the office did an excellent job, he assessed, of strewing the notes so they made little sense when examined individually.

Fueled by coffee, Tackett sat at his desk, continuing to rummage through the three stacks of files and papers removed from the crime scene.

Bloom's sister noted that his trusty briefcase was nowhere to be found when she came into the office for an interview. Though the messy conditions made it near impossible for an outsider to determine the office's state, she told Tackett nothing else appeared to be missing through misty eyes.

Despite Bloom's occupation, no one knew of any major enemies. Most of his cases were high dollar, both in his fees and the clients he represented. Rich people, whether employers or the exposed victims, didn't tend to seek retribution, for fear of worse consequences and exposure.

Based on the private investigator's scribbles, Tackett discovered the man had tracked a dozen mysterious deaths in Indiana and neighboring states. It appeared Clouse had also asked him to track the whereabouts and activities of the mansion incident survivors.

Considering two of them now worked for him, it seemed Clouse had adapted a motto of keeping his potential enemies closer than his friends.

Feeling a bit overwhelmed by all of the names and dates logged into Bloom's notes, Tackett tried doing background checks to the best of his ability. He didn't particularly want to contact Clouse, partly for personal reasons, but also because he couldn't rule out his former neighbor as a suspect.

He doubted Clouse had any part in Bloom's murder, but he couldn't officially prove or disprove hunches without solid evidence.

Bloom apparently spent very little time researching the mansion survivors, ruling out most of them except for two.

Jana Privett and Dave McCully.

His notes indicated Jana worked for the man responsible for the fiasco at the mansion, a murderer of at least three people, though she denied having any prior knowledge of his homicidal tendencies. Witness accounts said she fought valiantly to save her own life, as well as twelve others. She moved away from Indiana after a brief meeting with Clouse and his wife.

Tackett found it interesting that Bloom noted the meeting, perhaps to create a time line, or to cover Clouse from future lawsuits.

McCully's name had some interesting notions sketched beside and below it. A fairly successful man in his own right, the bluegrass singer had recorded several albums with his family and on his own. Several survivors testified to him having, or claiming to have, some form of psychic abilities.

Tackett grunted at the thought, not being one to believe in psychic abilities, ghosts, or monsters. The only monsters he'd ever encountered could be arrested, thumped, or killed. While one such person nearly took his life in an Ohio restroom, Tackett found some comfort in knowing that man was six feet below a tombstone.

Unlike Clouse, he didn't necessarily believe anyone could return from the dead. Tackett required visual proof, like Clouse and others claimed to have, before believing urban legends.

Regardless of what he believed, the detective required facts, including strong motive, to discover who murdered Ray Bloom.

Based on the attack perpetrated through the second story window, Tackett had to suspect the killer wasn't welcome in the office, perhaps one of Bloom's past sore spots. Whenever a private investigator's office lights were on, they could be depended upon to answer the door in hopes of finding a new client standing on the other side.

Either the killer wasn't welcome, or couldn't risk being seen by anyone in the area. Using a grappling hook to climb two floors upward in plain view of traffic didn't seem like an intelligent alternative, Tackett thought.

As he took a sip of coffee, a uniformed officer dropped a police report duplicate atop his desk in passing.

"Figured you could use more paperwork," the officer said with a chuckle.

"Yeah. Thanks a lot."

Tackett glanced at it, figuring it was something connected with one of his other open cases, then noticed it was from Orange County, regarding an intruder at Clouse's hotel.

Over the next five minutes he read the details of the intrusion with great interest before finding a strange detail that caught his attention.

"Brown dust," he muttered to himself, snatching the crime scene photos from his case off the desktop.

Near the front door, the crime scene technician found specks of brown dust that everyone had written off as some form of tracked mud. Tackett swiped the phone from its receiver, using the speed dial to call the technician's cell phone.

"I don't have the lab results back, if that's what you want," Rob Lowrey answered.

"Great talking to you, too, Rob. I just need to know if you swabbed any of that brown dust we found outside the Bloom crime scene."

"Of course," Lowrey said as though Tackett spoke preposterously.

"Did you send it to the lab?"

"I sent some of it, but I doubt there'll be a rush to get results."

"Okay. That's all I needed."

Knowing Lowrey would likely hang up on him, Tackett slammed the phone down first. They tolerated one another because their positions required them to, but beyond the crime scenes they shared, they never spoke informally.

Taking up the phone, he decided to give Roland Brown in Orange County a quick call to compare notes before sifting through more paperwork.

***

Clouse, Jane, and Randy Niemeyer stood beside the bed when Tim finally began to stir, affirming their hopes for a complete recovery from whatever ordeal left him roadside the prior evening.

His blue eyes fluttered open momentarily before focusing on his hosts, one at a time.

"What's everyone staring at?" he finally asked, propping himself onto his elbows with a smile. "Is it really you guys, or am I dreaming?"

"It's really us," Randy said, clasping his brother's hand as he moved onto the edge of the bed.

Clouse hesitated, unsure if he could trust his own eyes. For five years he had fought to subdue memories of his high school friend to avoid the hurt they brought him. So many friends had been sacrificed for no reason, and not by any of his doing.

Finally stepping forward, he took Tim's opposite side, deciding to let the brothers talk before he spoke. The room filled with uneasiness the way a sinking ship takes on water through gashed seams. No one seemed to know the next appropriate statement to continue their conversation.

"How long's it been?" Tim inquired, lying flat on the bed once again.

He still looked somewhat fatigued to Clouse.

"Since what?" Randy asked.

"Since that night."

Now the discomfort level drew near lethal proportions.

"Almost five years," Clouse answered as sensitively as possible. "What on earth happened to you, Tim? We laid you to rest just days after that Halloween."

Tim closed his eyes, reliving the painful moment. While his friends and family shared emotional pain, he was the one stabbed approximately two dozen times.

"Maybe we shouldn't go into that right now," Jane suggested.

"You're right. I'm sorry, Tim."

"Are you hungry, big brother?" Randy asked.

"Not really," Tim answered slowly, traces of his Southern accent coming through. "Ah'm still so tired. The last couple days since they moved me from that cell are a blur."

Clouse looked toward the nearby restroom.

"We've brought in everything you need when you're up to it, Tim. You can shave and shower, cut your hair, and pick out some clothes from the shops downstairs."

"Where the hell am I anyway?"

"You're in the West Baden Springs Hotel, buddy."

Tim propped himself up once more, looking around.

"I still own the place," Clouse revealed. "Even fixed it up a little more."

Almost as though he hadn't heard his friend, Tim's eyes scanned the room more intensely.

"Where's Vicky? And the kids?"

No one really had a good answer, especially since no one had bothered contacting Tim's former wife. So far as she knew, Tim left her a widow with two children when Martin Smith's goons murdered him.

"Vicky remarried about two years ago," Randy finally answered reluctantly.

Tim seemed stunned, but only for a few seconds.

"I always wondered what was going on with all you guys while I was in that cell."

"You were in that cell the whole time?" Clouse asked.

"That cell or another one just like it. They moved me a few times."

"They?" Randy asked.

"Well, I assume it was more than one, but only one guy brought me food and bedding."

Reaching into one of his pockets, Randy pulled out a photograph of the deceased Nathan Runnels.

"This guy?"

Tim stared at the image momentarily, possibly struggling because Runnels wore his police uniform in the photo, including the forest ranger style hat.

"Yeah. He's the one."

"Guys, why don't we give Tim some time to get cleaned up," Jane suggested. "Maybe he'll work up an appetite and we can talk over dinner in the café."

As the group started to leave, a concerned look crossed Tim's face.

"What's wrong?" Clouse asked him.

"You guys aren't going far, are ya?"

"We'll be right next door, Tim. I've got all kinds of security in the building, including a few guys on this floor. No one is getting close to you without us knowing it."

He appeared satisfied with the answer, breathing a sigh of relief.

"Ah'll see you guys in a little bit."

***

Over the course of the next hour, Niemeyer trimmed his hair just short of the scalp with an electric hair trimmer, shaved his beard down to a full goatee, and took the longest shower of his life. He searched the closet, finding several shirts, blue jeans, slacks, tennis shoes, and a pair of black dress shoes.

During the shower he sobbed as he thought of being free, finally having the rest of his life before him. He occasionally wept the first few years after his friends buried him, but he eventually hardened, believing his captors would find him dead in his cell before they ever let him go.

His life as he knew it ceased to exist that fateful Halloween night. Trapped with only his thoughts in a cell smaller than most bedrooms, he ate whenever food was provided, read on the rare occasions a magazine or book came his way, and eventually lost hope of ever seeing the outside world.

Treated like a cross between a dangerous criminal and a feral animal, his life was constantly monitored by a security camera, though escape seemed impossible. Only once in a great while was his bedding or clothing changed, typically at gunpoint. Not once had he been allowed to leave the cell, and his captor never divulged one shred of information.

Because only one person ever took care of him, Niemeyer worried constantly that something tragic might happen to the stranger, leaving him to starve while the rest of the world lived in ignorance of his plight.

The few times he was moved were blank spots in his memory. He suspected Runnels used some form of gas on him to put him into a deep sleep before transporting him. Niemeyer's memories all came from within prison bars, except when he dreamed or daydreamed his way into another place and time.

He thought about his parents, his brothers, Vicky, his children, and his friends many times over while in captivity. Thus far, the news hadn't been good regarding a return to normal life. While people wanted to know how his five years went, he couldn't begin to imagine the events and news he had missed.

After dressing in a golf shirt, slacks, and the black shoes, he perused a few magazines and newspapers left by his bed. Wasting a few more minutes, he jumped on the computer to access the internet, eventually searching for and finding some cologne in the bathroom. While the extensive shower cured most of his odor problems, he wanted to be certain before eating dinner with the others.

It occurred to him he had missed dental checkups, vision tests, renewing his driver's license, and all kinds of tasks that annoyed most people. Five years of missing his kids grow up was a lifetime, considering they were both about to enter high school. Soccer games, baseball, basketball, and who knew how many other activities Vicky attended while he rotted in a cage.

During that time he mentally constructed a list of things he wanted to do when and if he finally escaped, none of which included staying at a hotel having dinner with his best friend. He wanted to, but he couldn't bring himself to blame

Clouse for all of his problems. They had been good friends since high school, and the troubles Clouse stumbled into were none of his own doing.

Still, Niemeyer had risked his life for his friend, and lost years of his own life when six strange cult members attacked him. Everyone wanted to know what happened that night, and he honestly couldn't tell them.

He remembered, and often relived, the agony of being stabbed repeatedly shortly after making an ATM transaction. After looking at Randy, still seated in his truck, Niemeyer slumped to the ground as he lost consciousness, and presumably his life.

An unknown amount of time passed before he awoke inside his first cell, completely healed from the wounds. Knowing the attack was no dream, he searched for scars, finding only a few minor marks around his abdomen. His survival and miraculous healing were just another part of the larger mystery.

Giving a sigh, he moved away from the computer.

Finally running out of things to do, Niemeyer opened the door, stepping into the hallway to find two armed men standing near the main elevator door. He looked around, realizing his friend had changed more of the hotel since the last time he visited.

Finding the door to the suite open, he stepped inside, finding his brother talking with their hosts.

"Hey, Tim," Randy said as he stood, anxiously crossing the room.

He wrapped his arms around Niemeyer in a bear hug that nearly took his breath.

"Easy there, little brother."

"Ready for some grub?" Clouse asked.

"Sure," Niemeyer lied.

He didn't feel particularly hungry for food, so much as companionship.

Niemeyer observed a rather large bodyguard keeping watch over the children like a lioness might protect her young. A few minutes later he rode the elevator to the lobby with Clouse, Jane and his brother. Scenes of the atrium flashed through the elevator's windows, bringing back memories of its beauty.

When they stepped into the lobby, he found it fully furnished and more beautiful than ever.

"You do all this?" he asked Clouse.

"Jane came up with a lot of the decor, but we put a lot of work into it."

A few minutes later they were seated in the restaurant. Niemeyer and his brother studied the menu while the Clouses ordered drinks for the group.

"I haven't had good food in forever."

Niemeyer found his brother staring at him between glances at the menu.

"Something the matter?"

"I just can't believe this is real."

"Neither can I."

"You don't seem very enthused," Jane noted.

"Sorry. I'm just anxious to see the kids."

Randy grimaced slightly.

"All in good time, my brother."

"Is he a good man?"

"Come again?"

"Vicky's new husband."

"I suppose. I wasn't exactly invited to the wedding, Tim."

Niemeyer gave him a scrutinizing look.

"What the hell's happened to our family?"

"Nothing. No one blamed Vicky for getting remarried, but I think she felt a little bad."

"What about Mom and Dad? Are they doing okay?"

"Yeah. I'll take you over there this afternoon."

"Have you even told anyone I'm back?"

Randy hesitated.

"It was all so sudden, Tim. I didn't want to get anyone's hopes up, so I didn't tell anyone until I was sure you were going to wake up."

"But you *did* tell someone...right?"

"No. Not yet. I guess it'll be a surprise."

Clouse smirked.

"You'll be lucky if your folks don't have a stroke when they see Tim."

Niemeyer folded his hands before him, burying his face in them with frustration.

"This isn't anything like I thought it would be if I got out of there," he confessed. "I had a million scenarios thought up with hugs and kisses and Christmas trees with snow outside, but nothing like this."

"Are you disappointed?" Clouse asked with genuine curiosity.

"No. I mean I'm among friends, which is what counts. I was hoping maybe everyone thought I was a missing person, not lying six feet under."

"You never had any outside contact?" Jane asked.

"One person brought me the few things a person needs to survive, but other than that, I had no clue what was going on outside of that cell."

A few minutes later a waiter took their orders. After thinking about it, everything on the menu sounded good to Niemeyer. Some of the things served to him during his incarceration were barely a step above generic dog food. He found foods on the menu that might have made him salivate like a starved pet prior to his freedom.

He finally settled on the rib eye steak over smoked salmon, with garlic mashed potatoes and southwestern egg rolls.

"I don't want my first good meal to have anything to do with vegetables," he said aside to his brother.

Randy smirked.

"You always were all about meat and potatoes."

"Do you remember anything about last night?" Clouse asked, obviously not wanting to interrogate his friend heavily during dinner.

"Not really. The last thing I remember is being in a new cell for only a day or two, then waking up where you guys found me. They probably drugged me again."

Clouse appeared genuinely concerned.

"That not the answer you wanted to hear?" Niemeyer asked somewhat pointedly.

"It's just that if Runnels was your keeper all this time, and he died before your release, someone else is still out there who knows about all of this."

Randy cleared his throat with a purpose.

"Hey, we're just glad to have you back, Tim. There'll be time to catch everything up later."

Clouse nodded.

"I'm sorry, Tim. I don't mean to pick at you, but we've had some problems around here lately. I really *am* thrilled that you're back."

"Thanks, Paul. It's good to be back."

When their second round of drinks came, Clouse raised his to propose an informal toast. When the others joined him, he finally spoke.

"To my high school buddy Tim. It's good to have you back."

"And to many happy years to come," Randy added as everyone tapped glasses.

Niemeyer didn't feel particularly happy at the moment. He had no wife, no home, and no one even knew he was alive except for the people surrounding him. Life over the coming days and weeks was going to be a major adjustment period for absolutely everyone, and he still had no explanation why.

He still had five years of local, national, and family events to catch up on, so he decided not to dwell on how he came to be home. Instead, he planned on enjoying it.

Chapter 22

Mark Teakon wasn't sure he trusted the man seated across from him in a local mom and pop café.

An expert in antiquities and classic writings, Teakon knew about exotic finds from across the world, but none more dangerous than what Alan Rawlings had asked him to locate.

"I can't believe my contacts in the FBI, Secret Service, and CIA couldn't locate this item for me, but you've done it, Mr. Teakon," Rawlings said over a steaming cup of coffee.

Teakon knew very little about the man, except that he was a former government spook of some sort. Now he worked freelance jobs, the kind people were killed over if they knew too many details.

He guessed Rawlings to be in his mid-forties, finding the allure of the private market much more appealing than a government check. Very fit, with prematurely graying hair, Rawlings dressed nicely with a tie and khaki slacks. Despite the warm weather, he wore a navy blue sport coat meant to conceal the firearm he carried rather than provide a dapper appearance.

Far away from his Massachusetts home, Teakon didn't feel entirely comfortable around Rawlings. For the better part of a week, the two had played a sort of cat and mouse game, giving out only uncompromising details about their work, and their objectives.

Quite simply, Rawlings was offering a fair amount of money for Teakon to provide him with the name of the man who held a particular antique in his possession. Uncertain of Rawlings' intentions, Teakon agreed to the deal under particular conditions. As a gatekeeper of sorts, Teakon held certain information back.

Some he maintained within his mind, while the important parts remained locked inside a special book inaccessible to the outside world.

"We've come all this way to Arizona, Mr. Rawlings, and it's time we divulge some certain truths to one another."

Teakon taught history at a local university in his hometown, loving his use of large words, partially for conversational leverage.

"What you want to know is who I represent, and what I intend to do once I find the person who owns the cube, right?"

Teakon nodded.

"You see, it isn't just me who monitors these objects, Mr. Rawlings. Even if something happens to me, there will be someone to track the ownership of this object."

"I believe you, and I have no intention of harming you, or anyone else if it can be helped. I spent two years tracking this cube without success, and you led me here within a day's time. Can I ask how you do it?"

"You still haven't answered my other question."

"I don't know my employer's identity."

"Then he used a middleman? That could be even more dangerous."

"No. No middleman. Only a letter and some cash."

"What kind of letter?"

Teakon sipped some iced tea while Rawlings pulled an envelope from his shirt pocket, unfolding a letter from its protective sheath.

He pushed it across the table to Teakon, who read its contents over the next several minutes. The contents of the letter basically stated that the individual wished to find a red cube, possibly embedded within an antique. It provided only a cell phone contact number which was not to be called unless the object was found.

The letter went on to state the dangers of the object, and its possible owner wanting to keep it. While it didn't give many specifics, it gave Rawlings permission to use his discretion in obtaining the object, because the owner would not want to surrender it or sell it.

"Use your discretion?" Teakon questioned. "Is that like a license to kill?"

Rawlings returned a crooked smirk.

"Something like that. It also means I can entirely avoid confrontation whenever possible."

Before its closing, the letter went on to state that the object was dangerous in the wrong hands, but the sender intended to put it away forever to keep it safe from corrupt people.

"Do you believe this?" Teakon asked, pointing out the specific line.

"I know I believe in making a living. Eventually I have to meet this man, so I'll decide then what the best course of action is."

Teakon tried to suppress his amusement at Rawlings' ignorance.

"Do you have faith, Mr. Rawlings?"

"I don't go to church, if that's what you mean."

"I mean to ask if you believe in God, a heaven and hell, those sorts of things."

Rawlings nodded.

"I was raised by Baptist parents in the Georgia hills, so yes, I have knowledge and some belief in scripture."

"Some?"

"The Bible isn't infallible, Mr. Teakon. It is a collection of stories, after all."

"That may be true, but I have a story for you, and exactly what it is you're tracking. See, your employer didn't disclose certain truths to you about what the object really is, or where it came from. Your employer could be someone who was scarred by one of these objects and genuinely wants it put away, or he could be someone who wants it for personal gain."

"I take it this is more than just a private auction piece that someone wants returned."

"Much more, Mr. Rawlings. Much more. Do you care to know exactly what it is you're about to obtain?"

"I've waited this long. Another few minutes isn't going to kill me."

"Good, because you'll probably want to know some of this, and exactly what you'll be confronting in Mr. Pershing."

"As in Graham Pershing?" Rawlings asked with an arched eyebrow.

"Yes, but we'll get to that in a moment."

Teakon hadn't yet revealed the name for his own safety, and because he wanted to feel out Rawlings first. He still wasn't convinced the man was anything more than a hired mercenary, but he still had lots of security checkpoints to protect himself.

He readied himself to tell the entire tale of the 13 cubes from beginning to end if time permitted.

***

As a precaution, Tackett decided to speak with each of the mansion survivors. In part, he wanted their recollections from the event, and to verify their current whereabouts.

Dan Duncan and Craig Jennings were easy, considering they worked for Paul Clouse at the hotel. He tracked down Red Sanders, Jana Privett, and Keith Sanders rather easily. They all had very little to add to his investigation. Frank Oswalt provided no real clues, but he did give the detective a cell phone number for Dave McCully, the most elusive member of the group.

The only one of them with any celebrity status to speak of, McCully toured with his father's bluegrass group throughout the country. Finding him without a contact number or a tour schedule was nearly impossible.

Considering the late morning hour, he suspected the musician was either on the road or preparing for a concert, so he dialed the number.

After two rings, someone picked up on the other end, answering hesitantly.

"Hello?"

"Mr. McCully?"

"Yes."

"My name is Troy Tackett. I'm with the Monroe County Police Department in Bloomington, Indiana."

"Something tells me you aren't calling to ask for an autograph."

"No. Not exactly. I've been through the reports from your incident at the mansion in West Baden a few years back. We've had some local trouble there again, so I was wondering if there was anything you might recall that you forgot in your earlier interviews."

"I think I pretty much covered everything the previous six times I've been interviewed."

McCully didn't have a Southern accent, which surprised the detective a bit.

"Have you ever met Paul Clouse, the owner of the hotel you looked at?"

"No."

"Have you been back to Indiana since the incident two years ago?"

"Once for a concert in Nashville. Am I a suspect in your investigation?"

"I'm simply wanting some information, which will hopefully eliminate you as a suspect and allow me to move forward."

"I left there two years ago, Detective Tackett, with a rather sour taste in my mouth and no apologies from anyone. I'm bitter, but there's no way I'm going to seek revenge against anyone for the actions of one insane person."

"Considering your rugged tour schedule, I doubt you could make the time to visit our fine state. I'd appreciate a call back if you think of anything else from your ordeal a few years back."

"Can I ask exactly what you're investigating?"

Tackett thought he heard sounds of the highway from the other end of the line. McCully was likely traveling in a tour bus, or stopped somewhere for a moment.

"There was a murder in Bloomington that might be linked to the hotel ownership."

"Not much of a surprise, I guess."

Swiveling in his office chair, Tackett looked outside his window as gray clouds drifted across the sky. It seemed a downpour was likely coming his way within the hour.

Appropriate, he thought, considering his somber mood.

"Can I ask you something off the record before I let you go?"

A few seconds passed before McCully answered.

"Sure."

"I've been told you have certain, um, abilities. Is there anything you can tell me, anything you've, uh, seen that you can tell me about."

"If I do, are you going to believe me or call me a crackpot?"

"After what I've heard and seen this week, I'll believe almost anything."

"Anyone around that hotel is in grave danger, Detective. I heard the mansion got torn down, but there's still someone carrying on Bell's work."

Tackett wasn't sure how to phrase the next question without it sounding pointed.

"Have you *seen* anything that might tell me who I'm looking for?"

"I've been seeing lots of things lately, and hearing screams in the night. Now that I've been there, it just doesn't stop, and I can't tell if it's past, present, or future. If I were you, detective, I wouldn't set foot near that place if you value your life."

Tackett wasn't sure how to respond. He certainly valued his life, but he also enjoyed having steady employment. Keeping his job meant following through on the leads in his case.

"Thanks for your time, Mr. McCully," Tackett managed to say, still stunned by the man's chilling words.

As the bluegrass singer hung up the phone, Tackett felt absolutely no doubt about the man's belief that the hotel was dangerous. Still, he knew the danger existed only from the people in and around it. He wasn't about to let Ray Bloom's death go unsolved, and in the process, he might end Paul Clouse's problems once and for all.

Chapter 23

Teakon sipped his tea deeply before beginning the story. Rawlings didn't appear quite as calm, now that he knew the identity of the red cube's possessor, his thoughts distracting him from their conversation.

"In all, there are 13 of these cubes," Teakon began. "They were constructed shortly after the first World War by wealthy businessmen who wanted more out of their already extravagant lives."

"Why?"

"Why does anyone want more? I suppose they lacked moral fiber, but what they did was basically the single most dangerous and apprehensible act of the Twentieth Century."

"Strange that no one ever heard about it."

Teakon wished Rawlings would shut up and let him finish the story, but he simply humored him like a parent might a misbehaving child.

"One doesn't make it public knowledge when one owns one of these cubes, Mr. Rawlings. This group contracted a jeweler to make 13 unbelievably beautiful, shimmering cubes from the finest gems across the globe. Little more than a pawn in their scheme, the jeweler fulfilled their order, not knowing the intent of the objects until they were finished.

"He created a ledger specifically to commemorate the event, placing all 13 names of the men, accompanied by which cube they received, inside an otherwise blank, leather bound book. In the meantime, Thomas Ellington, the leader of the conspirators, organized a contract signing with the Prince of Darkness, to curse all 13 cubes, thus giving them each special abilities."

Rawlings had to stifle a laugh to avoid the other café patrons from looking their way.

"First of all, you're going through this fairy tale a bit too fast, and secondly, I can't believe a word of it."

"You'd better believe it, Mr. Rawlings," Teakon stated, daring to point a finger at the man, his look deadly serious. "If you pay Pershing a visit without the information I'm about to give you, you'll be buried somewhere in the back of his property without ever having a chance to defend yourself."

"I don't like threats, Teakon."

"Not a threat. Fact."

Teakon had to pause as their waitress brought them refills.

"The reason you don't hear much about cursed objects is because everyone without a conscience wants to own one. They provide power, youth, control beyond imagination, Mr. Rawlings. Each of these cubes possesses a distinct ability, given only to its wielder."

Giving a short sigh, Rawlings looked down to the table, apparently losing interest because he didn't believe Teakon's story.

"Do you think I just pulled Pershing's name out of thin air?" Teakon asked to counter his inattentiveness. "I don't have your contacts, or the mafia, or even a good psychic, but I do know Pershing is the man with that cube. And he's not going to hand it over to you if you ask nicely. He'll have his people take you out back and shoot you like a dog. I know a little bit about these people, too, Mr. Rawlings. Not in the same way you do, but because they all operate in the same way. They're the same as the original 13 in their own way."

Rawlings had returned his full attention to Teakon after the sermon.

"Then how do you propose I go about obtaining the cube? And how in the fuck did you find out Pershing has it?"

"I was getting to that part of my story before you so rudely interrupted. You see, the jeweler wasn't a stupid man, and he suspected his own life was in peril, so he placed his leather bound book in a secret compartment beneath the glass and marble container holding the cubes. He was right, as the group shot him, then set fire to his store to cover up their evil deed. But the book, with their names etched inside, became part of the curse placed on the cubes. Every time someone new takes possession of one of the cubes, his or her name is etched within the book's pages. The handwriting is that of the jeweler, keeping tabs on the people who possess such evil, to ensure no one person gains possession of all thirteen."

At this point, Rawlings was simply humoring him, openly ready to confront Pershing on his own.

"If all 13 are ever brought together, by one possessor, mankind, and the world around him, would cease to exist as we know it. Armageddon doesn't even begin to describe the magnitude of what catastrophes would encircle our planet."

"Then why would anyone be stupid enough to bring them together."

"Ignorance and greed will fuel people to own them all, Mr. Rawlings. Besides, the possessor of all 13 would be protected from harm, left to rule over whatever ruins remained strewn across the wasteland known as Earth."

Rawlings sat back momentarily in thought.

"So you're implying you possess the jeweler's book, which enables you to know the identity of all the cube holders?"

"I'm implying nothing."

"So now you're going to be close-lipped about this," Rawlings said with a chuckle.

"The book is protected by no less than a dozen protective measures, but it does exist. I don't have anything to fear by admitting its existence."

Rawlings gave him a quirky look.

"What if someone were to torture you? To make you give them the book?"

"As I said, the book is protected by numerous codes and devices, most of which will kill the man who doesn't get them right. My colleagues and I are prepared to die at the hands of our own measures, rather than let the book fall into the wrong hands."

"That sounds a bit fanatical."

"Not if you've seen what I've seen, Mr. Rawlings."

Rawlings shoved himself back from the table.

"I think I've heard enough, Mr. Teakon. You'll get your cut when I receive payment from my employer."

"I'm not so concerned about any cut right now, so much as I am about your safety. If you rush into this without a plan, Pershing won't hesitate to kill you. We both know exactly what the man is about."

"Yeah. I guess I can exercise some of the judgment my employer permitted me to use when I find him then, can't I?"

Without another word, Rawlings left the café, jumped into his SUV, then sped down the road. Teakon watched him drive away momentarily, then opened his cell phone to speed dial a familiar number. Being so close to the action wasn't something he sought, but he wasn't about to squander the chance to make certain one of the cubes was yanked from evil hands.

"Greg, we may have a little problem," Teakon said when someone picked up on the other end.

***

While Randy left the hotel to call for a family meeting, Clouse drove his friend to Bloomington to buy some new clothes. It was decided during breakfast that Randy needed to prepare the Niemeyer family for the shock that his brother was alive, rather than simply surprise everyone.

"Yuh really don't have to do this, Paul," Niemeyer complained from the passenger's seat of Clouse's pickup truck, his accent returning more consistently.

"Nonsense. You're starting over, Tim. It's the least I can do, especially since you'll be seeing your family in a few hours."

"Do I really have nothin' left in the world?" Niemeyer asked almost blankly. "It feels like I lost my house to a fire."

"When Vicky thought you were gone, she sold all of your things. Jane and I helped her through some of the tough times."

"I appreciate that."

Watching some of the businesses and shops just off the highway blur past him, Clouse kept one hand on the wheel while he drank from a water bottle.

"What did I miss after that night?" Niemeyer finally asked to break the silence.

"You want celebrity gossip or local news?"

"Nah. I want to know about that night. Who tried to kill me, and why."

Clouse spent a few minutes explaining how Martin Smith's faction, the Coven, stabbed him repeatedly that night. From there, he explained how Smith faked his own death, used a cursed object to rejuvenate himself, then sought revenge against Clouse and his remaining friends.

"Smith was kind of a dick, wasn't he?" Niemeyer asked.

"That's putting it lightly. Absolutely all of the bullshit we went through was because of him. He used everyone around the hotel as his pawns to find the cursed object."

Niemeyer shot him a quizzical glance.

"Ah'm still not sure I can believe a household item gave Smith that much power."

"I've done research on cursed objects, Tim. More often than not, they're standard items that are cursed with satanic power to do human bidding. Obviously there's a downside to using the things, but Smith didn't care. He planned to live forever."

"So what happened to him?"

"We had a standoff at the hotel. He almost killed Randy and Jane, but in the end he died by his favorite method of taking lives when I stabbed him in the guts."

Niemeyer hesitated before asking his next question.

"How did I survive, Paul? I don't remember a thing until I woke up in a cell."

"I'm sure it was part of Smith's plan, Tim. I can't even fathom a guess why he went through all that trouble. He caused us all a lot of emotional pain, but maybe he wanted you as some kind of backup plan."

"Five years," Niemeyer mumbled.

"I'm sorry, Tim. I really am."

"Yuh know, for years I kind of blamed you for not coming and getting me out of there. But you didn't know. I know that now. Truth is, I didn't really know what happened to me after the stabbing. Five years is a long time to dwell on things, and I guess I had a lot of hatred inside me. That's not very Christian, is it?"

"No one could blame you," Clouse said softly. "The point is that you're here now, and you still have a lot of life ahead of you."

"What life? My kids might not want anything to do with me."

"I can't say how people are going to respond to you being back, Tim, but that's one door that'll never close. Believe me, your kids are going to be thrilled to see you."

"God, I hope you're right."

Now Clouse decided to ask a painful question.

"What was it like in that cell for five years?"

"What do you mean?"

"Did you ever get out? Ever get anything to read? Was it anything like prison?"

Niemeyer stared blankly at the floorboard.

"It was far worse than prison. I had human contact about once a day, and usually it was just for food. He hardly ever let me read anything, and I didn't get showers or real exercise. I did pushups and crunches to pass the time, but there were times I thought about wrapping that sheet around my neck and ending it all."

Saying nothing, Clouse began realizing the hell his friend had endured. Losing five years of freedom was bad enough, but being sheltered from human contact of any kind sounded unbearable.

"I begged the guy to talk to me," Niemeyer said. "He wasn't totally cold, but I think he was afraid of getting to know me. It seemed like he was my keeper, and nothing more."

"Maybe he worked for Smith."

"A thousand theories went through my head, but I never got any answers."

"You didn't have the whole story, either."

"Was my funeral nice? Was I actually in the casket?"

Clouse started to chuckle before clamping his own mouth shut. It wasn't every day such questions were thrown his way.

"Yeah, you were in the casket. It was nice, Tim, it was nice. It was awful damn sad, though, too. First Ken, then you. My whole world caved in around me the night you were stabbed."

"Ah'm just glad to be out of there, Paul. I can't wait to see my family again."

Clouse said nothing, taking an exit to Highway 46 as Niemeyer perked up.

"This isn't the mall."

"Nah. That would be a girls' day out, old buddy. I'm getting you a welcome back present that you can really use."

Clouse pulled into the nearby Harley-Davidson dealership a few minutes later. Niemeyer had lived fairly well when he owned his own construction business, buying extras like a camper and his own motorcycle. Vicky often complained that their closets were about to burst from all the shirts, baseball caps, and accessories he stored within their sliding doors.

Like a kid inside a toy store, Niemeyer searched every rack, examining new shirts and gear with wide eyes once they stepped inside.

"Whatever you want, pick it out, Tim."

"Paul, I can't," Niemeyer said hesitantly.

"I'm serious, Tim. Money is no object. Pick out whatever you want because I'm buying."

Niemeyer absorbed the words, picking conservatively until Clouse prodded him to pick out more items. In all, his friend grabbed a handful of shirts, some headgear, and a few jackets.

"You can't be wearing all of this stuff unless you have a bike," Clouse said as they placed the wares upon the counter.

"Paul, yuh can't do this. Seriously."

"You've got five years of living to make up for, buddy. Go pick out a bike so you can ride it to your folks' house in style."

Niemeyer's eyes misted a bit as he gave Clouse a quick hug.

"I owe you big time, Paul," he said just above a whisper.

"You don't owe me shit. If anything, it's me who owes you for what you went through. You were the best friend I could have asked for when the chips were down."

Niemeyer began looking over the used bikes after a momentary hesitation.

"New, Tim, new."

Niemeyer chuckled.

"I think I like this one," he said, standing next to a barely used Softail Custom from the current year.

"We just had a customer trade that in yesterday," a salesman said, approaching the two shoppers. "Barely used it before he decided on one of the anniversary models."

"It's only got twelve-hundred miles on it," Niemeyer said softly, examining every inch of the beautiful black and silver bike. "Lots of chrome, too."

Clouse took the salesman aside.

"My friend has a previous engagement to attend to. I don't need a whole lot of paperwork tying us up, and I want him to ride that bike out of here today."

"Sir, it could take a while for a loan of that size to-"

"Cash."

"What?"

"I'm paying cash for everything. I want my friend to have his gear and his bike ready to go within the hour if you want my business. No bullshit, just the title and a full tank."

The salesman gave a cautious smile.

"Let me get started on the paperwork, sir. What was your name again?"

"Don't worry about my name," Clouse said, wanting to avoid a slew of thankful dealership phone calls later.

He planned to put everything in Niemeyer's name anyhow, since it was *his* bike.

"I think I love this bike," Niemeyer said, throwing an assertive arm around his friend's shoulder as he had in the old days.

"I know you do, Tim. We're getting the paperwork drawn up so you can ride it out of here."

Niemeyer looked at him, almost lost in the moment, or perhaps flashing back to the steel and concrete cell that crushed his hopes and dreams for so long.

"You sure about all this?"

"Tim, I'm sure. Life's been good to me, sort of, so it's the least I can do. I don't want you to have to worry about a thing. Just enjoy yourself and the time with your family."

"I don't have the words, Paul."

Clouse shrugged.

"We've been friends since before high school, Tim. There isn't anything I wouldn't do for you."

"Thanks."

"You're welcome. Now let's get some of this paperwork signed so you can see your folks. And we need to get you a helmet so you don't splatter your head on your first day of freedom."

Niemeyer shook his head.

"How about a skullcap? They look cooler."

"Again, back to keeping your thick skull intact, ol' buddy. You killed too many brain cells when we were kids. I hate to see you lose any more."

"Maybe a nice vest, too," Niemeyer said, meandering toward the clothes. "Can't have a protected skull if I'm just going to scuff up my back."

"How about avoiding crashes altogether?" Clouse chided, following his friend through the open aisle.

Niemeyer avoided answering the question until he reached the footwear.

"Toes need protecting, too, Paul."

Clouse laughed as Niemeyer examined the new styles of steel-toed Harley boots.

"Have at it, Tim. I'll go start on the paperwork so we get out of here before dark."

A confused look crossed his friend's face.

"I don't even have a license, do I?"

"Oh, shit. I doubt it, buddy. We'll have to get you insured, too. I can give you a lift to your family. The last place you probably want to end up is jail for riding without a license."

Niemeyer grunted to himself.

"Isn't that the truth."

Chapter 24

Using his connections, Rawlings discovered Graham Pershing's current residence, and a little about the man's agenda. A notorious local mob boss, Pershing made his money illegally through nearly every established means imaginable.

Living outside a small Arizona town, he owned a moderate mansion complete with indoor/outdoor pool, workout center, a six-car garage, and even a helicopter pad. Partially hidden by reddish mountain terrain, the estate constantly remained guarded by at least half a dozen henchmen.

Most were part of Pershing's numerous illegal operations, though some would freelance between his employment and regular jobs that furthered his causes.

For years the FBI had kept tabs on him, suspecting his involvement in dozens of ordered executions. He also smuggled drugs and dealt with slave trade according to their records. Shielded by layers of employees, middlemen, and henchmen, solid proof never linked itself to Pershing for police to make an arrest.

What few witnesses emerged over the years either disappeared or wound up in gutters, ponds, or trash bins. No one dared risk testifying against Pershing now, fearing he controlled area police and businesses.

Rawlings stood on a rock overlooking the ranch Pershing called home. Only wisps of clouds appeared in the otherwise clear blue sky. The sun's rays already had him sweating profusely, so he wiped his forehead before focusing on his agenda.

Using high-powered binoculars, he watched for activity on the outskirts of the property. He noticed two guards wearing fairly casual attire, carrying rather large semi-automatic rifles as they patrolled the area.

While he wasn't one to pass judgment and stereotype others, he suspected most of Pershing's employees were soulless grunts who lived for money and pleasure. No one with morals, or a conscience, worked for such a notorious thug. They also didn't carry guns for self-preservation.

Rawlings had a choice to make. Storming the grounds didn't sound very prudent, even with the element of surprise. Taking Pershing away from his home wouldn't be easy, since the guards likely traveled with him. Timing was important, because Pershing didn't necessarily keep the target with him at all times. There could be a safe to crack, or a hiding place to locate before acquiring the cube.

He spent a few hours conducting surveillance on the property, watching guards come and go. When two large vehicles left the grounds, leaving red dust behind them as they headed for town, Rawlings decided to make his move.

Only one armed guard remained outside the house, so he decided to set to work disabling the power, phone, and cable lines, to ensure no outside communications existed. His own cell phone didn't have any reception, so he suspected a land line was their only means of calling out. Thanks to his connections, one handheld computer instantly shut down the entire network with the right passwords already programmed into its memory.

Rawlings watched the guard turn around, reacting to a noise, or a change in lighting. Reasonably certain a generator would kick on to restore some power and lighting, Rawlings moved toward his borrowed vehicle for a closer look.

Working alone against Pershing's resources wasn't the smartest move, he decided, but a necessary tactic nonetheless. He didn't mind sharing the money by employing others to help him, but his employer made it clear the object in question wasn't to be discussed with anyone else unless absolutely necessary.

Teakon proved necessary, though his words weren't the least bit comforting. Rawlings had lied to him in part about the arrangement with his employer, mainly for his employer's protection. Though he really didn't know the man's name, Rawlings had spoken with him several times over the phone, and met with him in person only once.

With an array of firearms and tools at his side, Rawlings drove to the open gates of the mansion, snagging a tranquilizer pistol from the collection. He didn't want to take human life unless necessary, though Pershing's crew likely deserved euthanasia from top to bottom.

Speeding up as he passed through the main gate, Rawlings prepared for light resistance, shooting the first guard in the shoulder with the tranquilizer to avoid any body armor. The man barely glanced in shock at the dart's tail end before collapsing in a heap to the dusty ground.

Closer to the mansion, grass had been expertly planted to provide a traditional look to the untraditional home.

Rawlings pulled around the circular driveway, aiming the disabling gun at the unfortunate soul about to cross through the front door's threshold. Upon first glance, only one person stepped outside, followed by four others, including Pershing himself.

Dressed in slacks, a tan button-up shirt, and a black sport coat, Pershing looked the part of a Miami drug lord, rather than an organized crime leader in Arizona. His black hair was cut short, suited for the climate, but his dark, penetrating eyes worried Rawlings the most.

A knot swelled in his throat, then ran its course to his stomach as Rawlings realized his visit was expected. Knowing Pershing's reputation, he decided surrender was a futile option, so he raised his tranquilizer gun, downing another henchman before throwing the car into reverse.

Now Pershing's smug look manifested into anger as he shouted orders.

"Stop him! Don't kill him! Stop him!"

Bullets riddled the car, including the tires, as Rawlings tried backing away from the deadly projectiles. Two tires immediately burst, leaving the car virtually crippled, and his life in grave danger. The only reason Pershing might want him alive was to extract information from him via torture.

In no mood to experience bodily harm, Rawlings plucked a MAC-10 from the seat beside him, sending lethal bursts into the small group. If they were willing to help Pershing kill him, they deserved no mercy. Everyone ducked for cover, some getting winged by the bullets, buying Rawlings a bit more escape time.

"Get up you pussies!" Pershing screamed until Rawlings fired a second volley his way.

Knowing the vehicle was incapable of making a full escape, Rawlings had only seconds to decide his next move. He opted to step from the car, toting several firearms with him. He fired the last rounds from the MAC-10, disabling the remaining henchmen long enough for him to take cover behind the car.

Throwing the submachine gun to the ground, Rawlings took up an AR-34 rifle, aiming it toward Pershing.

"The cube," he demanded.

"Who sent you?" Pershing asked with a sneer. "You're not the first, but I plan on making you the last."

"The cube, now, or you won't get the chance."

Pershing reached into his sport coat, retrieving the light red object, embedded within a glass case. It glimmered in the sunlight, causing Rawlings to turn away from its blinding reflection momentarily. When his attention returned, he never knew his mind had been seized by a greater power from within the cursed object.

He only knew his will was no longer his own, and Teakon's words were one-hundred percent accurate.

"Tell me your name," Pershing stated sternly.

"Alan Rawlings," the former government agent heard himself say without willing his body to utter the words.

"Who sent you?"

By now some of the henchmen were staggering to their feet, some bleeding, others just scraped up from diving to the concrete. Inside, Rawlings began fearing for his life as the gun he held dropped to the ground uselessly. He felt as helpless as a cow trapped within a fiery barn, unable to defend himself or escape.

"I don't know his name."

"Don't know," Pershing pondered aloud. "Your usefulness is dwindling, Mr. Rawlings. I suggest you go jump off the cliff about half a mile that way."

Pershing nodded the direction and Rawlings felt his legs taking him there as his mind wondered what the afterlife was like. No doubt remained within his mind that he was about to plummet to his death after the half-mile walk. The only questions were how long it would take to get there and how far to the ground.

Watching Rawlings walk toward certain death, Pershing chuckled to himself momentarily. He didn't particularly enjoy putting people to death, but he didn't hate it either. In the name of business he did whatever was required of him to survive and keep his secrets. The fact that Rawlings knew about his cursed object concerned him, though in a limited way. *Individuals* sent mercenaries like him after the cube, not corporations or agencies.

Still, his men now knew more than he wanted them to about his business. He didn't trust anyone regarding his secret, and its power, so he casually picked up an automatic weapon from a fallen henchman, thinking their newfound knowledge came from his own carelessness. Suspecting he had used the cube's power earlier than he needed to, Pershing created his own new dilemma.

Figuring he had no better opportunities coming his way, he turned the gun on his remaining henchmen, mowing them down as blood particles danced through the air. Their final cries of pain were brief as the bullets tore through their flesh, muscle, and bone.

The droplets disturbed the dusty ground as they landed beside the falling bodies of Pershing's former employees. A cleanup crew could take care of the bodies without question, for their usual fee. Rawlings, on the other hand, could rot away at the base of the cliff as buzzards picked away at his flesh.

Stealing a glance toward Rawlings, he found his victim almost halfway to the deadly drop. As he looked out toward the virtually unused highway, Pershing saw a glimmer of light, possibly from a discarded piece of glass.

Or a gun scope.

The sound of long-range rifle reached his ears a fraction of a second before a shell penetrated his left eye socket, dropping him beside his fallen henchmen.

***

With Clouse out all day, and his wife dealing with other matters regarding Tim Niemeyer's sudden return, Parish shouldered the load with the kids into the afternoon. He understood his job description as a bodyguard and babysitter combination, but some days tried his patience more than others.

Zach and Katie never directly gave him problems, though the attention they received from guests and the media sometimes gave him fits. After the invasion of his workplace the other day, Parish felt especially on edge. He started looking at fellow employees a bit suspiciously, questioning which of them might be on someone else's payroll.

Even the simple task of getting his morning coffee felt a bit stressful because he found himself looking around the restaurant, studying faces and mannerisms.

Growing tired of being imprisoned on the sixth floor, the kids convinced Parish to take them outside. His last standing orders from Mrs. Clouse were to keep them on the grounds, which provided ample acreage for them to scurry around, so long as they remained in his sight.

"You two stay close to me, understand?" he stated more than asked as the elevator descended effortlessly from the top floor.

Both nodded, eager to escape the stuffy confines of the suite. Parish had noticed fresh air entered the hotel only through open windows, and disappeared quickly.

When Parish crossed the lobby with the children he drew the usual stares. Everyone always wondered why a large man dressed in a suit walked two kids everywhere. The gun often bulged from his jacket, probably inciting mafia-related rumors. Much like a Secret Service agent, he let his eyes dance from person to person, making certain no one was lying in wait to harm or abduct the children.

"You might want to hold up a second," Craig Jennings said, virtually jogging to catch up to the trio from the atrium.

"What's wrong?"

"News media outside. They're wanting an interview."

"This is private property, Craig. You can kick them out."

Not the least bit concerned about adult conversation, the kids continued toward the door.

"Stop," Parish commanded, freezing them both in their tracks.

Unlike his own children, they listened to him with unwavering faithfulness. Because he and his wife shared different philosophies on discipline, Parish found his own children listened to him only part of the time. He was surprised his friends hadn't signed his family up for some televised psychology show to resolve their parenting issues.

"What the hell is going on, Craig?" Parish asked a bit more forcefully than he intended to. "This is a business. We can't have the media running around here."

"Mr. Clouse wants everything to appear status quo. I was just about to step outside and do an impromptu press conference. I was just warning you so you didn't go out that way."

Parish suddenly realized he had overreacted a bit, jumping down Jennings' throat for no good reason.

"Sorry, Craig. Things have been a little crazy since the incident."

"It's okay. I'll take care of things out here if you guys want to slip out the back way."

"Sure."

Avoiding the two lobby entrances altogether, Parish took the kids through the kitchen and into the side lot, which allowed them to run around the front, or into the garden if the media people were occupied. Instead, the kids opted to run up the hill toward the reserved valet parking area.

"Stay away from the cars," he warned as they dashed through the lot toward the observation building offset from the regular and valet lots.

He hated sounding like a nag, but everything around him posed a danger if someone wanted to abduct the children. Watching them run around the small observation building, Parish realized how close they were for not being blood-related. Of course they had very few people in their lives other than hotel employees and their parents, so their environment likely forced them to depend upon one another.

Glancing from the kids to the truck service entrance, Parish thought he saw someone moving through the bushes in the foliage behind the hotel. Assured Zach and Katie were occupied and still safe, he took a few steps up the concrete driveway, seeing a black material flapping in the breeze from a distant tree.

"Craig, can you or one of the guys come out back a moment?" he inquired over the radio.

"What's your location?" Jennings himself replied.

"Near the observation building. There's something that needs checked out, and I've got the kids."

"Clear. Be right there."

Parish stood like an Irish setter on point, staring at the hill's crest. The more he stared, the more he believed it was something discarded, perhaps a trash bag, dangling from a tree limb. The sky had grown overcast, making it more difficult to spot details against the dark background.

He listened to the kids playing, oblivious to his findings, as they dashed around the rounded building. Turning around to check on them, he saw Zach reaching for the doorknob on the building. Parish thought the building was supposed to be locked, typically used to store custodial tools and replacement trash bags, but it opened for Zach, and someone emerged from the doorway holding a dark object in one hand.

Zach and Katie both shrieked, obviously not expecting someone to be lurking inside the building.

With no regard for his own safety, Parish darted forward as the person reached for Zach, the dark object still in his right hand. Time did not permit the bodyguard to reach for his own weapon, so he struck the person viciously with his left hand as the intruder touched Zach's shoulder.

As the man tumbled to the ground, an expensive-looking camera rolled from his right hand, hitting the ground hard, but not breaking. Parish stood above him, finding time to draw his own weapon as Jennings rushed to his side. Training his pistol on the intruder, Parish brushed the children behind him with his free arm.

"Who are you?" he demanded of the stranger.

"Evan Parsons. I'm with the *Courier-Journal*. There's no need for guns here."

"I'll be the judge of that."

"My camera," Parsons said, picking it up to examine it. "You better hope this isn't broken."

"And you better hope I don't sneeze real hard or my finger might seize up. You've got about five seconds to prove you're who you say, or I call the cops."

Rubbing his jaw painfully with his right hand, Parsons slowly reached behind him to produce identification that confirmed his statement. Jennings examined it, handing it to Parish for a look before tossing it back to the ground.

"What the hell were you doing in there?" Jennings asked almost as gruffly as Parish was about to.

"I was hoping to get some good shots. You know, get a scoop on the other papers. I'm only part-time, so I need some exclusives to get a real gig."

Parish looked to Jennings, who didn't look the least bit impressed by the story. He was the authority over the property and those who inhabited it, so Parish waited for him to make a decision, still training his gun on the photographer.

"Is it really necessary for your goon to point that at me?" Parsons complained a second time.

"Yes," Parish answered for Jennings.

"Todd, maybe you should take the kids inside."

"I'll wait here, thanks."

Parish didn't want to usurp Jennings' authority, but he didn't want to see Parsons released without a few more solid answers.

"Why were you hiding in there?" he asked. "This is the back of the hotel."

"All the better to see something unusual. I heard a lot of the old murders happened back here."

"Untrue," Jennings said, now souring more toward the intruder. "And if that were true, why place yourself in harm's way?"

"Like I said, I need a break. I figured if no one saw me inside that building I'd have a better shot of spotting something gritty."

Parish replaced his firearm, letting the kids move to his side. He worked his left hand behind him so that no one else noticed. It stung from striking the photographer, but he didn't want the kids to worry, and he didn't want Parsons to know it hurt.

"We should call the police," he suggested to Jennings.

"That's not necessary," Parsons insisted, suddenly sounding a bit desperate.

"Why hide back here?" Jennings demanded. "What's the big story you expect to find?"

"You've got a missing security guard, presumably dead, you had a mystery man invade the hotel after getting past security checks of all kinds, and now there's word that Clouse's best buddy is back from the dead. How can there *not* be a story around here?"

Jennings stiffened, arriving at a decision.

"This may be a public hotel, but it is private property. Either stick with your media buddies or stay off the property."

Pleasantly surprised by the man's backbone, Parish couldn't have said it better himself. He placed a hand on a shoulder of each child, sneaking a look up the hill behind him. Whatever black cloth had been fluttering in the wind was no longer in sight. Perhaps it had blown away, or maybe it was indeed a loose trash bag.

As Parish ushered the kids toward the hotel, he stole a glimpse of Parsons examining his camera for damage before walking a defeated stride toward the hotel lobby. He could tell the kids weren't excited about going inside, but they knew the next logical step without Parish saying one word. Jennings had already disappeared, probably to fend off the remainder of the media people near the lobby.

"I'm sorry you guys had to see that," Parish said as he unlocked a maintenance door that took them through the kitchen area.

He knew every square inch of the hotel, typically keeping them from public view whenever possible.

"It's okay," Katie replied, though sounding a bit down.

After they passed through the kitchen and dining room, Parish led them into the ground level where a furnished lobby greeted them.

"What can I do to make it up to you guys? And no more ice-cream or your parents are going to fire me."

Both kids giggled because they knew Parish losing his job was completely dependent on their parents running the idea past them first.

"Can we go swimming?" Zach asked, his blue eyes virtually pleading.

"You think this looks good in swim trunks?" Parish retorted, looking down toward his belly.

Again the kids snickered because they knew he was going to let them swim, though he wasn't going to partake. Part of his unstated job description was keeping them reasonably happy at all times so long as their happiness didn't endanger them.

As they rode the elevator to the sixth floor, Parish couldn't help but wonder what the strange black object was, and where it went. His job wasn't to solve mysteries, but self-preservation seemed to dictate he learn something about the ever-changing circumstances around him.

Looking out the elevator window to the atrium below, he patted the firearm at his side for reassurance.

Chapter 25

Mark Teakon approached the bodies of Pershing and his henchmen cautiously, uncertain if one of them might still have some life left. Small pools of blood formed near most of the bodies, while trickles of drying blood clung to the chins and cheeks of a few. Teakon felt a bit sick to his stomach, partly because his associate had killed men to get the necessary results, but also because such evil men used cursed objects in the first place. He knelt down beside Pershing, scooping up the cursed cube.

One look at Rawlings revealed he hadn't stopped just because the command's issuer lie dead. While Teakon had the ability to track people who possessed the cursed objects by name, his knowledge of their workings was limited to a few texts, interviews, and personal experience. The few times he encountered the cubes provided him with his first looks at them. Either he overcame the odds or he didn't with each encounter, but he always brought backup and a solid plan with him.

Glancing behind him, Teakon found Greg Slone making his way down the rocky bank across the highway, carrying his sniper rifle with him. A former military marksman, Slone provided a very secure addition to Teakon's fold when he agreed to help track down the cursed objects. The money wasn't great, but after several scrutinizing interviews, Teakon determined he was a zealot for the cause.

Near death experiences such as this only made their trio a bit closer, although their third member was plotting their next move in their New England hometown.

"I could have used someone to interrogate," Teakon commented when Slone stopped a few feet behind him.

"And I'm sure one of them would have loved you as a hostage, Mark. You brought me on board to protect you and Julie, so that's what I do."

"I know," Teakon mumbled, wishing they could find a balance between collecting information and personal safety.

Slone stepped around the bodies, checking each of them for any remaining shred of life. Satisfied, he slung his rifle around his back, pulling the semi-automatic pistol holstered at his side to a ready position.

"I'm checking inside," he reported, taking two steps toward the doorway before hesitating. "You fetching your boy or letting him walk off the cliff?"

Teakon grunted, then began the arduous walk toward Rawlings, still uncertain whether he could reverse the order Pershing gave. More often than not, the cursed objects directly linked themselves to their possessors, which should have severed the link between Rawlings and his directive.

Finding it necessary to break into a jog before Rawlings walked off the cliff, Teakon intercepted him less than fifteen steps short of the edge. Standing in the man's way, Teakon gripped both of his shoulders, pushing against him to break the trance.

His method failed as Rawlings continued trudging forward.

Teakon pushed back to no avail, finally slapping Rawlings hard across the face, stunning him enough to slow him. It took another two slaps to bring the man to a stop, and out of the trance, only three paces short of the dropping point.

Rawlings looked around in confusion as Teakon stepped to his side, away from the deadly cliff. He no longer had Slone to protect him, so he took precautions in case Rawlings reacted violently. No set of circumstances regarding the cursed cubes ever seemed remotely the same, but Teakon took some comfort as a gleam from the house caught his eye. Slone had returned outside, now aiming his sniper rifle toward the two men at the cliff's edge for a look.

"You with me?" Teakon finally asked after a few tense seconds.

"What happened?" Rawlings asked.

Teakon explained the cube's hold over Rawlings after Pershing gave the order. Though he seemed reluctant to accept the truth at first, Rawlings finally remembered.

"I would have jumped," he said, daring to stare off the cliff's edge.

"Yes."

"And the cube?"

"Safe."

Teakon wasn't going to reveal any further information, hoping Rawlings would be thankful simply to have his life.

"And Pershing?"

"He won't be bothering anyone else."

It took some time, but the two men returned to the gruesome scene along the driveway. Rawlings looked somewhat surprised that Pershing and all of his henchmen were dead, though far from shocked.

"You guys take this cube hunting thing seriously," he commented.

"Very," Slone answered. "We need to be departing the premises, Mark."

Teakon nodded.

"This is where we part ways, Mr. Rawlings. I hope your employer is understanding."

"I guess he'll have to be. It's been an education, no matter what happens."

Rawlings looked at the bodies and weapons strewn across the pavement and dirt. For a moment Teakon thought he might try and stop them for the cube, but he appeared thankful for the life-saving assist. Slone kept a trained eye on him as they walked up the road toward their car just in case.

"He knows about us," Slone commented with an underlying tone.

"We can't go whacking everyone who knows a little something about us or the cubes, Greg," Teakon warned. "It's bad enough we have to take life at all."

"The greater good, Mark. That's what you told me when we first met."

Teakon felt sweat dripping down his forehead and chest, not so much from the dry desert heat as the toll each recovery took on him. He felt nervous before, during, and for a few days after each event. Luckily he had Slone for cold and calculating brawn and Julie for devising and maintaining their bookstore and antique dealership front.

Looking back one last time, he wondered how Rawlings planned to leave the premises with his vehicle broken down. If no police were summoned, a resourceful man such as Rawlings had plenty of time to find alternate transportation and fabricate a story. Teakon imagined the man probably had some of the up-front funds from his assignment remaining.

"What's next for us?" Slone asked once they reached their rental vehicle.

"We get home and see what Julie says our options are. Saving the world requires funding, my boy."

Slone packed his firearms in the trunk, which they would dispose of before returning the car and flying home. Covering their tracks completely was impossible, but the group made it difficult to trace their whereabouts and activities. Teakon pulled the cube from his shirt pocket, examined it, and dropped it into a black cloth draw-string bag. In theory, collecting just one of the objects and hiding it kept the world safe, but Teakon was raised to be thorough in everything he set out to do.

While he had concerns about Rawlings, and the man's employer, knowing about the cursed cubes, Teakon didn't have the stomach for tying up loose ends. If trouble came his way, Slone dealt with it accordingly, but becoming mercenaries defeated their original charter.

"What do we do with that?" Slone asked once they were both seated inside the car, referring to the cube.

"I'll find a safe place for it."

He didn't like telling Slone or Julie about the details, mainly for their safety. If he was the only one who knew where the objects were placed then he could take such secrets to the grave, even if someone tortured him first.

Always thinking ahead, Julie had booked them separate flights to and from the West Coast. The move also gave time for Slone to clean things up on his end, particularly since his weaponry was bought on the black market discreetly.

Teakon didn't particularly like operating outside of the law, but discretion was an absolute must. He felt working for a higher power superseded any man-made laws because the cursed objects stood in defiance of the church and God Himself. If Teakon and his team didn't make an effort to recover them, someone with sinister plans might make a similar attempt, or the cubes might be used to take countless lives.

"You want me to drop you off at the airport and take care of things?" Slone asked as sandy scenery passed them in a blur.

"I hope by 'take care of things' you mean the weapons and car only."

"I suppose," Slone grumbled.

Sometimes Teakon didn't know how seriously to take Slone's replies because the man was constantly cynical, accompanied by dry humor.

He only knew at this point he wanted to be home, able to sleep in his warm bed inside his refurbished Victorian home, or letting his dog outside for a walk around the block. His two children had moved away after completing college, leaving him alone to conduct his work. If not for his wife passing away at the hands of a cursed object, Teakon might never have taken up such a dangerous cause.

Glancing behind him, he thought about Rawlings before laying his head back to rest a few minutes before they reached the city limits.

***

As much as Jane Clouse hated leaving her kids alone for a minute, she felt equal concern for her husband after the recent turn of events. She marched through the casino toward the offices in the back, prepared to take action before more threats entered either of her hotels, or the casino itself.

Passing through an employee doorway, she checked the camera room, finding one of the senior security staff monitoring casino activity from a swivel chair.

"Hello, Mrs. Clouse," he said, barely shifting his eyes away from the screens to address her.

"Is Daniels here?"

"If he's not in his office he probably stepped outside for a minute."

Jane checked his office, finding it locked with no answer when she knocked.

She hadn't seen Daniels on the way in, but she doubted he would leave for the day so early. After doing a quick walkthrough of the casino, trying to avoid the lights and carnival sounds, she walked past security, finding Daniels outside a side door as he finished a cigarette, snuffing the butt as he exhaled upward.

One of the hotel employees who had joined him outside quickly scurried off when he spied Jane coming toward them.

"To what do I owe the pleasure?" Daniels asked.

"I need you to do something for me, Mark."

"Is this business, or off the record?"

"Off the record, and you're probably not going to like it."

Jane and Daniels had always been cordial since he and her husband were practically best friends. Other than the life-threatening ordeals they survived together, she saw very little in common between them. She didn't particularly like Clouse throwing him a bone after his divorce, because business and friends made bad bedfellows. They had bought Daniels and Cindy a waterside home when they were married, which Jane considered more than generous toward any friend.

In a manner of speaking, she felt Daniels owed her family for being so kind to him. By the sour look on his face, he seemed to sense the favor about to be asked of him.

"What do you want from me, Jane?"

No trace of friendliness remained in his expression because he knew she wasn't there for his benefit.

"It's occurred to me that some strange things have been happening at the other hotel lately, and I think Paul has turned a blind eye to a few things."

"Such as?"

"The bulletproof man who tried to kidnap my kids, Tim Niemeyer's sudden return, and the lack of evidence unearthed by local police. Randy Niemeyer is so giddy he can't see straight to investigate anything, and Troy Tackett virtually hates us, so he's not much help."

"And your private investigator was murdered," Daniels added. "Are you ordering me to be your next sacrificial lamb? Because that's not part of my job description."

"I'm asking you to discreetly check on a few things. You've got your police contacts, and I'm sure you've made new friends since working here."

Daniels sighed heavily, openly disturbed by the request.

"This is for Paul, not for me. He's too consumed with Tim's return and getting the hotel to stay afloat to look over his own shoulder."

"What do you want me to look at?"

"Maybe you can see if Tackett has any information about Bloom's murder, or why Tim is suddenly back from the dead. It just seems funny that Randy is mailed a video of his brother, and Tim winds up on our front lawn a few days later."

"Are you saying you don't trust the brothers?"

Jane shook her head.

"I don't know who to trust right now. We both know Smith had lots of backup plans before his death and we've already fallen behind whatever this is."

"We don't know this is Smith."

"You're right. We don't know what or who this is, but you can probably find out."

"Is this an order?"

"No. This is for Paul, your friend who's done so much to help you out."

Daniels sneered, wiping his expression clean within a second's time.

"I'll admit I appreciate everything you've both done for me, but giving my life isn't the repayment I had in mind."

"I'm not asking for repayment. This is all about protecting my husband, protecting all of us, and bringing this whole thing to an end. I would *never* send you on a suicide mission."

Daniels stared toward the French Lick resort behind him, rubbing his hand across his mouth and jaw in frustration.

"I'll make a few calls. If I come up with anything I'll e-mail you so Paul doesn't find out."

"Thank you for doing this, and for keeping it under wraps."

"This is for Paul. Make no mistake about it."

Jane appreciated that Daniels was a man of few words, satisfied that he maintained loyalty to her husband. She didn't particularly enjoy putting him in such a position, but Jane had few law enforcement avenues, and even fewer people that she trusted.

"Take care, Mark," Jane said before walking toward her car.

Daniels watched her momentarily, wondering what her intentions were, and why she chose to single him out. He felt he owed Paul Clouse for quite a few things, but Daniels had suffered during the course of the hotel murders only because he was ordered to investigate them almost seven years prior. His life had been in danger several times by scythe, gun, and knife.

Prior to the past week he might have thrown caution to the wayside a bit more rashly, but recent talks with Cindy seemed far more amicable. He didn't want to trick himself into thinking they were getting back together just yet, but helping Jane in any way meant doing exactly what Cindy hated most.

Something about the events at the hotel, and Ray Bloom's murder, didn't quite add up. In the past, the people behind the murders typically made them spectacles for the press and locals to gossip about. This time someone had a more secretive agenda, skulking behind the scenes with an ultimate evil intent yet to be revealed.

Daniels examined the hotel and casino surrounding him, wondering who might be responsible, hoping Smith really hadn't found a way to regenerate himself as mansion witnesses believed. Reaching inside his sport coat, he fished for a cigarette to calm his nerves before returning inside. Dealing with dozens of employees and potentially cheating guests suddenly seemed easy compared to what Jane asked of him. Falling back on his experience as a detective, he decided to check on those around him, at both hotels, knowing the past troubles stemmed from familiar people.

He lit up, staring in the direction of the West Baden hotel down the road, deciding where to start his search.

Chapter 26

After spending some time with his family, Tim Niemeyer accepted a dinner invitation to dine with Clouse and his family at the hotel. Clouse had given him the okay to bring any of his family members he wanted to, so he brought his parents.

While the kids had room service with their current chaperone, since Parish was done for the day, Clouse and Jane sat at a large round table with Niemeyer and his parents, who were obviously thrilled about his return. They also seemed to enjoy the hotel atmosphere, their eyes darting from the conversation to the chef preparing a nearby couple's food just feet away from them behind a small, clear partition about the size of a bank teller window.

"So Randy couldn't make it?" Clouse asked his friend.

"Nah. He's spending time with the wife and kids."

Within a few minutes the entire group had put in their drink and dinner orders. Clouse found it difficult to engage his guests in conversation because they kept watching the chef prepare their food. For ordinary hotel guests, seats beside the chef cost extra because it was such a privilege to see gourmet food being prepared.

"Sorry," Martha Niemeyer said when she noticed Clouse and Jane waiting for her to speak again. "It's just such an amazing place you have here."

"Thank you," Jane said graciously with a smile.

Clouse knew she had put on a front lately with all of the strange events at the hotel. So far, their idea of protection by surrounding themselves with others had proven effective, but her patience wore thin when the kids were targeted.

As part of the invitation, Clouse had invited Niemeyer's parents to spend the night at the hotel. They insisted on dressing up for dinner, much to Niemeyer's chagrin, though Clouse wasn't particularly thrilled about donning a suit, either. He found a charcoal gray suit that fit, wearing a pair of eel-skin black cowboy boots. Jane chose an emerald green dress that hugged her curves well. Around her neck was a multi-tiered gold chain with inlaid black pearls and diamonds that glistened even in the restaurant's low light.

"I got my driver's license," Niemeyer said with a grin. "My life's almost back to normal."

His look went from jovial to moderately somber.

"Except my wife is remarried and my kids don't know what to think."

"They'll come around," Niemeyer's father, Charlie, told him with a pat on the back.

"You ready to ride that Harley?" Clouse asked, trying to change the subject.

"Am I ever," Niemeyer replied with renewed enthusiasm.

"It's in the garage whenever you want it," Clouse offered.

"How is your health?" Jane asked, steering away from manly subjects.

"I feel good. Haven't had time for a checkup yet, and without any insurance I can't afford the hospital."

Jane set down her glass of red wine, giving him a reassuring smile.

"Stop by the clinic and I'll get you a full exam, plus blood work."

"You flirting with my friends, dear?" Clouse joked, drawing a snicker from Niemeyer.

A few minutes later their meals arrived, but Niemeyer ate slowly, a look of concern crossing his face.

"Penny for your thoughts, buddy," Clouse said.

"I've just been catching up on some news and rumors, Paul. I'd like to have a talk with you sometime about a few things."

"Sure."

Niemeyer's parents took note of the uncomfortable silence at the table a few seconds afterward until Martha spoke.

"We really appreciate you letting us spend the night. We've been wanting to get down here for so long and just haven't had the chance."

"We're glad to have you," Jane said. "I can't imagine how happy you must be to have Tim back."

"We're tickled," Charlie answered. "Five years ago it was the worst time of our lives. First Ken, then our boy. We were worried to death about the two of you after that."

Clouse had grown up around the Niemeyers, considering them an extension of his own family. During their high school years, Clouse, Niemeyer, and Ken Kaiser were virtually inseparable. They had sleep overs on weekends, played sports together at the local youth centers and city parks, and had a ritual of eating out every Friday night after school. All three had clean fun, leaving their parents little to worry about because they never did drugs or fell into the wrong crowd.

Clouse felt he had grown up right, hoping Zach and Katie might someday get a taste of what a normal life felt like. Caught between teaching them values and protecting them from the boogeyman lurking around every corner, he simply hoped they didn't need psychiatric help when they reached high school.

Some tense feelings existed between Clouse's family and the families of Ken Kaiser and Tim Niemeyer after they were both reported dead as a result of their friendship with Clouse. Tackett also grew distant, leaving him with no friends or neighbors who cared. He threw himself into raising his kids, salvaging the hotel, and remaining by Jane's side because she had stuck by him.

A wave of relief came over him when his friend turned up alive. Though Clouse and Kaiser had remained closer friends over the years, he missed Niemeyer's on and off again accent, and the man's quirky one-liners.

"I've got a little surprise for you, Tim," he said, spying Dan Duncan coming toward them with a small box. "Everyone, this is my manager here at the hotel, Dan Duncan."

After everyone exchanged pleasantries, Dan held out the box toward Niemeyer, then opened it as smoothly as a game show host displaying a prize.

"I heard you used to like these, so I picked out some good ones at one of our local shops for you."

"Wow," Niemeyer said, fingering one of the dozen cigars inside the small rose-wood humidor. "Haven't had one of these in about-"

"Five years?" Clouse finished for him.

"These are some of the finest available," Duncan added. "And this is all yours, compliments of the house."

"Thank you," Niemeyer said as his mother rolled her eyes.

"I was hoping he might forget all about those things."

Niemeyer flashed her a quick smile.

"You've got to enjoy the finer things in life, Mother."

***

Determined to get a few good shots for his newspaper, or any tabloids willing to pay for them, Parsons remained in the wooded shadows behind the hotel. He had returned, setting up a telephoto lens on the hillside near the parking lot when no one was looking, simply waiting for interesting shots.

He desperately wanted a photo of Tim Niemeyer, a man currently considered a hot topic in the local press. His prayers were answered when he zoomed into the restaurant, finding the Clouse family dining with Tim Niemeyer and an older couple. His heartbeat doubled instantly as he tried to seat himself comfortably on the leafy ground to settle in for some good photo opportunities.

Now growing dark outside with the sun setting, Parsons could easily see inside the restaurant through windows with undrawn shades. He had already set his camera on a tripod, able to use a manual release cord if he wanted to shoot a picture without touching the unit. It was one of the few techniques that worked in any low light setting.

He observed the group ordering, then eating, occasionally snapping pictures that looked appropriate for sale or print. Feeling his patience was paying dividends, he focused on the task at hand, not worried about video cameras or bodyguards this time. His jaw ached from the earlier punch, causing him to wish he could catch the bodyguard responsible in a precarious position.

This time around, Parsons had a perfect hiding spot to himself. After parking his car, he walked directly to the woods behind the parking lots, then hiked to a spot clear enough for photography, but bushy enough to conceal him from security and the valets.

Parsons continued to photograph the dinner scene until the sound of twigs snapping behind him caught his attention. He turned, careful not to disturb his steadied camera, but saw no one there, and nothing unusual, considering the weather was clear and pleasant.

Returning his attention to the restaurant, he started to look through his camera, adjusting the focus toward Tim Niemeyer, when something blacked out his lens.

Looking up, he saw a black-clad figure standing over him, figuring security had discovered him. Parsons tried formulating an excuse about why he would be in the bushes when the man grabbed him, yanking him to his feet. Now Parsons noticed the figure wore a black mask beneath a hood of the same color, raising his anxiety considerably.

"I didn't mean any harm," he said in protest to whatever the mystery man had in mind. "My editor knows I'm here."

Now the figure produced a knife from beneath the drooping sleeve of his right arm. Parsons simply stared with wide eyes, fearing for his life.

Unsure of who would want to harm him, or why, he took a step back, catching his foot on some thick vines or roots lying atop the ground. He started to fall on his back, but the figure caught him by the shirt, pulling him to an upright position before thrusting the knife into his abdomen. Parsons started to let an agonized scream escape his lips, but the assailant cupped his mouth violently before repeating several stabs to his stomach and ribs.

Feeling his life quickly ebb away, Parsons collapsed to the ground clutching his stomach, hearing the grass crunch around him. His assailant removed his camera from the tripod, standing over him momentarily as though examining his handiwork. He then searched Parsons' pockets for car keys, finding them momentarily before grabbing the photographer's shirt once more. This time, however, he dragged Parsons along the dewy ground toward the parking lot as consciousness wavered for the photographer.

Blood swirled around his innards, some of it leaking to the outside, creating a red trail along the leaves and shrubs lining the ground. He didn't know how much longer he would hold out before expiring, but Parsons wished he had chosen a different career path.

The last thing he saw was an overhead light from one of the parking lot globes that shimmered like the path to a heavenly gate. He hoped it wasn't just his imagination playing one last trick on him.

***

Shortly after dusk, Clouse rocked on a veranda chair in the warm spring air as Duncan and his high school buddy smoked cigars near the balcony railing. He wished grave concerns hadn't returned to his life on a regular basis, but supposed worries were inevitable.

While most people fretted about taxes, house payments, and stress at work, Clouse woke up every morning, wondering if he or a member of his family might be targeted for death. If not for the mystery surrounding Smith's possible return at the mansion two years prior, he might have slept easier at night, and men like Todd Parish might be working elsewhere.

Niemeyer's parents took an impromptu tour with Jane, thrilled she was going to tell them the history of the building and all of the behind-the-scene secrets of what it took to rebuild it. Clouse had only been dating his wife when the hotel was first restored, but she was part of the creative force behind the second restoration once they decided to open a casino.

"Life is good again, Paul," Niemeyer said, exhaling a stream of gray smoke toward the veranda roof. "Five years in captivity drains a man of ambitions, but you never forget the good stuff."

Duncan gave him a perplexed look.

"Five years? That's a long time."

Clouse was glad Duncan had volunteered to stay over, hoping the gift to Niemeyer might expedite the psychological healing process for his friend. Having Duncan, Jennings, and other familiar faces around him kept Clouse feeling a bit safer from the world beyond his hotel property.

If he thought too deeply about it, his logic appeared flawed because most of the past problems occurred *at* the hotel.

"Randy wants to talk to me about my ordeal tomorrow," Niemeyer revealed. "Says he wants me to officially identify the guy who fed me in the cell so they can make a case of it."

"I'm a little bit surprised he isn't by your side at all times."

"He got some bad news. Effective Monday, he's being taken out of the drug task force and placed in the detectives division."

"You make it sound like a bad thing."

"He's not happy about it. They'll make him mop up old cases."

"Maybe he'll be in a position to find out who was behind your abduction."

Duncan listened to their conversation, though he tried to shield his interest by staring into the garden. He drew on his cigar before looking to the headlights coming their way along the brick path.

Someone was checking in late.

"You going to carry their bags?" Clouse joked.

"I'll leave that to the kids."

Though Duncan performed his managerial duties exceptionally well, he barely knew how to turn a computer on, much less check guests in, or solve any of their problems electronically. He made efforts to learn, but some of the hotel software continued to elude him.

"I am going to take a look out back before I head out for the night," Duncan said, strolling toward the back end of the veranda.

"Take care, Dan," Clouse said.

"Good meeting you," Niemeyer added.

"Likewise."

Duncan walked to the end of the veranda, swallowed by darkness as Niemeyer slumped into a rocking chair a few feet away from his friend.

"Something on your mind?" Clouse inquired.

Niemeyer let a sigh escape before answering.

"I guess this isn't the life I thought I'd be coming back to."

"How's that?"

"I didn't expect the kids to be so freaked out when they saw me, Paul. I always figured Vicky would move on, find someone new, but the kids..."

"So the meeting didn't go as well as you'd hoped?"

Niemeyer waved a frustrated hand against the air.

"You know, I just wanted to come back and start a normal life, but everything requires an appointment, and it's almost like starting over from birth. I can't even drop in to see the kids without calling first, like Ah'm divorced, or some convict. And, you know, it really bothers me that I can't remember what happened to me that night after I lost consciousness."

"Don't let it eat at you. What matters is that you got a second chance, Tim. It might not be perfect, but it's what you make of it. You still have friends and family who care about you. Vicky and the kids will come around when they're ready."

"What if I hadn't come back at all? Maybe things would be better for everyone."

"Don't say that, Tim. Things are never perfect, even in everyday life."

"What about this?" Niemeyer asked, waving his arm across the span of the garden. "You fell into something good with all of this."

Clouse scoffed at the words.

"It's both a blessing and a curse, my friend. I've been looking over my shoulder ever since I got the place."

"I've had some time to digest things since returning from the dead, Paul. Do you think it's possible Smith had something to do with what happened to me?"

"He had some contingency plans, so anything is possible. But if that's the case, the person monitoring you had no reason to keep you locked up when Smith really died."

"Except to blackmail you."

"Maybe, but why would he wait so long to blackmail me?"

Niemeyer shrugged helplessly.

"I see you've beefed up security around here."

"With the hotel open, I can't screen who comes and goes around here, so we hired experienced people to protect the kids and watch over the guests."

"Hardly sounds like living to me if you're that worried all the time."

"There are some things about Smith you never got to see. He and his minions are the only threat to me and my family."

Niemeyer directed his blue eyes Clouse's way with a hard, questioning stare.

"Can there be any of them left?"

"It's hard telling. He hired a number of people to bring him back."

Both men sat silently a moment, staring into the starry night above the garden.

"I'm worried about you, buddy," Clouse finally said. "You're welcome to stay here as long as you want. I know you want to be around family, but it might be safer for everyone involved if you're here."

"My parents and Randy can put me up. I feel like staying here would kind of be another prison. No offense."

"None taken. But you're welcome anytime."

"Thanks. You know, I'm still worried about the fact that this former state trooper was dead before I got dumped outside your hotel. It's hard to believe Smith had that many resources."

"He had a legion of followers before he died, so who's to say he didn't reform the Coven before I killed him?"

"You and I know something about the importance of life, but he had no regard for anyone but himself, did he?"

"No, he didn't. He had me fooled for years, Tim. His actions cost me a lot of anguish, including losing you and Ken. I've never forgiven myself for what happened to you guys, so there won't be any mercy given to anyone left on Smith's payroll."

Niemeyer looked around the veranda, then up to the decorative light fixtures glowing above them.

"I haven't told my parents any of this. They're just so happy to have me back, and happy to be *here*, that I didn't have the heart to say anything."

"Just enjoy tonight, my friend," Clouse said, leaning back comfortably in his chair. "That's all you gotta do."

Chapter 27

Clouse showered the next morning after Jane went downstairs to give Niemeyer's parents a daytime tour of the gardens. He wanted to be present when Niemeyer saw his new motorcycle for the first time out of the dealership, but stopped to look at his secondary cell phone. It had an unchecked voice mail, and the number came back to someone both familiar and very important.

To keep himself safely distanced from Rawlings, in case someone compromised the man's investigation, Clouse purchased a disposable cell phone for only their conversations. He didn't want any direct links to him or his family in case something happened to the investigator. Removing the phone from its charger, Clouse stepped through the living room with only blue jeans and socks toward his bedroom.

"Good morning, Todd," he said to Parish, who watched over the kids as they raced one another in a video game.

"Morning, sir," Parish answered. "Any major plans for the day?"

Parish often inquired out of professional courtesy so he didn't overstep his bounds with the kids.

"Not yet, but that may be about to change," Clouse replied, holding up the cell phone.

Stepping outside the suite, he checked the message, which came from Alan Rawlings, indicating Clouse needed to call him immediately. The call went rather badly on Clouse's end, considering he anticipated good news regarding the cursed object. Though he hadn't formally devised a plan to recover and hide all of the cubes, he figured Rawlings was the man to get him a good start. Involving more people meant adding to the risk factors of greed and potential loss of human life.

Rawlings informed him about Teakon, the bloodshed at Pershing's house, and the complete loss of the cube.

"When you hired me, I didn't believe a word you said about its importance," Rawlings confessed after his relaying the information. "Now I'm sold."

Clouse didn't particularly care about the man's opinion at the moment.

He wanted facts.

"This *Teakon*. What's his angle?"

"I think he wants the things for the right reasons. To hide, or possibly disperse them."

Clouse thought of the terrible repercussions if the opposite scenario played out. Bringing together the cubes might spell disaster on a global level.

"This book of his. What did he say about it?"

Rawlings spent a few minutes explaining the book's tracking ability regarding the cubes. Clouse wondered if it was just a matter of time before Teakon came looking for him.

Or perhaps he already had, explaining some of the recent strange events.

"And he said this book was part of the curse?"

"He did."

Clouse questioned whether Mark Teakon was friend or foe, which meant a world of difference whether the man possessed that book or not.

Over the next few minutes Rawlings relayed the entire curse saga to Clouse, which explained a few issues, but opened up new questions at the same time.

"How do I find this guy?"

"I found him through one of my contacts. The only thing I have is a phone number, because we met at a neutral site in Baltimore. He lives somewhere on the East Coast, but he doesn't leave much of a trail."

"Smart man. Maybe he has family members on the titles of his house and vehicles. I can track him down."

"Sir, with all due respect-"

"I said I could track him, Alan. You've done a great job getting me this far, and I'll be sending you adequate payment for time and effort spent."

Both of them knew the agreement was payment in full only when the cube was delivered to Clouse.

"Is this a sympathy bonus or a severance package?"

"Neither," Clouse said, strolling toward a window that overlooked the atrium with people milling about five stories below him. "It's half of what pay you would have received if the cube had been placed in my hand. I'll let you know when your services are required again."

Clouse severed the call before Rawlings could object further. He clipped the phone to his side before returning to the living room where he called the kids over to him.

Realizing he had neglected them earlier, he gave them each a quick hug.

"I'm going to be downstairs with Tim for a little while. You guys be okay with Todd?"

They both nodded quickly and affirmatively.

"Good. Mom and I will see you in a little bit."

With Jane's ex-husband out of the picture, seldom finding time to see his daughter, both kids had grown accustomed to having a single family. Katie often called Clouse her father, while Zach considered Jane his mother, having lost his natural mother at a very young age.

A few minutes later Clouse found Niemeyer on the veranda staring out at the garden where Jane was showing his parents some of the blossoming plants.

"I thought maybe you'd sleep in," he told his friend.

"Too nice a morning for that. I loved the room, Paul. You've really outdone yourself the way you fixed up this place."

"Thanks. You ready to see that Harley again?"

Niemeyer lit up like a halogen bulb.

"I thought you'd never ask."

***

Along the first floor of the hotel, Daniels walked from the valet area toward Jennings' office to compare their findings. Both had spent countless hours reviewing every single employee hired since the casino opened.

Reaching the office, Daniels gave a brief rap on the doorway, stepping in before Jennings had time to invite him as he looked up from some memos.

"Have a seat, Mark," Jennings said with a wave of his arm.

Today he wore blue jeans and a golf shirt with an official resort emblem on the chest. He looked a bit fatigued, as though he hadn't slept well the night before. Massaging his eyes, cheeks, and neck, Jennings set aside his memos for a stack of reports.

"Hitting the greens later?" Daniels inquired.

"Hadn't planned to. I wanted to get some sleep today but the wife has other plans for me."

Daniels flopped his own thick packet of files atop the desk.

"I'm coming up empty on my end," he revealed. "I've checked and rechecked every person I've hired since the casino opened. Every person who had high level casino access was hired by me personally, and I had a hand in every interview."

"Pretty much the same story on my end. I can't vouch for hotel staff on the cleaning and cooking end, but my people all seem to check out. I even double-checked references, addresses, and everything."

"Does Duncan have a hand in all of his hires?"

"Probably not. He's a busy guy, plus he barely knows what a computer is."

"That could be our problem," Daniels thought aloud. "Or maybe this person simply figured out how to get into our system."

"That's not likely."

"Oh? You can say that after Jon Lopez appeared in our system after you say you deleted him?"

"I *did* delete him. Even if he hadn't quit or disappeared, it's safer to put them back into the system than run a security risk. And what exactly are you implying?"

"That our security system isn't flawless. Who designed that system anyway?"

Jennings looked incredulous as though a frying pan had struck him in the face because the thought had never crossed his mind.

"Mr. Clouse hired some company to write the software."

"Maybe we should check into that."

"The more time we spend checking on everything, the more this person, or persons, will infiltrate what defenses we have."

Daniels couldn't argue the point. Both he and Jennings had jobs to do without playing detective on the side. He planned on honoring Jane's request to dig up other clues without overextending himself. His life provided him with enough problems outside of work, so jeopardizing his career, and perhaps his life, didn't bode well for making his situation better.

"Any other ideas for making this place safer?" Jennings asked.

"Carry your gun with you at all times. You're going to have to watch the employees here, and French Lick."

Daniels smirked.

"You do know how to use your firearm, right?"

Jennings sighed in response.

"You're not the only one who survived an ordeal around here, my friend. I don't plan on seeing myself or anyone else harmed, so if I need to hire more security, so be it. And, yes, I do know how to fire my gun."

"I'm getting back to work, but I'll let you know if anything comes up."

"Sounds good. I'm going to enjoy what's left of my day off."

Daniels left the room wondering whom he dared trust. He knew it only took one person to disrupt life as he and everyone around him knew it. If that one person had access to their security system, no one was safe. Partly out of survival instinct, he didn't consider anyone working around him as competent as himself. While he wasn't arrogant about his abilities and knowledge, Daniels performed his job thoroughly at all times.

He couldn't trust others at the hotels and casino to do the same.

Passing the lobby, he noticed Clouse and Niemeyer standing near one of the doors in conversation. Daniels couldn't help but wonder why Niemeyer was suddenly back in the picture. Perhaps it was coincidence, but he doubted it. He wondered if Niemeyer was part of the problem, or a cleverly placed decoy meant to throw everyone off balance.

Daniels was present during the calling hours and the funeral. Like everyone else, he was convinced beyond any reasonable doubt the man was dead and buried. The horrific tale told by Randy Niemeyer, along with video from the ATM security camera, left little doubt Tim Niemeyer died an agonizing death at the hands of six people.

Yet the man stood less than twenty feet from him, beyond an authentic antique window.

Deciding to leave before the two friends spotted him, fearing an awkward conversation, Daniels made his way toward the rear entrance with his files in hand.

He still had a busy day ahead of him.

Chapter 28

Troy Tackett knew he wasn't going to like the crime scene one bit when he received a call about a body found in the woods surrounding Lake Monroe. A popular camping, fishing, and boating resort during the warm summer hours, the lake hosted hundreds on a daily basis during the peak season.

He had just started making evening plans as his morning shift drew to a close, but a call concerning a corpse missing its right hand came in. One of the local conservation officers answered the call when a couple hiking near the lake followed a stench to the body. Tackett received a few details from the officer discreetly over one of their unmonitored tactical channels, knowing they had found Jon Lopez before he left the station.

After navigating his way through several dirt roads, he found himself less than a quarter mile from the lake where the scene had already been taped off by a road officer. The officer brought him up to speed by relaying what the witnesses said, while preparing him for the deteriorated condition of the body.

"That the couple?" Tackett asked, looking over toward a man and woman younger than himself dressed for hiking and camping, their packs lying on the ground beside them.

"That's them. They didn't see anyone else back here."

"Why would they?" Tackett asked himself more than his fellow county officer. "Our stiff has been here a while."

Were he a betting man, the detective would lay odds that Lopez had been there about a week, dating back to the night he disappeared.

"Just take their information and cut 'em loose," Tackett instructed the officer so he could turn his attention to the body.

Luckily for him a gentle breeze carried most of the foul odor of the body in the opposite direction. Certainly no stranger to bodies, Tackett found the tiny bottle of peppermint oil he always kept with him in a pouch beside his spare ammunition. Dabbing some under his nose, he examined the body from a safe distance, looking for visible evidence, including footprints or discarded items.

He knew his department's other forensic technician was already making his way down, so Tackett waited another five minutes for Henry 'Hank' Ziegler to arrive in his marked van.

"Long time no see," Tackett commented, since the two had shared a quick lunch together in town earlier that day.

"Sorry I'm running behind. I was running a test in the lab when the call came in."

Only a few years away from retirement, Ziegler was one of the most professional officers Tackett had ever worked beside. He knew forensics like nobody's business, and gave Tackett several pointers in detective work shortly after his promotion. Ziegler's strands of gray hair fluttered in the gentle breeze as his brown eyes scanned the ground like a hawk searching for prey.

While some of the younger technicians in the area were territorial, Ziegler didn't mind help on a scene as long as officers weren't blatantly stupid about their techniques. He respected Tackett enough that he didn't mind the detective poking around the scene before he arrived.

"See anything?" he asked finally.

"I didn't get too close, Hank. This is related to something else I've got, so I didn't take any chances."

Ziegler nodded.

"Not surprising, there aren't any footprints."

They were surrounded by tall grass, rocks ranging from pebbles to small boulders, and dirt that had gone from a hardened state to mud and back again.

"Any DNA will probably be inadmissible," Ziegler muttered, though this wasn't news to Tackett.

"I'll settle for a solid lead at the moment."

After putting on latex gloves and foot covers, Ziegler offered Tackett the same items, then proceeded to check around the crime scene with the detective in tow. Occasionally snapping pictures and grunting to himself as he went, Ziegler convinced Tackett he had found something of interest.

When Ziegler was in the zone, no one questioned him or his methods until the examination was complete.

Tackett finally got his first close-up look at Lopez's body when Ziegler photographed it from a few feet away. For the most part, the remains were bloated bluish-gray flesh, ravaged by scavengers and birds. If not for the neatly severed forearm, Tackett might have thought a scavenger ripped the hand off for supper. He tried looking for any distinguishing features along the body, but even the eye sockets were overcome with puffy flesh.

Being in the warm, moist outdoors had taken a toll on the body rather quickly. While the body was still clothed, the flesh ran over parts of the cloth like the top of a muffin over its paper bottom. In a few areas the skin had split open from exposure to the elements, much like an overdone hotdog. Tackett recognized the tattered remains of the uniform as the type Clouse's security people wore at both of his hotels.

"Poor sap," he muttered.

"What?" Ziegler asked.

"Nothing. Sorry, Hank."

Tackett eventually chose to watch Ziegler work from a distance to give the man some peace and quiet. Leaning against the front of his marked Ford Explorer, Tackett opened a pouch of chewing tobacco, stuffing a wad into his mouth before spitting brown juice to the ground a few seconds later.

"I thought you were quitting that," Ziegler commented when he returned a few minutes later.

"I was going to lose a few pounds, too, but shit happens."

Tackett spat another trail of brown refuse toward the ground. He had learned long ago how to talk around the wad jutting from his cheek, his voice changing very little.

"Find anything of interest?"

"I only found one piece of physical evidence," Ziegler answered, holding up a sealed plastic bag with a brown substance that looked like dirt within it.

"Is that mud?" Tackett asked, drawing closer for a personal examination.

"It's flaky, unlike dirt, and there were trace amounts on his shirt and pants. It would have blown away if it hadn't gotten embedded in his blood."

Tackett's mind immediately went back to the brown specks found at the hotel when Clouse's bodyguard was attacked by an intruder.

"That might be the same thing they found at the West Baden Springs Hotel last week," Tackett revealed. "Can you check with the state lab for comparison?"

"What did they find at the hotel?"

"They thought it was flecks of dead skin."

"If that's what this is, I can have them do a comparison, but unless you have a suspect in mind, I can't get a rush on the results. You already know that, Troy."

Tackett thought back to the talk he had with Clouse. Logic, reason, and his police training all told him what Clouse spoke of was impossible, but he also knew irrefutable facts to the contrary. Martin Smith somehow shaved decades off his age before dying for real, and Clouse's bodyguard emptied a full clip into someone, including head shots, before that person fled from the suite.

"You have someone in mind, don't you?" Ziegler asked with a knowing look.

"I do, but it'll be hard to match."

"Why's that?"

"The man I have in mind is supposed to be dead."

***

Tackett worked in conjunction with the coroner's office over the next hour, finally leaving the scene once he and Ziegler were satisfied with their investigation. The deputy coroner who responded officially declared Lopez dead before delving into his portion of the investigation, which included identifying the dead security guard.

Lopez had identification inside his wallet, along with nearly one-hundred dollars in cash. His murder certainly wasn't a botched mugging, or some random killing. The deputy coroner filled out some paperwork, bagged any loose items, and began the search for the next of kin needing notification.

Ziegler promised to put a rush on the evidence to the state lab in the morning, despite Tackett refusing to reveal whom he thought the DNA belonged to.

"You're obstructing justice in your own way," he lectured the detective.

"No one would believe me, Hank."

"They won't if you don't say it."

"This person is dead and buried, and there's no way to draw his DNA anyway."

Ziegler's face twisted in confusion.

"A ghost killed this guy and attacked people at the hotel?"

"See? Right there, you're already putting me in a padded room."

Holding up his hands defensively, Ziegler walked away to gather his equipment.

Now Tackett drew near his county home, ready to put his workday behind him. He wanted to contact authorities in Orange County, and possibly Craig Jennings at the hotel, but didn't want to risk word leaking out before Lopez's family was notified.

Sifting through Ray Bloom's paperwork hadn't proven to be a picnic either, and he saw absolutely no traces of targeted people, or their birth dates, in any of the records so far. Perhaps killing the private investigator and stealing his paperwork cut off all traces of another crime.

As he pulled into the long driveway leading to his house, Tackett's Golden Retriever, Rusty, greeted him at the halfway point, running alongside the truck to the house. Tackett stepped from his police vehicle, petting and lightly smacking the dog's side playfully.

"What's going on, boy?"

Though he refused to admit it to anyone else, the detective lived with a sense of paranoia after surviving what should have been a mortal stabbing. Had he not been wearing a rodeo vest to break it in, the knife certainly would have struck vital organs and caused internal bleeding enough to doom him before help arrived.

He made certain to have a loyal dog around at all times, kept his home security system armed around the clock, and slept with a gun under his pillow. His incident alone didn't haunt him so much as the fact that people around Paul Clouse tended to get killed, and if they survived, they often died during subsequent attempts.

It took the detective only a few minutes to replace his good clothes with jeans and old boots to do some work around the barn after he fed the horses and barn cats. As he walked toward the barn, thunder clapped in the distance, followed by a lightning strike that seemed to land in the middle of his largest field, though he knew it was miles away.

"Guess we're in for a storm," he told his dog, yanking open the barn door, which slid to one side after undoing the latch.

Tackett managed to feed the cats and his two horses while the storm drew closer. When the fourth set of rolling thunder sounded, followed by another electrical discharge from the sky, the lights flickered momentarily. Barely able to grab the closest rechargeable light before his barn went completely dark, Tackett felt grateful he never needed to navigate his barn in complete darkness again.

Rusty made a low moan as the thunder sounded again, but Tackett was already exiting the barn. Clouds had obscured any chance of viewing his property by starlight, including his house. His powerful flashlight and the occasional lightning bolts were the only thing able to create visibility as the sky unleashed a powerful rain upon Monroe County.

"Fuck," Tackett muttered as he unlocked his front door, absently fumbling for the security system knocked out by the power.

Realizing he was in for a boring evening, the detective made his way through the house, finding himself in a moment of weakness, wishing he were still married. His marriage, which happened in his late twenties, lasted only a few years. He had one daughter he saw whenever possible, providing the only remaining contact with his ex-wife. Seeing his little girl made life worth living, but his ex simply reminded him of how incompatible he had become in relationships.

He envied his former neighbor sometimes. The man had found true love twice in his life, and despite their hardships, Jane stuck by his side at all times.

Tackett set the flashlight beside his bed once more to change into sweat pants and an old shirt, deciding to call it a night early, since he couldn't do any work until the power was restored. In the outskirts of the county, it might take some time before the problem was tracked down.

As he finished changing, he heard Rusty whimper from the other room.

"Boy?" he called.

Rusty didn't run to him or make any further noise.

Tackett stood from the edge of his bed as lightning flashed outside, illuminating his house for the briefest of moments. Carrying the flashlight in one hand, he grabbed his service weapon with the other from the nearby night stand. As silently as possible, Tackett crept from his bedroom into the living room, shining the light before him in a sweeping pattern.

"Boy?"

Rusty rushed to his side from behind a couch as lightning flashed again, startling Tackett enough that his heart skipped a beat. At that moment he heard his cell phone ring from the kitchen where he had plugged it into the charger earlier.

"Tackett," he answered, still trying to catch his breath from the scare.

"Troy, this is Barry Waterson from the state police lab. Sorry to call so late, but I found a few interesting details about some samples that were dropped off last week."

"Oh?"

"Ziegler gave me a heads-up about some brown skin flakes you guys found on a body today, which got me to thinking. They had the same thing a week ago when that bodyguard was attacked at the West Baden hotel, right?"

"So I've heard," Tackett answered somewhat neutrally, since he hadn't actually worked the case.

"They had a similar reported substance two years ago at that mansion disaster just up the road from the hotel, so I did some digging, and found the old sample. And guess what, my preliminary tests show the two actually match up."

Not good, Tackett thought, not daring utter the words aloud.

"Is it human DNA?"

"It is. There's no question about it."

"Have you found a match yet?"

"I've checked the databases, but nothing came of it."

The state and national databases covered only the criminal element, typically any prisoners incarcerated over three months for particular crimes. Tackett's prime suspect had never been in jail, much less prison, leaving his primary concern unaddressed.

"Do you have someone you like for these cases?" Waterson inquired.

"I might. Can I get back with you tomorrow?"

Chapter 29

Daniels decided where he wanted to start his new investigation the next morning. He hadn't done real police work in almost two years, and worse yet, he had no official backing this time around. He had contacts, and hopefully they would provide the answers and access he needed.

Shirking his duties wasn't something he relished, but Clouse was too preoccupied to notice if he was gone an hour or two at a time. Besides, Daniels had the freedom to create his own schedule, giving him a reasonable excuse if he was asked about his whereabouts.

He started his morning by arriving at work and calling Randy Niemeyer from the list of contacts he had established with Clouse's help. The contacts, mostly survivors from past dealings with Martin Smith, were there in case he ever needed information regarding new developments. The numbers were also provided in case of an emergency, which seemed to be more necessary with each passing day.

Remembering that Niemeyer, according to Clouse, had been placed in the investigations division, Daniels tried him there first. Another officer answered the line, but Niemeyer came on a minute or so later.

"Niemeyer."

"Randy, it's Mark Daniels."

"Good morning, Mark. Can't say I expected to hear from you on my first day back to work."

"I hate to bother you, but I need to ask you a few questions."

Niemeyer let a silence linger between them momentarily.

"I thought you gave up the detective business for greener pastures."

"So did I, but I've been given a private assignment. I need to ask you about Nathan Runnels."

"I didn't really know him. I wasn't on very long when he quit, and we worked in different posts."

"Who could tell me about him?"

"He worked at the Jasper Post. There's only about five guys who work out of there, so a few of them probably remember him. Dale Greene is in charge of the post, and he's been there for years."

"I'm thinking I've met him," Daniels said, recalling some seminars, and even his original case at the West Baden Springs Hotel, where they had worked together.

A short time later the former detective found himself driving toward Jasper in the remains of the previous night's storm front. Rain spattered against the windshield and wipers of the company car he borrowed to make the drive. He certainly wasn't putting miles on his own vehicle, or buying gas, to do errands for Jane Clouse.

He didn't know much about the Jasper Post, but apparently they indeed ran with a total of four troopers and one detective. Considering the post covered six counties in all, he found the number of troopers rather surprising. Daniels wished he could have simply phoned Lieutenant Greene, but without his credentials backing him, a personal visit seemed in order.

A trooper working post command, considered dispatch at most police stations, greeted him, then called for the lieutenant. Daniels felt fortunate Greene wasn't preoccupied, since he was arriving unannounced, though he doubted the troopers saw much action in the primarily rural counties they patrolled.

When Greene first stepped into view from the office he reminded Daniels of the troopers used in billboard ads when police agencies were actively recruiting. Although he didn't have his park ranger style hat with him, Greene wore a perfectly pressed uniform, complete with brass adornments and appropriate patches. His brown hair was parted neatly to one side, graying slightly at the temples, and he carried himself with a distinguished air, openly evident through his upright posture.

Daniels reintroduced himself, finding his right hand clasped in Greene's five-fingered vice as the post commander gave him a curious look.

"I remember you from some of our cases," Greene said, "but I thought you left the detective business to run the casino in Orange County."

"I left to head up security at the casino, and I'm actually not here on official business."

"Oh?"

Daniels followed Greene back to his office where both men took a seat. The lieutenant didn't appear comfortable behind his desk, as though he missed the freedom that routine patrols offered. He put forth a brave front, but seconds into their conversation he shifted uneasily in no part because of his company.

"I was wondering if I could ask you about Nathan Runnels."

"I thought this wasn't official business," Greene countered. "The man was murdered just a few days ago."

"I'm aware of that, but I'm not interested in his death. I have reason to believe he quit here to work in the, uh, *private* sector."

Greene grimaced, as though the statement touched on something he already suspected.

"Nathan wasn't exactly your average cop," the lieutenant began. "In fact, I wondered on several occasions how he even passed our interviews and the psych test."

Daniels waited patiently for him to continue.

"He was somewhat of a loner, even more so than most of us. Didn't particularly socialize with us, didn't really do his job very well, either."

"How's that?"

"Hardly ever wrote tickets, never came to department functions, and hated being told what to do. It was like someone *made* him come here."

Daniels had a gut feeling the pieces were about to fall into place as Greene shifted uncomfortably in his chair once more.

"I hate being stuck in an office all day," he commented, noticing Daniels' stare. "So if you're not curious about who killed him, what do you want to know?"

Now Daniels didn't feel entirely comfortable.

"I have reason to believe he might have been responsible for someone's disappearance a few years back."

"Got proof of this?"

"Only someone's word. Runnels may have been paid a nice sum of money to watch over an abducted person, which could explain why he left so abruptly. Can you tell me how exactly he left the department?"

Greene started to reach for the filing cabinet and stopped suddenly, as though he didn't need any consultation.

"His file says he left under good terms, with no outstanding issues, but it felt funny when he handed me a letter of resignation and his two-week notice. Didn't say he had something else lined up, or that he was going to miss the job, or anything. The kid just shrugged his shoulders and said he was leaving."

"You never heard anything through the grapevine?"

"Nah. No one really knew him, so after his two weeks were up he just sort of vanished."

Greene gave him a cagy stare, his experience and insight probing Daniels and his motives like X-ray vision.

"There's something you're not telling me about this, isn't there?"

"Like I said, there's nothing I can prove. I'm just trying to make sure the person Runnels might have been working for doesn't cause more trouble around the casino."

"Who might he have been working for?"

"You wouldn't believe me if I told you," Daniels said, standing up. "I thank you for your time, Dale."

"Maybe I'll come down to your casino when the governor gives us a raise."

Daniels gave a quick smile, knowing every new Indiana governor promised the state police great things, then failed to deliver once they gained office.

"Guess I'll see you when we get a new governor, then."

***

Clouse felt somewhat relieved that his friend had gone back to stay with his parents in the Bedford area, though life at the hotel felt a bit more empty without Niemeyer around. He wished both of his best friends were around to see the hotel and how well he had done for himself. Considering Niemeyer missed five years of normal life, it still felt like both he and Kaiser were lost to him.

As he walked through the lobby, sealed coffee mug in hand, Clouse stopped to look at the beautifully redone stained glass windows the Jesuits installed during their tenure before he was born. Money, hotel ownership, and prestige failed to fill the void of friends and family lost over the past six years. He sometimes missed his old career as a firefighter. Things were simple in the brotherhood where the guys, and a few women, put their lives in one another's hands. His colleagues learned quickly whom they could rely upon to join them inside a blazing house with property and lives on the line.

Clouse no longer felt that security. His new empire consisted of a few remaining friends, several hand-picked employees, and people placed on his payroll simply to keep them from suing for damages. Even if someone brought him Martin Smith's body and the remains were cremated into particles smaller than sand, he wasn't sure his sense of security would ever return.

Blame cast invisible shadows all around him.

The stained glass windows came from the Jesuits, which also spawned trouble in the form of Father Ernest. From Ernest came the orphan who eventually changed his identity to Martin Smith, then Smith hired people who made the rest of Clouse's life a living hell. At this point, Clouse had no intention of putting more innocent people in harm's way. He didn't consider his life worth more than that of others, which stemmed from his willingness to put himself in danger to save others years prior.

Taking a sip of coffee, Clouse spied Craig Jennings entering the lobby with a concerned look and a hurried pace.

"Good morning, Craig."

"Good morning, sir. There's a development I wanted you to hear about before I acted on it."

Clouse noticed no other employees were within earshot, but he guided Jennings toward the far side of the room anyway.

"The Louisville newspaper called me about an hour ago to let me know one of their photographers never returned after our press conference a few days back."

"It took them that long to notice he was missing?"

Clouse felt concern over anyone missing from his grounds, but questioned why the newspaper would take so long to report it.

"Are the authorities involved?"

"Not yet. It was a courtesy call on their part, wanting to know if we'd seen anything."

"This isn't the guy Todd clocked, is it?"

Jennings nodded reluctantly.

Groaning aloud, Clouse sensed trouble brewing on his property.

"When did you last see this reporter?"

"I kindly told him to leave the grounds. Todd and the kids were right behind me."

"So you didn't actually escort him off the grounds?"

Jennings directed his eyes toward the carpeting.

"Before we call the police, or the newspaper, I want you and your crew to scour every inch of the grounds. Look for any signs of the guy, Craig. His car, his equipment, or God forbid, his body."

Jennings swallowed hard at the prospect of a murder on the grounds. He had already found himself at death's doorstep once before.

"I'll go talk to Todd and see what he knows," Clouse added. "Let me know what you find."

"Yes, sir."

Jennings retreated toward his office to gather the limited security forces on duty at the hotel. Most of the security worked at the casino and the other hotel, except for Clouse's own bodyguards. As he walked toward the elevator, Clouse considered putting them on the scent of the photographer's trail, but decided against it in case the entire disappearance was a ruse to trick him into doing just that.

As he rode the elevator up, Clouse wondered why anyone would target a photographer unless the man saw something he wasn't supposed to. Killing Lopez made sense to gain entry, but a newspaper man hardly seemed worth the risk.

Clouse passed a security guard once he reached the sixth floor, receiving a courteous nod before he stepped into the suite. Jane was working on the computer while the kids watched television, so Clouse motioned for Parish to join him in the hallway.

"Something wrong?" Jane inquired, taking notice.

"Everything's fine. I just need to ask Todd something."

As though contradicting his own words, Clouse shut the door behind them.

"Sir?" Parish asked with concern.

"The reporter who was here the other day, Todd, what happened?"

Parish scowled.

"I drilled him after he scared the kids half to death. At first I thought he had a gun the way he burst out of the observatory with something in his hand."

"And after that?"

"I took the kids inside once Jennings asked him to leave the grounds."

"And you didn't do anything else to him?"

Parish appeared stunned at the question, perhaps even a bit hurt that Clouse second-guessed him.

"Sir, I didn't have time to. My priority was to get the kids upstairs and away from any other media hounds."

Clouse figured as much, but had to hear the answer for himself.

"Is something wrong, sir?"

"The photographer apparently never returned to work. No one's heard from him."

"Sir, I swear I didn't-"

"I know, Todd. Before anyone gets too excited, I wanted to hear your version of things."

Parish still appeared to be plagued by something.

"What's wrong?" Clouse asked.

"Do you think something bad happened to him? Here?"

Clouse dared not answer such a question. He wanted to believe it was just a coincidence, but experience told him to think more realistically.

"I'll let you get back to work," he said instead.

"Yes, sir," Parish said before returning to the suite.

Clouse decided to see how the search was going downstairs. He wasn't sure if not knowing was worse than having a corpse turn up when he least expected it later. After the attack on Parish during the failed abduction, Clouse wondered exactly what the intruder had in mind. If someone had indeed returned to the grounds to carry out more sinister actions, Clouse had good reason for concern.

Not knowing what the assailant wanted, he considered taking an extended vacation away from West Baden until things blew over. Doing so, however, only put off what he was destined to confront in due time.

Running meant putting other innocent lives in danger and his conscience was already stained with the deaths of his friends and coworkers from years past, as well as the five years Niemeyer lost. Though he dared not tell his wife, Clouse had some feelers out, checking on Mark Teakon and some of the mysteries surrounding the trespassers at the hotel.

He hoped to hear something before anyone else suffered at the hands of the madman behind the untold plan.

***

Jennings had organized his two men working security at the West Baden hotel, and two from French Lick who weren't assigned to a particular post, to search the grounds with him. They began with the front of the hotel, walking out to the highway across the freshly mowed grounds where a golf course once existed.

Two of the men fanned out toward the sunken garden while the other two walked toward the parking lot behind the hotel.

Jennings monitored from the veranda area as he looked for clues closer to the hotel. Unfortunately, the grounds included the new golf course down the road, shared by the two hotels, and even the stables down a winding gravel path. He planned to save the obscure areas for last, in case nothing turned up along the yards.

He met up with the two men who went toward the parking lot, helping them check the old Jesuit observatory building, then the parking lot itself. Paying little attention to the vehicles, the trio ventured into the grass directly behind the hotel. The path leading up to the long since dismantled church was overgrown with weeds, and rapidly deteriorating because the concrete stairway remains were either crumbling, or covered with moss and mud.

The other two officers had wandered toward the far end of the garden, reporting through radio contact that they saw nothing out of place.

Jennings watched the two officers in his proximity climb the treacherous hill while he searched the tall grass below them.

"Be careful," he called to them.

He noticed the valets giving them strange looks from beneath the decorative awning at the hotel's rear entrance.

After taking a look up the hill to verify they were safe, Jennings walked along the grass, spotting several strange indentations only a few feet apart. Kneeling down, he traced the disturbed grass blades with his fingertips, trying to figure out what had made the marks. Several footsteps and trampled grass indicated activity in the vicinity, though it took Jennings a moment to guess what created the mess.

"A tripod."

Perhaps the photographer had snuck onto the grounds after the request that he leave.

Jennings searched the immediate area, finding a number of grass blades covered with dark streaks that felt sticky to the touch. Realizing the streaks stuck to his hand on contact, with a reddish color, he wiped his fingers clean behind him.

Walking in a crouched position to follow what appeared to be a bloody trail, Jennings found himself nearing the parking lot about a minute later. Much of the blood seemed to coincide with occasional flattened patches of grass, as though something, or someone, had been dragged toward the parking lot.

The security supervisor felt his stomach tighten like a wrung washcloth as he neared the lot. At the concrete edge the trail suddenly stopped cold, leaving Jennings to begin searching around the dozen or so vehicles in the immediate area. He thought once of calling to the two men atop the hill, then considered the possibility of them finding more evidence. Instead, he weaved through the vehicles parked in the lot, shifting glances between them and the concrete for evidence.

He began to suspect someone had injured or murdered the photographer, then dragged his body to the parking lot's edge through the cover of shrubs, weeds, and perhaps darkness, to a tarp or a waiting vehicle. Not so much as a speck of blood appeared in the lot, prompting him to give up until he spied something odd in the nearby employee parking area.

Several moderate stains appeared on the back of a sand-colored, small SUV that caught his attention. As he neared the vehicle, Jennings examined the substance more closely, discovering a similar color and texture to the blood in the grass blades.

A hand clasped his shoulder, startling him as he whirled around to find the two security officers behind him.

"Find anything, Mr. Jennings?" one asked.

"I found blood in the grass over there," Jennings replied, pointing to the area, "and some more right here."

"Whose vehicle is it?"

"It belongs to Todd Parish," Jennings answered with a grim look that matched his tone.

Chapter 30

Clouse absolutely hated the idea of interrogating one of his own employees, particularly after the loyalty Parish had shown. Jennings thoroughly and calmly explained the situation to Clouse and Jane, which led them to call upon one of the other security officers to stay with the kids while the couple and Jennings summoned Parish downstairs to one of the vacant conference rooms along the ground level.

While Jennings wasn't Parish's direct supervisor, he was the one who made the discovery, and ultimately made the decision of whether or not to involve authorities. Clouse wanted him there to direct the questioning, because he didn't want to interrogate one of his favorite employees personally. Still, he needed to know without a doubt whether Parish was any kind of threat to the family, or employees at the hotel.

When Parish entered the room apprehensively, he looked to each face, trying to gauge their reactions. No one dared breathe, waiting for someone else to utter the first word.

"Have a seat, Todd," Jennings finally said, using the phrase that often led to terrible consequences.

Everyone else had chosen one of the sixteen seats in the room, none very close to anyone else, though Parish seemed to have one side of the room to himself as he chose a chair on the closer side of the table. He sat, his gaze going directly to Clouse.

"What's this about?"

"We found blood behind the building," Jennings said before Clouse mustered enough courage to piece together a statement. "We have reason to believe the photographer set up a tripod out back and staked out the hotel itself for a photo op."

"And what does any of this have to do with me?"

"We found blood on the back of your vehicle. Dried blood."

A stupefied look crossed the bodyguard's face.

"I have nothing to do with that guy disappearing," Parish said adamantly. "If there's blood on my car, it can't be his."

"I hope not," Jennings said, "because I'm about to call the authorities and have them comb the scene out back."

Parish put his head in his hands briefly, then looked between Clouse and Jane.

"I have nothing to do with this."

"Then you have nothing to worry about," Jane said somewhat frigidly, as though she might doubt Parish's innocence.

She seemed to have lost patience for everyone lately.

"We don't have confirmation of anything right now," Clouse said, trying to ease the tension all four people felt. "Right now this photographer is technically a missing person."

"I don't like the idea of being the center of a crime scene," Parish said. "This is absolutely ridiculous."

"We need to get to the bottom of this," Clouse said. "The police can clear you and we can get down to the business of finding out who's behind all of this."

"Clear me? What if that blood is the photographer's? What if someone is trying to frame me?"

"There's no body as of yet," Jennings stated. "Maybe we're getting worked up over nothing if this is some kind of hoax."

"I don't think someone trying to abduct the children is a hoax," Jane said. "Tim Niemeyer being dropped off at our front doorstep wasn't very funny, either."

Clouse stood up to intercede this time.

"That's not what Craig meant, dear. We're getting off the subject, and perhaps it's time that Craig called the authorities to clear all of this up."

"On it," Jennings said before departing the conference room.

A moment of silence filled the room until Parish spoke again.

"I can't believe this. You two trust me with your children, but now you're pegging me for a killer?"

"Not at all," Jane said, her tone softening somewhat. "We know all about the tricks Smith and his group can play, so we want you cleared of any wrongdoing."

"What if the police find something?" Parish countered. "If this guy got upstairs, he can certainly plant something incriminating on me."

"That's what we have good lawyers for," Clouse said. "We're *not* going to let anything happen to you."

Parish hesitated before making another statement.

"Then why call the police at all? If this is a setup, can't we handle it internally?"

"Local police already mistrust us," Jane answered. "We have to keep them involved if we're going to receive help when we need it most."

Jennings returned a moment later.

"Sheriff Brown is personally coming to check out back."

Everyone exchanged uneasy glances, wondering what the sheriff might find.

***

Hotel employees tried not to watch as the sheriff scoured the grounds for any shred of evidence. He initially spoke to Clouse about calling in a forensics unit from the state police if his search warranted further examination, but thus far he had simply looked around, bagging a few interesting items along the way.

Curtains occasionally inched aside, along the upper floors, not because of open windows, but rather the curious guests and staff wanting a peek at the activity below. Some guests stared from the dining room windows, while others stepped out back near the valets for a gander. Clouse stood beside Parish, who tried to hide his trepidation, watching the sheriff's every move with quiet desperation.

During the course of the search, Clouse fielded a phone call from Randy Niemeyer.

"I have some bad news," the state trooper began.

"I can't get enough of that this week," Clouse answered sarcastically.

"We went through Nathan Runnels' place, but someone beat us to it. The place was completely ransacked."

"You think Runnels had something of interest?"

"If he did, it's long gone by now. We've checked his house, vehicles, phone records, bank accounts, you name it. Nothing."

Clouse thought momentarily as Brown knelt beside the area where the indentations were made along the hill.

"How can someone be so careful all that time, then be so careless to ransom out your brother?"

"Hard telling. Maybe too much time had passed and he thought he was in the clear. My brother can be a pain in the ass to take care of."

"And why kill Tim if you can eventually get money out of him, right?"

"Something like that. But someone didn't like Runnels' extracurricular activities."

"Obviously not. Have you found anyone who knew the man? Maybe knew some of his other friends?"

Now Brown followed the blood trail toward the parking lot, stopping a few times along the way.

"Whoever trashed his place made sure we didn't connect the dots, Paul."

"Neighbors?"

"His closest neighbor lived about half a mile away. Said Runnels kept to himself."

"Great. A hermit kidnapper."

"I'll let you know if we find anything else. Now that I'm back in detectives I should be on top of things."

"Take care."

Clouse shut his phone as Brown motioned for Parish to join him at the base of the bloody vehicle.

"Can you pop the back open, son?" the sheriff asked the reluctant bodyguard.

Parish pulled the keyless remote from his pocket, hesitated momentarily, then pushed the button. As the hatch slowly opened upward, Clouse and Jennings joined the other two men to see nothing except standard items in the rear of Parish's vehicle.

Breathing a sigh of relief, Parish put his keys away.

"I don't know what to make of it," Brown said, taking Clouse and Jennings aside. "Someone bled around here, but it's certainly not conclusive enough for me to call in more people. I'll fill out a report and save the blood samples I collected, but there's not much else I can do."

"Thanks, Sheriff," Clouse said, shaking the man's hand.

"No problem. I'm just a call away if you need me."

Clouse next addressed Parish.

"Todd, your two days off are coming up, but I want you to take a few extra."

"But, sir—"

"No 'buts,' Todd. If someone is setting you up, it's better you're not here to play the victim."

Parish appeared especially concerned, if not insulted.

"This isn't a trust issue, is it?"

"Absolutely not," Clouse said earnestly, meaning it. "Spend some time with your kids and enjoy them for a few days. Get your mind off of this place."

Letting a grin slip past his tense exterior, Parish seemed to believe his boss, finally relaxing a bit.

"Can I finish out the day? Your kids wouldn't forgive me if I just took off."

"Absolutely. See you upstairs."

As Parish returned to duty inside the hotel, Clouse scanned the windows, seeing the peepers had diminished with the sheriff's departure, though speculation was due to run wild inside the building.

Clouse looked to his wife and sighed.

"I'm glad we're too far out of the way for the tabloids to pick on us."

"Me too," she said, giving him a hug. "I'm glad they didn't find anything in Todd's truck."

"Yeah, but that leaves us with a lot of unanswered questions, and considering we're about to be voted into the Top 10 Worst American Employer's poll, it'll be tougher to get answers. Working for us is riskier than the military these days."

"We're not responsible for this any more than we were responsible for making Smith what he was."

"Or is."

Both stared at the hillside, pondering what misfortune lie ahead for them and the hotel.

Chapter 31

Daniels spent part of his day tracking down leads on any of the ongoing investigations through a number of contacts. He hated "wasting" his return favors for Jane's quest, finally deciding there wasn't going to be a more urgent time to use them. Friends in the police and the media were unable to provide him with many new answers about Ray Bloom's murder, Lopez's disappearance, or Nathan Runnels.

Strangely enough, there was some coverage of the massacre near the West Coast that Clouse had mentioned to him. Daniels wondered if his friend was getting in over his head by trying to contact people willing to take so many lives. He knew from personal experience that cursed objects provided motivation for unparalleled violence and trickery.

Now he sat behind the sidelines at a picnic table, beneath a large pine tree, watching another soccer match. Most of the parents stood near the sidelines, cheering on their children from a closer proximity, but Daniels wasn't much for making a scene, or being seen unnecessarily. With his sport coat set beside him, he lit a cigarette as he watched the soccer game with moderate interest when his mind wasn't wandering to the concerns surrounding his job.

"Penny for your thoughts," Cindy said, surprising him a bit as he crushed the last of his cigarette beneath his shoe.

"You probably wouldn't want to know," he answered, his eyes still trained on the game.

After a few minutes of casual watching, she spoke again.

"Maybe I asked too much of you before, Mark. You shut me out of your world, and when you finally opened up it was more than I could bear."

"It's the same old shit, different job. I'm not sure you'd want to know who's making my life miserable now."

"You'd be surprised."

"I would too, if I knew who it was, but I don't have a clue."

He watched the game a moment more as the kids all ran over to their coach between periods.

"It's funny that Paul and Jane seem to have it all, but there's always someone who doesn't want them happy."

"What about you?"

"What about me?"

"Are you happy?"

Daniels wondered if the question stemmed from genuine concern or came loaded.

"I like the job, and I liked how things had calmed down, but it seems like this bullshit never ends."

"That wasn't really an answer, Mark."

"Do you want me to spill my guts here, Cindy?"

"I want you to be open and honest. There are things between us that went unsaid when we split up."

Daniels chuckled.

"You mean when you left me. That's how I remember it going down."

"And maybe that's what I wanted to hear. Maybe I didn't give you enough time to come around. Or maybe I was unhappy and just thinking of myself."

Drawing a deep breath, Daniels decided to be entirely honest and open, knowing he might never have another opportunity.

"My life hasn't been the same since the divorce, Cindy. You know I tend to dwell on things, and my new job took priority for a while, but I never put off the kids, and I've never left you holding the bag since we split up. The fact is, I wonder almost daily why we didn't give it more time. Why *you* didn't give *me* more time. It felt like you were off to do these great things in your life and I was just holding you back. I wanted that for you, but I wanted to be there to see it, too."

Cindy started to reply, but Daniels held up his hand to stop her.

"I don't date anymore, I barely have a life outside of work, and when I do, it's with the kids. Things are just incomplete for me, and I feel too old, or maybe just too stuck in my ways, to start over. It takes two to make it work, so if you're asking if I'd give us a second chance, I'd do it in a heartbeat. But if you're just asking to make me feel better, or lead me on with some false hope, then please don't ask me to be this forward again."

"I don't want the kids confused," Cindy said. "I don't want to get their hopes up for nothing."

"So we're both going to live in misery until they finish high school? There are options like counseling, God forbid."

"That's exactly the attitude that drove us apart in the first place."

"If I'm willing to change, where does that leave us now?"

Cindy softened a bit toward him.

"That leaves us closer than we were five minutes ago."

***

Sheriff Brown returned home shortly after a brief supper in town, prepared to pack for a three-day police leadership conference in Dayton, Ohio. He pulled into his driveway, unlocked his front door, then stepped inside the quiet house. Divorced twice before being elected sheriff, he hadn't found the time or energy to seek a relationship, so he lived alone.

Setting his keys on the kitchen counter, he checked his messages, then called to confirm his reservation in Dayton. He had the choice of leaving that evening, or rising very early in the morning.

As he removed his duty shirt, Brown thought about his day, the trip to West Baden in particular. Two years ago he had found himself near death at the mansion when the hotel and casino package were fair game in the market. He hadn't forgotten one bit of the experience, and vowed to keep a close eye on the troubled hotel during his term.

Brown took a quick shower, barely catching a phone call from his son as he scurried through the living room immediately following to scoop up the phone.

"What's up, boy?"

"Not much, Dad. I didn't get to ask you what happened at the hotel since I was on that wreck all afternoon."

A three-car wreck just outside of Paoli had required Arlan's attention for nearly an hour, while the paperwork took twice as long.

"Nothing you'll see on the news, I suppose. They had a blood trail and thought it might be the missing reporter."

"Any word on him?"

"Nope. Something fishy is going on over there, I'll tell you that."

"Anything you need taken care of the next few days?"

Brown reached into his refrigerator for a beer, ready to kick back the remainder of the night and begin an early morning drive.

"This place will be fine, and I know you guys can handle the department just fine for three days."

"Why do you need a leadership seminar anyway? We're in Orange County for Christ's sake."

"The perks are fantastic, my boy. Free drinks, free goodies, you name it. Might even get you a deal on dry-cleaning."

Arlan seldom ironed his uniforms properly, despite his father constantly nagging him about looking good in the public eye.

"Funny, Dad. Have a good trip, and give me a shout tomorrow night if you get the chance."

"Will do. Keep an eye on those hotels while I'm gone. Some weird shit is going on near that casino lately."

"Okay," Arlan assured him. "Drive safe."

Brown hung up the phone, hearing a noise from outside that sounded like wooden planks dropping on one another. It just so happened the sheriff had been storing both firewood and some spare boards behind his house.

He quickly threw on old jeans and a stained shirt before grabbing his shotgun and heading out the door. Cautiously making his way around the house, Brown looked around each corner before stepping, though he saw no one on his property and no sign of a disturbance. He considered calling for backup, but didn't want to be the butt of anyone's joke when the sheriff had to call for the police.

His mind suddenly thought back to the trespasser on his property within the last month, wondering if the person failed to attain his objective the first time. Keeping his shotgun close, Brown wondered what kind of intruder waited until a person was home to make his move.

The dangerous kind.

When he reached the far end of his house's rear side, Brown studied the wood pile, then the scrap timber stacked beside the wall. Nothing looked out of place to him until he saw a bare tree stump where his old ax typically rested. Drawing closer, he hoped it had fallen beside the old stump, or perhaps he put it in the shed and forgot about it.

No, he decided, he never put the rusty thing away. He just sharpened the blade and kept on using it.

Based on recent events around the hotel, Brown decided to swallow his pride and call for help, even if he simply called Arlan or another off-duty officer. He turned to retreat to the front side of his house when, unseen by him, a dark figure emerged from behind one of the nearby trees, hitting him in the back of the skull with the blunt side of the ax, making the afternoon sky the last thing he saw as he fell to the mossy earth.

***

When the sheriff awoke from his assault, he felt his head spinning, finding the sky above him a bit darker as dusk loomed over the county. Still outside, and still behind his house, Brown tried to move, discovering he could not. He looked to his sides, finding both hands bound to sturdy pieces of wood on their respective sides. His feet were also bound together, then tied to a stake a few feet straight below, so he couldn't swing them in any fashion.

In the middle of nowhere, with no neighbors or stragglers close enough to hear cries for help, Brown realized he was at the mercy of whomever had struck him down. His head ached, and the trees around him appeared to be swaying, as did the clouds above, but he knew the optical illusions were part of the concussion he felt certain the killer gave him.

He heard someone rummaging through his house because one of the nearby windows was open. A few minutes later he heard a truck door shut after the person exited through the front. The killer wanted something from him, and Brown doubted his usefulness was going to be extended beyond the next half hour.

Clothed in the bare minimum, Brown struggled against the ropes, having no knife, no nearby weapons, and very little hope. He thrashed up and down to try loosening the ropes against the board, but only furthered the damage to his skull instead.

Groaning to himself, the sheriff tried to regain his senses, but found himself trapped and at the mercy of the killer as a figure dressed from head to toe in black rounded the corner. Brown vowed often that he would never beg and plead if put in a life and death situation, but it didn't sound so bad at the moment. If nothing else, he needed to stall for time, though he doubted anyone was visiting his property as a potential savior anytime soon.

"You don't have to kill me," Brown said. "I haven't seen you. Take what you want and go."

Instead of complying, the figure stood over him with the ax, shaking his head negatively in a slow, taunting fashion. He then held up a set of keys with a security card attached to the key chain. Brown stared, trying to identify the keys through hazy vision, until he realized they were access keys to both hotels and the casino.

Unfortunately for the killer, most of the high security access points were inaccessible without further security measures being met.

Moving briskly around the sheriff's upper half, the cloaked figure pulled a rag from within his costume, quickly stuffing it into Brown's mouth to serve as a gag. Brown couldn't understand the need for silence unless the killer actually planned to let him live.

Next, the figure placed an extra board beneath the piece of wood holding the sheriff's right arm out to his side. As the killer grabbed for the ax once more, Brown knew exactly what this diabolical person had in mind as he struggled to free himself, his muffled cries barely escaping the gag. Whatever happened to Jon Lopez seemed to be the same fate awaiting him and his appendage.

When the ax swung toward his arm, Brown turned away, trying in vain to pull his arm with him, but the blade found its mark at the center of his forearm. He heard the snap of the two primary forearm bones, screaming in agony through the gag, which suppressed his audible sounds to about a thirty-yard radius, likely heard by only a few startled woodland creatures.

Thin strips of skin and muscle tissue barely kept the arm attached at first, but the killer made several shorter swings, taking the hand as a souvenir and an access point to the hotel. Brown watched as blood spurted from the remains of his right arm for a few seconds, then shock began to set in as the blood slowed to a trickle. He moaned agonizingly into the gag, trying to keep his focus in case the killer simply left him for dead.

His only chance for survival was escaping his bindings and calling for assistance. Neither step seemed very plausible at the moment as the killer stuffed his severed hand into a bag to preserve it. Brown's consciousness teetered on the brink a few minutes later, after the killer had walked around to the front. The disguised figure returned a few minutes later, ax in hand.

Brown's eyelids fluttered as the ax raised above the killer's head, then came straight down toward his neck.

Chapter 32

Clouse's contacts came through for him, which put him on a flight to Amherst, Massachusetts by late afternoon. Not only did Mark Teakon teach business on the Amherst College campus, but he also lived in the town, running a local business with two associates. Clouse pulled some strings at the airport, got a ticket on the next flight out, and traveled light to ensure a swift arrival and departure.

For Clouse, sending a surrogate negotiator was not an option, because he trusted very few people, and what he planned to propose was for Teakon's ears only.

Based on what Rawlings told him, Clouse suspected he knew the business's true purpose, which might shatter the town's belief system if they ever found out. At this point, Clouse hoped his investigator's theory about Teakon proved accurate, because he hadn't brought backup, and only Jane and Daniels knew where he was heading.

"It's a day trip," he told Daniels before departing the hotel, shortly after lunch.

"This is foolish, Paul," Daniels responded as they stood to the side of the casino. "You've done some stupid things before, but this takes the cake."

"This could be the answer to all of my problems, Mark."

"And it could be your funeral I'm attending next if you're wrong. This place is falling into chaos and you want to take off?"

"One day, Mark. You and Craig can take care of things while I'm gone."

"You mean to say I can. Jennings is glorified mall security at best, and you just laid off the guardian of your children."

Clouse chuckled.

"I gave him a few extra days off. We've got other people to protect the kids. Why are you so worked up about this?"

"Something about this whole thing stinks, Paul. Just be careful."

His friend's words stuck with him as Clouse rented a car, then followed the navigation system's directions to the campus. A few friendly students provided him instructions on how to find Teakon's building, then he walked across the beautiful grounds, wondering if Teakon taught summer courses or focused on other activities during the warm months.

He found his answer a few minutes later posted on the man's door that provided contact numbers if students needed to reach him during the summer months. Obviously he was spending his time elsewhere, perhaps even burying a recently recovered cursed cube.

Clouse referred to his information before driving to a neighborhood bookstore where Teakon and his associates reportedly sold books and some antiquities. If Rawlings was incorrect in his assessment, and Teakon's store was simply a front for selling cursed objects, Clouse would do just as well drawing a red target on his forehead.

As he stood outside the bookstore, which looked almost as large as the national chains, and none too shabby, Clouse peered inside to see a young lady assisting a few customers. Looking at their store hours, he wanted an opportunity to speak with her, or hopefully Teakon, because the store closed in less than fifteen minutes.

Sucking in a deep breath, he opened the door to step inside.

***

Ron Edwards had been hired by Paul Clouse to watch over his parents, John and Helen, after the attack on Todd Parish at the hotel. Edwards knew sketchy details about the attack, but he was fine with receiving checks for basically babysitting a retired couple. He and his partner, Bobby Mueller, took turns with another pair of ex-military bodyguards, working 12-hour shifts.

"You want some more coffee?" Mueller asked from the passenger seat of the sedan they used to monitor the house.

"Nah, I'm good."

While Edwards was reasonably new to the protection business, Mueller had worked as a police officer after serving in the Gulf War. He was honorably discharged from the U.S. Army, though he left the Indianapolis Police Department under far different circumstances. Rumors of battery on arrested subjects gained him a reputation as a protector not afraid to use force when necessary.

Edwards found him to be tolerable, and even friendly most of the time. Mueller didn't speak much about his past, acting professionally toward anyone who wasn't a problem or a threat. He even learned a few things from his partner, considering he had only done some celebrity events around Indianapolis and Chicago. Edwards typically chaperoned important people from their flight to the event, then back again. He sometimes carried a weapon, but most of his work consisted of shooing the press and leading the way through seemingly immovable crowds.

During his time with Clouse's parents, Edwards had learned quite a bit about them. Despite their son's fortune, they chose to remain in their old farmhouse, which made guarding them a bit more difficult. For the most part the couple stayed at home, Helen usually baking goodies, or brewing coffee for her new protectors. The couple freely admitted they hated having protection at all, though they were extremely friendly toward the armed staff that dressed much like Secret Service personnel.

Mueller stared out the window before glancing at a magazine by the car's dome light. Outside, thunder grumbled in the distance as lightning illuminated a strangely purple sky with brief glimpses of yellow-green grass that looked unnatural, like an old television with poor tint and hue adjustments, during the brief illuminations.

"We're under a tornado watch," Mueller grunted, taking a sip of coffee.

Edwards had left the car running for the radio, some lighting, and to operate the wipers as heavy rains poured across the normally dusty driveway, as though dumped from a large bucket. Another round of lightning illuminated the old white barn across the yard, which remained structurally intact to the say the least, despite nearing the 100-year mark. An open door and two windows along the narrow wall's upper level made it look a bit like a jack-o-lantern the briefest of seconds when the weather brought it to light.

On this particular evening, Helen had baked them some gingerbread cookies, so Edwards nibbled on one as his eyes panned the long driveway. Though the couple had invited them to stay inside, Clouse insisted they keep vigil from a distance so his parents weren't disturbed any more than necessary. Being "rude" to their protectors seemed to bother the couple even more, but Edwards and Mueller were professional enough to manufacture excuses why they needed to remain outside.

After a few minutes, Edwards started feeling unusually groggy, almost unnaturally. He exercised often and made certain to get enough sleep, so he wasn't sure why he felt so sluggish so early in the evening. A glance over to Mueller told him he wasn't alone as his partner shook his head just to stay awake.

"You want to check our tailpipe?" Edwards asked, recalling a story about a police officer pulling over in the dead of winter to do a report, then dying inside his patrol car because his tailpipe was packed full of snow.

"Flip you for it," Mueller countered.

"It's on your side, Bob."

"Why don't we just roll down the window until this rain lets up?"

"Great. Then we can be overcome *and* drowned like rats."

Mueller rolled his window down partway, allowing the rain to pour inside as though it had been invited.

"Shit."

As Mueller turned to say something else to his partner, a knife cut the rain through the open window, then slid across Mueller's throat in a quick, steady motion.

"Holy!" Edwards managed to stammer as his partner gurgled his last audible sounds, clutching his throat to stop the escaping blood from taking his life with it.

Instinctively, Edwards reached for his gun while opening the door simultaneously, refusing to be a stationary target. He immediately regretted the move as he stepped into the rain, barely able to see a few feet in front of him, with no sign of the killer anywhere. He hadn't seen anything except a forearm and the glimmer of a bladed weapon, so the only thing he knew about the attacker was that he, or she, was Caucasian.

As the rainfall instantly drenched him, Edwards fought to keep his eyes open and focused against the harsh wind and elements. He stepped away from the car in case the killer had slid underneath, waiting to slit his Achilles tendons. His heart thumped against his chest as he breathed heavily, despite trying to remain calm, barely able to do so with his partner's fresh corpse seated in the car.

Stepping sideways around the car, Edwards monitored the area around him as he searched for the attacker. When he reached the rear portion, he found the tailpipe blocked by a rag stuffed completely into the opening.

Holding his gun in a ready position, Edwards glanced around the car and the grounds, finding no sign of the assailant. He thought about the house, seeing the kitchen light still on through one of the windows. It was early enough that the

Clouses were still up, likely watching television, but he didn't believe for one second the killer was going to ignore him to seek cover near the house.

Lightning flashed around him, but the illumination didn't help Edwards spy the killer. His cell phone remained strapped to his side, but coverage was iffy when the sky wasn't overcast, so he didn't risk trying a phone call in the downpour. Instead, he remained a safe distance from the car as he walked backward toward the house, still unable to see any sign of his partner's killer. As he neared the door, another bolt of lightning struck nearby, allowing him to see the bloody line across Mueller's neck as the man's eyes remained open.

I don't want to wind up like that, Edwards thought to himself, seriously doubting for the first time in his life he might survive a particular incident. Not only did he have to warn the couple inside the house, but needed to use their phone to call for police without fear of the line cutting out.

Reaching the house a moment later, Edwards turned to knock frantically on the door, finding the metal door locked after flinging open the storm door. He turned periodically to make certain no one was sneaking up behind him as John Clouse stood from a living room chair which seemed a mile away to the protective guard.

"Come on," Edwards urged frantically, his attention diverted more and more from the dangers behind him as John neared the door.

When the door finally opened, John's face went from bewilderment to terror in the matter of a second.

"Look out!"

Edwards tried spinning around to defend himself, but the curved blade of a modified small scythe stuck in the lower right portion of his back, pinning him against the house. Overcome with unimaginable pain as the blade pierced several vital organs, Edwards slumped to both knees, still trying to turn for an opportunity to fire at his attacker. For his trouble, Edwards received a steel-toed boot to the head that sent his skull forcefully into the doorway, knocking him cold.

With both security men out of the way, the killer was now free to complete his primary objective without interference.

Chapter 33

It took some time for Clouse to convince Greg Slone and Julie Knowles that it was in everyone's best interest that he speak to Mark Teakon personally. They closed down the store before Julie went into the back to find Teakon, who was organizing some books and updating records. Slone kept a shrewd eye on Clouse the entire time, which put him on par with the information Clouse had on the man.

Once Clouse decided to spend the money on a private investigator on the East Coast, it took a matter of slightly more than a day for him to have everything he wanted. While receiving the facts in expedited form was refreshing and helpful, it made him wonder how easily the secretive trio might be discovered by the wrong people.

When Teakon finally walked through a large curtain used to divide the front from their offices in the rear, formal introductions were made all the way around.

"So you're the man who hired Rawlings?" Teakon inquired, taking a seat across from Clouse.

"Yes. It seems we were after the same thing, and I hope for the same reason."

"I'm not exactly sure what you're after, Mr. Clouse."

"Then I'll get straight to the point. Either we both want to see these things put away for good, or you're about to order Mr. Slone to put a bullet in my head."

Teakon sat back with an uncertain smile crossing his face.

"Well, that's not about to happen, and I was wondering about your motivation. Your type is usually just the person we have to do battle with to get these things out of harm's way."

"My type?" Clouse questioned, knowing Teakon meant people with money. "Let me tell you a little story about how I came in contact with these things and how they've practically ruined my life in every possible sense."

Clouse spent nearly half an hour reliving the condensed version of the hell Smith and his minions had put him through. The deaths of colleagues, friends, and family members had left his life shattered, despite the millions he inherited. Even now he was forced to live in isolation and seclusion, protected day and night by people he hoped he could trust.

"So you see, my life isn't worth living until I'm rid of Smith and his curse once and for all," Clouse added. "I can only imagine how many other lives, how many families, have been touched by these...*things.*"

"I take it you aren't here to ask us to sell your autobiography," Teakon commented. "How can we help?"

"One, by educating me on what I'm dealing with, and two, by making certain it ends up far away from the wrong people once I recover it."

"You said you've dealt with two of these," Teakon said, scratching his bearded chin. "You buried the first?"

"Beneath a building and several tons of concrete. It should be safe there for years to come."

"But the second cube is giving you trouble," Teakon restated more than asked. "It disappeared from the mansion along with Smith's body?"

"Yes."

Teakon stood, went to the back and returned a few minutes later with a rather thick, leather-bound book. He thumbed through the pages until he found something that caught his attention.

"We should begin assisting you immediately," Teakon said after reading a few passages.

"I don't want help recovering it, Mr. Teakon."

The man raised an eyebrow at the statement.

"Then what exactly do you want us for?"

"I want you to discard this cube when I get it back, then I want to hire you to find the rest of these things and deal with them accordingly."

"You have to understand one thing, Mr. Clouse. While human lives may be lost, the cubes are spread throughout the world, meaning there is no danger of them ever being brought together."

"If I found you this easily, Mr. Teakon, what do you think someone else is going to do when they discover you're recovering them at a leisurely pace? I'm giving you a chance to go on the offensive and recover these things sooner rather than later. If what Rawlings told me is true, the paper trail ends with the last owner, and if you have the book, that makes you reasonably safe, doesn't it?"

"It's a bit more complicated than that, Mr. Clouse."

"Paul."

"Paul, while these aren't well-guarded secrets to us, they are well-guarded in the physical sense. Getting the latest cube from Pershing was nearly a complete disaster. Had the man hired better protection, or thought of-"

"But he didn't, did he? I want to provide you with the financial means to hunt these things down and disperse them to places they'll never be found."

The look of concern didn't leave Teakon's face for one second.

"Let's look at the immediate future first. You have two cubes in your immediate area, one hidden, and one a major danger to you and your loved ones. I'm not sure you've truly conceived what you might be up against."

"I've become painfully aware the past two years that Martin Smith had several backup plans in the wings."

"I'm referring to the cube," Teakon said with some apprehension. "It only takes one death for this thing to bring back one life. What condition the revived corpses are in may be in question, but if Smith walked out of the mansion two years ago *with* the cube, he could have a virtual army of the living dead assisting him."

Clouse shook his head.

"He keeps things low-key because he wants his life back. If what you say is true, and Bryan Bell's blood entered Smith through the cube, then he could very well be alive. And all this time I thought it took the ritual he designed to make it work."

"No," Teakon said. "The ritual he performed, had it gone correctly, was to bring him back to life and fully restore him. Chances are, whatever condition he was in when the cube did its thing, is how he looks today."

Suddenly it made sense to Clouse why dust scattered when Parish shot the mysterious intruder, and why he wouldn't die. The mansion survivors reported Smith's corpse as being little more than a bag of bones with deteriorated muscle and skin in some overlying areas. Without the ritual, he was a hideous shadow of his former self, forced to take revenge in secret.

But if the ritual failed, why had a dozen or so strangers from nearby states been abducted with matching birth dates from the mansion scare survivors?

Smith wanted an accomplice to help him carry out his revenge. Someone who might despise Clouse and hate being dead as much as Smith did.

"Oh, no," Clouse muttered, terrible fears running through his mind.

"What's the matter?" Teakon asked.

"I've got to get home right away. I appreciate the insight, but you may have just opened my eyes to a terrible truth right in front of me all along."

"Want some help? We can continue this conversation on the way."

"It's better I do this alone, Mr. Teakon. If I survive all of this, we definitely need to finish this talk."

Clouse gathered up what little paperwork he had brought with him, barely taking notice of the three people staring at him with questioning, perhaps suspicious, eyes.

He didn't care at this point. His primary concern was getting his family out of harm's way before Smith turned up the heat on his evil plan.

***

Troy Tackett found himself centered in the middle of another disaster related to Paul Clouse. A bodyguard had managed to call 911 after surviving a serious stabbing in the middle of his lower back. The first arriving patrolman found the man still alive, though his partner in the car was far from it.

With his consciousness wavering, Edwards wasn't able to provide much information, but authorities knew John and Helen Clouse were missing, presumed abducted.

The patrolman knew about Tackett's open investigation with the Bloom murder, so he asked his dispatcher to page the detective. Much to Tackett's chagrin, his worst fears were realized because Clouse's parents were missing, their kitchen floor a wet mix of rain and blood.

Since the only confirmed murder was technically outside, the scene being saturated with rain water, Tackett moved carefully about inside. He treated the case like an abduction, which he suspected it was, allowing him to move a bit more freely inside without fear of disturbing evidence.

With Edwards on his way to the emergency room, Tackett had to rely upon instinct while hoping some form of evidence might present itself. He stepped carefully around the kitchen area, finding the television still on inside the living room.

The killer had to have taken out the two security people first, but Edwards was likely alerted when his partner was killed. Footsteps other than those of the patrolman led up to the residence, barely visible through the rain-soaked mud outside.

Why hadn't Edwards simply used a cell phone to call for help?

Tackett noticed the damage to the exterior where the bladed weapon had penetrated the man's abdomen from the back, then lodged itself in the house. It left damage to the siding and a blood stain that couldn't easily be washed away because it sat beneath a short awning.

Pulling out his cell phone, Tackett found his reception bars toggling between one and zero, meaning he probably couldn't get a signal strong enough for an outgoing call. The house phone sat on the floor where Edwards had left it after struggling to dial for help. Tackett wondered if the phone had been knocked there by a struggling family member, or if Edwards had to reach up to the wall unit to retrieve it.

With everyone else preoccupied outside, Tackett searched the house from top to bottom for clues. Visible footsteps didn't extend past the kitchen, and the couple's belongings were all still inside the house. The detective figured they were taken exactly as they were dressed by the abductor, based on the fact their clothes were still laid out on a bed upstairs and their wallets and cash remained behind.

Obligation forced him to investigate the murder a short distance from the house, but he wanted to contact his former neighbor first to let him know the circumstances. Already wearing a latex glove, Tackett looked up the phone number in his cell phone index, using the house's landline to dial Paul Clouse.

Chapter 34

Tim Niemeyer had taken as much of being cooped up with his parents as he could tolerate. After borrowing his father's old pickup truck he headed into Bedford with a loaded debit card Clouse had given to him until he got on his feet again.

Despite his life returning to some sense of normalcy, Niemeyer still didn't have his own business, a marriage, or even a relationship with his kids as of yet. At least he had family and friends who supported him, even if they felt a bit strange that they had buried him and now he was back, like in some cheesy soap opera plot.

A flood of bad memories ran through his mind on his way into town. He passed the old Hilton property, which he learned the surviving family members were hoping to auction or sell by year's end. The old hotel ruins remained atop the grounds, deteriorating further with each passing season. Though Niemeyer wouldn't have minded obtaining the land, he wasn't sure he had the ambition required to build a house on the property or develop it himself.

He was plagued with more important matters at the moment.

Deciding he wanted a bite to eat, he stopped at an ATM in downtown Bedford to withdraw some cash with the debit card. He parked the truck and waited for an older lady to finish her transaction before stepping out. Dressed in jeans and a Harley shirt, he stepped onto the curb with a black motorcycle boot, freezing in his tracks as his mind vividly recalled the fateful night.

Every so often he felt the pain of a sharpened blade stabbing his stomach or sides, only to find his mind playing tricks on him. He looked down at his shirt, afraid he might see blood seeping from a hole, but his body was fully intact.

Shaking off the thought of six dark figures lurking in the bushes and nearby vehicles, he stepped forward to make the transaction. A cold sweat caused him to shiver the virtual eternity it took the computer to ask him questions, then process his transaction.

Niemeyer walked back to the truck, got in, then breathed a sigh of relief as he backed away from the bank.

He drove a few blocks west, grabbed a bite to eat, and decided he felt restless enough to kill some more time before driving home. His parents had treated him like an infant needing constant care, simply worried that something else might happen to him. Niemeyer felt thankful for his freedom, but he planned to treat each day like a blessing, not worrying about if and when something dreadful might happen.

His new cell phone rang at his side, so he pulled into a gas station parking lot to answer the call.

"Hello?"

"What are you doing, big brother?"

"What's going on, detective?"

Randy sighed audibly with a groan.

"I'm hating this new position. It sucks having regular hours."

"Try not working at all and having everyone think you're a charity case."

"Speaking of my favorite charity case, Mom and Dad said you went into town. Want to meet up somewhere?"

Niemeyer had already eaten, and the entertainment options, even in town, were very limited.

"Well, I'm pretty much done here. Want to meet up with the folks?"

Randy replied with a sickened bellow.

"So I can watch them fall over one another trying to wait on you?"

"Do I detect a bit of jealousy?"

"Uh, no, you do not."

"Just the same, why don't you meet me there in about fifteen minutes?"

"You got it."

Niemeyer pulled out of the gas station, heading out of town along the county road that led to his parents' house until he noticed a haze wafting across the road ahead of him. Still about a mile away from his parents' house, he drove through the foggy substance until he came upon an automobile accident.

A car had embedded its front end into a large tree, now forked around it with smoke rolling from the engine compartment. Niemeyer pulled to the side of the road, feeling adrenaline surge through his body as he tried contemplating what to do next. He had no public safety experience like his two chums from high school, but he knew enough from talking to them.

"Assess the scene," he mumbled to himself as he approached the car, reaching for his cell phone because he knew a call was going to be necessary.

A woman younger than himself was slumped over the front wheel, bleeding profusely from her head. Her eyes were closed, and she appeared to be motionless, though Niemeyer didn't figure the accident, while severe, was enough to kill someone.

"Ma'am, can ya hear me?" he asked with no response.

"She won't be hearing anyone ever again," a voice said from behind Niemeyer.

He started to turn to see what kind of callous bastard would say such a thing, but a shovel landed squarely against the back of his head before he moved more than a few inches. Not entirely knocked out from the blow, Niemeyer felt himself fall to the ground, then the sensation of someone grabbing him by the feet and dragging him toward the pickup truck. He lost a few seconds of time, either from blacking out, or the pain of the blow to his skull. A strange stinging sensation throbbed in his left shoulder, but he couldn't touch it, or even move for that matter.

Bordering on unconsciousness, Niemeyer wondered if he had been drugged after the shovel struck him. Strangely, he could open his eyes a little, and feel most everything happening to him, but he couldn't move.

He was unceremoniously tossed into the truck bed like a sack of garbage, then gagged and tied, as though he might overcome his helpless condition at any moment. A crude vinyl tarp was thrown over him before his assailant started the truck, driving it down the road as though it had never stopped.

***

Clouse received the news about his parents shortly after his plane touched the ground and he was able to turn on his cell phone to retrieve messages. Tackett hadn't provided details, but spoke of an incident at his childhood home. He did mention that Clouse's parents were not found at the farmhouse.

"What happened?" Clouse asked into the phone, walking briskly toward his truck in the parking lot.

"We're still checking things over," Tackett answered. "One of the security guys you put on your folks is dead, and the other is barely hanging on at the hospital."

Clouse grimaced at the thought of his parents becoming part of the plot against him. He doubted they had been harmed, because they were likely the bargaining chips used to replace his children. Still, not knowing the truth was already making him a nervous wreck. He was too close to making his own plan operational, but this threatened everything set in place.

"Any sign of my parents?" Clouse asked as he found his truck, then jumped inside to find it hotter and muggier than the outside.

"None. All of their belongings are here, Paul. I think someone took them after taking out the two guards."

"And I think I know who, Troy."

"Don't go there, Paul. You don't know for sure."

"I don't? Then what's been building up for weeks at the hotel? Smith is alive and he wants back at me for killing him."

Tackett said nothing for a few seconds. He had already admitted to believing at least part of Clouse's story, but he didn't have Teakon's confirmation that Smith was in all likelihood alive and able to take human life again.

"If Smith has your parents, where would he take them?"

"I have no idea. He's had two years to plan whatever he's doing, and he's practically immortal in his condition."

Clouse started his truck, ready to begin making his way home. At the late hour he expected light traffic, short of any traffic wrecks, so he could make good time. Things at the hotel were going to be quiet during the middle of the week, and his corporate staff at the hotel was already gone for the night.

"There's got to be someone you can call for help," Tackett insisted.

"Who? *Ghost Busters*? Come on, Troy. I've only got one authority on this sort of thing, and I just left him in Massachusetts."

"Then maybe you should fly him out here."

"Maybe I should," Clouse thought aloud. "I'm certain Smith is going to contact me shortly with instructions."

"What could he possibly want?"

"Oh, the same old thing. 'How about I kill you and let your parents live', or 'I'd like to have my other cube back so I can kill you and everyone you know before I reclaim my old life'."

"This is serious, Paul."

"I'm *being* serious, Troy. We're not going to sit down over afternoon tea and discuss this like gentlemen. He's compromised my defenses, so the ball is in his court."

Tackett had no immediate response.

"If you need anything, you call me."

"You've done plenty, which is more than I'd ever ask of a former neighbor. For your own good, stay out of this, Troy. Take care of yourself."

"You, too."

"And for both our sakes, this conversation never took place. Just tell them you got my voice mail or we're both going to have a lot of explaining to do."

Tackett gave a subtle groan.

"Understood."

Clouse finally navigated his way out of the airport, then to the nearest freeway. He was well over an hour from the hotel, with little else to do except dwell on his situation.

He thought about calling Mark Teakon, but the man didn't fully grasp the situation. Clouse had enough resources to take care of any problem himself, but he needed to figure out Smith's game before he acted.

He felt positive Smith was alive and behind the abduction. Somehow he had known it the moment he discovered the man's body was missing from the mansion two years prior. It took what felt like an eternity for Rawlings to track down Teakon, and that delay may have cost Clouse dearly in the present.

He considered calling everyone on his staff to put them at high alert, then decided against it since Smith already had leverage over him. With Parish off for the next few days, he decided to call Jane to fill her in and make certain the kids were safe. He hated treating them like prisoners since they were well-behaved and easy going. They loved Parish to no end, which often proved difficult keeping them close by and safe when he wasn't around.

Clouse believed his employee had nothing to do with the photographer's disappearance, but giving him an extra two days off suddenly felt foolhardy considering the danger posed to his family.

Picking his phone up from the console beside him, he called the sixth floor suite's number to speak with his wife.

***

Jane had spent much of her day with the kids around the hotel instead of working at the clinic or securing her family's future safety like she wanted. She knew harassing Daniels was a surefire way to create friction between her and her husband, but no one else she trusted had connections like the former detective.

While Clouse wasn't in denial, he wasn't as proactive as Jane wanted him to be. Instead of hiring certified professionals to protect them and their interests, he felt obligated to employ people their situation had wronged. He made absolutely certain their high level employees were trustworthy, but even honest people had a price.

The kids busied themselves playing an online learning game on the computer while Jane tidied up the kitchen area, wondering why she hadn't heard from Clouse since he landed in Massachusetts. As though on cue, the cordless phone beside her rang. She recognized the number as her husband's cell phone, then answered the call.

"Any news?" she asked, bypassing normal formalities.

"Bad news, as always."

Clouse explained his parents were missing, and a few details about the meeting with Teakon.

"That's terrible about your parents, Paul. What are we going to do?"

"What *can* we do? I know that son-of-a-bitch has them, Jane. He'll call when he's ready to do business."

Jane turned away from the kids, lowering her voice.

"You sound awfully assured for someone whose parents are presumed kidnapped."

"Losing my head isn't going to help, dear. He couldn't get the kids, so he did the next best thing. I should have seen this coming."

"You did see it coming. Why else would you have put a security detail on your parents?"

"And now one's dead and the other might be by tomorrow morning. I'm about ready to give Smith that cube and his fucking money and be done with it."

Closing her eyes momentarily, Jane understood his frustration, but didn't share the sentiment.

"After everything he's done to us for his own personal gain the last thing we need to do is give in to his demands. Did that professor have any answers for you?"

"None that help us in the here and now, but I still have a few tricks up my sleeve."

Jane looked to the kids, finding them both preoccupied with the computer game.

"What aren't you telling me?"

"Smith isn't working alone. What Bloom found out about the deaths wasn't directly related to Smith. In theory, he was brought back to life two years ago, so the sacrificial deaths wouldn't have been for him."

"If that's the case, who would he bring back?"

"Who conveniently appeared at our doorstep about a week ago?"

Jane refused to believe Tim Niemeyer had an evil bone in his body. Smith had no reason to bring him back, because Niemeyer would surely refuse to help the man in any way.

"Tim would never hurt you. You've known him since high school, Paul."

"I want to believe he was locked away for five years, but five years is a long time to keep someone in captivity. At best, Tim is an innocent pawn in this whole thing."

Considering everything they had been through as a couple, Jane understood his mistrust.

"We can talk about this when you get home. Where are you?"

"Just south of Indianapolis."

"I'll put the kids to bed, then we'll put our heads together and make a plan."

"Sounds good. I love you."

"Love you, too."

Jane hung up the phone, ready to give the order for the kids to brush their teeth and get dressed for bed until a commotion outside the main door caught her attention. Only one guard ever remained on duty upstairs this late at night, leaving Jane to feel like some mafia princess who constantly needed protection from rival mob bosses.

The sound also drew the attention of Katie and Zach, but Jane held up a hand for them to stay put. She had crossed half of the living room when the door burst open and an ominous figure stood in the threshold, a bloody knife in one hand, and a severed hand in the other.

"Oh my God," Jane muttered, recognizing the figure once he took a step inside. "Not you."

Chapter 35

When Clouse arrived at the hotel almost two hours later, due to traffic delays, he entered through the valet area, crossing the dimmed atrium toward the front desk. After nine o'clock the overhead lights in the atrium were turned down to allow guests a good night's sleep, and couples a chance to snuggle in the oversized lounge chairs.

"Do I have any messages?" he asked Sonya, one of his veteran hotel receptionists who always recognized him with a friendly smile.

"No, Mr. Clouse. Do you want me to page you if anything important comes in?"

"Definitely."

He hesitated before heading for the elevator.

"Has anyone, um, strange come through here tonight?"

Sonya gave him a curious look in return.

"I haven't seen anyone except guests come through here."

"Thank you, Sonya."

Clouse took the elevator to the sixth floor, finding small pools of blood accompanying the ding of the elevator door opening. His eyes followed the thin red trail to a body lying reasonably close to the suite entrance. His heart immediately began racing as he knelt beside the prone body of the lone security guard keeping watch over his family that evening. The blood trail ended at the guard's body because he had been stabbed hard, deep, and repeatedly in the abdomen, assuring certain death within seconds.

Ahead of him, Clouse found the door to the suite wide-open and a severed hand lying just inside the door. For all of his foresight, he suddenly felt staggered by the horrific events telling a tale around him.

Clouse half-expected to find his family inside the suite, perhaps in one of the bedrooms, slaughtered like lambs. His worst possible fear had been realized in one night, because everyone dear to him had been violated in some way by Smith and the man's cronies. He searched each and every room quickly and thoroughly, finding them empty. Breathing a partial sigh of relief, Clouse picked up the phone to call the authorities, wondering if he dared tie himself up with interviews and paperwork if Smith finally chose to contact him.

He set the receiver down, staring at the phone momentarily before it rang, startling him. Swallowing hard, he answered.

"Hello?"

"Hello, Paul. Remember me?"

Clouse thought of a number of comebacks, most of the four-letter variety, he wanted to tell Martin Smith at that moment, remembering the old man in good times and murderous times.

"Tell me my family is alright," he demanded with as stern a tone as he could muster.

"It's like a reunion over here. If only you were here to join us."

"Just say where and when."

Smith laughed in a way that only the insane might understand, except he wasn't crazy. He was overcome with greed and a strange immortal power.

"I wouldn't call the police if I were you. They'd only complicate our situation."

"My people have seen me enter the hotel. That might look kind of funny, considering there's a murdered employee right outside my door."

"That's not my problem."

"No, because you *are* the problem. Tell me what you want, Martin."

Clouse looked out a nearby window, wondering if he was being monitored. Based on the conversation, he felt certain Smith was keeping tabs on him somehow.

"We should meet tomorrow morning."

"What's wrong with tonight?"

"I want to see the look on your face clearly when I make my demands."

Clouse sucked in a breath, and some of his pride.

"Whatever you want. Just don't hurt any of them."

"That's more like it. Lay low for the night and I'll call your cell phone in the morning."

Clouse heard the click, standing motionless for a moment before collecting his thoughts. At least everyone in his family was safe, and Smith had to keep them that way or he lost his bargaining leverage.

Taking a few minutes to check around the suite, Clouse found that Jane's cell phone and purse were left behind. If Smith had been careless enough to let someone bring their cell phone along, authorities could track it to a specific location.

But Smith wasn't stupid or careless, and Clouse knew his parents' phones were left at their old house.

"Think," he told himself, then began formulating a plan of action.

He decided to stay in his suite at French Lick for the night, continuing to plan a counterstrike against Smith. When trouble first began at the hotel, he took precautions he hoped were about to pay for themselves. He felt terrible that human life was lost once again in Smith's greedy attempt to live forever, but Clouse planned to end the good doctor's tyranny once and for all.

Chapter 36

When Craig Jennings arrived at work the next morning he found several police cars parked to the side and the rear of the hotel. Shaking his head, he stepped inside to see what trouble awaited him this time.

A commotion in the front lobby caught his attention first and foremost, with police interviewing several hotel staff members. He saw one of the front desk receptionists point his way while talking to an officer, obviously informing the county officer that the head of security just walked inside.

At the moment he wanted to crawl into a corner and hide for about two hours. No one deserved to be tormented by police and whatever crime they were investigating at seven in the morning. Fulfilling his duty, he stepped over to speak with the county officer and a state police investigator.

"What's going on?" he asked the investigator as a forensics technician pulled up outside, unloading some of his equipment.

Now Jennings really felt worried. The investigator, who quickly introduced himself as Scott Benson, took him to the side before speaking.

"There was a murder on the sixth floor overnight."

"Sixth floor?" Jennings asked hesitantly.

"One of your security personnel was stabbed repeatedly with a knife."

"Dan Musgrave," Jennings said, knowing who worked upstairs from a schedule he and Clouse produced each week.

They only did so because Clouse had his own private security team, but sometimes Jennings' people worked security outside the suite. In this case one of his people had apparently lost his life.

"Was he the only person up there?" Jennings inquired, beginning to feel lightheaded.

"We did a full search of the floor and found no one else. Doesn't the Clouse family live up there?"

Jennings nodded, gravely concerned for the safety of his employer's family.

"We've had some trouble here lately. I'm starting to fear the worst."

"We found a single blood trail, and there was a severed hand used to bypass the code on the door."

"Severed hand?" Jennings asked slowly, not sure he wanted to know the details.

"We weren't sure where it came from, but we also found a slide key nearby."

"Those are individually coded. I should be able to tell you who it belonged to."

Jennings walked with the investigator, answering questions as best he could, until the man gave him the coded card to analyze through his computer. Only after he put on latex gloves was Jennings allowed to swipe it through the computer in his office for identification. It took less than a second for the computer to register the encoded number and inform him whom the card was issued to.

"Roland Brown."

"The sheriff?"

"The cards work only in conjunction with fingerprints, so that has to be his hand you found."

Benson used his radio to request one of his fellow troopers to check on the whereabouts of the sheriff immediately, even if it meant traveling to his residence.

Jennings suddenly felt ill. He had seen the sheriff firsthand yesterday, seriously doubting the man had cause to chop off his own hand. The pit of his stomach started to ache as he thought about the prospect of a murder spree like the one he endured two years prior. As though on cue, Dan Duncan stuck his head in the door, just arriving to begin his workday.

"Something I should know about?" he asked.

Jennings introduced the investigator to Duncan, giving the manager a quick summary of the morning find.

"Have you heard from Mr. Clouse?" Duncan asked Jennings, momentarily turning his back to Benson.

"We haven't heard from any of them, Dan. I'm a little bit worried that some-one might have taken them."

Both he and Duncan typically left the hotel after standard business hours, neither of them ever going upstairs unless called upon. For all they knew, something could have happened to the family the previous afternoon.

"Who was the last person to see any sign of the family?" Benson asked.

Both men shrugged.

"Mr. Clouse left on business to Massachusetts yesterday afternoon," Jennings answered. "I believe Mrs. Clouse brought the kids down for a late lunch, but that's the last I saw of them."

"I was in meetings all day yesterday," Duncan stated, as though feeling the need to establish his alibi early.

Jennings shot him a sour look before addressing the detective.

"We have cameras throughout the hotel if you want to review them."

"I would like that very much. Do you have cameras on the upper floor as well?"

"Well, some. Mr. Clouse didn't want us watching over him like hawks, so he only put them in hallways and common areas."

"Common areas?"

"Near his conference room and the workout facility. Places like that."

"Is that footage monitored around the clock?"

"No. My personnel make rounds inside the hotel and around the grounds, only occasionally monitoring the video during the week. We record the footage into the hard drive in case there's an issue that requires further review later."

"You said that was your protocol during the week. What about weekends?"

"On weekends I have an extra man who helps walk the grounds and spends more time viewing the monitors."

"And how many people might know your standard protocol?"

Jennings shrugged.

"Anyone who works here knows my staff. If they were observant they would probably be able to pick up on our habits."

"While we're waiting for the forensics team to arrive, can I have a look at your video footage from last night?"

Jennings nodded, picking up the phone to call one of his security staff. He requested the man join them in the video room, right beside his office, as soon as possible.

"Most of my people are better with computers than I am," he admitted to the detective. "I'll let Benny walk you through whatever areas you want to see. He's the guy who usually monitors the screens for me."

Benson nodded.

"Just show me the way."

Jennings and Duncan walked with him to the adjacent office, then to the monitor room, which realistically only held two people comfortably. Benny Martinez, known as Benny the Bull around the hotel, arrived a few minutes later to work with Benson once they were introduced.

"Let me know if there's anything else you need," Jennings offered before leaving with Duncan at his side.

The two returned to the lobby, a scene of employees talking with police officers in different areas from the front desk to lounging chairs on the opposite end of the lobby. Jennings imagined the staff from the prior evening might be of more assistance, so he offered to call some of the employees for a nearby deputy.

"Please do," the officer replied.

It took him a moment, but Jennings recognized the man as Arlan Brown, the sheriff's son who survived the mansion killings with both he and Duncan. Since Benson had called a trooper to check on the sheriff, the son likely had no idea his father was in grave danger or dead.

Brown seemed to recognize him as well, but said nothing, because the survivors didn't need to state anything to understand their link.

As Jennings approached the desk to ask Duncan's head receptionist to begin calling in employees who worked the night before, she handed him a note first. He made his request, then stepped away from the desk, Duncan still following him like a homeless puppy. Under normal circumstances Duncan acted as an intelligent, capable businessman, but out of his element he sometimes acted lost.

"Does this have to do with that photographer?" he asked.

"Probably not, Dan."

"What are we going to do?" Duncan persisted as Jennings walked into the atrium, trying to free himself from the pressure cooker with stained glass windows and a front desk.

"The first thing I'm going to do is try contacting the Clouses to see if there's any chance they weren't upstairs when that happened."

About to pluck his cell phone from its carrying case, Jennings stopped to open the note labeled "urgent" addressed to him. With Duncan looking over his shoulder, Jennings read the note from Paul Clouse that he wanted both he and Duncan to meet him behind the hotel near the old Jesuit observatory. He asked that they tell no one else, and only the two of them meet with him because there was still hidden danger. Handwritten, the note was signed in last name only at the bottom, in writing that Jennings believed was that of his employer.

"Why out back?" Duncan questioned aloud.

"Maybe he didn't dare leave the grounds. How should I know?"

Jennings weighed the situation over momentarily, wondering if he dared go to his office to retrieve his gun. Seldom did he take it home, because he already had guns inside his house and his wife didn't like the idea of him leaving a gun and holster draped over a chair when he arrived home each night. Retrieving the gun, however, meant possibly getting caught up with more police interviews, and he felt the letter was genuine.

Stuffing it into his sport coat pocket, Jennings headed toward the nearby springs entrance that led to the parking lot. He waved to the valets as he stepped outside, though they seemed more preoccupied with getting their impending checkouts organized than fraternizing with the head of security.

Jennings tried looking inconspicuous as he and Duncan walked up the hill toward the parking lot, reaching the observatory within a few minutes. He found it strange that the building was locked from the outside as he jiggled the sturdy gray lock. Grunting to himself, he looked around the area for any sign of his employer.

When a white van drew near the pair, Jennings thought very little of it until the driver stepped out, aiming a silenced firearm at them. He immediately recognized the man as an employee from inside the hotel, but couldn't readily place which department or area the man worked within.

"Gentlemen, would you please step inside the van? I have someone who would love to see you on Mr. Clouse's behalf."

The question was apparently rhetorical, considering a firearm remained pointed at them.

"Who are you?" Jennings dared ask. "Really?"

Now the young man smiled.

"If you think back, I'm sure you'll remember me from some years ago. But we have all day to discuss the past. You can either step into the van, or you can stain Mr. Clouse's beautiful blacktop with your blood."

Jennings suddenly wished he had retrieved his firearm because this man wasn't about to frisk them. At this point, he had little choice except to comply, because he had little doubt regarding the man's intentions. Duncan's expression was a cross between surprised and dumbfounded because they had actually fallen for the ruse.

With no time left to stall, and no one to see their predicament from a vehicle or the valet area a hundred yards away, they reluctantly stepped into the van. Jennings discovered a strong metal cage separating them from the driver, like those used in vehicles transporting prisoners from jail to a work site or another facility. As they drove past the valet area, the young men working there had no idea of their plight, or the danger their employer might be facing.

***

Though completely unaware of what Jennings and Duncan were experiencing, Clouse felt just as much a prisoner in the suite of his other hotel. He hadn't answered any phone calls, about thirty in all, and with the exception of about a two-hour window when exhaustion caught up with him, he hadn't slept.

He had, however, created a plan of action with several layers based upon what he figured Smith had in mind.

After taking a quick shower, finding a fresh change of clothes, then gathering his belongings, Clouse wanted to escape the hotel without notice. Based on the volume of phone calls, he figured the gruesome discovery had police and staff swarming throughout the other hotel, wondering what happened to him and his family.

He hoped the confusion bought him enough time to get clear of the area, then follow Smith's impending instructions. So far, none of the missed calls matched the number Smith used to call him the night before.

Clouse took up his paperwork from the bed before opening the front door to leave the room. He found the space before him clear until he stepped into the hall, coming face to face with an old friend.

"What are you doing here, Mark?"

"Seems you have some trouble at your other hotel," Daniels noted. "Feel like sharing?"

"I didn't want to get you involved, Mark."

Clouse started to walk away from his friend, but Daniels snagged him by the arm.

"I wouldn't go that way."

"Reporters?"

"And lots of cops. I told some white lies to keep them off you awhile. Come on."

Daniels directed him through a series of hallways that would eventually take them to the parking lot with minimal attention.

"We can take my car," he offered.

"I don't want you involved in this, Mark. There's no telling what Smith has in mind, and I'm not putting you at risk again."

"Who else do you have?"

Clouse stopped in the middle of the hallway.

"No one. Randy Niemeyer left me a message saying Tim never made it home last night and his cell phone was found near a car wreck. If I hadn't been so stupid, I might have realized what Smith was up to a long time ago."

"This is no time to beat yourself up, Paul. I know I've bitched and complained about helping you before, but if we can end this I say we do it."

"I'm still waiting for him to call. If he doesn't know you're with me, it might be to my advantage."

"You want to split up once we get to the parking lot?"

"Let me go first. I'll call you when I know something."

Daniels nodded, letting Clouse finish the remainder of the journey on his own.

When Clouse stepped into the parking lot, he could already feel the muggy nature of the morning air. The thunderstorms had passed, leaving a warm, sticky air in their wake. Cautiously making his way toward his truck, Clouse found no police around the parking garage, and no road blocks out front. They were still in the initial stages of their investigation, so he decided to proceed before they began a thorough search for him inside.

Thankful he had the foresight to park amongst other vehicles on the second level, Clouse prayed he hadn't drawn any attention to himself coming to or leaving the French Lick hotel.

A few minutes later he watched the grounds shrink in his rearview mirror without anyone having noticed his departure. Driving deeper into French Lick, he heard his phone ring beside him. This time he recognized the incoming phone number from the night before.

"Yes?" he answered, knowing it was Smith.

"You mind well, Paul. Perhaps it's time we met face to face. All of your friends and family are waiting."

"Just say when and where."

"How about the site of my old mansion? It brings back such fond memories."

"I want to see my family."

"I'm a reasonable man. Choose one of your friends or family members and I'll bring them along to prove my sincerity."

Somehow Clouse doubted any sincerity from the man he once trusted like a grandfather.

"Bring my son."

Clouse had two good reasons for requesting Zach. It wouldn't raise any concern on Smith's part, and he could implement the first, and potentially most important, part of his plan. He found the first available parking lot to turn his truck around, then pulled in, waiting to see if Smith had any further instructions.

"Be there in half an hour. Alone."

Clouse heard the click on the other end, prompting him to immediately call Daniels.

"What's the word?" his friend asked.

"Smith has called me from the same number twice. Cell phones can be traced, right?"

"Of course. We usually have to work with the phone company to get an exact location."

"Do you have contacts who can do that?"

"You're talking about letting the cat out of the bag, Paul."

Clouse stopped in another parking lot, realizing he had plenty of time to reach the mansion only a mile away. He wondered if Smith had given him such a lengthy time to throw him off track. For all he knew, Smith was keeping everyone near French Lick or West Baden instead of a safe distance away.

"Cat out of the bag?"

"If we let anyone outside of our circle know about this, there's the chance Smith could find out."

Clouse recalled his troubles with Smith's Coven in years past. Though he suspected most of those people were dead, or focusing on different projects, he couldn't take the risk. Only one safe solution presented itself.

"I'm going to call Randy Niemeyer, Mark."

"He could get the job done, but can he keep it quiet?"

"To get his brother back, he'll do whatever it takes."

Daniels said nothing for a moment while Clouse heard slot machines in the background. He wondered how his friend could hear anything while standing inside the casino.

"Call him, then. Hey, what did Smith tell you?"

"He wants to meet in half an hour. He's bringing Zach on good faith."

"There's no such thing with him, Paul. You need some backup?"

"No. He wants me alone."

"I don't like the sound of this."

"Neither do I, but what choice do I have? He's not going to hurt me as long as he wants something from me."

"What if he takes you? I'd never be able to find you in time."

Clouse watched traffic go by momentarily, letting his friend's statement sink in.

"He won't take me. He would have already if he wanted to."

"Just be careful."

"Always am."

Clouse disconnected the call, phoning Randy Niemeyer next, trying to formulate the exact words he needed to bring the state trooper on board.

"It's about time you got around to calling me back," Randy complained upon answering his cell phone.

"I'm sorry to call you like this, Randy, but if you want Tim back, I think I have a way."

Chapter 37

By the time half an hour passed, Clouse stood at the ruins of the old mansion with an envisioned plan, hoping it went off without a hitch.

Not even the basement of the mansion was spared in the demolition process. Every piece of furniture, kitchen appliance, and utensil was removed before dirt was poured into the basement foundation from wall to wall. Covered completely by earth and the grass seed planted over it, the remains were untraceable to the naked eye. Clouse still owned the empty field to ensure no one tampered with the grounds, attempting to resurrect the mansion's evil power.

He stood on the grounds only a few minutes before he began pacing along the grass, beginning to wear down a path when his cell phone rang.

"Caught by a train?" he asked Smith sarcastically after a look at his watch revealed the former doctor was now ten minutes late.

"I've changed my mind about the terms of our arrangement. I want you to see the lengths I've gone just to ensure your cooperation."

"My cooperation in what? You've never stated your terms."

"I want my cube back," Smith hissed over the line. "And you're going to deliver it to me personally, or I'll begin systematically murdering everyone you've ever cared about."

"I'm not doubting you. You've proven your complete lack of conscience several times over. I don't have ready access to the cube, Smith."

"That's why we're having a little face to face talk so I can prove that delays in delivering the cube will cost you dearly."

Clouse swallowed hard, though he wasn't willing to lose control just yet. He needed to play the game to reach the desired ending.

"Where do you want me to go?"

"The gang's all here at the old Homestead Hotel. Why don't you join us?"

Clouse knew plans to convert the old hotel into apartments had either fallen through or slowed to a crawl. Located directly across the highway from the West Baden Springs hotel, the Homestead put forth a renovated exterior, though the inside remained gutted. No one currently visited the hotel, making it a quality hideaway for Smith and any prisoners he gathered along the way.

"Don't bother calling the police or tracing my calls, Paul. After we conduct our business, I'll be covering my tracks and moving to another location."

"I just want to know that everyone is alive, and I don't want them harmed. Do what you want to me, but leave them alone."

"Their condition will depend entirely on you. I'll see you in a few minutes."

Clouse closed his phone, then walked briskly toward his truck, taking a longer glance at the grounds than he meant to, as though looking for inspiration. He finally looked above him toward the clearing sky.

"I could use some help down here, big guy."

He drove directly to the Homestead, pulling around back where a large van was parked completely out of view to anyone driving past the front. The thought of a trap crossed his mind, but he reasoned that Smith could easily have killed or abducted him if given enough time.

No, Smith wanted his cube back, and only Clouse knew its location. Even Daniels, whom he believed was his last trusted friend at the time he buried the cube, didn't know the details for his own protection. If Teakon was right, Smith needed the cube to complete his transformation back to his vigorous youthful form.

Clouse hesitantly stepped through the open backdoor of the old hotel, the morning light barely daring to follow him inside. Shadows and darkness took some getting used to with boards and dark draperies hung to protect most of the hotel's new windows. Though the building had lots of square footage, common sense told Clouse any prisoners weren't going to be at the far reaches because Smith might need to move them at a moment's notice.

He walked along the main hallway, checking room to room until he saw a thin beam of light emerge from a doorway down the hall. Quickly walking to it, he opened the door to a scene that stopped him cold. Smith hadn't bluffed when he said he held all of the pieces in this game of human chess.

Clouse saw most of his family gagged and bound throughout the room, all of them seated against walls on the uncomfortably bare floor. His parents, Jane, Zach, Katie, Tim Niemeyer, and Duncan were all safely distanced from Smith for the moment, their eyes all looking longingly his way for a savior. It was Craig Jennings that Smith chose to make an example of, and in a most distressing way.

Centered in the lengthy room, Smith held a knife to Jennings' throat as the head of Clouse's hotel security was on his knees, hands knotted behind him. The room itself was too dim for Clouse to make out Smith's features, and the man was cloaked beneath a thick brown robe anyhow. He wondered if the robe was inspired by the Jesuits, based on the time Smith spent with them a lifetime ago.

Smith ran a gloved hand over the bald area of Jennings' head, though the action was meant for intimidation, without one shred of compassion.

"So soft and smooth, just like a newborn's, and just as easily smashed in."

Jennings quivered slightly as Smith continued to handle him like a child might a new, interesting pet. Clouse wouldn't have blamed the man one bit for wetting himself in front of everyone, but Jennings held it together, hoping he wasn't the first casualty in the war of cursed objects.

"I'm here, Smith," Clouse said. "What do you want?"

"I want to tell you all about my grand adventures the last two years, and what's brought us to this point."

"Can we just skip it and get to the part where I fetch the cube for you and you let all of my friends and family go?"

Smith laughed, almost like a cackle, sending a shiver up Clouse's spine. This thing before him wasn't human except in shape. Smith's mind was warped and twisted to new extremes, his desire for eternal life and power fueling his every action. Clouse doubted there was any chance he was going to let anyone inside the room live once his possession was returned to him.

Clouse looked around, wondering how Smith had possibly subdued and moved them all by himself.

"Right now you're probably thinking about attacking me and ending this ordeal, aren't you?" Smith inquired tauntingly. "Is the life of Mr. Jennings something you're willing to sacrifice to save your family?"

Clouse stood his ground a moment, finally looking to the floor in despair.

"No."

"I'm not here alone, Paul. As you might have guessed, based on your recently deceased private investigator's findings, I brought someone back to help me."

If he had to guess, Clouse would have guessed Smith brought back his son, better known as Ryan Andrews. Everyone else in the world either feared or loathed Smith for what he'd done, and Tim Niemeyer was eliminated by default, since he remained restrained in a corner.

Clouse didn't have to contemplate the answer very long as a fully rejuvenated and alive Ryan Andrews stepped through a door on the other side of the room. Though it took twelve innocent lives to bring him back in such healthy condition, Clouse doubted it mattered one iota to Smith or his son.

"Long time no see, Paul," Andrews commented, walking dangerously close to Zach as a scare tactic. "Funny that you never noticed me hard at work around your hotel, but I guess you're just too much of a rich snob to pay attention to the hired help."

Clouse chided himself for not recognizing Andrews earlier, feeling certain Smith's son had never actually allowed himself to be spotted at the hotel.

Even if Clouse had been foolhardy enough to bring a firearm, killing Smith was an impossibility while the man was still in a life and death limbo. He had no choice except to hear Smith's demands and chose the best course of action once he left.

"As you may have figured out, my Coven isn't dead," Smith began his personal tale. "Bryan Bell gave his life two years ago for the betterment of my organization."

Clouse scoffed at the notion, shaking his head.

"I was alive and conscious of everything around me, but I had no way of completing the transformation since I wasn't brought back according to the ritual."

"You mean the ritual that requires twelve people to die so you can have your selfish life back?"

"Watch your tone," Andrews said, kneeling down beside Zach, causing the boy to shy away from him.

"It's okay, Zach," Clouse promised, holding his hand out toward his son to show support.

"To think, I once trusted *you* like a son, Paul," Smith said.

"You mean the era you were setting me up to be your scapegoat during your search for cursed objects? I remember all the good times we had, you abducting my entire family and plotting to kill us all so you could conveniently get your fortune back."

"You have such a negative slant on things, Paul. You're forgetting how I got rid of all of your problems for you."

Clouse stared intensely enough to burn a hole through Smith and his costume. Because of the man before him, Clouse lost his best friend, nearly lost his son twice, and became the victim of numerous lawsuits and slander that cost him financially and in reputation.

"I remember you getting rid of my problems, alright, Doc. Like the way you conveniently set things up for junior over there to kill his own mother if things didn't go as planned."

Smith looked from Jennings, who was now distraught that Clouse was bad-mouthing the man with a knife to his throat, to Andrews. A look of grave concern crossed Andrews' face as he stood and took a few steps away from Zach. Clouse had dropped a bombshell that might put them at odds, though he hadn't intended to do so just yet.

"What's he talking about?" Andrews demanded. "I thought you said my mother died during childbirth."

"Don't listen to him," Smith countered. "He's just trying to pit us against one another. I wouldn't lie to you about that."

"You have quite the track record for speaking the truth," Clouse chimed in. "Why should your son be any different?"

"You shut up!" Smith screamed with a pointed finger, stepping forward enough that his hood fell back, revealing his hideous facial features for the first time.

Everyone in the room gasped through their gags, and even Clouse had to take a step back as Smith pulled the gloves from his hands, completing the tormented picture with his bony brown hands. Jennings breathed a sigh of relief now that he was removed from immediate danger.

"You see, this is what you did to me," Smith said with a seething tone.

His face, or what remained of it, was little more than mummified skin atop bones. The flesh and muscle tissue had deteriorated to such a degree that his entire body was brown and flaky, the decomposition process halted only by the evil power that gave him life through Bryan Bell's death.

Even Smith's eyes had a brown hue throughout the pupils and irises, and his nose had shrunken to little more than a nub without the supporting cartilage. He had no hair to speak of, short of a few dark strands that twirled like pigtails from his head. His cheeks were sunken, with barely any flesh left to form them. Most strangely of all, his neck appeared about as thick as that of a terminal cancer patient wasting away by the day. Clouse doubted the man had much physical power at all, which explained why Parish had fended him off during the attack at the suite.

Ever the theatrical genius, Smith had accomplished what he wanted. No one except Clouse was thinking about the fact that Joan Landamere was Andrews' biological mother, and for the moment that seemed fine.

Clouse would use that piece of information again when the time was right.

"Are you happy," Smith sneered at him, "to see me this disfigured?"

"You're where you are because of your own actions, Martin. I didn't ask you to murder people and come back to this world. But I would like to know what you did with my buddy Tim."

Smith drew an awkward smile, difficult to recognize because he barely had lips enough to generate distinguishable facial expressions.

"You want to know why your friend isn't six feet under after my Coven stabbed him repeatedly in front of his dear brother?"

One look to Niemeyer showed he wanted to know the truth as well, and he tried saying so through the gag that muffled his words. Clouse could only look into his friend's blue eyes and hope the truth wasn't going to be agonizing for either of them.

"The fact of the matter is simple. After the embalming process was finished, I reversed the procedure that evening in the funeral home, then used the cube to bring him back to life. He was immediately drugged to sell his death through the calling hours, then his body removed from the coffin just before the funeral. It wasn't easy to pull off, but a rather simple plan if I do say so myself."

"Why bring him back at all if you ordered the hit on him?"

"It occurred to me I needed to shock you in a major way, but then I had second thoughts about protecting my own future interests. If I was going through all of the trouble to make certain I came back to life if things went badly, I needed some form of leverage to use against you. Nathan Runnels was a plant in the right place at the right time all along, so when I died, he knew exactly what to do."

"Then why did you kill him?"

"He got greedy. When it seemed I wasn't coming back, he decided to sell you back your friend, but I wasn't having any of that. Runnels wanted to risk everything I had planned before my death for financial gain. It seems he had a habit of spending cash rather freely at your casino."

"So you cost my friend five years of his life, then gave him back to me on a whim?"

"Hardly on a whim. I wanted to remind you how it feels to have something precious, only to have it ripped away a second time."

Clouse found it interesting that Smith wasn't entirely convinced his own planning would work, which explained how shards of his Coven carried on without him.

"You see, your friend truly was dead for a period of about two days. Enough time that I dare say his soul left his body."

He turned to Niemeyer.

"Like me, you have no soul left to give the Lord, my friend."

Niemeyer struggled against his bonds, trying to yell several choice four-letter words at Smith through the gag, but the ropes held him in check.

Clouse glanced at Andrews, who continued to eye his father suspiciously. Glad the seed of doubt was planted, Clouse decided to act on the next part of his plan.

"I want to see my son before I go."

Smith held his arm out toward Zach, allowing Clouse to walk toward the boy as Andrews stepped away.

When Clouse knelt beside his son, he also looked to Katie and Jane nearby.

"I'm going to get you all out of this, I promise."

He made certain to give his wife a reassuring look since he now had a plan in mind.

Next, he clasped his son's shoulders.

"Zach, stay strong and I'll be back soon. I'm not going to let anything happen to you."

His past experiences with danger, and with Smith, toughened Zach up, but he remained on the verge of tears, unable to free his arms to embrace his father.

"Hang in there, son. I'll be back soon."

Clouse stood, intentionally brushing his right hand against the left side front pocket of his son's blue jeans to tuck something inside the pocket, unseen to Smith and Andrews. Zach started to look down, but Clouse took hold of his head, quickly planting a kiss on his forehead to mask their actions.

Standing up, Clouse returned to the center of the room.

"I'll get your cube, but it may take some time. It's buried."

"I don't want your excuses," Smith said. "I want my cube back."

"I can have it tomorrow."

"You have unlimited resources. I want it by this afternoon."

Clouse held up his hands in frustration.

"It's just not that simple."

Andrews walked over, handing Smith a silenced pistol.

"For every two hours I don't have that cube, I kill someone, Paul. I can start with menial employees like Mr. Jennings, then work my way up to family members from there. Do I make myself clear?"

"Crystal."

Clouse started toward the door, not wanting to waste any time in the recovery effort, but Smith stopped him short.

"Oh, Paul."

Clouse turned around to find Smith aiming the gun at various people throughout the room, making each of them cringe in turn.

"I'm going to give you a little incentive to hurry along your way."

He turned suddenly on Dan Duncan, seated beside Clouse's parents, firing a shot into the man's lower stomach area. His actions drew a grunt, followed by a pained moan, from Duncan as everyone stared in awe.

"You son-of-a-bitch," Clouse muttered, trying to determine the severity of Duncan's injuries.

"He'll survive, maybe a few hours, maybe even a day," Smith taunted. "But why wait to see what happens to him, Paul. Bring me the cube and everyone goes home happy. I know what a burden it can be searching for a new manager, but then again, Duncan was given his job to keep him from suing you, wasn't he?"

Duncan continued to groan as he struggled to find a moderately comfortable position with his new wound.

"If I get some assurances the cube is on the way, maybe I'll let your beautiful wife tend to his injury. I would do it myself, but alas..."

Smith held up one of his hands, allowing a fleck of skin to teeter toward the floor like a fallen leaf.

Clouse turned to begin his quest.

"I'll be in touch," Smith called, his voice eerily cheerful as though he hadn't just shot a man.

Instead of giving in, Clouse departed the hotel without another word. Luckily he had the foresight to know what Smith wanted, ordering a construction owner to begin digging beneath the building where the cube was buried.

The building, one of several he and Jane had constructed for their business ventures after Smith was killed, remained vacant at the moment. Their business, bought out by another company, moved to Georgia, leaving the building vacant with a for sale or lease sign in the slightly overgrown front yard.

Recovering the buried chest containing the cube, however, wasn't an easy task. The simpler way might have been tearing down the building and digging up the chest, but after speaking with a local construction owner, Clouse decided on another method.

Tunneling.

Based on the depth and thickness of the concrete, the construction expert figured they could reach the chest within a matter of hours, possibly a day at most if complications arose. Luckily for Clouse he took the initiative to set this up the night before, paying the man a hefty sum in advance to begin tunneling for the box before daybreak.

Clouse wanted no questions asked, and the chest to remain unopened. While the construction owner said he would conduct the dig personally, he figured it might take a few hours to bring the equipment up from Louisville.

The last contact Clouse had with the man was around five that morning, and he was informed that the equipment was at the site and work was under way. Though he wanted to drive to the site and see how the work was coming, he didn't feel very trusting of Smith. The man seemed eager to brag about his Coven and their extensive work for him. If Smith still had loyal agents, they might be watching Clouse's every move.

Thinking on his feet, Clouse came up with a solution to his problem before reaching the town limits. He reached for his cell phone, deciding it was time to call for some assistance.

Chapter 38

Daniels realized Jane had been right about approaching him for help in seeking answers, because her intuition obviously served her well. He didn't particularly like the idea of putting himself at risk, especially with the possibility of getting back together with Cindy growing more probable with each encounter.

A lack of time prevented him from digging up very many answers, but he remained loyal to his friend. When Clouse called him with a request for help, Daniels readily agreed, helping Clouse put a plan into action.

Now parked along a dirt turnaround point, Daniels watched his friend drive past on a primarily desolate county road. Remaining in his spot, Daniels felt like a fisherman waiting for the first nibble. When a gray Cadillac passed about a minute later, he felt certain someone had taken the bait, but he needed to be positive before acting.

As part of their plan, Clouse went up the road, turned around, then headed back the way he came, going nowhere near the grounds where the cube was buried.

Daniels saw his friend drive past, waited patiently once again, then watched the Cadillac drive past, with less time differential than the first pass. He pulled out, hoping Clouse remembered to slow down so the car trailing him would follow suit. Clouse remembered, giving Daniels an opportunity to memorize the license plate and call Randy Niemeyer after turning right on another county road to avoid suspicion.

"What have you got?" Randy asked after answering his cell phone.

"Paul is definitely being followed. I need you to run this plate and see who it comes back to."

Daniels read him the plate number, waiting a few minutes as Randy processed the number in his patrol car's computer system.

"Comes back to a Stephen Ellis. Nice address in the Bloomington area."

"Big surprise there."

"Probably a doctor. Want me to find a reason to pull him over?"

"No. He'd just call Smith as soon as you cut him loose. I think I have a better idea."

***

Dressed in his full duty uniform as Clouse requested, Randy had already arrived in the West Baden area when Daniels called him. After listening to Daniels' idea, he sped down a county road hoping to intersect Clouse at just the right spot.

Clouse had brought him into the fold that morning, leaving a package for him at the French Lick Springs Hotel. Now that he understood the plan, and more importantly, believed in it, the state trooper simply wanted to see his brother safe and sound once more. What Clouse left him at the hotel gave him some assurance that his wish was an almost certain probability.

Driving to a four-way stop sign almost two miles away from the casino, Randy waited for Clouse to drive through it, as planned, allowing himself to get pulled over. Stepping from his patrol car, Randy went through the motions of speaking to Clouse, pretending to ask for his license and registration as the trailing car passed them both at a slow pace.

"Is he looking?" Randy asked Clouse.

"Yeah."

At this point the trooper had to make certain the Cadillac's driver didn't see his face, just in case Smith had told him about Clouse's potential allies. He lowered his head, pretending to read the information as the driver passed.

"Let me know when he's out of sight," Randy instructed.

It took about a minute before the car was a mere dot in the distance, but Clouse finally nodded, then got out of his truck. He followed Randy to the car, jumping into the passenger's seat before the state trooper quickly turned them around.

"You good with all of this?" Clouse asked.

"Not that I have much choice, but it sounds like you have the bases covered."

If everything went well, they would be out of sight within seconds, leaving the driver of the other car to wait momentarily before cautiously inspecting Clouse's truck. By the time he figured out Clouse wasn't in the truck, they would be safely heading toward the buried chest.

"Where's the package?" Clouse inquired.

Randy thumbed toward the back seat, allowing Clouse to reach back and snag the opened brown package, which revealed a small laptop computer containing specific hardware and programming.

Clouse opened it, turned it on, and loaded up the main program to begin tracking Smith's whereabouts. He had placed a tracking device, no larger than a watch battery, within Zach's blue jeans, allowing him to follow his son wherever Smith took him. Clouse had also left a tracking device within his own pockets in case Smith abducted him, or forced him somewhere against his will. Randy could have followed the signal based on the quickly jotted instructions included with the computer.

"Are they mobile?" Randy asked.

"Looks like it. They're on the outskirts of French Lick according to the GPS map."

"Tell me again why I'm putting my career on the line instead of calling in my people and the local police."

"Because Smith can't be bargained with. He also can't be killed with conventional weapons, so he has absolutely nothing to lose."

Grunting to himself, Randy continued to drive as Clouse fed him instructions.

"We're not going to intercept Smith, are we?"

"No. We need the cube just in case things don't go as planned."

"You could be playing right into his hands. For all we know, he could have a tracker on you."

Clouse suspected his truck might have been tagged, which allowed the Cadillac's driver to remain a safe distance behind. Smith covered all bases when he planned something, but Clouse had remained one step ahead this time.

He had filled in Daniels and Randy about the stipulations Smith gave him, including the situation and the identities of those abducted by Smith and his son. While he hated leaving Duncan in such a dire predicament, Clouse knew he needed the bargaining chip or everyone might be lost before he found an opportunity to act.

Still unsure of how he wanted to proceed, Clouse at least had some help on his side, and possibly more waiting in the wings.

"Can your system pinpoint where they are?" Randy asked.

"Down to the address numbers. As long as Zach has that chip in his pants, we'll find them."

Considering the cube's hiding place was located north of Orange County, it was going to take longer than Clouse wanted to arrive. While he had informed the state trooper beside him of almost every detail, he hadn't told him that his brother was one of the first people on the chopping block if Smith didn't have the cube soon. At the moment, he hoped the construction owner hadn't lied to him about getting the cube in less time by tunneling.

Deciding to find out, Clouse gave the man a call.

"Johnson Construction," he answered after three rings.

"David, this is Paul Clouse. How's the dig coming along?"

"Well, the machine broke down just as I was getting close to the building's underbelly."

Clouse's heart skipped a beat as he envisioned everyone he cared about lying in a pool of blood. Smith's impossible deadline had become just that.

"What's the plan?" Clouse asked. "I'm kind of in a time crunch here."

"I've already got mechanics working on the thing," Johnson revealed. "They were on standby all along since these things are notorious for breaking down."

Clouse expected little more than his standard bad luck all around, including the machine he depended upon to save his family.

"It's become even more important that I recover that chest in a hurry," Clouse stated earnestly. "Is there anything I can do to help speed up the process?"

"Nah," Johnson said as though any urgency mattered little. "We'll be digging again before you know it."

"Good, because I'm on my way there. I'll see you in about half an hour."

He closed the phone, deciding he had better things to do than hold up Johnson, including getting the remainder of his plan moving forward. He also had a backup plan or two formulated in case the cube wasn't readily accessible.

"I take it that didn't go so well?" Randy commented, now cruising along the highway at speeds only a state trooper dared travel without fear of being pulled over.

"No. It didn't."

"How are you so sure Smith won't kill everyone just for the fun of it?"

"Because he knows I'll want a guarantee before I deal the cube away. And lugging dead weight around is a lot tougher than having mobile prisoners."

"That sounds cold, you know."

"I'm sorry to sound that way, especially since he has my family, but I find myself thinking like him just to outwit him."

Clouse looked at the computer, finding the signal had stopped at the far end of French Lick, past the casino, and away from West Baden. He pointed out the given address to Randy, allowing the trooper to examine it when they stopped for a red light.

"Edge of downtown?" he guessed aloud.

"That's what I'm thinking," Clouse replied, "but I can't place the building."

Using his computer terminal, which served many functions for state troopers, Randy typed in the address as he accelerated from the now green light, able to type and drive at the same time.

"There," he said, turning the terminal toward Clouse a few seconds later.

"The old civic center," Clouse thought aloud, based on what the computer search engine had revealed. "May I?"

Randy nodded, allowing Clouse to access the computer further, revealing even more information.

"The old civic center was once a saloon," he summarized aloud for Randy's benefit. "The original building was torn down shortly before World War II and the site went between ownerships for almost a decade before the town bought the property for public use. It was a playground for a few years, then redeveloped for use as a community center."

"Do we really need the history lesson?" Randy complained.

"If we're going to this place, we need to know exactly what we're getting into. Anyway, the community center had several wings, including a theater for community and school plays. Part of it burned down in 1983, leaving just the theater portion, the basement, several changing rooms, and a small lobby that was rebuilt and expanded."

"Sounds like a great setting for *Phantom of the Opera*."

"Probably why Smith chose it. I'm a little bit surprised he picked something so close to the hotel. With two years of planning, I figured he'd be more original."

"Maybe he wants it close to the hotel on purpose."

"He always was kind of nostalgic, wasn't he? I remember the good ol' days when he tried to slit my throat at the hotel to get back at you."

"Those were good times," Clouse said, faking a reminiscent tone, pulling out his cell phone to make a few important calls.

Now that everything seemed to be falling into place, except delivery of the cube, he wanted to have everyone prepared for the inevitable confrontation with Smith.

Chapter 39

When Clouse first saw the equipment David Johnson had set up at his old business building, he questioned the effectiveness of the man's plan almost immediately. After stepping from the patrol car, he walked around the building to the back where Johnson had set up the entry point along a hill.

Clouse liked that Johnson had chosen the most direct route to the chest, based on the three-meter hole started along the hill where perfect grass once grew. A tube less than two feet in diameter fed out from the hole, releasing moist dirt from its tail in a continual stream. From within the manmade tunnel, Clouse heard the machine in action, its engine whining like any piece of heavy machinery struggling with a load.

"At least he's back to work," Randy said with a hopeful shrug.

"If I call him it would just slow him down, so I guess we wait."

Nearly twenty arduous minutes later Johnson emerged from the tunnel on foot, collapsing the now empty return tube upon itself. When he saw Clouse standing nearby, he smiled, walking over to shake the millionaire's hand.

"Not another technical difficulty, I hope," Clouse said.

"Nope. My machine just tapped your buried chest, literally, so I'm about to back it out and let you get your prize."

Clouse fought to keep from showing emotion, but inwardly he was ecstatic. He still had time to meet Smith's insane deadline and possibly save everyone inside the old civic center.

Minutes passed like hours as he waited for Johnson to back the machine out of the dirt tunnel. When it finally emerged, hind-end first, Clouse found it to look somewhat like the drilling machines used in action movies, mobile with the assistance of a large industrial tread, similar to those used on military tanks. Unlike its movie counterparts, the machine didn't have a large steel drill attached to the front that spun in one direction. Instead, it had one centered drill that bore through the dirt, surrounded by three rotating steel arms that fed the dirt into a disposal tube as the machine made progress.

Johnson stepped away from his machine, labeled the RT-7 in blue paint along either side, handed Clouse a flashlight, then waved his arm toward the tunnel entrance.

"There's a shovel over there if you want it," Johnson offered.

Clouse grabbed it on his way into the tunnel, finding himself in the darkest walkway he'd ever experienced. In the fire department he was too thick and tall to do much confined space work, but the few times he'd worked in attics or tunnels paled in comparison to the dark, wet feeling of this area.

Immediately consumed by darkness, he kept the flashlight's beam aimed ahead of him, following the treaded path left by the machine. Though he felt somewhat nervous that ten tons of concrete rested mere feet above him, he was equally apprehensive about seeing and touching the cube again.

For a tiny, unassuming object, it fascinated men with its power, taking hold of their desires and fears simultaneously. Clouse only saw the red cube, embedded within a wooden cross, after his last confrontation with Smith. He managed to put the object within a box, then inside the chest, until he found the appropriate time and place to bury the entire package. At the time, he planned for the thing to remain safely tucked away from human hands forever, or at least until he discovered a safer place to store it.

It took just over a minute for him to reach his destination, but the light showed him exactly where one of the side handles for the chest was located, still partially covered in dirt. Feeling like Indiana Jones, he reached up cautiously for the handle, discovering the chest began to pull toward him with very little urging. When it seemed the handle was about to twist completely free from the box and break, Clouse picked up the shovel and began freeing the packed dirt around the chest.

A minute later he had the chest freed from its dirt casing, dropping the case beside him on the ground. Because it was buried in such a safe place, he never bothered putting a lock on the case, so it opened freely for him, revealing a shiny red cube still encased within the middle of a wooden crucifix. What a paradox, Clouse thought, that the two objects should be merged together.

He removed the cross before making his way back to the entrance, hopeful that he could stop Smith before anyone else was injured or killed. The man didn't deserve to live, much less have use of such a powerful weapon.

As Clouse neared the entrance, the daylight stung his eyes after being in complete darkness for so long. At first he didn't see Randy Niemeyer or David Johnson standing within his line of vision, but as he stepped out from the tunnel he found them both with arms raised, slightly to his right. Turning around from sheer instinct, he saw an older, slightly overweight man holding them captive with a pistol.

"I'll take that cube," the man stated coldly.

***

Clouse immediately knew this was the man following him earlier. He wore a blue dress shirt under a gray suit without a tie, and the shirt was drenched in sweat. A thick fringe of gray hair horseshoed his otherwise bald head and his glasses were somewhat fogged from the humid morning air. He looked far too distinguished and well-off to be in legion with Smith, but apparently that was the case.

"Mr. Ellis, I presume?"

"Dr. Ellis, actually. Martin gave me specific instructions on how to deal with you."

Johnson grew fidgety, standing only a few feet from Clouse.

"I didn't sign on for this, Clouse."

"Just stay put and shut up, and we'll be out of this in a minute."

"I'm afraid none of you will be going anywhere," Ellis announced, overhearing them. "That little tunnel of yours is the perfect place for an accident to claim the three of you."

Ellis used the gun as a pointer, ushering them toward the tunnel.

"He doesn't look very steady with that thing," Randy noted, but Clouse had already considered trying to disarm the doctor, and decided against it.

"What are you a doctor of exactly?" he inquired instead.

"Pathology."

That made perfect sense, considering how Smith had rearranged dead people at various times and tinkered with bodies conveniently.

"You two get inside," he ordered Randy and Clouse, who reluctantly entered the fresh tunnel, remaining near the entrance. "And you are going to block their path with your vehicle, at least ten feet inside," he said to Johnson who now looked purely bewildered at the turn of events.

"He's going to kill him, isn't he?" Randy asked Clouse.

"Probably."

Clouse decided to stall for time.

"You can't leave us in here to starve, Ellis."

"I could, but Martin wants to come deal with you himself. After I call him, he'll tie up any loose ends, then come and pay you his final respects."

"Shit," Randy said, frustrated that they were as trapped as their family members.

"Once we get shut in, there's no way out of this," Clouse informed him. "We can't let him make that call."

"I can rush him," Randy said, an unusually crazed look in his eyes.

"No. Wait until Johnson gets close with the drill. I doubt Ellis is a crack shot with that gun."

They watched as Johnson climbed aboard his machine, started it, and drove it at a snail's pace in their direction.

"Where's *your* gun, Randy?"

"He made me toss it to him on the hill. I think he threw it toward my car."

The car was halfway around the building, which meant his gun was virtually irretrievable, even if they escaped the tunnel. Ellis could probably wing one or both of them, given enough chances to fire.

Within a minute Johnson had drawn near the two trapped men. His machine was within five feet of the entrance when Clouse decided something had to be done, or everyone at the old theater was going to die within the hour.

"If we get behind the machine, we can make a break for the other side of the building," Clouse suggested. "He can't get us both if we get to cover fast enough."

Clouse glanced at the machine itself, where Johnson was reasonably protected by the metal cage around him. Because it dug into all kinds of surfaces, he was enclosed within the device, possibly able to lock himself inside. Feeling somewhat better that the innocent man was protected, Clouse placed a hand on Randy's shoulder as they prepared to run for their lives the long way around the building.

He wondered exactly what they were going to do if they managed to escape, but they had to try. Smith wasn't going to win this easily, Clouse thought angrily, looking at the machine now only a foot from the entrance.

They had just stepped from the tunnel, fully prepared to run, when Ellis' eyes grew wide with terror as he trained his gun at something atop the hill. A bullet ripped through his chest, bringing forth a brief yelp before his body slumped to the ground in an awkward heap. Clouse slid around the machine, still ducked for cover, when he found his friend standing atop the hill, replacing his firearm to its side holster.

Daniels didn't appear the least bit happy about taking a human life, though his loyalty to Clouse and a desire to end this ordeal compelled him to act.

"Thank God, Mark."

"Bet you're glad you gave me directions."

"That's an understatement. This prick was going to bury us and tell Smith to kill everyone else in French Lick."

Daniels looked to his watch.

"We don't have much time, Paul."

Clouse surveyed the area, recovering the crucifix while Randy found his gun atop the hill. Johnson simply stumbled out of his machine, wondering what form of craziness just occurred around him as Clouse scooped up Ellis' cell phone for monitoring purposes.

"We'll settle up later, Dave," Clouse promised. "I'm sorry about this, but there's no time to explain. I told you it was a matter of life or death when I hired you, and I wasn't kidding."

"Come on," Daniels prodded as Johnson stood by his machine, a stunned look still crossing his face.

While Daniels hopped into his own vehicle, Clouse decided to ride with Randy once more. They were in a race against time, and on a collision course with Smith in a showdown that Clouse hoped they could win with the element of surprise.

Chapter 40

On the way back to French Lick, Clouse looked to Ellis' phone as it rang, but he didn't answer it. A few seconds after it stopped ringing, his cell phone rang with a different phone number than before. Clouse now knew the man was smart enough to change cell phones to avoid being tracked to one location.

Little did he know he'd already been tracked a different way.

"Yes?" Clouse answered.

"Just thought I would check up on my favorite pupil," Smith said over the line.

"I'm doing fine," Clouse simply answered, wondering if Smith dared inquire about the last of his Coven.

He didn't, likely guessing Ellis was indisposed one way or another if he wasn't answering his phone.

"Do you have my property?"

"I'm on my way back, so don't hurt anyone."

"I wouldn't dream of it if we have an understanding. Where do you want to meet?"

"Somewhere where the two of us can have some privacy. We have so much to talk about."

Clouse's mind raced for an ideal spot that benefitted him, but he felt certain Smith already had something in mind.

"Why don't we meet in the hotel's basement, Martin? It's a place you're awfully at home with, and maybe I could hand you the keys to the place."

"I don't much care for your tone, Paul. Maybe someplace a little more fitting is in order, like the cemetery where I was buried the first time around. One hour. Alone. Bring my crucifix, or everyone you hold dear will be a distant memory."

Clouse shut his phone after a click came from the other end.

"Well?" Randy asked.

"Good news and bad, my friend. He wants to meet me alone, away from the others, but I think he has something special planned for me."

"If he's meeting you, that leaves just his son to guard Tim and your family. We should be able to handle him, especially if he doesn't know we're coming."

"That's true. And he's mortal, so bullets will work on him. The problem I have is that bullets don't hurt Smith, and I don't know what does."

He opened his cell phone once more.

"Who you calling now?"

"Someone who can give me some answers. I hope."

***

Clouse received at least some of the answers he needed, then told the others to go on without him as he took his truck to meet Smith. Based on the meeting place, a private cemetery on the south end of Monroe County, he needed to make good time to meet Smith's deadline. He assumed Smith wasn't lying, picked up his truck on the way back toward French Lick, then went his separate way as Randy Niemeyer and Daniels met up with Todd Parish at the West Baden hotel.

Parish readily agreed to assist the group, to get Zach and Katie back by any means possible. Ignoring his usual dress code, Parish dressed completely in black, like he was getting ready to run with a SWAT team, right down to the multi-pocketed BDU pants. He listened while Randy filled him in on the day's events and what to expect when they reached the old civic center. Daniels, standing over a nearby table in the hotel lobby, studied some blueprints they obtained from the local French Lick library's architectural archives.

Daniels listened intermittently to their conversation, trying to decipher which of the blueprints still held true, because they were drawn before the devastating fire claimed portions of the building.

"Can we assume Andrews is alone?" Daniels asked Randy once he was through catching Parish up on their woes.

"We can't assume anything after that guy had a gun on us at Clouse's old building."

"We're going to be armed," Parish stated. "If Andrews isn't like his pops, then we can deal with him."

"But not at the expense of the hostages. I'm not putting my brother's safety at risk for anything."

Daniels was somewhat surprised that the state trooper was willing to be so patient with his brother at Smith's mercy. He had indeed matured over the past few years, developing patience and caution that came with age and his police training.

"Are we ready to do this?" Parish asked, looking to the other two men for approval since they were a bit more official than him in the legal world.

A few minutes later the three were parked about a block away from the civic center, pulling weapons from the trunk of Daniels' car, checking their ammunition and making certain they were prepared and protected. Luckily they were shielded from public view, so no one would call the police when they spied three heavily-armed men roaming the streets.

Parish removed a large semi-automatic rifle from inside a protective black cloth with a magazine already loaded into its center.

"What the hell is that?" Daniels asked as the bodyguard checked over his weapon that looked like it belonged in a war video game.

"An AR-15. It's the civilian version of the M-16."

"Civilian, huh?"

"Yeah. No joke."

Parish put on a pair of black leather gloves once he finished inspecting the weapon, and though he said nothing, it dawned on Daniels that the man really liked black.

"You're really into this, aren't you?" Daniels asked, eyeing his attire from top to bottom.

"Sorry, I guess I left my forcible entry attire manual at home," Parish replied sarcastically. "There wasn't exactly room for a lot of details when Mr. Clouse called me."

"Are you two about ready?" Randy asked testily.

Daniels nodded, and the three of them headed toward the civic center with Daniels taking the lead. While it looked like they were heading for a major Hollywood showdown at first, all three approached the building with caution from the only alley that kept them hidden.

Separate from most of the other local downtown buildings, the civic center was overshadowed by its only neighbor, a tall defunct business building. For security reasons, the building had only one entrance with a set of double doors. One of the theater's sides had an emergency exit, but it didn't have any kind of access handles from the outside.

"What now?" Parish asked Daniels as they stood beside the front double doors.

Daniels knew going through the front wasn't wise, in case Andrews found a good spot in which to monitor the prisoners and the single access point.

"I wish Paul was here. He used to break into buildings for a living."

"Don't you cop types do that, too?" Parish asked.

"Only the testosterone-enriched SWAT guys. And they don't exactly do it quietly."

Parish looked at the front entrance, then stepped to the side of the building with the fire exit. He returned with a sly grin, cracking the knuckles on one fist with his open hand.

"That door back there is made of wood. Old wood."

"Even if it's made of paper that doesn't help if we're going to get shot the second we walk through it," Daniels argued.

"Yeah, but if there's a distraction up front, I could bust through that thing in a heartbeat, and maybe get the jump on Andrews."

"You've got a family. Sure you want to do this?"

"I'm a big target, but I'm not stupid. And the longer we wait, the worse this could get."

Daniels pulled out a copy of the building's blueprint, using his intuition and experience to guess where Andrews might be hiding inside.

"This is the best vantage point I can find," he said, pointing to public seating entrance doors inside. "He could watch the stage and the front doors from that spot. If these are still accurate, the side door would be out of his view from there, but he'll be able to hear almost anything we do."

"If you two can rattle the front doors, I can get in the side," Parish lobbied for his plan once again.

"Be prepared for anything, Todd. He may not be expecting us, but he might have planted traps just the same."

Parish nodded while Daniels continued to examine the layout.

"If I had to guess, I'm betting he's keeping everyone below the stage level. There's a storage area down there with only one way in or out. There's probably a door he could block to keep them inside."

"What if he's down there with them?" Randy asked. "Will he even hear anything we do?"

Daniels shrugged.

"There are a lot of what ifs, Randy. We've got numbers on our side, but we don't know what he has, so both of you be careful. Todd, when you leave this spot, count to thirty, then see if you can get inside that door. We'll make some noise up front and see if we can get inside, too."

Parish nodded and started walking toward the building's side, holding his rifle in a ready position in case he found something inside.

Daniels admired the man, putting his life on the line for two kids who were not his own. Parish had always said nothing would happen to them on his watch, and now Daniels believed the bodyguard lived and breathed his own philosophy.

Now Daniels turned to the uniformed man beside him.

"Let's do some knocking, Randy."

***

Jane remembered being ushered roughly into the civic center by Ryan Andrews, past the auditorium seating with an overhead chandelier dimmed to the minimum. The sides were lined with light fixtures designed to look like candles, with flicker bulbs installed. Only about half of the lights in the place worked, testament to the fact that the building had been primarily neglected the past few years.

Community funding had dried up, and while she and her husband planned to aid in the restoration of the old center, they had been busy with other things lately.

Like staying alive.

Now stuck in the storage area of the basement with the others, Jane had no real way of communicating with the prisoners around her. Still bound and gagged, at least she could see since Andrews had removed everyone's blindfolds so they could make their way downstairs.

Though Smith hadn't killed any of them yet, keeping his word thus far, Dan Duncan wasn't doing well. Andrews had helped him walk to the storage area only to shove him down the steps where the door was closed swiftly behind the group. Now Duncan was mumbling incoherently, on the brink of an unconsciousness from which he likely wouldn't awaken. Most of his injuries were internal, but Jane knew if she could free herself, she might be able to at least assess him. She held out hope that help might arrive, or her husband might outwit Smith.

A single bulb lit the room, but their eyes had adjusted to the near dark conditions. Apparently Andrews hadn't given much thought to keeping them apart, or had better things to do, because each of them were able to scoot along the floor. Jane took advantage of this fact by moving toward Craig Jennings. They didn't need to speak for Jennings to understand that she needed her hands to examine Duncan.

Jennings and Duncan had survived the mansion incident together before working closely at the hotel, even forming a loose friendship away from business. He began undoing Jane's bonds, though the knots seemed to trick him momentarily. With Jane unable to verbally direct him, he struggled for nearly two minutes before undoing the thick knot, allowing her to shake off the remaining rope. She untied her feet before running to Duncan, ignoring the others for the moment.

If Andrews came back and saw them untied, he might begin shooting first and asking questions later. She could always go back to faking being a model prisoner if she heard him coming.

"Dan, can you hear me?" she asked after pulling down her gag.

Duncan groaned inaudibly a moment, fighting to focus his eyes on her.

"It burns," he finally said, clutching his abdomen where the bullet entered.

Jane slowly rolled him over, finding the bullet hadn't exited, meaning it remained lodged inside his internal organs somewhere. Regardless of its location, it was eventually going to kill him with the internal bleeding it created unless he received medical attention. Jane was in no position to operate on him in the confines of a theater basement.

"Hang in there," she said before crossing the small room to converse with Jennings, pulling down his gag.

"We have to get out of here," he said immediately.

"Andrews has a gun."

"He can't shoot *all* of us."

"Are you positive of that?"

Jennings shrugged as much as his bonds allowed.

"Dan is going to die if we don't get him out of here."

"We could all die if we try it without a plan."

Jennings looked both determined and angry at the same time.

"I don't want to be shot like a dog, Mrs. Clouse. Not like this."

Jane agreed, beginning to undo the ropes binding him when a violent crashing noise drew everyone's attention upward.

Perhaps their prayers had been answered.

Chapter 41

All during the drive to the private cemetery, Clouse had tried to envision the place in his mind from his only previous visit. He kept remembering Smith's casket lowering into the ground, at the time feeling burdened and sad because he had trusted and loved the man like a grandfather. He couldn't remember enough of the cemetery to feel comfortable, so he relegated himself to believing Smith had the advantage, which meant he needed to be sharp.

Even if he died battling Smith, he believed his family would survive because he trusted Daniels, Parish, and Randy Niemeyer to overwhelm Andrews and free the prisoners.

He parked outside the cemetery entrance in a gravel area, approaching the front gate slowly as he examined the cemetery and the woods behind it. Seeing no one, he knelt down just outside the main entrance, which gave a foreboding "no trespassing" feel without the benefit of words. He examined the grass for foot traffic, finding the entirely green path very much intact.

The front gate consisted of black wrought iron bars that stood about twice his height. A perimeter fence, also black and about waist-high, surrounded the cemetery to protect about two dozen tombstones within its confines. A fairly exclusive place to be buried, the graveyard included bodies over a century old.

Set off the road far enough that it worried Clouse, the cemetery had an eerie look to it, even in late spring. A large, dead tree with absolutely no leaves and a number of crooked branches stood ominously to one side of the small field. Clouse half expected to see crows with glowing red eyes perched upon its branches, but there were no birds, and no sounds coming from anywhere within the fenced area.

In the far corner, Clouse spied what he thought was a living person for a second, but as he closed the gap, he noticed a faded, tattered, white dress blowing in the gentle breeze upon what might once have been a living person. He cautiously approached the mummified looking remains, noticing an open grave behind the staged corpse. His mind traveled back to a battle inside an open grave with a cloaked figure that nearly killed him.

Clouse heard a voice that froze him in his tracks, bringing his mind back to the current danger.

"Paul, why did you let me die?"

He hesitated, looking from side to side, certain the voice hadn't come from the body before him. Somehow the haunting words reminded him of how familiar the dress looked, but the eerie familiarity of the voice stopped him cold.

"Angie?"

As impossible as it seemed, he stared at the seemingly floating corpse, wondering if it might actually be his deceased first wife. While Smith hadn't committed the murder, he certainly knew enough about Clouse's misery at the time to play on his emotions.

"I was so good to you, Paul," the voice came from nearby once again as Clouse froze at how eerily close it sounded to Angie. "You left me to die, didn't you?"

Realizing this was all Smith's doing, real or not, Clouse ignored the voice he knew couldn't be Angie's, searching the area for clues. Focusing on the open grave nearby, he carefully peered inside, finding a speaker box of some sort, explaining where the voice originated. Still, Smith was nowhere to be found.

"Where are you, Smith?" he called out, knowing no one else would hear the sound of his voice.

It occurred to him that Smith might have duped him into visiting the cemetery as a form of mental torture. Doing so might have given the sinister man a chance to do something with his captives, but he knew Smith was desperate for the cube's power. Smith might have been virtually impervious to harm in his current form, but Clouse figured his strength was significantly diminished from his days as a living person.

He wasn't willing to bank on that presumption, however.

"Smith?" Clouse called again, a rumbling growl in his voice this time.

He turned around from the grave, surveying the area, suddenly nervous that Smith bought enough time to harm those close to him, or move them again.

Could he have located the tracker in Zach's pants and broken the original deal? Had he been lying all along to lure Clouse away from the nucleus of his evil plan?

"Why, Paul?" the voice called again. "Why did you let me die?"

"You're not real," Clouse said to himself more than the mysterious recording, unwilling to look any more closely at the body.

He now knew it was propped up by some kind of metallic brace, keeping it in place while the dress flapped in the wind. Smith had spared no time or expense in setting up this disturbing scene, though Clouse had yet to figure out why. Still unsettled by the scene before him, Clouse failed to notice the false floor in the open grave move aside as Smith crawled out of the hole like some zombie emerging from eternal rest. Grabbing a nearby shovel, Smith swung as Clouse heard the noise and turned around, rendering the younger man unconscious.

"Time to pay the piper, Paul," Smith said, standing over Clouse's prone form.

***

Everything seemed to be going according to plan when Parish kicked in the emergency exit door on the civic center's side. Daniels and Niemeyer had carried through on their intentions to make noise at just the right moment, but Parish found himself in a dangerous situation the second he stepped inside.

Engulfed by darkness and silence, he knew the daylight behind him made him a perfect target for Andrews. Unable to see any booby traps, or even step freely without fear of running into objects, he hesitated momentarily, hoping his two partners might find their way inside. He found himself completely blind within this new environment.

Parish found himself unable to adapt to the intentionally darkened inside of the theater, bumping into a row of seats only a few steps away from the door. He tried steadying himself after nearly tripping over a broken seat, hearing a low electronic hum from about ten feet away as he stood up, readying the AR-15.

"Who's there?"

Before he could react, much less think about reacting, he felt his body stiffen in intense pain, as though every muscle had simultaneously succumbed to one mammoth charley horse. No longer in control of his own actions, Parish dropped his gun, falling awkwardly into the seats, realizing he had just been taken down by a stun gun.

Experience and prior training let him know exactly what to expect from the weapon being used on him. Typical guns used by police use small metal prongs, or hooks, that latch into the skin, then deliver a shock for five seconds. The user then has the option of extending the shock another five seconds by squeezing the trigger, or subduing the victim another way. Most guns also have the option of manually stopping the shock before five seconds are up, but this was not one of those cases.

By the time Parish figured out exactly what his body was experiencing, five seconds had passed, along with two swift kicks from his assailant to his abdomen. As the shocks ceased, Parish started reaching for the man he suspected to be Andrews, but another shock stiffened his body with intense pain.

One benefit of the stun gun, that he didn't much care for at the moment, was the ability for the user to touch or handle the victim while the shock was being administered.

Parish received two more kicks, and a solid punch to the chin while still under the gun's paralyzing effects. He hated being helpless to defend himself, much less reach his gun, with so many lives at stake. If Daniels and Niemeyer didn't get inside soon, Andrews was going to finish him one way or another.

As the shocks stopped a second time, Andrews hovered over him. Parish tried catching his breath from the stiff blows, finding that the wind being knocked out of him was just as paralyzing as the shocks.

"You should have learned your lesson when my father let you live the first time," Andrews said, holding a large knife over Parish as he taunted him. "Now you have to face me, and I'm younger and stronger than ever before."

"Good for you," Parish said, reaching for the hooks leeched into his chest.

Another shock prevented him from freeing himself as Andrews slowly bent over, aiming the knife toward his throat.

"Stop right there!" Randy Niemeyer's voice boomed from behind Andrews, causing the murderous man to stop short of slitting Parish's throat.

Still winded, Parish reached up, pulling the probes from his chest to ensure he didn't receive further punishment. Andrews complied, putting up his hands, still wearing a smug grin across his face.

"You can't stop it," he said assuredly.

"Stop what?" Daniels demanded angrily.

"What's going to happen to your friend. You can kill me, but after my father gets the cube back from Clouse this will all start again, and again, until you are *all* dead and we're the only ones left."

"You sound awfully sure of yourself," Randy sneered. "Where's my brother and the others?"

Parish couldn't utter a warning fast enough as the click of a revolver near the state trooper's left ear caused both he and Daniels to slowly turn. While Parish had no idea who the slightly overweight, older man behind them was, they seemed to instantly recognize him through surprised gazes.

"Ellis," Daniels said disdainfully. "Didn't I shoot you already?"

"It's called body armor," the doctor said with a grin, obviously very smug about his own foresight. "One would think a former police officer might remember to wear some, or at least check a gunshot victim more thoroughly."

Forced to lie still on the ground while events around him unfolded, Parish thought about his sidearm, still holstered readily at his side. Though Andrews was armed only with a knife, so far as he knew, Parish didn't want to jeopardize Daniels or Niemeyer to save himself. At this point, however, he found no sound alternatives, considering he was the only one left with an accessible weapon.

He waited for Andrews to move toward the AR-15, but the man seemed to be in no hurry to arm himself, and he had yet to notice Parish's extra firearm in the darkened room.

Seconds ticked away, feeling like forever, before a squeaking noise caught everyone's attention from the stage portion of the theater. Though he wasn't positive, Parish thought it sounded like a door opening.

Andrews swiped up the AR-15 as he stomped down the sloped aisle toward the stage to see what caused the disturbance. Ellis also cocked his head to see if the prisoners had somehow escaped, or another person dared interrupt their scheme.

Parish seized the momentary distraction by positioning himself for a clear shot at Ellis before reaching for his sidearm. His clip-on holster had no tricky security restraints like those of officers on police departments, so he undid the latch in one motion, pulled the gun, then fired one shot a Ellis' chest to stagger him, then another into his head, all within a second's time.

"Guess they don't make body armor to cover that inflated head of yours," Parish thought aloud, already repositioning himself to fire at Andrews, but the man had already ducked behind some old props on the stage. "Get to some cover, guys."

Concerned with the present, Parish would deal with the consequences of his actions at a later time if they survived this ordeal.

Daniels and Niemeyer found separate pillars in the back to separate themselves from Andrews and any potential gunfire. Parish scurried behind some nearby seating, but Andrews wasn't budging, despite superior firepower. In the background he heard Niemeyer calling for backup and an ambulance on his radio, meaning the conflict was either going to end shortly, or become a hostage situation.

Andrews probably didn't want to risk opening fire inside the civic center for fear that he might run out of ammunition before completing his objective of killing the hostages.

Getting himself into a low crouch, Parish started moving toward the stage, trying to use the seating for cover. He wasn't about to have his own weapon used as a murderous tool if he could prevent it. As he neared the stage, Parish saw Andrews emerge briefly from behind his cover, then dart for the door that led downstairs where the prisoners were likely being held.

All three men had noticed his movement, simultaneously rushing the stage. Andrews had already proven he had no qualms about dying because of his confidence in Smith's plan. If he reached the hostages before they could stop him, Andrews would kill each and every one of them before turning his weapon on the three men pursuing him.

After all, he had nothing to lose except his life, and he had already lost that once.

Chapter 42

Clouse woke up in a haze, feeling grass beneath him as he looked up to see the decayed corpse floating above him. He directed his eyes around him, finding Smith dressed in his black garb looming overhead.

"Where is my crucifix?" Smith demanded, bending over so Clouse could clearly see the black mask beneath the cloak and hood.

"How stupid do you think I am?" Clouse retorted, his head still pounding from the shovel's blow.

"You were stupid enough to come out here alone. And you were stupid enough to trust that I would keep my end of the bargain. Soon my son will eliminate your friends and family, leaving just me to reclaim my fortune and my hotel."

"You have a shitty way of negotiating, Smith. If you kill us all, you won't find your cube."

Smith chuckled maniacally.

"I have forever to search, Paul. You aren't intelligent enough to hide it somewhere that I can't find it. And I already have the green cube, the one that brought my son back to me. I can bring back an army of searchers if need be."

"You don't like giving me credit, do you?" Clouse stated, sitting up to find his arms bound behind him with some kind of twine. "This is going to end once and for all."

"You're in no position to make threats, much less act against me," Smith said calmly, pulling a medium-sized scythe from behind him. "I have a feeling your threshold for pain isn't nearly what it used to be. You've grown soft with my money."

"And you've grown overconfident with all of your schemes. Seems you're just about out of hirelings and backup plans."

Smith held the weapon across his chest.

"Luckily I won't need any more plans after I get done carving up your flesh. You'll tell me everything, or you'll bleed to death slowly right here, where no one can help you."

Smith raised the scythe, prepared to bring it down upon Clouse into an undisclosed body part, but the would-be murderer barely had the physical ability to lift the bulky weapon over his head. Since his legs were free, Clouse began scooting toward him in an attempt to trip him up, but Smith was quick to react, bringing the sharp end of the blade down into the meaty part of Clouse's left leg.

Clouse cried out in pain as Smith twisted the weapon in an attempt to dislodge it for another swing. Blood seeped from the new gash with no available means of controlling the reddish flow available to him.

"Tell me where it is, or this continues," Smith warned.

"Never."

"This will be painful, Paul. It can end right now if you want it to."

Clouse looked to the feminine body beside him, angered that Smith would defile his first wife's corpse in such a way. He knew without a doubt it was Angie, because Smith wouldn't stop at just a simple hoax. To complete his circle of revenge, the pain had to be mental in addition to the physical pain and bleeding.

"I'm so sorry," Clouse said softly to his deceased first wife as Smith dislodged the scythe from his leg for another long swing downward.

Clouse yelped from the pain once more, but as Smith lifted the weapon a second time, Clouse found himself in range to deliver a swift kick that sent the living corpse tumbling to the ground. The scythe fell forward, barely missing Clouse's skull before lodging itself in the soft earth behind him.

He immediately began rubbing his bonds against the blade, hearing the durable twine snap several times as each strand was split apart. Smith immediately regained his footing, grabbing for the scythe, but Clouse kicked him again, sending him tumbling backward, end over end until he came to a stop.

"Seems another plan of yours has backfired, *Martin*."

"Just try and kill me, Paul. See which one of us lasts longer."

Clouse took up the scythe, swinging it through what would have been Smith's abdomen, if the man possessed a normal human body. Smith hunched forward, as though in agony from the blow, the blade completely through his dried remains.

He waited a few seconds to let Clouse think he had dealt a crushing blow before letting out a sinister cackle. Already expecting as much, Clouse tripped him again by kicking him in the legs, sending Smith falling to his back. Instead of attempting another offensive move, Clouse hammered the scythe further into the ground, through Smith, by stepping on it with his boot.

With the blade embedded into the ground, Smith found himself unable to pry it loose to free himself. Clouse limped toward his truck without any real urgency, prepared to thoroughly do whatever it took to finish the job.

"Running won't save you, Paul," Smith taunted. "You can't escape fate."

"You're absolutely right, Martin," Clouse called back without turning around. "It's time I faced up to it and put you to rest."

When he reached his truck, Clouse checked the back to make certain the materials he required were still intact and ready for use. He had made one stop during his trip to the cemetery, suspecting what Smith had in store for him, simply hoping he guessed correctly.

Finding his purchases in the truck bed, he checked to make certain Smith was still pinned down before climbing inside. As he started the truck, a wave of relief engulfed him that the end of his ordeal was within reach.

***

Parish climbed onto the stage before Daniels and Niemeyer caught up with him, but he had to move cautiously because locating the downstairs storage area access for real wasn't as easy as looking at blueprints.

He brushed aside curtains, dodged props, and listened for any sign of Andrews as he made his way around the stage. Both of his temporary partners climbed up the stage, making more noise than he might have hoped from them. He realized the three of them clustered together made for an easy target, so he threw caution aside before they caught up with him, finding a closed wooden door marked with red lettering that read "Storage" as well as an arrow pointing down.

"This is it," he announced a mere second or two before gunfire erupted below them, sending the three men scurrying away from the doorway until they realized the bullets weren't coming their way.

Instead of one short burst, the gun fired several clustered bursts in a row before finally stopping altogether. Each of the three men drew to the side of the door in case the gun was now aimed their way. Parish reached for the doorknob, swinging it open so Niemeyer could take the lead and aim his service weapon down the stairs.

From his vantage point, Parish found no lighting along the stairwell as Niemeyer struggled to see to the bottom. For all they knew, Andrews continued to wait for them, which meant a stalemate. Of course, he could also be finishing off the last of the victims by hand instead, meaning the time left to stop him only grew shorter.

"Screw it," Randy said, charging down the stairs to see what fate awaited them.

Parish followed both men, finding a corner only a few feet after the bottom of the stairs that puzzled them with another mystery. Around the corner was another short hallway that led to the storage room's access. At this point they were met with complete silence, waiting for a sign, a noise, anything that might indicate safety ahead of them.

Daniels looked around them for something useful, his eyes finally settling on a medium-sized mirror hung above the trio. He took it down, then carefully slid it into the hallway, keeping it on its base to give them a safe view down the hall without exposing themselves to Andrews.

"The door is open," he muttered, though Parish and Niemeyer had already seen the same thing.

Each of them sucked in a breath, wondering if they were about to find a room full of bloodshed, or Andrews armed to the teeth in a corner, waiting to pepper them with gunfire.

"Tim?" Niemeyer called, the grimace on his face telling the tale that he prayed against all hope his brother was alive and well.

A few tense seconds passed as the mirror fell to the floor, shattering upon impact. All three men clutched their guns, preparing to confront Andrews if necessary.

"Randy?" a familiar voice called back. "That you?"

"You okay, big brother?"

"We're fine. We need some medical help for Dan."

"It's on the way, Tim. Where's Andrews?"

"Oh, he's in here with us."

Parish followed Niemeyer into the room following his brother's cryptic words. The dimmed storage room painted quite a disturbing picture in a single glance.

Jane Clouse continued to monitor Dan Duncan's condition, using a cloth to apply pressure against his gunshot wound. The kids sat huddled against their grandparents nearby, while Jennings and Tim Niemeyer stood watch over the body of Ryan Andrews only a few feet from the door. Their positioning looked like a cross between cautious prison guards and hunters standing over their trophy kill.

As Daniels knelt down to examine Andrews, Parish peered over his shoulder, finding the more dangerous end of a claw hammer still lodged in the back of the man's head. Andrews remained in the same crumpled position in which he fell from the attack. Randy Niemeyer stepped over the body, throwing his arms around his older brother, clutching him for several emotional seconds before letting go.

"What happened?" Daniels asked no one in particular.

"We managed to get free," Jennings began, "but we knew he was going to be back, so we barricaded the door. He couldn't get inside, so he opened fire on the door before kicking his way through the shredded boxes he disintegrated. We armed ourselves with whatever we could find, so when he busted through, I struck him with that hammer I found in one of the crates. He was holding a gun."

Jennings had added the last statement softly, as though his actions required justification.

"We know, Craig," Daniels said sympathetically.

"We had to dig through the boxes to find anything useful," Tim Niemeyer further explained. "He probably thought it was all just props and costumes, but there was a small toolbox buried in one of them."

Jane looked up from Duncan long enough to ask one question.

"Has anyone heard from Paul?"

Everyone looked at one another, then directed their guilty consciences toward the floor.

"Where is he? Mark, tell me where he is."

"He went to confront Smith. Alone."

The room remained silent until approaching sirens cut through the air. Everyone watched with heavy hearts as Jane tended to Duncan, each of them wondering how her husband would fare against one of the most evil men in the world.

Randy Niemeyer suddenly perked up, looking to Jane.

"Paul has a second tracker on him," he informed her, "but he's a county away from here. I can get to him if I have someone to navigate the computer tracking software for me."

"I'll do it," his brother volunteered.

"Thank you," Jane said to Tim before he stepped over Andrews to follow his brother.

He nodded in return before disappearing through the door, leaving an opening for the kids to rush over to Parish.

"You guys okay?" their bodyguard asked, kneeling so they could wrap their arms around him.

They both nodded affirmatively, silently thanking him for finding them.

"I'm so sorry I wasn't there for you guys," he said genuinely. "But I'm here now, and I won't let anything bad happen to either of you."

Zach looked up to him.

"Is my dad okay?"

"I hope so, Zach. Your dad is tough."

Parish wondered, like everyone else in the room, exactly how Clouse could outwit Smith, considering the man had two years of planning backing him. If anyone knew Smith for what he was, however, Paul Clouse certainly did.

***

Clouse drove the truck closer to the cemetery entrance so his necessary items were easily accessible. He stepped from the truck, approaching Smith cautiously, but not as apprehensively as before.

"Why did you have to dig up Angie's body?" he asked Smith, who remained pinned to the ground by the scythe's blade.

"Perhaps for the same reason you murdered my son," Smith said, carrying on the conversation awkwardly from his restrained position. "Emotional distress."

"Two problems with that, Smith," Clouse said as he loosened the scythe from the ground, prepared to drag Smith to another location. "One, I killed your son in self-defense, and two, you were supposed to be dead at the hands of the man I later found out was indeed your son."

Clouse worked the scythe's handle up and down like an old water pump until the blade broke loose from the ground. He started to tote Smith toward the open grave, favoring his bad leg until a sharp pain shot through the back of his right leg's calve muscle. Clouse fell to the ground, clutching his new injury as Smith held a double-bladed knife in a threatening way, advancing toward him.

The scythe still jutted from Smith's chest, forcing him to walk awkwardly. Clouse felt fortunate his Achilles heel hadn't been slit, or his own mobility would have been severely impaired. Of course his boots prevented direct access to his heels, leaving Smith the single option of stabbing into the back of his leg instead.

"We can do this all day, Paul. I won't tire, and you can't hurt me. Just tell me where the cube is, and I'll be on my way to murder your family."

"I think you're going to be unpleasantly surprised on both fronts," Clouse replied, still applying pressure to the new stab wound.

He tore off part of his shirt, quickly tying the cloth around his leg to maintain some pressure because he needed his hands free to combat Smith. Just as he finished tying it into place, Smith brought the knife down toward his chest, but Clouse fought him off, clasping Smith's bony wrist as they struggled for the blade.

While Clouse had the strength advantage, Smith maintained leverage over him, trying to force the blade into his chest with both hands and all of his weight. Already injured and bleeding from the two wounds, Clouse felt somewhat woozy as the knife slowly crept toward his heart. Calling upon his last physical reserves, Clouse used both of his hands to twist the weapon free from Smith's grasp, knocking it several feet away.

Smith fought and kicked, but in his literally deteriorated condition, he was no match for Clouse physically. Wracked with pain in both of his legs, Clouse stood, dragging the scythe's handle laboriously toward the open grave.

"Go ahead, Paul. Bury me. See what good it does you."

Fed up with Smith's taunts, Clouse slung him into the grave, letting the weapon fall in with him. He then limped toward his truck, hoping for no more surprises from Smith or anyone else. Stopping short of the truck, he knelt beside the cemetery entrance, picking up the crucifix he had left there when originally scanning the area for trouble. He brought it in case it became necessary to produce the weapon to save his family, but the situation never warranted him giving it to Smith.

Reaching into the bed of his truck, he pulled out a full gasoline can before trudging back to the grave. He peered inside, finding Smith attempting to crawl out of the hole, which was literally six feet deep without his makeshift covering in place. Clouse had no idea who had been inside the grave, or even if it was a legitimate plot, but it mattered little at this point.

Perhaps Smith intended to bury Clouse in the hole, but Clouse had the opposite result in mind as he booted Smith back to the bottom of the grave. Without studying Smith or the opening, he popped the cap off the gas can's nozzle, then poured the entire canister's contents into the hole.

"You can't stop me, Paul!" Smith screamed from below.

"I know a little something about fire, Martin, and I'm pretty sure this will hurt."

Clouse pulled a lighter from inside his blue jeans pocket, tore a piece of the tattered dress from Angie's corpse, then lit it. Assured the fire was steadily burning, he threw the cloth into the grave, instantly finding flames shooting upward like a miniature explosion. Not daring to peer into the hole, for fear of searing his eyebrows, he limped toward his truck for the next batch of items he needed to complete the job.

An initial scream from below hurt Clouse's ears, and he wasn't so certain no one else heard it. The shrieking stopped suddenly as only the sound of fire entered his ears, except it was closing in on him. Clouse slowly turned, finding Smith out of the grave, the scythe no longer buried in his chest as he dripped flaming portions of tissue and flesh to the ground.

"You can't stop me, Paul," Smith goaded, despite the fact he was disintegrating from the fire engulfing his body.

He looked something like the poorly done special effects in old movies with flames covering him from head to toe, except he was the opposite of the stuntmen carrying out such daring feats. Instead of big and bulky, he was little more than a scarecrow's size, thinning more by the second.

Clouse took up a shovel, charging Smith as he let the weapon fly from side to side, striking the overconfident man in the torso and head, backing him toward the hole. Clouse dared not touch him, fearing the gas and fire would instantly ignite him as well. After a few swings the shovel caught fire, but Smith was staggered, mere inches from the deep grave.

"I'm sending you back to hell for all the shit you've put me through, Martin. Damn you for ever dragging me into this."

At this point Smith simply stood and watched him, if his eyes hadn't been charred beyond proper usage. For all Clouse knew, the man couldn't hear him, either.

"You could have picked anyone else, but you sunk your claws into me. You and Landamere both. I hope you both rot in hell for what you've done."

Clouse swung the shovel with all of his might, aiming to decapitate Smith, but the shovel connected with the remains of Smith's shoulder instead, sending him flailing into the grave.

He heard Smith scream out in pain, cursing his name several times until all sounds from the grave subsided. Clouse carried over several buckets of water, along with concrete mix, wanting to make certain Smith never returned from the dead again. After a few minutes of continuous burning, his dry skin and tissue had gone up like paper, leaving little physical material in the wake of the fire that began dying within minutes of ignition.

When Clouse finally looked down, he took a defensive stance, wondering if Smith might have defied death once more, but only ashes covered the bottom, some still glowing orange. The false floor Smith initially used to conceal himself had also burned away. Clouse saw its thin wood on end, completely engulfed, before it collapsed into the grave with Smith.

Clouse didn't have the heart to touch Angie's body, much less replace it where it belonged, knowing he could hire such a dirty job out for the sake of making certain no one disturbed Smith's new resting place.

If no one knew about it, no one could dig him up again.

Before finalizing the deed, putting his past to rest for good, Clouse retrieved his phone from the truck, deciding to call Randy Niemeyer to make certain everything had gone well on the other end.

"You alive?" Niemeyer asked when he answered his phone.

"Yeah, I'm good. Did you and Mark take care of Andrews?"

"He's no longer a problem. Everyone is fine except Duncan. They're flying him to Methodist to remove the bullet."

"God be with him."

"You take care of Smith?"

"I'm finishing up with him right now. He won't be bothering us again."

"Better I don't ask?"

"That's probably for the best. You don't have to come up here, Randy. I've got it handled."

"I've got a big ol' country boy who wants to see you."

Clouse grinned.

"Can you guys handle things in French Lick until I get back? Tell Tim he can kick me in the shins later for putting him through all of this."

Niemeyer chuckled.

"He's probably going to bear hug the air out of you instead. We have a lot of explaining and paperwork ahead of us, so we'll head back."

"I don't want any paperwork on this end, Randy. We never had this conversation, and I went to meet Andrews' fellow conspirator who never showed up."

"Got it. See you later."

"Count on it. Take care."

Clouse slit open a bag of concrete mix, wanting a solid layer atop Smith before replacing the remainder of the loose dirt. He limped along, dripping blood every so often, wanting to see his family in the worst way, but knowing he needed to finish the task ahead of him to keep them safe.

He looked skyward, hoping all of the fear and apprehension was behind him. Feeling confident the last of the Coven died with Ellis, he wanted to resume a normal life again, whatever that meant these days. There would always be people wanting to swindle him out of money, take advantage of his wealth, or bear ill-will against him, but no one could match the extremes Smith put him through.

He looked forward to spending time with his family more than anything. For the first time, owning the hotel might feel like the right thing to do, though he wasn't certain he wanted to live like a prisoner on the sixth floor any longer.

Time healed all wounds, and for Clouse, it provided opportunities for redemption. He wanted to provide for his friends and family, because in the end they mattered to him more than anything else that came and went in his life.

Epilogue

By July most everything had settled down around the hotel. Clouse had his lawyers perform a great deal of damage control, even as the media hounded everyone in his camp for information. As usual, the police were reasonably uncertain how to fill out their reports due to the unusual circumstances of dead people making threatening appearances.

Angie's body was returned to its original grave with no fanfare. Clouse ultimately decided that her family would only be hurt by the prospect of burying her again, and he didn't want the police treating her like common evidence. Clouse found someone respectable to put her back, which allowed his tales to the authorities to hold merit.

Despite his efforts, the usual repercussions came about, with families wanting to sue him for damages regarding their murdered loved ones. Arlan Brown stayed away from the hotel completely after the death of his father. He didn't sue, but there was no love lost between him and anyone at the hotel after the misery both the hotel and the mansion caused him.

Dan Duncan survived his surgery, remaining in the hospital nine days to heal his wounds. Clouse covered every bill, visiting his hotel manager several times after Duncan was transferred to Bloomington from Indianapolis. Not one to lie around very long, Duncan was ready to come back to work already, but the doctor's orders kept him from doing so for another week.

Clouse had decided to move away from the hotel after discussing the possibility with Jane, but they wanted to take their time, possibly building a new house not far from their hotels and the casino.

At the moment he was celebrating life by throwing a July 4th party for all of his friends and family at the West Baden Springs Hotel, in addition to any lingering guests from the previous evening. He spent much of the morning greeting guests and conversing with his friends. His parents stopped by briefly, but left because his mother wanted to go flower shopping at a nearby garden store. John Clouse rolled his eyes because he would have preferred seeing his son and the Niemeyer family longer, but his marriage had lasted because he and Helen made concessions for one another.

The afternoon sun beat down on guests as they ate hotdogs and hamburgers along the veranda, while kids and parents alike played volleyball in the field near the sunken garden. Some took advantage of the unlocked gate to the outdoor pool, swimming or sunning in the beautiful weather.

A kickball game was starting in the front yard, so Clouse had changed from his usual attire to shorts and tennis shoes. Zach and Katie had begged him all morning to play kickball with them, so he talked Jane into playing as well. Their family life needed some repair, so their time together was all the more precious.

Clouse sat on a bench along the veranda, tying his tennis shoes as Parish took his side, back to wearing his suit and shined shoes on a regular basis. He sometimes donned sunglasses to give himself a Secret Service appearance whenever photographers were around.

"Everything okay, Todd?"

"Fine, sir. Now that we've weathered the media storm these past few weeks, I wonder how much longer my services will be required."

Clouse scoffed.

"You think my kids would ever let me hear the end of it if I let you go? Just because Smith and his son are gone doesn't mean there's no danger out there."

"Yes, sir."

"Todd, you're practically part of this family. You can stop calling me 'sir' at any time."

"No, sir."

Clouse grinned, looking up to the guardian of his children. Parish let a slight smirk slip, but only for a second.

"Todd, I'm suggesting you head down to the front lawn to keep an eye on the kids," Clouse said in a very informal tone. "And I'm suggesting you take off your socks and shoes, because they'll probably want you on their team."

Parish got the meaning that his boss wanted him to lighten up a bit, breathing a sigh of relief that his job was no longer such a figurative pressure cooker.

"Yes, sir."

Some changes required more time than others, Clouse decided.

Parish sauntered toward the front lawn where bases had been set up for the impending game. The kids greeted him halfway, walking and jumping alongside him with excitement that he was going to participate in their game.

"They really *wouldn't* forgive us, would they?" Jane asked, sitting beside her husband, putting her head on his shoulder.

She had done a wonderful job nursing his injured legs after the hospital finished stitching up both wounds, allowing him to participate fully in the holiday festivities.

"Todd is part of our tribe, no matter what," Clouse said. "Ours is a terrible club to join, but I'm thankful to be surrounded by such great people."

Clouse thought about the other people in his life. At the other end of the veranda he saw Daniels speaking with Tim and Randy Niemeyer. He relished his opportunity at a second chance to befriend Tim and make up for lost time. To show his appreciation, Clouse helped his friend get back everything he owned before his abduction and apparent resurrection. Once again Niemeyer was opening his own construction business, not allowing Clouse to pamper him to no end.

He needed training and updates on building codes and new laws, but Clouse helped him fund new and used equipment so he could take on jobs he was already sanctioned to carry out. In the meantime, Clouse had begun negotiations with the heirs of the Beverly Hilton property to purchase the old hotel grounds for his friend. Niemeyer had no idea, so Clouse decided to save the surprise for the right moment, perhaps even Christmas. By then Niemeyer might have some money saved back to build a house, and perhaps the bond with his kids might return. They were coming around to the fact their father was alive and well, but slow to let him into their lives on a regular basis.

Daniels broke away from the Niemeyer brothers, greeting Cindy along the hotel's brick path. They talked momentarily before heading around the back of the hotel, presumably so he could give her a tour of the place.

"Aren't they adorable?" Jane said as Clouse took her hand.

"I suppose so. It's good to see them together again."

Though wedding bells were miles down the road, the estranged couple had decided to at least give their relationship one more try. Clouse had sensed misery in Daniels from the day the couple separated until recently when they began speaking openly again. Their separation was a major reason he offered his friend the casino job. Daniels needed something to preoccupy him from the divorce proceedings while providing him a healthier salary on which to survive.

After speaking with the police several times, Clouse arranged a meeting for Mark Teakon to dispose of the two cursed cubes. Clouse and Daniels recovered the green cube Smith had been using after a little detective work. They tracked Andrews through his falsified hotel application, visiting several apartment complexes until they found the correct one where Smith and his son had been residing.

Clouse provided Teakon with plenty of funding to ensure the cubes were hidden at opposite ends of the planet. As long as they were well outside of Indiana, Clouse really didn't care to know anything else about their history or future.

Clouse wished to speak with Teakon further, once the cubes were hidden away, about tracking the other cubes. Teakon seemed agreeable, so long as he ultimately had the power to make decisions based on the dangers of such journeys. Clouse simply wanted to keep innocent people from sharing his pain by removing the cubes from dangerous hands.

Craig Jennings returned from the ball diamond, looking a bit stiff as he climbed the stairs toward the veranda. He wore baseball pants and an old, faded jersey, along with a Chicago Cubs baseball cap.

"I think this'll be the last year for this sort of thing," he commented in passing before opening a nearby door. "I'll be in the hot tub if anyone needs me."

The hotel staff had put together a few softball teams, and Jennings captained his security force against the younger valet and cleaning staff. Clouse and Jane shared a brief laugh, partly at the expense of his pain, but also because the hotel was finally a normal place to live and work.

Only department heads and Clouse's personal security staff were allowed to use the exercise facilities, including the pool and hot tub, so long as they didn't abuse the privilege. If everyone was given free use of equipment, nothing would ever get done around the hotel. Clouse treated everyone who worked for him very well, including full benefits and good pay, but he wanted to go the extra mile for his leaders.

"You ready to play some kickball?" Jane asked, nudging him with her elbow.

"As I'm ever going to be."

Clouse stood, following his wife down the veranda stairs. He reached the bottom, then looked up to the always gorgeous view of the two towers closest to him.

In the past, he might have expected to see a shadow pass by one of the windows, or some ghostly image of a deceased loved one, but no longer.

He planned to enjoy his early retirement without fear or repercussions the right way, taking care of those who were always there for him. Most people envied him for his riches, or the time he could devote to his family, but Clouse didn't really care what those people thought.

He had more than earned the right to do as he pleased.

THE DOOMSDAY CLOCK:

Book Six of the West Baden Murders Series

Dedication

This book is dedicated to my good friend Shane Buis who was taken from us too soon. No one was ever a greater help to me on my West Baden projects than Shane, and these books are better for having been touched by him.

Thanks

Thanks to Brad Wiemer, Barb Caster, Nannette Bell, David Blackford, Korby Sommers, Stephanie Barber, Steve DeLisle, Mike Ritchie, Tim Lee, Rick Shellabarger, Deron Clark, Brian Kidd, and Aaron "Tex" Standridge for their assistance.

Special thanks to Kendrick Shadoan at KLS Digital for creating the cover, handling photography, and doing a great job as always.

Visit www.klsdigital.com

Chapter 1

Todd Parish felt certain he was going to die.

Bobbing up and down on a fishing boat in the middle of October wasn't his idea of fun, but it was his job. He wasn't on a fishing trawler for fame and glory on some television show, though his assignment felt equally dangerous. Working for a billionaire he respected and admired, Parish put his life on the line for more than just a paycheck. Being one of the good guys, he wanted to do his part in hiding a majorly evil force from the world and those who would use it.

Even kill for it.

Named the *Shamrock* because its new owner wanted to pay tribute to his Irish heritage, the one-hundred-seventy-four foot trawler cut through the worst of seas without falter. Painted black with green accents, the former U.S. Navy vessel cost Henry Flanagan a small fortune four years earlier. Tired of fishing for someone else, the experienced deckhand became a green captain when he purchased the boat from a retiring captain. Though some of the superstitious fishermen thought it bad luck to repaint and rename a ship, Flanagan did just that.

Built in 1945 to serve the U.S. Navy as a fuel oil barge, the *YO-204*, like its *YO-65* class sister ships, served no real purpose to the military after World War II drew to an end. Many of the oiler boats were sunk to create artificial reefs, or used for target practice during military maneuvers. The *YO-204* escaped such a fate by random chance until it was sold in 1976 to a crab boat captain who wanted to replace his old boat. Its holding tanks were converted for storing crab and creating additional engine room, and the boat was christened *Sea Lady* by its new owner. The rest, Flanagan stated, was history.

Normally a bodyguard for his employer's son and stepdaughter, Parish took the special assignment after a sit-down meeting with the man. The terms were clear, extra pay was provided, which he considered hazard pay, and Parish was off to Alaska for the start of cod fishing season. Though he and the two men accompanying him bought a fishing vessel and its captain for the week, their intention wasn't to take anything from the sea, but rather discard a cursed item almost a century old.

Standing on the starboard side of the boat, Parish found himself clinging to the equipment normally used to lure and ensnare unsuspecting crab. Feeling rather seasick, he questioned how much longer his stomach could hold out before he upchucked over the side. Trying to keep his mind from dwelling upon the churning in his stomach, he stared up at the night sky. Instead of clear skies containing stars that winked at him, the night sky cast down angry freezing rain, adding dampness to the already brisk air. Knowing he couldn't have custom ordered more horrendous weather conditions, Parish shuddered momentarily, folding his arms as a small wave sloshed over the side. His gear blocked most of the sea water, but some droplets sneaked through small exposures, causing him to curse under his breath.

Carrying a Glock 22 semi-automatic in his shoulder holster, Parish felt like a polar bear, wearing a thick rugged weather jacket and a stocking cap. He also donned insulated rubber gloves the minute he stepped outside for some fresh air, rather than stinking up the living quarters if he vomited. A fear of the trawler being struck by a rogue wave with him trapped inside replayed through his mind, so he felt safer standing outside. He chalked up his worries to inexperience on the sea.

"You okay?" Mark Teakon asked, startling him as he joined Parish at the side railing.

"I've been better," Parish admitted.

"It's easier if you take something for it."

"Already have," Parish grumbled unhappily.

Teakon, a history professor at Amherst College in Massachusetts, partnered with Parish's employer to dispose of two gemlike cubes. While Teakon's hired gun tagged along, currently below decks, Parish acted as an armed witness to protect the cube onboard from falling into the wrong hands. The *Shamrock* needed to travel to the central most part of the Bering Sea before they tossed it overboard.

More than just a professor, Teakon took on the responsibility of hunting down cursed objects across the globe, making himself an expert on their history through written texts and experience. The death of his wife at the hands of someone possessing a cursed object prompted his research, understanding, and desire to hunt them down, keeping his teaching job as a cover once his new passion consumed him.

"How much longer before we reach the drop area?" Parish inquired.

They had already been at sea over a day.

"Another couple hours and we should be to the deepest waters."

What little bit Parish knew of the Bering Sea included the fact that it was split by an Alaskan and Russian divide. The bottom held shelves of varying depths, so Teakon wanted to find the deepest area possible before discarding the cursed object. While he asked the captain's opinion, it seemed the professor had an area in mind before they ever launched from the Alaskan coast.

Nearing sixty years of age, Teakon stood several inches shorter than Parish with a full beard peppered with brown and gray hairs. His thick head of similarly colored hair was tucked beneath a navy blue stocking cap. Reaching into the pocket of his dark pea coat, which stuck out near the waistline from his protruding belly, Teakon produced a small metallic box slightly larger than a jewelry box for a wedding ring. Constructed of lead to conceal the colorful object inside, the box felt heavy when Teakon handed it to him. Parish hated touching the cubes, having done so only a few times, because he knew what evil their users carried out to reap sinister benefits.

He still found it difficult to believe such tiny objects created so much havoc around the world, quickly handing the box back to the professor. Cursed objects offer their users a specific benefit, always requiring a sacrifice of some sort, which in this case was human life. When Parish took the job of bodyguard to two children, he was warned of danger, though he never expected such a heavy burden. Given several chances to quit or be reassigned, he chose the most dangerous possible assignment, looking at the bigger picture. With a wife and two children of his own, he wanted the world to be a safer place for them, so he put his own life at risk.

As the boat bounced from striking a wave crest, Parish clasped a bundle of nearby ropes attached to a pulley system from fear of tumbling over the side. Cursing himself for volunteering to board a boat, he wished they could have rented a helicopter or small plane and dropped the cube into the tumultuous water. Doing so, however, would have put them all at risk because certain individuals and groups wanted to possess the cubes. Renting one of the few local aircrafts risked drawing attention to their small group, so Teakon opted to lease one of the dozens of fishing trawlers heading to sea. Parish didn't much care for flying, either, so his prospects for comfortable travel appeared bleak either way.

"I can't wait to be off this thing," Parish stated sourly.

Teakon chuckled.

"It's the only way, Todd. Mr. Clouse and I agreed to this location specifically because we knew the cube would churn on the bottom until it fell into a ravine deep enough to keep it forever."

"Nothing's forever," Parish said grimly.

"Yeah, I know," Teakon conceded. "Some scientists believe man crossed the Bering Strait on foot during the last ice age, migrating from Asia to North America. Though we'll never see it, the Earth is constantly shifting and adjusting."

"Dust in the wind, right?"

Teakon nodded.

"Something like that. Are you a religious man, Todd?"

"Yes. I go to church on Sundays and say my prayers."

"Has your experience with these objects changed your perspective?"

"It's affirmed my beliefs," Parish said before another small wave jolted the boat, causing him to tighten his death grip on the ropes. "If there was no heaven and hell, where would such evil objects come from?"

Teakon never found time enough to reply as the distant sound of helicopter rotors pierced the turbulent sloshing of waves against the trawler and the deafening rain around them. Parish immediately suspected the aircraft was closer than the sound indicated, proven correct when he spied red and white lights overhead in the distance.

Greg Slone, a former military man who protected Teakon on the more dangerous assignments, appeared in the doorway from the staging area where deckhands often changed their gear. Dressed for the inclement weather, carrying an automatic weapon like the guns often toted by SWAT team members, he tilted his head toward the sound.

"If that's not the Coast Guard, we're in trouble," Slone stated with his usual stone-faced expression, pulling a pair of binoculars from his gear to examine the helicopter more closely. "Shit."

Teakon turned pale, obviously not expecting to have their transportation discovered, much less invaded, before disposing of the cube. He looked over the side of the boat as though contemplating tossing the encased cube immediately.

"You have to," Parish insisted.

Instead, Teakon looked to Slone for advice.

"Modified civilian chopper," Slone reported. "At least four onboard."

"They have to be searching blindly," Parish reasoned aloud. "How could they know which boat we took?"

"The name on the side is a start if someone blabbed about three guys leasing a boat without a crew."

Either someone in the helicopter knew the boat by name, or the aircraft simply went from boat to boat, hoping to spy Teakon or Slone. Parish might not have been on their radar, but no crew working on the decks and three men dressed for mountain hiking instead of fishing was a dead giveaway.

"We need to get below decks," he said. "Maybe they'll think the crew is sleeping after unloading the equipment."

No equipment remained aboard the deck, only because it was removed before the *Shamrock* ever left the Dutch Harbor. Even so, Teakon didn't appear convinced.

"If I get trapped down there, I can't throw this thing over the side before they snag it."

Teakon looked shaken well beyond any panic threshold Parish recalled witnessing in the man. Like a scared, cornered rat, the professor didn't know which direction to run. Completely out of his element, Teakon didn't move until Slone snagged him by the arm as the helicopter drew dangerously close.

"They know it's us!" he yelled over the howling wind to Parish. "They've already seen the boat's name and they're still coming."

"Ditch the cube!" Parish insisted to Teakon, still seeing indecision in the man's eyes. "Throw it and get to safety. I'm going to get the captain and get ready to abandon ship."

Slone's expression showed that he didn't like any part of Parish's intentions.

"Getting in a raft will make us a big floating target. We need to make a stand."

Teakon didn't look so certain. Reaching into his pocket, he tossed Parish the encased cube.

"Do it," he said before allowing Slone to stow him inside the closest doorway.

Parish held the small box in his hand, staring at it momentarily before ascending the stairs to speak with the captain. Teakon neglected to inform the captain of their real intentions, simply paying him well with money provided through Parish's employer. Assuring the captain they weren't dumping weapons or bodies at sea seemed to ease his conscience. Paying him double the amount he received for a week's worth of fishing also swung him to their side in a hurry. It only took one witness saying Captain Henry Flanagan left the docks without a crew to start a firestorm of rumors.

Barely twisting the handle before bursting through the door, Parish received a stunned look from the captain. Dressed for the warm interior of the cabin, Flanagan wore beige cargo pants and a black turtleneck sweater. Getting ready for a long season of catching crab a week at a time, returning to unload, and crab fishing all over again, the captain had begun growing a beard that appeared a few days old.

"What's wrong?" Flanagan asked quickly.

"We have company."

Looking out the window through the driving rain, the captain discovered the helicopter closing in on the boat's position. Despite the unusual circumstances of their voyage, Flanagan insisted his three visitors learn about the safety and escape measures aboard his vessel. Each of them tried on a survival suit before learning where the two inflatable rafts were stowed and how to deploy them.

"Unfriendly company?" Flanagan inquired with grave concern, letting his boat battle the waves momentarily without his guidance.

"You could say that. We'll probably need to abandon ship."

"You're kidding me, right?" the captain asked with bewilderment. "I'm not leaving a boat that costs five times more than my house."

"They'll kill you and leave you to go down with your ship."

"Boat," Flanagan corrected him, despite the dire circumstances surrounding them. "I didn't sign on for letting my boat sink, or being shot at by pirates."

Thinking fast, Parish tried outsmarting the invaders at their own game. He knew they wanted the cube at all costs, likely unconcerned with human life in the process.

"Can you turn off the power from in here?" he asked the captain a few seconds later when an idea came to him.

"I can shut down the engine and most of the lights."

"And no one else can start it if you take the key, right?" Parish asked, seeing the helicopter approaching the bow, slowing so its crew could scale down to the boat using the ropes that dropped a few seconds later.

"If I have the key, the boat won't work for anyone else," Flanagan assured him.

"Good. Shut everything down that you can and follow me."

Looking at him with uncertain green eyes momentarily, the captain flipped a number of switches that threw the deck and the cabin into darkness. Only a few marker lights and the helicopter's spotlights illuminated the trawler and the rough seas around it. Flanagan took the keys from the ignition console, looking to Parish as a dim glow penetrated the front window.

"I don't like this," he stated.

"It's the best chance we have. If it works, you might not lose your boat in the process. I need you to grab each of us a survival suit and get one of the life rafts ready. Don't inflate it until I tell you to."

"And what are you going to do?"

"Try and keep these fuckers from setting foot on your vessel if I can help it."

Parish followed Flanagan out the cabin door, immediately pulled his semi-automatic from the shoulder holster beneath his coat. Wishing he possessed heavier firepower aboard the trawler, he noticed Slone taking cover below the metal stairs. Slone took aim, as did Parish, waiting for the mercenaries to reveal themselves as armed and dangerous before opening fire. Only when four men dressed in black began descending the ropes, firearms slung around their shoulders, did Parish fire shots that seemed to have little effect on his targets.

He quickly realized they wore body armor, so he aimed for the legs of one man, hitting him somewhere close to the knee. Unable to hear the man's painful yelp, Parish spied a burst of blood emitting from his target, confirming the hit. All four of his enemies descended the ropes with precision speed, hitting the boat deck within seconds. Safely behind the metal stairs and the corner of the cabin, Parish exposed his body just long enough to take a few shots, immediately seeing two of the men targeting Slone.

Automatic gunfire forced Parish to take cover behind the corner as bullets ricocheted off the stairs. Apparently sharing the same idea, Slone took down one of the intruders with a shot to the thigh, providing the injured man's partner time to target him in the process. Slone tried ducking for some nearby pallets, but shots rang out before he left his partial cover behind structural metal beams. Parish watched the man's shoulder flinch awkwardly as a bullet entered and passed through Slone's flesh. Several more followed, burying themselves in the man's chest, finishing him as he slumped to the deck.

Now two angry wounded men, and their two uninjured partners, turned their attention to Parish, whose cover wouldn't suffice once they rounded the cabin and opened fire. He hoped Flanagan was making headway with the survival suits and the inflatable raft. Enclosed on all sides, including the top, the modern escape raft was meant to help survivors battle the cold, summon assistance, and travel under limited power. Most importantly to Parish was the full enclosure, which kept the assault team and helicopter pilot from peering inside.

Doubting the captain had ample time to fulfill his hurried assignment, Parish debated how to buy Flanagan time without getting himself killed when the unexpected happened. Teakon burst out of the metal door below, throwing his hands up as though in surrender. All four mercenaries froze at the sight of the unarmed man who ran to Slone's side, checking his vitals. Parish knew, as did Teakon, that Slone was beyond saving. Teakon gave Parish the subtlest of hopeless looks in the dim lighting, tilting his head toward the back of the boat, before standing and producing a sidearm as he neared the port side of the trawler. Knowing immediately that Teakon meant for him to break for it, and discard the cube if the feat hadn't already been accomplished, Parish stood just long enough to see another innocent man's death.

Teakon took aim at the four men, holding the gun in his right hand as he reached into his pocket and pulled out a small object, holding it over the railing momentarily to tease his adversaries. He allowed them little more than a glance to speculate whether he held the cube or not, before releasing the object. A satisfied grin crossed his face, as though quashing their objective with his efforts, but making his life worthless in the process. He fired two shots that hit nothing solid before all four mercenaries opened fire on him, striking him once or twice before he tumbled over the railing. Parish saw the man's heels swing upward as Teakon fell headfirst off the boat, instantly swallowed up by the rough seas that gladly devoured any victim who came their way.

"Inflate it!" Parish yelled, finding Flanagan in the back of the boat already inside a survival suit.

With a simple push of a button, the enclosed raft inflated itself with an internal pump like some kind of bouncing castle at the county fair. Parish stood guard, watching the corner like a hawk for anyone brazen enough to peer around it. No helmet was going to stop a bullet at such close range and the mercenaries intended to survive so they could spend their blood money. Ignoring the hissing sound behind him, Parish reached back with his left hand until he felt Flanagan close enough for conversation.

"You have a storage hatch right below us, don't you?"

"Yeah," Flanagan replied, apparently unhappy with the realization of Parish's plan. "We'll be fish in a barrel if they search it."

Parish noticed the helicopter had fallen back to a surveillance position to provide better lighting for the mercenaries. Knowing these men wanted the cube at any cost he prayed his diversion was enough to distract them while he put a secondary plan into action.

"Push it in," he said in a hushed voice to the captain, who shoved the life raft over the side without exposing himself to the helicopter's lights.

It took less than ten seconds for Flanagan to pop open the hatch to the empty storage area and the two men to jump inside before the mercenaries rounded the corner. Parish had snagged the survival suit left for him by Flanagan, dragging it down with him out of sight so the mercenaries didn't grow suspicious.

Reeking of long dead fish and their organs used for bait, the hold overwhelmed Parish momentarily, but he quickly grew accustomed to the smell. Feeling like he was imprisoned within a sensory deprivation chamber, Parish discovered smell was about his only useful sense because he couldn't see anything, and all around him metal kept him tucked tightly into place.

Prompted by information relayed to them from the pilot, the men immediately dashed to the opposite side of the boat, seeing the orange inflatable raft bobbing along the waves. Standing nearly eight feet tall, with a zippered top that kept water out in case of listing, the raft also kept anyone from readily seeing inside.

Regretting that he never found ample opportunity to toss the encased cube over the side without being seen, Parish needed only a few seconds on the deck to carry out Teakon's final wish. The tromping of footsteps and rain hitting the metal hatch above made him feel like a refugee in hiding from a death squad, tapping and probing for his presence. Parish couldn't see Flanagan's eyes in the darkness, but he suspected they were either closed in prayer or wide-open with anticipation.

"Check this entire boat," one of the mercenaries barked above them. "If they're in that raft we'll chase it down with the chopper."

"We could just shoot it," another voice said.

"And risk losing the objective? You care to explain that to the man who hired us?"

"You mean the man we've never seen?" the second mercenary grunted.

Both men paused, which concerned Parish gravely. Unable to see a thing in the darkness, he heard both of them shuffle around above him before stepping off the cover. He readied his firearm when they attempted to yank the handles to the hatch, but the handles locked automatically when shut into place. With no locks on the inside, Parish and Flanagan were literally trapped inside the hold until the doors were forced open or Parish shot the locks. One of the first things Parish and Slone had done when they boarded the boat was memorize every square foot of storage and equipment, taking nothing for granted.

Hoping Flanagan didn't make a peep, Parish waited a few agonizing seconds until the mercenaries stopped tugging on the hatch, realizing they weren't getting in very easily.

"Let's check over the rest of the boat," the leader said as thunder rolled in the background.

It took several agonizing minutes, but Parish waited for a sign that the four men were done with their evil deed. He wondered if Teakon's sacrifice gave them the impression the cube was already overboard, curtailing their exhaustive search for the cube or additional human life. He knew at some point they were going to have to check every crevice in the boat, but they risked the life raft getting away because it wasn't traceable by using radar like the trawler. Parish grew more nervous by the minute, trying to steady his nerves for the captain's sake, but Flanagan stood silently beside him in the darkness.

"Is this your grand plan?" Flanagan finally asked just above a whisper with an edgy tone. "To get us shot like dogs down here?"

"Patience," Parish whispered back. "They need to locate the survival raft or risk losing it. They *have* to leave soon."

Being trapped in a storage locker the size of a bedroom closet almost made Parish forget about his seasickness. The turbulent waves didn't seem so bad within a confined space, plus he needed to use his senses to stay alive. He listened attentively for what seemed like five minutes before the four men met just outside the cabin above the two trapped men.

"You two stay here and continue the search of the boat," the leader said. "Starks and I are going to chase down that life raft with the chopper. Remember, we're looking for that cube. Any people you find aren't useful once they give you information."

"Understood."

Parish felt some relief that the two injured men were conducting the local search. He waited until he heard the helicopter leave in the direction of the life raft before grabbing the survival suit at his feet.

"It's about time for us to get out of here," he informed Flanagan. "Where's that other life raft?"

"Right beside this hold. If you fire that gun, they're going to hear it."

"What choice do I have?" Parish said more than asked, feeling the first of the locks by hand before taking aim in the darkness.

He suspected the two gimpy hired guns were below decks, conducting a more thorough search. Waiting until thunder masked his movements, he fired a shot that disabled the first locking mechanism. He located the other lock and fired again within seconds as thunder continued to roll ominously in the distance, hoping noise didn't carry particularly well through the vessel's metal hull.

Climbing out of the hold, Parish quickly donned his survival suit, feeling like a seal out of water, barely able to move. Flanagan wasted no time retrieving the second life raft, monitoring the area around them while Parish pulled the last of the suit over his thick waistline. Intentionally keeping his right arm out of the survival suit's sleeve, Parish vigilantly positioned himself to watch for the two mercenaries while the captain inflated the craft.

"It's ready," he said after half a minute or so. "I'm unzipping one side because we'll have to swim for it once we're in the water."

"Get in and I'll push it over," Parish said, wishing they had thrown it overboard when it was only partially inflated. He spotted several synthetic ropes tied to the raft, serving as tethers so a swimmer could stay in contact with the inflatable vessel even if he couldn't climb aboard. "I'm a certified diver."

Flanagan eyeballed him skeptically, probably due to Parish's husky form.

"Seriously," Parish assured him. "Now get in before you get us both shot."

Climbing inside the orange device, Flanagan positioned himself in a corner of the rectangular craft before Parish muscled it from the deck to the railing. He strained momentarily to clear the railing and direct the life raft away from some rather precarious edged metal along the side of the boat before releasing it. Securing his firearm in its holster, he zipped up his coat before he finished donning the survival suit, including the hood that slipped over his head once he removed his stocking cap and stuffed it inside the suit. Assured that the cube remained in his pants pocket with a quick pat, he leapt over the side, securing one of the life raft's handles as he hit the water with his right hand. Had he missed, he and Flanagan might have drifted apart, becoming additional casualties claimed by the rough seas.

Parish quickly realized the survival suit did not shield him from the elements completely as the biting cold of the sloshing water touched him like sharp fingernails clawing at his skin. Simply meant to slow the hazardous effects of the water, the suits bought the wearer about an hour before hypothermia set in. Bodily functions shut down as the body went into shock, leaving only a corpse inside an orange floating marker for Coast Guard helicopters to find.

Putting such thoughts out of his mind, Parish tugged on the tethered line, willing himself closer to the inflatable craft as it washed further away from the trawler. The rain continued to pour, as though sent along with the mercenaries to prevent him from escaping. Flanagan unzipped the side closest to him, stretching out an arm to help Parish climb inside to safety. After clinging to the base of the unzipped side, Parish kicked to pull himself inside, finally relieved when his entirely body wasn't touching the Bering Sea.

By no means comfortable, the cramped space inside the vessel was dark and cold, but mostly free of water save the droplets the two men brought inside with them. Parish landed against the solidly inflated wall of the craft, watching the *Shamrock* drift further away from them as Flanagan securely zipped the opposite side.

"We're pretty much done in now," the captain bemoaned as he slumped against a different side of the life raft. "We didn't even get a mayday off before leaving."

"We'll be fine," Parish assured him, unzipping his survival suit far enough to reach inside and pull out a small device.

"What's that?"

"A transmitter. The second I activate it, my boss knows to send the Coast Guard after us by tracking its frequency."

"This thing can transmit for help," Flanagan stated sourly. "I was more worried about getting back to my boat."

"You've got insurance, don't you?"

"Yes, but losing a week or two during the crab season is financially disastrous. I've got a crew depending on me to help them feed their families."

"We might still recover her, but we can't transmit for help until our company leaves. If they can track us, they won't hesitate to shoot us and sink every last piece of evidence. Besides, my employer will take care of your losses if we don't find her."

Flanagan's expression softened in the extremely dim lighting just a bit.

"Sorry about your buddies."

"They were colleagues, but they were good colleagues," Parish admitted, learning how admirable Slone and Teakon were during the brief time he spent with them.

He dug into his survival suit, finding the lead box inside a pocket before pulling it out. The box's pointy corner had been digging into his skin the entire time as a painful reminder of the task at hand.

"It's all about this, of all things," Parish lamented, opening the box to reveal a green cube created from an emerald.

Even in darkness it seemed to glow, seeking attention from the outside world. Like a siren, it lured men to its beauty, but it didn't kill them outright. Men killed one another to fuel the evil cube and possess it for their betterment.

"What is it?" Flanagan asked, stunned by its beauty. "Is it like that rock from the *Titanic* movie?"

"No. It's pure evil."

Parish closed the lead box, wondering if he dared throw it to the sea since Teakon led the mercenaries to think it was dropped within a mile of their present location. Even with modern technology, finding a tiny lead box on the bottom of the ocean was like the old adage of finding a needle in a haystack. Torn between the risk of carrying it longer, or daring bring it back to Indiana with him for a later second attempt, Parish decided to let the sea have it as an offering. He unzipped the nearest opening before tossing the encased cube to the water, verifying that nothing stopped the waves from devouring it.

"Why did you do that?" Flanagan asked, dumbfounded that someone would discard what looked like a harmless, beautiful gem to such a fate.

"Because it's my job."

Hoping their life raft quickly became the figurative needle, Parish settled into his spot as comfortably as the elements allowed. The two men needed to wait for the helicopter to come and go once more, if they could even hear it over the weather and rough seas, before transmitting for assistance. Built to endure the choppy waters, the life raft could outlast a human being in the elements, so Parish planned on waiting as long as possible before tripping the transmitter.

Taking a deep breath, he felt some relief that his job was accomplished, though the deaths of Slone and Teakon weighed heavily on his conscience. He wondered how the mercenary crew tracked them down, knowing that any investigation on his part endangered his employer's wishes for secrecy.

Placing his head against the hard rubber base of the inflatable interior, Parish tried to get some rest before summoning the Coast Guard.

Chapter 2

Parish officially survived his incident of terror when he and Flanagan were picked up by the Coast Guard. It took a few days, but he returned home to Orange County in Southern Indiana. Originally from the area, Parish felt a rush of relief when his flight arrived in Indianapolis, and overcome with joy when he found his wife and two children at home awaiting his return.

He met with his employer first thing the next morning, giving Paul Clouse details about the trip to Alaska and the outcome. Despite numerous other issues clogging his calendar, Clouse listened attentively to the information, openly disturbed about the deaths of Slone and Teakon. He expressed relief that Parish survived the horrific ordeal, blaming himself for not being more prudent before sending the trio to Alaska. Clouse excused himself from Parish only a few minutes after learning the details of the trip, saying he planned to assist the families with funeral costs.

It wasn't until almost two weeks later, on a Friday, that he requested to sit down with Parish once again. On Halloween of all days, Parish met with Clouse at the man's prized West Baden Springs Hotel in the grand atrium. The two briefly shook hands as Clouse suggested they take their conversation inside one of the available conference rooms along the ground floor.

Nearing forty years in age, Clouse lived a charmed life in the eyes of some, but Parish knew the hardships the man endured from the moment he ever stepped foot inside the one-of-a-kind domed hotel. Rising from part-time architect to the man who owned the building, Clouse lost a number of friends, permanently, living in fear that his family might be targeted by the types of individuals Parish encountered on the trawler.

"You know what day this is," Clouse began when they sat across from one another on the narrow side of the long conference table.

"Halloween, sir."

"And you know about my history with this holiday, so I'm hoping for an uneventful Halloween."

"Yes, sir."

At one time Clouse informed Parish, eventually insisting, that he could call him by his first name, but Parish remained constantly respectful, raised to act accordingly by his parents. Clouse had since given up trying to dissuade his family's bodyguard from changing his ways.

Standing just over six feet, Clouse remained very trim and toned from daily workouts. His full head of brown hair was parted to one side, while a mustache of the same color resided on his upper lip. From looking at him, no one knew he had inherited land and assets totaling in the low billions. A very down to earth boss, Clouse formerly worked as a professional firefighter, so he came from a normal background. Wearing blue jeans, a flannel shirt over his T-shirt, and what appeared to be brown hiking boots, he appeared ready for a walk with his wife along the trails.

"It seems the Coven, or some organization just like them, has an interest in the cubes," Clouse said almost dejectedly. "I'm working on patching our relationship with Julie Knowles after her two partners were killed in Alaska."

The Coven, a group created by Clouse's former arch nemesis, sought to obtain a few of the cursed cubes for their evil purposes. Led by Martin Smith, the group members seemed to disappear after Smith's death less than a year prior. Clouse partnered with Mark Teakon and his associates to ensure the cursed objects stayed out of malicious hands. Julie Knowles served as their local partner in Massachusetts, never working in the field to recover or hide the objects. Her bond with Clouse wasn't very well established, because Clouse often worked with the professor instead.

"We have to reorganize this whole thing, and not just with Julie," Clouse stated. "There's a more worldly force than Smith could ever put together going after these things."

Parish cleared his throat.

"I seem to recall Teakon stating something about Armageddon if the cubes were ever brought together."

Clouse's blue eyes met his with cognitive recognition.

"I can't imagine why anyone would want to literally end the world, but maybe this group has plans to capture all of the cubes. It seems Teakon might have held out on some important information."

"Or maybe he just didn't know the whole story. He seemed awfully trusting of me to dispose of the emerald cube."

"No offense, but it sounds like he was in a pinch."

"None taken, sir."

Clouse rubbed his chin momentarily in thought.

"We need to work with Julie more closely if we're going to discover who these people are and what they want. This is going to take more than a handful of us stumbling around, trying to figure out who's after the cubes."

"A task force, sir?"

"We need a group effort, whatever we call it."

"I'm in, sir. Whatever you need."

Parish realized too late he probably sounded like a suck-up, trying to get in the boss's good graces with his quick response.

"No, Todd. You've done plenty, and you've got a family. I'm not putting you in danger again."

"Sir, you know I'm loyal to this cause, and to you. Keeping these objects from falling in the wrong hands makes my job easier because I know your family is safe."

Clouse forced a grin.

"You know, when I picked you to watch over my kids, I knew you were a good man who was loyal to his own family, Todd. Coming back here and working for your father was noble, because you put your family first."

"You're leaving out the part where I was flat broke, sir," Parish added, drawing a genuine smile from Clouse.

"While that may be true, you had experiences that could have landed you a job with better pay, in far larger places than French Lick. What I'm trying to say is I knew you were a good find on my part, but you've far exceeded my expectations with your loyalty."

"And with all due respect, I want to see this through, Mr. Clouse. I know I can't keep up with the former military types you'll have to hire, but I can represent your interests in the field."

Clouse openly gave the option some thought.

"I'll consider it. My conscience can't take much more strain, Todd. I've lost enough friends to this madness, and I'll be damned if I put the people I employ in harm's way."

"Sir, I'm not exactly a babe in the woods. You've sent me to a dozen schools and seminars, which I considered preparation for retrieving these objects."

Clouse stood.

"Let's take a walk, Todd."

Parish followed his boss out of the conference room, wondering if he was about to get reprimanded or their conversation was getting deeper.

Following Clouse into the rounded atrium, Parish tried to avoid looking up at the six stories of rooms and balconies above him. A mammoth skylight built into the ceiling provided rays of sun that lit the atrium where people sat in plush furniture, played chess at tables along the walls, or sat outside the hotel's bar named after a previous owner. Though Clouse had moved his family out of their sixth floor suite several months prior, memories still flooded Parish's mind of guarding the man's children at the hotel.

"Seven years ago to the day my life changed drastically," Clouse admitted. "My wife was murdered and I found myself the pawn in a game I didn't understand."

Parish simply hung his head, already knowing much of the story from hearsay. Not once had he ever thought of his boss as pompous or pampered. He knew of the ordeals plaguing Paul Clouse from the man's occasional melancholy state and what visitors and friends stated. Parish wasn't around during much of the man's troubles with Martin Smith, but the newspaper articles tried making sense of the murders surrounding the hotel seven years prior.

Making a game effort to report the truth, the newspaper and television reporters lacked inside knowledge about the cursed objects and what motivated the Coven.

"The reason I tell you this, Todd, is because it needs to end. It needs to end now. No one else should have to go through the hell of these past seven years."

"Sir, you still have two of the cubes. Isn't keeping those safe from harm enough?"

"I have one of the cubes and Julie has one," Clouse corrected. "And while she may have the power of tracking the cubes, who's to say any of us are safe from harm? They tracked your group down in Alaska, which means these people know who we are. I say it's time to start hitting back and using my resources."

"That will just put your family at risk again, sir," Parish said with genuine concern, following his employer from the atrium to the hallway that never ended, simply curving around the atrium's outer wall in a full circle.

"I know, which is why I'm going to get a few key people in place and put them under the radar the next few months."

"What about you?"

"I'll disappear, too. If all goes well, I'll have someone in place that Julie Knowles trusts so we can move forward with a search for the cubes."

Parish wasn't sure he agreed with such a bold move for a couple of reasons. One, it put the lives of many good people in jeopardy by searching for the cubes. Two, gathering the cubes seemed to play into the hands of their enemy. If some evil entity truly wanted to gather thirteen cursed objects for the sole purpose of ending the world, putting the cubes in one spot would make their objective easier if they discovered the hiding spot. Obviously, hiding the cursed objects didn't work very well, as Parish learned in Alaska, but at least the emerald cube was out of harm's way. While the cubes remained in the hands of corrupt individuals, lives would certainly be lost to fuel the cursed objects and use their powers, but Parish felt that letting sleeping dogs lie seemed the better course of action for the greater good.

"Don't get me wrong, Todd," Clouse said. "I want out of the cube hunting business once and for all, but I'm the last one who gives a shit about finding them who has the financial backing. I'm flying to Amherst to speak with Julie in person, and I want you to come with me."

"Me, sir? Why, if I may ask?"

"Because Julie doesn't seem to trust you very well after losing Teakon. I need to put her fears to rest if we're going to move forward."

Parish didn't feel particularly happy about the mistrust, but he understood since he and Julie Knowles had never met. He felt like a bargaining chip, though he trusted his employer implicitly not to make him a sacrificial lamb.

"I'm looking to hire a few trusted individuals who can devote their time to finding these objects and hide them away."

"How exactly does one interview for such a job, sir?"

"There is no interview process. The three individuals I have in mind are perfect candidates. I've had Mark scoping out hundreds of candidates since we last dealt with Martin Smith and his people. These three will either say yes or no to the proposition."

Clouse referred to Mark Daniels, his good friend in charge of casino security at the other major hotel he owned just down the road from the dome. A former police officer and detective, Daniels knew of the cursed objects, and more importantly, how to conduct background checks without drawing attention to their cause.

The two men eventually stepped onto the hotel's veranda where rocking chairs allowed guests to stare out at the waning beauty of the sunken garden. A fountain sprayed several streams of water into its own base which would soon be drained and the water supply shut down for winter. Parish leaned on the railing, staring at the green garden momentarily as Clouse relaxed his shoulder against a support beam.

"So, are you up for flying to Massachusetts?" Clouse asked.

Still not fond of flying, Parish didn't let his feelings show.

"When do we depart, sir?"

"Tomorrow morning if that works for you. The sooner the better."

Parish knew Clouse wouldn't keep them away very long. He often did daytrips for business, typically booking commercial flights with little notice, or leasing a local pilot if the flight wasn't more than a state or two away. Somewhat curious about how events were about to unfold, Parish wanted to stay in the loop. He also wanted to assure Julie Knowles he took the necessary measures to dispose of the cube, making the most of Teakon's sacrifice.

"I'll be ready tomorrow whenever you need me, sir."

Clouse nodded with satisfaction.

"Someone will call you with the details."

Chapter 3

Glad that Clouse didn't ask him to carry out chauffeur duties when they arrived in Massachusetts and rented a car, Parish simply took in the beautiful New England fall view while his boss drove. Orange leaves often lasted about two weeks around French Lick, never equaling the quantity or quality of what he saw beyond his passenger window. The sun glowed in the early afternoon hour, giving a false impression that the beautiful fall day felt warm and cozy. In truth, Parish and his employer dressed for the weather, Clouse wearing a brown leather jacket that shielded him from the biting wind when they stepped from the passenger jet an hour earlier.

Riding along the downtown area of the quaint college town gave Parish a good view of the brick buildings. Considered a small city with less than 40,000 residents, Amherst provided a quiet setting for students, limited in crime and violence. It also provided a perfect front for Mark Teakon and his associates to conduct their search for cubes touched by the devil himself.

Clouse pulled up to a bookstore along the main drag that appeared to cater toward all readers, rather than the student clientele. With a brick façade painted beige, the store looked inviting with two large picture windows looking in and a hanging sign that read "The Book Nook" in green lettering. It hardly appeared like camouflage for a vault beneath the ground floor that harbored cursed objects and their dirty secrets.

But Parish knew it was exactly that the second he saw it from Clouse's description of his one and only previous visit.

Feeling his stomach tighten as he followed his employer to the door, Parish felt apprehensive, like a police officer about to tell a family member a loved one was dead. Julie Knowles already knew this, but the bodyguard knew he needed to spill details, painful even for him, to satisfy her. Because everyone on Clouse's payroll survived Halloween without any incidents, Parish took this as a good omen heading into the winter months.

A tiny bell rang when Clouse opened the front door, alerting a young woman behind the counter to their presence. She recognized Clouse immediately before casting a skeptical eye toward Parish, who opted to wear a suit rather than dress down for the occasion. He typically donned a suit to alert reporters and curious onlookers to the fact that he was protecting the Clouse family. Like a Secret Service agent, he stood out like a sore thumb, but similarly he carried firearms to protect those he served.

The store looked more like a small-town library than a book store with its old wooden shelves lining the walls, with a few islands centered along the old hardwood floors. Parish heard the floors creak when he stepped onto certain boards, possibly acting as a subtle security measure for the owners. A few reading tables with chairs, all wooden, were off to one side, while a cash register occupied a sturdy counter on the opposite end. Lights hung from the high ceilings above on poles, like classic gymnasium lighting.

Barely older than a college graduate, Julie wore her creamed coffee brown hair out to her shoulders, sporting glasses that made her appear studious. Upon seeing her visitors, she stepped from behind the counter, setting down a rather thick log book of some sort. Rather petite, she gave an aura that indicated she was still someone to be reckoned with in any arena. Parish said nothing as Clouse introduced him, though he nodded courteously when they all went to sit at a large reading table with six chairs surrounding it.

Julie sat closest to Clouse, looking him in the eye when she spoke.

"I'll let you know exactly where our arrangement stands when I hear from Mr. Parish about exactly what happened to my two colleagues."

Parish wondered if Teakon had recruited her from one of his history classes, perhaps mentoring her in more than just history. He quickly put such a tarnished thought behind him, wishing to retain his belief that Teakon was a heroic man of virtue.

"I certainly hope our arrangement hasn't been compromised," Clouse said adamantly. "This was a terrible loss for all of us, but Mark envisioned us starting something that would protect people from these cubes for all time."

Folding her hands, Julie said nothing as she looked to Parish, patiently waiting for him to begin his tale. He tried to give her every detail of the journey, especially focusing on the invasion of the trawler and how Teakon and Slone perished. Living through the ordeal proved no easy feat, but retelling the tale without breaking down was equally difficult. Parish wasn't one to show his emotions while at work, but he struggled to maintain his composure when relaying how Teakon sacrificed himself to ensure Parish had a fighting chance to survive or at least dispose of the cube.

"That sounds like Mark," Julie concurred when Parish finished detailing the events, staring down at his hands before forcing his eyes closed to shut out the dire images.

Her eyes appeared misty, conveying her feelings for the man who mentored her into such a dark and mysterious world. Parish knew saving the planet from destruction and its people from being victims of homicide to power the cubes was no light task. The details of her partnership with Teakon and Slone still eluded the bodyguard, because even Clouse never learned much about the trio. Parish felt especially protective of his boss for that reason, knowing partnerships sometimes ended badly, possibly with betrayal.

"So where do we stand now, Julie?" Clouse dared ask.

"I trust you," she answered, looking to both Clouse and Parish. "Both of you. As much as I want out of this dirty business of hunting down the cubes, it's come to my attention that we have a much graver problem than anyone suspected."

Parish stiffened, already under the impression their dire situation couldn't grow much darker. He hated being on the outside looking in throughout so much of the search. Clouse had hired outside help before with mixed results. Only somewhat effective in obtaining results and the cubes themselves, the method left a gaping hole in the trust department between Clouse and those he already employed who knew the secret.

Hopefully the three that he and Mark Daniels researched were the perfect hybrid of trustworthy and incorruptible personalities required for such a job.

"Hunting down the cubes is risky," Julie stated. "Mark knew this, and you butted heads with him on the subject, Mr. Clouse. While I'm not a fan of hunting them down, it has come to my attention that another group will stop at nothing to own them all. You and I both know that can never happen because of the hazardous implications involved. We've all heard the predictions running rampant about

2012 ending the world as we know it. While that statement may be off, give or take a few years, the end could come in the form of these thirteen cubes."

"You're the expert, Julie," Clouse admitted. "We need you to lead us on this, especially with Mark gone."

"I've been going through Mark's research and conducting my own. There's one cube in particular that concerns me, because it could ruin everything we've worked so hard to prevent."

"What does it do?" Parish inquired, feeling his stomach tighten.

"It apparently allows the user to teleport through time," Julie said, taking a deep breath with a gravely concerned expression. "I received a document stating as much in the mail. Mark had a solid lead about a man involved with this particular cube and bid on the man's effects at an estate auction. Considering how little he paid for it, I don't think anyone else knew about our inside information."

Clouse rubbed his cheeks and chin nervously, realizing the ramifications of such power.

"How do we know it hasn't already altered this continuity as we know it?"

"We don't for certain, but it seems unlikely the cube was ever used, because a group secured it soon after its creation. A group very similar to our own."

"And they publicized their existence in a document?"

"No," Julie said, letting a grin slip for the first time since their meeting began. "This was a letter from one member to another, stating in rather vague terms they were transferring possession of the cube from one member to another for safe keeping. The content infers that they were safeguarding the cube from worldly forces that wanted to own it."

"But thanks to your book, you know who's possessed the cube over the years," Clouse stated with an airy wave of his right hand.

"That's true, but we've hit a dead-end at some point."

Parish knew from Clouse's description that a leather-bound book was created with the cubes, bearing the names of the original owners. Apparently slipped into the original spell or curse with the cubes, the book then became part of the legacy, bearing the name of each new owner of each distinct cube. Teakon always said the writing appeared in the book, not by human hand, but from the devil himself when each cube changed ownership.

"What kind of dead-end?" Parish asked, still somewhat skeptical about the powers of the old book.

"It seems the same individual has possessed the cube for the last forty years or so," Julie informed him. "The problem is the man disappeared immediately after he took possession of the cube."

"He went into hiding?" Clouse asked with a raised eyebrow.

"I don't think so. From what little bit I've gathered, it seemed his identity was probably compromised and wherever his body may be, the cube is probably nearby. This isn't fact, so don't get me wrong, but the trail ends with this man."

Clouse sat pensively a moment, folding his hands. Parish knew from working for the man so long that his employer's mental wheels were churning. When it came to the cursed objects and protecting his family, Paul Clouse always had plans in place.

"There may be a way around this issue," he finally said. "Are we in agreement that this time cube *needs* to be found by us first?"

"Absolutely," Julie replied earnestly.

"I've been conducting background checks on three types of people who may be of use to us in locating and retrieving the cubes," Clouse admitted. "I wasn't going to move forward without your blessing, but I've picked my three people and still need to sit down with them. This is important, because one of them is a psychic who might be able to locate this particular cube if we can get her on the trail."

Julie didn't bother hiding her concern.

"Bringing new people into the fold could be very dangerous."

"I understand that, but you and I alone cannot go hunting down these objects. Nor can we simply sit back and watch them being harvested by this other group. No matter the cost, we need to maintain at least a few of these cursed objects so the endgame can't be reached."

"I trust you've researched your three people?"

"Very much. I'm ready to sit down with them and make sure they're right for this before putting them to work."

"That's fine, but I'd like to have some input and feedback on the situation. You, I can trust, but not three new people all at once. This partnership can't be a one-way street."

"Agreed," Clouse stated. "We need each other more than ever."

"I'll help as best I can from here, but the time cube is our priority."

Clouse gave her a mock grin.

"Then *time* is of the essence. Maybe it's time we talk some more about the details."

***

Parish stepped outside the store to let Clouse discuss the new game plan with Julie. He loved the look of a colorful autumn, finding the weather more suitable to football than sightseeing. Even the local smells were like something out of an antique or candle shop, like burning wood from a fireplace and freshly baked goods from a coffee shop just down the street.

Because he hadn't worn an overcoat, and therefore found no place to stuff his hands, he slipped on black leather gloves to shield them from the cold. Every inch of exposed flesh felt chilled to the bone after his ordeal on the Bering Sea. Spending several hours bobbing in a life raft so close to freezing water changed his physical tolerance to the cold. Maybe his mind subliminally exaggerated the experience, but Parish didn't care to ever see the ocean again.

He felt better knowing Julie believed and trusted him, but he still wasn't thrilled about even more people joining their secretive group. The objects they collected tempted people, especially those weak in morals and mind, to fall prey to their own desires. In a mortal world, such people jumped at the opportunity to prolong their lives, renew their youth, or any number of unspoken benefits.

Taking a stroll down the picturesque street, Parish thought about the incident on the Bering Sea and how the Coast Guard finally pulled him and Flanagan aboard their ship. It didn't take long for their helicopter to track down the man's boat, which miraculously remained afloat after being completely abandoned. Parish didn't care to join the captain when he was reunited with his trawler, but being stuck at the Coast Guard base for hours of interviews made him privy to information.

He spoke with Flanagan only once at length, but the captain informed him the entire ship looked as though burglars had overturned it. Anything that wasn't bolted down was strewn across the floors and decks, while the engine room required some repairs before the boat's engines could be started again.

"Those sons-of-bitches probably did a hundred-thousand dollars in damage to my crab boat," the captain had revealed when they sat on a hallway bench, each holding a steaming cup of coffee.

"I'll let my boss know. I'm sure he'll compensate you for whatever the insurance doesn't cover."

"That's a relief," Flanagan said sarcastically. "The next time someone offers to buy my services I'm going to respectfully decline."

Thankfully the captain provided very few details to the authorities, which allowed Parish to put a spin on his version of the story. Luckily Parish hadn't given the captain details in the first place, so the man only knew about the events he witnessed. With all other witnesses either dead or gone, he became the primary resource for the investigators. Parish absolutely could not reveal anything about his true purpose for traveling along the Bering Sea. Thankfully, dropping his employer's name bought him a lot of credibility, so his tale about doing some seafaring research narrowly flew. He said he wasn't sure why people invaded the boat, chalking it up to an unusual band of pirates.

Parish wasn't accustomed to dealing with authorities, much less lying to them with cover stories, but he believed Clouse saved him, at least from a frustrating life of obscurity. Assisting the man with his quest to rid to world of its greatest evil felt like the least Parish could do. He rather enjoyed his usual job of keeping watch over the children, but loved the opportunities to travel. He didn't hope for danger, but kept vigilant for the rare occasions when it came his way.

Patiently waiting for his employer, Parish walked to a nearby park bench, taking a seat as he watched a young couple sitting a few benches down from him. Despite the light, steady breeze, he was able to overhear them talking about wedding plans and the young woman finishing her college courses in the spring. He thought about Mark Teakon and how so many students were probably going to miss him on campus, possibly holding vigils to honor him. He knew Julie missed her mentor, and though she didn't say much about Slone and his gruff personality the same surely went for him.

The young couple playfully tapped one another on their noses and kissed like puppies, very brief but without fear of showing their affection, or worrying about who might be observing them. How lucky they are, Parish thought of them, remembering when he dated his wife and felt the same way. Maturity dulled some of the playfulness, but he still felt passionate about wanting to spend the rest of his life with her and watch his children grow into young adults.

He watched the young couple literally put their foreheads together and talk lovingly in whispers. Parish wished his problems could be as simple as theirs. If only they knew how their life issues paled in comparison to the unseen dangers all around them, they might rethink their future together. Such people had it good and never knew it, living obliviously at a young age. Parish thought like them once, but his views on strangers and their motivations differed after meeting some very evil people over the past few years. He wanted the world to become a safe place once again so he could feel comfortable taking his wife and children on vacations and out in public. While he didn't usher them into the house at all times, Parish took measures to keep them safe without revealing the dangers of his job.

He believed in Clouse, and considered himself game for whatever plan the man conceived to keep the cursed objects out of evil hands. At the moment Parish simply wanted to get back to Indiana and slide into his normal routine for a while.

Chapter 4

Despite the passing of Halloween, roller coasters and other rides continued to run at the theme park known as Great Realms at the edge of Mason, Ohio. Management decided to get one last weekend out of the season before closing down for winter and beginning construction on the park's new ride. Ground had already been cleared, and the concrete stabilizing pillars placed along the dirt-covered land for a new roller coaster.

Clay Branson didn't much care about the business end of the theme park.

His concerns centered mainly around his new life in Mason and the past he left behind. Just young enough to leave his job as a police officer in Northeastern Indiana and join the Mason Police Department, he loved everything about his new life. Working as a local police officer provided him with a second job as park security during the operating months. It also allowed him to spend time with his fiancée, who happened to be the daughter of the park owners.

Clay didn't move a state away on a whim, or to endear himself to the Trimble family. After he helped alleviate a major threat at the park, he returned to see Casey Trimble several times on dates, knowing he wanted to spend time with her. Though she was nearly ten years his junior, he loved how she handled herself at twenty-five years of age. Bold and daring, she saw through bullshit and admired people who mirrored her good values. Clay shared her values because of his job, and because he hoped to outlast the trouble from his past that haunted him.

Walking along the main drag where half a dozen fountains spouted water into the air, adding to the cool breeze wafting across the park, Clay observed his surroundings. People packed the park, hoping for a few last roller coaster rides or memories with their children before the park went into hibernation. Now in his second season with the park, Clay adapted to the routine rather easily. He was being groomed for the head of security position due to open in another year or two when the man holding the position retired.

Strangely enough, Casey's parents had begun training her for every job in the park when she reached the legal working age. She loved and respected her fellow employees, whether she ran the rides or vended candy from an enclosed stand. He loved her more than words could describe, as much as he loved his first wife and child who were taken from him forever in Japan.

Clay sauntered along the paved walkway, trying to forget his years in the Orient. As a teenager he wanted to escape his overbearing police officer father and the home life he thought was so bad. He learned many things, including some very powerful tactics that his *sensei* taught with traditional means. A master of martial arts and hundreds of weapons, Clay knew how to kill a man with little more than a finger, but such knowledge never clouded his judgment or moral fiber. He trickled the information about his past to Casey through conversation, letting her digest it a piece at a time, fearing he might lose her otherwise.

Though his past wasn't sordid through actions he initiated, Clay had killed men in the name of self-defense. Strangely enough, some of the men he lived and trained with in Japan were the same people who tried to kill him within the span of a year.

Things had quieted down recently, allowing him to proceed with his engagement to Casey and their wedding plans. As he passed a coffee shop along the end of the main strip, Clay detected someone waiting for him around the corner. Casey always liked to try taking him by surprise, making it her little game with him. It never worked, because his heightened sense of his surroundings clued him in about danger and other strong emotions in his vicinity. He wasn't psychic, but his training in Japan opened up his mind in ways he never thought possible.

When he rounded the corner he caught Casey in a hug before she even had time to surprise him. She giggled in response, allowing him to embrace her and plant a quick kiss on her lips. With so many people in the park, he hated looking irresponsible considering he wore the park's police uniform. She typically took her duties more seriously as well, but the end of the season was upon them.

"I can't believe today's our last day," she said, walking with him toward the kiddie area of the park. "What are we going to do with all of our time?"

Clay grinned.

"I can think of some things."

Casey returned a playful, yet slightly naughty look.

Young, vibrant, and intelligent, Casey showed remarkable wisdom for her age. Able to read people and their intentions from a mile away, she trusted Clay implicitly, which he earned by never betraying her trust.

Wearing a park uniform that indicated she was working a vending stand at least part of the day, Casey had let her strawberry blond hair down to her shoulders. She smiled easily, making her face a virtual ray of sunshine in Clay's eyes. Slender and athletic, Casey showed an interest in learning some of the arts Clay had mastered in Japan, but he wasn't ready to take on a student quite yet with so many events consuming their schedules. He wanted her to learn for her own betterment, and to be able to better defend herself, because he wasn't certain the danger from his past was behind him.

"How's your day?" he asked, looking from her to the closest ride in the children's area.

"I've been selling cotton candy and pretzels to hyperactive kids. I need Tylenol in a bad way."

Clay chuckled, taking hold of Casey's hand. They walked along the side, so most patrons weren't going to notice their affection in the wake of their own jubilation.

"When are your parents going to rescue you from unruly children and greasy food?"

"Oh, they imprison me in the front office from time to time because they know I'm happy anywhere. I've been here for the ups and downs, so I'm happy just taking my time and learning everything. There are close to a thousand employees who depend on us to give them a paycheck every two weeks."

"I'm privileged to be one of them," Clay said sincerely with a smile. "Meeting you was the one good thing that happened to me the first day I came to this park."

He referred to the day when he and some friends stopped a terrorist incident at the park, all because someone wanted to end Clay's life in an elaborate plan. That day remained a blur in his memory most of the time, because he hated recalling the specifics. Casey's trust in him, a complete stranger at the time, gave him the means to secure the park and eliminate his adversaries.

"How long is your break?" Clay asked his fiancée.

"I'm the floater today. Only got a few minutes before I head to the candy store."

"More sugar and kids. Should I draw you a hot bath tonight?"

Casey looked up to him lovingly.

"Maybe a nice dinner out will make me feel better."

"That can be arranged," Clay said as they stopped walking. "Maybe we can have something sweet for dessert."

Casey reached around his neck, pulling him in for a long kiss without fear of who might be watching them.

"That's just a preview, stud," she said before turning to head for her next work station.

"I like it," Clay said under his breath.

He continued walking through the park, making his presence known when necessary. A few times he overheard parents telling their children they would have the park officer arrest them if they continued to act unruly. Clay hated people telling children such things, because he didn't want kids living in fear of police officers dragging them away. Ending negative stereotypes about police officers was nearly impossible, so he certainly didn't like it when people contributed to them unwittingly.

Sounds of rides spinning and roaring entered his ears, along with delighted screams from numerous children. So late in the season the costumed mascots didn't walk around receiving hugs or taking pictures with the children, but colors still flooded the kiddie area like a rainbow was shot down by a rocket, raining pieces across the theme park. He heard contemporary pop music playing in the background, though it didn't seem quite as appropriate in the cool fall air as it did during the sweltering summer days when the park was wall to wall people.

During the winter months a skeleton security crew remained at the park while the office personnel worked intermittently. Not until the early months of the following year would human resources begin the hiring process for the next season. Clay expected to work some security during the winter, possibly learning from their security director to bide his time.

Passing through the colorful rides with their lights and localized music and carnival sounds, Clay reached the opposite end of the kiddie area where a wide concrete path led to the waterpark. A train also made a circuit around half of the park, transporting guests to the waterpark or a faux western town where shootouts occurred on the hour between actors. Soon after Clay crossed the tracks that intersected the walkway he looked up to an old wooden fortress covered in ivy with a sign that hung crookedly on its one remaining metal clasp.

A few people passed him, walking the other way, but otherwise he was alone on the concrete path. With the waterpark and western attraction closed for the year, few people found any reason to take the train or walk away from the park's open attractions. Clay's eyes refused to leave the fort, not because it was such a neat vintage attraction, but rather because he sensed something dangerous nearby. Feeling certain he was an intended target, he reached toward his firearm just before the gleam of a gun scope caught his eye from the fortress's top area.

Clay dove for some nearby bushes, hearing the distinct sound of a suppressed firearm from above. He hit the ground, tucking and rolling as he did so, feeling no shooting pain or blood oozing from a fresh wound. Regaining his footing, Clay drew his sidearm as he pressed his back to the building. The shooter likely knew he missed the shot, meaning he would opt to retreat hastily or return to ground level in order to try finishing his assignment.

Listening intently, Clay heard nothing for a few seconds before the rustling of the ivy from within gave the would-be assassin's movements away. Three wooden walls comprised the fort, leaving the fourth area completely open for showman-ship purposes when the western town actors wanted to use it. Now entangled in a cat and mouse game, Clay moved along the wall without a sound, keeping his gun in a ready position.

Edging his way toward the open area, Clay continued to listen for move-ment inside. Uncertain whether his attacker was a traditional assassin or someone trained like himself, he exercised caution. Carrying nothing except his firearm and a metal ASP baton, his arsenal felt a bit lacking without any projectile weapons or blades. Spotting a tree at the end of the wall, he darted forward before the gunman tried shooting him through the wall, diving behind the tree for cover. Peering around the side, he found the man inside the three-walled fortress training a silenced pistol in his direction.

Able to use the tree to block his entire body when he stood upright, Clay heard two shots emerge from the pistol. The tree absorbed both bullets, buying him some time to reach up for a branch before tugging himself upward into a flip that landed him atop the branch. Using his new vantage point, Clay kept his fire-arm at his side, wanting to know why this man targeted him specifically. Killing the would-be assassin produced an adverse result, so Clay safely peered around the tree, trying to locate the man's knee for a quick disabling shot.

Seeing nothing before him, Clay heard no heavy breathing or running through the tall grass, so he quickly determined the man was close to the tree. In one motion he dropped down, grasping the branch while maintaining his grip on the gun, swinging his legs where he believed the man was hiding on the other side of the tree. Hitting nothing except air, Clay landed on the ground, immediately sensing danger behind him, so he rolled sideways behind the tree once again as two more quieted shots rang out from the man's gun.

He grasped the extendable baton from his gun belt, shook his hand to extend it, and whipped his arm behind him, around the tree, striking something solid and drawing a pained groan. Hurt but not disabled, the man stumbled from behind the tree, still trying to train his gun on Clay, holding the side of his head. Clay continued to circle around the tree, away from the gun until he found an opportunity to swing the baton around the tree again, striking the man's left hand, which dropped the gun after a nerve ending was struck.

Already knowing this man was not trained in the ancient art of *ninjutsu*, Clay pounced like a cat, flooring the man in one move from behind the tree. Holding the end of the baton against the man's throat, Clay made certain no one was walking the nearby path before beginning his interrogation.

"Talk, or this baton can go through your vocal cords, or your carotid artery, with a simple push. Who sent you to kill me?"

"Some Japanese guy," the man gasped, obviously not doubting the threat.

"What Japanese guy?" Clay asked, putting pressure on the baton.

He knew about a dozen men from Japan who weren't happy with him being the star pupil of their class when they carried on an ancient Japanese tradition. Being the only American among them didn't do much for his popularity, but he excelled because he knew of nothing else to focus on at that time.

"Some old Japanese guy met me in San Francisco," the man stammered as Clay applied more pressure with the baton. "He paid me half up front to kill you and your uncle in Muncie."

"Bill?" Clay asked, feeling an emotional spike that emanated from genuine concern. "God help you if you touched him."

"I didn't," the paid assassin replied, trying to squirm away from the baton's force. "The old man said your uncle knew too much and needed to die, but he insisted you go first."

Clay had an idea of who paid the man to kill them both as the pieces fell together in his mind. After two previous attempts on his life by his former fellow students failed, he began to question how they located him and their ulterior motives for trying to kill him. His relationship with Bill had grown a bit more distant after the last attempt on his life, because Bill hid information from him for his benefit. Inquiries about Bill's silence went unanswered to the point that they stopped talking altogether. Clay's move to Ohio simply added to the ease of them not communicating, though Clay very much wanted to confront Bill after this near death experience.

Forcefully flipping the man to his stomach, Clay applied handcuffs to his wrists before radioing his fellow park security officers for backup. He wasn't exactly sure what he wanted to tell them except that the gunman tried to shoot him with a rifle. How the man bypassed any of the gates with a loaded weapon eluded Clay, but he didn't plan on sticking around for the interrogation personally.

After explaining the situation as briefly as possible to authorities, he planned on paying his uncle a visit after a two-hour drive to his hometown.

Chapter 5

It wasn't until late Sunday evening when Clay arrived in Muncie, Indiana to find the college town the same as ever. Actually deemed a small city, home to Ball State University, Muncie was all Clay ever knew during his formative childhood years. The son of a city police officer who spent very little time around their home, Clay found alternative methods of entertaining himself during his teenage years, finally forming a bond with a man who worked for his father around the house. After several serious discussions between Clay, his parents, and Ryo Nosagi, it was decided that Clay would travel to Japan for mentoring from Nosagi.

Casey sounded disappointed when he tracked her down inside the theme park before leaving, simply stating a family issue required his attention in Indiana. She knew his father was in poor health, so she gave her blessing, and Clay said nothing to indicate a different reason for leaving. Coming from such a tightknit family, she held out hope that Clay might put aside his differences with his father before it was too late, but he couldn't share her optimism. Too many bad childhood memories kept him from ever truly forgiving the man.

Clay found Bill home by himself when he reached the country home his uncle had purchased soon after landing his job at the local hospital as the head of maintenance. Bill's life became an endless sequence of meetings, phone calls, and overseeing inventory between employees dropping in to ask questions or receive orders. Before Clay moved to Ohio, he changed Bill's life by entering him into the secretive world of *ninjutsu*, teaching him in his customized *dojo*.

"This is unexpected," Bill said when he answered the front door to the four-bedroom home that included an in-ground pool and hot tub before he added a three-car garage and coy pond in the front.

"Is Emily due back soon?"

"She just left for a business trip. Come inside."

Bill stood a few inches taller than Clay, remaining in excellent physical condition for a man in his mid-forties. He dressed casually at home with blue jeans and a flannel shirt to fend off the cooler weather. As he led Clay toward the immaculate, well-furnished living room, Bill looked back at his nephew with deep blue eyes through his eyeglasses. Not one to conform to trends, he still wore his brown hair parted to one side while a thick mustache of the same color covered his upper lip.

"You should've called if you were coming home," Bill said as he dropped into a loveseat.

Clay chose a recliner, unsure of where to start a conversation with his uncle. He needed to know the truth, and rather quickly, if he planned on preventing any further attempts on his life.

"I'm not exactly here for a social visit," Clay said up front.

"Oh?" Bill asked with genuine surprise.

The fire in the fireplace behind him warmed the entire room, completing the Terry Redlin cozy painting feel of the entire property.

"A man tried to kill me at the theme park today."

"Kill you?"

"I'm pretty sure you know where this is going, Bill. It's a repeat of what happened a few years ago, except this guy was paid to single me out. His orders were to end your existence once he finished with me."

Bill took a deep, unsettled breath, cupping his chin and cheeks a bit nervously.

"Care to explain why someone might have a need to kill you?" Clay pressed. "Maybe something you knew that someone couldn't afford to have leaked?"

Reflecting back to the night in question, Bill took a moment to collect himself before speaking.

"When that guy at the park thought he had me all but dead he made a confession, Clay."

"You mean the one you emptied a full magazine into?"

"Yeah, that one. Anyway, he confessed who hired him to carry out the attack against the theme park and your buddies."

Clay cleared his throat emphatically.

"And you couldn't find reason enough to tell me that someone might try and take my life in the future?"

"I didn't think you wanted to hear the truth."

"That the man who taught me everything I know, including the principles I live my life by, wants me dead?"

"How did you know?" Bill asked, unable to look his nephew in the eyes.

"Intuition. I looked at the pieces and nothing seemed to fit. There wasn't a real motive for these guys to come after me, because their type only cares about using their training for profit. It dawned on me that maybe I was being tested, then it occurred to me that I was asked to travel to Japan under false pretenses altogether."

Bill looked to him with grave concern, biting his lower lip.

"There's a lot more to this than you know, Clay. After the incident at the park, I did some pondering too. You and I growing distant is my fault, and it's because I feel a strong sense of guilt for not stepping in sooner."

"How could you have stepped in sooner? You helped save thousands at the park that day."

"That's not what I mean. I should have known better, and I should've stopped your father from sending you to Japan."

Recently Clay's father had taken a turn for the worse regarding his overall health. Slowed by a stroke at age sixty, only two years after retirement, the senior Branson found himself virtually confined to his home. Clay's relationship with his father was always distant, icy at times, so he didn't play the part of the dutiful son and rush home to check on his father, though he did phone regularly. And though he hated to think in a hateful manner, he supposed karma caught up with the old man at long last.

"Did you ever question why your father had a Japanese man doing handiwork around the house?" Bill asked.

"I suppose it crossed my mind, but I wasn't even twenty yet, Bill. A lot of things distracted me back then. What are you trying to tell me?"

Bill hesitated momentarily, looking to the ceiling.

"I wasn't in the picture back then, but I think your father was into something illegal that involved imports and exports. Your *sensei* was part of whatever he was doing, but they put on a front to fool everyone else."

"And you never said anything about this sooner?"

"I never connected the dots until the attack at the park when I found out Nosagi was behind the attempts on your life. After that I did a little research and asked your mother a few things. It didn't take a genius to figure out what your father did back then. Your buddy had some overseas connections he used to import new drugs into our country."

"So all that time I spent on the drug task force, stopping drugs between here, Gary, and Chicago, was in part because of my father's dealings?"

"That's a safe bet, but it's not the worst part."

Clay's face wrinkled in confusion, wondering what could be worse than his own father turning his back on every vow he took when the city swore him in as a police officer. In better economic times, Clay's task force put a stop to the heavy drug trafficking between Muncie and the northern cities. Clay moved to Ohio around the time the police chief disbanded much of his group, mainly due to financial cutbacks and a mayor who didn't much care for public safety.

Bill stood to tend to the fire, using a poker to move the log into a better position to intensify the flame. The fire tamed the dampness choking the fall air, at least inside Bill's house, while providing a warmth that electric and gas heaters imitated poorly.

"At this point I've practically disowned your father," Bill admitted. "Based on my dealings with him back in the day, and talks with your mom, I think your father sent you away for his own benefit."

"Yeah, so I'd be out of his hair."

"No, so you could learn to be an assassin and work for him when you came back."

"What?" Clay asked incredulously.

"Why else would Nosagi whisk you away to Japan, train you to do all of those things, and create this huge façade, Clay? He set you up with the perfect, quintessential life over there only to rip it away from you? *He* murdered your wife and son, Clay. Nosagi has been behind everything that's happened to you since you graduated high school."

Feeling like he was standing in some movie revelation moment where the camera quickly distanced itself from the shocked main character, Clay found himself figuratively slapped in the face.

"I'm sorry, Clay," Bill said compassionately. "I didn't tell you this before because I was afraid that going public with any of it might put you in even more danger. I'm really sorry."

"So am I," Clay muttered, barely able to digest so much negativity at once.

In the matter of one day his life went from walking on air to plummeting toward the earth without a parachute. He knew his life could never be the same, much less normal, until he located Nosagi and dealt with him.

Permanently.

Uncertain whether or not he was capable of killing his former mentor, Clay knew he needed to confront the man. Living the remainder of his life with Casey wasn't an option if he found himself looking over his shoulder every hour of every day.

"I'm going to find him," Clay vowed aloud.

"If I can help in any way, name it."

Clay wasn't certain how he felt about his uncle at the moment. While Bill kept certain truths from him, it seemed his uncle did so with Clay's best interest in mind. The man had always been more like a big brother than an uncle to him, treating him very well when he lived in the Muncie area. Even so, Clay decided he needed to return to his new home to check on Casey and begin his search for Ryo Nosagi.

"I've got to go, Bill."

"Don't leave like this," Bill said just short of pleading. "If you're pissed at me, just tell me."

"I don't know how I feel right now."

Clay stood to walk to the doorway where Bill intercepted him by blocking the door with his arm.

"If you find him, I'll help you any way I can, Clay. I want to make this right between us."

"We'll see," Clay answered neutrally, brushing his uncle's arm aside as he stepped outside to drive home.

Finding Nosagi was probably going to be difficult, and might even require him traveling to Japan. He didn't live in some soap opera where he could conveniently take time off work, or simply pick up another job if he quit the police department. With limited options, Clay needed to make some important decisions concerning his life and his future very quickly.

Chapter 6

Russ Greene couldn't believe how the past few months drastically altered his life. His career, retirement plans, and ambitions of putting evildoers behind bars for the United States Marshals Service abruptly came to an end. Luckily for him the occasional exciting fugitive chase, bank robbery cases, and constant battle against drug dealers and their labs ended on his own terms when a more lucrative job offer came his way.

Approached by Paul Clouse in the middle of November, Greene listened to the man's sales pitch about thirteen cursed cubes with skepticism and minimal interest, believing he was flown to Massachusetts as part of some television hoax show. Even when Julie Knowles chimed in with information and some of the history her group endured getting the cubes back, he wasn't convinced. While obituaries of Greg Slone and Mark Teakon backed their story to some extent, making him feel for them, it wasn't until they showed him a cube and the leather-bound book that Greene found himself convinced.

The book's writing revealed Julie as the latest possessor of the cube, but when she handed the cube to Clouse the book scrawled Clouse's name immediately in immaculate handwriting at that very moment. Seeing the writing live and in person, Greene felt certain his eyes grew as big as saucers. He doubted some kind of magic trick was responsible for the ghostly script before him, so it took only a little more description of their personal experiences with the cubes, followed by their impending hunt, to convince him to join their team.

Clouse also revealed to him that the cursed objects were indestructible when he took a hammer to one of them, causing it no damage whatsoever. It seemed Greene had a lot to learn about his new occupation because it dealt with religion and specifically the occult. The notion of Satan himself cursing objects in some sort of pact felt foreign, if not impossible, but Greene felt this new knowledge backed general religious beliefs.

Basically wanting Greene to replace Teakon as the leader of the hunting operation, Clouse offered him far more money than the government could dream of providing. There wasn't a pension per se, and the risk sounded steep, but the reward to someone as morally sound as Greene far outweighed the danger.

Working the private sector never crossed his mind because he loved his job, but the thought of stopping possibly the greatest source of evil in the world intrigued him.

Greene found himself accepting the job the day after the meeting in Massachusetts because there were no attachments to hold him back. It appeared Clouse knew he wasn't married, had no children, and wasn't in a serious relationship at the moment. Clouse also revealed that he knew of Greene's moral fiber through his lack of an arrest record, his unblemished personnel file, his responsible finances, and the fact that he lived tobacco and alcohol free.

"I want someone I can trust, who won't be distracted by vices," Clouse revealed during their conversation.

Greene felt certain the man possessed better means of background checks than the government, but he supposed money provided such assets. Clouse never went into details about his riches, or how he obtained them, but he made it clear he possessed financing enough to conduct a full hunt and retrieval of each cube.

Conducting his own research, Greene learned a few things about Clouse, though sorting fact from myth proved difficult. The media was never fed complete stories, and apparently the local police were shielded from the unbelievable truth as well. Greene used his credentials one last time to conduct the check on his new boss before turning in his badge and firearm to his lieutenant with his immediate resignation. His sudden departure shocked his fellow employees and his lieutenant, but Greene refused to provide any reasons or information, simply stating he took a job in the private sector.

A whirlwind of information swept over him in a short time, including the fact that Clouse wanted to hire two more necessary individuals to complete the team. Greene reviewed the two selections with his employer, agreeing with the picks completely as his faith in Clouse grew. They agreed that Clouse's choice to replace Greg Slone with a new, well-rounded expert in survival and weapons could wait because they needed someone with a specific talent to help them find the suddenly valuable time cube.

Because the cube's owner disappeared decades earlier without a trace, only one realistic option remained for the group to track the cube. While Greene found himself unfamiliar with psychics, and highly skeptical, Clouse assured him the process worked with the correct person using his or her talents. The two discussed the religious ramifications of using a medium in their quest, knowing the Bible plainly stated interactions with such people were taboo.

Now, in the middle of December, Greene found Liz Harper by his side in Schaumburg, a Chicago suburb, looking for their first major clue in the search for the time cube. Though he had yet to see Liz in action with her psychic abilities, her résumé looked impressive. She worked with police agencies in searches for missing persons and those responsible for committing unsolved murders.

Clouse made certain she never touched any of the cubes or the leather-bound book during the interview process. When Greene inquired why, Clouse explained contact with any of the objects involved in the curse might send a flurry of images through her mind about the origins of the cubes and the book. He wanted all of her concentration, and her abilities, focused on finding the most dangerous of the bunch once she accepted the position on their team.

He quickly discovered very little rattled Liz, as though she had seen the same types of gruesome scenes he had as a law enforcement officer. In a manner of speaking he supposed she had through her visions, but visions failed to provide the odors associated with death, or the shock of seeing a corpse waiting around a corner when it wasn't expected. Seeing such things in a third person capacity also removed the element of danger from the equation.

A native Californian, Liz acted down-to-earth for someone with such extraordinary abilities. She dressed like a gypsy at times, wearing dark tops and colorful shawls with dark slacks or long skirts. Today, with snowfall steadily falling around the Chicago area, she sat in the passenger seat of their rental car wearing a winter coat with a shawl of orange and black swirled colors. Her black hair was tied in a bun atop her head, held in place by a scarf as though she were an elderly lady heading out for a BINGO night on the town.

In truth, Liz was several years short of middle-age, choosing to put forth an eccentric appearance to match her talent.

"How do we handle this?" Liz inquired as Greene turned down the street toward the house in question.

"What do you mean?"

"I mean you no longer have a badge and I'm not exactly a poster child for civilian search advocate groups."

"We've been through this already," Greene said with a sigh. "Thomas Ervin, an officer with the Chicago Police Department, disappeared in 1979. Our information tells us he was the last one to possess the time cube, guarding it against those who wanted it for their own purposes. It seems soon after the cube was created, someone from this department has always kept it safe from groups like the Coven that Mr. Clouse dealt with. We're about to visit Trudy, his sister who never married, to see if we can gather any additional information, or you can do your thing."

"That still doesn't explain what you told her."

Greene peered intently out the side of the windshield, searching for the appropriate house number. In the older neighborhood all of the houses ran together, literally a few feet apart from one another with short fences across the front that held mailboxes.

"She believes we're with an advocate group, as you alluded to, dedicated to searching for missing persons. What do you need from her to do your thing? Because I'm just here as a mouthpiece."

"Don't worry about me. I'll get what I need from her and hopefully we can get a lead."

"We need one," Greene grumbled as he pulled in front of the correct house, a residence with metal siding painted yellow that appeared in desperate need of a facelift.

Liz followed Greene to the front door where he knocked, waiting patiently a moment until a thin woman with glasses opened the door and examined them with a hint of mistrust, as though they might be there to eat her.

"Ms. Ervin, I'm Russ Greene, and this is my associate Elizabeth Harper. I spoke with you about our group and possibly starting a search for your brother."

"Come in."

Liz tried giving him a skeptical look, indicating she thought this woman was a complete weirdo, but Greene turned away before Trudy saw him acknowledge anything. While she looked a bit like Adrian from the early *Rocky* movies, Trudy had yet to prove she was anything more than a single hermit surrounded by thousands of strangers.

"I'm not sure how you can help," Trudy said as they followed her inside the well-kept, yet dated residence. "My brother's been gone the better part of thirty years."

"He disappeared without a trace," Greene stated. "We specialize in generating a trail where the police and other agencies have failed through less conventional means."

"This house was his, you know," Trudy said with a hint of sadness in her voice. "When Mom passed away it fell to me."

Greene began to surmise the reasons for her lonely life, having everyone she cared about dying or disappearing in time. From the looks of the house's décor and the dated walls and carpeting, Greene believed Trudy froze herself in a time when her family surrounded her and she knew happiness.

"What can you tell me about the days leading up to your brother's disappearance?" Greene inquired as they all took a seat in the living room.

"Nothing, really. He went to work that week like usual, and he even called me the day before he disappeared."

"Did he seem upset?"

"No. It was an ordinary conversation. Look, I've been over this with the police a dozen times. Don't you know all of this already?"

Greene shifted his position, trying to find some sort of comfort level without a badge and holstered gun to provide authority and backing in his new career.

"I have an idea, but I'm not privy to the police reports, Ms. Ervin. It's important I have an understanding what led up to his disappearance."

"Do you have anything that belonged to your brother?" Liz asked without hesitation or any provocation.

Trudy simply gave her a stunned look in return.

"Maybe an article of clothing or a household item he owned," Liz continued, not fazed one bit.

"How does this help at all?" Trudy questioned.

"Liz can see things that other people don't," Greene explained ambiguously.

"Like a psychic?" Trudy asked excitedly, a mix of bewilderment and glee showing in her face.

Greene felt like he was sitting between padded rooms in a psychiatric ward. Often called upon to deal with unusual individuals during his marshal days, he knew how to exercise patience, but not how to deal with the supernatural element he now hunted.

"Exactly like that," Liz said, picking up on Trudy's intrigue like a relay runner grabbing a baton.

"I've always wondered when they might bring a psychic into the mix," Trudy said elatedly, standing to search for an item.

I'm in hell, Greene thought, figuring he was dealing with this bizarre woman in the slimmest of chances that he might advance his hopeless search. He wasn't a big fan of Liz yet, though that might change in a heartbeat if she proved herself worthy of Clouse's blessing.

Trudy returned a minute or so later carrying a display case full of badges that she set upon her lap as she took a seat. Carefully opening the box, as though it contained ancient, valuable relics, Trudy plucked a silver badge in the shape of a star from its resting place. She looked at it momentarily, openly missing her brother as she stared at one of the few things he left behind in the wake of his disappearance.

"May I?" Liz asked, tentatively reaching for the badge.

Trudy nodded, reluctantly relinquishing custody of the silver star as though it might vanish any moment.

Liz took hold of the badge, barely able to clasp it within her hand before her body jolted slightly and her mind took her to a different place.

Chapter 7

When Thomas Ervin took over the responsibility of caring for the most dangerous object in the world, he knew little about its history or the unheralded organization that chose him for the job. He only knew that five Chicago police officers comprised the group, and they monitored his progress on the department for several years before choosing him.

Once he passed several initiation phases, including extensive interviews and trust tests, Ervin was given the cube and told to hide it somewhere safe and tell no one where he placed it.

Ever.

The responsibility fell to him until one of the five died and they began the search for someone new to protect the cube. A heavy commitment fell on Ervin, one that required sacrifices similar to those of a Catholic priest. His life surrounded the defense of that cube, not allowing him to have relationships or stray very far from Chicago because he needed to remain in close proximity of the cursed object.

Continuing to live an everyday life by reporting to work and occasionally heading to taverns with his friends, Ervin checked on the safety of his albatross from time to time. Guarding the most dangerous object in the world while unable to tell anyone about his efforts became somewhat of a burden sometimes, but he understood his silence kept the world safe. He hungered for knowledge about the cube and the sister cubes he merely heard rumblings about from his fellow protectors.

After finishing his afternoon shift Ervin decided to drive around to clear his mind. A night of frustrating calls had left his blood pressure elevated, so he decided to cool off before heading to his dark and empty house for the night. He drove through Chicago en route to Schaumburg, deciding to drive a bit further before reaching his house. For some reason he felt impulsive about checking on the cube, as though it called to him for some reason.

Cursed objects took on a life of their own, as though programmed during their creation to lure weak-willed men and women to them like sirens at sea. In this case the cubes shimmered and glowed when touched, somehow projecting their abilities into the minds of those who held them. Ervin avoided handling the cube after his first few unsettling experiences, or donned gloves when he found a need to touch the square gem. Still in uniform, he already wore leather gloves, along with the leather duty jacket that creaked whenever he shifted in the driver's seat of his 1973 blue Plymouth Roadrunner.

Lucky to not be driving through drifting snow, Ervin felt certain his late November run to the county road where he kept the cube hidden would be the last until springtime. It took nearly twenty minutes to escape the confines of Schaumburg, and another twenty to reach an old bridge he remembered from his childhood. Numerous trips to visit his grandparents on weekends left the haunting vision of the decaying bridge imprinted in his memory. A short bridge constructed atop a stone foundation in the 1940s, the structure's days appeared numbered, so Ervin monitored county contracts and construction projects with great interest in case it was due to be replaced or demolished.

Gone were the street lamps, passing trains, and the criminal element that kept Ervin busy on a daily basis. Only trees, open fields, and the occasional residence created his current scenery, relaxing him a bit despite the frigid temperatures going head-to-head with his car's heater. Ervin eventually found the road that led to the bridge, turning the steering wheel with an open palm, grinning to himself. Visiting the bridge felt like going home again, stirring childhood memories for him each and every time.

Careful to check behind him every few miles to ensure no one followed him, or accidentally stumbled upon him requesting directions, Ervin pulled to the side of the road just short of the bridge. He stepped out of his car, slapped in the face by the biting wind and frigid temperatures. Thankful the blizzard conditions of the previous year weren't back, he walked toward the bridge, hearing the crunch of frozen grass and small rocks beneath his shined work shoes. He wore his regulation hat for the little warmth it provided his head, zipping his jacket a bit higher as he walked.

Thinking he heard the rumble of a car motor in the distance, Ervin stopped in his tracks, spinning to look for headlights. He spied nothing in the distance, no longer hearing anything aside from the wind through the nearby trees. Thinking his head was still swimming with the noises of the city, he grunted to himself before continuing his walk.

When he reached the beginning of the bridge, Ervin carefully stepped down the embankment, avoiding any loose rocks that might send him tumbling like a dislodged boulder. While the bridge itself rested on concrete, the ends were made of decorative rocks that began to loosen over the years as their mortar gave way. From his childhood days, Ervin knew that certain rocks came out with little more than a tap. Once he decided to make this the cube's hiding place, he expedited the process of breaking the seal, memorizing exactly where he placed the cube once he dug out a tiny cove for it.

Most of the rocks were light in color, with a handful in the medium gray range, and a few more that appeared dark gray in daylight or moonlight. Ervin counted the dark rocks from the leftmost edge until he got to the fourteenth one that resided just above his head. Using his height as a vertical marker and the memorized number as the horizontal reference, Ervin worked the dark rock about twice the size of his fist free from its resting place, reaching behind it to find a tiny deer skin pouch he once purchased from a rural flea market. He originally stuffed the cube inside the pouch to keep it from shimmering at him, like a wink from an attractive woman, whenever he laid eyes upon it.

Temptation to alter the course of time enters any rational person's thoughts from time to time, so Ervin didn't want any coercion from an inanimate object. As he pulled the pouch from its resting place for a quick look at the dark blue object, he heard a vehicle approaching slowly from the same direction he traveled. Suspecting the worst out of necessity, he stuffed the pouch into a jacket pocket, believing anyone who put forth the effort to tail him would not rest until they examined the area after murdering him anyway.

For all he knew, someone was above checking on his car, wondering if it was abandoned by the side of the road. He only thought of the worst scenario for self-preservation purposes. Ervin walked a longer way around the side of the bridge before scaling a nearby dirt hill to ground level with the bridge itself. Finding a car parked beside his Roadrunner, he dashed to a nearby large rock and ducked behind it.

Two men stepped from the car, looking very official as though they worked for the federal government. Both wore fedoras and dark suits with heavy overcoats. Ervin suddenly felt positive the two men had followed him by shutting down the headlights to their Ford LTD sedan. They looked like serious characters, especially when they both looked cautiously around as they stepped from the car, one even drawing a firearm without provocation. Ervin felt positive the backseat or trunk was reserved for him, with or without a bullet in his skull.

He now faced two major threats. One, he needed to place the cube in a new hiding place immediately, provided he survived this encounter. Two, if these two men knew about him, and more importantly, the cube, someone likely sold Ervin out to the government or another agency. The only people who supposedly knew about the cube were Ervin and his four fellow police officers.

If he couldn't trust them, he needed to dispose of the cube forever and tell no one about his experiences.

Unless these men did something careless, like distance themselves from their car enough for him to make an escape, Ervin suspected he might be involved in a shootout within minutes. He simply waited and watched as the men exchanged glances before walking in different directions. Wondering momentarily if they were robots, able to communicate without speaking before carrying out their orders, Ervin crouched behind the rock, reaching for his sidearm as one of the men walked in his direction.

Neither man glanced around in search of him, which only reinforced his opinion that his pursuers were androids or aliens, using technology beyond his comprehension. Ervin quickly shook off the notion, figuring the agents developed their plan before stepping from the vehicle. Government spooks or not, they were not allowed to lay hands on the cube, even if it forced the Chicago cop to use deadly force.

It took less than a minute for each man to reach one side of the bridge. The one not holding his firearm pulled out a flashlight, turning it on and shining it down to the bottom. Ervin knew their search was quickly going to reveal he wasn't there, meaning they wouldn't hazard the steep walk to the bottom. He decided he needed to make a run for it, and quickly, if he wanted to avoid a firefight.

Darting from behind the large rock, he cut across the short field to his car, drawing the attention of the two men almost immediately. Closer to the cars than his pursuers, Ervin drew his firearm and fired into the right front tire of their car before jumping into the Roadrunner. Not daring to look ahead, the cube's guardian slid his ready key into the car's ignition, hearing it roar to life before he looked up and noticed the two men drawing down on him, their firearms trained at his front windshield.

"Shit," he muttered, throwing the car into reverse, narrowly missing the LTD behind him as he backed a safe distance down the road before pulling the steering wheel hard to the right.

Not one shot was fired as Ervin slammed his foot on the gas pedal, putting the bridge behind him in a hurry. He breathed a sigh of relief as his mind raced to contemplate the next logical move. Hiding the cube was his priority, and Ervin knew to have contingency plans for virtually every situation, but executing them in the dead of night wasn't a cinch.

After a few miles Ervin began to slow his car, not wanting to draw attention to himself. The last thing he wanted was a documented stop by local law enforcement, or even a random passerby recalling that he spied a speeding Roadrunner in the overnight hours. While spending a few minutes deciding which of his next hiding locations he wanted to use, Ervin glanced behind him, thinking he noticed a glimmer of metal in the unusually intense moonlight. Seeing no headlights, he began thinking his imagination was getting the better of him when he felt his body lurch forward from a rear impact.

Shaking off the initial shock rather quickly, Ervin stomped the gas once again, seeing no headlights behind him. Either the two men were certified in race car pit stops, to change a tire so quickly, or a backup team took over in the pursuit.

Still highly familiar with his surroundings, Ervin pushed the knob for his own headlights, turning them off before he veered into a field. A cat and mouse game ensued with neither vehicle yielding to the darkness, so the young police officer knew only time and fate separated one of the vehicles from hitting a large object that disabled it. Luckily the moonlight lit the field fairly well, and though Ervin probably passed the field hundreds of times over the years he didn't know every square foot of it by any means.

He knew of a large tree near the center of the field, so he drove toward it, hoping to pull off a feat that might get him out of his current predicament. While the bumps and small rocks took a toll on his car, he simply hoped it could outrun the LTD, or at least outlast it. Unwilling to blink for fear he might crash and make himself a sitting duck, Ervin slowed just slightly until he saw the tree atop the next hill. He headed directly toward it, gaining speed despite the protests from his car whenever it struck a dirt mound or rock, lifting it a few inches off the ground.

Figuring he might be sentencing his car to death, Ervin continued pushing its limits, drawing dangerously close to the tree. He waited until he was within ten feet of it, hoping the men behind him were too distracted to see the danger, before swerving hard to the right. Ervin's racing heart virtually jolted within his chest when he heard a horrific crash behind him. The sounds of metal twisting and snapping reached his ears when the heavy engine block collided with the unmoving tree trunk, the speed of the impact alone compressing the car like a squeezed accordion.

Ervin brought his car to a stop, trying to catch his breath from the nerve-wracking ordeal momentarily as he stared in the rearview mirror. Smoke or steam rose from the engine block as the pungent smell of antifreeze was carried his way with the light breeze. The brake lights on the LTD glowed an eerie red, as though the driver's foot might be stuck in position, or his body was crumpled entirely beneath the dash. Still shaking from adrenaline and the experience that brought him closer to death than anything in his entire life, Ervin reached under the seat for a spare revolver he kept with him at all times.

His four fellow protectors told him to *never* tie himself to any situation by firing his issued sidearm outside of his workplace. Science was on the verge of breakthroughs in DNA and forensic technologies, including firearms analysis. They kept up on such technology, often attending seminars and workshops to remain ahead of adversaries who wanted the cube.

Flinging his door open, Ervin decided to provide some fast closure to the situation before someone noticed the scene from the normally quiet road. Already marching with a purpose toward the disabled LTD when his door shut itself on the rebound, Ervin kept the spare firearm clutched in his right hand as he walked. Despite approaching the passenger's side, he saw the driver more clearly, slumped over the wheel, his mouth agape while his fedora hung limply to the opposite side, one edge still pinned between the steering wheel and the man's head.

Drawing closer to the vehicle, Ervin saw only a little bit of the passenger's back because the man appeared pressed against the dash, probably not wearing his seatbelt during the pursuit. Ervin was now within ten feet of the vehicle, raising his firearm to ensure the two men reported nothing to whomever sent them. He hated the idea of killing in cold blood, if the two men weren't already dead, but he understood the importance of keeping the cube safe from evildoers.

Within a second, as though he had played possum the entire time, the passenger sat back in his seat, taking aim at Ervin with a revolver. Ervin found himself unable to pull the trigger before the other man fired at him, but he delivered a fatal shot a split-second after the man's bullet struck his abdomen. Immediately clutching the wound, Ervin staggered forward, seeing that his bullet entered the man's forehead, killing him instantly as wide eyes returned his stare. The driver showed no signs of life in the forms of movement or even breathing, but Ervin fired a bullet into the vehicle, striking the side of the man's head just the same to ensure the two men didn't follow him or summon help.

Blood trickled from his wound as Ervin painfully returned to his Roadrunner, determined to hide the cube before seeking medical assistance. His mind raced for anywhere nearby where he might dump the cube, ensuring its safety, until he could return to it. Driving toward the road, determined to distance himself from the bloodshed behind him, Ervin thought of two possibilities in the form of a pond and a quarry less than a mile from where his grandparents once lived. After his grandfather passed away, his grandmother moved in with the family for a time, but they eventually placed her in a nursing home. Ervin supposed he chose the area to hide the cube because it provided him with an excuse to revisit his childhood from time to time.

He considered the pond a better hiding spot, because it spanned a few football fields in length, often used for swimming or fishing recreationally during the summer months by the owners and their friends. While the cube would certainly be hidden better there, Ervin considered the task of finding it again rather daunting. Besides, the pond remained highly visible from the road and neighboring houses, meaning he couldn't risk getting caught trespassing while trying to retrieve it.

The quarry, however, remained filled with stagnant water all year round. Somewhat deep, at least from what he'd heard, the pit provided direct access to the cube at the bottom through a simple, strategic dive. Ervin knew two of his fellow protectors were certified divers, and if he didn't want to enlist their help by revealing his blunder, he felt certain he could take a crash course in diving.

Now driving toward the quarry, Ervin felt a bit dizzy. He reached for the concealed cube, stuffing it into an inner pocket within his duty jacket. Fighting to stave off the fatigue and blood loss that required his body to rest, he steered off the county road onto a dirt road that went uphill toward a metal gated fence. A construction company occupied the property during Ervin's childhood, but he seemed to recall his grandfather saying they dug for coal or minerals there once.

Uncertain of what entity owned the property, Ervin knew he hadn't seen another person step foot on it in years. Looters and vandals sometimes broke in for a look, so obviously someone monitored the area because a new lock always appeared on the mesh wire fence at the end of the dirt road.

Ervin cut the lock with a pair of bolt cutters he kept in his truck for just such occasions before returning to his car, feeling drained of all energy. He needed to conduct his business and leave the property to avoid the risk of passing out and being found by the keeper of the grounds. More importantly, he needed to ditch the cube, so he drove a few donuts along the dirt-covered grounds to make it look as though teenagers were driving recklessly on the property, then steered directly toward the quarry where the ground was solid enough to avoid leaving tire tracks.

Nothing really blocked the entrance to the quarry, because the fence that once surrounded the property fell into disrepair years prior, and the watery pit actually resided a little more than twenty feet below the edge of the property. Ervin simply needed to drive to the edge of the property, step from his car, and drop the cube into the dark water below. Instead, he succumbed to the gunshot wound, feeling his head swirl before it fell back against the seat while his foot remained pressed against the accelerator.

Brief sounds entered his ears during his semi-conscious state, including glass cracking and shattering, along with water gushing nearby. He awoke once to find himself surrounded by complete darkness with freezing water up to his chest, still seated inside the Roadrunner. Wanting nothing more than to fight his way out of the dire predicament, Ervin felt his body betray him, lethargic and exhausted to the point that he barely felt the deadly chill of the water. He tried the door, finding the water pressure holding it in place against his diminished attempts to escape. Knowing an air pocket would remain in place for hours, possibly days, within the car, Ervin drifted into a permanent, peaceful slumber with false hope.

Chapter 8

Clay Branson continued to work part-time at the theme park, despite the season ending. All year round the property required security forces to keep trespassers away, because people wanted to sneak peeks at the coming year's new ride being constructed, or simply walk the grounds without crowds around. Clay could appreciate that sentiment, hating the hot summer days where he felt like an ant amongst millions of other ants, simply trying to plow his way through the wall of people.

The fact that Nosagi wanted him dead continued to plague him, though he didn't spend every minute of every day consumed with revenge or worry, especially around his fiancée. He hated keeping secrets from her, but telling her about Nosagi endangered her if Clay confronted his former master and failed.

Clay had other worries as his father's health declined, though he still refused to return home. He remained angry at his uncle for keeping secrets and nearly getting him killed, but mainly for keeping secrets.

Dressed for the cooler weather, Clay walked along the main drag where people first entered the theme park, trying the door to every restaurant and gift shop as he headed toward the rides. Quiet and abandoned for the winter, the rides often stood against the elements without coverings while their trains were taken to the maintenance shops for an overhaul. Mechanics and security guards occupied the park during the winter months until directors and managers returned in early spring.

No snow fell from the sky in the greater Cincinnati area, but the wind chilled to the bone. Clay hated doing foot patrols, but he couldn't inspect every inch of the property on a four-wheeler, or in one of the marked park police vehicles.

Shivering slightly, Clay moved to the end of the main drag toward the mammoth observation tower. During the season two elevators took guests to the top where they could gaze across the entire park, well above all of the rides and games. Several coin-operated telescopes were fixed along the security railing for better views of whatever guests wanted to see.

Clay simply stared upward, unable to see the telescopes from the ground, though he recalled several romantic encounters with Casey atop the tower after park hours.

His radio crackled momentarily before the voice of a fellow Mason police officer who worked security at the park called for him.

"Clay, I've got some people here at the employee gate who want to talk to you."

"Did they say who they were?" Clay asked, possessing no clue about who might want to speak with him.

"No, but they want me to tell you they have information about some guy named Nosagi," the officer asked more than stated.

Curiosity and a bit of shock caused him to stiffen when he heard the words.

"Please send them to our office, Cal," Clay replied after a few seconds.

Apprehensive, yet chomping at the bit to hear news of his former mentor, Clay fought the urge to powerwalk or run toward the security building. Hidden behind the high fences that separated the patrons from the inner workings, the security office sat apart from the other management facilities.

His instincts told him anyone wanting to kill him probably wouldn't stop at one of the main gates to announce their presence, but Clay wondered if anyone who knew about Nosagi could be on his side of the law. He crossed the median, circumventing the five large fountains normally surrounded by a large pool of water. Fenced in to keep guests away from the water, the fountains changed colors at night thanks to waterproof lights at their bases during the summer.

When he reached the office, Clay used his staff identification card to let himself in with a swipe through the electronic reader. He paced the floor a few minutes until Cal Unger brought a husky man in a suit and another man dressed in casual attire. The second man introduced himself as Paul Clouse, and the man who looked like a bodyguard as his associate Todd Parish.

Once Unger left, Clay offered the men seats in a nearby conference room where he sat across the table from them for observational and self-preservation purposes.

"How can I help you?" he asked, directing his question toward Clouse.

"I'm here to offer you a job," Clouse answered without hesitation. "There's no sense beating around the bush because I need your skill set to retrieve something important."

"What does this have to do with Nosagi?"

"Your former teacher has possession of the object I need."

Clay found himself somewhat confused because of the vague statements coming his way. The last thing he expected when he woke up and worked out that morning was a job offer and the chance to find his former mentor, but it sounded like both opportunities landed at his door.

"It sounds like I need to hear this from the beginning," he finally said.

Clouse spent nearly half an hour telling him a tale of how a friend betrayed his trust, all in the name of obtaining a red cube that gave the possessor back his or her youth if used regularly. He went on to tell about meeting Mark Teakon, and how the professor showed him that the red cube was only the beginning. By the time talk of a leather-bound book came up, Clay felt highly skeptical of the entire saga. Clouse proved he knew quite a bit about Nosagi and the man's plan to train assassins and use them for his own benefit.

"How exactly did I land on your radar?" Clay asked the question that was skimmed over during Clouse's talk.

"The terrorist incident was very public news," Clouse answered. "It didn't take much beyond a traditional background check to learn about your time in Japan, and the other terrorist incident in your hometown. The rest of the story just fell into place."

Clay rubbed his chin, still a bit skeptical about the man before him and the story he brought with him.

"So I'm to believe my former *sensei* possesses a cursed object in addition to heading up a criminal organization?" Clay questioned once Clouse finished, though he already knew the latter statement held true.

"He's isolated himself on an island just off the coast of South America," Clouse stated, unwavering in his composure. "The locals thought it was cursed before he arrived, and now they warn everyone to stay clear of the island."

"Why is that?"

"Because everyone who steps foot on the island dies, Mr. Branson. I know Nosagi possesses a cube that allows him to turn dead or inanimate objects into creatures that carry out his bidding. For every person he murders, he gains a new servant unable to question orders or be anything but loyal to his every command."

"This just seems a bit farfetched to me," Clay said hesitantly. "You're asking me to give up my life here to track down some cube and my former teacher who may or may not be where you say he is."

Clouse provided a weak grin.

"I understand your skepticism. At first I was the same way, which is why I brought you proof of Nosagi's whereabouts."

Clouse nodded to Parish, who opened a briefcase and pulled out a thin stack of photographs showing habitation on the island in the form of a lodge or retreat of some sort. In one of them, Clay could make out a man of Oriental descent relaxing on a lounge chair of some sort, surrounded by henchmen that looked unusually proportioned. Considering the image was taken from above, and so far away, Clay questioned the details, wondering if the photograph was some sort of hoax.

Any doubts were erased when he saw the next photograph, quite possibly taken from a boat anchored offshore. Clay saw what appeared to be the same man strolling along the sand near the water's edge. He stared downward, providing no clear look at his face, but the next few images showed him lifting his head to stare out to sea, providing a perfect look at his features. Though aged almost fifteen years, the man was indeed the instructor who misled Clay, murdered members of his family, and failed in turning him into the assassin he dreamed of leasing out for murders and thefts.

"This is no easy undertaking," Clouse said, seeing Clay's face flush with anger. "Just to get to Nosagi you'll have to literally fight off the army he's amassed over the past year."

"Why hole up on an island?" Clay asked no one in particular.

"He still has communication set up with his employees. If he learns that my group is aware of his possession of the cube, he'll certainly send someone after us. It's a perfect way for him to conduct business while staying off the radar."

"How did he come into possession of this cursed object?" Clay asked, though he still couldn't believe he was inquiring about something that sounded like it came from an original movie on the Science Fiction Channel.

Clouse tapped his fingers on the conference table a moment, looking to a list from his briefcase.

"Does the name Quinton Shelby Lucas sound familiar?"

"No."

"We think Nosagi assassinated him personally for some reason, probably stumbling upon the cube at the man's estate. The cubes tend to make their presence known when there's a chance someone new is willing to use them."

Clay gave a quizzical look, though he refused to inquire further. Only one thing consumed his mind at the moment.

Nosagi.

"I need to make some arrangements at work, but I want you to take me to this island."

"I'm not asking you to simply do this one job for me," Clouse said. "There are thirteen of these things, and I'm assembling a team to help me track them down before the wrong people find them."

"I have a good thing going here," Clay stated. "With Nosagi gone, I can finally live without looking over my shoulder. If I survive this confrontation, I'll bring you back your cube, but that's all I can promise at this point."

"I pay well," Clouse added. "Well enough for you to quit your job, help me with this, and continue your internship toward the security director's position."

Clay mentally admitted the man did thorough homework, though he still wasn't sold on the supernatural aspect of the job.

Clouse seemed to sense he wasn't going to budge on his stand regarding the one-time partnership to retrieve the cube, drawing a deep, patient breath.

"Fair enough," he said. "I'll take you to Nosagi, but you'll be accompanied by Todd here. Consider the job a trial basis, and once you see what I've told you is entirely true, we'll have a position waiting for you whenever you choose to join us."

"I work better alone," Clay said, looking toward Parish. "Other people will slow me down and endanger us all."

"Believe me, I don't plan on getting off the boat once we're there," Parish assured him with a serious look and tone.

"In that case," Clay said, "I have someone I want to bring along as well to make sure everyone is adequately represented."

Clouse smiled, but it faded quickly.

"Sounds like we have a deal. Make your arrangements and let me know when you're ready to head south."

"Soon," Clay assured him. "You're the small miracle I was waiting for, but I hope you don't harbor secrets like Nosagi, or it'll be you that I come after next."

"After what I've been through, I don't fear much," Clouse replied evenly. "I also have no reason to lie to people who think as I do. We're willing to risk our lives to keep the world safe from these *objects*, and I believe you'll come to think as we do."

"We'll see about that. I'm just glad my passport is in order. With luck, I won't need my affairs in order."

Clouse stood for them all to shake hands briefly.

"With luck, we'll all be standing here in a few weeks thankful to be alive."

All of them knew that failure on Clay's part might create a trickle effect that put Nosagi on the path of each and every one of Clouse's employees until he felt satisfied he was no longer a target. Clouse understood a toll needed to be paid for him to gather all of the cubes, but he hoped to avoid the steep price of human life whenever possible.

Chapter 9

"So what did you see?" Trudy asked with a hopeful gleam in her eyes.

"Nothing," Liz lied perfectly, not displaying any signs that she was still shaken by the events that entered her mind from the past. "I thought I had something there for a second, but it was a false triggering."

"Do you want to try a different badge?" Trudy offered, holding up the case with eyes that pleaded for Liz to make another attempt.

Liz honestly wanted to get out of the house immediately to jot down what she saw during the vision, but she wasn't about to arouse suspicion by doing so. She touched another badge, then another, truly getting no further results the second, third, or fourth time around. She finally shook her head negatively, prompting Trudy to stare despondently toward the floor.

"I'm sorry."

"It's okay. I guess I was just hoping for answers after all these years."

"We're not done searching just because Liz couldn't get something," Greene said, taking the pressure off his colleague. "There are other ways to find Tom. Somewhere, someone knows something."

Trudy looked up, on the verge of tears.

"I hope so. The one thing I have left is the hope that one day he'll walk through that door. Everyone says there's always hope until they find him, well, you know."

Greene nodded understandingly.

"I've seen crazier things happen."

It took a few minutes to settle Trudy down and guarantee her they would inform her of any findings before Greene and Liz left the house. Liz felt absolutely terrible for hiding her incredible new discovery from Trudy, but her reasons for doing so eased her guilty conscience. She knew danger followed their investigation wherever it went, and they were probably about to begin a paper trail that led to the quarry where Thomas Ervin met his end.

Snow continued to spit from the sky, landing on Liz as Greene opened the passenger side door for her. She buckled her seatbelt as Greene slid into the opposite seat, placing the key in the ignition before looking her way with an expectant look.

"You saw something, didn't you?"

"I saw quite a bit actually. Can we just get out of here?"

As Greene drove them toward some of the main roads, Liz informed him of what she saw during the vision. When she finished, Greene stared out the windshield at the snow splattering against the warm glass, pensively breathing.

"We need to find that quarry without calling attention to ourselves," he said at last. "If we go poking around, that's dangerous for everyone involved."

"The library," Liz suggested. "We look up some county geography without asking anyone or using the internet and we find out where there was a quarry, or we look for businesses that went under just south of Chicago."

"That could take some time."

"It beats having men with guns come after us or Trudy."

Liz hated the thought of placing Trudy in danger. Greene told her to assume everything they did was being monitored, because another group was simply waiting to swipe the cubes from them the minute they surfaced. The time cube, in the wrong hands, could simply end their existence at any point in time if their adversaries gained control of it.

Greene programmed their GPS to search for nearby libraries, coming up with several branches in Chicago and a few south of the city.

"The larger branches are more likely to have good resources," Greene stated.

"But the county libraries take more pride in their history," Liz countered. "I worked at a library for three years."

Perusing the options, Liz finally found one near the area she believed Tom Ervin drove to on the night he died. She would know from some of the landmarks when they neared the library, so she chose the Naperville Public Library.

"This one," she said, touching the screen to indicate where she wanted Greene to drive them. "If we're lucky, I'll recognize something along the way."

"A lot can change in thirty years."

"I know. It was dark and there weren't many landmarks, but if we find that bridge, I think I can navigate us to the quarry. And if we get to the library first, so be it."

Greene didn't appear as assured as Liz felt. She knew roads changed, and the occasional new building was erected, but she doubted the rural landscape changed drastically over the course of the past three decades. A strange feeling that they were being tailed kept nagging at her thoughts. If Clouse possessed the resources to conduct elaborate background checks on people and learn their traits, certainly other people and organizations were capable of doing the same thing.

Through the side window she observed the landscape transition from the cold industrial setting of factories and old brick houses to winding country roads and trees bare for the winter. Christmas was less than two weeks away, with a strong possibility it might be snowy white, unlike holidays from her childhood. No loving husband or boyfriend awaited her with open arms, or any children who stared eagerly beneath the tree for a wrapped surprise. Twice Liz had opened herself up fully for a relationship that appeared to be sailing toward marriage, but twice she found herself disappointed.

At times her gift felt like a curse, so she kept quiet about it for the longest time until recurring visions virtually forced her to aid the police in the search for a missing seven-year-old who was kidnapped. That particular story ended happily, with the boy returned to his parents, though most cases Liz assisted on didn't give families the conclusion they prayed would come. Liz hoped closure was enough for them, but she never kept in touch with families once they were given final word of their loved ones. She found the ordeal painful enough without trying to create bonds that served as painful reminders of those she couldn't help.

"We're here," Greene said after what seemed like only minutes because Liz had drifted off to sleep, the flurries outside putting her under their hypnotic spell.

The brisk air refreshed her when she opened the car door, like a bucket of water to the face. She followed Greene up the sidewalk, walking through the door as he opened it for her. Beneath his gruff exterior, including the thick beard and brown eyes that often narrowed, like those of a predatory animal seeking prey, Greene acted the part of a gentleman. She wondered if he felt somewhat helpless with the federal government behind him, though she suspected he didn't encounter the bottom of the criminal barrel in Nashville, Tennessee.

She felt safe with him, not in the romantic sense of *The Bodyguard*, but rather the professional detachment Kevin Costner's character showed initially. Greene appeared capable in every facet, which explained why Clouse chose him to head up their team, but something about his personality remained vacant.

One instant of physical contact might reveal his entire past to her, but Liz didn't want to know intimate details about her colleague. It was better, she decided, to let nature take its course and see if he spoke more about his background.

"Where to?" Greene asked once they found themselves inside the comfort and warmth of the public library.

"I'm going to see if they have a local or state publication area. You might want to try periodicals and check out defunct construction companies from the 70s."

Greene nodded before beginning his search for old newspapers, which Liz hoped might be loaded onto microfiche for ease and timesavings. She found the library indeed kept an Illinois Room loaded with books new and old that covered local and state events. Picking out several hardcover books that showed promise, she leafed through them for pictures or information about local quarries. Strangely, her vision failed to show her a single road sign, or any markings along the property where Thomas Ervin took his final breaths.

She wondered if they might have better luck simply driving around the county roads until she found a familiar landmark. Daylight disappeared around suppertime in the afternoon, which meant their window of opportunity was dwindling. The gray, gloomy skies permeated the library's interior, trying to down her mood and make her listless. Liz refused to give in, knowing she was so close to finding Thomas Ervin and bringing closure to his sister. She understood the score, meaning Trudy couldn't know any information until the cube was recovered. Many more lives were at stake if secrecy wasn't maintained until the blue square was in safe hands.

Receiving an answer to her query was as simple as asking a local what construction company once housed its operation atop a hill with a nearby quarry, but Liz understood that any paper trail or witnesses to their search could lead the wrong people back to them.

Or the cube.

She continued flipping through the pages of a county history book that covered buildings, outbuildings, and historical sites that had come and gone over the decades. Deciphering the age of any building during the course of a vision never proved easy, so she started at the turn of the Twentieth Century to avoid missing any useful information in case the building she saw replaced an older structure.

A strange sense that someone was watching her crept into her mind. Looking up, she saw the perpetual gloom outside, but she felt a presence behind her. Placing her hands over the book pages, she turned to look both ways behind her seat, finding no one in the room with her. No one stood at the framed entrance looking in, but she still sensed something, or someone, nearby with ill intent.

She wondered if the unseen, virtually unknown enemy might have contracted someone like her to give them an insider's advantage. Fighting the urge to find Greene, Liz cursed herself for acting like a scared schoolgirl as she turned the pages briskly. A shadow to her right caused her to look to the doorway as a librarian stood there with a friendly smile.

"Finding everything okay?"

"I think so," Liz answered as positively as she could muster.

"If you need anything, just let us know."

"Thank you."

Liz decided the book was written, or at least published on a local level. Someone invested a lot of time into the research of information and collection of photographs for the hardcover book. She looked through the images covering the first few decades, figuring a construction business in the county wasn't likely passed down through several generations. Based on the area's appearance in her vision, it was plausible the business opened and closed within a year or two.

Growing impatient and feeling on edge from the thought of being observed, Liz fought to keep her concentration on the pages, flipping through the 1940s and 1950s rather quickly. A strange sense that she was drawing near an answer caused her to examine each page a bit more thoroughly, even reading instead of skimming the text.

When Liz reached the year 1964 in the book, she found a familiar building pictured atop a hill listed as Clausen Excavation, which probably meant they bid out contracts for construction, or possibly dug for minerals where the quarry later existed. She now knew the location existed in the southern part of DuPage County, and amazingly the address was listed in a column right beside the photograph.

Pulling a scrap piece of paper from her handbag, Liz jotted down some information despite immediately committing the address to memory.

She closed the book with both hands, causing a clapping sound before she returned it to the shelf, disobeying library rules about not re-shelving books. She intentionally placed it far away from its original position, going through the trouble of turning the flat side toward her as she hid it behind a row of tall books. If anyone tried tracing her tracks, they weren't going to have an easy time of it.

As Liz left the room to find Greene, he walked the floor rather briskly toward her, a disconcerted look etched across his face.

"What's the matter?" she asked.

"We need to leave. *Now.*"

Liz was about to ask for elaboration when he took her by the wrist and led her toward the exit. She spied two men in dark suits exiting a black sedan through the door's glass just before Greene pulled her against a nearby wall, motioning for her to keep quiet with a finger to his lips. Concealed behind some shelving, they observed the two men walking through the entrance from a side view. Only when the men passed the front desk did Greene take Liz by the hand and dart out the entrance with her in tow.

"They could be looking for an overdue book repeat offender," Liz suggested jokingly as she opened the passenger side door.

"Fat chance," Greene retorted. "I've seen enough government spooks to know their kind."

Liz thought the men looked eerily like the mysterious men who chased Thomas Ervin through the very county where she now found herself teamed with Greene. They didn't wear fedoras, but they shared the same shrewd, dark eyes.

"They were packing guns," Greene informed her.

"How do you know that?"

"I'm trained to notice details, Liz. If I missed a suspect with a gun in my former life, he might shoot me in the back later."

He started the car, trying to back out of the parking lot undetected, but the two men burst through the front door at the moment the rental car hit the open road. Greene muttered a curse word under his breath before gunning the accelerator to put some distance between them and their new stalkers.

"These guys remind me a lot of the men who were after Tom Ervin," she confessed.

"That's not a good thing, considering how he ended up."

Greene took some corners rather hard, trying to remove them from the sight of their pursuers. Liz kept looking over her shoulder, seeing the black car quite a distance behind during the first few turns. It took a sharp right turn away from the business district for Greene to lose them as he parked the car behind a large dirt hill beside a vacant lot.

"Why would they risk coming after us in the open like that?" she questioned.

Not even breathing heavily for having narrowly escaped torture or death, Greene maintained his professional composure, again affirming why Clouse chose him over dozens of candidates to lead the search.

"That's awfully brazen," Greene admitted. "Whoever controls this particular cube literally controls the destiny for billions of people over time. And I struck out in the periodical section. I was standing to stretch my legs when I saw them pull up outside."

Liz gave him a cagy grin.

"I didn't strike out. In fact, I know exactly where to find the remains of Mr. Ervin."

"That's good news," Greene said, smiling for the first time the entire day. "Now we have to tread carefully."

Liz considered telling him about the feeling she was psychically being spied upon, but she wasn't certain she believed it herself. While it explained how the men were suddenly acutely aware of their location, she felt Greene was still put off by her abilities. The idea of her gift acting as a figurative modem, sending and receiving information, had never crossed her mind. While she didn't want to place their objective in jeopardy, Liz needed more proof before spilling the beans about her theory.

Right now she simply wanted to get Clouse the information and let him create a strategy for retrieving the most dangerous object in the world.

Chapter 10

Harlan Samuel Stone found himself working in the offices of the FBI in Albuquerque, New Mexico. Somewhat new to the Bureau, Stone found the job to his liking, though he wanted a transfer to his home state of Texas in the next few years.

Like many people born south of the Mason-Dixon Line, Stone was given two names that rolled off his mother's tongue whenever he did something wrong as a child. He couldn't count the number of times he heard "Harlan Samuel!" during his childhood. By his teenage years Stone grew to hate the sound of both names, so he tried whenever possible to have friends and schoolmates call him by his last name or the ever-popular "Stoney" nickname.

No longer in the Hoover days, agents enjoyed a more casual atmosphere at work. Though much of the work was white collar in nature, Stone found it a welcome change from patrol duties in Houston. Sitting at his desk, perusing a case file regarding an abduction that crossed state borders between Arizona and New Mexico, Stone fought the urge to prop his feet atop the desk for more comfortable reading. Civilians worked in the office, and both suspects and witnesses crossed the FBI offices, so he dared not visibly relax.

At home it wasn't uncommon for him to kick back on the front porch and watch the world pass him by. In the county he saw more activity from wildlife than people and traffic, which suited him just fine.

"Still daydreaming that we'll get assigned to that case?" Dom Givens asked, seated at the desk across from Stone.

"Why does the SAC hate us so much?" Stone asked, putting on his glasses with his free hand to see his colleague more clearly.

Stone referred to Bryson Elliot, the Special Agent in Charge of their field office.

"What you mean to ask is why does he hate *you* so much? I got nothin' in it."

Givens was a black man born and raised in California who volunteered for an assignment in New Mexico because his wife's family resided in Santa Fe. He and Stone got along very well, often working cases together, but Stone openly disliked the SAC, which meant he and Givens shared joint punishment.

Stone tossed the file atop the desk in disgust, wanting to investigate more than his desk and the nearest restroom. After a stint of tedious surveillance duty on a man suspected of aiding his brother-in-law with hacking a local government website, Stone found himself in possession of a list of potential terrorism suspects. Ordinarily the assignment might be invigorating, but he quickly discovered different lists were assigned to each team and his suspects were the least threatening, and least likely to be affiliated with terrorists.

He currently hated life.

"Where did you get that file anyway?" Givens asked.

"I lifted it off of Harrison's desk. I feel like one of those people who have to read fiction to escape their humdrum lives."

"Your life will be a lot more exciting in the unemployment line, Harlan Samuel."

Stone gave a sharp-edged grin.

"I'll keep that in mind, Dom. What kind of respectable mother names her son Dom anyway? I've been meaning to call your mom and ask her. It sounds like you should be doing hits for the mob."

Givens shook his index finger at Stone. The two often chided one another over their personal lives to relieve work tension.

"Oh, so you think I should be a Tyrell, or maybe a Jermaine? Something a little more urban, like maybe Darnell that says I just missed the cut for the NBA? You know Dom is short for Dominic, right?"

"I'm well aware as you've told me a dozen times or better. It just never gets old getting a rise out of you."

"You ain't seen a rise out of me, Harlan Samuel."

"I never should have told you my middle name."

Givens grinned mischievously.

"Your dear mother did the honors when she told me all about your upbringing."

"She's getting coal for Mother's Day."

Stone picked up the file, walking it back to his fellow agent's desk where it belonged. It burned him that the SAC disliked him because he didn't hide the fact that he was a proud Texan currently stuck one state away. When he started with the branch, Stone put the other agents to shame with his tenacity and fearless attitude. He didn't care what parts of town he entered, or what prominent citizens he needed to interrogate to solve a case. Things only got better when the powers that be paired him with Givens, thinking the two were destined to mix like oil and water. And while a complete stranger might think they hated one another to the core sometimes, they actually enjoyed working as a team.

"You are such a racist," Givens joked when Stone returned to his desk.

"How can you say that? You're the one renaming yourself. Besides, I've eaten what your wife calls barbeque and said nothing derogatory about it."

"You Texans and your food," Givens said, shaking his head.

"We do it right over there. I can't help that you yuppies from California only eat nuts and berries."

"There you go again, Stoney. You just see me as Trivette to your Walker."

"Hey, Trivette was smart."

"And I'm not?"

Stone threw up his hands.

"I wasn't saying that! I'm just saying give the man some credit."

One of the female agents walked past the duo, giving them a quizzical stare.

"Don't you two have anything better to do than insult one another's heritage?"

"Actually, we're about due to violate some poor schmuck's civil rights because Lord Elliot deems it necessary," Stone answered.

He was about to make another comment sure to land him in hot water with the SAC when the phone atop his desk rang. Based on the ring, he knew the call was from within the building, and not from an outsider. Scooping it from the receiver, he wondered if Elliot was spying on him with hopes of accumulating enough dirt to fire him.

"Stone."

"Harlan, it's Sandy. Can you come to my desk, hon?"

"Sure," he replied to Elliot's secretary, wondering if he was about to be terminated after all.

Unlike Elliot, Sandy Newberry was a joy to be around on a daily basis. She had worked under two previous administrators, admitting to Stone that Elliot displayed the most temperamental personality of the three. She gave Stone insight about the reasons Elliot probably didn't like him, but none of it eased the tension because Stone wasn't about to change to appease his boss.

Despite his comment a moment earlier, Stone wasn't doing any fieldwork because of the late afternoon hour. He planned on heading home to see his wife soon because Elliot never gave him meaningful work that inspired him to work long hours. Stone played along, not wishing to lose his job, though he wished he could wriggle out from beneath the SAC's thumb long enough to get a transfer to his home state.

Elliot enjoyed tormenting him too much for that to happen anytime soon.

"What was the call about?" Givens questioned.

"Sandy had something for me. Maybe Bryson took an early retirement."

"The boy needs to."

Stone gave a halfhearted smile as he stood, ready to face whatever new punishment the SAC wanted to hand him.

Wearing dress slacks with a starched white shirt, Stone resembled the old-school FBI most agents fought to abolish. On this day he wore a tie bearing the Texas state flag in its bold red, white, and blue colors wrapped several times around the accessory. He wore a western style belt, since buckles were frowned upon at the workplace, though he did opt to wear shined black cowboy boots instead of shoes.

"It's no wonder he hates me," Stone said under his breath as he walked down the hallway, the clopping sound of his boots preceding him as he entered the SAC's office.

Relieved to see Elliot's door shut, and the lights off, Stone gave Sandy a smile as he placed both arms on her desk and leaned forward slightly.

"How's my favorite cowboy?" she asked in a slightly more cheerful tone than usual, indicating she indeed had good news.

"I reckon I'm doing fine," he said, intentionally letting his drawl slip.

He fought to suppress his accent and language on a daily basis because he couldn't be taken seriously as a federal agent if he spoke words like "y'all" and "cattywompus" on a regular basis. Only Sandy and his wife saw Stone's natural demeanor because he felt comfortable around them.

"What's the news, darlin'?" Stone asked.

"You're going to Washington."

"Washington?" Stone retorted, taken aback. "What the hell for?"

"I don't know. The Deputy Director wants to meet with you personally."

Stone waited for the punch line, or someone to call him to let him off the hook from whatever prank they were pulling. No agent in the field met with the Director or Deputy Director, or anyone higher than their SAC for that matter. Considering the unremarkable nature of his career lately, Stone couldn't fathom why anyone with clout would want to meet with him. Anyone with dreams and ambitions at work the past few months had avoided him like the plague.

"You're serious?" he finally asked, raising an eyebrow while doing his best to give a penetrating stare.

"Yes," Sandy said with a chuckle. "You're on the eight o'clock flight from Albuquerque International to Washington National."

He felt certain his jaw dropped, giving him the dumbfounded look he felt through and through.

"What? Tonight?"

"Can't keep the Deputy Director waiting, Stoney. He wants to meet with you immediately."

Stone looked to his watch, realizing he might need to use his credentials just to ensure he made the flight. Just over three hours to go home, pack, change, and make it through the airport security checkpoints didn't seem feasible, but he sensed urgency enough to make it happen.

"Here's your flight information," Sandy said, handing him a packet.

He leafed through the paperwork as though it might be a hoax, or part of some delusional dream, finding it completely authentic.

"Thanks," he said, starting to walk away almost absentmindedly.

"Don't forget us little people when you get your office with a view."

"Yeah, right," Stone said with a laugh as he picked up his pace, ready to see what new chapter awaited him.

***

Amazed he didn't have to catch a connecting flight, Stone decided the Deputy Director truly wanted to see him right away. He read two newspapers during the flight, tried to sleep, and even watched the in-flight movie just to pass the time, hoping to keep his nervous jitters at bay. Barely able to remember running home to pack, Stone felt as though a hurricane carried him through packing a small suitcase, quickly explaining the surprise to his wife, and finally to the airport where he used his credentials to bypass several levels of security so he could travel armed.

Stone soon discovered the small airliner was nearly filled to capacity, explaining why it never landed until reaching Washington D.C. Most of the people were dressed for business, obviously part of the Washington crowd. Based on observations alone, he figured at least two Congressmen were flying with him, talking with their aides during much of the flight.

Thanks to a phone call from Sandy, Stone found a rental car waiting for him at the airport. While his travels never took him to the nation's capital, Stone followed directions well, so he soon found his way to the hotel where he was booked, which also happened to be where the Deputy Director requested to meet him.

Bright, dazzling lights weren't new to the federal agent, but Stone found himself swelling with pride just stepping foot in Washington. To think, dozens of United States Presidents lived and served there, monuments and treasures were housed within the sacred city, and even the tragic events of 9/11 had touched the city with the icy finger of death. It was almost immediately after the terrorist attacks that the FBI went from chasing white-collar criminals to battling terrorism and tracking down spies.

Somewhat disappointed that Alan Stewart didn't request a meeting at FBI Headquarters, Stone figured the man had his reasons, particularly since the time change meant the midnight hour had come and gone a few hours prior.

He found himself wondering what kind of FBI leader summoned a typical everyday agent for a late night meeting outside of official offices, though he tried to avoid dwelling on the topic.

Even the adrenaline from anticipating the meeting failed to keep fatigue from setting in as Stone pulled into the hotel parking lot. He received a parking voucher, parked the rental in the nearby parking lot, then walked toward the hotel with a purpose. Sixteen stories loomed above him, but Stone observed an outdoor pool, closed for the winter, adjacent to an interior lounge housing a pool, sauna, and hot tub. A few signs indicated the hotel restaurant, which included a bar, remained open for another hour. It looked high dollar to Stone, but for some reason he expected he might find his answers waiting inside.

Instead of entering the restaurant, Stone walked through the one remaining unlocked door toward the front desk to check in. He decided to test the waters, wanting to spy the Deputy Director before Stewart laid eyes on him. Besides, he didn't want to act anxious, even if the anticipation was eating him from within. His armpits felt damp and sticky from both excitement and nervousness, considering Stone had never been summoned by anyone higher than his direct supervisors before.

A few minutes later he pocketed two keycards to his room before turning around to find a man wearing a suit standing behind him. While the Bureau had changed significantly over the past few decades, he felt certain the man wasn't seasoned enough to hold an administrative position in the organization.

"Please follow me, Agent Stone," the man said immediately with no introduction.

Still carrying his small suitcase, Stone followed the stranger into the restaurant, directly over to the bar. The man ducked into a segregated room momentarily before emerging to wave Stone into the same area. He let Stone pass, standing erectly at the door like a security agent, so Stone set the suitcase at his feet before entering the room with a single covered table.

A well-dressed man with salt and pepper hair stood to shake hands with Stone, a very wide smile crossing his lips.

"Agent Stone, Alan Stewart," he said, introducing himself.

"Deputy Director," Stone replied respectfully. "It's good to meet you."

"Have a seat," Stewart offered. "Would you like a drink?"

Stone gave him a skeptical look, wondering if business hours were truly over considering the apparent urgency of the meeting.

"You're off the clock," the Deputy Director stated.

"In that case I'll take a draft beer."

"I had you pegged for more of a scotch man," Stewart stated before calling out their drink order to the bartender just outside the isolated room.

"Only when things aren't going so well," Stone replied.

The agent escorting Stewart brought in their drinks momentarily. Stone only took a swig when the Deputy Director raised his glass, feeling like he might explode from curiosity.

"I have a new job title for you, if you're willing to accept it," Stewart said, cutting to the chase before taking another healthy drink from the glass.

Stone took a deep breath, trying to find the right words to speak.

"I know, you're wondering why you of all people," Stewart stated for him.

"You read my mind."

"It's not just one reason, Harlan. You've had ambitions since you were a teenager that still haven't materialized. First and foremost, you joined the Houston Police Department hoping to make your way into the Texas Rangers someday. In order to bolster your résumé, you worked your way into the Bureau so you could gain experience in investigations. Do I paint a reasonably accurate picture so far?"

"You're not too far off," Stone replied, not thrilled about having his failed ambitions laid out before him.

"Freshly married, you just turned thirty-six, and you have a supervisor who isn't thrilled about your aggressive tactics or your stand on your home state because he favors the Oklahoma Sooners. You want action, but Elliot holds you back because of some weak grudge. Your record is impeccable, you possess a bachelor's degree in law enforcement from Texas State University, and you dress like us old-timers. I see you left your boots behind in lieu of shined shoes, which I hope you didn't do on my account."

Stone gave a sheepish grin, hating how right the man was about every detail. Stewart possessed ideal intelligence about Stone, as though he'd taken a personal interest in him for quite some time.

"You don't need to hide who you are around me," Stewart said with a dismissive wave of his hand. "There's no need to hide your accent or dress differently for my sake. I want to offer you an assignment that will take you off the grid and put you working directly under me. You'll be a rogue agent of sorts, watching highly dangerous individuals for the sake of national security. That is, assuming of course, that you're interested in hearing about this position."

"You have my attention, sir. But this sounds like more surveillance."

"It's not just monitoring their activities, Harlan. These people are after lethal weapons of mass destruction and they're Americans, just like us. I'm asking you to put a stop to domestic terrorism by any means. There's no need for me to butter you up, but you're an expert marksman, you speak Spanish well enough, and you've studied both jujitsu and tae kwon do, so I know you can take care of yourself. Are you up for some action?"

Stone didn't like the vague nature of his assignment, but he supposed he could sort out the details later. Working directly under the Deputy Director promised a lot of clout for his future with the Bureau, and anywhere else he chose to seek employment.

"You do this, and do it well, and I'll see what we can do about getting you in with the Rangers, if that's what you still want."

Taking a hearty swig from the beer, Stone looked Stewart in the eye with subtle delight that came from ascension to better places.

"I'm in, sir."

"Good," Stewart said, leaning back with a smile. "I hope your passport is in order, because you're going to South America in the very near future."

Stone tilted his head in curiosity, wondering just how far his new position was going to take him in both position and geographical locations.

Chapter 11

Todd Parish decided he liked being on a fishing trawler better than bobbing and weaving on the Pacific Ocean west of Peru. While Clouse had arranged reasonable travel conditions that kept Parish, Clay Branson, and Bill Branson out of the public eye, Parish still felt certain they were being followed.

One positive aspect was that Clouse decided to wait until after the Christmas holiday to send the trio on this particular mission. Nosagi wasn't going anywhere, and another pressing matter regarding a different cube came to Clouse's attention. It seemed the other situation required assistance from lawyers, and some research into property rights before a plan was formed.

Strangely enough, the current mission lacked thorough planning, only because no one ever laid eyes on the island and survived. Satellite images and distant photographs provided very little intelligence about the nature of Nosagi's defense. Parish hated being outnumbered, feeling that the Bransons brought a different agenda with them, though Bill didn't seem thrilled about giving up a weekend to assist in the effort. His nephew kept saying something about Bill owing him, though Parish knew none of the details.

After Clouse's personal pilot flew them to South America in a private jet, the gear was unloaded without much inspection by local officials. They seemed more interested in the money tossed their way to help unload the disguised gear and place it on the boat the group rented. Each of the three men dressed the part, acting as though they were fishing at some company's expense, but the gear was not fishing poles, lures, and bait. Instead, a variety of weapons and equipment remained inside the packs until the boat was at sea.

Not a large boat by any means, the fishing vessel fought the ocean surface the entire way, occasionally feeling like a toy being pushed back by the choppy waves. More than half an hour passed before anyone even spoke, creating even more tension between the three men who felt unhappy about the trip for various reasons. Parish busied himself by pulling his familiar AR-15 from a footlocker, checking it for damage while making certain the spare magazines were all present. Bill steered the boat toward their designated location, using a small GPS mounted beside the steering wheel to guide him.

"I'm still not happy with you dragging me along on this," Bill said heatedly to his nephew, as though the statement required some built up courage on his part. "When I offered my assistance, I didn't think you'd honestly drag me this close to your mentor. You're damn lucky I have a passport."

"And you're damn lucky I'm alive after what you pulled," Clay retorted, seated on an overturned crate as he inspected some gear. "I could've ended this a long time ago if you had said something."

Parish tried not to listen, but with only three of them on a medium-sized fishing boat he found it hard to ignore conversation.

"The locals call this place *la isla de la muerte*, Clay," Bill said, his voice trembling with concern. "Do you know what that means?"

"The island of the dead," Parish stated, casually inspecting his Glock sidearm. "I heard some fishermen saying to avoid the area before we left."

"I *know* what it means," Bill said with open frustration, shooting Parish a testy look as his nephew said nothing, simply checking over his own array of bladed weapons. "I just want to know why we're doing this, or why we couldn't just leave well enough alone."

"You didn't tell him?" Parish asked Clay, concerned that Bill really had no idea what he was motoring toward.

Clay looked up without so much as a grin.

"You mean your ghost tale about cursed objects and zombies running around the island? Of course not."

"What is he talking about?" Bill asked Clay, who simply shrugged both of his companions off, focusing on his weapons instead.

"It's a little hard to explain," Parish began, "but my group is chasing after thirteen cursed objects that individually do a lot of harm, but together might bring about the end of the world."

"I've heard of cursed objects," Bill replied, flushing red in his face before turning his attention to his nephew. "And you failed to bring this up, Clay?"

"The way you failed to mention my mentor is secretly the leader of an assassination guild?" Clay fired back, standing to get face to face with his uncle.

Parish spotted something in the distance, feeling certain they were approaching their target island.

"I hate to break up this family squabble, but I think we're within range."

All three men stood silently a moment, staring toward the small island with limited greenery, some natural rock structures, and possibly some sand near the water. It hardly looked like paradise, but the island didn't show obvious signs of peril or death. Only the sloshing of small waves licking the boat and the purring of the boat's motor broke the silence momentarily until Bill broke the silence.

"What exactly is the plan?"

"I'm going alone to confront Nosagi. If I survive, I'm bringing Mr. Parish here a souvenir to take home to his boss."

"Are you sure you want to go alone?" Parish questioned. "I'm not sure you're comprehending the serious nature of what you're going to find on that island."

Clay shook his head negatively.

"Regardless of what I find on that island, it's going to be made from organic material. I think I can take care of anything organic with this."

Holding up a modified, razor-sharp *katana* with a slightly shortened blade, Clay slid it into its sheath before packing the sword and other weapons into a small pack he then placed on his back for easy transit. Parish observed him putting on a modified gun belt that holstered a semi-automatic Glock 17 on each side. What little glimpse Parish got caused him to believe the guns were modified to house larger, more deadly rounds. Perhaps Clay worried about more than just reanimated corpses after all.

"Sure you don't want any backup?" Parish asked.

"I'm sure. If I'm successful, I'll shoot up a flare to let you know. Give me an hour, and if you haven't gotten a sign, you two better get out of here."

Parish hated the idea of standing by, but he knew what kind of culture Clay and his former mentor lived and breathed. A common man posed little threat to those trained in the ancient art of assassination. He wondered how Clay entered such a life as an American, but he figured he and Bill had plenty of time to discuss matters once Clay departed for the island.

With each passing second the boat drew closer to the island, which now had a background of dark, ominous clouds. Distant thunder rolled, adding to the trepidation of the moment, each of the men now having some understanding of the danger ahead.

"This should be good," Clay said quietly when the boat was within swimming distance of the island.

Despite the choppy water and hidden dangers on land, Clay made certain his weapons were securely attached to his modified backpack and gun belt before diving in without another word.

"Is he always like that?" Parish asked Bill.

"He's a bit embittered lately. A lot of that is my fault."

"My employer seemed to think he's the best man for the job, even if Clay doesn't."

"Oh, he's good alright. I just hope he's aware of the danger his former mentor poses. The man has tried to kill him twice now."

"Let's hope the third time isn't a charm."

***

In a move to conserve energy, Clay only paddled when the tide carried him toward the shore because each time it returned the water erased some of his progress. Truth be told, he didn't want to believe a legion of the undead awaited him ashore, but the battle with Nosagi was certain to take a toll on his body. Any additional surprises required expending energy before the life and death struggle, so he decided to let the tide work for him.

His thoughts drifted to Casey momentarily, and how he longed to see her again. Clay quickly put his emotions to bed, knowing they sapped his focus like a leech. Confronting Nosagi and surviving the encounter required every ounce of his concentration and mental sharpness he could muster.

While the ground froze solid close to Cincinnati, Clay found the water approaching the island warm like a soothing outdoor bath. He sensed grave danger once the tide washed him closer to the shore, his feet touching the jagged rocky bottom for the first time since leaping from the boat. Wearing athletic shoes that were a new hybrid for water and land, often used by triathlon competitors, Clay avoided scrapes or cuts along his feet. Had he chosen to don the traditional clothing he wore in Japan, like the ninja footwear known as the *ikitabi*, his chances of being battered and bruised would have gone up significantly.

He hoped nothing happened to his uncle, or Parish, because he felt completely responsible. If the choice were his, he would have come alone to confront Nosagi, but Clouse wasn't going to provide him with the location unless he brought Parish.

A bargain was a bargain.

Wearing a form of durable hiking shorts, along with a tank top, Clay remained comfortable, though he felt like he was betraying some of the traditions he learned in the Orient. He supposed his mentor had long since abandoned some of those same principles, so he didn't dwell on his thoughts. He hoped his clothing might dry out before he confronted Nosagi, but he wasn't wasting one precious second standing on the beach. About twenty feet of bleached sand awaited Clay, scrunching beneath his feet as he walked toward the thicket of trees awaiting him. The rocks, as it turned out, were a small mountain of sorts beyond the wooded area on the opposite end of the island.

And while the island wasn't very large, the wooded area ahead showed Clay no visible end. He trudged across the remainder of the beach, entering a labyrinth of trees, vines, and various shrubs that failed to make room for any kind of manmade trail. Clay was almost certain the intelligence was entirely false, or they picked the wrong island to land upon when he spied activity ahead.

Oh, crap, Clay thought as numerous figures appeared from behind trees and large rocks. He quickly assessed the situation, memorizing the position of each human figure while conducting a head count. Clay found eleven figures from left to right, none of them still among the living based on the level of decay on each body. Each of the reanimated dead stared at him with blank, glassy eyes, silent as they stood in place, as though awaiting a command. Tattered clothing dripped from each of the male zombies, a few of them holding firearms while the rest gripped rocks or heavy sticks.

"Guess they weren't lying," Clay said to himself, reaching behind him to pull his sword from its scabbard with deliberation.

Utilizing a different strategy than usual, since the undead couldn't be killed, Clay needed to blind his adversaries so they couldn't attack in mass, or track him. Beyond that, he needed to disable them, which might require a bit more analysis and experimentation. Clay scooped up several rocks from the sand as he picked up his pace, jogging toward the leftmost adversaries partially obscured by the vegetation. The second from the left wielded an automatic weapon of some sort, so Clay flung the rocks toward its eye sockets, hitting the mark just enough to throw the military uniformed zombie's head back. Already at a full sprint, Clay ignored the undead flanking his left and right, charging instead toward the armed threat in the center. His *katana* found its mark, severing the head and both hands in one swift motion as the body parts and rifle fell to the ground.

Checking for booby-traps in the woods while being pursued, even for someone with Clay's skill set and sense of danger, wasn't a wise move. He decided to stand his ground at the edge of the woods, using limited cover to engage the small army that had already begun closing on his position with the disabling of their first member. The headless, handless body still squirmed and moved on the ground, determined to the last to assault Clay in some fashion. Ignoring it, Clay beheaded the body to his left, then another one to his right before they could strike him with blunt weapons.

The familiar sound of a gun clacking reached his ears, so Clay dove into the brush for cover, able to see one of the other animated dead pointing another automatic weapon in his direction. Bullets sprayed the shrubs where Clay initially ducked for cover, but he continued to move into the woods like a snake keeping contact with the ground. Only able to obey simple commands, the undead minion continued firing in exactly the same spot until the magazine ran empty a few seconds later. Clay emerged from the woods like a charging predator from the African safari, cutting down more of the enslaved men who weren't at peace. Heads, hands, and the occasional foot landed atop the beach with minimal red splatters, since the lifeblood belonging to the mindless slaves stopped flowing weeks and months prior.

Like a whirlwind, Clay spun, sliced, and observed with uncannily trained diligence as his body stayed in motion. He noticed one of the remaining undead gripping a sidearm, raising it to take aim as Clay downed one of his fellow zombies with a precision slice of the neck using the *katana*. All of the undead minions moved stiffly, as though simply commanded to defend the interior of the woods from which they emerged. An ordinary man, even a soldier, could easily be outnumbered and murdered by the mob while carrying standard firearms. Explosives, or a sword for that matter, changed the odds considerably.

Seeing the gun aimed in his direction, Clay grabbed a headless corpse before it collapsed, using it as a shield to absorb the bullets. He could have thrown a weapon to blind or disable the armed dead man, but Clay knew once the bullets were spent, he needed only expend enough energy to chop off potentially harmful body parts before proceeding into the woods.

Ironically, the corpse appeared to have been shot or stabbed in the chest, one eye now drooping from its socket. His once beige dress pants were torn and tattered below the knees, while his white dress shirt indicated previous struggles because of the brown and green stains permanently etched within its fabric. The dead man's skin, now a pallid greenish color from its original olive shade, showed minimal signs of decay, as though the animated dead's regular movement kept it from falling apart. The collective made no sounds, like the moaning and groaning zombies make in horror movies, which caused Clay to believe Nosagi somehow instructed them on exactly how to behave and defend the island when he took control of them.

Clay threw the bullet-riddled body to the ground before using his sword to continue mowing through the legion of the undead. It took less than a minute for him to leave a trail of body parts in his wake before he stood on the beach, observing his work to ensure no stragglers remained. Convinced none of the former human beings were left standing, Clay prepared to enter the woods when the sound of plant life being trampled reached his eardrums. Holding his *katana* before him, Clay looked at the second defense wave reaching the edge of the woods, far more dangerous than the first because it wasn't made of flesh and blood.

"Shit," he muttered, seeing more undead and nearly a dozen tribal statues ready to pulverize him.

Chapter 12

It took a good five minutes before Parish or Bill looked at one another or spoke. They busied themselves with cleaning weapons or checking gauges on the boat. Both worried about the outcome on the island for different reasons. Perhaps those reasons kept them from speaking cordially, or Bill simply remained upset for being dragged along on a highly dangerous trip. From what Parish learned, Bill possessed no military or police background, and his engineering degree helped little on an uncharted island.

"This whole cursed object issue," Bill finally said, sauntering toward Parish who continued to inspect his AR-15. "Is it the real deal, or were you just trying to exaggerate the danger to get Clay onboard?"

By now Parish had changed clothes, wearing a black flak vest over a black shirt and tech pants that provided plenty of pockets. Several knives and other assorted weapons were stuffed into the vest and Parish's gun belt. He also kept an additional survival knife strapped to his leg with a Velcro sheath. Staying vigilant in case anything followed Clay from the island, or Clay didn't come back at all, Parish continued preparing for the worst possible scenario.

"It's not my story to sell," Parish answered without looking up from his gun. "But if it makes you feel better, I've seen the objects up close and personal."

"What do they do?"

"They cause men to kill one another for personal gain. There are thirteen of them, and each one does something different."

Bill put his hands up to his head in frustration.

"This is all too much. It's bad enough Clay's mentor wants him dead and then I find out he's mixed up in cursed objects? This can't be happening."

"Take it easy," Parish said, putting forth some compassion. "Clay is going to take care of Nosagi, get the cube, and the world will be a little safer."

"And that's why you're putting together a weapons depot over there?"

Parish grinned.

"What can I say? I like my guns."

Standing, Parish looked to the island, seeing the blue-green water move toward the island before returning. The boat, now anchored, continued to bob gently as the dark clouds in the background appeared to be moving beyond the island instead of heading their way.

"How much trouble could my nephew be in?"

"It's hard telling," Parish answered. "We're not sure how long Nosagi has been holed up on the island, or *why* for that matter."

"How the hell does he get supplies?"

"He must have transportation, but we never spotted any planes or boats in our images."

Parish wondered how many tourists had traveled to the island, only to find a nasty surprise awaiting them. Surely search parties went looking for the missing tourists and locals, only to find themselves victims of Nosagi's traps.

Gunfire suddenly erupted, shattering any preemptive thoughts that might have been forming in Parish's mind. He scooped up nearby high-power binoculars, observing Clay's progress on the island as he emerged from a thicket of shrubs, tearing into what appeared to be human forms standing stiffly on the beach. No one with any sense of tactics simply stood in place with a blunt weapon, Parish deduced, until he saw the group act collectively, trying to bring Clay down by converging upon him.

"Should we do something?" Bill asked, peering through a second set of binoculars.

"I think he's got it handled."

"It's my fault he's in this predicament."

"Sounds like he would have come after Nosagi regardless of when he found out the truth," Parish said calmly, observing Clay cut down the undead as though they were store mannequins.

A different splashing sound than the water lapping the boat reached Parish's ears, distracting him from the beach battle. He held the binoculars at his chest, scanning the water for any kind of intrusion, wondering if something from the island detected their presence. Few dangerous ocean creatures resided near the island, and Parish doubted any sharks or large sea dwellers were going to attack a recreational boat. He leaned over the rear of the boat, looking for anything foreign in the water. The boat wasn't close enough to shore for him to see the seabed, but Parish saw some ripples coming around the back of the boat, as though something in the water took time enough to observe them.

"What is it?" Bill asked.

"I'm not sure, but I don't think we're alone."

Parish started to reach for the AR-15 to provide some firepower against whatever object was large enough to create wave-like ripples if it showed itself. He failed to make it before a large anaconda with numerous injuries to its exterior surfaced along the boat's aft end. Mesmerized by the grand scale of the serpent, Parish continued to slowly reach his right arm toward the rifle, studying the exterior of the serpent.

Probably twenty feet in length, the snake slithered in a swimming motion along the water's surface, but Parish noticed something not quite right.

"Holy shit," Bill muttered, catching a glimpse of the reptile for the first time.

"It's not alive," Parish said, taking notice of the pale skin and multiple wounds along the scales and flesh. "It's reanimated just like the hoard Clay is facing."

Not only was the exterior flesh damaged, but several gaping holes appeared a few feet behind the head, near the halfway mark, and closer to the tail. Such wounds in any organism were fatal, confirming Parish's statements. His firearms weren't going to kill something already dead, though bullets might rip apart the snake's long frame enough that it fell apart when it tried to attack them.

"It can't get us up here, can it?" Bill asked, backing away from the railing.

"Don't be so sure," Parish answered, touching the AR-15's cool metal as the head of the snake launched from the water directly toward him.

He tried to retreat from the surprising attack, but the decaying mouth of the snake, without the restrictions that living muscles and tendons brought about, snagged him by the head and shoulders. Without time to react, Parish found himself pulled into the water as the snake immediately tried to wrap itself around his torso. The same freedom that didn't restrict its mouth from opening prevented it from truly constricting around him, though it held his right arm in place so he couldn't swim very well using conventional strokes.

Apparently content just to sink to the bottom and drown Parish, the reanimated anaconda didn't readjust its position until Parish wriggled his arm free from the loose grip. Considering he barely took a breath before the sneak attack, Parish fought and kicked his way toward the surface, reaching it seconds later. He gasped for a breath of fresh air, finding Bill scrambling for a weapon or method to combat their adversary. Unfortunately for Parish his efforts to survive allowed the deceased guardian to reposition its body for a different sort of attack.

Parish felt additional weight on his legs as he fought to stay near the surface, grasping for the boat's rear railing. He clutched the railing at the very second he lost the ability to kick because pressure surrounded his legs, immobilizing them rather effectively.

"Find something sharp," Parish stammered before the snake yanked him underwater once more.

The pressure that started around his legs now moved up to his waistline, and Parish realized he was being swallowed by the anaconda. He knew under ordinary circumstances the pressure of the animal's muscles crushed ingested prey, suffocating it if necessary before digestion began. In this case, however, the muscles fit like a stretched sock, effective enough to swallow him easily, but incapable of constricting or putting crushing force on him.

Parish fought to reach the water's surface once more, but after a few decisive gulps, the snake swallowed him whole. He felt his captor swimming toward the sea floor, apparently making a second effort at drowning him. Parish fought against the skin, testing how much play the dead tissue provided him for movement.

Suddenly the anaconda changed directions and swam toward the surface, allowing him a breath through one of the three gaping wounds along the skin when it rose above the water. Trying not to panic, Parish thought of only one reason the snake might choose to surface over attempting to drown him.

It wanted to ensnare Bill Branson and get a double kill for its efforts.

***

Though Bill might have looked like a panicked mouse trying to escape being a serpent's lunch, his experiences with danger and near death helped him keep his wits about him. He searched the boat for weapons other than firearms, or something to help him trap the reanimated beast. He quickly located a machete used for cutting tangled lines or burdensome dock moorings, scooping it up before returning to the boat's aft section.

Several seconds passed without any sign of Parish or the anaconda, including any kind of splashing or bubbles from beneath. Bill almost wrote off his traveling companion when the snake surfaced in search of something.

Him.

Half of the snake was bloated, indicating it had swallowed something. At first Bill figured Parish was a goner, either drowned or suffocated by the snake's tissues conforming to his body and leaving no air pockets to breathe. A few seconds later, however, Bill felt his heart race at the fact he wasn't necessarily alone in his struggle against the undead creature just yet.

Bill could barely see Parish's face through one of the gaping wounds along the snake's body, trying to breathe before the animal dove below the surface again. The outline of Parish's fingertips along the snake's loosely fitting skin showed as ten bumps and a bit of his palm pushing against the skin to keep it from suffocating him further. He attempted to speak through the hole as the anaconda spotted Bill before advancing toward the boat, its tail end swishing back and forth in the water. It swam almost as easily as a water moccasin, somehow retaining its instincts for pursuit and devouring prey.

"Grab something-"

The snake dove beneath the surface, swimming under the boat, which cut off Parish's message. Apparently looking to surprise Bill, or find the easiest way to snatch him from the safety of the boat, the anaconda surfaced along the port side.

"Cut its head off," Parish managed to state before the serpent took him beneath the water again.

Bill stared at the machete in his hand momentarily, seeing a problem with Parish's suggestion, in that Parish remained close to the serpent's head instead of sliding further into the lengthy form. He couldn't say that he blamed him, considering one of the few holes from which to breathe was located directly behind the head with those formerly beady eyes that now appeared glazed with a blue film.

"Come get some," Bill muttered angrily, locking eyes with the island's guardian.

Unaware of the dangerous machete in Bill's right hand, or unconcerned, the undead serpent lunged toward the back of the boat, opening its mouth widely in an attempt to snag Bill. Ducking while he backed away simultaneously, Bill lost his balance, falling to the deck as the bladed weapon fell beside him. Fortunate the machete didn't cost him any fingers, Bill stayed low, grabbing the weapon as he prepared for another round with the beast. He chose to stand in the center of the deck where he was best able to spot his attacker and parry if necessary.

He felt perspiration dripping down his forehead and cheeks as his eyeglasses began fogging up to the point that he could barely see. Holding the machete defensively in front of him, Bill listened for sounds, focusing with the one sense as Clay taught him about when they were still on good terms. Valuing the lessons Clay gave him with instruction on weapons and mental awareness alike, Bill could never devote himself to the warrior's code like his nephew. Clay spent four years in Japan living and breathing the old rituals of the samurai and ninja, continuing to practice to this day on a daily basis.

When the snake appeared for its next attack, Bill raised the machete, prepared to chop off its head, or slash it in the mouth to cut the cheeks and weaken the jaw mechanism. About to bring the figurative hammer down on the serpent's jawline, Bill saw the beast open its mouth for another attack. At the top of its throat Bill spied black hair surrounding a bald spot that could only belong to Parish. Bill delayed his attack long enough that the anaconda snapped at him, barely missing his leg. If he found himself caught by the dead reptile, Bill imagined he would be swallowed, crammed into the lengthy belly as he compressed an already miserable Parish toward the tail.

Bill decided if the creature made the mistake of revealing its hind end to him, he would chop it off and provide Parish an alternate escape route. For the moment, however, he simply needed to survive the attacks to keep Parish's hopes for escape alive.

Chapter 13

Clay found one redeeming fact with the emergence of his latest adversaries from the wooded area. If they were roaming through the vegetation, it seemed unlikely traps and snares awaited him within the shaded areas, so he trudged forward to confront them in the available cover.

Uncertain whether the tribal statues before him were native to the island, or something Nosagi brought with him, Clay knew his swords were practically useless against their carved stone forms. Barely sapped of energy from the first round, he suspected the second wave wasn't going to be so easy. None of the zombies held firearms this time, but every one of them grasped blunt or bladed weapons. Clay stole a glance at the statues, which looked harmless with their awkwardly wide mouths, oval-shaped heads, and lightly detailed chests and arms. They barely possessed true legs, most of them lumbering behind the zombies, indicating they were by no means agile.

Hoping this might indeed be the last wave, Clay started for the zombies before half of them even began raising their knives, swords, and thick branches toward him. Immediately beheading the first, he adeptly sliced diagonally through the chest of the next one, rending it useless as the two pieces fell to the ground along with an arm victimized by the *katana*. He tore through several more undead bodies, laying them to waste as the statues drew closer, beginning to surround him so he couldn't simply run into the woods.

Finding a semi-circle around him, his options were to fight or retreat to the ocean behind him. If Clay chose to, he figured he could dodge and weave through the small army, but he didn't want to discover more enemies in the woods with this group behind him. He also didn't want them to turn their attention to his uncle and Parish, who were probably growing bored with guard duty on the boat.

The entire experience felt surreal to him, like being on the set of some fantasy adventure movie. Such things couldn't be real, despite what Clouse had said about the cubes and their mystical powers. Clay now understood the depth of Nosagi's evil, fueling a controlled rage inside him to reach his former mentor and bring his reign of terror crashing down.

A few straggler zombies waited behind the line of statues, some of which were the size of an average man, while a few stood almost eight feet tall. Clay slipped his sword into its scabbard along his back, reaching to his sides where he drew the two Glock pistols and began firing into the faces and necks of the first two statues, hoping those were weak points. One of the statues disintegrated, crumbling to the ground in a heap of broken pebbles. The other continued marching toward him, but he jumped to kick it just above the torso, sending it back into a small boulder that caused it to lose balance. Falling to its back, the statue also crumbled into loose mortar and rock shards.

Figuring a lead pipe might be his best weapon against the unnatural monsters, Clay needed to settle for the available objects nearby, or his firearms. The statues tried to surround him, but their plodding steps kept them from making a solid perimeter. Holding a Glock in each hand, Clay fired at two more of the statues, using more ammunition this time before they crumbled to the ground. Two of them staggered toward him simultaneously, raising their club and spear respectively to smash him into paste if they found their mark. Waiting until the last possible second, Clay rolled out of the way, watching the two statues bring their weapons down upon one another. Both shattered almost immediately, their pieces tumbling into small rock piles along the beach. The tide would eventually take them home to the bottom of the sea, but Clay still had four more statues and five zombies to eliminate before moving into the woods.

A frontal roll put him past the statues, allowing him to holster the guns and cut through two more zombies with his *katana*. Deep down he knew the tissue and flesh his sword cut through were once living human beings. Strangely enough, some of them died trying to put an end to Nosagi's rule over the island. Clay's blade beheaded yet another zombie dressed in battle fatigues that probably worked as a solider for hire or served in a military group.

Another zombie raised a club of some sort against him, but Clay sliced cleanly through the forearm, dropping it and the weapon to the ground. In the return motion, he severed the head, rendering the body useless as a defense mechanism. He barely detected the motion of a statue behind him until the shadow loomed over him and the heavy footsteps caused the ground beneath his feet to tremble like an earthquake tremor.

He sidestepped a clubbing blow from the statue's stone axe, intentionally backing toward the last remaining zombie, a woman dressed in the remains of a skirt and blouse. Obviously a tourist who chose the wrong destination with her group, her glossy, cold eyes stared at Clay ravenously, wanting to bite, claw, or assault him with her large knife to inflict damage. When Clay felt the earth shake beneath his feet a second time, he dodged the blow from behind, watching the stone axe crush the zombie beneath its unforgiving weight. Little more than a puddle of dark blood and strips of flesh emerged from the weapon before it was pulled from the ground. The human tissue mixed with the sand, creating a colorful decoration of natural colors, spelled the end of the zombie adversaries.

More importantly, Clay used the precious seconds to draw the Glocks because four statues remained to end his existence. While they weren't nimble, the statues only needed to graze Clay to strike a killing blow or set him up for certain death with a secondary hit. He walked backwards toward the wooded area, firing his guns at one of the statues, using six bullets total to crumble its aged form to the sandy beach.

Out of bullets in one gun, he decided to exchange both magazines for the full ones at his side. Clay quickly ejected both magazines to the ground, dodging a stone mace in the process as two of the taller statues closed in on his location. The one busied itself retrieving its mace from the sand as the two both swung their weapons toward Clay. He rolled away from the danger as their weapons collided with one another, shattering instantly. Both statues lost parts of their arms in the process, which failed to deter them from focusing on Clay. All four stony figures directed their focus on him as he finished inserting both fresh magazines. Questioning whether three-dozen rounds were enough to down all four statues, Clay took aim at the first one's neck, trying to separate the head from the torso. The feat required only six bullets before the head plopped to the ground and the body crashed beside it in dozens of pieces.

Three statues remained as adrenaline pumped through every fiber of Clay's body. Dodging a swing from the closest piece of living art, Clay felt a bit friskier, delivering a sidekick to the abdomen area hoping to save some ammunition. Such a kick to the sternum of a human being shattered the bone, incapacitating or killing the recipient. This blow did little to weaken the stability of the statue, and in return Clay received a curious tilt of the head from the unusually disproportioned figure.

Strange, Clay thought, that any of the reanimated objects contained any traces of personality. He wondered if Nosagi was able to program them like robots or train them like attack dogs with various traits. Living isolated on an island, the man probably had nothing except time on his hands to play with his new toys.

As one of the other statues took a swing at him, Clay avoided the blow by closing the distance between them, leaping toward the chest of the tribal statue to launch himself toward one of the other two. He kicked a different statue this time with significantly different results. The statue itself looked down to its chest, its wide oval mouth seemingly registering surprise as a large crack began around the nipple line. Quickly spreading across the chest and down to the rocky stomach, the crack caused the dismantling of the statue as it broke into two pieces that landed atop a fallen counterpart in a shattered heap.

Clay took aim at the closer of the two remaining statues, firing both guns simultaneously into its head and neck, trying to take it down. The head broke away from the neck, falling to the ground almost immediately, but the statue continued toward him, toting a dangerous sword made of solid rock. It took a giant swing downward, allowing Clay to evasively roll to his right before shooting it in the knee, crippling it by dropping it to its remaining knee. Instead of wasting ammunition in an attempt to break it apart, Clay shot out the other knee to immobilize the statue while he dealt with its partner.

Refusing to give up, the statue pulled itself forward using the sword as a cane of sorts to drag its body along. Clay ignored it, methodically shooting into every body part of the one remaining whole statue. It flinched as though feeling each bullet penetrate its natural armor, holding a short spear it wanted to aim at Clay. Weakened by stress cracks in various areas, the statue survived one kicked from him as it missed with a swinging spear. Clay dodged a downward swing of the spear, which the statue used like a sword, before kicking upward into its lower chest. Stopping in its tracks as though making a horrific discovery, the statue looked down at its compromised torso before crumbling into smaller stones.

Dropping his guns to the sand momentarily, Clay picked up a black rock the size of a softball and hurled it at the struggling legless statue with his left arm. The stone hit the statue in the shoulder blade, starting a crack that resounded throughout its body until it literally fell into dust that mingled with the beach sand. Giving a brief sigh under his breath, Clay took up his Glock firearms, stuffing them into their holsters before trudging toward the trees.

He stiffened at the sound of screeches from some form of primates ringing through the trees toward his direction.

"Damn it."

***

After several short bursts of breathing when the anaconda surfaced, Parish decided he couldn't wait for Bill to assist him. For some reason, the undead serpent seemed to employ a game plan that kept it from getting chopped up while securing its prisoner. Based on the way it chose to surface repeatedly, the snake obviously had ideas of attacking Bill Branson.

Trying to communicate with Bill cost him valuable seconds he could have spent attempting to free himself from the belly of the deceased creature. Parish tested the elasticity of the skin restraining him, realizing his arms and legs were able to move slowly beneath the weight of the thick skin. Between the water gushing inside and the natural deterioration of the intestinal track, Parish felt slime all around him, penetrating his clothing while further slowing the ability to feel around his surroundings.

When the snake surfaced again to stab at Bill with its mouth, Parish sucked in a deep breath as his right hand slid close to his waistline. The serpent's skin pressed Parish's hand against his own body, making it difficult to reach the survival knife strapped to his right leg. The two smaller knives sheathed within his survival vest were fine for minor cutting or close-up combat, but they weren't heavy enough to filet the anaconda's skin to facilitate his escape.

Reaching the knife proved difficult as the snake thrashed around, constantly trying to reposition its head to attack Bill or find a better attack zone around the boat. Even as his hand neared the survival knife Parish worried about how to unsheathe it without cutting himself initially or when he turned it into the decayed flesh of the serpent.

Constant pressure from the thick flesh and the water surrounding the anaconda left Parish feeling as though g-forces were compressing his own hand against his body. This time the serpent remained beneath the surface a longer period of time, as though realizing it needed to incapacitate its first victim before pursuing another. Parish knew he had about thirty seconds before his body began screaming for air, so he doubled his efforts to free the survival knife.

When the pressure seemed to intensify, Parish questioned whether the undead creature was taking him deeper, or possibly out to sea. Grunting to himself, he slid his hand down his stomach, then along his waistline, before using his elbow to shove out the skin surrounding him just enough for his hand to find the knife handle.

Clutching it like the lifeline is was, Parish pulled the edged weapon from the sheath before finding it incredibly difficult to turn the blade to an effective position. He could feel the serpent kicking toward a destination with renewed effort, pitting itself against Parish's resourcefulness. Clearing the sheath at last, the knife's tip found its way into the soft, slick skin of the anaconda, piercing the inner and outer layers almost simultaneously. Water immediately gushed through the slit, leaving Parish fewer tiny pockets of precious air from which to breathe.

He wasted absolutely no time in running the sharp edge of the knife upward through the skin, creating a hotdog bun effect that provided him a nice opening from which he could escape. Parish barely remembered to take a deep breath before thrusting himself through the large gash to the saltwater freedom awaiting him.

Surrounded by darkness and water, Parish required several seconds to regain his senses because the surface wasn't even visible. Mentally cursing to himself, he began kicking toward the surface, praying enough air remained within his lungs for him to complete the journey. He worried that he might be too far from the island, or the boat, to help either Branson. Too far out and he might be washed out to sea with little hope of reaching any form of safety.

His thoughts quickly returned to the dilemma at hand when he spied daylight above him and something brushed against his leg. Parish immediately knew the anaconda wasn't giving up on sending him to the bottom of the Atlantic, but his lungs were burning too badly to combat the island's guardian until he drew a breath of fresh air.

Feeling a tug at his leg from the snake trying to wrap itself around him, despite the gash lining most of its side, Parish kicked his feet desperately toward the surface. He kept the survival knife clutched in his right hand in case the serpent made a frontal attack. Parish was on the verge of sucking in water because his body demanded he breathe, unconcerned with what gas or fluid entered his lungs.

At the same instant the anaconda wrapped around his leg to tug him down to the bottom, Parish felt the sweet relief of fresh air. His face broke the rolling liquid plane just long enough for him to take a breath before his adversary pulled him under. Without so much as a glimpse of his surroundings, Parish found himself encumbered by darkness once again. He pulled his leg upward, dragging the insistent serpent with it as he tried remaining close to the surface.

Parish jabbed at his attacker with the knife, striking it several times in the face before catching the knife inside its mouth. He pulled the blade toward him, ripping the upper portion of the snake's head down the middle, effectively ceasing its ability to grasp anything with its mouth or small teeth. Able to wriggle his leg free, Parish surged toward the surface again, thrilled when the sun and warm air greeted him. He wildly twisted his body, looking for anything that resembled land or a boat, finding both directly to his right. Wasting less than a second, Parish began swimming toward the boat where he saw Bill Branson frantically scanning the water for him or the anaconda.

"Bill!" he called out, wanting his only salvation to know his location before the snake attacked him again.

Between the wind and choppy water, Parish's cries for help went unheard as he felt something rub his left leg. Knowing the serpent wanted to wrap itself around parts of his body for another assault, Parish began swimming toward the boat with determination.

Almost twenty strokes toward his destination, Parish felt a tug at his leg, but he shrugged it off, determined to reach solid footing before making a stand. By now Bill had spotted him, desperately searching for a weapon or some sort of pole to help Parish aboard the boat. Still a good forty yards from the boat, Parish felt his body betraying him as each stroke felt a bit heavier than the last.

Having the anaconda tug at his leg like a needy child certainly didn't help matters, but he dug down for some reserve energy. Each foot closer to the anchored boat drove Parish that much harder, especially with the tide giving him a gentle push from behind. He felt especially fortunate the damage to the snake kept it from grabbing him tightly enough to pull him too far under the surface for him to recover.

His arms felt like they were each carrying weight bands, growing heavier with each stroke, but refused to give up after surviving the snake's deadly attacks and the incident on the fishing trawler in October. In the back of his mind, Parish grew concerned that Clay might not outlast whatever awaited him on the island, which in turn endangered the two men awaiting his return at sea.

Parish finally neared the boat as the serpent repeatedly tried to wrap around his leg and pull him beneath the surface. Bill reached down for him without assistance from an oar, pole, or anything else. Parish missed clasping his hand the first time as the anaconda pulled him down, likely reminding Bill of several scenes from the *Jaws* movies. He heard Clay's uncle calling his name from beneath the surface, so he kicked his way upward, immediately reaching his hand upward in desperation. When he felt Bill clasp his hand and wrist between both of his hands, Parish tried helping however he could, relieved that true safety was inches away.

Trying to land his feet against the boat to help lessen the burden of his weight for Bill, Parish felt his already waterlogged boots barely getting any traction against the smooth side. Now a stationary target, Parish found his own body being used as a rope in a tug of war between Bill and the serpent. He pushed against the boat and upward with his one free leg, trying to tip the battle in Bill's favor.

Bill braced himself against the inside of the boat, pulling with every bit of strength he possessed until both Parish and the anaconda tumbled into the boat with him. A "holy shit" moment occurred between all three parties as Bill and Parish exchanged stupefied looks and the serpent simply looked between them with glassy eyes at the sides of its split head. Parish tried standing to attack the creature with his survival knife, but he slipped on the wet deck, falling directly on his hindquarters.

As he scrambled to regain his footing, Parish found his feet slipping in some kind of liquid oozing from the anaconda, causing him to fall repeatedly like a comical cartoon character. Before he was able to stand on his own, Bill had grabbed the nearby machete and crossed the deck with purpose before swinging the weapon downward. The move lodged the machete in the wooden surface, but not before severing the head of the anaconda, essentially rendering it useless. For good measure, Bill pried the weapon loose to repeat his swing several times over, leaving the serpent in half a dozen pieces before hurling them over the side of the boat with a disgusted expression. Parish helped throw the last few meaty chunks into the sea, watching them slowly sink to the bottom as he breathed a sigh of relief.

"Thank you."

"You're welcome," Bill replied, visibly shaken by the bizarre experience. "We need to check on Clay."

Scooping up some binoculars, Bill looked toward the island, seeing nothing except the carnage left behind by his nephew.

"We'll just be in his way," Parish stated, continuing to drip water onto the deck.

"I know," Bill said with quiet resolve. "We'd probably get killed or taken hostage, which would complicate things."

It took nearly every trick in the book for Parish to survive one adversary, so he couldn't imagine confronting numerous undead people and creatures. Both he and Bill were virtually panting from the deadly confrontation, and Parish felt absolutely drained of energy and fighting spirit. He questioned Clay's chances of survival, envisioning Bill reluctantly steering the boat away from the island when the one-hour timeline expired.

Just the same, Parish picked up the other set of binoculars to observe Clay's progress, hoping against all odds his gut instinct proved incorrect.

Chapter 14

Unsure of what to expect, Clay kept his *katana* drawn at his side. Based on the lack of sound from the human zombies, he wondered if the primate sounds were from living or dead beings. Considering Nosagi's ability to manipulate and train those around him, Clay wasn't going to be surprised by whatever he saw.

Leaving the beach behind, Clay trudged into the woods to find several small monkeys hopping in the trees above. Snarling, they appeared bent on attacking him, and the glaze in their eyes indicated someone beat him to ending their lives. The first jumped to a tree just in front of him, about fifteen feet above Clay. It landed on a branch, stared at him less than a second, and leapt toward him bearing its teeth with intentions of sinking them into his throat.

Able to slice a baseball into two perfectly equal halves with his sword, when thrown by a professional pitcher, Clay easily timed the speed and trajectory of the attacking primate. What felt like a touch of overkill under ordinary circumstances proved necessary as he basically let the undead animal cut itself in half from head to toe. Clay needed only flick the sword to the correct angle as the monkey's momentum sent it through the blade.

The other two waited mere seconds before initiating an attack on him, but Clay beheaded one as it jumped to the ground, using it as a launching pad to propel itself toward him. Its larger partner jumped down from a branch, ducking and rolling his first swing of the *katana*. Clay wondered if the captive undead creatures learned from the deaths of their colleagues and other observations during training or battles.

Whatever it learned the first time around didn't help when it attacked again, charging at Clay. It ducked and rolled similarly to Clay's defensive movements against the statues, making a fatal mistake by duplicating the direction and landing spot it chose the first time around. One clean swing through the waistline cut the primate in half, but before the two pieces even began their descent toward the earth Clay provided a vertical cut with the sword that turned two pieces into four.

Barely taking a breath after the latest wave of attackers, Clay continued walking deeper into the woods, which were hardly as dense as they looked from a distance. He saw a clearing ahead, almost immediately, that indicated what little civilization the island offered awaited him momentarily.

His heartbeat doubled the instant he spied a man knelt down in a small dirt circle on the far end of the clearing. For some reason the clearing housed only a few deteriorating stone structures in the center, which might have been altars that outlasted the elements over the years.

As the storm clouds drifted away, a sunbeam hit the center of the clearing with perfect timing. Clay observed the gray-haired man from a distance as he meditated from the kneeling position. Immediately sensing a ruse, since no one with hearing could have missed the commotion on the beach, Clay cautiously stepped forward. His heightened senses detected danger, though strangely enough it wasn't from the man he assumed was his mentor less than a football field's distance from him.

From the corner of his eye Clay spied someone else entering the fray to his left. As though sent at the perfect moment to answer his question, a flawless figure, dressed completely in formfitting white stood before him. Armed as well as Clay, and with similar weaponry, the woman possessed full locks of blond hair and an expression that indicated she knew how to use blades.

"I didn't realize Nosagi needed a bodyguard," Clay said, fishing for information, hoping to find a way around another obstacle.

"He doesn't," the woman replied in a self-assured voice, though she didn't strike him as the mercenary for hire type.

"Then maybe you should step aside and let me do what needs to be done."

"I don't think so. Like it or not, I have a partnership with your former mentor, so I can't let anything happen to him."

Clay twirled the *katana's* handle in his right hand momentarily.

"You realize this may not end well for you."

"I'll take my chances. Nosagi trained me, and I suspect you're a little rusty, if not fatigued from your exercise on the beach."

The man across the clearing stood at last, walking into the opposite side of the woods without so much as looking behind him. Clay started in his direction, but the woman drew her own sword, moving his way with foreboding steps. Deciding he needed to solve one problem at a time, Clay drew a deep breath, meditating momentarily without carrying out any *kuji-in.* To a ninja, the *kuji-in* were hand signals used to draw focus or a particular state of mind necessary to carry out a particular task.

He had spent some time on the boat drawing his focus before swimming to shore and dispatching the numerous guardians. Making a costly mistake after coming this far wasn't in his plans, but he desperately wanted to know if the man who just left the area was indeed his former mentor.

Taking a risk, Clay sprinted past the woman, counting on his senses to alert him to any danger approaching from behind. If she was truly trained by Nosagi, she knew how to use any number of throwing weapons. She would also possess excellent conditioning, much like Clay, who now counted on his to get him across the clearing.

Instead of hurling weapons at him, she took chase, using a shorter route to cut him off before he entered the woods on the opposite side. Clay engaged her as their swords crossed, discovering she knew her techniques exceptionally well. Considering their craft relied more upon finesse and cunning than brute strength Clay needed to consider her a worthy adversary until he learned otherwise.

Clay crossed his blade with hers momentarily until he found a defensive position, his back facing the direction he wanted to travel.

"I don't know what he's paying you, but it can't be worth risking your life for him."

"He's not paying me at all," the woman said before taking a deliberate cut at Clay's head which he blocked with his blade.

"Then he's lied to you. He does that exceptionally well."

She took several shots at him with her blade, which Clay deflected. He wanted to know details about her relationship with Nosagi, but time was running out to catch his former mentor if it was indeed Nosagi who fled, and not some kind of body double.

Backing away from her to provide adequate spacing, Clay pulled a silver sphere the size of a gumball from a storage pouch along his waistline. Within a split-second Clay pulled the device and threw it against the ground where a vertical plume of yellowish smoke flowed skyward. Typically used to create distractions, smoke bombs provided ninjas an escape from their enemies. With only one true direction he wanted to travel, Clay simply needed to provide a head start, rather than escape altogether.

By the time the smoke reached its full capacity, Clay was already covered by the trees. He quickly scanned the area, seeing gigantic rocks to his left and more trees and brush to his right. Directly ahead he spied water, and bobbing at a crudely constructed dock he noticed a pleasure boat fully capable of sailing the ocean tides.

He saw the same man undoing the moorings, readying the boat for a quick escape. The Nosagi Clay once knew never ran from a fight, but he also thought the man was upstanding and truthful. He almost yelled to distract the man momentarily, but he quickly decided against it. He couldn't afford to let the woman know his location, if she didn't already, and he wanted an opportunity to take at least one shot at Nosagi.

Clay sheathed his sword with practiced ease, into the pack behind him. From another pouch along his cloth belt, he pulled out two *shuriken* stars, throwing them simultaneously at the man undoing the line. Having little doubt the man was his former mentor, or an evil minion at the very least, Clay watched the four-sided blades spin through the air until the man drew a sword from his side, deflecting one while torqueing his body to dodge the other completely.

Nosagi, Clay thought, seeing the man's face for the first time. Though aged almost fifteen years, the face looked much like he last saw it. Gray hair had replaced much of the black, leaving it peppered, but Clay knew not to believe the man's advanced age made him any less dangerous.

The brown eyes narrowed with disdain when they locked with Clay's blue eyes, registering the indisputable fact that he recognized his former pupil. He stepped into the boat with an eerie calmness, as though leaving for vacation in the Bahamas rather than eluding a battle that might take his life. His eyes flickered, in less than a blink, beyond Clay's left shoulder indicating something closing in on his former protégé. A smug grin crossed his face before he eased the boat away from the wooden dock.

Ordinarily Clay might have taken more time to note some details about the direction of Nosagi's departure but he knew the mysterious woman was behind him. Clay stopped running only to duck in the same instant as two metal spears about six inches in length flew over him. He remembered Nosagi teaching him the same offensive technique years prior, rather satisfied the man hadn't taught new tricks to his recent students.

After several assassination attempts on his life, Clay knew he either had to reason with this woman or kill her. With Casey in his life, Clay could hardly afford to look over his shoulder on a daily basis and live a normal life. Both Clay and the woman in white stopped running on the beach beside the dock, drawing their blades once more as the sound of a boat motor grew more distant.

"This isn't necessary," Clay said, circling her with his *katana* held defensively before him.

"You talk too much," the woman replied, attacking him with her blade, Clay easily deflecting it the first few passes.

She read his defense, swinging low instead which threw him off-balance. He blocked the low swing, leaving his torso and arms for attack, which allowed her to graze his shoulder with a quick adjustment of her sword. Clay blocked the backstroke, ignoring the stinging sensation that accompanied the fresh cut. Taking to the offensive, Clay swung his *katana* in several different directions, one stroke after another, keeping his adversary in a defensive position until he managed to position his blade beneath hers, knocking it upward and out of her hands. Her grip had loosened ever so slightly because the tip of his sword drew dangerously close to her fingers during the last exchange.

Finding an opportunity to end the conflict if the woman's skills weren't on par with his, Clay thrust the blade's tip toward her face. Keeping her palms flat, she caught the sword between her hands, preventing Clay from striking the killing blow. Placing both hands on the hilt for better strength and leverage distribution, Clay pushed the blade toward her, but she backed away, keeping them at the same pace until the *katana* struck a tropical tree behind her as she ducked away from the blade.

Leaving the sword momentarily, Clay engaged her in hand-to-hand combat as she deflected several of his punches and kicks until he landed a glancing blow alongside her face. Stunned only a second at best, she managed to avoid a square punch aimed for her sternum as she did a backflip that might make most professional gymnasts green with envy. Determined to find a way to disable or kill her so he could pursue Nosagi, Clay prepared to draw another weapon from his pack when she launched a smoke bomb of her own, disappearing from sight behind the cloud of manmade smoke.

Clay might have missed her altogether except his sharp hearing detected the brief and subdued sound of a splash near the dock. He started toward the unsafe looking structure, stopping in his tracks when a Jet Ski emerged from beneath the wooden planks, taking off in the same direction Nosagi chose to travel. It seemed they had formed a contingency plan to meet up in case the island's guardians failed to eliminate Clay.

Grunting angrily to himself, Clay sprinted through the clearing once more, not slowing a bit until he reached the opposite end of the beach. He ran into the water until it reached his waist, slowing his progress to a crawl. From there he dove into the sea, battling the current as he swam toward the boat ahead of him, praying a chance to catch Nosagi presented itself.

He knew better than to swim directly against the current, so Clay took an angle that approached a corner of the boat so the gentle waves didn't constantly bat him backwards. As he drew nearer the vessel, concern grew in his mind because he didn't see Parish or his uncle. Though he doubted Nosagi dared take the time to harm either of them, Clay's former mentor obviously harbored little concern when he sent people to assassinate Clay and eliminated the police officer's friends and family in the past.

When he finally threw an arm over the boat and began pulling himself aboard, Clay found his uncle seated on the deck with his back against the rail, trying to catch his breath. Several small chunks of what looked like a giant chopped up eel dotted the deck near his feet.

"What happened here?"

"Giant undead anaconda," Bill answered. "Turns out the guy who hired you wasn't lying."

"That's an understatement. Where's Parish?"

As though on cue, Parish emerged from the housing quarters with a few firearms and a second machete in his arms.

"Good to see you made it back," he said upon seeing Clay, setting down the array of weaponry. "How did you make out?"

"We need to head that way," Clay said, pointing the direction. "Nosagi has an assistant and they both took off toward the mainland."

Bill scrambled to his feet, taking the helm as he quickly gave the boat full power and steered in the indicated direction.

"Assistant, huh?" Parish asked, taking Clay's side as they both stared ahead, hoping to catch Nosagi for different reasons.

"He'll say whatever it takes to land a capable apprentice. I'm sure he's fed her worse lies than he told me years ago."

Clay's anger stemmed from more than just the four years he spent overseas. His own father let him fall victim to a lie, for the betterment of a drug empire, no less. The law and Clay's own moral code kept him from seeking revenge on a family member, especially since his father was dying, so he focused his attention on Nosagi.

Evidence of Nosagi's sociopathic nature lay strewn across the island behind Clay in the form of over a dozen human beings the man killed just to build his own enslaved army. Clay wasn't sure if their boat could catch Nosagi and the mysterious woman, but if they didn't, the chances of finding him again were slim at best. Already well behind his former mentor, Clay felt certain his only hope of finding them would be if they landed in a major port. Realistically, the dock the trio launched from was about the only official landing for fishermen and commercial vehicles that could be reached from the island on a standard tank of fuel.

He doubted Nosagi was foolish enough to show his face in the villages, knowing Clay or other entities might be tracking him. And a few hours later the group would come to realize Nosagi and the woman vanished without a trace.

Chapter 15

From his front row seat in a four-seat 1969 Cessna, Harlan Stone had seen virtually everything from a distance. Using high-powered binoculars, Stone observed the anaconda attack, and Clay Branson surviving a hoard of strange-acting humans and mobile statues. He wished he could have recorded the entire incident from start to finish, but maintaining a healthy distance from the scene to keep his involvement secret was his highest priority.

Managing to use his credentials at the airport in order to learn where Branson and his friends were heading, Stone quickly booked a flight to South America. Stewart arranged for both boat and air travel in the meantime, instructing Stone to follow the group wherever they went. He also made certain the agent knew to remain unseen.

With the nearest cell phone tower possibly a hundred miles away, Stone used a satellite phone to call his employer as the pilot began circling the island with every living being now heading for the mainland. The pilot, a local man who commonly rented his plane and piloting skills to Americans, spoke decent enough English for Stone to communicate.

"Keep circling," he said, making a stirring motion with his finger to illustrate his wishes.

Stone pulled out a digital camera as his satellite phone tried to make contact with Stewart. Snapping some pictures with a telephoto lens, Stone knew there would never be detail or clarity enough to explain what he actually saw, but the numerous bodies lying on the beach told a story of their own.

Although the freelance pilot said absolutely nothing, as though completely oblivious to what he had witnessed, Stone had little doubt the man saw the same exact scenario without the benefit of binoculars. No stranger to assisting the FBI and CIA, the man likely knew talking about many of the stings and surveillance missions he piloted would end badly for him.

Stone managed to snap about four shots before his supervisor answered his cell phone.

"Stewart."

"Boss, you're not going to believe what I just witnessed."

"Where did Branson go? That's what I need to know first and foremost."

"He came out to this island a few hours from the mainland. I'm not even sure you're going to believe what happened when he got here."

"Try me."

Stone took a few more pictures as he cupped the phone between his ear and shoulder, trying to avoid missing some prime images.

"He fought off these people, but they weren't exactly normal."

"Not normal? How so?"

"Well, they looked like they were in a trance, or under direction from something. Almost like zombies."

"Interesting," Stewart replied without the slightest hint of growing interest in his voice.

"And these stone statues were walking toward him, but he shot most of them and took them down. It was the most uncanny thing I've ever seen."

Stone tried to maintain his composure, but he still couldn't believe his own eyes and mind to accurately recount the bizarre scenario. He felt like a kid peeking through a wall and seeing some monumental event only the adults were supposed to know about.

"Where is Branson now?" Stewart asked, unfazed by the information.

"He met up with the other two men and took chase after another boat."

"Follow him."

"What about the other vessel?"

"Don't worry about it. Just keep tabs on Branson and don't let him make you."

Not wanting to question his boss, or endanger his new position, Stone hated to ask questions of Stewart, but the man's behavior struck him as odd.

"Sir, I basically just watched him cut down fourteen or so people and you're acting like it's an everyday occurrence."

"There are two problems, Agent Stone. One, those probably weren't people as you and I would classify people. I'll explain that when you get back. And two, you're far, far away from our jurisdiction, so you are to simply follow him and report back to me. Is that understood?"

"Yes, sir."

Stone severed the connection before having the pilot circle the island four more times, closer with each pass, as the agent snapped more pictures of the carnage below. He wondered what business Branson had with the two people on the opposite end of the island and why they took off individually. He also questioned Alan Stewart's motives for having him conduct this unorthodox surveillance and giving him partial answers to his inquiries.

Catching up with any vessels traveling along the water wasn't going to be difficult for the small plane. Stone needed to assess the situation and make certain he guessed where Branson's party was going to land so he could beat them to their destination. Making a landing at the airport would take up precious minutes, even before Stone drove his rental vehicle to the dock to locate Branson once more.

Based on the way things ended on the island, however, he doubted the subject of his observations was about to do anything noteworthy.

Only time would tell.

Chapter 16

All of January and half of February passed with no luck for Russ Greene on the cube hunting front. After the Bransons and Parish lost Nosagi in South America, the deceitful Japanese native disappeared from sight with his new apprentice. The entire group knew it might be mere weeks or months before numerous people disappeared from a particular geographical area again, leading them straight to him.

In the meantime, Julie Knowles conducted some research that led her to believe another cube was being used for financial gain, particularly during prime sporting events. It seemed a certain man was winning rather big on a consistent basis at the horse tracks particularly, and the name mentioned in a newspaper article matched the one etched in Julie's cursed ledger.

Greene worked with Julie, attempting to locate the lucky better whose known total winnings netted at least twenty million dollars. Their search reached a dead-end rather quickly when they discovered he abandoned his modest house in Missouri after the newspaper article publicized his good fortune.

"Lucky my ass," Greene said of the man's attributing his winnings to good fortune.

Though he placed bets all over the country, the man seemed to have a penchant for the Kentucky Derby each May. Finding him wasn't going to be easy, considering he could live anywhere and simply pay for everything from food to living quarters with cash. He didn't have a cell phone on record and hadn't used a credit card since the article went public. Greene credited the man for knowing how to live off the grid, but he needed to find him soon, and with good reason.

Not one to place all of his eggs in one basket, Greene developed a plan with Julie's assistance too elaborate to set into place at the last minute. He planned on continuing to track the man known as Lincoln Daine through every means possible while asking Clouse for financial assistance to execute his plan. Although Greene no longer possessed federal powers to do much on his own, he maintained several excellent contacts and knew a plethora of ways in the private sector to track individuals. He found himself working more like a private investigator without his credentials, but serving a greater good made the sacrifice worthwhile.

The only other front requiring his attention was the time cube outside of Chicago. Clouse worked in secret to find what individual or entity owned the land. Greene's instincts told him to put a small army on the grounds before they even acquired the land to protect the cube, but Clouse and Julie felt it wiser to simply stay as far away from the property as possible. Clouse also ordered his attorneys to put feelers out on dozens of properties in the greater Chicago area to create a smokescreen in case someone monitored their activities.

Greene doubted there was any "in case" about it. He felt certain every hotel employee confirmed to do more than sweep floors, wait tables, and work a hotel desk was under observation of some sort from a separate group.

With the onset of a harsh winter in upper Illinois, Greene doubted anyone was going to easily access the filled in area where Thomas Ervin and his car had rested for the better part of three decades. Clouse had sent one of his employees on a fieldtrip to the property in secret for a detailed report about the property's condition, because any public actions taken through lawyers endangered the harvesting of the time cube. Little had changed about the property over the years, except that the quarry was now filled in with dirt, likely for safety reasons.

Greene felt compelled to assume the cube was still inside or near the car through gut instinct. If the world had indeed been altered by someone's use of the time cube, Greene supposed he would have no knowledge of an altered time continuum because life as he formerly knew it would be erased worldwide.

Implications from the cube's use were mindboggling, so he tried to avoid dwelling upon such thoughts for very long. Instead, he focused on obtaining the other cubes and making the world a safer place.

Liz returned to California temporarily, mainly to get enough belongings for a move to Indiana. Greene considered it important for the team to remain within close proximity because he never knew what information might come their way suddenly. Clay Branson returned to Ohio, his future with the group still unclear because his sole motivation to align himself with them disappeared with Nosagi and his new apprentice. Julie remained closer to the East Coast because her secure facility housed the cubes the group captured. Right now the number remained staggeringly low because of the fiasco in Alaska and the complete failure when it came to landing any new cubes.

Sitting in his apartment, because a permanent house made him easier to find, Greene stared out the window at the outskirts of Bloomington. The adjacent parking lot and several trees provided a bland late morning view, but Greene intended to unpack only what he needed and move again soon. He refused to house near the campus of Indiana University, preferring quick access to county roads and highways. Plans of housing the group together, once the team was comprised, ran through his mind. Being in charge of a one-of-a-kind unit provided him with numerous challenges, sometimes making him question whether or not he was capable of completing such a daunting task for Clouse.

Growing up in the farmland of Montgomery County in Tennessee, Greene dreamed of escaping and working in the big city. His uncle worked as a deputy, which inspired him to look to law enforcement for a career that guaranteed an escape from plowing fields and harvesting corn and other crops. He remembered the man visiting their farm, laying his gun belt across the table after a long day's work to join the family for summer sometimes. As a boy, Greene thought the sight of his uncle in uniform, toting a firearm, was like something out of the movies. He paid his dues, struggling through four years of college in the Nashville area after high school, driven by his lifelong dream.

He could have gained experience with a local police department instead of attending college, but Greene wanted to understand the outside world. Besides, he didn't want to linger around his home area, especially as a deputy who garnered no respect from the public. He aspired to work somewhere where the world was indeed his playground and he wouldn't feel confined.

Not every night was devoted to homework and studying, but Greene stayed the course and finished his four years with a respectable GPA and an understanding of social behavior away from the farm. He worked in Arizona and Oregon a few years before finally returning home to Tennessee, discontented with the lifestyle outside of his home state. Working in Nashville, a city filled with iconic outward appearances, taught him that not everyone in the Music City was charming both inside and out.

And then came Paul Clouse with a job offer that took him to an even darker place.

Greene peered at a nearby calendar, realizing just over a month remained before the Sunland Derby took place in New Mexico. His elaborate plan required a number of calculated guesses to prove correct, along with a little luck. Even if the initial phase of the plan went according to his projections, the latter part could fail utterly and cost Clouse a lot of money. While Clouse had openly stated money was no object when hunting the cubes, he tended to prefer sure bets to a longshot. This plan fell somewhere in the middle.

Before calling his employer for a blank check, Greene decided to make a different kind of call. He hated dragging any of his former colleagues into the mess he now called a career, but the federal government possessed better resources for finding missing people and criminals than any local agencies or freelancers like himself.

Scooping the cordless phone from its charger, he decided to use a landline rather than a cell phone, again erring on the side of caution. Unsure whether his former colleague would help him, or if Daine could even be found, Greene suspected his next call was to his employer asking for some financing after he provided a convincing narrative.

***

In a complete departure from his normal afternoon, Chase Dalton found himself seated at his desk in Estes Kefauver Federal Building. The building housed numerous courts, along with the United States Marshals Service, which currently employed him. Working in downtown Nashville came with some perks, but Dalton liked the nightlife and the Music City's atmosphere more than anything.

Not a conformist by nature, he hated wearing a tie and slacks to work on a daily basis, but until Casual Friday made a comeback he saw no alternative. With his sport coat draped over the chair behind him, Dalton typed a report into his computer regarding a prisoner transport that went wrong for local authorities. The prisoner escaped custody, but Dalton and another marshal found him within hours by visiting the man's usual haunts. He felt certain the paperwork was going to take longer than the search itself, but Dalton needed to know details if any aspect of the case ever appeared in a courtroom.

"You meeting us at Miss Kitty's later?" one of his colleagues asked on his way through the office, referring to a downtown tavern.

"Maybe," Dalton answered neutrally. "Depends on what the girlfriend wants to do."

His fellow marshal made the sound of a whip snapping while giving a smirk as he exited the office.

Dalton rolled his eyes, returning his attention to the report, which neared completion.

For almost the first time that week the clouds gave way to some rays of sun, providing a bit of warmth and a glimmer of the spring season to come. Dalton's back felt warm from the natural light piercing the window behind him as he typed, wondering how soon he could change into regular clothes for the evening.

It took another five minutes for him to read over the report and finally officially enter it into his departmental database. His lieutenant had mentioned several other assignments that needed attention, though not urgently, so Dalton thought about checking into those when his phone rang.

"United States Marshals Office," he answered officially. "Deputy Marshal Dalton speaking."

"You sound like you're ready for the weekend," a familiar voice replied.

"Russ? That you, you sly dog?"

"The one and only."

"I *am* ready for the weekend. What has you calling from Hawaii, or wherever you moved to?"

"I wish," Greene scoffed. "You wouldn't trade me jobs for anything if you knew what I was doing."

Dalton always wondered exactly why his former partner did leave the marshals service. Everyone knew it was a private sector job, but the man never gave one single hint about exactly what the job entailed. Even Secret Service agents were able to talk about what they did, even if they refused to provide details.

What could possibly be so secret that Greene took a vow of silence regarding his new career?

"So where are you calling from?" Dalton asked.

"Indiana at the moment."

"How are you supposed to protect the president from there?"

Greene chuckled.

"He's here to speak about his new corn-based weapon of mass destruction."

"Incredible stuff. I'd like an autograph sometime."

"I'll see what I can do," Greene replied, unable to stifle a brief laugh.

Dalton remembered why he and Russ Greene worked so well together. Both grew up with something missing in their lives. Greene longed for the city as a teenager, feeling more enslaved every season he worked with his parents on their farm. Dalton lost both of his parents at the age of ten in a tragic car crash. He finished out the remainder of his formative years in West Virginia living with his grandparents. Given all of the love and support a boy could ever want from his grandparents, Dalton longed for an escape to something bigger and better, often entertaining himself with police dramas and true crime books.

During his college internship at a local police department, Dalton forged a friendship with a veteran West Virginia state trooper. The man, who became a surrogate uncle of sorts to him, recommended joining the FBI or the U.S. Marshals as a job that could take him away from the state that haunted him with memories of his parents. Though the trooper eventually retired, Dalton kept in close touch with him over the years, thankful for the man's advice and understanding.

Perhaps Dalton saw some of the trooper's traits in Greene, including unequalled work ethic and a certain stubborn nature that could only come from someone who no longer accepted denial. No matter how many rules and regulations slowed Greene, the man obtained results time after time by circumventing the red tape.

"I'm actually calling for a favor," Greene said, returning Dalton to the present from memory lane.

"I should have known there was a reason I'm just now hearing from you after *months* of silence."

"It's been a busy couple of months. I'm trying to track down a missing person, Chase."

Dalton tapped a pen atop his desk momentarily, wondering why his former colleague couldn't track such a person himself.

"Missing person, eh?"

"I've tapped out my resources on this end. You're my last resort before I have to make a big play I'd prefer not to."

"Am I allowed to ask questions?"

"The less you know the better."

Dalton sighed.

"Is he even a real missing person?"

"He is, but he might be voluntarily out of sight because he's done some bad things."

"Fine," Dalton said, figuring he owed Greene at least one favor from their days of working together. "What's the name?"

"Lincoln Daine."

Greene spelled the last name, since the spelling wasn't common.

"You going to rescue me from government work one of these days, big shot?"

"I could probably use someone with your qualifications. There's no turning back once you agree to this job though."

Dalton grunted to himself, waiting for the computer to come up with information about Daine. Short of opening an investigation, Dalton could only search basic information about Daine as a person of interest. Missing persons were typically dealt with by state police or the FBI as the marshals focused on fugitives, prisoner transportation, and court security. They occasionally worked in asset forfeiture or bank robberies when the FBI was busy with homeland security, but Dalton seldom witnessed much excitement.

Before he could contemplate Greene's casual offer, Dalton's computer screen blinked, displaying some basic information about Daine.

"He looks squeaky clean, Russ. It gives an address."

"Old news. He's on the lam. Does it give any relatives or contacts?"

"No. No criminal record means we don't have his network, but you already know that. What are you really wanting, old friend?"

"I need to find him. The man has a track record of winning big at races and disappearing."

"And you think he has a little help on the side?"

"Something like that, yes. He's careful not to use credit cards or a registered cell phone."

"Then why call me at all?"

"Just hoping for a longshot. Also, he uses a bookie in the Nashville area sometimes."

"How does that help?"

"He bets on football and basketball every so often, and he has to be present."

Dalton grumbled audibly.

"Give me the name and I'll visit the guy if I find time."

Greene provided the name and location of the bookie, not certain himself if Daine ever used the same betting source twice. He seemed excessively cautious about covering his tracks, as though he knew his habits might get him discovered by someone wanting the cube.

"I owe you," Greene said.

"I know. And I have a feeling I'm going to regret doing this."

Chapter 17

It took Dalton only two days to report back to Greene that the bookie had evidently moved to a new location. Though he felt confident he could track the man down, Dalton said he probably needed another few days to a week.

Unwilling to let fate decide his chances of success, Greene went to Clouse with his plan, asking for some heavy financial assistance and permission to use or hire a few people for a few months. His plan involved getting a horse, with long-shot odds, to the Kentucky Derby in May. Any number of hurdles stood before him, but once Clouse gave a green light on the financial end, Greene needed only buy into an existing horse already on the cusp of being Derby material and get it to Louisville by hook or crook.

To ensure all parties involved were represented, Greene accepted Matt Teakon for the sake of Julie Knowles, and a man by the name of Craig Jennings on Clouse's behalf. Matt Teakon had worked with Julie and his uncle, Mark Teakon, on several dangerous encounters before Clouse formed an alliance with their group, so the younger Teakon was very much trusted by Julie.

Jennings worked under Clouse at the West Baden Springs Hotel and French Lick Springs Resort as the head of security. While Jennings did not oversee the casino security, he often kept busy during the tourism season at both hotels. Events like vintage baseball, hot air balloon rides, golf tournaments, train rides on the Monon, weddings, and concerts kept Jennings occupied.

"I feel ridiculous," Craig Jennings said, standing front and center before the track at Sunland Park Racetrack & Casino in New Mexico.

Formerly a shop teacher before Clouse hired him to head up security at the hotels, Jennings lived in the country and disliked big city life. It wasn't uncommon for him to wear cowboy boots to church or even jump in and sing with the gospel band occasionally, but he didn't feel comfortable at the moment.

"Suck it up," Matt Teakon replied. "I'm a fish out of water, too, you know."

Both men wore black slacks, black cowboy boots, and black leather blazers along with black cowboy hats. Only Teakon's red dress shirt and gold bolo tie provided contrast on his part, while Jennings wore a bolo with a large turquoise stone centered in silver over his white shirt. Neither spoke with a New Mexico drawl, and neither felt confident acting their parts, much less speaking differently, so Greene told them they were posing as investors who had brought their business to New Mexico a year ago.

Jennings wished his employer had come down personally to play the part, but he knew Clouse was needed elsewhere much of the time. At least Clouse once owned a horse or two and liked wearing boots.

"Hell, the only reason they picked me for this was because they needed someone who knew the situation," Jennings complained, keeping his voice low as a preliminary heat of horses stampeded around the track.

"There aren't many of us, with good reason."

It took Greene some time to train both men what to do during their time in New Mexico, because he never planned to travel with them. He had other matters to attend to in Illinois, so he arranged for Jennings to pose as a co-owner of a horse named Desert Phantom, a three-year-old chestnut colt. The horse had performed well enough in other races that if it placed in the Sunland Derby it stood an excellent chance of being invited to the Kentucky Derby. While Teakon possessed almost expert knowledge of horses from growing up in the Midwest, he didn't feel comfortable or qualified to act as a racehorse trainer. In turn, Greene asked him to pose as Jennings' ranch manager, which worked out perfectly since the horse already resided at the original owner's ranch. No one would ever ask to see Jennings' ranch that in fact did not exist.

Greene discovered that Margaret Stough had exhausted most of her funds just getting Phantom into several key races. Between training, travel expenses, and the entry fees, she could not afford to enter him in the Sunland Derby, one of the most important prep races for the Kentucky Derby. Greene fronted Jennings the money to pose as someone interested in a benefactor position with the horse, basically taking a co-ownership position through the racing season to give Phantom a chance at the most prestigious race in the world.

Margaret wasn't anxious to accept a partner, but she needed the financial assistance after several banks turned her down and other owners shot her lowball offers for the colt. Now eighty-five, she didn't get around very well so she liked the idea of Jennings being the front man for the horse when the media came around. He promised her he could handle the responsibility, a lump forming in his throat during their entire conversation.

Now committed to his double life, Jennings watched as the results from the last race were posted on the electronic scoreboard. He dreaded the thought of his new colt failing miserably during the final race for numerous reasons. Strangely, he felt an attachment to Phantom, and to Margaret, even after being affiliated with both for less than three weeks. It turned out the trainer was about the best choice possible because he only worked with a few horses, and devoted much of his time to Margaret's colt. Not that Jennings truly possessed control over who trained the horse, but he felt certain changing trainers would lead to certain disaster.

It didn't take a racehorse expert to understand only a fool tinkered with something that didn't require fixing.

Jennings also found himself adapting to Mark Teakon's nephew, who apparently assisted the Massachusetts group in hunting the cubes from time to time. He already knew details about the cursed objects that made him an immediate fit with both groups. Close to six feet in height, Teakon possessed brown hair and a full goatee that encircled his lips. A divorcee who recently left a civilian job at a military research facility, Teakon gave up good pay and security for the betterment of the planet. Capable of working with his hands and understanding a wide array of machinery, Teakon seemed to know a little bit about every topic he and Jennings discussed. He often advised Jennings on the way of horses and ranch life, encouraging him to at least understand ranch life so the workers respected him a little bit.

Returning his attention to his attire, Jennings abided by Margaret's wishes for him to dress like a gentleman from New Mexico with some class. He grew out his beard, finding a greater mix of gray with his normal brown hair this time. With little more than a fringe of hair left atop his head, he actually felt somewhat thankful the assignment required him to wear a Stetson.

Feeling a bit more tense as the race drew nearer, Jennings found his stomach in knots all morning long, partly from hoping his ruse worked, but also because he wanted to win the race and potentially put another cube in safe haven. Only a handful of Paul Clouse's friends and employees knew about the dangerous objects, though Jennings woke up most mornings wishing he had never accidentally stumbled into a convoluted plan to use one of them at the cost of a dozen or so lives. Fortunately the plan didn't reach its lethal conclusion, though a number of people died in the process. From time to time Jennings woke suddenly in the middle of night, his bed sheets soaked with sweat after reliving the horror in his dreams.

"You okay?" Teakon asked, breaking Jennings' trance.

"Fine. Just nervous about the race is all."

Surrounded by thousands of people wanting to watch the race, despite the cool, windy weather, the two men passed the time by reading the program or watching the other races. They didn't bother mingling with the nearby people, since most of them were simply spectators and not fellow owners. In the past few weeks they learned that March nights in New Mexico were below freezing and it took until lunchtime for the temperatures to swing to sixty or seventy degrees.

Jennings hadn't asked Teakon much about his uncle's life, and even less about the man's death in the Bering Sea. Considering Teakon volunteered little information about either situation, and seemed short whenever either topic was brought up, Jennings only asked a few questions before giving up completely.

Trust wasn't easy between the two men because they represented different factions searching for the same thing. No one was really certain Clouse and Julie trusted one another, but they worked together for the sake of Mark Teakon. Jennings knew Clouse surrendered the cubes to the deceased college professor, affirming his belief in his employer's intentions. He wanted to believe the cubes were being cast out of society's reach one at a time, never to be seen again, but nagging feelings otherwise haunted him.

"It's too bad Margaret couldn't come," Teakon said, making small talk at this point.

Her nerves, more than her health, kept her from attending the race. Despite investing so much money into Phantom and bringing him to this race, she let Jennings confront the press, assuring him she would make the trip to Louisville if their horse was invited.

Two more preliminary races started and finished before Jennings and Teakon watched Desert Phantom being led by one of the stable hands, his jockey already in the saddle. Jennings knew little about the jockey, Johnny Gomez, except that Margaret placed complete faith in him. The man had lost his last two racing gigs to more seasoned riders, but Margaret loved the way he handled horses, often reading their desires. He seemed to have a knack for keeping them safely in the middle of the pack once a race started, only letting them put on a burst of speed when he felt they were ready for a charge but not in danger of petering out.

Jennings had the option of standing almost anywhere along the track, on the upper balcony where the VIP tent was located, or inside the casino. A far cry from Churchill Downs where the stands towered above and around the oval racetrack, this track provided what appeared to be a pen between the casino and the racetrack itself, complete with solid white fencing as tall as most men but easy to see through. The announcer who called the races reported that an estimated nineteen thousand people showed up to watch the day's events and place wagers.

The casino, honoring local heritage, was painted burnt orange, red clay, and turquoise on the exterior, giving it a strident appearance that visitors found difficult to miss. Jennings turned to admire the décor before returning his attention to the impending race, knowing his horse needed to finish at least fourth to accumulate enough earnings to make the big dance.

Wins at the Silver Deputy Stakes and the Grey Stakes the year prior provided him with enough earnings to come this far, but he needed nearly another $100,000 to be one of the twenty horses eligible to run in Kentucky. His last race ended badly when he placed second to last on a different New Mexico track. Margaret's financial troubles apparently led to subpar travel conditions and a lapse in training when she couldn't afford trainer Jeff Slaton's services for a few weeks. He cut her some slack and stayed with the horse whenever possible, but he took some paying jobs that kept him away from the ranch more often.

"If he doesn't place at least third, all of this is down the drain," Jennings muttered, knowing the winner earned $400,000, second place $176,000, and third place $96,000.

All three positions were enough to take the group east, but only Phantom could decide his own fate. Jennings sucked in a deep breath as the horses were led to the starting gate. In this race only a dozen horses ran, and there wasn't quite so much spectacle, like the promenade or jockey group photograph as there was in Kentucky. Jennings hoped, prayed even, that he was going to see Churchill Downs from the inside. While it wasn't a childhood dream by any means, he thought bringing a racehorse to the track would certainly be a lifetime accomplishment. His primary motivation stemmed from wanting to find another cube and keep it from doing anyone else harm.

"This is it," Teakon said before drawing a deep, calming breath. "In two minutes we'll know if we just wasted two weeks of our lives."

Jennings couldn't bring himself to utter a reply, simply content to watch the horses being loaded one at a time into the starting gate. Phantom drew the third door from the gate, which historically speaking wasn't bad luck. Being on the outside meant a horse needed to make up more ground and work its way toward the inner rail, which often drained any reserves the horses might need during the final turn. Drawing the innermost slot sometimes pinned an aggressive horse against the railing as it struggled to keep up with the pack. Most horses needed only a little bumping and kicking to break their routine and demoralize them to the point that they fell back and refused to run hard.

One of the horses refused to settle in the gate easily, detaining the race start momentarily. It finally entered the gate, led by one of the track workers dressed from head to toe in green coveralls and a baseball cap. Phantom was loaded next without a hitch, leaving only two more horses before the race began along the dirt track.

Although he wasn't Catholic, Jennings made a sign of the cross as he watched the final horse being loaded, knowing the race start was mere seconds away. When the bell rang to signal the race start, Jennings found himself startled because his eyes were locked on the third stall, hoping Phantom could beat eleven other horses and take first place. Admonishing himself for being a bit greedy, Jennings knew enough purse money to take them to Louisville would suffice, but he wanted Margaret to fare well.

Every gate opened, releasing the twelve horses in Phantom's heat. They all emerged cleanly, remaining in a tight pack until two horses dropped back around the first turn. Jennings virtually pressed against the white fence for a look at the track, finding it difficult to see much along the same level as the horses, with dust floating behind the field. Suddenly the VIP tent above sounded like a much better idea, though several monitors provided an excellent view as a video camera followed the leaders.

Every sense felt heightened as Jennings tried to follow the race on the monitor once the horses ran along the back straightaway. Listening to the announcer give a play-by-play was about the only way to keep track of the positions at this point.

Teakon shook his arm and pumped his fist with excitement.

"Hear that? He's moving up the pack!"

Jennings tried listening intently but the man spoke like an auctioneer, rattling off names and positions. On the monitor, he spotted Phantom's blue saddle blanket with the embroidered number three centered in the pack. His eyes locked on the colt, watching it run steadily with five other horses centered between two leaders and the stragglers. The thunderous clop of four dozen hooves had diminished to a distant echo after the horses made the first turn, but Jennings found new sounds in the form of betters and spectators all around him cheering for their picks.

By the end of the opposite straightaway Phantom began moving toward the front of the central pack, but Jennings knew Gomez was battling to hold the horse back. In a mere two weeks Jennings learned the horse had incredible spirit, but the jockey's job was to ensure the colt's determination didn't outlast his body. It wasn't until the pack rounded the last turn that Gomez finally let Phantom surge forward. He began fist pumping as he saw Phantom begin to leave the pack behind him, on pace to catch the two leaders by the finish line.

"Come on," Jennings muttered as Teakon clutched his arm harder this time from the sheer excitement both of them felt.

Phantom overtook the entire center pack, assuring a third place finish at worst if nothing disastrous happened. Jennings rather hoped Gomez didn't push him harder for first place after seeing broken legs and other injuries on televised horseraces. The thought of Phantom suffering such an injury, which in turn required immediate euthanizing, entered his mind for the briefest of seconds. Margaret's dreams would be crushed in an instant, the chance to find the cube in Louisville would die on the dirt track, and evil would indeed triumph.

Jennings watched the horse battle forward during the final stretch, suddenly contending for first place without Gomez even using the whip in his right hand. Obviously Gomez felt content with third place, or sensed the horse didn't want to slow, so he just let Phantom run his own race.

"He's going to do it," Teakon said, putting a fist up to his mouth as his brown eyes stared down the track.

Phantom overtook the second place horse with less than fifty yards to the finish line, creating a frenzied crowd. Jennings started jumping up and down in place a bit when he saw Phantom chase down the leader with less than twenty yards to go. He couldn't imagine what momentum the group would carry with them to Kentucky if Phantom finished first, but he soon discovered it wasn't meant to be. Phantom came within a nose of catching the first place horse, just short of a photo finish, easily securing second place.

Jennings and Teakon exchanged mixed looks of excitement and grave concern after seeing the finish. They were indeed heading to Louisville without much fanfare, which suited their secretive task of locating a certain gambler and the cube he used for financial gain after murdering someone each time.

Based on the reception Clay received at the island west of South America and Parish's experience on the Bering Sea, they anticipated they might not be the only ones heading to the Kentucky Derby.

Chapter 18

Paul Clouse learned to keep secrets well over the years, even from his own family. His parents knew little of his ordeals, and now in their retirement years, they needed to be content and happy instead of worried about him. While his self-appointed position as the guardian of cursed cubes put them in danger a few times, he shielded them from the majority of the truth on a regular basis.

When he told his wife, Jane, of his plan to recover the time cube himself, she thought he was losing his mind, but he told her he was going to disappear in a few days and use some unorthodox methods of travel to avoid detection. Feeling certain his every move was being watched by a certain entity that may or may not have been the Coven he dealt with previously, Clouse played it smart regarding the time cube.

Not only did he have his people look into numerous properties around the Chicago area to create a figurative smokescreen, but he also kept the property Liz located under wraps by using a different lawyer, from Chicago, to inquire about the property. Under orders to keep his mouth shut to everyone, including his secretary, wife, and office partners, the lawyer found the property was owned by an investor who failed to do anything useful with it in a decade.

Clouse discreetly had the lawyer approach the man as a contractor who wanted an area for storage. Though the land was nearly impassible from the vegetation growing around it, and the main building showing signs of wear from neglect, the property still seemed passable for storage or light construction work. Names were signed along the dotted lines shortly after the new year and Clouse let none of his people step foot near the property. He figured the best way to keep his secret safe was to let his adversaries follow him and his people while they conducted everyday business.

Not until early April, when the ink on the property thoroughly dried and the weather took away the bitter ice and snow from Northern Illinois did he finally decide to act.

It took more willpower than Clouse expected to leave his property in the middle of the night without kissing his wife and children goodbye. He drove to the train station in Indianapolis, buying a ticket for Massachusetts, which indicated he was sneaking off to see Julie Knowles. Clouse rather hoped anyone observing his actions believed he was carrying on an affair with the young woman. Whatever his followers thought of such a trip didn't much matter to him so long as they believed he was indeed traveling east. In truth, he bought a train ticket from an individual to Chicago discreetly, rather than purchase it at the sales window.

By morning light he stepped from the train, rented a car and drove it to a busy hotel in downtown Chicago. He didn't formally check in because he wanted no paper trail of his travels. Aiming to simply lose any tenacious followers, Clouse hailed a cab from the hotel's courtesy phone, asking for the driver to meet him around back. From there Clouse met with the attorney who purchased the property for him, asking the man to personally drive him to the property, hoping his actions were enough to provide him with privacy for the next day or two.

"You sure you don't want me to stay?" the lawyer asked when Clouse stepped from the car, leaving the door open to converse momentarily.

"I'll be fine. You did get me everything I asked for, right?"

"Of course."

Clouse paid the man handsomely for both legal and errand boy services. His demands certainly weren't outlandish, though the attorney likely found them highly specific.

"I'm just worried about you being out here all alone. How will I know when to come get you?"

Clouse looked up at the partially cloudy morning sky. Puffy white clouds with hints of gray glided across the blue background, gently propelled by an early April breeze. Stubborn hills of snow remained on the grounds, the air cool enough that Clouse opted to wear a fall jacket with a thermal layer. He wore three layers of shirts beneath the jacket, and some insulating legwear beneath his blue jeans. Some snacks, a winter cap and two pairs of gloves were tucked into the pack he brought. He learned on the fire department to always keep an extra pair of gloves handy at all times.

"Come and get me tomorrow morning around this time."

"You're sure?" his attorney asked, his eyebrows arched as though he questioned his best client's rationale.

If not his sanity.

"Positive. See you tomorrow."

Clouse shut the door, watching and listening carefully as the man drove his Lexus down the hill, away from the old construction hub. He wanted to know the sounds of a vehicle approaching, though Clouse supposed he lacked adequate hiding spots if anyone decided to visit him. His pack also carried his cell phone, though he removed the battery from the back before leaving his mansion. Knowing the government or other entities might trace him through the phone communicating with cell phone towers, he decided to bring it for an emergency situation only.

Quickly surveying the property and the equipment left by a rental company through the attorney's orders, Clouse found everything in order. While he trusted his team, Clouse couldn't take the chance of someone else finding the most important of the cubes and using it to his or her advantage. He supposed Greene or Liz could have already unearthed the time cube, but they obviously hadn't, which only raised their stock in his eyes.

Clouse spent almost half an hour climbing down to the spot where the quarry once rested dangerously below the construction headquarters. Several young saplings took residence where water once pooled near the steep natural wall. A few shrubs dotted the dirt wall, which looked almost directly vertical from below. Behind him, a farmer's field stood barren with the previous fall's stalks still clinging to the ground, dead and tan. Because the former quarry belonged on the land Clouse purchased, a small access path stemmed from the main road heading up the hill. The construction company had left an excavator and some hand tools there for Clouse to use, per the attorney's orders.

With limited experience in construction equipment, Clouse carefully positioned the excavator until he got the hang of using the articulating arm. Saying he mastered the machine would have been a gross overstatement of his abilities, but he found himself digging in the quarry area within an hour. All the while he felt more than slightly disturbed about intruding upon a grave. Knowing Thomas Ervin believed in the same principles, and wanted to keep the cube safe from evildoers, drove Clouse onward.

Working up a sweat in no time, Clouse removed the trees, shrubs, and several large rocks before getting to his true purpose. He dug almost twenty feet before he found a need to locate the 3D imaging metal detector the rental company left on the trailer. Not the easiest tool in the world to use, the detector finally provided a range of colors across the screen for Clouse to decipher any objects below him and their depth. The detector promised a range of sixty meters below the ground, though Clouse figured that was under ideal conditions.

He found himself surrounded by virtually the opposite scenario thirty years after Thomas Ervin disappeared.

Despite nature's barricades, Clouse discovered that much of his already dug hole was directly over a large object, which he imagined was a Ford LTD. Ladders stood with the remaining construction equipment when he felt the need to climb down, but more digging needed to be done before he planned on shoveling his way into the vintage car.

Wiping the sweat from his brow, Clouse took a moment to observe the area surrounding him. Very isolated from the city, this wooded area provided the sort of peace and serenity he once found at the West Baden Springs Hotel on the team that helped restore the building. After years of living and working in Bloomington, near the Indiana University campus, he loved traveling an hour south to work at the dome. Unfortunately the job, and the building itself in some ways, led to the darkest days of his life after his first wife was murdered.

Clouse found his name centered in the investigation, eventually cleared thanks to help from a man he now considered a close friend. Angie's murder, and the subsequent events, took him down some dark roads as he discovered the Coven and at the heart of the group, a man he considered a benefactor, friend, and mentor. While that man now lay six feet deep with a slab of concrete covering his charred remains, Clouse carried on his war against the cubes and those who intended to use them for personal gain.

He suffered terrible losses over the years, similar to mounting casualties during times of war. His first wife, his best friend, the family dog, and countless friends and acquaintances did nothing to deserve death. Their only "crime" was affiliation with Paul Clouse, and for that many of them were taken from him too soon. Much of this happened before Clouse even knew the extent or power of the cubes, and subsequently dedicated much of his life to harvesting them for safekeeping.

Hanging his head momentarily, Clouse prayed he wouldn't lose more. A man of religious convictions, he wanted to believe the Lord above was watching over him and approving of his methods. He treasured the friends and family left around him, and he conducted such costly work to maintain their safety.

"Back to work," he muttered as he climbed into the excavator's cab, ready to dig another ten feet before breaking out the shovels.

He spent another twenty minutes trying to fine-tune the digging above where the detector showed the car's location. From there, he created a jagged, staggered side, almost like crude stairs, so the ladder wasn't his only method of entry or exiting the now thirty foot deep hole. Finally the metal teeth at the end of the articulating arm struck something more solid than dirt with a clunk that was unmistakably metal. Clouse breathed a sigh of relief, feeling sorrow simultaneously because he knew he was going to be the first person to lay eyes on Thomas Ervin in decades.

Using the arm to carefully dig a trench around the car, about four feet further down, Clouse worked until the LTD's slightly raised hind end was free. For some reason the car came to rest at an angle, probably due to a large rock or another object dropped into the quarry. Clouse could examine the bottom of the car to find out definitively, but he didn't much care about conducting a forensic analysis.

Jumping from the excavator's cab, he positioned the ladder down one of the more vertical sides of the large hole. He also took a braided rope the rental company provided, tying it to the excavator's arm before throwing the opposite end down the embankment. Being stuck in a hole during a frigid spring evening didn't sound particularly good for his health, so he wanted multiple exits in place. Carrying a shovel with him, he finally descended the ladder until he reached the secondary level just above the car. Assured the rope was in place, he jumped down to the car, taking a moment to admire the courage Ervin put forth in defending the cursed object. Desecrating one's grave wasn't something Clouse took lightly, especially since he and Ervin were kindred spirits.

Positive he wasn't going to like what he found regarding the body's condition, Clouse warily dug around the driver's side door to free more of the sediment from his path. A layer of silt continued to cling to the car's shell from its time underwater, preventing a good look inside. He refused to wipe off the windows for a peek, though doing so would have given him an immediate view of the body's condition. Showing restraint, he spent about fifteen minutes shoveling dirt to the side until he freed the door enough to open it.

Unsure of exactly when the quarry was filled in with dirt, Clouse found two things very interesting about the LTD. One, the door actually opened despite some rust to the body and the uncoated metal hinges. The second and possibly more amazing find was an absolute lack of dirt and mud inside the vehicle.

No water remained inside the vehicle as the years slowly evaporated it into the surrounding dirt particles. Clouse could only assume the dirt dumped into the quarry to fill it turned to mud immediately upon impact with the water, keeping it from breaking the car's rear and side glass. The intact car preserved the terrible odor associated with death, coupled with the mustiness and rot accumulated from the car itself.

Groaning as he covered his mouth and nose with his forearm, Clouse coughed a few times when the permeating smell reached his throat and lungs. He suddenly wished he hadn't overlooked requesting a form of self-contained breathing apparatus like he once used as a firefighter.

Stepping to the inner portion of the door, Clouse finally looked inside the car, immediately seeing a skeleton positioned in the driver's seat. The lower jaw was dropped, giving the impression Ervin's bones spied something ghastly in front of the car. Clouse knew without tendons and muscle tissue, the bone simply fell out of place over the years. No muscle remained and the bones looked surprisingly clean despite their surroundings. While the bones showed only minor yellowing, Clouse discovered most of Ervin's clothing was deteriorated. Nothing stopped water scavengers, then earthworms, from getting their fill over three decades.

About the only thing left was Ervin's duty jacket, and even it remained tattered. Fighting off the urge to vomit from the cocktail of odors entering his nostrils, Clouse dared reach inside the car to probe the jacket with one hand, searching for the inside pocket that housed the cube according to Liz's vision. He found no pocket, but only because the material inside had succumbed to the elements, likely letting the cube fall to a different position.

"Oh, great," Clouse grumbled as he searched around the body for the object.

After searching between the bony legs, around the seat, and just to the right of the body, he finally spied a glimmer from the passenger's side floorboard. The cubes wanted to be noticed, so some unsuspecting soul might use them, and this dark blue cube glistened at him where no light entered to illuminate it.

At him.

Clouse never mistook the purpose of the cubes, or the fact that they knew how to toy with human emotions. Considering himself immune to their charms, he treated them like an abusive parent might an insolent child.

No longer did the protective pouch cover its nature, but it never escaped Thomas Ervin's watchful eye. Clouse reached over the man's remains, careful not to disturb the bones as he plucked the cube from the far corner. He pocketed the evil object, wishing cursed objects could be destroyed, but indestructibility was somehow woven into the original curse ceremony.

Taking a final look into the car, Clouse prayed for Tom Ervin that the man found peace in the afterlife. He shut the car door slowly with his mood deeply somber, wishing things hadn't ended so badly for the devoted cop and protector of mankind.

Clouse decided to leave the area alone and report the discovery of the body to the authorities. Trudy, the man's only surviving relative, deserved the truth after so many years of Ervin's disappearance remaining a mystery. Of course Clouse needed to sugarcoat certain parts of the discovery to avoid talking about his true reasons for using excavation equipment. He suspected a few members of the Chicago Police Department might want to have a talk with him regarding the cube. They would have to use careful wording when probing to see if he found the blue object, and Clouse suspected he might be forthcoming with the entire truth.

A number of variables needed to occur before such a conversation ever took place.

Now barely lunchtime, Clouse locked up the equipment and set everything back where he found it for the rental company to retrieve. He needed to remain hidden until morning with the cube, hoping no one figured out his plan or came to get him. So long as he left the cell phone separate from its battery and remained indoors, his chances remained good to excellent.

His major dilemma became where to hide the cube once he left Illinois. Dumping it into an ocean no longer seemed practical, leaving him to wonder if he might have been smarter to leave it in Thomas Ervin's care. Fortunately nothing pressing awaited him in the near future, giving Clouse time enough to ponder alternative areas in which to hide the cursed object.

Clouse gave the equipment and the partially buried car one last glance before heading up the access road. He planned to rough it overnight in the old building overhead, likely haunted by dreams of Thomas Ervin in life and death. Like the Chicago police officer, Clouse now felt the overwhelming responsibility of guarding the cube looming over him like a dark cloud with unforeseen consequences.

Chapter 19

When Chase Dalton finally tracked down the bookie he believed his friend was searching for, he waited until Saturday before venturing into the man's lair. Calling it a place of business, apartment, or living space felt too generous to the marshal. Basically a closet in the back of a convenience store, the room provided both the privacy and secrecy the bookie needed to conduct business. His friend at the front counter only let people through who knew the right thing to say, and fortunately for Dalton an informant provided him with both the location and information.

He dressed much like he might during the week because betters came in all shapes and sizes. A sport coat covered the firearm at his side, and Dalton's credentials remained safely tucked inside a pocket. Walking down a street that appeared far different than most people envisioned when they thought of Nashville, Dalton felt his sport coat flap when the gusty breeze struck it. Strangely, the street appeared mostly deserted with people emerging from one door just long enough to duck into another.

Dalton immediately regarded the store as a dive fit for roaches and vermin with only half of the overhead lights working and a perpetual stench that resembled body odor. Shelves and racks weren't fully stocked, and most of the food items had packaging that looked faded or damaged. He didn't look around very long because the clerk eyed him suspiciously the second he stepped through the front door. The deputy marshal approached the counter with a sense of purpose, deciding not to waste additional time.

"Remember the Titans," he stated the password, which related to the Tennessee Titans football team.

Though the man continued providing a suspicious stare, he let Dalton walk around the counter toward the back room. He gave three knocks with his knuckles in a rhythmic pattern before opening the door, indicating with an open hand for Dalton to enter.

Seated behind a small wooden desk in an otherwise empty room, a haggard man with weathered skin and pale blue eyes barely looked in his direction before focusing his attention on a spreadsheet with numerous columns. Disheveled thinning gray hair covered the man's head and he reeked of stale cigarette smoke. His hands trembled slightly as he jotted something on the spreadsheet, a cell phone held against his right ear by his bony shoulder.

He murmured a name that sounded like a racing horse because it was three words in length before jotting down a number and someone's last name on the paper. Only when he confirmed the name and amount did he end the phone call and look up to Dalton a second time.

"And how can I help you?"

"By telling me about one of your clients named Lincoln Daine."

"Who's asking?"

"Someone who owes a friend a huge favor. I just need to know the last time you heard from him and I leave your place of business alone."

Dalton moved his sport coat aside just enough to display the firearm and the badge he attached to his belt.

"Fucking great," the man sighed.

"Daine," Dalton urged, poking his finger onto the spreadsheet.

"It's been months," the bookie answered without shifting his eyes away from the marshal. "The guy moves around constantly."

"But he always comes back. Certainly a man of your caliber, with such lucrative clients, has the means to reach his clients when something good comes along."

The bookie shook his head.

"Daine comes in when he wants to. He knows the score, and the state of Tennessee isn't usually the place to win big."

Dalton wasn't convinced, so he put forth an expression to indicate he wasn't leaving without at least a little cooperation from the bookie. He didn't envision the man keeping a Rolodex of clients in a penthouse office downtown so he needed information here and now.

Getting a bit more serious, Dalton made a fist before slamming it down on the table where the bookie sat. While his actions failed to frighten the man into talking, the sudden sound of gunfire behind the deputy marshal drew a shocked expression from the bookie as Dalton reached for his sidearm.

Putting his right arm behind him with an open hand, Dalton indicated for the bookie to stay put as he drew his officially issued firearm. He figured someone was conducting a robbery on the store, though he couldn't imagine why anyone would bother knocking off such a rundown business. Holding his firearm at his side, the marshal cautiously turned the doorknob, opening the door just enough for a peek into the cluttered store. He barely put his face to the opening when the butt of a shotgun rammed through the opening, striking him in the forehead.

Dalton fell to the floor in a heap, still semiconscious from the blow. He heard some sounds, but everything reaching his ears sounded garbled while his vision was blurred and fading fast. Between the two senses he was able to determine the man with the shotgun taking aim at the bookie, the bookie pleading for his life, and the sound of the shotgun being fired that caused Dalton's ears to begin ringing more than before.

The bookie's lifeless body fell to the ground beside the marshal, his eyes wide open with a death stare. His chest was red and bloodied from the shotgun pellets, chunks of flesh and clothing dangling with the fresh, dripping blood. Dalton saw the man's killer kneel beside the fresh corpse, pulling something from his own pocket that he touched to the bookie's blood before uttering some words.

"I wish to take the form of this man," is what it sounded like he said, but the statement made no sense to the marshal.

Dalton fumbled for his gun, now unable to find it beside him, as the gunman turned his attention to him. Certain this was the end of his life, but uncertain why, the marshal watched the man reach toward him with whatever object he used to touch the bookie's blood.

***

When Dalton awoke from the unconscious state he fell into at the convenience store he found his ears ringing, his vision still a bit fuzzy, and his head aching as though he'd suffered a concussion from the shotgun blow. Amazed to be alive after the bizarre events that transpired inside the convenience store, Dalton blinked what seemed like a thousand times before his eyes finally stayed open to take in the room around him.

He couldn't recall if he regained consciousness at any point, so Dalton wondered how far removed he was from Tennessee, if at all, and if the day was still

Saturday. Feeling somewhat groggy, as though drugs were used to maintain his helpless state, the deputy marshal struggled against his bonds. The familiar clanking of handcuffs reached his ears when he realized his hands were bound together in addition to being bonded with a separate chain to the solid metal chair where he sat.

His feet were also shackled to the chair, which reminded him of a throne because the back sat as tall as most people. Its comfortable padding provided little relief to Dalton as the metal frame refused to budge, even against his considerable strength. At least his eyes finally began to take in the scenery around him, even if he couldn't get up for a closer look.

Otherwise devoid of furniture, the room felt cool and humid with its solid slab floor, indicating Dalton was probably being held on a ground floor. He only knew it wasn't a basement because of the window just behind him to the left. Some dark red drapes that looked decades old from their pattern covered part of the window, allowing some daylight inside. Dalton thought it was a late afternoon sun based on the reddish glare, though he found his eyes equally drawn to the cobwebs and dust clinging to the old curtains.

The walls were covered with vintage Victorian wallpaper consisting of gold and red patterns that complimented the drapes. Above him, intricate engravings showed through the gray shade of the ceiling tiles, causing Dalton to wonder if he was trapped inside an old mansion or the dressing room of a closed down performance theater. No sign of electricity came from the light bulb over him or beneath the door behind him when he strained his neck to look.

Completely helpless, Dalton couldn't even budge the chair once he braced his feet against the ground, much less knock it over. Stripped of his firearm, keys, and any other loose articles, Dalton possessed nothing useful to expedite his escape. The thought of the bookie being blown away in front of him crossed his mind, making him wonder why he was spared at all.

Another ten minutes passed as Dalton cleared his head and found his vision growing better with each passing second. When the door finally opened behind him, Dalton expected to be executed swiftly, or dragged from the room for use as a bargaining chip in some kind of ransom scheme.

Instead, he came face-to-face with himself.

Himself.

"What do you think?" the stranger who looked like him asked, the voice exactly like Dalton's own.

Speechless, Dalton felt certain he was in one of the *Terminator* movies about to be executed and replaced by some machine or clone.

"Before I begin asking you questions that you will answer, I'm going to explain the situation to you," the stranger said, kneeling down in front of Dalton. "You're here because of your friend Greene, and I need him to think that I'm you."

Dalton said nothing, his mind racing for answers. Having his friend's name thrown in the mix only confused him further. What the hell had Greene gotten himself into in the private sector?

"I barely even know Greene," Dalton lied, drawing a smile from his twin self, which gave him the creeps.

"That's not true, and I'm banking on the fact that Greene will offer you a job in your time of need. See, you're about to leave your job with the government and ask your old friend for a job."

Dalton scowled, knowing he was about to be pried open like a can of sardines for information. Though he hated the idea of bringing harm to Greene in any way, he wished to keep all of his body parts intact, hoping for an escape attempt at some point.

"I want to know everything," the mystery man said ominously, leaning forward until their faces were inches apart. "Every detail about your work with Greene, every drink you two shared in a bar. If I'm going to live your life I need to know about your personal life, especially pertaining to Russ Greene."

"How are you even capable of this?"

"Forgive my bad manners. I intended to explain this in detail before starting the interrogation."

Dalton said nothing, just waiting for some answers.

"This little object," the man said, holding up a cube the color of a tangerine, "gives me the ability to look and sound just like whomever I choose."

Sitting back with a stonewalled expression, Dalton said nothing, immediately disbelieving whatever this identical stranger said.

"It's not a genie, however, Mr. Dalton. It requires a sacrifice each time I want to use it, and your buddy is hunting down these cubes and everyone who possesses one. It's only a matter of time before he and I meet face-to-face, and I want it to be on *my* terms."

"What the hell are you going to do?" Dalton asked, his concern escalating for his former colleague.

"I'm going to kill him, of course. Or rather *you're* going to kill him."

"Bastard!" Dalton shouted, trying to buck the restraints that held him in place against the sturdy chair.

"Don't worry. He won't die right away. I need to earn his trust, and for that I need your assistance. Only then can I find out where he's hiding the rest of these delightful little cubes so my organization can take what's truly our birthright."

Dalton still couldn't believe a single word entering his ears, but the proof stood directly before him. How else could the man look and sound identical to him? Even the best technology created by the government showed telltale flaws in the field.

"You're insane," he muttered anyway, trying to provoke a response.

"No, I'm not. It's only too bad your friend didn't trust you enough to bring you with him, or you'd know the truth."

Reaching for a leather handbag behind him, the man drew a pad of paper, a pen, and lastly a knife that appeared surgical in nature, setting each to his right side in order. With the dark, narrowing eyes of a serpent he looked directly at Dalton.

"Shall we begin?"

Chapter 20

During the last week of April a number of important items required Russ Greene's attention. He chose to stay in the sixth floor of the West Baden Springs Hotel with his employer's blessing simply to plan for the Kentucky Derby and several other pressing issues.

Liz finally made a permanent move from California to Indiana, based on his recommendation. After proving her worth with the Thomas Ervin saga, Greene spoke with Clouse about bringing the entire team closer in proximity. Clay Branson, still a rogue by comparison, remained in Mason, Ohio without much commitment to the cause. Greene suspected the man might disavow the group completely once he relocated and settled the score with his former mentor.

Putting aside his feelings toward Branson, Greene opted to speak with Clouse about the most important of the cubes privately. His employer traveled to the hotel, meeting him at Ballard's Bar in the grand atrium of the resort around lunchtime. Though the bar was not entirely secluded, both men felt safe in the hotel because the likelihood of someone listening to their conversation or observing them seemed remote. After all, Clouse owned the hotel, and therefore all of the security cameras, personnel, and establishments within it.

"Where do we stand with our overall objectives?" Clouse asked once the two men shook hands and sat at a table with bottles of beer before them.

"We stand to lose or gain a lot in the next two weeks," Greene answered. "Right now we still possess enough of the cubes to ensure the world is safe."

"Have you done any further research?" Clouse asked before taking a swig of beer.

"Enough to know that you are labeled as the possessor of one of the cubes," Greene answered without fear of retaliation from his boss.

He didn't much care what Clouse thought of his opinion at this point, grasping the notion that their quest far exceeded the worth of either man.

"For now it stays in my possession," Clouse answered firmly. "It's safe."

"Safe from whom? There are people who would kill in the blink of an eye to possess that thing. They would gladly abduct your family and fillet them in front of you until you surrendered it."

"Point taken," Clouse said calmly. "And so long as no one except you and Julie know that I possess it, I shouldn't have much to worry about."

"Oh?" Greene asked, sitting back to create some distance from his employer. "And what if you were to use the cube? Maybe take a trip back in time and save your first wife? Or your best buddy from high school?"

Clouse barely raised an eyebrow as his glare relayed his opinion on the matter.

"I didn't bring you into the fold to serve as my backup conscience, Russ. While I appreciate everything you and the team have done thus far, that cube stays with me until we can guarantee it doesn't fall into the wrong hands."

"That's the problem with cursed objects. They never go away."

Both men took a drink from their beers, trying to calculate what the other was thinking.

"I simply didn't appreciate being left out of the loop," Greene stated for the record.

"That's understandable, Russ. But you've got to understand that a game changer like the time cube isn't something I can just toss into a local safe and forget about. Believe me, if I had plans to do something about the past, it would already be done. I've suffered a lot of losses the past ten years, but it's brought me to this point where I can actually do something good that affects, if not saves, billions of lives."

Greene understood Clouse's point, knowing that meant the book linked to all thirteen cubes became equally essential from a protection standpoint. For the past few months a thirst for knowledge about the cubes ate at Greene from the inside, not because he sought their power, but because he knew great leaders understood their enemy.

"I doubt this is the last time we'll be having a conversation about that cube," he informed Clouse.

"I certainly hope not, and I'm very open to ideas about keeping it safe well beyond our years."

"Tom Ervin certainly did a good job," Greene said with a sharp edge to his tone.

Clouse caught the meaning, though he masked his feelings about the thought of sacrificing himself in a dark and lonely grave with the cube.

"No disrespect, boss, but when you said you wanted me to keep the cubes safe from everyone because you trusted me implicitly, I thought you meant *everyone*."

"I thought I did, but for now this is the exception to the rule."

Thumbing his beer bottle momentarily, Clouse looked more at ease about the situation, understanding Greene's perspective.

"Aside from questioning my moral fiber, what else is on your mind, Russ?"

"I want to let Liz get more involved."

"More involved?"

"Until now we've been operating on conjecture, a handful of documents, some research Mark Teakon conducted, and a book that may or may not be our ally. I want her to handle some of these objects and see if she can tell us where they came from, and maybe something more about them."

Clouse held his beer, stared at it momentarily in thought, and finally put it down to look Greene in the eye.

"That can be a dangerous game, especially if what she said is remotely true about someone tapping into her thoughts. We don't know if the other side has someone with equal or greater ability than hers."

"We also don't know if the other side possesses three-quarters of the cubes, preparing to murder us in our sleep so they can carry out their plan."

"I leave it up to you," Clouse said, holding up both hands. "Just know there are significant risks if the other side gains an understanding of things. Right now we have a strategic advantage because we possess the book. If they find out about it, a lot more people will die."

Greene nodded.

"We already know they're watching our every move, which is why we can't safely dispose of the cubes. Maybe it's time to start learning who our enemy truly is."

"How so?"

"We set up stings all the time when I worked for the government," Greene said with a cagy smile. "Maybe we can lure someone into a trap and get them to talk."

"If the other side can play dirty, I don't see a problem with that."

Clouse held up his bottle and Greene tapped it with his. Aside from the recent sneaky stint, Greene liked and respected his employer wholeheartedly.

***

Near the end of the conversation with Clouse, Greene received a call from Chase Dalton in which his former colleague asked to meet with him in person.

"It's urgent," Dalton said in a hushed voice, as though someone nearby might be eavesdropping.

Greene offered to travel to Tennessee, but Dalton countered, saying he could make it to Indiana by nightfall. Deciding it wasn't any big deal, Greene provided his friend with the name and address of the hotel. He then made arrangements with Dan Duncan, the hotel manager, to put Dalton up for the night before returning to some paperwork to pass the time.

During the day he made plans for the Kentucky Derby, along with potential ideas to dispose of the remaining cubes where no one could find them. He felt a lot more pressure doing his current job than he ever experienced working for the government. While some of the names written in Julie's book let him know who possessed the cursed objects, in some cases he found absolutely no information about the people through his research. Searching for people seemed much easier with government computers, informants, and anonymous tips.

Uncertain whether or not his friend would call or simply show up, Greene remained inside the hotel most of the day. He left once to buy a deep-dish pizza down the street at one of the local pizzerias, choosing to escape the hotel walls in lieu of the fine dining along the ground floor.

The sun began setting around the time Greene stepped onto the hotel's veranda, admiring the serenity around him, wishing more moments in his life could feel so care free. Much of the day he found his mind wandering to what kind of trouble Dalton stepped into that required a face-to-face talk with him. Dalton was never one to deviate too far from the rulebook at work, and he never dabbled in illicit activities outside of work.

Greene's stomach grumbled because lunch at the pizza joint was almost eight hours behind him. He decided to hold out in order to show his friend some good hospitality in the French Lick area when Dalton arrived.

Some of his planning on the hotel's sixth floor put him in contact with Liz a few different times. Both were currently staying there for different reasons. Liz had yet to find an apartment or house locally, which Dalton attributed to her being a picky California girl. Greene simply needed to remain close to most of his team, and West Baden provided a solid base of operations.

Paul Clouse and his family once lived in the sixth floor suite of the hotel because it provided them safe haven from the public and anyone wanting to harm them. More than once people had tried using Clouse's family as leverage against him to obtain one of the cursed cubes, which forced his retreat into the hotel. While the hotel itself initiated many of the problems in Clouse's life, he felt the public setting provided protection, and the isolated sixth floor made it easy for his bodyguards and hotel security to protect his family.

Because none of the hotel's two-hundred-forty-six rooms took up space on the ground floor, each of the other five floors housed over fifty rooms each. Much of the top floor's space was transformed into a suite sectioned off from the other rooms initially. When Clouse moved his family there, the entire floor was transformed into a penthouse of sorts, complete with workout facility, dining areas, special guest rooms, and office space. While its rounded hallways comprised a massive amount of square footage, the segmented areas made it feasible that Greene and Liz might not spy one another during the course of a single day.

Looking out to the sunken garden, Greene paced the veranda's tile surface momentarily before taking a seat on one of the white rocking chairs placed behind the railing. Often sure to keep busy every second of the day, Greene found the sensation of simple relaxation rather foreign. Even now he wanted to look anxiously over his shoulder, feeling certain someone was spying on him or preparing to assault him in search of the cubes.

He sometimes wondered who Clouse's alternate choice for his job might have been. None of the people Clouse researched were revealed to one another, but Greene felt certain he, Liz, and Clay Branson were the man's top picks with good reason.

When Greene decided to stroll around the back of the hotel, he noticed the bulbs in the Victorian green lamp posts coming to life, illuminating the brick drive and the garden area. He saw a couple about to take a carriage ride, one of the many perks about staying at the hotel. Between the stables, two major golf courses, the spas, the casino, and a theme park just over half an hour away, people found numerous reasons to spend the night.

Spying headlights approaching as he walked along the driveway, Greene stepped aside to look at the vehicle. Because it wasn't quite dark outside yet, he was able to see inside the government-issued sedan, noticing his friend Chase Dalton. For some reason Dalton didn't even look around, much less notice Greene right beside him. He continued to drive toward the parking lot, so Greene chose to follow on foot. Thinking his buddy might have suffered from fatigue during the long drive from Tennessee, Greene decided to lend a hand and carry some luggage.

He passed the valet area, which Dalton had also bypassed, heading directly to the regular parking lot. Following the sidewalk up to the parking area, he found Dalton unloading a suitcase from the trunk of the sedan, wearing slacks and a dress shirt minus the tie. He appeared tired, but not haggard as he set the suitcase on the ground to shut the trunk.

"Want some help with that?" Greene asked.

"No, I'm good," Dalton said in a tone that indicated he didn't know who was speaking to him, possibly thinking a valet was searching for an easy tip.

When he did finally turn around, he noticed Greene standing there and stuck out his hand after a few seconds. They shook hands, which Greene considered a new concept only because they were always so casual around the office. Of course he hadn't seen Dalton in months and their relationship was no longer based on their occupations.

"Good to see you, Russ."

"Likewise, Chase. You drove right past me back there."

"Sorry about that. I'm just so tuckered out after this drive I wasn't even looking."

Greene noticed his friend only brought a small suitcase, doubting Dalton planned on staying long.

"Traveling light, I see."

"Yeah," Dalton answered with a weak smile. "This all came unexpectedly. Boy, have I got a tale to tell you."

"You can tell me over dinner because I'm starved. What sounds good?"

"What do you have here?" Dalton asked. "On second thought, anything sounds good as long as it goes with beer."

Greene thumbed toward the hotel.

"There's a bar inside that serves a couple dishes."

***

Greene waited until his friend settled into his room and changed clothes before meeting him at Ballard's Bar. Part of the bar sat just inside the atrium with traditional barstools and a television usually tuned to sports of some kind. The outer portion was located inside the atrium itself and provided nearly two-dozen seats for guests to sample some of the spirits or get a bite to eat. Little more than appetizers rounded out the menu, but it was decent food and usually served quickly.

"So what's this big story of yours?" Greene inquired. "You had me half scared to death when you called."

"I don't even know where to begin," Dalton said, shaking his head.

In detail, the man weaved a story that captivated Greene during the entire telling.

Dalton relayed how he was ambushed at the convenience store, kidnapped, and brought face to face with himself in a musty old room. The entire telling took nearly twenty minutes, during which onion rings and potato skins came and grew cold because neither man touched them. As Greene heard that one of the cubes was responsible for his friend's peril, he felt partially responsible, swelling with the notion he needed to retrieve that cursed object at any cost.

"How the hell did you get out of there?" he finally asked, knowing the details leading up to confinement in a smelly room.

"That's the tricky part," Dalton confessed, finally munching on an onion ring. "The guy had some henchmen watching over me because he wanted to use me for information to infiltrate our department."

Greene didn't take offense to the implication he still worked for the government because he hadn't been gone terribly long.

"It was just like in the movies. When they let me go to the bathroom I overpowered one of them and got his gun. After that I just made a run for it and called you when I got far enough away from their hideout."

Unsure of what to say because the last portion of his friend's testimony seemed rather brief, while the rest was filled with details, Greene simply tipped his beer bottle to his lips. As though on cue, Liz crossed the atrium, taking notice of their conversation. She appeared unsure of whether or not to join them, so he waved her over before making proper introductions.

"Liz assists me in my new job," Greene added as she took a seat at the table.

Despite Dalton telling him one of the cubes was responsible for his current predicament, Greene didn't reveal his new line of work. He felt an obligation to explain the truth to his former colleague, yet he didn't want Dalton placed in additional danger.

"Are you ever going to tell me exactly what you left a perfectly good government job for?"

Liz gave Greene a smirk, as though daring him to speak the truth.

An awkward silence encompassed the table momentarily until Dalton spoke.

"I'm sorry to bring all this trouble up here, Russ. I was hoping maybe you'd be able to help me get to the bottom of this issue with the guy looking identical to me."

"Well, there's a lot to be said about plastic surgery these days."

"And sound like me, too?"

Greene looked away uncomfortably, not wanting to speak on the subject with Liz present. He wasn't certain he ever wanted to speak to anyone outside of his current group about what he did for a living again. His earlier meeting with Clouse only compounded the issues already swirling through his mind.

"Maybe we should talk more about this in the morning," he finally suggested. "We're probably a little too amped up to keep talking business."

Dalton nodded.

"I appreciate everything you've done for me, Russ. I just didn't know where else to turn because no one else would believe me."

"Well, that's quite a story you've got, old friend," Greene said neutrally. "I won't be far, Chase. Get some rest and we'll talk some more in the morning."

Dalton stood, giving Greene a friendly nod before finally shaking hands with Liz. From the corner of his eye Greene noticed Liz tense the briefest of moments when physical contact was made. She didn't flinch like Dalton's skin was cold, or from static electricity. No, Greene decided immediately, Liz *saw* something beyond the physical world.

She played down the minimal change in behavior immediately, and Dalton seemed none the wiser about any indiscretion on her part.

Greene watched as Dalton gave them a quick wave before heading toward one of the large doorways to find an elevator. He waited until the man disappeared from sight before looking to Liz with anticipation that she met with a knowing gaze. Greene found it uncanny how they already knew one another so well that he didn't even have to speak to receive the answer he needed.

"That isn't your friend," she said evenly, though her words came with a hint of sadness. "What he spoke wasn't entirely untrue, but it was from your friend's perspective, and he was the perpetrator."

Somehow Greene sensed the truth, even before Liz uttered the words. The Chase Dalton he knew wasn't forgetful or impersonal. Had he not been informed, however, Greene might have eventually bought into the ruse.

"Is Chase…?"

Greene couldn't finish the sentence, already feeling the heavy burden of befriending anyone because friends easily became targets.

"He's alive so far as I could tell," Liz answered. "This man, whoever he is, possesses one of the cubes."

Greene reasoned that the man wanted inside information through joining Clouse's team, using the connection between Dalton and Greene as the means. His mind, working like an analytical computer at times, couldn't help but wonder if there was a connection between this imposter and Lincoln Daine. After all, Dalton went looking for Daine as a favor to his former colleague. Thinking beyond the surface layer, Greene wondered if he had spoken to the real Dalton at all, and perhaps this man was Daine, or an accomplice.

Either way he needed to act and act soon.

"Act casual and walk with me to the garden," Greene asked of Liz, who complied without hesitation.

The two walked across the atrium, finding themselves outside a few minutes later, away from snooping eyes and ears.

"What else did you see beyond what he told me? And how did you know what he told me anyway?"

"I could sense what he told you in the vision. He's keeping your friend prisoner down there in case he stumbles and needs information. There are armed men at the location."

"Anything else? Could you see the cube?"

"Yes. He held it in front of your friend, telling him everything about it. I think Chase is in grave danger."

"That goes without saying."

Greene knew the imposter would never reveal everything to Dalton unless he planned to dispose of him soon after.

"Your friend found the bookie, but the whole thing was a trap," Liz said, trying to remember details from the lightning flash of information. "It was in a convenience store, and the way they took him seemed well-organized as though they planned it in advance."

Suspecting the link between Daine and this imposter might now lead to a larger organization, Greene wondered how to proceed. He wasn't willing to gamble with Dalton's life, but he needed to ensure the villainous group learned nothing about his intentions or his people.

"Do you know where they're holding Dalton?"

"By sight," Liz answered. "I could guide you there when we get close. It looked like downtown Nashville, but not the better part."

Greene had some general ideas of ideal hiding spots. He didn't want to rely upon Liz to direct him, because he hated putting her in any kind of danger.

"What are you going to do?" Liz asked, her concern showing over the glowering look crossing his face.

"What needs to be done," he answered simply. "Thank you, Liz. I'm going to recommend you get a good night's rest because we may be heading south in the morning."

Greene hoped to discover his friend's location through other means, but that required the execution of a quickly assembled plan.

Chapter 21

Due to a stroke of luck Greene altered his plan slightly, putting it into action just after midnight.

Liz knew this because he called her less than half an hour after their talk outside the hotel. He told her to pack lightly for an overnight trip to Nashville with Todd Parish. While Parish wasn't technically part of their group, he often came in handy for last minute assignments. He brought a rental car by the hotel close to one in the morning and picked up Liz for an overnight drive to Tennessee.

She now found herself in the passenger's seat beside Parish, waiting for something that Parish had yet to divulge. Looking to the sky Liz discovered a nearly cloudless blue above her before looking down to the dashboard clock.

8:13 a.m.

"Not to sound like a broken record, but exactly what are we waiting for?" she inquired.

Parish parked about one block away from the building she identified as the old theatre where the real Dalton was being held. In a neglected portion of the downtown area, away from newer construction, taverns, and neon lights, the theatre looked like an oversized house with faded red and gold paint. The roof showed major wear as a few large areas no longer contained shingles, and some of the windows contained holes the size of baseballs and small rocks. Signs on the front door and a few of the lower level windows indicated the place was condemned, and likely up for demolition. Parish simply grunted when they drove by slowly the first time, possibly thinking the signs were forgeries.

"We're waiting for someone else to show up," Parish answered. "I'm just here for backup purposes."

"Is it Clay Branson?"

Parish looked at her as though slightly surprised and impressed at her intuition.

"How did you dupe him into helping out again?" Liz wondered aloud.

"*I* didn't do anything. There's only one thing that man wants, and Russ offered it to him."

Liz scoffed at the notion.

"I don't recall us locating Nosagi for him a second time."

"No, but if Russ is correct, we're facing off with a criminal element, and not just individuals. It stands to reason that Nosagi might be part of that clan."

"Something tells me Clay was fed less than the entire truth, which means my fearless leader will have to answer for it later."

Parish grinned slightly.

"That's *his* problem. If our part goes well here, he might not have much to worry about. We need Dalton back before he can proceed with his plan at the hotel."

Liz immediately grew concerned.

"And who's backing him up if you're here?"

"No one so far as I know. He's a big boy who can take care of himself."

Hoping Greene didn't do anything rash, Liz wondered exactly what he planned to do with the imposter. From her vision she knew the imposter was dangerous and just as analytical as her team leader. The one thing he lacked, however, was compassion because he showed about as much remorse for murdering the convenience store clerk as some people displayed after swatting a mosquito.

Leaving the car turned off for obvious reasons, Parish rolled down the window only to have someone pop up from below a few seconds later, startling both he and Liz. Parish actually gave a little yelp until he discovered their visitor was none other than the man they expected.

"That wasn't necessary," Parish berated Clay.

"But it was fun," Clay replied while Parish caught his breath and Liz chuckled at the husky bodyguard's demeanor.

"Bet you're fun at horror movies," she commented.

"I've *lived* horror movies, thank you."

Parish looked feverishly around both sides and behind him.

"What the hell did you drive?"

"I'm two blocks down," Clay answered. "I didn't think it was a smart idea to look like we're having a block party outside the place."

Parish scowled at the implication he parked too close to the theatre.

"Anything changed?" Clay asked.

"We haven't seen a thing."

"Then they're all inside, which makes it a bit difficult, especially in broad daylight."

"Greene wants this to be completely non-lethal, too. We don't need any police looking for us, even if we are doing the right thing."

Clay soured a bit.

"He says it's the right thing, and he says he'll get me Nosagi, but I'm probably better off hunting him down myself. And what is it with everyone assuming I'm some kind of murderous bastard because of my particular skill set?"

"Weren't your kind paid assassins back in the day? And didn't your *sensei* train most of your clan to maim and kill?"

"Touché."

"Boys, can we get to the business at hand so we can head home?" Liz interjected.

Clay looked to the theatre nearly ten seconds, analyzing it.

"Give me five minutes and I should have Greene's buddy out of there."

For the first time Liz noticed he was dressed primarily in black with a holstered sidearm on his left side. A few weapon handles emerged from around his shoulders, indicating he brought several bladed weapons and possibly more interesting goodies with him.

"What do you want from me?" Parish asked Clay, wanting to be part of the action after driving nearly six hours south.

"Stay here and watch her. I'll handle this."

"Excuse me?" Liz asked defensively, but Clay was already across the street, making a stealthy approach to the theatre.

She folded her arms unhappily.

"You men are all alike."

"Yeah," Parish replied without much empathy, watching Clay until he disappeared behind some overgrown shrubs. "We're insufferable."

***

Clay started by walking from the side of the theatre to the rear, listening intently at each window. He only heard the sound of distant voices at a window near the rear, where he guessed the old dressing room might be located. Because human beings, even paid underlings, were social creatures, he figured most of the men guarding Dalton were gathered in one area, content to check on the prisoner every so often or conduct rounds.

The nature of the building limited the number of windows, particularly along the auditorium and stage areas within. Clay decided to search for access to the basement, figuring the building would have such an area due to its age. Overgrown shrubs and untended grass made it nearly impossible to search anything directly against the building, but he finally found one small window that disclosed a basement indeed existed. Unsure of exactly what purpose the window served, Clay realized it was too small to serve as emergency egress and not attractive enough to add to the building's décor.

Suspecting no direct access existed from outside the building, like some old farm house with a stairwell leading down to the cellar, Clay decided to try the window. He needed the element of surprise, so barging through a door, or trying to scale a wall to the second floor meant taking a huge risk.

Hardly anyone ever guarded a basement.

Placing his body between the shrubs and the small window, Clay made certain he wasn't visible from any first or second story windows before using the blade of a throwing knife to work on the old window's weakened metal clasp lock. It took mere seconds before the lock gave way, which implied the previous owners relied upon some form of security device they disabled before surrendering the premises. Unfortunately the window tilted inside, so Clay forced its hinges beyond their capacity, breaking their thin metal before pulling the window outside and discarding it. He now needed to work quickly due to the minimal chance someone spotted the glass missing through the thick shrubbery.

With the difficult part out of the way, Clay removed the small utility pack from his back, placing it to one side of the window before peering inside. Just enough light entered behind him to illuminate the concrete floor almost eight feet below. Aside from an old wooden chair no furnishings showed themselves, so Clay clutched his pack and slid his body through the narrow opening. He barely fit, letting his feet enter first, followed by his legs and torso as he clutched the window's frame with conditioned fingers.

Once inside, his feet silently hit the floor as he scooped up his weapons pack and slung it around his back once more. As both a police officer and an unwittingly trained assassin, he had dealt with fellow killers and the worst of criminals in the past. Along the way a few Special Forces types had crossed his path and Clay handled them just fine as well. He suspected these were probably locally hired guns, though he knew not to underestimate them. Despite his training and abilities, Clay could be taken down by a well-placed blade or bullet.

Discovering the basement was immense, probably the full length and width of the building above, Clay wasted little time looking around except to find a route upstairs. A few tattered costumes remained along one rack, probably ravaged by moths overs the years, appearing rather faded.

When Clay discovered the stairwell, he struggled to see details in the low lighting. He tested the old, creaky wood with one foot, finding it both noisy and in slight disrepair. Finding a way around using the stairs directly, he placed his feet on the large boards to either side of the stairs, which supported the stairwell, and began ascending toward the door above. He avoided using the hand railings altogether, compensating with his practiced balance to steady himself with posture and foot strength.

One major disadvantage about not having many windows along the theatre walls was the inability to assess his location. Clay suspected he wasn't near the room where he overheard conversation based on his proximity to the access window. More than likely the basement stairs led to the backstage area, which only made sense. If so, he expected to find an area engulfed with darkness, but there was only one way to know.

He turned the knob, pushing the door into whatever room awaited him, indeed finding darkness ahead. A squeaking noise accompanied the door's movement, so Clay quickly leapt into the room ahead, discovering it was one side of the main stage. Looking around, he found no one waiting for him as voices carried from a nearby room. Suspecting the men might do routine patrols, or check on their prisoner, Clay drew a *kusari-fundo* from his pack for defense. Basically a chain with two weighted ends, the weapon provided non-lethal means of subduing an adversary without creating a commotion. Entirely customized by Clay, the two weighted ends actually served as handles capable of containing the short chain when pushed together to comprise one longer handle.

Clay left the handle intact, ready to pull the ends apart in a split-second if need be. He silently walked toward the conversation, wishing to know how many potential enemies awaited him. Brushing past some levers and old backdrops lining a wall, he spied into one of the old dressing rooms, finding three men playing cards around an end table layered in dust. Seeing no sense in attacking them if he could simply sneak Dalton out of the building, he continued his search through the ground floor, finding only empty rooms until he came upon a set of stairs leading upward.

He ascended them, only to discover they made both a creaking and a clopping noise simultaneously, prompting someone above him to speak.

"About time you came to relieve me."

The voice came from around a banister and the speaker remained out of view until a person drew near the top stair. Clay debated whether to make a hasty retreat or continue onward toward an inevitable confrontation. His major concern stemmed from the other three hired guns overhearing a struggle, but they were practically halfway across the large building.

Clay decided to confront the lone guard in the hope of freeing Dalton the easy way.

He decided to flatten his profile against the wall of the stairwell, hoping the guard might get antsy and look over the side. It took mere seconds for the man to grumble and mutter something under his breath before stomping a few steps away from his post to look over the banister. Listening intently to the footsteps, Clay determined his adversary planned to simply look over the edge because the steps sounded linear.

Already set, Clay pulled apart the two handles and purposefully threw the center of the chain upward in practically one motion. Timing the henchman's arrival perfectly, Clay watched the U-shaped end of the chain seat itself around the man's neck. Originally intending to pull the man down to his level, Clay changed plans when the man immediately began to squirm before the chain was able to grow taut against the nape of his neck. Instead, Clay let his own weight tug the man's head against the solid wooden banister, stunning him momentarily as the chain released its hold.

Quick as a cat, Clay ascended the stairs, jumping the banister's railing like a cowboy jumping a fence. The man had barely grunted when his head hit the wood, but he was about to shout for help after regaining his wits. Clay delivered a form of sidekick that connected with the man's abdomen, both knocking him back and deflating any chance of audibly signaling his buddies.

Still holding the *kusari-fundo* like a coiled snake in his left hand, Clay unraveled enough of it to swing the short section of chain at the man's head, knocking him to the ground with a gash to his left temple. Only when Clay dropped down and wrapped the chain around the man's neck to subdue him and quickly render him unconscious through oxygen deprivation did he take time to truly examine the thug to understand the nature of the men guarding Dalton.

Dressed in dark slacks with Italian loafers, the man wore a pastel purple shirt with the sleeves rolled up to his elbows. A silk tie of purple and glistening gold trim gave Clay the impression these weren't common gang members, but rather up and coming mafia types. He suspected these men were soldiers trying to make their way to a higher rank in whatever family employed them. The sidearm tucked into the man's belt along his back never became a factor, but Clay pulled it out and discarded it just the same.

The struggle lasted mere seconds before the well-dressed man gurgled for air one last time before going completely limp. His arms fell by his side, and Clay laid him on the hard wooden floor after ensuring he wasn't dead or dying. Years often passed between actual life and death combat for Clay, and though he maintained his skills, he knew a fine line existed between incapacitating someone and killing them.

Standing, Clay found three closed doors surrounding him. He was about to reach for the first knob when he heard a commotion coming his way like a herd of buffalo. Shouts of panic and anger reached his ears, meaning somehow the other three men were alerted to his presence. How mattered little, because now Dalton's rescue became that much harder.

"Crap," Clay muttered, looking around for the best area to make a stand.

Chapter 22

With only seconds to decide how best to defend himself and combat three armed men, Clay dragged the unconscious sentry close to the banister. Wanting all eyes to immediately shift to their fallen comrade, he flipped the switch for the hallway light, creating near darkness except for a thin morning light piercing the maroon curtains in the only hallway window.

Clutching the chained weapon between his hands, Clay pressed his body flat against the floor along the banister, waiting for the three henchmen to draw closer. He assumed an unconscious position in case he was spotted, just to further confuse them. In seconds they reached the second story, clambering for better positions to examine their fallen colleague as they made nervous comments. If they were able to see in the nearly completely darkened hallway, none of them made mention of Clay. It took a few valuable seconds for any of them to consider that the darkness around them and their buddy's condition wasn't a natural occurrence.

By then it was too late.

Despite all three men already having their weapons drawn, Clay closed his eyes after hiding beside the banister to adapt them to the darkness, simply relying upon sound. When he sprung from his position, Clay struck the man farthest to his left, sending him tumbling down the staircase. He used the chain casing for the strike, leaving the chain itself free for him to swing and wrap around the second man's gun hand. Once the chain was knotted into position, Clay yanked it upward, removing the gun from play before he kicked the man in the sternum. Clay barely took time to watch the man's back strike the solid wall behind him before turning his full attention to the last henchman.

Hearing the grunt followed by the thud of the second man, Clay assumed a gun was already trained on him even before he glanced at the last of the trio. Luckily during the last kick Clay hadn't stood idly by, choosing rather to swing the chain simultaneously in the direction of the last henchman. Taking his best guess at where the man's gun was pointed, Clay aimed the chain, learning within a second's time he came close enough.

Grazing the man's hand just hard enough to deflect it before the trigger could be squeezed, a battle tested Clay wasted no time or movement. Pouncing like a cat toward the mentally stunned henchman, he pinned the gun against the man's chest before hitting some nerves that loosened his grip on the firearm. From there Clay plucked the sidearm away from the hired gun, which left him vulnerable momentarily as he slid it down the hallway floor.

A bit more feisty and intelligent than the other two, the third man rammed his head against Clay's to cause separation. Clay stumbled back a few steps, feeling pain something like an ice-cream headache as the man lunged at his jaw with a fist. Though he sidestepped the first swing, Clay couldn't avoid getting socked in the stomach with the opposite fist. Luckily his abdominal muscles didn't have much give, so the blow barely registered.

Clay grasped one handle from his chained weapon before swinging it across the man's jaw, breaking it just beneath the chin. He waited less than a second before clipping the side of his adversary's temple with the hard casing. The man simply grunted, tough as nails, so Clay raised a knee to his sternum, forcing every bit of remaining air from his lungs.

Despite the setback, the henchman clasped Clay's shirt in two places, hurling him against the wall with a thud. Another knee to the chest caused him to lurch forward, however, allowing Clay to throw the chain around his neck and draw it tight. While he preferred a quicker method of subduing this subpar sentry like his buddies, Clay felt thankful for the opportunity to simply end their skirmish.

Within a few seconds Clay had chased the remaining oxygen supply from the man's lungs through careful manipulation of the chain. Assured the man was simply unconscious and still breathing with a look at rise and fall of the chest, Clay made certain the other two mafia types weren't moving before entering the room containing Chase Dalton.

"Based on the ruckus can I assume you're here to save me?" the government employee asked.

"You can, and your buddy Greene is ultimately to thank," Clay answered as he undid the restraints binding Dalton to the chair using his personal handcuff key.

Dalton's face displayed signs of being beaten with a swollen lower lip and bruising on his right cheek. Clay didn't bother asking if the mafia wannabe goons roughed him up, because he suspected he already knew the answer. One of the man's brown eyes carried a purple hue all around it while a thin gash was prominent along the top of Dalton's scalp because his ordinarily shaved head was grown out to stubble after the rough few days since his abduction.

Shaking his numb hands loose, Dalton rubbed the reddened areas where the restraints had dug into his skin. It required a minute for the marshal to get circulation in his legs from sitting so long, but he finally stood under his own power before following Clay out of the room.

"Some handiwork," he noted as they passed the four unconscious forms along the upstairs floor.

Clay said nothing as he led the man out the front door and down the street to where Parish and Liz remained vigilant from their vehicle.

"That was a little longer than five minutes," Parish chided, keeping a straight face.

"It beats you shooting up the place, or getting in my way."

"Boys," Liz interjected sternly, reminding them of the bigger picture.

"They'll get you to safety," Clay said when Dalton offered a handshake as thanks.

Clay shook his hand, but his mind was already motoring ahead toward his next move. He wanted to know Nosagi's location more than anything else, and he was promised that and more information once Dalton was rescued. He didn't care who Greene needed to torture for details, or how he went about it, so long as the information was obtained.

Before walking away, he observed Parish pulling out his phone and sending a text message of some sort. He could only assume the man was informing Greene that their operation went successfully.

Clay hoped to hear his own good news in the near future.

***

In the overnight hours Greene decided to make some changes. He started by shaving his beard, leaving his face completely clear of hair. The lack of sleep left his eyes a bit puffy and red when he looked into the mirror. Accustomed to long nights from his government work, between stakeouts and surprise raids on criminals, Greene kept his body fueled with coffee and energy drinks. When he did take a catnap his cell phone remained by his side at full volume to ensure he didn't miss any messages or calls.

Just before nine that morning, Greene finally received a text message from Parish that their mission was accomplished and Dalton safely with them. Standing in the sunken garden, Greene looked around at the plant life beginning to turn green with the warmer weather. Less than a month prior he might have seen his breath in the early morning hours, but just a week away from the Kentucky Derby and another potential opportunity at securing one of the cubes, a warm breeze brushed against his bare forearms.

He walked inside, calling up to the pretender's room, acting as casual as humanly possible given the circumstances. Stating that he found some answers to the man's problems, he asked to meet him in the basement, which contained the larger conference rooms within the hotel. He then asked Dan Duncan, the hotel's manager, to assist Craig Jennings in a thorough search of the false Dalton's room.

"Gladly," Duncan answered from behind his office desk before standing to march toward the security director's office.

Jennings happened to be in town for a few days despite the Kentucky Derby occupying much of his time recently. With Louisville only an hour away, Jennings found time to conduct research at the hotel when he wasn't with his horse's training staff. Acting the part of the owner, he left Teakon to monitor the staff and manage the day-to-day affairs in Kentucky where Phantom was currently residing.

Both Duncan and Jennings had participated in the cursed object game long enough to know what needed doing. They were up to speed on the situation with Dalton and the imposter, which solidified their understanding of the urgency to find the cube. If the man escaped he could literally assume the identity of the first person he made contact with and murdered.

A few minutes later Greene took a seat in one of the comfy leather chairs surrounding a small oval conference table. Although the smallest of the conference rooms in the basement, containing only a dozen seats, this particular room contained the most technological equipment, often used by Clouse to hold staff meetings and sometimes secretive meetings. Because the nature of the latter meetings required nothing spoken to leave the room, it was often swept for listening devices, and the walls and ceiling were redone with soundproof materials once Clouse began his quest to collect all of the cubes.

Greene waited less than five minutes before the imposter who stole his former colleague's identity walked in with a wide smile, apparently anticipating an offer to join the team or at least learn some answers about his unsuspecting enemies.

Strangely enough, Greene expected the exact same thing from this encounter.

"What's up?" the stranger asked, looking around the conference room as though it suddenly occurred to him that the isolated room was an unusual place for a personal discussion.

"Have a seat," Greene offered, waving his arm toward one of the comfortable chairs.

Remaining calm while the imposter reluctantly walked toward a chair, Greene held up a remote control to press a button that activated the metal bars that secured the conference room doors. Clouse had them installed to ensure meetings remained private, but the room doubled as a panic room of sorts. A far cry from the security of Fort Knox, the room offered limited protection until authorities were summoned or an alternate escape route presented itself.

"What's that about?" the man asked with a stunned look after hearing the metal bars lock into place.

"A form of security," Greene answered, standing as he pulled a silenced pistol from the back of his belt. "This room was built so no sound could escape. I suggest you answer my questions honestly, or you'll be on the receiving end of as many bullets as it requires."

The man sucked in a deep, cautious breath, refusing to break character just yet.

"Russ, we've known one another for years," he said with a look of grave concern. "Why are you doing this?"

Without moving more than a few inches, Greene fired a bullet into the man's right knee, drawing a pained cry immediately. The man clutched his knee as he leaned forward, coming just short of tumbling to the floor in a crumpled heap. He continued to moan and groan in agony, finally shooting a hateful glare in Greene's direction.

"I don't even care to know your name," Greene said. "Yet."

"If I tell you anything they won't let me leave these grounds alive."

"I doubt that," Greene said with a suspicious smirk. "Your group can't be that well-connected."

"We're far more expansive than you could ever imagine. The incident last October was just the first phase of things to come."

Now Greene's suspicions were proven true. A collective of rich, connected individuals seeking the cubes for themselves put his people and his employer in grave danger. He needed to know what people comprised the roster of such a group or he'd spend an eternity trying to locate them individually. He wasn't sure if they possessed any of the cursed objects, and if they didn't, their names would not appear in the manifest.

"I need to know everything," he demanded evenly.

"You can't let me live any more than they can. Just shoot me now and be done with it."

Greene took aim at the imposter's other knee and fired a round that connected with flesh and bone. Again the man screamed in agony, clutching the new injury before looking to the door as though thinking of escape or some kind of impending rescue.

"Regardless of my plans for you, this can go rather quickly or be painfully dragged out," Greene stated grimly, still not visualizing the endgame of his plan beyond this interrogation.

He knew leaving an exact clone, in appearance anyway, of his good friend wasn't a good idea if he located the cube. And if this individual used the cube to alter his identity again he might prove impossible to find. Greene decided he needed to extract any possible information in his present situation or risk staying a step or two behind the coalition trying to undermine everything he struggled to preserve.

"You don't deserve to live," he admitted to the stranger, "and it's dangerous for me to allow you to. After all, you've killed countless people for your own benefit."

"Then stop beating around the fucking bush and execute me because I'm not telling you anything," the man sneered.

"Why?" Greene asked before pausing. "Why would you stick up for people who only do harm to others? You don't have any desire for redemption?"

"Redemption?" the stranger laughed through the pain. "If you knew the things I've done, the events I've conspired in, you'd know there's no such thing."

Having no experience in psychology, and painfully aware that his interrogation skills from his marshal days didn't apply, Greene saw few options remaining. He could continue to search for a shred of human decency in this imposter or simply apply various forms of torture until answers spilled forth. With the carpet a complete loss and no one hearing the disturbance as of yet, Greene found no reason to deviate from his original plan.

His cell phone vibrated at his side, indicating a call or text message was being received. Plucking it from his side, Greene found a new message awaiting him from Craig Jennings.

Found it.

"It seems my colleagues have found your cube."

"Good for you," the man replied without any real emotion. "Now kill me or get me some medical attention."

Greene shook his head.

"You're not getting off that easily. Tell me more about this group of yours or the next bullet finds its way into your nut sack."

The man's eyes shifted uneasily toward his genitalia, obviously weighing over how much pain he wanted to withstand before his death or release. Short-term pain before death might be tolerable, but complete loss of a man's genitals, followed by years of life without sex if he survived, likely gave him something to consider.

Considering Greene's reputation didn't peg him as a murderous type, the imposter probably figured his chance of survival as reasonable. If the collective who sought the cubes truly did their homework they would know the former government man went by the book. His work history got him noticed by Clouse, but Greene's attitude changed when he was put in charge of saving the world on a regular basis.

Before he could continue pressing the threat of immorally neutering the man, Greene's cell phone buzzed with a new text message from Jennings.

Come out here. Dan can watch him.

Stepping outside the conference room momentarily after he unlocked the door, Greene found both Jennings and Dan Duncan waiting in the hallway. He slapped his gun into the hotel manager's hand, looking Duncan in the eyes.

"He shouldn't be able to walk, but if he tries just shoot him in the leg again."

Duncan nodded with approval.

While he wasn't cut out for adventurous work like some of Clouse's employees, Duncan understood the mission statement because cursed objects nearly cost him his life twice. None too tall, he possessed a potbelly his sport coats concealed fairly well. His sand-colored hair showed some graying in the temples much like the flecks of gray that appeared more prominent in his mustache over time.

"What's wrong?" Greene asked Jennings as Duncan slipped inside the conference room before someone noticed their impromptu gathering.

Jennings let a grin slip.

"We found some interesting things in his room that might give you some inside knowledge about our friend in there. I left them up there if you care to have a gander."

"Let's take a walk," Greene said, adjusting his tie and dress shirt before they went upstairs, assured no blood droplets stained his clothes from the interrogation.

Chapter 23

A pair of black cowboy boots clopped against the wooden floor of the old theatre as Stone stepped inside the back entrance where Clay Branson and Chase Dalton had departed just minutes earlier. Confident he would locate Branson with minimal effort soon enough, the FBI agent surveyed the ground level, finding several pieces of information including the abducted man's name and some contact information pinned to a board that he pocketed. Deciding the building had been chosen because of its abandoned nature, Stone headed upstairs where he heard minimal commotion. He put aside his main objective by simply taking time to enter the building instead of following Branson. Out of professional curiosity, Stone wanted to know what kind of death and destruction his target left in his wake this time.

With his hand atop his firearm, prepared to draw the instant he spied danger, Stone slowly ascended the stairs to discover one of the four downed henchmen coming to, fumbling for the cell phone inside his sport coat. By the time he regained his senses enough to see the FBI agent reaching the second floor, Stone kicked the man in the head hard enough to render him unconscious again.

"Stay down, son," Stone said, reaching for his own cell phone to touch base with his agency benefactor.

He placed his boot heel on the next man in line to make sure he wasn't going to regain consciousness, while watching over the rest of the hallway area. All four were still breathing, but it didn't look as though they'd be leaving the premises anytime soon. Moving on, Stone took in the musty smell of the theatre, seeing dust linger in the wake of a sunbeam emitting through a set of dingy curtains. Beyond the dust he noticed a heavy chair with handcuffs still drooping from the arms, and the agent began to piece together exactly why Branson traveled to Tennessee.

Feeling a step behind the Ohio cop and two steps behind the man who directed his actions, Stone wanted some truthful answers. Branson's actions didn't mirror those of an evil man, rescuing a federal marshal from local thugs, or traveling to a different continent to disable a few dozen living dead. Stewart fed him information only as it became necessary, but he did tell Stone the undead were a menace created by the man Branson was tracking.

What disturbed Stone most was the fact that no one else was after this man, or that Stewart sat on such information like a mother hen waiting for the right governmental eggs to hatch. Stewart simply told him the information, and the Oriental suspect, were not their agency's problem. Stone began to question the man's integrity and loyalty, which in turn led him to question his own. Above everything else, Stone wanted answers, which meant continuing to follow orders and document his actions, even if those actions incriminated him down the line.

When the time came, Stone planned to choose his allegiance accordingly, hoping his choice benefitted his career, but only if he remained on the right side of the law.

He crouched down, looking for any further clues along the floor. Finding nothing of use, Stone plucked his cell phone from his side, deciding to call Stewart to report his findings and see if the Deputy Director fed him any new information.

"Stewart," his boss said after one ring.

"Branson just rescued someone from this old theatre in downtown Nashville," Stone reported, returning to the hallway.

"So he's working with them," Stewart muttered just above a whisper.

"With who?"

"Nothing for you to worry about."

Strange, Stone thought, that Stewart wanted no additional information or details, almost as though he knew about the abduction of Dalton and the possibility of a rescue attempt. The feeling he was being used always resided in the back of the agent's mind, but now he felt like an absolute pawn in some kind of grander scheme.

Though he wasn't the most ethical agent in FBI history, Stone thought more highly of his abilities than to serve as someone's lapdog.

"Where is Branson now?" Stewart inquired as Stone walked along the hallway, kicking one of the henchmen in the head as he regained consciousness, losing it just as quickly.

"Heading back to Ohio," Stone lied, simply assuming the man would return to the same area as always.

Branson lived a very open life, working for the local police department and the theme park security force where it appeared he was being groomed to take over. During the course of his time around the theme park Stone had learned some interesting things by talking to some of the locals.

He sauntered down the stairwell, remaining vigilant as he cupped the phone to his ear, heading for the rear exit.

"I'm heading back to Ohio unless there's something else you need done," Stone said once he stepped into the overgrown lot behind the building.

"Just keep up the good work, Harlan. I've got an important meeting today and things may be looking up for both of us very soon."

Stone heard background noise from Stewart's end, guessing the man might be walking through an airport. Sounds of garbled voices and an announcement being made over an intercom reached his ears. He sometimes wished he could tail Stewart to discover what business the Deputy Director conducted on a daily basis.

When he reached his most recent rental car, Stone slid inside the driver's seat. Before he started the ignition he looked to his right where several yellowing newspapers sat atop the seat. Spending so much time in Mason, Ohio left him with time on his hands while Clay Branson worked shifts at the theme park or patrolled in the city. By happenstance Stone stumbled upon some information during a noontime lunch when two park employees discussed an FBI agent who visited Great Realms and helped avert a terrorist takeover. Upon further digging, Stone learned that Jack Turpin, the FBI agent in question, spoke with Clay Branson during the day of the major incident.

Rumor had it that Turpin offered Branson a position within the FBI, which one theme park employee believed was a "rogue agent" position in the Los Angeles branch of the Bureau. At the time Alan Stewart was the assistant director of the branch, and apparently Branson turned down the offer to stay in Mason. Now it seemed someone else was courting the cop for his unique services, but that didn't explain Stewart's continued interest in the man.

The obvious solution to Stone's new dilemma was to find Turpin, a colleague within the Bureau, and inquire innocently about the theme park incident. Turpin, a fellow Texan who worked with the Houston Police Department before joining the Bureau, would certainly speak freely about their home state and share work stories.

Picking up the top newspaper, Stone sighed from frustration because learning the truth never proved an easy task. His ideal solution wasn't feasible because Turpin retired from the FBI that past November only to fall victim to a fatal car accident in January at the age of fifty-five. And while the reported account made the accident seem completely legitimate, Stone doubted a man with Turpin's knowledge, experience, and good health was involved in a one-vehicle accident without some kind of external factor being discovered.

Putting the newspaper down, Stone decided to continue his dual investigation carefully or risk winding up in some mysterious "accident" down the road.

Starting the car, Stone picked up the phone to call his wife. He hadn't spoken to her since the previous day and he needed a reassuring voice before moving forward with some potentially life-altering decisions.

***

"Who the fuck is this guy?" Greene asked, palming a handful of various licenses and ID badges from numerous states and companies.

"I thought you might want to see this before you proceeded," Jennings said. "With some of this information you might be able to piece together some of his movements."

"It'll take weeks or months to get what we need, Craig," Greene grumbled. "We need to know something so we don't walk into the Derby blindly next week."

Greene tossed the laminated identifications atop the unmade bed, thinking he might try retrieving some fingerprints or DNA from them. If the cursed object allowed the imposter to completely impersonate people, he was going to know exactly what identities the man had assumed. If his own DNA or fingerprints were left behind, Greene could figure out the imposter's identity and use the information against him, which required days or weeks. However, the effort would link him to other key figures that impeded Greene's mission to obtain and dispose of the cubes.

Lit by natural daylight from the glass door panels facing into the atrium, the luxury room looked immaculate other than the bed being used overnight. Majestic and clean, all of the rooms were held to high standards in Clouse's hotel, but Greene was going to ensure this room wasn't touched by the staff until he retrieved everything he needed.

"Here's this," Jennings said, handing him a yellow cube that gleamed a momentary wink at Greene when it touched his hand. "We found it tucked between the matresses."

Ignoring the cursed object's beauty and charms, Greene stuffed the cube into his right pocket, imagining the countless lives that might be saved once he locked it away.

"We need to collect his belongings," he informed Jennings. "Everything. And use latex gloves so we don't get our prints on anything."

Jennings nodded.

"You still have friends who can do that stuff?"

"I gave up a government job, but I still have connections. Given the importance of knowing what this guy knows, I'll find a way to identify him."

"The methodical torture method isn't going so well?"

Greene returned a sly grin.

"It's just getting started."

"Probably for the best if I don't ask any questions?"

"Probably."

Jennings stuffed his hands into his pockets, continuing to glance around the room, including the open suitcase sitting atop a chair in the corner.

"This guy probably has ties to Lincoln Daine, doesn't he?"

"It would explain why he intercepted my buddy in Nashville. If that's the case, they're both part of the larger group he alluded to, which might include Clay's mentor."

"If they're obsessed with getting all of the cubes they have to be planning to combine them. That can't be a good thing."

Greene only knew of rumors about what might occur when the cubes came together. Mark Teakon's research was considerably incomplete, which worried him greatly. Most of the man's findings stemmed from discovered letters, diary pages, and a few personal interviews that often came secondhand at best. None of the accounts painted a remotely optimistic picture about the end result if the cubes were brought together.

Only one true way to discover the truth occurred to Greene and it meant traveling back to when the cubes were created or originally conceived by the group that possessed them first. Unwilling to use the time cube, which Clouse kept hidden anyway, he figured Liz might be able to envision the crucial events if she came in contact with one of the cubes. Using the time cube was immoral and dangerous, but asking Liz to subject her mind to one of the gravest events of all time wasn't easy to ask.

Greene knew there might come a time when he needed to ask Liz for that sacrifice, but he prayed for another solution to present itself first.

"Can you get everything together and store it on the sixth floor?" he asked of Jennings.

"Sure. I'll get it handled."

"Thanks."

Greene headed out the door, prepared to continue the interrogation until he learned about the dangers still lurking, waiting for his team at every turn.

And possibly the Kentucky Derby.

With a chance to secure a majority of the cubes at his fingertips, Greene wasn't about to take any chances. Now on the verge of breaking open the major secrets that eluded him, Greene wanted to shut down the syndicate opposing him and guarantee world safety. He didn't like the idea of conducting an illegal interview at the hotel, but moving the imposter opened an entirely new set of problems.

He needed to wrap up the interrogation soon since Dalton was coming back from Tennessee with Liz and Parish. Curiosity ate away at his mind when he wondered what kind of havoc the imposter wreaked upon Dalton's career and personal life. Either way, Greene planned on knowing all kinds of answers within a few hours.

Chapter 24

Greene returned to the conference room only to find a bizarre scene awaiting him. Standing beside the door Duncan continued to hold the loaned firearm, but the imposter was lying face down on the ground beside the chair where he initially sat.

Without speaking, Greene simply looked to the hotel manager who gave a helpless shrug as he returned the gun by slapping it into Greene's palm.

"He just fell over," Duncan said without empathy. "Probably faking."

"Thanks, Dan," Greene said as the manager let himself out.

Taking a slow walk toward the downed villain, Greene held the pistol in a ready position near his waistline. He didn't hold it defensively, but rather in a spot where he could hold it over the imposter while he spoke his mind.

"If you're going to play games and pull this shit there's no reason for me to prolong double tapping you in the head right now."

Very little blood pooled on the floor beside the imposter because Greene made certain not to fire at major arteries or blood vessels when he shot the man's knees. After momentary thoughts of kicking the man, Greene simply fired a silenced shot into the floor, bringing a flinch from the man in response.

"Feel free to get back in the chair."

"I can't," the man moaned, beginning to stir as he propped his upper body on his elbows, struggling to move along the carpet.

"Then you can just sit there because I'm not touching you, but you're going to answer my questions."

"Just shoot me and be done with it."

"It's not going to be that easy. Obviously there's no sense appealing to your morality so this will just be long and painful. And since I'm not very experienced in torture it'll just take all the longer."

The man shot him a detestable glance the likes of which Greene never saw from the real Chase Dalton.

"Do your worst then."

"I don't have to," Greene confessed. "I've got your fingerprints and DNA from the items you left upstairs. Even if the fingerprints aren't your own, I'm positive the DNA is still yours, which means I'll soon know who you are and I'll know about everyone in your life."

"And what? You'll go after my family? You don't have balls enough for that."

"Try me. And what do you have to gain protecting people who want to destroy the world for personal gain anyway? You're not going to be around to see any of it."

"I have plenty of incentive because you don't have a clue what you're dealing with. You've been two steps behind this entire time."

"But I've got *you*, don't I?"

Greene turned for the door, prepared to get to work by obtaining the man's DNA from the samples Jennings removed from the room. He didn't particularly like the idea of submitting the fingerprints in case he somehow implicated Dalton in something illegal that the imposter might have carried out.

"They aren't your friends," he said, turning around to address the imposter one last time. "And if history is any indicator, they won't have your back once you're incarcerated or dead."

"It beats selling out to tree-hugging pussies like you."

Greene gave a sly smirk.

"We'll see."

***

Nearly six hours later Greene had sent the DNA samples to an FBI contact out of Indianapolis for comparison to a national database. He wasn't expecting a miracle, knowing even a rush on the sample meant weeks or months of waiting. Even so, he needed to explore every avenue to discover the imposter's true identity and trace the man's steps backwards to establish his contacts and family.

Keeping the prisoner under wraps proved moderately difficult considering business as usual allowed several corporations to hold meetings in the other conference rooms. Duncan and Jennings took turns monitoring the imposter, who wasn't very mobile with a bullet in each leg, while Greene collected, stored, and shipped the DNA samples. In the meantime men and women dressed in business attire wandered through the hallways, unaware of the grave situation occurring mere feet from their meetings.

Greene made very little progress during the interrogation, often being belittled or called names by the man who possessed the information he required. Walking a fine line between incapacitating the man and inflicting pain kept him from drawing additional blood. Unfortunately the mental aspect of torture put him no closer to the truth, so he found himself walking out of the room more often than he cared to.

On this return trip, however, he walked into a scene he never expected after making certain the hallway was clear before opening the door.

While Dan Duncan stood beside the door, the imposter was lying face down beside the conference table, arms sprawled outward. He looked as though he wanted to move, to be anywhere except the position he was frozen in atop the carpeted floor. Unable to even turn his head to look at Greene, the imposter found a handful of new issues to overcome if he wanted his inevitable death or freedom.

Stripped down from head to toe, except for his underwear, the man was lying helplessly along the floor with numerous thin needles protruding from his skin. To someone with lesser knowledge it might appear he was literally pinned to the floor, but Greene immediately saw the source of the needles and understood why the man was incapable of movement.

"Having fun?" he asked Clay Branson, who knelt beside the man, examining the needles and their placement.

"Get him off me!" the man demanded. "I'll tell you whatever you want to know!"

Greene sauntered over to the imposter.

"Why the change of heart? I thought you were a stone, incapable of being broken."

Seeing Branson at the hotel came as a surprise, but Greene decided to play along with it since his unwilling guest was in genuine distress.

"What seems to be the problem?"

"I can't feel my legs! I can't feel anything!"

Branson leaned over to needlessly speak softly to the prisoner.

"You're not going to feel it when I cut off your balls either. After that, it's on to your toes, one at a time."

"Can I talk to you for a minute before you get to cutting our friend apart?" Greene asked more casually than he felt.

"Sure."

Greene gave Duncan a nod that he could take off, and the hotel manager gladly did just that. Branson followed Greene into the hallway once Duncan left, leaving the hapless imposter screaming inside. Thankful no one else heard the cries while the door remained open a few seconds, Greene couldn't help but like Branson's style.

"Dare I ask why you're here?"

"To get results. Your people let the word slip about this guy and I figured I'm not getting a better chance to learn where my former mentor is holed up."

"Feel free, but there's a lot more at stake here. Can I count on your help until I'm finished with him?"

"The needles pull right out. Once I warm him up you won't need a thing."

"I'll take that as a no," Greene said, opening the door to the conference room.

"We can take turns," Branson counteroffered.

"What exactly did you do to him?" Greene asked, blocking the doorway with his arm.

"Nerves in the human body are a tricky thing. They can take away all feeling or inflict a lot of pain when pierced just right."

Greene couldn't help but draw a grin as he allowed Branson to walk in first.

Their prisoner grunted and groaned, struggling to move, now stripped of his free will and command over his own body. Though Greene couldn't grasp his associate's knowledge and control over nerve endings, he felt somewhat assured they were about to receive solid answers because the imposter showed true panic for the first time.

"Get these things out of me! I'll tell you anything you want!"

Branson made no effort to hurry to the man's side, letting the psychological impact burrow just a bit further.

"Doesn't deprivation of the senses usually take longer to kick in?" Greene asked Branson rather casually.

"Usually. Part of my training was to build immunity to having none of my senses available. Then you get pretenders like this guy who need every advantage to make their way in the world."

Reaching down, he tinkered with one of the thin needles ever so slightly, causing a yelp from their prisoner.

"Anything you want," he pleaded once more.

"You know what we want," Greene said. "I need names and places of people who possess the other cubes."

"Particularly Nosagi," Branson chimed in. "Have you heard that name?"

"That's about the only name I *have* heard," the man confessed, looking between his two interrogators. "I talked to him a week ago and I'm supposed to meet with one of his representatives in a few days."

"When and where?"

"I wrote it down. It's in my luggage somewhere."

Greene confirmed the information with a discreet nod.

"What was the meeting about?" he pressed.

"Something about getting the cubes and their owners together. I think they were going to shoot me an offer for mine."

Or just shoot him Greene thought with a major concern in mind. He wondered how anyone other than his own group knew about the imposter or his cursed object. Until a few days ago this man was off their radar and Greene still hadn't learned his identity though it dawned on him he might find out from Julie Knowles through Clouse the name of this man without confirmation from DNA or fingerprint testing. He chastised himself for not thinking of such a solution earlier, but the day hadn't exactly been normal.

For some reason Clouse didn't like Greene having direct contact with Julie more than necessary. To Greene it felt like an us-versus-them team effort between the people who had survived horrific experiences with the cubes and those he hired to combat and eliminate the greater threat.

"I need the information for that meeting," Branson stated, looking to Greene.

"You'll get it. I need to know for certain if there are more of these people associated with him."

"There aren't," the imposter answered emphatically. "They said they tracked me through some kind of psychic or something."

Greene felt figuratively stabbed through the heart. Liz had proven herself invaluable to the cause over the months, but if the enemy employed a psychic of their own, and he or she was somehow more effective, then Liz's fears of being mentally invaded might prove true. Even worse, if she was accidentally providing information through mental wavelengths, the entire team was in jeopardy.

A year prior he might have thought his mind was coming unraveled at the thought of psychic powers and their various abilities. Liz proved him wrong almost immediately, but he relied upon her experiences to guide him through the rest of the psychic world.

"Why didn't they just kill you?" Greene inquired of his prisoner, still thinking something about the man's answers felt misleading.

"They knew they couldn't find me because I kept changing identities. They said their psychic saw my phone number in a vision and I could either sell them the cube and live or they would hunt me down. The whole reason I kidnapped your buddy was because I wanted your resources to check on these people."

"If you were posing as Chase you could've looked all of that up yourself."

"I don't have his training. I needed you for that."

"I'm not sure I believe that. You probably tortured him and asked him some questions in Tennessee."

"I roughed him up, but he wouldn't sell you out. That's why I came here in disguise. I've answered your questions, so can you let me up now please?"

"No. Did these other cube holders say why they wanted your cube?"

"*No.* The conversation wasn't exactly friendly."

"And you just agreed to a meeting based on a phone conversation?" Branson asked curiously, though Greene knew he was itching to see the information about the meeting.

"They mailed me a severed hand."

Greene looked to Branson, wondering if the hand in question might be from an island located in South America. For all he knew, the statement, or the imposter's entire testimony, might be one big lie.

"If you were counting on me to get you information, why did you have goons guarding him in Tennessee? Why didn't you just kill him like you apparently do with everyone else in your path?"

Instead of answering, the imposter struggled against his bonds and the nerve-deadening pins that pierced his skin, grunting and groaning.

"I guess someone isn't ready to tell the truth yet," Greene stated before turning his attention to Branson. "Ready for a look at that note about the meeting?"

"Sure."

Greene felt a bit foolish for assuming the man would break so easily. He knew the man had masterminded Dalton's abduction with some kind of inside information, but the slip about a psychic worried him. Extremely few people knew about the cubes, and even fewer knew about Clouse and his team created to hunt them.

Only those people, with ill intent, possessed motive to infiltrate the small group and learn its secrets.

He didn't feel very reassured about extracting answers from the man after evaluating the current state of affairs. Branson didn't seem the least bit deterred by the turn of events or the possibility that the stated meeting might not even be a true, scheduled event.

"Don't sweat it," Branson said evenly. "He's going to crack eventually, even if it takes a little more prodding on our part."

Greene wasn't sure exactly what his uncommitted ally meant, but he hoped the prophetic words came true.

Chapter 25

"Mother fucker," Greene muttered when they went through the imposter's belongings and discovered everything that the man said was apparently a lie.

Even the slip of paper with a date and time turned out to be some kind of meeting or appointment that had already occurred.

"I'm about to go medieval on his ass," Branson said sourly.

"I'm running out of reasons to stop you. We need answers without calling a lot of attention to ourselves. This hotel is still my boss's place of business."

Standing on the furthest floor from the basement, Greene realized he needed to take an elevator down immediately. Because Parish, Liz, and the real Dalton were on their way to the hotel he wanted to clear up any unfinished business beforehand.

With the man paralyzed by Branson's needles there was no need to leave someone in the room to guard him. Greene stood silently beside Branson during the elevator ride until the doors opened on the first floor. Because they took the passenger elevator and not the service elevator the first floor was the final descending stop.

When the door opened Greene stepped toward the basement access door but Branson lingered momentarily, staring at something he spied through the large doorway into the hotel atrium.

"What's wrong?" Greene asked, stopping midstride.

"Nothing. I'll catch up with you in a minute."

Taking only a few seconds to stare into the atrium, Greene saw about half a dozen guests milling around as the morning sun illuminated the round area through the glass atop the dome. He also noticed a blonde wearing sports clothing that hugged her athletic figure crossing the atrium toward the opposite entryway.

Branson appeared fixated on her above all else, which Greene found strange considering he was in a phenomenal situation with his impending marriage and he was the one more intent on interrogating their suspect.

Grunting to himself, Greene walked to the metal door that pushed open, allowing him access to the basement after walking down some carpeted stairs. He bypassed a few of the conference rooms, finding one filled to capacity with some investment group before reaching the locked room where he left the imposter.

Strangely the room was no longer locked and the door appeared ajar a few inches, splintered wood marring the side where the lock and doorknob once worked to keep it shut.

"Fuck."

Reaching beneath the back of his sport coat, Greene drew his firearm after a quick glance revealed no one else occupied the surrounding hallway. Holding the gun in a ready position he kicked the door gently with his right foot, allowing it to swing open slowly, but silently.

Only the muffled voices of the group a few doors down provided any noise along the basement. Greene felt unnerved as he peered around both sides of the doorway, seeing no one inside except his prisoner lying in the center of the floor with a weapon of some sort sticking out of his back. Assured no danger lurked inside the room, he stepped forward to examine the body, noticing a short sword of some kind went completely through the chest of the imposter, still standing erect because the pointed end remained embedded in the floor.

Kneeling beside the body, Greene realized the man never had a chance with the paralyzing needles throughout his body and two disabled legs to boot. He felt like an accomplice to murder even though he didn't stab the man through the heart and run like a thief in the night.

A small pool of blood surrounded the wound along the back, soaking into the imposter's shirt as the man lay lifeless. He imagined the carpet was absorbing the blood on the opposite side, but Clouse could seal off the room and have everything repaired. Greene wondered whether to call the police or simply dump the body because the man looked identical to his friend. That particular decision could wait as Greene refused to be mesmerized by the strange homicide.

The wound looked clean, very professional in nature and Greene suddenly understood what Branson might have thought he spotted in the atrium. He also learned some truths the man now revealed in death that he hadn't spoken in life. Either he was in cahoots with the organization competing for the cubes and they ensured his silence through murder or they really were tracking him. Greene doubted the latter scenario, suspecting the man worked for the group and figured he could infiltrate Clouse's fold by getting close to Greene and learning all of his secrets.

He wondered if the imposter simply followed Dalton until the time to strike arrived or if the villainous bunch knew about Lincoln Daine as well. If so, he might find the Kentucky Derby far more dangerous than he originally anticipated, having to watch for so many adversaries.

For now he simply needed to provide Branson with some backup and make sure the conference room remained secure. With cell phone numbers for both Duncan and Jennings he decided to call the hotel manager, hoping Duncan knew how to fix the door jamb without hiring it done and hiding the body.

As he pushed to dial the man's cell phone number, Greene felt reasonably assured the businessman grew up working for a living before he made his money. He found it strange that a millionaire like Duncan felt content running the daily affairs of a grand hotel, but he supposed many people held a fascination for the West Baden Springs Hotel.

"Duncan," the manager answered momentarily.

"Dan, I need you to come downstairs and secure the conference room."

"Again?" Duncan bellyached.

"Yeah, and that's not the worst of it," Greene said as he walked briskly toward the stairwell. "Our prisoner is no longer alive."

"You *killed* him?" Duncan asked in a hushed voice as though he might be near eavesdroppers.

"No, but someone didn't want him talking to us."

Greene opened the metal exit door, securing it behind him as best he could before darting up the stairs toward the ground level.

"So you *let* someone kill him? I'm trying to run a business here and I don't need you conducting guerrilla warfare tactics down there."

Feeling certain he would smack the hotel manager if he was present, Greene didn't have time for questions about his methods.

"You have a bigger problem in that the assassin might still be on the grounds."

"Fantastic," Duncan replied sourly. "What do you need me to do?"

"Quit bellyaching and get down here, would you? We're on the same team."

"If you say so. I'll get it handled."

Ending the call and clipping his phone along his belt, Greene pushed through the door on the ground floor, taking his best guess where Branson might have traveled during the past few minutes. The parking lot felt like his best hunch, so Greene headed toward the exit doors nearest the valet stand.

***

While Greene continued toward the basement, Clay followed the blonde he spied in the atrium toward the exit she chose. He remembered her from the island, feeling confident she hadn't spotted him, though she acted wary of her surroundings as though suspicious he might be somewhere nearby.

Occasionally she glanced behind her, but Clay made certain to follow her from a distance, his mind already contemplating the possibilities of how to confront her. As she passed the concierge desk and a bellhop station he saw guests milling about. He knew guests were certainly outside waiting for a shuttle bus to the casino and valets often stood at their outdoor station during favorable weather.

He envisioned a public scene where he tried to confront her and she jumped in the car to escape. From there he would certainly jump atop the car without the benefit of weapons and attempt to subdue her. Disadvantaged because she possessed weapons and a one-ton rental car, Clay would inevitably be shaken from the moving vehicle at best. Experience told him a rental or a stolen car awaited her in the parking lot, so when she exited the double sliding glass doors, he remained inside and veered right to find Craig Jennings' office.

Without knocking he threw the door open, drawing wide eyes from Jennings who shifted in his seat to see who dared barge into his office. His fingers remained poised above his computer keyboard, his expression not particularly endearing once he recognized his visitor.

"I need a view of the parking lot from your security camera," Clay said without hesitation.

"What?"

"Parking lot. Now. This is an emergency."

Jennings typed in a command through his keyboard with heavy fingers, pulling up a view of multiple cameras throughout the hotel's interior and parking lot. With minimal movement of his mouse and a few typed commands Jennings narrowed the screen of twelve images to only two cameras that displayed the parking lot.

Clay's eyes feverishly searched the screen as he made his way around the desk for a better view. He spotted the woman making her way toward the edge of the lot, taking a precautionary glance behind her.

"Those cameras can zoom in, right?"

"Sure," Jennings answered. "What do you need?"

"I need the license plate of whatever car she gets into."

Clay watched with Jennings just long enough to see her enter into a silver Toyota as though she had just finished lunch with a friend instead of murdering someone. He didn't need to see the body downstairs to know why she came to the hotel and what she'd done. Confronting her in the parking lot wasn't wise because he wasn't armed and so many witnesses meant police intervention within minutes.

The moment he verified the car's make and model Clay darted from the office and ran down the hallway toward the lobby entrance, almost knocking over a meandering guest in the process. He reached the door, peering outside without opening it to see if his adversary chose to leave through the main brick road entrance or the side entrance often used by service vehicles.

He watched the car drive down the lesser used side entrance, wondering if she meant to head to Louisville instead of Indianapolis. Granted, smaller airports existed in between either city, but Clay figured she was flying commercial somewhere, possibly even out of the country. Instead of making a scene he bet on a hunch that such a new rental car was equipped with some sort of GPS tracking from the manufacturer or the rental company. While his job provided him the means to contact various companies and check on the license plate he knew a federal agent possessed better means.

Without investigative status on his department, Clay had no rational explanation why he would request a vehicle be tracked. His come and go status lately hadn't left him in the department's good graces, so he decided not to rock the boat until he was ready to assume the security helm at the theme park.

A few minutes later he found Greene in the atrium speaking with the real Chase Dalton. Both seemed pleased to see Clay had returned with no injuries.

"Your head of security helped me get the plate number," Clay informed Greene. "I need to track it down, especially if it's a rental car heading to the airport."

Greene grimaced a bit.

"I've about extended all of my favors. It won't be easy."

Clay immediately regretted not jumping on the car and taking his chances.

"The imposter didn't wreck my career, so I'll give the office a call," Dalton offered. "Even if we can't track the car directly, we'll know where it's going."

"And that's all I need," Clay said, his heart racing in anticipation of drawing closer to his former mentor.

Chapter 26

By Friday Craig Jennings and Matt Teakon started their third morning in Louisville, though only their second with the horse from New Mexico. Trainer Jeff Slaton wanted Desert Phantom's comfort level transitioned perfectly from the rugged terrain and hot weather to bluegrass and comfortable air.

Jennings felt a chill in the morning air, just after dawn, when he and Teakon leaned on the track railing to watch their horse run like dutiful owners. Truth be told, they felt less like owners than security guards, vigilant at every turn for the man known as Lincoln Daine. Greene bet on a longshot that the man was going to target the race, which seemed plausible with so many opportunities to accomplish his goal.

Security at the track was excellent, with state troopers and local police officers standing by around the clock. Security cameras provided additional comfort for most owners and trainers, but Jennings saw far too many random people sauntering around the grounds. The press was allowed inside in limited numbers, but every team seemed to have numerous trainers and assistants walking around with the certified special laminated badges hung around their necks.

"Seems like everyone around here has a badge," Jennings said, thumbing his own.

Today he wore a pair of old brown cowboy boots, blue jeans, and a work shirt, along with a straw cowboy hat, which he tilted back for a better view of the track. Teakon dressed similarly, opting for his black hat as he watched Johnny Gomez start along the backstretch to see how Phantom performed on the dirt surface on his second day. When Gomez reached a designated mark along the track Teakon started a stopwatch to time the horse, hoping for moderate improvement over the previous day's mark.

"We didn't really expect Daine to show up early anyway," Teakon noted. "We're here on the off chance he's infiltrated someone's team."

"Doesn't sound like he's a natural horse person, so that seems doubtful."

"You just called the kettle black."

"I never said *I* was a natural horse person, did I?"

Jennings watched his own breath in the chilly morning air, figuring the sun would end such a phenomenon when it peeked above the horizon momentarily. Morning workouts ran smoothly, one assigned horse after another, the jockeys often scrambling to find the next of their multiple horses they were riding over the weekend. After the running of the Kentucky Oaks finished later that day Jennings figured his visual list of suspects would be cut in half because only the jockeys and a few owners needed to stick around.

He heard the click of the stopwatch as Phantom thundered past, his hooves clopping and kicking up dirt, barely visible in the low lighting.

"Better," Teakon said when he looked at the time. "I find myself wanting this horse to win for Margaret's sake, but not at the expense of someone's life."

"That's why we're here, remember?"

"Of course I do. It just sucks that we have to go through the motions when we could be looking for this Daine guy."

Jennings knew their objective was secondary because Greene and Liz were around the grounds as well, unrestricted as they mingled with everyone from owners to police officers. Greene expected to make friends easily with his background as a marshal, posing as security for Jennings and Margaret. Liz, on the other hand, remained by his side pretending to be Jennings' longtime girlfriend. For the assignment Jennings had removed his wedding band and convinced his wife to stay home for her own good. He felt bad quashing her enthusiasm about going to the Derby, but he explained it was related to his job and not entirely safe.

So far as she knew he headed up the hotel security force because he never revealed the rare occasions he hunted down cubes with Clouse's team. He felt terrible for making excuses when he went on "business trips" but Jennings knew the risk and he wasn't putting her in harm's way.

At first she questioned how a high school shop teacher received an offer for a job doing security, much less leading the force, when he possessed no law enforcement experience. Jennings tried to tell her his military experience gave him an edge and that Clouse felt bad about the experience that accidentally brought Jennings onto his property and nearly caused his death. In truth, Clouse felt hiring the man and giving him a good paycheck beat leaving the lingering chance that Jennings might sue him, and they both knew it.

Truth be told, Jennings actually enjoyed the unspoken half of his job, feeling somewhat like a secret agent out of a movie or a comic book. He experienced events both rewarding and sorrowful that the average person couldn't fathom seeing during a lifetime. Knowing what the cursed cubes could do firsthand, and how they corrupted men, he harbored no regrets about hunting them down and making the world a safer place.

"You okay?" Teakon asked as Jennings watched their jockey ride Phantom to a nearby exit, dismounting as one of the stable hands took the reins.

"I'm good," Jennings replied, reaching into his shirt pocket for a canister of dip.

He popped the top, snagging a pinch between his forefinger and thumb from the canister before inserting it between his bottom lip and gums. As he shook any fine tobacco fragments from his finger he caught Teakon giving him a disapproving look.

"You know the Mexicans aren't going to respect you any more for doing that."

"I'm just trying to fit in, Matt. I don't know horses like you do, and our staff thinks I'm a worthless blob who just buys other people's horses to make a quick buck."

"Well, give them some credit. They're judging based on what they see of us."

"You know, I quit this stuff years ago, but I just want them to think I'm an everyday guy so we can get some help from them."

Teakon gave him a cagy smirk.

"I've already got their trust, so just leave it to me, oh rich and powerful snobby horse owner."

Jennings shook his head dejectedly, knowing he couldn't fit in, and somewhat glad their ruse was likely up after the impending weekend, regardless of the outcome. He spit brown tobacco juice with precision aim at the nearby dirt, a little upset that the experience of his habit hadn't ever entirely left him.

Both men reluctantly left the railing, understanding the need to return to their true assignment, though hating to leave the fairytale behind. Jennings turned his head to spit toward the edge of the track, catching the beauty of the infield as the morning sun began to illuminate some of the awe-striking grounds around them.

Manicured to perfection, the lawn would have to endure dozens of racing teams trampling on it over the weekend as they took center stage on the winner's circle.

A newspaper photographer approached the pair, asking if he might get a picture of the owner leading the horse back to the barn for a photo opportunity. Sheer willpower kept Jennings from stiffening like a board at the thought of taking hold of the reins. He knew the Hispanic stable hands already lacked respect for him and he pictured this going badly in two possible ways. One, he added fuel to the fire by figuratively pushing them aside to fuel his own ego in their eyes. Two, he took the reins and horse pulled away from him, or worse, Phantom reared on his hind legs and thrashed as though a gunshot had rang out and frightened him.

He was still fishing for excuses when Teakon nodded positively to the reporter and guided him toward the reins.

"This is good public relations," he whispered.

"If the horse doesn't kill me."

Jennings felt certain he saw a narrowing of Rodrigo's eyes and a thin smirk when he took the reins from Margaret's stable hand, as though the experienced horseman somehow knew one of Jennings' two fears was about to reach fruition. He tried to act naturally when he took the reins, knowing he wasn't a complete stranger to Phantom.

He was more like the divorced father who saw the young horse on weekends and the occasional holiday.

By no means an ordinary horse in any sense of the word, Phantom knew the people he liked and those he did not, and Jennings had never truly tested the strength of their bond. With internal trepidation he took the leather reins and calmly gave a gentle tug, waiting for the horse to either fling him into the air or follow obediently.

On several occasions he had rubbed Phantom's head or spoken to the horse, but never had Jennings attempted to lead him anywhere or expect that he could. He envisioned a scene where the horse whipped his head to one side, sending his pretend owner through the air like some cartoon character who landed with a mushroomed orange explosion fifty feet away in the infield. Of course all of this was greatly exaggerated within his mind and turned out to be completely unsubstantiated when Phantom obeyed the gentle tug of the reins and followed him toward the stable he temporarily called home.

Much to his surprise, the horse even gave him a friendly nudge along his spine that startled Jennings. Luckily the cameras failed to catch his surprise, allowing him to retain his calm demeanor publically.

A few minutes later the photo opportunity concluded and the employees took the racehorse aside for a thorough bath before stalling him. Jennings and Teakon watched from a short distance, finding another fence to lean upon as their eyes occasionally drifted in search of shady individuals. So far neither had come across anyone they thought looked peculiar, lacing their minds with doubts about finding Daine before he struck. They really didn't know what the man looked like, and Daine choosing the Derby to make a small fortune in the first place began to seem doubtful.

"How does it feel to be such an underdog story?" Teakon finally asked to break the tension of their assignment, considering they were fifty-one to one odds almost from the beginning.

"It makes me nervous. I worry that Greene is wrong about this guy showing up this weekend, but I worry even more that he will. At heart I'm still a shop teacher, not a cop or some vigilante. What if we can't stop this guy?"

"We can only do our best. For a shop teacher you're not doing too badly around the horse."

Jennings grinned slightly.

"I don't know much about horses. You can show 'em, you can race 'em, and in a pinch you can eat 'em. That's about the extent of my knowledge."

Teakon couldn't help but chuckle.

"I'm sure everyone else down here takes your philosophy to heart."

Taking one last look around, Jennings decided their time might be better spent away from the racehorse, looking for potential suspects. He motioned for Teakon to follow him, knowing either way his part in the charade concluded the following afternoon.

***

It turned out the mysterious lady indeed headed to Louisville, but not to flee the crime scene or return to Nosagi. Quite the opposite, she settled in near Churchill Downs, spending her time surveying the grounds and preparing for the same exact mission Greene and his people were planning to execute.

Obtaining the cursed cube from Lincoln Daine.

Any doubts Clay harbored that this woman was sinister were erased with the death of the imposter and her trek to Louisville. She, and any associates who might remain hidden from view, possessed a tremendous threat to Greene and his people. While Clay might not have eagerly jumped on board with Clouse's group he understood and believed in their quest. Because of that, he needed to eliminate any threat that might bring harm to the group.

After feeling assured the mysterious blonde wasn't leaving the area anytime soon, Clay used some stealth to borrow a master keycard from one of the cleaning ladies in the hotel directly across from Nosagi's apprentice. He observed her until he was satisfied about her habits, deciding against his better judgment to approach her first. It wasn't in his nature to simply assassinate people without first knowing they truly deserved death. In this case he might have confronted her in any number of vacated areas but he wanted to learn what he could about his former mentor first.

Against every natural instinct, Clay casually walked into the hotel lobby, spotting her seated in the bar beyond the front desk. She often chose a seat that gave her a view of the racing grounds and the front lobby. He assumed she remained vigilant for Lincoln Daine, because Clay would use the same tactic if he wasn't tailing someone else at the moment.

In a public place she might be able to murder an average person without calling attention to herself, but Clay knew the tricks of the trade, even creating a few of his own over the years.

Dressed in khaki pants and a short sleeved button-up shirt that screamed tourist, he crossed the lobby and entered the bar, immediately drawing her attention. Acting far too casually upon spying him, she recognized him and Clay knew it, which made his direct approach that much easier. She continued to act aloof and calm until the moment he pulled up a chair, only then shooting him a stare that questioned his brazen nature.

"That was some interesting handiwork in French Lick," he said while sitting, wondering if she possessed the will to murder innocent people as well.

"I thought it was West Baden," she answered smoothly, her eyes looking toward the entrance instead of him. "You're way out of your league tailing me here."

"I don't think so. If Nosagi didn't teach you adequately you won't last two minutes against me."

Despite his words, Clay knew better, considering her his equal instead of underestimating her.

She finally made eye contact, revealing a sinister grin amplified by the glossy red lipstick she wore. Her low-cut beige dress revealed the tops of her breasts, and Clay fought to avoiding looking down because he knew this woman was a praying mantis, just waiting for a male to show weakness before slaying him. A small, matching purse sat atop the table, causing Clay to wonder what goodies she harbored inside. He wasn't completely weaponless, carrying a few small knives with him and a *shuriken* star in his breast pocket.

"Oh, he told me all about you," she revealed. "How he tricked you into joining the fold because you were noble to a fault."

"Did he tell you how he murdered my wife and son?"

She looked him directly in the eyes without blinking or faltering.

"Yes," she said so matter-of-factly that he knew this woman's veins ran cold with the same ice water that fueled Nosagi. "He also told me you ran back to America like the pathetic coward you are."

Clay refused to let her words intimidate or infuriate him. So far his probe for information brought him more than he expected, so he decided to let her continue speaking.

"And how did you become his prized student?"

"He recruited me after one of his students attempted to rape me and I killed him. See, I wasn't as hard to turn as you because I was tired of the world stomping me into the ground."

"Poor you," Clay said sarcastically. "Becoming a professional criminal and assassin is a long ways off from staking your claim in the world."

"You wouldn't understand, coming from a loving home, never living on the streets wondering where your next meal might come from, or if you could find somewhere to stay out of the cold."

While his right hand gripped the knife in his pocket Clay gave her a cold stare. The bar conversation around them hadn't changed in the least, meaning no one took notice of their discussion. The televisions in the background drowned out most of the chatter taking place, though this woman surely drew several pairs of eyes due to her striking appearance.

"You seem to have done well for yourself," Clay evaluated aloud.

"I'll be doing better once I eliminate you from this assignment."

"You can still walk away from this, and from *him*. It's only a matter of time before I find him and kill him and whoever stands in my way."

"The man did you a favor and you want to kill him?"

"He murdered my family."

"Technically he didn't," she reiterated a partial truth. "You can't tell me you were too naïve not to know exactly what kind of techniques he was teaching you and how they were used in the field."

"He told me he upheld a centuries-old tradition by teaching us those methods. I read the history and I understood why ninja clans existed."

"Nosagi never lied to you. Your father sent you over there for a reason. He saw the potential in you to deviate from the law because you were a troublemaker. You let both of your father figures down."

"Neither of them were father figures in the real sense, and you know that. I hardly came from a *loving* home as you describe it."

"It was your own fault for not embracing what they provided for you. When I kill you, your failure will come full circle, won't it?"

Clay smirked.

"I can see there's no changing your mind, so when and where are we doing this?"

"There's a hospitality area on the second floor of this hotel. I suggest we make use of it after it closes tonight."

"I'm not too fond of security cameras. How about the tennis courts behind the hotel?"

"Too bad you're so shy, but that works for me."

The irony of how inhospitable the sporting area would be when the two brandished weapons later that evening was lost on Clay because he only thought of drawing one step closer to Nosagi and destroying his former *sensei*.

"I'll see you this evening," he said before standing, leaving the bar with his senses attuned to his surroundings in case the woman tried any form of stealthy attack.

She did not, and Clay knew his death meant failure, if not annihilation, for Greene and his team on race day.

Chapter 27

While he hoped Greene and the group might have located Lincoln Daine by that evening, Clay learned otherwise when he spied Craig Jennings taking a break from the search. Standing high in the seats within Churchill Downs, Clay saw the man looking out to the infield, his body language indicating disappointment and frustration.

Clay exited the grounds as easily as he had slipped inside, using both his stealth and experience in police techniques to avoid security measures. Destiny awaited him a short jog away at the hotel where he planned on confronting Nosagi's latest follower. He saw little point in reasoning with her now that he knew her heart was contaminated. Killing her served little purpose other than sending a message to Nosagi and protecting the group intending to find Lincoln Daine for all the right reasons.

Determined, yet not led by blind fury, Clay reached the tennis courts minutes after the sun set, leaving only artificial lighting to guide him. He carried numerous weapons which he picked up from a hiding spot shortly after exiting the racing grounds. His pack contained bladed weapons, some blunt weaponry meant to conceal additional damage dealers, and several throwing stars and blades.

He waited less than a minute before she emerged from the darkness, wearing the same black garb as him, meant to conceal their identity and their movements under the cover of darkness. They stood on opposite ends of the tennis court, within a makeshift fighting cage made of mesh wire, only a net separating them.

Clay drew his sword and scabbard from his side, prepared to set them beside him as he engaged in the ritual known as *kuji-in*. A time-honored tradition, the *kuji-in* served as the strength of the warrior, evoking various powers in the person who summoned them to enhance the senses or physical traits of the recipient. As he prepared to bow respectfully to his adversary, another tradition Clay was taught, he noticed she made no movement to carry out the ritual, or show him respect.

"I'm not into traditions," she said almost haughtily. "You can delay the inevitable if you want to, or we can get this over with."

Unfortunately traditions were drilled into him by Nosagi, but Clay knew they were one of the few truths the man taught him. Either the man personally grew tired of traditions himself or he picked students who wanted everything here and now like the new generation. Or perhaps the student pool wasn't quite so plentiful for a man who lived on the run from authorities and cursed object hunters alike.

Clay slowly drew his customized *katana* from its scabbard, letting the covering hit the tennis court with little more than a hushed clank.

"Since I'll be dead momentarily you wouldn't mind revealing where our master is, would you?" he inquired.

In reply she gave a cagy grin that he read through her eyes since the black mask covered the rest of her beautiful face.

"Either way he'll find you."

Before Clay decided on any further words to speak she charged him, leaping over the net as he blocked the swing of her sword with his own, immediately falling into a defensive stance. Though he understood Nosagi taught many of his students similarly, Clay didn't want to assume this mystery woman didn't bring something new to the table.

They crossed swords several more times, each deflecting the other's offensive attacks until Clay performed a backflip over the tennis net to distance himself momentarily while he thought of a new strategy. Putting an end to any further interference, the woman sliced the net cleanly with her sword before attacking Clay, keeping him from deciding on any long-term offensive maneuvers.

Darting toward the nearby mesh wire fence, Clay leaped just high enough to gain a step along the fence and propel himself into a backflip as the woman chased him, narrowly missing his feet with her sword when he initiated the move. Landing on his feet, Clay crouched down, taking a swipe at her feet with his own sword. She jumped to dodge the first pass of the sword but Clay's expert handling of the weapon allowed him to flip the blade for a backhanded swing as expertly as a cheerleader twirls a baton. In one fluid motion the sword acted as an extension of his forearm on the backswing, but his target had already floated backwards, landing on her hands like a gymnast, still clutching the sword as she followed through with a backflip of her own.

Clay gave chase, swinging twice more before she was on her feet and deflecting his attacks. Luckily no one had spotted their activity yet, despite all of the area hotels weathering one of their busiest nights of the year. Even more fortunate was the fact no one opted to play tennis in the courtyard, leaving them to conduct their deadly business in private.

Already deciding the mystery woman was seasoned enough to hold her own in combat, Clay continued to test her abilities, seeing nothing from her that threatened his existence just yet. Luckily the tennis courts provided nowhere to run or hide, providing a contest based on skill and experience without trickery.

As though reading Clay's thoughts, the woman dropped a smoke bomb on the ground, creating a plume of gray smoke that concealed her movements. Often used as a tool for escape or repositioning, smoke bombs provided means for survival or a cheap advantage. Clay suspected she wanted to use immoral means to end his life, so he backed away from the temporary distraction instead of charging toward it.

He quickly realized she had jumped along one side of the fence, looming above him. With one hand clutching her sword and the other clinging to the mesh wire like a fly on a wall, she leapt toward him after shifting the sword to both hands. Clay blocked the powerful strike with his own sword, losing it in the process as it bounced several feet away atop the green court.

Without hesitation the woman went for the kill, lunging her sword directly at him, forcing Clay to duck before bobbing and weaving a few more times while the razor sharp blade missed his cranium by inches. He wanted to reach behind him for a replacement weapon but time didn't permit if he wanted to keep his head attached to his neck.

Clay now knew she was excessively aggressive, not patient enough to wait for a true kill shot. She might have finished a common security guard or lesser military man with her tactics, but Clay was neither of those. He rolled back, reaching into his small pack concurrently to pull out a light wooden cane in the process. Relatively harmless in appearance, the cane was a custom weapon Clay liked to employ, slightly less than two feet in length.

The woman made two cuts with the sword toward Clay's torso the second his momentum stopped. He blocked both death blows consecutively with the customized baton, backing off just slightly to pull it open, revealing a chain hiding within. Quickly twirling one end of the chain, he threw it as his adversary attempted to launch another attack at him, catching the sword in the links before pulling it from her grasp. Irritated, but far from finished, she pulled two wooden canes from her side, pressing upward on levers that produced short blades, like small sickles, atop the shafts. Known as a *kusari-gama*, the cane was much like Clay's weapon in that it concealed yet another weapon.

She swung both bladed canes down upon Clay, forcing him to use the chain for defensive purposes momentarily. The blades were only about half a foot in length, but plenty long and sharp enough to end his existence if they struck any number of crucial spots on his body. After a few blocks of the blades Clay rolled to his right, sending one end of the chain like a lightning bolt toward the woman's left leg, tripping her when he tugged it close to his body without hesitation.

Having no weapon prepared to throw, or a blade of his own readily in hand, he decided to make a bold move and step forward. Still on her back, the woman slashed at him with the *kusari-gama*, allowing him to use the opposite end of the chain to ensnare it before it cut into his knee like a prize bullfighter might use a whip. Taking another step forward, he anticipated that she might try and strike even lower, but his chain was quicker, wrapping the weapon tightly and leaving her weapons useless within her hands.

He attempted to carry out a handstand to relocate behind her for a finishing blow but she scurried out of the way before he completed the move, abandoning her weapons in the process.

Clay landed close enough to his discarded sword that he picked it up, turning just in time to block an attack from a short sword the woman had pulled from a small pack on her back. He knew she was trained exceptionally well by Nosagi, and being female presented no hindrances to her assaults or defense. He wondered which of them was going to find an opening first to finish the other, still determined to survive if only to find his former mentor.

***

Harlan Stone entered the hotel where the mystery woman was staying, under orders to examine her room. Because Stewart wanted him to keep a low profile, Stone gave up his usual duds for a Hawaiian shirt, khaki shorts, and leather sandals. He also wore a floppy straw hat and sunglasses, sure to carry a drink with him as he entered the lobby, giving the appearance he was returning from a nearby party of some sort.

He detested entering the building unarmed, and hated acting the part of a drunken tourist almost as much.

Noticing only one hostess occupying the desk at the late hour, he decided to try the easiest approach first. Stewart had provided him with a few gadgets that left him feeling like a secret agent, including a small device that read swipe card readers. Able to copy data from a card, the little machine also possessed the capability of inserting an attached card into a machine and accessing any local database. In this case, Stone hoped it would snatch all of the available room number passwords, or at least obtain a master code of some sort. Simply inserting the card into a room lock might eventually crack a simple numeric code, but Stone couldn't risk being seen loitering in a hallway.

A pretty girl in her early twenties manned the front desk, but Stone decided flirting wasn't the best method if he wanted access to the card reader sitting beside her computer terminal. He didn't have time, and the agent was fully capable of weaving a lie on the spur of the moment when necessary.

"Can I get a few towels?" he asked, heavily leaning on the desk while purposely slurring his speech.

"Certainly," the young woman answered hesitantly, veiling a concerned look while openly buying his façade as a lush.

She walked back to a room, providing him enough time to insert the false card into the reader, letting the miniature computer begin its penetration of their software. With the room only a few feet behind her the hostess returned in less than ten seconds, which didn't provide Stone with much assurance his device completed its scan.

"There you are," she said, setting the towels beside him as he swayed slightly, carrying on with the inebriated act, praying she didn't look down to her computer terminal.

He decided to keep her eyes focused on him by engaging her in conversation momentarily.

"There is one *hell* of a party out there," he said slowly, basing his actions on how his college buddies back in Texas acted back in the day.

"That's nice, sir," she said, trying to deflect her attention away from him.

No one else approached the desk, so any and all stalling fell to him.

"You know my wife didn't come because of her allergies?" he asked. "Who does that? Skips the Kentucky Derby because of allergies?"

The hostess shrugged, and Stone could tell she was growing uncomfortable, so he decided to try a different approach before security sauntered their way. Hotels were certain to have extra security with the biggest event of the year in town. Stone hoped the person watching the cameras wasn't very attentive, or found something better to do than watch him hack their computer system.

"Can I get one more towel?" he asked her nicely, indicating he was ready to leave her alone if she complied.

He staggered a bit against the counter until she turned her back, immediately reaching for his device and hiding it between the two towels atop the counter. She returned and he nodded thanks before walking unsteadily toward the elevators. With numerous people coming and going, he simply walked into the first available car with a family of four, asking them to push the fourth floor for him. The elevators required a room key, but Stone didn't want to pull out the strange spy gadget in front of anyone, so he let them use their key.

When the doors slid open a few seconds later he stepped onto the fourth floor, counting the windows from one end of the floor to the other once he determined the correct side. From spying outside and watching Clay Branson's movements he knew the correct room when facing it. Now he simply mirrored his technique, knowing which direction he stared from in the various spots where he conducted a stakeout.

Finding what he felt certain was the correct room, he inserted the modified card rather than knocking. He knew the room's occupant was busy confronting Clay Branson outside, and knocking only made him look suspicious to any neighbors or security cameras. Covering his actions with his body the best he could, Stone waited only a few seconds before the device transmitted the numeric code to the attached swipe card and the door lock mechanism turned green.

"Presto," he said, opening the door as he slipped inside.

The curtains were drawn and the bed was made as though the room was awaiting a new occupant. Stone pulled a pair of latex gloves from his right pocket, snapping them over his hands before he touched anything. Amazingly, the bathroom held nothing of interest as the soaps and shampoo bottles remained sealed. Only a small handbag occupied one side of the bed when he scoured the room for evidence of life. He knelt beside it, painfully aware of the fact this woman was trained much like Branson. And while Stone didn't know exactly where the two received their training, or what purpose it ultimately served, he respected their skills, knowing both were secretive and deadly.

Checking to make certain his latex gloves were free of tears, he kept his distance while unzipping the travel bag with an outstretched arm. No booby-traps sprung upward, so he grew a bit more brazen and looked inside. Finding clothing on top, he carefully peeled back the items, discovering a cell phone and numerous identifications underneath.

He decided to call his boss before making any moves, uncertain of exactly what Stewart wanted done with the find.

At this point Stone wasn't feeling very trusting of the Deputy Director because the man refused to provide him with any details while the agent risked his life simply tracking Clay Branson. Granted, the man led a boring life while in Ohio, but Stone knew something was gravely awry when the man battled hordes of undead and locked swords with a woman trained in the deadly arts.

Thanks to some other electronic devices he overheard their conversation that morning, which left him ample time to set up a video recorder pointed toward the tennis courts. He didn't expect great clarity in the dark through a mesh wire fence, but Stone simply wanted to know how the skirmish ended.

Regardless of the outcome he planned on spending a few days in Texas while Branson was either laid to rest or returned to Ohio. Stone didn't really have an opinion of the man because observation alone didn't really speak to the man's character, good or bad.

"Stewart," he heard the Deputy Director say over the phone momentarily.

"I'm in your mystery woman's room. She travels light."

"Does she have a name?"

"Try a dozen or so."

A pause crossed the line momentarily.

"Collect everything and send it to me."

Stone wasn't one to question orders, but he felt rather unethical simply stealing a person's belongings without legal backing.

"Don't I need a warrant? Or something? This isn't exactly legal."

"I will *make* it legal."

Stone knew the words meant for him to carry out the order or find himself unemployed, or dusting an FBI records room somewhere in Alaska. He shut down his phone, suddenly disliking the idea of lingering in the room. Taking up the bag, he exited the room hastily, wondering how the battle in the courtyard was taking shape.

Chapter 28

By the time thunder grumbled in the skies above, the thunderstorm was already upon the greater Louisville area. Clay didn't have time to analyze the weather, or the impact upon the running of the Kentucky Derby the next day, because his life depended on his full concentration of the ongoing battle in the tennis courts.

Both combatants were back to using swords, using what few openings presented themselves to swing at limbs. Thus far Clay and the mysterious woman had both evaded major damage from weaponry, but as she swung her sword at Clay's feet he leapt over it, taking a quick cut at her neck which she ducked before their swords clashed again. While their weapons remained intermingled Clay kicked the side of her knee before using her thigh to launch himself into a backflip, creating some space.

She barely registered any pain from the blow because she had moved her knee just enough to lessen the impact. And she swung the sword while he was in mid-air, but he blocked the attack with his own sword, landing on his feet as she took another sweeping swing that caught the top of his thighs. As the black material split apart, Clay's legs looked as though someone had painted the upper portion of his thighs with a red paintbrush stroke. Perfectly symmetrical, and ordinarily a painful sting, they went ignored as Clay continued to move, tossing his sword behind him before carrying out three consecutive backflips toward the discarded weapon and a mesh wire wall.

Clay noticed during the rotation on his third backflip that the woman wasn't going to allow him to land and scoop up his weapon as he planned. In less than a split-second he conceived a plan to catch her sword's blade with his palms when she struck it toward his face, but he abandoned the notion just as quickly for a riskier gamble.

Hesitating ever so slightly, he waited for the blade to slice downward, aimed for his back while he was still in mid-flip. Relying completely on instinct and past practice, because his head faced the opposite direction, Clay used his feet to clasp the blade and yank it upward in one motion.

Ordinarily the move might have failed utterly, but Nosagi trained Clay to stop a blade between his palms and certainly taught this woman Clay's usual defensive tactics. She was playing right into his habits until he switched up his defensive move at the last second, thwarting whatever chain of moves she planned to use against him.

Now the sword flew above both of them, ripe for the taking. The woman glanced upward to time its descent, providing Clay an opportunity to kick her in the chest, connecting lightly enough that she stumbled a few feet back. He grabbed the sword from the air, sweeping the blade toward her neck, but she recovered enough to anticipate the move, rolling to her left.

Carrying out a sequence of moves, slashes and stabs that all missed because she backed away and evaded them, Clay refused to grow frustrated, keeping his focus on the battle. Strength didn't win these contests, but rather skill, agility, and mental toughness. Basically unarmed, and running out of room as her back drew closer to a fence, the woman threw another smoke bomb on the ground close to Clay, disorienting him momentarily while she scrambled for a new offensive position.

Heavy rain cut loose after the concocted distraction hit the ground, drenching Clay almost immediately. Despite the smoke bomb and raindrops pelting him from above, he kept a clear mind, sensing she might make an attempt to snag his discarded sword rather than draw a new weapon from her arsenal. Considering his back was now turned to his own sword, the move seemed logical, and a sense of immediate danger equivalent to flashing red lights and a blaring siren in his mind warned him of unseen peril.

Based on where his sword landed, he knew she couldn't have leapt at him from atop the fence, so he plunged his current sword behind him, along his right side, knowing how a right-handed person like herself would attempt to slice diagonally through his shoulder blade. Lessening the chance of a blade potentially cutting through him, Clay backed up as he thrust the sword behind him, feeling it plunge into something solid.

All at once he felt the pressure on the sword change as the weight of something tilted the blade slightly. An audible gasp behind him indicated he struck home with the weapon, carving into the mystery woman's intestines to the point that only immediate medical attention might save her.

Retracting the blade as he turned around to face her, Clay discovered his hunch proved accurate. Had he guessed incorrectly on any number of fronts it might be him bleeding profusely as his blood mixed with the rainwater standing atop the green tennis courts. She clutched her wound after dropping Clay's sword to the ground with a muffled clanking sound. Feeling little emotion about mortally wounding the student of his sworn enemy, Clay watched her slump to her knees as the rain continued to soak him. Both combatants understood their skirmish had reached a conclusion as the thunder rolled in the distance.

As the woman took in deeper and deeper breaths, her body trying to compensate for the lack of blood and her heart pumping faster, Clay wondered where her life had taken such a bad turn. She removed the mask portion of her *shinobi shōzoku* as her arm felt limp to her side, still clutching the covering.

"Finish it," she muttered, blood still streaming from the fresh wound onto the already wet tennis court.

"Where is he?" Clay inquired first, removing his own mask, feeling raindrops run freely down his face and into the curves of his lips.

His hair pressed flat against his scalp as though molded into place. The cloth from his outfit stuck to his skin like adhesive, feeling unusually chilly as the rain brought a cold front with it.

Adrenaline kept his battle wounds from bothering him just yet, but the time was coming when his nerves would break like a dam and let the pain come flooding inside.

"You won't find him," she answered plainly, no ambition left within her to lie or deceive Clay at this point.

"I will find him one way or another."

"If you do, it will be on *his* terms. Your new group is on a collision course with death itself. They're in over their heads, and even you can't save them."

She made it clear that Nosagi was part of a larger faction and not just living in isolation as some kind of marked man. Clay knew some difficult choices lay ahead of him, not only about his former mentor, but the fate of the world if Nosagi united his cursed cube with a dozen others. Greene was a hardened veteran agent of the federal government, but still a novice when it came to taking lives or understanding that the world around him contained a spiritual element very few people ever witnessed, much less understood.

Now coughing up blood, Nosagi's pupil wasn't long for the living world. She fell forward, assuming a position on all fours, still leaking blood from the wound and choking on the red fluid rising from within.

Unwilling to take a chance that this woman knew one of the dozens of tricks to induce herself into a coma and slow her heart rate to only a few beats a minute to stave off death, Clay raised the sword above his head. He waited only a few seconds before letting the blade cut through the rain and her neck, severing the head which bounced once atop the ground before coming to rest.

Clay felt no better, despite eliminating a major enemy, because a greater evil revealed itself, proving Greene completely right. Wanting nothing more than to return to Ohio and spend time with his fiancée, Clay felt obligated to stay in Louisville and ensure his allies completed their task. He knew all roads led to the cursed cubes, and from the cubes to the men responsible for endangering Greene's team.

And eventually those corrupt individuals led to Nosagi.

Clenching his fist, Clay set to picking up the discarded weapons quickly, trying to leave the scene looking like the brutal homicide of a Jane Doe. The rain helped wash away any potential DNA left behind, so he only concerned himself with loose weapons and the mask to the mystery woman's *shinobi shōzoku*. He didn't want investigators making any connections between her and the traditions he spent years learning.

At least not yet.

Knowing exactly where the woman stayed, Clay briefly considered sneaking into the hotel and seeing what information her room contained. He decided against the move, making Greene's people his priority and deciding this woman wasn't about to leave her real name lying around, much less information about Nosagi. Despite her strong front, the blonde knew she might not leave their battle alive, her thoughts mirroring Clay's concerns.

Utterly soaked, Clay trudged across the tennis courts, feeling fatigue and pain setting in as the adrenaline faded. He forced his mind to stay focused, checking the area around him for any potential witnesses, finding none. Only as he exited the mesh wire surroundings did he notice a man in the distance stumbling toward a dark sedan of some kind. The man took no notice of Clay, but the Ohio law enforcer recognized something about this individual, even in the dark and from a distance.

His gait.

Perhaps serving as a police officer, or the fact that he lived in constant paranoia since discovering Nosagi was corrupt heightened Clay's powers of observation, but he recognized this man simply by the way he walked. Despite the attempt to disguise his mannerisms, this man couldn't fool Clay because he had appeared in the police officer's daily routine several times over the past few months. Strangely, Clay remembered him from the theme park, the grocery store with Casey, and now a state away in Kentucky.

Retaining enough energy and mental stability to confront the man, Clay decided to put others before his personal vendetta, his instincts telling him this man wasn't an agent of Nosagi like the woman. Though he doubted the rugged man was entirely ethical and pure, Clay decided the inevitable confrontation could wait.

He studied the man momentarily, trying to avoid giving himself away in case a glance came his way. Clay carried on through the diminished downpour, hoping for a successful Kentucky Derby in more ways than one.

Chapter 29

By morning only a few clouds lingered over the Louisville sky, but the dirt track was reduced to mud, no matter how many times tractors dragged the surface. Mugginess lingered in the air as Craig Jennings paced in front of his horse's stall, still refusing to accept a true ownership role. Instead he felt helpless because he was forced to play the part while trying to track down a known murderer who possessed a deadly, corrupting force.

He and Matt Teakon were both dressed similarly to what they wore in New Mexico at the qualifying race. Wearing the black leather blazer again had already left him with sweaty armpits and an undershirt clinging to his chest. Fulfilling the wishes of the horse's true owner was the least of his worries as media coverage and the impending preliminary races left the stable area buzzing like a beehive.

Spying cameras from every major television network and several local affiliates, Jennings felt butterflies in his stomach because he knew Margaret Stough was going to make him the front man for the ownership team. He understood the role, knew what to say, and suspected he would legitimately be excited about seeing the horse run again, but felt guilty because he wasn't able to truly assist in the search for Daine.

"You're not helping matters," Teakon informed him, leaning his shoulder rather casually against a wooden post.

"And you're acting a bit nonchalant considering what we're here for."

Teakon withdrew from the post, leaning in once he ensured no one was within earshot in either direction.

"We're here to run a race and act the part of ownership first, search for the bad guy second. Greene and Liz and that theme park cop guy are handling that part of it. We just need to act naturally and not smother the horse. We're a fifty-one to one shot to win this thing, so if there's a payday to be made it's with Phantom."

"I'm still not happy about it. And the theme park guy isn't your average cop."

Jennings started to reach for the canister of tobacco residing in his white button-up shirt's front pocket but Teakon caught his arm.

"Cameras. Everywhere."

Jennings groaned aloud. Clasping the plastic canister fully within his palm, he transferred it to one of the blazer's slip pockets where it would remain out of sight and hopefully out of his mind.

"I told you it was a bad idea to start that again. The hired help doesn't notice anything we do."

"It's a little late for the lecture. My wife is going to kill me if she finds out."

"You haven't told her?"

"She nagged me to quit the first time, so there's no way I'll have a chew around the house."

Teakon chuckled.

"Sounds like you're heading for trouble."

I'm just kind of nervous with all of this around me," Jennings admitted.

"You have a right to be. No one in their right mind expects you to come all the way from New Mexico and be a natural."

When Teakon spoke the words "New Mexico" he held his fingers up as quotation marks to reinforce their assignment's true nature.

"Come on," Teakon encouraged, leading the way away from the stables as they walked toward the track.

Both wore special passes encased within plastic coverings around their necks for the local police and state troopers working security to see. No one questioned them, regardless of where they went, because they looked the part of horse owners, or at least someone who belonged behind the scenes.

Smells of horse manure faded, replaced by the scent of freshly cut flowers as the two men neared the outer rail. The majesty of Churchill Downs reached a new level as color splashed the grounds like a Thomas Kinkade painting. Certainly no stranger to weddings and funerals, Jennings had never laid eyes upon a collection of flowers that compared to the arrangements throughout the infield and surrounding the outbuildings. As people began filling the seats, the men wearing suits and the women donning dresses and a multitude of hats, the figurative rainbow grew more intense.

Only hardcore fans struck out this early in the morning because the real race didn't take place until late afternoon. Threats of a morning popup thunderstorm kept some spectators away, or at least closer to cover until the races began. The atmosphere, even in the morning light, felt overwhelming to Jennings. Only people like his true employer ever graced Millionaires Row atop the stands, and one needed some luck just to secure a regular seat and sip a mint julep.

Fiddling with his bolo tie, Jennings watched a few horses gallop past the rail some distance away as riders were forced to use the turf area inside the muddy track for morning runs. Tractors continued to tow using various components, trying to stir and flatten the mud with management hoping the track might dry out before the races began.

Acting as casually as possible, he turned around to look at the people around him, wondering if one of them had murder on his mind. Jennings knew any attack or murder within the grounds wouldn't go undetected for long, or possibly at all. Between security personnel and video cameras the notion seemed impossible, which made him wonder if Daine might kill someone before entering the grounds and put the cube's power to use once he came in contact with the horse.

Each cursed object's use varied from its siblings, and no one in his group knew exactly how this one worked. They assumed it worked by touching the intended recipient and passing the enhanced life force from the sacrificial victim, which required Daine to step foot within the most secure area of Churchill Downs. Greene knew this, so he and Liz planned to hover around the stables most of the day, looking for clues. Jennings had no idea where Clay Branson fit into the plan since he audibly committed just the night before.

Local news stations reported a murder down the road outside of a hotel, but the victim was a Jane Doe and police weren't revealing many details. Because of the secrecy on their part, the story quickly tapered off when coverage migrated to the famous horse track. What little backstory Jennings knew about Branson allowed him to surmise that Branson might have removed one adversary from the dangerous path Greene's group was treading. His review of the security footage at the hotel furthered his knowledge of Branson's personal quest, but he personally liked their chances of stopping Daine with the cop around.

"There aren't even any guarantees this will work," Teakon said, trying to reassure him. "This guy might bypass the Derby for something different."

"There aren't that many sports that offer this kind of payday, Matt. You're talking about one team versus another, or a boxer against one opponent. To pick the winner in a race, with so many variables, with so many betters lost in the shuffle, Daine could clean up. Besides, he hasn't struck in a very long time."

Teakon knew better than anyone except Julie Knowles that Daine wasn't lying in a ditch dead somewhere or the cursed ledger would have recorded a new owner for the cube. It made perfect sense for Daine to visit the Derby if only a laminated badge gained people access to the stables.

Both men knew their chances of being a true help to the team rested between slim and none, but their fictionalized roles brought Greene, Liz, and Clay Branson to the dance.

***

Liz acted the part of a horse owner's love interest, stroking the horse's long nose with her right hand after removing a white glove. While some might have thought she was acting dainty, she actually needed skin-to-skin contact with Phantom if any valuable information was available. Nothing happened, so she removed her hand, still smiling at the horse because he was a majestic creature.

"Nothing?" Greene asked beside her, playing his role as an unarmed bodyguard rather well, standing stiffly while wearing a gray suit with a peach-colored tie.

"No. Thankfully."

For her part, Liz wore a yellow sundress and a large white floppy hat adorned with a yellow ribbon. Small flowers of white, blue, and yellow were attached to the ribbon to the right side of the hat's front. A blue rose was pinned just over her left breast atop the dress, a touch she thought of while researching Derby attire online. She also opted to wear shoes with low heels, mainly for the sake of comfort throughout the day, and *not* because she planned on getting involved in any foot chases.

Concern grew throughout the group as minutes and hours passed with no results. Now close to noon, Liz and Greene had only come across Jennings and Teakon once because the two were caught up with interviews and paperwork. She felt bad for them because they spent much of their week in Louisville, going through the motions of ownership because Margaret Stough didn't arrive until Friday afternoon.

Then again, Liz thought, how many people experienced the behind-the-scenes atmosphere of the Kentucky Derby in person? She suspected the travel and worries over the horses racked the nerves of most owners and trainers, especially when the positioning draw took place the Wednesday prior to the Derby.

She felt some relief that she didn't have to fake being the horseman's girlfriend to the extent of giving him a hug or speaking at length. Liz harbored no resentment toward Jennings, but her experience as an actress was limited to a high school play, despite being a California girl. The less she needed to act a part, the better.

"What are we going to do now?" she asked Greene, who appeared on the verge of a meltdown.

Sweat appeared around the collar of his dress shirt, and the veins along his neck were thick and bulging from frustration.

"We can't linger around the horse," he answered, knowing Daine would abort his quest if he sensed people were looking for him, or authorities surrounded the area. "These passes let us roam around just about anywhere, so I suggest we take advantage of them."

Liz pulled out the most recent picture of Lincoln Daine that Chase Dalton was able to provide when Greene called him. Considering Daine had fallen off the radar the past few years, and hadn't been charged by any police agency of a crime, the picture appeared to be something Dalton obtained through unconventional means. He might have used a local police agency to contact the man's remaining family to ask for a photograph because the image appeared to be part of a larger family photo. Distorted and a bit fuzzy, it wasn't much help, but Greene appreciated his friend's effort.

Daine wore his brown hair in a ponytail back then, a five o'clock shadow covering his face. Reports of his more recent appearance stated he'd cleaned up and wore his hair more conventionally short, which basically reduced the photograph's usefulness significantly.

"Why couldn't Chase get a driver's license photo?" Liz inquired as they walked away from the stables.

"Because you need to open an investigation or an inquiry for something like that. It raises a lot of red flags and there will be bigger favors to ask of Chase in the future."

"Because getting this cube from Daine is secondary?"

"No, because I have you and that rogue cop here to help me, so I shouldn't even need the photo. I hope."

Liz looked around, realizing Clay Branson was supposed to be somewhere inside the facility but she hadn't seen him all morning.

"Are you sure he's here?"

"I left a pass for him at the front office," Greene said, leading the way toward the track where several trainers were being interviewed on camera. "There isn't a whole lot more I can do at this point."

They brushed past a few stable hands that looked like authentic horsemen with weathered straw hats and dirty blue jeans. A gate and security guards temporarily kept them from crossing into public view where the stable area met the track and its abundant seating. Liz instinctively checked to make certain her white gloves were snug atop her hands because she didn't want to accidentally touch random people and see aspects of their lives at the risk of blowing her cover.

Her gift didn't always work consistently, or when she wanted it to, but it seemed to present itself when necessary. As though guided by a higher power that wanted her to see certain events unfold, her visions seemed paced. Liz knew her mind couldn't take a flashflood of scenarios in a short amount of time, and she hated seeing the past of anyone she knew personally.

Therefore she avoided touching Greene like his body hosted some sort of world-ending bacteria.

Perhaps the circumstances of their working relationship clouded her judgment, especially since she'd never experienced true adventure before, but Liz rather liked Greene. He was athletic, sure of himself, and fueled by a desire to do right by the world and its inhabitants. None of the cases she assisted police with provided very much excitement because everything she saw or touched was very much removed from the crimes in question.

Greene still carried himself like a government official, often dressing in suits and walking with a rigid swagger. Liz couldn't help but feel safe around him, though it wasn't the emotional stability like a husband provided, or a physical form of protection from a habitually jealous boyfriend. She simply felt unequivocally secure having him near, but felt certain some deep, dark secret from his past might rush forward if they made physical contact.

"What's wrong?" he asked when she balked at walking into the courtyard that preceded the main track area.

An area absolutely packed with spectators and officials.

"Nothing. It's occurred to me that if Daine is going to access the horse he needs to get into the stable area. What if we're looking at this wrong and he's not just sneaking in here sometime today?"

Greene sensed she might be dodging the entire truth from the look on his face. He was trained, after all, to read the way people answered questions while observing their body language.

"Either way, we've come this far, so let's finish the ruse."

Truth be told, Liz wasn't sure she fit in with the well-dressed people standing around the race track. Sure, most of them were fakers, pretending they were rich and civilized for one day, probably returning to their day jobs come Monday morning. Liz envied them in a way, because she had no job beckoning her. Her days were spent searching out evil while putting herself at risk because Paul Clouse presented an offer that took her away from California and the so-called occupation she held there.

"Have I told you that you look great?" Greene asked, possibly sensing her reservations about stepping into public view.

"You're just saying that."

"No," he said emphatically, presenting one of his rare grins. "You look stunning, and if we weren't on duty I'd ask you to dinner at one of these fine Louisville restaurants."

Liz thought the offer sounded sincere, but Greene was known to prod and motivate his colleagues just short of manipulation. Her childhood left her with little self-confidence because she wasn't particularly athletic, wasn't confident speaking around groups, and did well in school, but never achieved the grades that brought scholarships her way. Her parents were supportive enough, but they worked constantly to put food on the table. They never aspired to work their way into the Hollywood scene as actors or writers. Their move to California from Iowa as young adults stemmed from a desire to see lights other than the flashing stoplight in the center of their hometown.

Her parents were simply stuck in a rut, unable to make a sound living or move somewhere else. In turn, Liz fell into their situation, trying to use her ability for good, but only alienating herself from society all the more while struggling to make a living with two or three jobs. With her father deceased from prostate cancer nearly two years now, and her mother's health deteriorating from constant work, Liz accepted Paul Clouse's offer to truly do good for people and to assist her struggling mother.

She remembered the fun times with her father when he took her on walks through the park, throwing a Frisbee on the beach, or fishing off the pier. Liz always considered the fun times she spent with her father rather simple, but as an adult she realized they were also affordable. She never knew they were poor growing up, and she didn't really care because her parents always stayed close to their only child.

Most people saw her and judged her immediately, using words, often hurtful adjectives, to describe her. Greene never addressed her negatively, or made light of her ability, even though she sensed he wasn't sure about its purity. Always inquisitive, he asked legitimate questions about her visions, instead of acting juvenile like some of the police officers she worked with in her home state.

Now he waited patiently for her at the threshold of a public domain she really didn't want to enter, but Liz knew he wouldn't stray far from her once they entered the courtyard. Because of their respective roles Greene couldn't hook his arm through hers and prove his words true, so Liz simply accepted the confidence boost and entered the courtyard for hundreds of people to see.

In the distance, dark clouds closed in from the west as the wind picked up slightly, threatening to ensure the race wasn't going to take place in dry, sunny conditions. Liz expected little else, considering the normal luck of their group.

Chapter 30

Harlan Stone might have felt bad about neglecting orders from his direct Bureau supervisor if not for the fact he questioned the man's intentions for him. Granted, his behavior toward the criminal element was far from angelic, but it was the criminal element after all. Stone didn't regard regular people with equal disdain, nor did he care to engage in activities that placed innocent people in jeopardy.

As he drove along the rural roads of Harris County, outside of Houston, Texas, Stone pondered exactly why Stewart asked him to monitor Clay Branson. At first Stone figured Branson was a dirty cop involved in some major criminal activity. The incident on the island, followed by the sword fight in the parking lot left him thinking otherwise. Branson showed no inclination toward illegal activity whenever he returned to Ohio, and his other activities certainly couldn't be defined as criminal.

Unfortunately Stewart wasn't very forthcoming with explanations of the bizarre events Stone witnessed. The apparent uprising of undead on the South American island, particularly, wasn't satisfactorily explained when Stone made inquiries. Stewart tried to say something to the effect of innocent people being brainwashed and Clay Branson cutting them down mercilessly, but what Stone viewed was *not* murder. The fact that statues and animals had also attacked the man indicated some rather dark forces were at work on that island.

In his experience he classified Branson's actions as self-defense.

Looking down to some scribbled notes in the passenger's seat, the agent figured he was close to his destination, finding a two-story faux brick house about half a mile down the road. Practically brand new, the house wasn't within sight of neighboring homes in any direction. A white picket fence literally crossed the front yard, hedging the mailbox on either side. Stone checked the address against the sheet of paper, verifying that he had arrived at the address of Jack Turpin's widow.

Deciding to avoid falling off the radar completely, Stone requested the weekend off from his direct supervisor to return to his home state. He threw in the statement that Clay Branson had returned to Ohio, a lie that served to accomplish his goal. And though he certainly planned on spending some time with family over the next few days, Stone decided to take advantage of the opportunity to learn something about his predecessor.

After his flight landed in Houston, Stone turned off his phone and disconnected the battery to ensure he left no digital trail. Though he required a rental car to make the rest of the journey, he put the tab on his own credit card, ensuring no one possessed the legal right to track him later.

He pulled into the finished driveway, wondering if Jack Turpin had spent the last of his savings on a house he barely called his own before his untimely death.

A garage that looked more like a workshop occupied the backyard, the rolling door open as sounds of heavy moving emerged. Stone approached the open door cautiously, hoping his information wasn't misleading. He hated the thought of making the trek into rural Harris County only to discover new ownership at the house.

"Hello?" he called upon reaching the large opening, seeing stacks of cardboard boxes inside, along with tools hung along the walls and a large table saw.

"Can I help you?" an attractive woman with black hair in her early forties asked as she maneuvered around the boxes to lay eyes upon her visitor.

She wore old blue jeans and a faded top appropriate for cleaning out a garage during a slow weekend.

Stone quickly removed the black cowboy hat from atop his head, holding it near his waistline respectfully. The woman looked him up and down, from his shined boots to the red and gray striped tie atop his white shirt. He decided he wanted to look the part of an FBI agent, even if his business here was personal.

The woman appeared stunned after staring at him momentarily, a curious look crossing her face.

"Are you with the Bureau?" she finally asked.

"Yes, ma'am."

Caught off-guard by her question, Stone failed to properly introduce himself, somewhat elated that he seemed to have found the right person.

"Oh, I'm sorry," he said, offering his hand. "Special Agent Harlan Stone."

She shook his hand, though her expression turned a bit wary.

"Kristina Turpin. I thought I was done with the Bureau after my husband died, but then they came around and asked even more questions this past winter."

"I'm here on more of a personal level," Stone confessed.

"Oh?" she asked, wiping her hands with a towel.

"It just recently came to my attention that I'm the man who took your husband's spot in the Bureau."

"His spot?" she questioned with raised eyebrows.

Stone decided to tread carefully, unsure of what Jack Turpin told his wife, or exactly when the couple met.

"When he worked in Los Angeles, Jack was part of a special division. If you don't mind me asking, when did the two of you meet?"

Kristina smiled.

"Let's head to the house so I can get us some tea."

"That sounds wonderful, ma'am."

"Please, call me Kris," she said, leading the way toward the front of the house where an open front porch awaited them.

Stone waited patiently while the widow stepped inside to make them some iced tea. When she returned the agent gladly accepted the tall glass from her, taking a seat on one of the two padded rocking chairs just outside the front door, placing his hat atop one knee. Though it wasn't protected by a screen, or otherwise enclosed, the porch provided shade in the form of a small awning. The concrete floor ensured the elements couldn't weather the surface or leave mold and mildew during any season. Stone had a feeling the house was custom built very recently for Turpin and his wife to enjoy after his retirement.

"Did you know my husband?" Kristina asked once she occupied the other seat.

"No. I just recently learned about him on an assignment."

"Jack was special," she revealed with affection. "He was an absolute gentleman who didn't speak unless he needed to."

Stone simply nodded before taking a sip of the tea.

"You remind me of him a little bit," she confessed. "He always wore his boots and spoke with a slow, thoughtful drawl."

Grinning, Stone thought of how much he fought to suppress his own accent, particularly when he traveled outside of his home state.

"We met when he came back to Houston for his father's funeral of all places," Kristina revealed. "I worked with his mother for a few years before she retired and she prodded him to date me. Jack wasn't keen on the idea after three previous marriages, so he tried to put me off by saying long distance relationships didn't work and he traveled all the time."

She took a sip from her own tea.

"I hate to bore you with the details, Agent Stone."

"You're not boring me at all, Mrs. Turpin."

"But I'm sure you're not here to listen to past romances."

"It's okay. Really. I'm still somewhat of a newlywed myself."

Kristina gave a smile of approval before continuing.

"I think Jack's mother continued to meddle because he finally dated me whenever he came back to Texas. We hit it off, but he was always secretive about his work, like he did something other than what I've always pictured FBI agents doing."

The irony wasn't wasted on Stone, who realized his recent activities were nowhere close to what he expected when he applied to the agency.

"Jack was a loving husband, but he always seemed to have a void in his life. He once told me he worked out of Los Angeles because the travel allowed him to search for his son. I don't think he liked the work, but he seemed determined to find his boy before he retired."

"Did he?"

"No. He found some decent leads in the Chicago area, but his son was adopted and grew up under a different name. Jack's first wife was murdered while he was overseas and his son was already in the foster system when he returned home. It sounded like someone adopted him quickly, which explains why Jack could never get him back, or find much information. But I think he was hurt that his son never looked for his natural parents."

"Maybe he did," Stone suggested. "The system doesn't make it easy to obtain information either way."

"Jack eventually let go of his dream and decided to retire, but he made it sound like retiring might be, well, dangerous."

"Dangerous?"

"I'm not sure that's the right word for it," Kristina said, taking another sip of tea. "Financially we were fine, even after beginning construction on the house, so I wasn't sure why he was concerned."

Stone began wondering if working as a rogue agent wasn't equivalent to being a made man in the mafia. Most people in that profession died as a result of their profession, sometimes by the hands of their own people if they tried to leave the criminal lifestyle.

"Do you have any idea what might have worried him? You're doing his job now, right? I mean I know you make enemies in your line of work, but I didn't think they dared come after FBI agents."

Stone decided not to shatter the illusion that standard criminals might have brought harm to her husband.

"That's really what I wanted to ask you about, Mrs. Turpin. Jack was only retired a few months before his accident. Had his behavior changed at all before his death?"

"Not really. Like I said, Jack was quiet about everything. If something was bothering him, he didn't always show it."

"And he never told you anything about the nature of his work?"

"No. Nothing specific about the cases he worked."

"Do you know for a fact that he worked cases?"

Kristina looked at him curiously.

"Jack never mentioned specifics, but he always implied he worked cases. Is that not what *you* do?"

"So far it's not what I do," Stone confessed. "Did any of Jack's old colleagues come to his funeral services?"

"Not really. Jack said he was recruited into the Bureau after his police and military days were over. He made it sound like he worked special cases and didn't really have too many colleagues."

"What about a man named Alan Stewart? Did he attend the services?"

Kristina shook her head negatively.

"No, but he did call. And he sent flowers. He said it was the least he could do."

Stone questioned how his boss knew about a retiree's death from so far away, especially considering the brief time Turpin spent with the Bureau.

Staring at her glass momentarily, the widow seemed to struggle to ask her next question because the answer might shatter her current beliefs.

"You think his car accident was no accident, don't you?"

Crafting his reply carefully, Stone knew this woman was his only hope of digging up the truth, and so far she hadn't provided any earthshattering information. Going to the local police, or questioning whoever performed the analysis of Turpin's vehicle was sure to raise some red flags, so Stone placed his hopes in the widow's answers.

He decided to answer her question with a question.

"They said Jack fell asleep at the wheel. Had you ever known him to do anything like that? Did he have health problems?"

"No," she answered, her voice a bit more despondent. "He was in phenomenal health for his age. And the few times he drank he certainly never drove. The medical examiner asked me about a thousand questions because I don't think he could find a reason for Jack hitting a tree the way he did."

"And he was pronounced dead at the scene?"

Kristina nodded solemnly.

"I have some concerns about my new position," Stone said slowly. "The less I tell you, the better, but if someone brought harm to your husband I *will* find them."

Stone told the absolute truth, because if he discovered someone within his organization targeted Turpin he would bring them to justice out of self-preservation. He had an idea that Stewart was using the rogue agent program to serve his own means, but Stone still didn't know why or how deep the potential corruption reached. He ran an incredible risk if he tried to investigate the situation himself.

"How do I reach you?" Kristina asked.

"You don't," Stone said vehemently. "I took great lengths to make certain no one knew I came here. If you were to contact me it might put us both in danger. Until I find some answers it's best we don't speak again."

Her expression grew rather grave.

"I didn't mean to worry you like this."

"Well you have, so it's a little bit late to apologize now."

"Again, sorry. Please don't go to anyone else with what I've told you. At this point I'm not sure who to trust, especially around here. Maybe this will all turn out to be nothing."

Stone wasn't particularly good at being reassuring, but he didn't want word of his visit to reach beyond the yard where he currently sat.

"I'm sorry to bring this to your doorstep, but you should be safe if you don't mention this to anyone."

"And what about you?" Kristina asked with open concern.

"I have to take my chances, but I can take care of myself."

Stone set the nearly empty glass of tea atop the porch railing and replaced his hat, hoping to make a quick exit. He only had a few days away from work to see his parents and contemplate the reasonable doubt regarding Jack Turpin's allegedly accidental death.

"Thanks for your time," he said, nodding as he touched the brim of his hat. "And for the tea."

"You're welcome. Just promise me you'll eventually let me know what you find out."

"When the smoke clears you'll be the first to know," he said with a grin.

Sauntering toward the rental car, Stone wondered if he was becoming soft, and if Jack Turpin had experienced a similar transition before someone likely staged his murder to look like an accident.

Chapter 31

Craig Jennings found it hard to concentrate on the task before him as reporters descended upon all of the horse owners and trainers like locusts. While the sounds of buzzing wings didn't enter his ears, their words certainly bounced around in his head and he knew more about horse racing than he ever cared to know.

As he walked from the horse stalls to the nearest bathroom he wondered how Lincoln Daine could ever *possibly* get close enough to Phantom to use the cursed object. Between the stationed state troopers and the press, it wasn't easy to go anywhere without a pass around one's neck. Most of the horses weren't accustomed to strangers, nor were they very receptive to being touched by anyone except their handlers. Some trainers hardly ever made physical contact with their horses, often leaving it to handlers or stable hands.

Jennings took notice that Jeff Slaton, Phantom's trainer, and the stable hands didn't stray far from the racehorse. During his morning run and the bath that followed, the men were always within sight of the stall. They occasionally fielded questions from fans or the press, or took turns getting a bite to eat, but someone was always nearby.

Stepping into the restroom area, Jennings found two urinals and two stalls, so he stepped up to a urinal and conducted his business, feeling certain he had the restroom to himself. Sidestepping the pressure of searching for Daine and avoiding the media felt good, and he certainly couldn't wait for the day to end so his life could return to normal.

Normal for him certainly wasn't the standard, but at least he landed in a comfort zone while working at the West Baden Springs Hotel.

After pulling up his zipper Jennings checked his watch, seeing the minute hand closing in on five o'clock. Already a preliminary race had been run on the soggy turf, meaning the time for Phantom to run drew ever closer.

Jennings quickly washed his hands, hearing the sound of everything he did reverberate in the restroom because it was so open, with solid walls on all sides. He dabbed some cold water on his face, looking up to the mirror to see the gray uniform of a state trooper standing almost directly behind him. Complete with the matching campaign hat with the flat brim that many troopers and military sergeants wore, the man stared directly into the mirror, studying something. The trooper hadn't made a move for the stall or one of the urinals, and he certainly could have used the second sink to wash his hands.

Startled a bit, Jennings turned to speak to the trooper but Teakon walked through the doorway first, giving the trooper a nod before addressing Jennings.

"You shouldn't run off like that, Craig. One of the ESPN reporters wants a word with you."

"I already did an interview with them," Jennings groaned, starting toward the door as he shook the remainder of the water from his clean hands.

Margaret was due to arrive any minute with her son, so Jennings wanted all of the interviews and showmanship finished quickly. She absolutely wanted to see Phantom before he ran, and stand in the grandstand during the race. Jennings had made all of her wishes a priority because he cared about the grandmotherly woman and wished her the best of luck with her prize racehorse. He just hoped any success on Phantom's part came via natural means.

Following Teakon back to the stall, Jennings suddenly contemplated why the state trooper stood so silently behind him in the restroom. The man never stated his business, if he indeed needed anything from the pretend horse owner. Jennings decided he was just overthinking the situation after so many hours of observation as security chief at the hotel. Shrugging to himself, he decided more pressing issues required his attention.

***

Lincoln Daine found it necessary to modify his original plan. He had spent the better part of the last year creating and modifying his Kentucky Derby heist while winning bets in lesser sports as means of support. He mentally prepared himself for the security presence, over one hundred thousand people in attendance, and the need to get close to whatever horse was the long shot after placing a major bet.

Two issues still plagued him so late in the afternoon. He hadn't been to the windows to place a bet, but only because he hadn't used his cursed cube on Desert Phantom quite yet. He originally planned to murder someone and take their life essence outside of Churchill Downs, but he decided to arrive early and scout the grounds and activities first. Dressed as a Kentucky State Trooper, he moved about freely without anyone questioning him. Somewhat surprised at his luck, he already possessed a cover story ready if a real trooper questioned him. He knew many of them came from all across the state to work security, so he had a fairly remote post and assignment ready to tell them in reply.

The uniform came from a trooper he deemed the right size and build almost seven months prior who lived outside of Lexington. Daine studied the single man's habits before breaking into his house one day when the trooper reported to work. The lack of household pets and a security alarm made for an easy entry without detection, and within ten minutes Daine possessed the items he needed, complete with hat and name badge. He truly hoped the real Mike Stephens wasn't assigned to the Derby, and even if he was, the chances of the trooper working around the stables seemed remote. The younger troopers were assigned more menial duties like traffic control and standing near the entrance gates.

He had thoughts of strangling the southwestern cowboy standing at the sink because a gunshot would create too much noise, but Daine couldn't afford a lasting struggle either. While the looks of the man dressed in black indicated wealth, Daine stood close enough to him to smell his cologne, which didn't smell like a designer brand. After years of socializing with people on both ends of the financial spectrum, Daine analyzed people by smell, attire, and posture almost instantly.

Taking a thoughtful breath, he tapped the knife folded in the pocket of the stolen pants, thinking he needed a weaker victim as he left the restroom. Selecting a victim and killing him or her wasn't the main problem because he needed somewhere to stash the body where it wouldn't be found for at least an hour or two following the primary race.

By then he planned to be driving through Ohio or Indiana to a new destination with a sizeable check. Daine needed somewhere quiet and secluded, not because he feared being discovered, but rather to avoid losing money to his recurring gambling habit. If not for that weakness he might have retired from the vicious cycle of taking human life to earn money a year ago.

He didn't especially like murdering people for personal gain, but putting his gambling habit to rest felt impossible. Perhaps the earthy-brown cube in his other pocket pushed him toward the card tables and slot machines because it could never be satiated. Daine didn't understand how an inanimate object could possess will or thoughts, but he knew the cube wasn't just a passive device, waiting listlessly for someone to use it.

Walking along the stables, Daine noticed people practically everywhere. And though no particular area housed a mob, it seemed owners, trainers, and reporters stood along every corner. He desperately needed to find someone isolated from the crowd and a seldom-traveled location in which to store a body. Forcing himself to watch rigidly while studying everyone around him, Daine acted the part well, having observed other police personnel throughout the day and watching video from the previous year's Derby.

Most of the police working security remained near what he assumed were assigned areas, so he dared not kick up dirt in the same locations too many times. Daine decided to walk around the stable buildings, along their sides that faced fencing and walls, hoping to locate a straggler who might be heading to a restroom or one of the lesser populated beverage and food areas.

Much of the ground consisted of packed dirt, sometimes atop concrete surfaces, and new, smooth blacktop occupied the areas closer to the gates for loading and unloading of livestock. For some reason the dirt around the stables didn't look nearly as milky as the track, but Daine wasn't taking in the sights. He watched every person within his peripheral vision to see where they were heading and if they might be an easy mark. He wanted the cube charged and ready for the second phase of his plan. The race was over an hour away, but the jockeys and owners took the horses out of the stalls well before that to parade them along the dirt track's straightaway toward the gates to be loaded for the Walkover.

Beginning to walk with urgency, Daine scoured the stall areas for *any* straggler far enough away from the noise of reporters and the security of other people milling around the stables. He felt like a lion, hunting for a gazelle separated from its pack, or injured to the point that it couldn't run very far. He passed a few stalls that weren't being used in one of the rear buildings before spying his quarry slowly shuffling toward a marked restroom area less than fifty feet from the last stable quarters.

"You'll do," Daine said under his breath, watching an older gentleman hobbling on a cane toward the bathroom with a hunched back.

He entertained visions of placing an "Out of Order" sign on the door once he finished the dirty business of murdering the old man to keep people from entering the restroom stall. The custodial closets usually weren't far from the restrooms, often seated in a small space between the men's and women's doorways.

Daine continued to study the old man, who shuffled along at a snail's pace, wearing new clothes, as though this might be his one and only Kentucky Derby. He might have been an owner's grandfather, or perhaps a ceremonial guest from one of the past Churchill Downs events, but Daine intended to make this the man's last appearance on the grounds. As the man finally slipped into the restroom, Daine trailed him to the door, planning to carry out what needed to be done before covering up his crime.

If all went according to plan, he would leave Churchill Downs with millions in just over an hour.

Chapter 32

By the time the procession for the Walkover lined up, Craig Jennings wanted to hang his head in failure, but he still had a part to play. Absolutely left in the dark because he'd been isolated from everyone in his camp, including Teakon, the pretend horse owner joined trainer Jeff Slaton and Manny Garcia. Garcia was the primary stable hand who spent the most time around Desert Phantom at the stall. Much like a colorful parade, trainers and some of the owner-ship camp walked counterclockwise around the track from the stables with their respective horses in front of the thousands in attendance. For some horses it was unnerving because many had never been in front of such a huge crowd and heard thunderous applause.

Jennings knew the Walkover was a cakewalk compared to the race itself when the jockeys and horses required every ounce of concentration.

Teakon had left his side to escort Margaret Stough and her son to the prime seats reserved for their entire party since they were owners. Eventually Jennings would join them to watch the race, unable to imagine how that moment was going to feel. Intuition told him either Daine succeeded in using the cube on the horse, or the killer decided to skip the race for some reason. Not hearing from Greene bothered him immensely, and no one had seen or heard from Clay Branson all day.

"You ready for this?" Slaton asked as they fell in line for the prestigious parade.

"As I'll ever be," Jennings answered.

Under ordinary circumstances owners spent their day hobnobbing with social-ites, placing bets, and drinking mint juleps or other various spirits. Because Slaton had recently pulled a muscle in his back he wasn't able to provide jockey Johnny Gomez with the traditional leg up when he mounted Phantom. Jennings volunteered, particularly since horse owners from the New Mexico area preferred to be hands-on in training and races whenever possible. Following such traditions kept Margaret happy, and Jennings felt morally obligated to abide by her wishes since she allowed Clouse and his people to enter the horse ownership aspect of her life.

"When do we meet up with Johnny?" Jennings inquired as the group slowly walked onto the track.

He looked across the crowded infield, spying the famous twin spires atop the grandstand roof. Sounds of the crowd reached their ears whenever the spectators seated there spied local favorites or some of the better known horses and trainers.

"He's with the other jockeys getting the traditional photo," Slaton replied. "We'll meet with him for final instructions shortly."

Jennings tried to take in the whirlwind of activity around him, still concerned about his overall objective lying in ruins like a train wreck. The not knowing pained him because on two previous occasions he had nearly fallen victim to the murderous ways of corrupted men possessing the cursed cubes.

Deciding he was powerless to do anything at this point, Jennings simply accepted his role, surrounded by overcast skies and a far weaker breeze than the morning brought. His black boots immediately took on a thin layer of dirt and mud as he found it slightly difficult to walk. While the track didn't have standing water, the muddy surface felt like quicksand, ready to plant him in the ground.

Numerous reporters walked in stride with trainers, asking each of them questions relating to their horse, or in some cases, their thoughts on their horse's chances of winning the Derby. Jennings fell back when an NBC analyst questioned Slaton about the trip from New Mexico and Phantom's up and down finishes the past year. Slaton handled the inquiry like a pro, furthering Jennings' assessment that the trainer knew his way around a racetrack, no matter how big the stakes.

Positive he was within view of the camera, Jennings really didn't have any other choice. Besides, it wasn't as though he led a secret life like the evil men who possessed the cubes, using disguises and manipulation as they made their way through life. Jennings simply stared straight ahead or looked at the chestnut colt walking in front of him, happy to let Slaton talk on national television.

When the reporter finally moved to the next interesting story behind them in line, Jennings glanced at the crowd, seeing lots of white and colorful dots, each representing a suit, hat, or dress of some kind. By this time there wasn't a vacant seat in Churchill Downs and a buzz of electricity ran through the crowd in anticipation of the annual race.

The procession ended when the groups entered a tunnel leading to the paddock area and walked their horses into tiny stalls. The stalls looked more like divider walls with decorative wooden backings and the name and number of each horse above its respective staging area. On Wednesday Jennings and Teakon had sat in a room with every other owner and trainer to learn which starting position they would receive through luck of the draw, or in some cases, bad luck of the draw. The team drew the number eight slot from a field of twenty, which Slaton informed them wasn't too bad. While no position proved overwhelmingly better for horses placing, Jennings knew the starting gates along the two ends were often recipes for disaster.

Shortly after reaching the temporary stalls the command for riders up was given and Jennings provided his jockey a leg up before breaking off to meet his group in the stands. His pass got him past security as the call to the post was trumpeted from across the dirt track. A friendly state trooper cleared a path for him at the entryway to the seating and pointed out the appropriate direction after Jennings provided the seat numbers. When he spotted Teakon, the two exchanged uneasy glances before Jennings stepped forward to give Margaret a reassuring hug and her son a handshake.

"It's the moment of truth," he said gently, giving her a genuine smile because he wanted her to own a champion thoroughbred. He then turned to Teakon on his other side. "No word at all?"

"Nothing," the man answered with a shrug.

"You both look so handsome," Margaret said, unaware of the turmoil both men felt regarding her horse.

Both uttered sheepish thanks, wondering how many people took notice of their black duds and cowboy hats. Jennings hadn't been in the seating area long enough to know how many other owners surrounded them but for Margaret's sake he was going to hoot and holler like a high school sports parent when the race started.

He heard an announcement being made about local sponsorship and the track management before the announcer asked everyone to rise for the sentimental singing of "My Old Kentucky Home" as a university band played the song. Teakon handed him a program that contained the song lyrics, so Jennings joined the thousands around him in song momentarily, realizing the song was one of loss, which he knew something about. As he belted out some off-key lyrics, Jennings noticed the horses beginning to amble toward the starting gate, and a knot formed in his stomach.

The breeze picked up as a floral smell crossed Jennings' nose once more, just as the sun broke temporarily through the clouds above.

"I'm so scared," Margaret confessed as the first of the horses were loaded into the gates.

"Me too," Jennings replied, though his fears stemmed from knowing a murderous bastard might still be on the loose.

Jennings suddenly wished he would have remembered binoculars, but a screen across from their seats provided a view of the action. Wasting little time, race officials ushered the horses into the green metal gates, closing them within the small area until all eighteen horses still entered in the contest were loaded. Two horses had been withdrawn for various health concerns over the past twenty-four hours, making the field smaller and the betting more interesting.

Barely two seconds passed after the last horse was loaded on the far end of the rail before the starting bell rang and the gates flew open with a thunderous gunshot noise. Jennings kept rocking between his boot heels and his toes as he looked from the track to the screen, seeing both provided him an ample view of the race as the horses all flew out of the starting gate almost all neck and neck.

The field quickly became a cluster as jockeys moved their horses toward the inside rail to shorten the running distance for their horses. Jennings searched for the horse with the "8" on his blanket, but the crowded field made it impossible to see any numbers. He changed his strategy, trying to decipher the blue and gold uniform Johnny Gomez wore out of the colorful pack as they streaked down the main straightway.

"I can't see him," Margaret's son said, trying to look through binoculars.

"There," Teakon spoke up, finally spotting their horse. "In the middle."

Jennings picked up on the colors about the same time his colleague spoke the words, finding Phantom and Gomez stuck between a few other horses. By the time the first turn came about, a few horses had already dropped off the pace, freeing up some space for the frontrunners. Gomez still didn't have anywhere to maneuver, but he kept Phantom safely in the center of the pack without brushing against any other horses and upsetting his own mount.

"Oh my," Margaret said, cupping her mouth and nose with her hands in nervous anticipation.

Feeling like his head was about to explode from the one-hundred-fifty-thousand voices reverberating around him, Jennings concentrated on locking his eyes onto the gold and blue silks worn by Johnny Gomez. As the pack rounded the first turn it grew difficult to track any individual horse because the group became one brown blur.

Turning his eyes to the screen, Jennings felt disheartened and happy at the same time when he saw Phantom in the middle of the pack when the group rounded the next bend. He noticed Gomez trying to hold the horse back because Phantom wanted to surge forward and the jockey was trying to conserve the horse's energy until the end. Jennings questioned just how much extra the colt might possess in his reserves.

Teakon nudged him in the ribs, apparently reaching the same conclusion.

"Johnny is really struggling with him, Craig."

"I noticed," Jennings replied just above a whisper. "It might be nothing. The horse likes to surge."

Grimacing, Teakon said nothing more as his eyes locked on the screen. He gnashed his teeth noticeably, nervous about the outcome like his undercover partner.

When the horses entered the backstretch, little changed except the third and fourth place horses were jostling for position. Phantom remained in the hunt, and when the horse to his left started to falter, Gomez moved him closer to the rail to shorten their ride to the finish line. He visibly continued to hold the thoroughbred back, even while entering the far turn as mud spat upward from every raised hoof. Jennings glanced at Margaret and her son, who both appeared to be holding their breath in anticipation of the impending photo finish. A few more horses had now dropped off for various reasons, but half of the eighteen starters still remained in contention for a place or showing.

Jennings watched the screen as the field rounded the bend into the final turn with a centralized cluster of horses still leaving little room for maneuvering. He spotted the horse he claimed to own in part on the screen, watching Phantom enter the last turn as Gomez finally turned him loose to use every bit of his energy reserve with half a mile left to run.

"Dear God," Teakon muttered as the jockey guided Phantom through two horses that ran dangerously close to the rail.

By comparison, they looked like their gas tanks had expired and Phantom had used a form of illegal booster fuel to overtake them. He passed them within seconds as he entered the straightaway, closing ground between his position and the five leaders remaining ahead of him. Jennings abandoned the screen as though it might deceive him in some way, wanting to see the finish with his own eyes since it would occur directly in front of him.

Down the final straightaway the horse closed the gap as though he was custom-built to run on muddy tracks. He passed the fifth place horse in seconds, securing the fourth position a few seconds later. Only a few lengths now separated him from the three leaders and Jennings unconsciously grasped Teakon's arm, shaking it just slightly from nervous anticipation.

"Hey!" Teakon said, though not in a scolding manner because the competitive bug had bitten him as well. "He might pull this off!"

Jennings stole a look at Margaret, who appeared on the verge of collapse from the excitement of her adopted colt making a name for itself and her family. She held her shaking hands before her, perhaps in prayer, as Phantom passed the third and second place horses almost in succession, leaving only the leader in front of him with less than two hundred yards to the finish.

Gomez barely used the jockey whip as Phantom naturally pressed forward, pressuring the leader almost immediately. For a few seconds they were neck and neck and Jennings felt his body tense from the excitement of being part of history, even if he wasn't a true contributor. They were seconds away from seeing the winner cross the finish line, and Jennings subconsciously grabbed hold of Teakon's arm once again, jumping up and down briefly like a kid about to receive a birthday present from behind a huge curtain.

Teakon didn't seem to mind, his own eyes locked on the horses as he clapped and whistled before holding clenched fists in front of him, channeling energy for Phantom to pull off the impossible.

Both of them observed the final one-hundred yards with baited breath, watching the other horse suddenly run out of steam while Phantom continued to press forward until the finish line where he finished by two lengths.

All around them the crowd went wild while Jennings and Teakon shared hugs with Margaret, her son, and virtually everyone around them. After receiving some high fives from the remainder of spectators and owners around them, the pretend owner and ranch manager locked eyes, exchanging concerned looks as the reality, or the possibility of a different reality, entered their minds. The only bright spot Jennings considered was that the thoroughbred didn't run away with the race like an illegally enhanced athlete might.

Regardless of what they thought, or how they felt, the two men were committed to trudging forward with the ceremony. Neither wanted to wait for the truth, especially if they were powerless to stop someone from being murdered right under their noses, but no one had called or sent a text message their way as of yet.

Jennings followed Margaret and her son toward the nearest exit as they were expected on the infield for photographs and interviews momentarily. Teakon followed without so much as a word, knowing full well what his uncle sacrificed to save lives, even giving his own in the process to protect others.

He wanted out of this dirty, dangerous business, but only if he knew others wouldn't suffer because of his self-indulgence.

Chapter 33

Greene knew from the moment the horses left their stables that his chances of finding Daine were practically nonexistent. He monitored Desert Phantom closely and never saw anyone other than the usual staff approach the horse before Margaret Stough's trainer and stable hands came to retrieve it for the procession leading into the race.

"This is hopeless," he muttered, watching several horses prance by as he and Liz watched from the side of one of the stable buildings.

"There isn't anything more we could have done," Liz said, touching his arm with her gloved hand.

Sometimes he wanted her to touch him with a bare hand, not because he sought intimate contact to advance their working relationship to a personal level, but because he simply felt shunned. Liz claimed she tried to avoid touching all people, but she made it a special point to never have contact with Greene. He couldn't recall any abnormally shameful event from his past, and there were no skeletons in the closet that might embarrass him. During their time together Greene told her about growing up in Tennessee, and passed a few hours talking about some of his more interesting cases with the federal government.

Liz touched the horse at a few different intervals, but nothing triggered her ability. Considering there was no science behind her visions, Greene wondered if maybe her powers simply didn't work, or required a recharging of some sort, but the possibility existed that Lincoln Daine never came to the Kentucky Derby, or he somehow slipped past them.

Or he simply chose a different horse on which to use his cursed object.

Neither of them gave up, even after the horses began the walk to the paddock as Liz set to touching the components of Phantom's stable while Greene followed the horse, monitoring the horse's surroundings like a Secret Service agent. His pass only got him so far, however, until the true security force halted him to let the procession pass through some gates. Since he wasn't part of any team, Greene was forced to wait where he stood, feeling his blood pressure rise. He couldn't move forward, and he couldn't readily get to the stands, so he decided his only option was to have Liz continue making contact with people and objects.

She complied, but it wasn't long before the introductions came over the speakers and Greene knew he was too far away from the action to make a difference in time. With glum expressions he and Liz listened to the race without watching, feeling content their secretive mission was a waste of time until the very end when Desert Phantom suddenly made a push to win the race by two lengths.

"Shit," Greene muttered, turning around to discover a sight that heightened his fears.

He found several state troopers and emergency medical technicians standing over a prone body beside one of the isolated restrooms. Drawing closer, Greene didn't want to interfere or draw their attention because he wanted to know if Daine found a victim prior to the race, or something completely unrelated occurred.

Gaining a better vantage point, Greene noticed the person lying on the ground was dressed in a Kentucky State Trooper uniform. His hands were tied behind his back and a wallet was placed atop his pants around the thigh area. One of the troopers picked it up to examine the contents, and Greene dared step close enough for a look, discovering a Tennessee driver's license with a picture of the man he knew as Lincoln Daine and a completely different name on the identification.

He moved back toward Liz before the authorities noticed him, hoping the troopers would reach the conclusion he easily came to with a mere glance.

One of them hunched over, comparing the name tag on the uniform to the identification in the wallet, shaking his head slowly. He handed the wallet to his fellow trooper and they shifted their stances enough that Greene noticed the man lying on the ground didn't appear to be conscious. In addition to that, his hands were also bound behind his back with plastic disposable restraints like the type police officers often used.

"Didn't one of our guys down south have his house broken into?" one of the troopers asked the other, receiving an affirmative nod in reply.

Greene felt newfound respect for Clay Branson because he never once saw the man on the premises that day, yet he felt certain the cop made good on his promise to assist with finding Daine. Apparently he went above and beyond his promise, apprehending the man without assistance and almost certainly saving a life in the process.

"I think our work is done here," he informed Liz, leading her away from the scene before more gawkers stopped to look.

"Did our invisible member strike?"

"It seems so."

Greene looked around, wondering if any security cameras in the area might have caught the events leading to the imposter state trooper's capture. He didn't immediately spy any equipment, but that didn't mean footage wouldn't be appearing on the evening news. The matter of retrieving the cube from Branson remained, but Greene felt safer knowing the cube was with him rather than Daine.

He led Liz to the ground level of the stands where they arrived just in time to see Jennings and Teakon standing beside the horse with Margaret Stough, her son, and the rest of their staff. The roses were already laid across Desert Phantom and the official photographs were being taken by a staff photographer while freelance and newspaper photographers took the best shots possible from further distances. Jennings and Teakon played their parts well, but Greene decided to let them off the hook by sending Jennings a text message so the pair could finally relax.

After this the winning team was escorted up the stairs of a pagoda where television crews surrounded them and the governor of Kentucky made what sounded like a speech for a television spot before handing Jennings the trophy. Jennings quickly passed off the golden icon to Margaret as the reporters asked him how he felt about joining the ownership team recently and winning the greatest race in the world. Extremely humble, he answered that he felt blessed to have helped Margaret bring her horse to Kentucky and that she deserved all of the credit. Bringing a flushed redness to her cheeks and a tear to her eye, Jennings had completed his job because Clouse would honor the agreement and allow her to buy back full rights to the horse.

Once the reporters asked Margaret and her son a few questions they switched to Jeff Slaton and Johnny Gomez who had made their way up the white ceremonial building as well. Greene watched Jennings read the text message on his phone from afar as a wave of relief crossed his face and he whispered the good news to Teakon.

A night of celebration and parties awaited the winning team and Greene wished he could join them, but his job came first. He needed to get Liz back to Indiana and make contact with Branson. From there he would hide the latest cube or surrender it to Clouse who usually turned any cursed objects over to Julie Knowles in Massachusetts.

He understood she kept watch over some kind of secret vault where all sorts of security measures kept anyone except her and a select few from entering and taking hold of the cursed objects hidden inside. Of course some of the select few were lost at sea when Clouse tried to send one of the cubes to the depths of the Bering Sea. Greene doubted some of his employer's planning, but he still felt confident Clouse meant well with his actions.

At least Greene could return to Indiana with good news for the man who signed his paychecks for a change.

Chapter 34

Matt Teakon survived a hellacious night of partying after Margaret Stough's horse won the Kentucky Derby. He barely consumed any spirits, but he awoke with a terrible headache the following morning, intensified by the fact that he only slept a few hours. And though he didn't directly participate in interviews with numerous morning shows and local networks, he stayed with Jennings until his cohort offered to drive them back to Indiana.

Another full day of rest prepared him for the trip to Amherst, Massachusetts where he was to deliver the latest cursed cube to Julie Knowles. Clay Branson handed the cube to Russ Greene rather unceremoniously before the group left Kentucky. He explained briefly how he simply disguised himself as a rather feeble old gentleman who relied on a cane to get around. Once Lincoln Daine revealed his true colors and attempted to murder Branson it was a simple feat for the trained assassin to subdue him and reveal the man's crimes by placing his wallet where authorities could readily retrieve it.

Everyone accustomed to locating the cursed cubes found Branson's demeanor difficult to read. They weren't certain if he was any closer to joining their cause or if he simply wanted to use them until he located Nosagi. Either way, the job was nearing completion. Teakon estimated they possessed all of the cubes except for two or three, not counting the one discarded into the unforgiving Bering Sea, which wasn't likely to see the light of day ever again.

"We're almost there," Julie Knowles said when she saw Teakon walk through the door with the cloth-covered cube.

He treated the cubes as living, breathing entities, never allowing them to see the light of day for fear they might turn men to stone like Medusa or lure them with a siren song to conduct evil deeds. It was the same reasoning his uncle used when he transported the cubes outside of their group's secret vault, placing them in a lead box that shielded them from human eyes and made them difficult to detect.

"A few more hazardous trips and we might lay hands on all of these," Teakon replied, handing the concealed cube to Julie.

She said nothing more, simply turning to head downstairs and place the cube in the vault where its siblings resided. Keeping them in one spot wasn't ideal, but the vault contained nearly a dozen safeguards against intruders that would kill anyone who tripped two of them in succession. Mark Teakon designed and practically built the entire level below the bookstore over the course of a few years before his death. His access to historical documents and people in the know provided him with knowledge about the cursed objects long before Paul Clouse's troubles with two particular cubes ever began.

"I got this letter from one of your uncle's old college contacts yesterday," Julie said upon returning and retrieving the sealed mail from beneath the old cash register.

"Thanks," Teakon replied, tucking the letter into his shirt pocket. "You could have opened this. Uncle Mark didn't have any secrets from you."

Julie simply shrugged, perhaps doing a kindness by letting Teakon feel connected to his uncle once more.

He normally dressed business casual regardless of his daily schedule, so Teakon continued to wear button-up shirts after the horse racing ruse ended. Khakis replaced his black jeans, and leather sandals took the place of cowboy boots the day after Desert Phantom made history. Add a cup of expensive coffee in one hand and he might pass for a campus regular like the professors.

"Have a look at that," he said, clenching his fist and moving it closer to Julie so she could view the new ring on his left hand a bit better.

Much like a Super Bowl championship ring, the large gold band was custom made for the ownership team of the Kentucky Derby almost immediately by a jewelry store in Louisville. Primarily gold with some silver trim and the championship trophy enclosed by a horseshoe in the center, the ring was full of detail, likely costing thousands to create. The current year and the words "Kentucky Derby" were wrapped around the top of the ring in a full circle.

"Very nice," Julie said, examining the ring closely. "About time you got some bling."

Teakon chuckled, fully aware that he didn't spend much money on his appearance after working on ranches in rural areas for so long.

Looking through the huge storefront windows, Teakon noticed a slightly purple hue overtaking the sky as dusk came to the East Coast. He walked toward the front door to flip the open sign over when he noticed a large black SUV stopping suddenly in the closest available parking space to the store. Most of the other shops lining the block closed around five, so he didn't understand why someone risked whiplash to take an unopposed parking spot. When four men, two of them armed with automatic weapons, stepped from the vehicle with unfriendly scowls, he received his answer and turned immediately to Julie.

"We need to get downstairs! Now!"

Julie barely found time enough to return a stunned look before Teakon clasped her by the arm and led her to the secret entrance behind the counter. Unlike the main entrance to the vault, this one took them directly to a lengthy panic room that required a code upon both entrance and exit. Short of military-grade weapons, no unwanted visitor could gain access to the room.

Teakon heard the front door being kicked in while he closed the secret entrance behind him. Sounds of wood splintering and glass shattering entered the store without hesitation, as though the thieves were confident they could simply snatch their objective within seconds and disappear. Following Julie down a dimly lit stairwell, he knew no one would be able to get to them or access the vault without making a major ruckus. With luck the brazen thieves might give up once they realized the difficulty of obtaining their prize.

Knowing robbers didn't knock off bookstores, even major chains, Teakon deduced someone was after the cubes specifically, which sent his mind racing. A very select few people knew about the cursed objects, so either a traitor betrayed their camp or a patient outsider was finally making a move.

When the pair reached the basement an imposing steel door awaited them with an electronic keypad beside it, slanted for easy use upon a slab jutting out from the door at hand level. The clomping of footsteps above them provided Julie with enough sense of urgency to type in her personal code quickly upon the keypad. After she pressed enter on the device the door swung open, granting the pair access to safety. Teakon hesitated only to wipe down the keypad with his shirt, trying to eliminate any material left from human fingers in case their visitors tried determining the code by using chemical means or a thermal detector.

"Who the hell could it be?" Julie asked as the door sealed shut behind them with the sound of hydraulics activating.

"I don't know," Teakon answered, looking to make certain both of the panic room doors were secure.

Aside from the one that took them upstairs, another door existed that opened in the heart of the vault, providing them virtually equal security inside its thick concrete walls. Mark Teakon spared no expense when building the shelter, and he considered every possible contingency, including betrayal from within. A number of failsafe options were installed that both the younger Teakon and Julie knew about, but neither expected anyone else to join them in the bowels of the bookstore. Though a phone seated in the center of the room provided access to 911 and police help, Teakon and Julie knew involving the police might cause trouble that outweighed any potential danger.

A dozen security measures separated the intruders from Teakon and Julie, but a noise caught Teakon's attention and his head snapped upward to look at one of the six monitors that watched and recorded various areas of the store on down to the vault. He saw the two armed men, now wearing masks and dressed in black, along with another masked man who seemed to be directing them. Touching his ear occasionally, the stranger acted as though he was talking to someone through an earpiece on his phone, directing the fourth individual to look ahead to the next trap.

"How do we pass through that?" he asked the fourth individual, who did not wear any disguise.

Feeling his body tense from concern and a sense of dread, Teakon realized the group had already penetrated two of the traps. He sucked in a deep breath, seeing something familiar about the fourth man, whose presence appeared to be against his will. Shaking his head negatively, he refused to say a word, but momentarily the unarmed man shoved his face up to a retinal scanner, letting the laser analyze his right eye.

"Dear God," Julie muttered quietly when she looked up to the same monitor. "It can't be."

"It is," Teakon conceded as the three villains passed the third defense system, dragging his unwilling uncle along with them. "Damn it."

How on earth Mark Teakon survived gunshot wounds, freezing water, and months under the radar, his nephew didn't pretend to have a clue. Either Todd Parish lied about the events aboard the *Shamrock*, or the bastards who nearly caused his demise scooped him from the deadly sea like a wounded sea lion. A completely unwilling participant in their scheme to bypass the security measures, Teakon said nothing and stood numbly beside the unarmed masked man. To his nephew, it almost seemed as though they had already extracted the information from him, but if that were the case, why would they bring him along?

"Oh, no," Teakon muttered nervously, three consecutive times, realizing exactly why his uncle remained alive as he saw the weathered, weary look scrawled across the man's face.

"What is it?" Julie asked, touching his arm.

"Remember that I told you Liz thought someone on the other side was getting into her mind?"

"Yes," Julie answered, though her shaky tone indicated she still didn't understand the problem.

"Whoever that guy is talking to is reading my uncle's mind in real time."

Julie muttered something that went unheard as Teakon contemplated several possible ideas to either save his uncle or rescue the cubes from evil clutches. There simply wasn't a way to disable two armed men to retrieve his uncle, and the elder Teakon would berate him for not putting the work of harboring the cursed objects first. But if he dared enter the vault, the chances of him collecting all of the cubes before the men entered the vault were slim. Julie's life also rested in his hands, and though she was committed to the cause, he wasn't going to see everything lost to the goons making their way closer to the vault.

"I'm going to grab a few of the cubes," he informed Julie, punching his personal code into the second door before she could stop him.

A beep and a hydraulic "whoosh" later placed him inside the vault where a musty smell hammered his nostrils. His uncle hadn't designed the vault with the idea of making a finished basement someday.

The large vault held several secured areas where the cubes were stored for safe keeping. Each of them required a keypad code for access, but the code was the same for each safe built into the walls of the vault. Figuring he could recover a few of the cubes, not being particularly picky about which ones he grabbed, Teakon left the door to the panic room open as he set to opening the first safe. Without looking, he snatched the cube from an elevated perch and performed exactly the same maneuver with the next closest safe, using up a valuable minute overall.

"Matt!" Julie screamed out the door at him, indicating he needed to return to the safety of the panic room.

Her shouted warning startled him, causing him to bobble both cubes before they eluded his grasp and landed on the floor with their coverings, one tumbling beneath a nearby table. Teakon knelt down to recover them but the immense main door to the vault made a stone-on-stone grinding sound as it slid to one side like some kind of Egyptian crypt from the movies. Suddenly confronted with the three men holding his uncle hostage, Teakon barely found time enough to dive for the door to the panic room before bullets struck the floor behind him.

Julie stepped forward to pull the door shut, sealing them safely inside as the gunmen rushed into the room. Regaining his footing, Teakon stared through the thick glass window into the eyes of the leader with the wireless phone device in his ear. The man said nothing momentarily as his henchmen tried opening the door with every means possible short of shooting at it. Apparently realizing the glass and both doors were virtually impenetrable, the trio turned their attention to Teakon's uncle.

Wasting little time, the three men searched the vault, discovering the safes lining the vault's walls. In the meantime, Teakon looked to the eyes of his uncle, finding them bloodshot, sunken, and defeated as the man stared into the concrete floor. Even while standing still his body seemed to sway slightly, indicating some form of drugs ran through his system. Either his abductors wanted him to speak, or think the truth, or they used a serum to keep him subdued. His skin appeared ashen and his drastic weight loss led his nephew to believe he'd been severely mistreated for months and kept alive simply as a source of information. Teakon's uncle deserved a better fate than this, but he could only stare at him through the security of the only window in the panic room. No matter what, he needed to make certain he survived with Julie to carry out his uncle's wishes.

He berated himself for dropping the two cubes before ducking into the room, but at least the evil group couldn't possess the entire collection, even if they cleaned out the vault.

"I'm sorry, Uncle Mark," he said through the glass, doubting his blood relative could hear him through the layers of protection.

For the first time his uncle looked up, looking to Teakon with the last of a defiant fire in his eyes, silently telling his nephew to stay strong no matter how far these armed bastards took this fight.

"How do I get into this safe?" the man with the phone earpiece asked their captive.

Mark Teakon tried to resist assisting the villainous men in any way, the strain showing on his face, but when his thoughts were plucked from the air like fireflies into a jar, his resistance was futile. Moments later the leader of the group typed in the correct number for the keypad of the safe, retrieving one of the cubes.

"Pick those up," the man ordered one of the henchmen who had been standing watch over the sealed door of the panic room.

Teakon knew it was a matter of time before the masked leader asked his uncle for the code to the panic room, but he already had an idea how to handle that predicament when it arose.

"Give me the code to this safe," the leader ordered the elder Teakon after he walked briskly to the next secure door along the wall. "It's the same, eh? I guess you never figured anyone would beat you at your own game and get down here."

Hanging his head, Teakon barely found strength enough to look at his uncle while the intruders went through the remaining safes and stole all seven of the cubes hidden within the basement of the bookstore. When he raised his head, several tears streamed from one eye as he looked to the man who helped mold him while fighting to keep the world safe from tyranny. No man could ask for a better role model than someone who sacrificed everything to keep others safe. If Mark Teakon possessed a weakness, he simply lacked the ruthlessness necessary to keep the cursed objects safe from greedy mercenaries.

Realizing no cavalry was coming for the two people locked in the panic room, the three men took their time until the leader walked behind Mark Teakon, virtually whispering his next phrase into the man's ears, feigning secrecy.

"I want to know how to get into that panic room so I can clean up this mess."

Knowing his uncle couldn't help but compromise his colleagues, Teakon reached for a lever seated just a foot or so away from the window. Observed by the man standing outside the window, who was likely receiving the information from his outside source, Teakon watched a sinister grin finally cross the man's lips. With Mark Teakon's code available to him, the leader of the trio reached for the keypad on the door, but as he touched the first number Teakon flipped the lever upward, effectively killing the power to the panic room, including the entry doors. The monitors, powered by a different circuit, continued to glow and illuminate the two people safely trapped inside the panic room.

Teakon watched the arrogant smirk twist into an angry scowl on the man's face.

"Open the door or your uncle dies," he threatened.

"You can't!" Julie insisted just above a whisper, gently touching his arm.

Keeping his hand on the lever, Teakon refused to throw it downward.

"I know."

Looking his uncle directly in the eye, he pressed his hand against the glass, and his uncle slowly did the same, overcoming whatever mind-numbing drugs they pumped into his veins at last. Both knew the move effectively signed the elder Teakon's death warrant, so they said a silent goodbye through the glass. Teakon felt tears trickle along his cheeks as the thought of losing his uncle a second time overwhelmed him. He found it difficult to look his uncle in the eyes due to guilt, but he understood the need to survive and carry out the man's lifelong mission.

"Goodbye," his uncle mouthed the word through the glass as a pistol was positioned behind his head.

Already knowing he was doomed, Mark Teakon barely uttered his farewell before his blood and brain matter stained the glass.

Teakon immediately turned away, breaking down as his back slumped against the wall and he slid to the ground, sobbing uncontrollably. He could only wait for his enemies to leave before briefly mourning his uncle and moving forward to pick up the pieces. Regrouping wasn't going to be easy, particularly with most of the cubes now in evil clutches. About the only saving grace was that they hadn't found the book that accompanied the cursed cubes, but if they were able to pluck thoughts like radio waves, Teakon couldn't even trust himself with knowledge.

"Damn it," he said, burying his head in his hands, feeling absolutely helpless.

Chapter 35

Despite the major setback, Julie and Teakon traveled to Indiana the next day to meet with Greene and Clouse to share their bad news in detail and hopefully learn something from the video footage shot while the two were trapped in the panic room. Toting a briefcase filled with their evidence and the leather-bound book containing the names of everyone that ever possessed a cube, Teakon crossed the atrium of Clouse's hotel with Julie by his side.

Knowing the police and the coroner's office would take the bookstore hostage, the two removed anything they might need from inside the building before calling for help the previous day. Julie also made copies of the footage from the security system's hard drive for them to keep because the police indeed confiscated the hard drive for their investigation. Talking to authorities wasn't easy, but Teakon kept his composure for the most part and explained that the thieves took valuable gemstones from the basement. He found he was able to provide a factual account of the events, simply leaving out the parts about cursed objects and psychics. When the police inquired about the stolen property, Teakon said custom gems were taken, which wasn't an untruth on his part.

When he thought about it, Teakon understood why the leader didn't ask how the group located the cubes. Any rational person would speculate about letters or diaries, possibly never suspecting a cursed ledger that kept track of the cubes. Regardless, the question was never brought up, but Teakon saw firsthand how effective the methods of his adversaries proved.

"You holding up okay?" Julie asked as they pushed open the door for the stairs descending into the basement.

"As good as could be expected I suppose."

He wasn't looking forward to attending a second funeral for his uncle. The first time emotionally tore him apart, but he hadn't witnessed his uncle's alleged death and there was no body. Now he bore witness to Mark Teakon's execution and wanted to divorce himself completely from the bookstore to avoid recalling the horrific image.

Questions remained about how his uncle survived a fall into freezing waters after being shot in the chest. Choppy water no less, Teakon thought as he remembered being told details of the trip by Clouse. Of course the details came second-hand from one of Clouse's paid henchmen, who happened to be standing outside of the secured conference room down the hallway from the stairs Julie and Teakon used.

"Go ahead," he told Julie. "I'll be right in."

Stopping directly in front of Todd Parish, Teakon drew close to the bodyguard until their noses were separated by only a few inches.

"You said my uncle died in front of you," Teakon virtually growled.

"I said your uncle was shot in the chest, maybe the shoulder, and toppled off the side of the boat," Parish answered evenly. "The chances of someone surviving in freezing water without the appropriate gear for more than a few minutes are thousands to one. So, yes, I assumed he was lost at sea."

"And you couldn't be bothered to check?"

Parish's expression grew outright perturbed.

"Bullets were flying in my general direction. Your uncle himself made it clear that disposing of that cube was the first and foremost priority."

"Dropping it to the bottom of the ocean was *his* job. *Yours* was to tag along and keep him safe at all costs."

"Look, I'm sorry for your loss, really I am, but there's no need to lay this at my doorstep."

"I disagree," Teakon said, feeling his face grow hot because any number of minimal differences on that fishing vessel might have left Mark Teakon alive and the cubes securely locked in the vault.

Frustration, more than anything, caused him to take issue with the bodyguard when he knew full well his uncle's mission meant more than his own existence. He was about to walk away and conduct himself properly when Parish decided to critique the situation further.

"Maybe you're just upset with yourself because you followed his orders and locked yourself inside a fortress instead of saving him."

The words infuriated Teakon to the point that he spun and lurched toward the collar area of the bodyguard's suit.

"You mother fucker!"

Each of them exchanged a few punches around the facial area, neither causing much damage from such close range, until Clouse emerged from the room to break up the skirmish. He pushed Teakon back before restraining Parish with his free arm.

"This is the *last* thing we need right now!" he scolded them both with his tone. "Placing blame isn't going to bring Mark or the cubes back. If we're going to do right by him, we need to work together and find the people behind yesterday's attack."

Parish simply scowled before walking into the conference room without another word. He wasn't about to disobey the man who signed his paychecks, but Teakon still felt he crossed the line by implying he cowered behind concrete walls while his uncle was murdered.

Closing the door so no one else inside the conference room could see them in the hallway, Clouse placed his hands on Teakon's shoulders.

"I know you're hurting, and I appreciate you coming here with everything you have. You have my condolences and prayers, Matt."

"Thanks. I'm not sure what hurts more, losing my uncle again, or failing him."

"We haven't failed yet. They don't have everything, and even if they do plan on bringing the cubes together they need to know the ritual."

"That's what scares me, too. We have a book, but we have no idea what those pricks really know."

"I know," Clouse said, stepping back with understanding and sympathy in his eyes. "But I have some ideas, and if these guys were desperate enough to invade your sanctity and put themselves on camera I have a feeling we can turn the tables on them."

Teakon nodded, suddenly feeling numb as he truly let the events of the past twenty-four hours enter his mind for the first time. Everything felt like one big blur, but dwelling on the invasion would keep him from concentrating on the moment and helping people who shared in his beliefs catch the men responsible. Still, he fully realized how close he came to dying the previous day at the hands of people who thought nothing of taking human life.

"Let's do this," Teakon said with as much resolve as his mind permitted.

***

Harlan Stone suspected his benefactor wanted to continue whatever secretive activities he was conducting without the agent's assistance. Though Alan Stewart claimed he needed to return Stone to his old position temporarily for his own good, the agent suspected otherwise. He considered the possibility that Stewart somehow learned about his field trip to Texas, or perhaps the Deputy Director found someone else to carry out his dirty work.

Being assigned Dom Givens as a partner made the transition a bit less traumatic, but Stone's mind constantly wandered. He questioned why he was relegated to New Mexico when Stewart could have easily assigned him to his home state instead. Something didn't add up, and he feared not reaching the conclusion in time to save some lives, including his own.

By placing Stone in New Mexico, Stewart could easily track his movements by monitoring the local Special Agent in Charge.

"You daydreaming again?" Dom Givens asked from the driver's seat of their assigned sedan.

"Nah," Stone answered, shaking off any lingering thoughts as he stared out the passenger window at the desert passing in a blur. "Explain to me again why Lord Asshole is sending us to a motel in the middle of nowhere again."

Givens chuckled.

"Supposedly an informant has red-hot information about a murder-for-hire and won't meet us anywhere else."

"Murder-for-hire?" Stone questioned. "Sounds a little highbrow for Elliot to entrust to the likes of us."

"He assigned it to *me*, partner, and I'm damn lucky he let me keep it. He still hates your pasty white ass."

"Glad to hear he hasn't smartened up."

Givens continued to drive, casually drooping his hand over the steering wheel as he grinned.

"You two are like oil and water. Why do you hate authority so much?"

"Maybe I've just never had a boss worth liking."

"Maybe you Texans are just as stubborn as the mules you ride."

"Oh?" Stone retorted with a chuckle. "At least we don't take surfboards to work like you California types. That way you save the planet by not using fuel while you're battling the evil known as commercialism."

"It helps us sleep easy at night," Givens said, playing along.

"Roller skating along the beach and chasing tail," Stone said dreamily. "Must be nice out there."

Givens laughed.

"Not nearly as fulfilling as bronc riding and cooking barbeque squirrel on the grill, I reckon."

"I can't believe you'd stereotype us Texans that way."

"Your grammar is proving me right. Besides, you're the most racist partner I've ever had the pleasure of being assigned."

Stone scoffed aloud.

"You call yourself all kinds of names and say I did it. That would make you clinically insane in the eyes of most quacks, my friend."

Stone stared out the window momentarily as the morning sky began to show the infant stages of a blue, cloudless canvas. He questioned how long his exile from specialty work might last, or if Stewart planned to disavow himself completely from the agent.

"So, what was your temporary new assignment all about?" Givens inquired.

Stone shrugged while he cleared his throat uncomfortably. He wasn't entirely proud of the body of work he carried out during his time in Ohio and Kentucky, but an unstated need for secrecy kept him from elaborating.

"Mostly surveillance details."

"They dragged you away on some super-secret assignment just to watch someone? They could have any field agent conduct surveillance."

"You calling me a liar?" Stone kidded with a raised eyebrow.

"I'm just saying that you're holding out on me. There's all kind of crazy talk around the office about you going to work for the big man in Washington. And the way you left with barely a word made me wonder if that shit was true."

"You're just reading too much into it, Dom. It was business-as-usual kind of stuff, but I'm sworn to secrecy."

"Can't even tell your partner?" Givens goaded him. "That's not right, Stoney."

Stone shifted uneasily in his seat. He felt a need to protect Givens by not telling him anything specific, considering the recent turn of events.

"I'm not trying to bust your balls," Givens finally said, relieving the tension. "It's good to have you back, partner."

"It's good to be back."

Stone looked out the window again, seeing nothing except dry, brown flatlands along the Chihuahuan Desert, sparsely dotted with plants that appeared near death. Now well south of Albuquerque, Stone didn't recognize the land or any recent landmarks. Of course he hadn't worked in the state very long, and neither had his partner, but Givens appeared to know exactly where they were heading without benefit of a navigation device.

"You know where we're going?" Stone questioned, looking over to his partner.

"Of course," Givens said confidently. "Matter of fact, it's dead ahead."

Staring ahead, Stone spotted what appeared to be the ruins of a very tiny town with a gas station and a motel readily visible. He thought a few dilapidated houses might have stood some distance behind the gas station, but it was impossible to tell until they drew closer. The entire scenario looked like one of those areas in a low-budget movie where scummy bad guys ambushed the heroes. He questioned why any informant would want to meet two federal agents in such a distant, isolated location.

Touching the firearm nestled along his side, he grew wary as they neared the strange little settlement.

Chapter 36

Clouse looked around the room once the doors were shut, essentially sealing everyone inside the conference room for a look at the video footage. No blood remained on the carpet, and the body of Chase Dalton's impersonator now resided in a shallow grave along the outskirts of some farmland in Monroe County. He decided to take care of the matter personally to avoid placing his friends and employees at risk.

Matt Teakon stood in a distant corner while Todd Parish sat at the table, closer to the screen, looking rather uneasy. Clouse knew all too well that frustration caused Teakon to lash out at Parish from having lost so many of his own close friends and family to heartless, greedy people he thought were allies.

No idle banter filled the room because the tense situation of losing Mark Teakon a second time, along with knowing all of their hard work had just gone down the drain, deflated a lot of spirits. No one, Clouse included, expected to find any evidence in the video to help them locate the people responsible for stealing the cursed objects.

Greene and Liz sat beside one another on the opposite side of the table, and Jennings attended the meeting in case he noticed anything familiar from his time at the race track. Despite an invitation to the gathering, Clay Branson failed to show, leading Clouse to question the man's devotion to anything except finding his former mentor. The glimmer of hope that stemmed from him retrieving the cube at Churchill Downs dissipated with him turning his back on the group once again.

For the first time in a long time Clouse began to lose hope regarding their mission. As long as men with evil in their hearts knew about the cubes the quest could never end.

Julie Knowles started the video footage, which ran through a projection machine onto the huge white wall it faced. Though painful to watch for everyone, the footage provided more detail than real life had for Julie and Teakon. While Teakon said a painful farewell to his uncle and avoided being killed, Julie worked her magic at the video surveillance controls, zooming in whenever possible on the bookstore assailants.

She started with the leader, confirming he was a Caucasian man somewhere around six feet tall, which they pretty much already knew. The microphones captured his voice, and they learned his eyes were a form of hazel. Aside from those few details, they knew nothing else about the man other than the fact he seemed to relish his authority.

"Anything?" Clouse asked Greene, whose eyes remained glued to the image of the man frozen on the wall.

"It's not much help," Greene admitted, "but I might have some contacts who can run his voice through an analyzer."

"Wouldn't you need a sample database for comparison?" Liz asked.

Her experience assisting with police provided some knowledge of their procedures on her part.

"My one buddy designed a program that can go through a sample database or check every single video that's uploaded online for a match. Unfortunately that can take a *very* long time to complete."

Julie allowed the video to continue, pausing as the screen showed a van outside of the bookstore, providing a full view of a man seated inside the passenger seat of the van. He spoke toward the dashboard every so often, indicating a communications radio was mounted there, or some form of speakerphone perhaps. It quickly became clear he was the man responding to the leader's inquiries from inside the bookstore's basement. All eyes slowly gravitated toward Liz, who understood the gravity of the situation because this unknown man was picking her brain for information. When the video came to a close-up of his face, Julie pushed pause, providing a detailed image of the man who likely caused the entire group so much grief.

Not exactly the face of a monster, the man appeared slightly heavyset and only confident when he spoke into the dashboard. When he sat, his body language indicated a timid, uncertain individual who placed his hands near his chest in a praying position, except that he left his fingers curled. His red hair was thinning atop his round face, and he appeared to still have childhood freckles dotting his face, despite an age Clouse guessed to be early twenties. The man spoke normally and clearly enough that everyone in the room came to realize the man before them likely possessed above average intelligence, but perhaps childhood obesity and incessant teasing made him antisocial.

Liz stared at his face, and though she put on a brave front, she felt intimidated because she knew nothing of this individual and it felt as though he had already violated her in every imaginable way.

"Can we locate that van?" she asked aloud with resolve.

"It's probably a rental," Greene surmised. "I'd imagine that we can."

"Think you might learn something if you lay a hand on it?" Clouse asked her.

"I hope so."

Everyone in the room suspected answers would never come that easily for them. They were at least one step behind the collective robbing all of the cubes, but just one fortunate break might put them back on even playing ground.

"You don't have to do that," Greene assured Liz in a hushed voice.

"I *need* to know. Flushing them out is the only way to stop them."

Once everyone stopped conversing, Julie started the video again, which showed closer, more detailed images of the two henchmen who also wore ski masks to hide their identities. One was a fairly stout, powerful white male who did not appear to have any facial hair beneath his mask because none showed when he adjusted the mask's fit a few times. He wasn't as tall as any of the other men in the room with him, but his rigid posture and confidence with an automatic weapon seemed to indicate he was possibly former military. Some soldiers returned from overseas to work at the postal service, or at some local government position, and some found higher wages as mercenaries.

Clouse stared intently at the second masked man, because he was the one who inevitably pulled a sidearm and ended Mark Teakon's life. Julie had already informed him of this, and he wanted to know the man's identity because anyone who killed such an idealist deserved the same in return.

Like the other henchman, this one never spoke a word, but he didn't stand or act as regimented as the first. He certainly didn't lack confidence, though, and when the time came to eliminate Mark Teakon he did not hesitate or question orders. In fact, it took little more than a word from the leader to prompt the act.

"Who are you?" Clouse questioned under his breath.

About the only two things he knew about the man were that he also had no facial hair, and his skin color was that of a black man.

***

A red light went off in the back of Harlan Stone's mind as his partner pulled past the decrepit gas station with its cracked front window, and a faded realtor sign residing unevenly in one corner. Amazingly the pumps were not removed, or even covered, and the price set on their gauges indicated the gas station hadn't functioned in nearly eight years. Even the plastic sign cover looming over the station barely hung by a screw, swinging with the breeze as though daring someone to saunter carefree beneath it.

While the idea of a motel and gas station in the middle of nowhere likely appealed to a weary traveler, Stone understood why it probably wasn't financially feasible to keep either business open with rising business costs. After a brief glance at the gas station, Stone quickly focused his attention on the motel about a hundred yards ahead of them on the opposite side of the road.

"I don't see anyone," he noted as Givens pulled the sedan closer to the front of the building.

The building consisted of one main stretch containing about ten rooms and a check-in window for the manager on duty. Another four rooms branched off from one corner, giving the motel an "L" shape. Faded to an unsightly olive green, the hotel walls were also trimmed with sand and cobwebs. The roof looked like it might collapse if anything heavier than a house cat dared step foot atop the gray shingles, and Stone couldn't help but suspect they were driving into some sort of trap.

"Let's drive around back and make sure we don't have any extra company," he suggested to Givens.

"You're awful jumpy today, partner."

"And you don't seem the least bit concerned about driving the better part of two hours to meet an informant. Is he thinking about settling down and owning a business here?"

Givens chuckled.

"Hard telling."

A drive around the rear of the motel revealed absolutely no vehicles parked on the property, so Givens checked behind the gas station and around the two small houses. The duo found no vehicles anywhere in the isolated settlement, leading Stone to question if their supervisor sent them on a wild goose chase. It wasn't above Elliot to punish him with nonsensical assignments, but typically Givens was spared the wrath of their egocentric leader. Despite his usual lack of common sense as an FBI supervisor, Elliot knew better than to tinker with Givens, fearful of a discrimination grievance landing atop his desk.

Following the full search of the area, Givens parked in front of the motel, putting the car in park before killing the engine.

"So we're just going to wait?" Stone asked as he raised his voice to ensure his objection was clearly heard.

"Maybe the guy's running late. What's got you so riled up today?"

"My patience with life in general is wearing thin."

"You're just mad because the wizard brought you back from Oz to work in the pits with the rest of us."

Stone grinned, rolling down the window to find the dry air already growing warm. Dressed in a long-sleeve shirt with a tie, as usual, he fully expected to be perspiring within minutes if he remained inside the stuffy car. He opened the door to stretch his legs and survey the area further.

"You thinking about buying some property out here?" Givens kidded.

"Not unless this place gets annexed by Texas."

Opting to stay in the sedan, Givens opened a booklet of some sort, studying its contents.

In the meantime, Stone walked along the front of the motel, his nostrils detecting a musty odor as his boots clopped along the dirty concrete landing. Naturally curious, and looking for anything to occupy his mind, he tried the door of the room closest to him, finding it open as it swung inside with a creak.

"That's not the least bit creepy," he muttered to himself, stepping inside the dark room.

Flipping the light switch provided no further benefit and the smell only intensified with the door open. Stone stood aside, letting natural light fill the room to reveal two beds and a nightstand covered with dust. No television or phone remained within the room, and Stone wasn't daring enough to look inside the bathroom. Instead, he stepped outside to find everything much the same, growing impatient with their directive, especially since Givens seemed so calm and collected.

Stone strolled toward the office area, peering inside the glass surrounding the small sliding door where the money was exchanged for a place to stay. Apparently the departing owners made certain to clean out their belongings before heading to whatever grand horizon awaited them.

Looking to Givens, Stone tapped the watch on his left hand with his two fore-fingers, indicating he was growing tired of waiting. His partner simply shrugged helplessly, quickly turning his attention to the radio to search for a working music station.

Refusing to stand around, Stone walked from one end of the motel to the other, enjoying the shade that the overhead awning provided. It wasn't until he reached the last room along the lengthy portion of the hotel that a strange sound reached his eardrums. Freezing like a statue, Stone listened intently for what sounded like a whimper, or perhaps a muffled cry for help. He slowly turned his head toward the final room as he reached for the doorknob, clasping the firearm holstered at his side. Deciding not to alarm his partner until he proved his imagi-nation wasn't working overtime, Stone pushed the door open as he drew the Glock 22 from his holster.

Seated in an old wooden chair, and strapped tightly to it with numerous syn-thetic ropes, Kristina Turpin looked to him with widened, desperate eyes, hoping he was there to rescue her rather than add to her torment. A gag encumbered her mouth, preventing her from elaborating upon the peril of her situation. Stone immediately deduced the events surrounding him, his gun clearing its holster too late to assist him as he heard someone step onto the motel's landing behind him.

"You were on the way up," Givens stated, his firearm trained on Stone's head when the agent dared steal a glance. "The boss had big plans for you until you went snooping around."

Stone let his firearm slide into the holster, though he refused to release it from his grip completely. Options raced through the agent's mind, but none of them provided safety for Kristina. Diving for cover put her in the line of fire and didn't necessarily remove him from harm. Turning around while raising his firearm would assuredly get him shot and killed, and curiosity compelled him to find out why Givens was working with Stewart.

He hated the idea of surrendering his firearm and practically signing his own death warrant. While he worried about his own survival, he felt obligated to pro-tect Kristina because he placed her in this precarious situation.

"Tell me, Dom, will my wife be okay after we're all said and done here?" Stone asked, his hand still seated atop his firearm.

The Glock remained in the holster, but loose of the security mechanism that kept the average person from disarming him.

"Oh, they'll find your body, partner. Eventually. She'll get your pension and wonder why you and another dead agent's wife were having a fling."

Stone gnashed his teeth, incensed that a dishonorable death awaited him. His hopes and aspirations for a greater career blinded him to whatever personal gains Stewart placed ahead of human life.

He remained halfway turned around, considering the possibility of testing his right arm's quickness. Knowing full well Givens wasn't going to let either of them leave the motel alive, Stone preferred going out shooting, rather than being shot like a rabid dog.

Kristina made muffled noises through her gag, but any pleas were lost on Givens. Only now did Stone realize the man played him, acting a role better than some Hollywood stars who took home Oscars. Stone looked into her eyes with a solemn indication that he was going to make the only play that might save them.

"You've got it all planned out, don't you?" Stone asked, trying to survey the area around him, realizing no cover existed, particularly while he stood in the open doorway.

"It'll all be covered at a higher level, but you needn't concern yourself with the details, Stoney."

Stone shook his head negatively, hoping his aim was true to atone for his mistakes the only way he knew how. He sucked in a deep breath, drawing his weapon as he turned to shoot down his own partner.

Before he even turned enough to think about firing a shot, he heard the sound of Givens' gun and felt the impact of a bullet entering his abdomen, followed by another round into his right shoulder. The second shot effectively forced Stone to drop his firearm because his fingers and arm felt a spasm go through them that loosened his grip. As he slumped against the doorway, Givens walked over to retrieve the Glock from the ground.

"You're fast, but even you aren't that fast," Givens commented with a confident laugh. "You see, our boss paired me with you to test you out. When I thought you might be the right material for our little team he gave you some simple tasks to test you out. But your little deviation to Texas let us know you were getting too curious for your own good."

Stone couldn't decide whether to clutch his shoulder or try applying pressure to his stomach wound. The shoulder wasn't going to bleed out, and most of his bleeding from the first bullet was occurring within his vital organs where he couldn't prevent his eventual death. Only a surgeon could save him at this point, but he didn't care about his own life so long as he found a way to stop Givens and Stewart from going further with their plan.

"You won't get away with whatever you're doing," Stone stated between labored breaths. "There are people who know."

"Oh, like Clay Branson, the man you did a piss poor job of watching? We have something special in store for him. And just yesterday we carried out the biggest part of our plan in Massachusetts. I've got a big payday coming my way. You would have, too, if you could've stuck to your orders."

"Stewart's going to fuck you hard in the ass, Dom. You're going to wind up in some roadside ditch once he gets what he wants."

Stone groaned, forced to clutch his stomach as the burning sensation inside began to spread. Kristina continued to sob and plead for mercy through her gag, but the words bounced off Givens like bullets hitting Superman.

"All that loss of blood is going to get to you, partner," Givens said. "We better wrap this up quickly, hadn't we?"

Stone gave him the middle finger in response, prompting a grin from Stewart's henchman before he lifted his gun and fired a bullet squarely into Kristina Turpin's forehead. Blood splattered upward before her head slumped forward and her body grew limp in the chair.

"You bastard!" Stone cried, trying to crawl toward Givens to get one last lick in before the man ended his life.

Instead, Givens forcefully kicked him in the shoulder, flipping him back toward the door and Kristina's body.

"You just killed her, buddy," Givens said. "That's what the report is going to read."

"You don't care about anything, do you?" Stone fired angrily, fighting through the pain.

"I care about cold, hard cash. And I mean it when I say you killed Kristina. If you hadn't gone to visit her, she never would've been the wiser about her husband's death. And she certainly wouldn't have contacted an old friend in the Bureau and asked for a second look into Jack's *accident*. But don't you worry about them finding anything new in Jack's death. When I took care of him I made sure it looked legit."

"You should be proud," Stone said sarcastically.

"Thanks. See, Jack was a bit of a loose cannon like you, so Stewart took a liking to him. He even sent Jack to Ohio to offer Clay Branson a spot in our little club, but Branson turned him down. Jack snapped a guy's neck while he was there, pretty much saving the day while he showed what a badass he was. It wasn't until Jack developed a conscience and started snooping that he became a threat."

Stone clutched his stomach, beginning to feel a little cold from the loss of internal blood.

"Stewart thought you were just the man to replace him. You weren't above bending a few rules, could handle a firearm pretty well, and you were even from Texas, just like Jack. But I guess he was wrong about you."

"You can go to hell, Dom. And take Stewart with you."

Givens simply smirked at his partner's final cliché statement, lifting his gun to fire the bullet that ended Stone's suffering.

A low whistling sound reached Stone's ears at the same instant the point of an arrow pierced Givens' chest, sticking out about three inches when it came to rest just below his sternum. Sucking in several labored breaths, the dying agent slowly looked down to the metal point jutting from his chest. A mixture of confusion and shock showed in his eyes as the firearm dropped from his right hand and his fingers reached up to touch the arrow as though it might be some form of illusion.

No sooner had he touched it than he fell to the ground in a heap, dead so far as Stone could tell. The agent strained to see his unknown savior beyond his dead partner's body, discovering little more than a silhouette because his consciousness faded with each passing second. Despite his best efforts, Stone failed to hold his head up long enough to identify the blurry figure walking his way. He passed out before knowing if the stranger intended to rush him to a hospital or wrap him up like a loose end by snuffing out his life.

Chapter 37

Clouse pulled Julie Knowles aside after the meeting, deciding he wanted to search for a different solution while his team attempted to locate the men responsible for stealing the cursed cubes. Nothing earthshattering came from the video, but at least Greene and Liz provided a glimmer of hope, especially if Greene's contacts located the van used in the heist.

Some of the group lingered in the room, talking amongst themselves, or returned to their duties if they worked at the West Baden Springs Hotel for Clouse. He and Julie stood in the hallway, away from prying eyes and eavesdroppers.

"What can you tell me about the origin of the cubes again?" he inquired.

"Just that they were created shortly after the end of World War I. Of course we know who all of the first thirteen conspirators were because of the book."

"And what's the exact date they were created?"

"December 17th of 1918. Why?"

Julie appeared perplexed that his inquiry was suddenly so important in the scheme of their current plans.

"Didn't you or Mark ever consider it odd that we had two of the cubes hovering around this particular area for years?"

Clouse spoke of the two small towns that housed numerous hotels when gambling was at its pinnacle.

"The thought crossed our minds, but we never had time to investigate it further. And no one ever stepped forward with historical information."

"Probably because everyone who knew about the cubes from the old days is dead. I know a little about where they've been, but I also know the history of this valley. Before Los Angeles, Chicago, and New York were the haunts for celebrities and millionaires, everyone who was anyone came down here for the healing waters or the gambling."

Catching on to what he was implying, Julie looked at Clouse with widening eyes.

"Could it be that simple?"

"It *could* be, but I can't guarantee the things were created right here in little old Orange County."

"Right in one of your hotels, perhaps?"

Clouse shrugged doubtfully.

"While some evidence has shown up here before, I don't think this is the place where they would have done the deed considering all of the foot traffic. I'm going to do some historical research and see about hotels, churches, and any businesses that might have been condemned, torn down, or maybe changed hands around that date or early 1919."

"Be careful," Julie said earnestly. "We don't know who's watching us these days."

"I know. I'm about to take precautions to hide my family, and until we find out more about this psychic helping the bad guys, I don't want to know where they are. I miss them like hell when we have to do this, but it's safer for everyone I know if they can't be kidnapped and used as pawns."

Julie gave him an empathetic look.

"I know you've been through this several times. It doesn't get any easier, does it?"

"No, but you've been through a lot yourself this past year. If we can all get on the same page, maybe we can end this once and for all."

"You're right. There can't be that many people left who know about the cubes if it's taken this long for someone to come after us."

"And I'll bet whoever's in charge of their organization isn't planning to leave any loose ends once he obtains the entire collection."

"Whoever these people are, they would never have gotten as far as they have without that psychic. If he can get inside Liz's mind, any of our minds for that matter, we'll never be safe."

"I know," Clouse said, hanging his head momentarily.

He felt as frustrated as anyone, thinking he was ahead of the game when he recruited Greene and Liz to assist him. Such a gift, almost a superpower of sorts, wasn't meant to be used for such evil purposes. All of his hard work, from hiring people to hunt for the cubes to aligning himself with Mark Teakon and his people, suddenly felt worthless. He found it strange how all of the wealth left to him by one of his former mentors could never make things right. Of course that mentor turned out to be pure evil, which also helped set the horrific events of Clouse's life in motion.

"You can't go back to that bookstore," Clouse stated more than suggested to Julie. "At least not until we're absolutely positive we've eliminated the problem."

"Which might be never. But don't worry, I don't plan on returning anytime soon."

"You're welcome to stay here as long as you want to. I'm going to be keeping more security on the grounds just to keep all of us safe, and I have room in the sixth floor suite."

Julie forced a grin.

"I appreciate it, but I still have work to finish in Massachusetts. Besides, they probably won't be targeting me now that they have what they came for."

"I certainly hope not, but I'll be glad to send some protection back with you."

"No thanks. I'm sure Matt's coming back with me."

Clouse nodded.

"Let me know if you change your mind."

Before their conversation could continue, Matt Teakon emerged from the conference room holding a letter in his right hand with a stunned look crossing his face.

"You two need to hear this right away."

"Is that the letter I handed you last night?" Julie asked.

"Yeah. And it talks about the time travel cube, and exactly how the thing works."

Clouse immediately felt a tingle run through his spine at the thought of knowing how the most important of the cursed objects functioned.

"Who is it from?" Julie asked.

All three of them took a quick look around, not wanting anyone else to hear the findings until they deciphered whether the letter was genuine or some sort of fabrication. Clouse thumbed the opposite direction since the other conference rooms weren't being used at the moment.

"We can duck in one of the other rooms."

Once inside the room, Clouse went to close the door just as Todd Parish walked past. The bodyguard looked inside, seeing his boss with Teakon which brought forth a slightly wounded expression. Parish simply ducked his head and continued walking without a word. Clouse might have offered words of reassurance any other time, but he needed to hear what news the letter brought their group.

"The letter comes from one of the former cube guardians my uncle had gotten in touch with," Teakon began. "Apparently this guy was the one who held the cube before Tom Ervin took over the task. There's a journal entry written by some guy named Gene Lusardi who monitored the cube during the Fifties. The whole package seems legitimate to me, and if so, it explains exactly how that thing works and the danger it poses."

"Can we read it?" Clouse asked politely.

"Sure," Teakon replied, handing it over without delay.

Clouse read the companion letter first, which stated what Teakon had told them in a lengthier format. The letter was addressed to Mark Teakon in regards to an earlier inquiry. Apparently Teakon had convinced them he knew about the cursed cubes and requested any information about the time cube that might complete his archives. It was brief, and written by someone other than Lusardi, to help explain that the journal was found in the man's house after he passed away by the protective group.

Beyond that was a diary entry on a page torn from what Clouse surmised was an old notebook of some kind. The yellowed paper appeared dated enough to have come from the Fifties, and the handwriting wasn't particularly easy to decipher in the modern age where cursive was becoming antiquated. Still, he set it on the table and read the front page as Julie's eyes followed the same lines, equally curious to learn what the entry beheld.

11-20-57

Today I had the cube with me at work because I planned to move it to a safe spot after my shift. I know writing about this goes against the secret code we swore when we were chosen to watch over this thing, but this is the only way to keep myself sane. Since this is the only entry I am making about the cube in detail, anyone reading this will probably think I've lost my mind anyway.

My shift went by without a hitch. Just a few domestic dispute calls and a traffic stop because the guy had let his license plates expire. I let him off with a warning. Nothing to write home about. I was about to take the cube to its new hiding spot when I stopped for some coffee and a sandwich at one of the deli shops on South Clark. Bought a turkey sub, not very Italian of me, I know, but those things are delicious! Had the bag and my thermos in hand as I'm walking out of the deli when I spot this guy running down the street with what looks to be a bank bag in one hand. I might not have thought much about it, but he kept stealing looks behind him and people were looking at me in my uniform expecting me to do something. Because of the cube I didn't really want to act, but didn't feel like I had much choice.

There's too much traffic, so I throw my coffee and sub into my car and start chasing the guy on foot, yelling for him to stop. Of course he doesn't, so here I am chasing him for the better part of three city blocks before he finally ducks between some buildings to shake me. I've been on the force too long for some novice robber to shake me. He decides to run down the alley between these two apartment buildings, which I already knew didn't go very far. To cut down on crime the owner of the buildings put up a fence that isn't particularly easy to scale. Knowing he wasn't going far, I entered the alley a bit more cautiously than usual in case he had a weapon.

Good thing I did, because he took two shots at me when he saw my shoulder poke around the corner. I'd been yelling at him the entire time to stop because I was a police officer, so I didn't see the need to say it again. Now I knew exactly where the shots came from, so I hunkered down and threw some pebbles around the corner to distract him. Maybe I forgot about the precious cargo I was carrying, or the nature of my job just took over, but I came around that corner and shot him twice in the chest. He dropped the gun and the bag of loot right away, and as I approached him I saw the guy take his last few breaths.

I started to think of where I might use a phone to call for backup, but something inside me thought about the cube and how it worked. Here I'd just killed this guy, and self-defense or not, I had a chance to see how this power worked. Looking back, I wished I hadn't done it, but I took the thing out and instinctively I knew what to do. I stared at it a second or two and it was like the damned thing told me what to do.

Feeling a bit ashamed, I started to look up at the apartments to see if anyone was watching. There was snow on the ground, so no one opened their windows, and most people were still at work, so I didn't see no one. At this point I didn't care, because if the cube really worked, I was about to travel back in time and I didn't know if I'd be coming back. I just knew I had to think of the time and place I wanted to travel to and rub the thing on this man's blood. Kind of like a sick version of Dorothy and her ruby shoes.

There was only one thing I wanted to go back in time and see. My father had been shot and killed as a Chicago police officer before I graduated high school. They arrested some black guy for the crime. Gordie Brown was his name, but he always swore innocence. Something about his testimony stuck with me, because he never changed a detail in his story, and no one ever connected him to my pop. It always stuck in my craw, so I decided to see exactly what happened that night and maybe save my old man if I could.

No sooner had I pulled the cube from my work jacket and touched the man's blood with it when my surroundings completely changed. Here I was in the summer of 1934, still wearing my uniform, watching my pop from about a hundred yards away as he pulled up to a building in a patrol car. It was surreal because it looked exactly like I remembered it during the Depression. I could even smell fresh-baked bread somewhere in the distance, which seemed strange because it was nighttime.

The area where my dad was shot was on the outskirts of town and I watched him get out of his patrol car and knock on the door of this little house kind of set apart from the rest of the neighborhood. It's dark out, and he seems impatient about something until a woman answers the door. She's wearing a nightgown and tells him to wait a minute at the door, or something like that. I couldn't hear exactly what they said, but I walked toward him to warn him about the danger, or at least get a closer look. There was this patch of trees and shrubs between me and pop, but I kept pressing onward, not sure what I would do or say when I reached him. What could I say to him that wouldn't sound completely insane in time to save him?

Dad, I'm from the future and I'm here to save you, but I don't know from what?

I only knew he was gunned down, and I wasn't convinced the police caught the right guy. It wasn't until I was older that I realized this was a white neighborhood. People like Gordie Brown didn't waltz into these neighborhoods, and they certainly didn't tote guns into these neighborhoods. They still don't. And Brown had no previous arrests or trouble with the law, and no witnesses ever reported him owning a gun, much less using one.

Something just never added up.

I had about a hundred feet left to walk when I saw this car pull up behind my pop's patrol car. Two men dressed in plain clothes stepped out and my father knew them because they started talking about work, so I knew they were cops. Probably investigators the way they were dressed. I stopped behind a bush, thinking my pop was safe for the moment when one of the guys pulls out a gun while he's talking shop and shoots my father twice in the chest without missing a beat. As my pop lays there bleeding, the two men grab the woman and take off in their car as though they had just made a delivery instead of shooting someone in cold blood.

Before the car was out of sight I ran up to see if Pop was still alive. Part of me wanted to see if I could save him, but I just wanted to touch something physically in the past, just to make sure it wasn't some kind of dream. Call me stupid or greedy, but I didn't want to just see it in my head. I wanted to feel something to make sure it was real, but I didn't want to risk changing the past. The guys warned me about how the cube could be used to change things in the past, even if the person using it didn't realize the smallest little thing could alter the present we know.

It barely makes sense to me, so I'm sure if someone else is reading this you're probably thinking I'm off my rocker.

When I got to Pop he was already gone. I tried to resist, but I touched the blood on his shirt and felt certain I was about to sob after reliving all of the pain again, but in an instant I was back in the present beside the guy I just shot in the alley. It took a minute, but I pulled myself together before some of the guys from my precinct showed up. I'm sure what I experienced in the past was real because I came back with Pop's blood on my fingertips. The cube is now in a new safe place where no one else will use it, but I'm going to make sure no one sees this journal while I'm alive. The guys will think I let them down if they ever find out.

I'm glad I didn't change anything the night Pop died because I might have changed my own future. It ain't perfect, but things have turned out pretty well for this cop's son. Good night.

"Am I the only one who read that with a Chicago accent in my head?" Clouse felt compelled to ask. "I kept thinking he was going to say Da Bears any second."

Julie gave him a shocked look for being so offbeat during such a serious moment, but Teakon shrugged with a mischievous smirk.

"I kind of thought the same thing."

"Seriously, you two," Julie said with exasperation. "We just learned a major piece of information and you're laughing it up?"

"Lighten up," Teakon said. "It's not like we can scramble the military over a diary page. But I do have proof that our man was telling the truth."

Teakon produced a document from his back pocket that he placed atop the conference table for them to peruse.

"That's the police report from the diary date that indicates Lusardi indeed shot one Ronald David Thompson who had just robbed a restaurant for their deposit bag at gunpoint."

"Do you trust its authenticity?" Clouse asked, turning more serious because he wanted to know the power of the one trump card he still held.

"I'm inclined to think so," Teakon replied, looking to Julie who agreed with a nod.

"So we can assume the thing gives the user about a five to ten minute window and brings them back to the present in whatever state the present is after time travel," Clouse deduced. "I can't even believe I'm speaking these words. This is the kind of shit you see in films, not what you picture yourself saving the world from."

All three stared at the paperwork momentarily, better informed, but no closer to resolving their other problems until the rest of the team made some headway. Clouse hoped for a lucky break in the near future or the world was in for a whole heap of trouble.

Chapter 38

Harlan Stone awoke to a daylight fringe around the room-darkening curtains inside what looked like a hospital room. He looked under the sheets, noticing he was wearing a hospital gown, feeling certain no underwear covered his privates beneath the disposable cloth. His right hand reached for his injured shoulder, followed by his abdomen, discovering both were repaired and covered with fresh dressings. Someone brought him to the hospital because he wouldn't have lasted much longer in the desert without assistance.

Lots of questions entered his mind, from who saved him, who brought him to the hospital, where the hospital was located, and whether or not Stewart sent someone else to finish the job Givens started.

Shifting his weight in the hospital bed, Stone found his two injured spots still tender after being surgically repaired. He wasn't attached to any monitors, though a device located on his right side provided the means to summon a nurse. None of his belongings except his eyeglasses surrounded him, so calling his wife with his cell phone wasn't an immediate option if he even dared try. Placing her in danger was the last thing he wanted because he took the risk of working for Stewart to benefit their marriage and lifestyle, especially if they chose to have children.

Stone was about to make an attempt to stand when the door opened, bringing forth a brunette dressed in a nurse's uniform who looked surprised to see him awake. He swiped his spectacles from atop the stand adjacent to the bed and put them on for a better look.

"Glad to see you finally joined us," she said, sauntering over to the bed.

She gave him a cursory examination, looking over his wounds before taking his pulse and checking his blood pressure.

"How did I get here?" Stone decided to ask, testing the waters to see how much information the staff would provide.

She responded with a suspicious stare as though he should already know the answer.

"Your friend brought you in after the search warrant execution went bad."

Is that how it went? Stone mentally questioned sarcastically, virtually confirming his suspicions that Clay Branson brought him in after sending an arrow through Givens' chest. How or why the dangerous man located him and decided to save him eluded the federal agent, but Stone felt certain Branson wanted information. All of his movements and phone calls away from Ohio stemmed from his search for one man.

Nosagi.

Stone had already witnessed what the trained assassin was capable of when he beheaded an even more mysterious killer in Louisville. After watching the video footage, Stone knew he wasn't a match for someone so capable of using firearms and handheld weapons. That kind of training required dedication and countless hours, above and beyond what any normal person in law enforcement endured after the academy.

"Have you seen my friend?" Stone inquired, not using a name because he wasn't going to blow Branson's cover story just yet.

"Not recently, but he was here this morning."

Stone looked at a clock, realizing a day had passed since the events in the desert.

"Where am I?"

"Roswell Regional," she answered casually. "I'm going to have the doctor come take a look at you, okay?"

"Sure," Stone answered almost absently, his mind already wandering.

A few minutes later the surgeon explained Stone's injuries and the surgery required to repair them. Surprisingly, he didn't probe or ask Stone anything, possibly deciding to let the agent heal before authorities bombarded him with questions about how he suffered his injuries.

"Have any police agencies been here?" Stone inquired.

"Local police were called since you were shot," the doctor replied as he stood to walk toward the door. "Your buddy talked to them and gave them the information. Don't you worry about any of that, Mr. Stone. Just get some rest so we can get you home."

At first Stone felt surprised that Branson used either of their real names, but the man probably used their police credentials to keep it under wraps, possibly spinning a story that someone might track them for retaliation. Strangely, Branson apparently tied their actions together, at least for the cover story, which meant he obviously didn't plan on murdering the agent and burying him in the desert.

At least Stone hoped that held true.

Settling in for a nap wasn't the wisest course of action, but Stone felt exhausted after the previous day's events and the toll the surgery took on his body. His eyelids grew heavy, and when the door opened again it revealed a very unwelcome sight to the practically helpless FBI agent.

Though he couldn't identify the beefy man dressed in the black suit, Stone knew this granite-faced individual couldn't be bargained with because he wasn't some local investigator sent to conduct an interview. No, Stone decided, this man was sent by Stewart to extract information and clean up any loose ends.

Loose ends like nosy agents who'd become expendable the past few days.

Finding it too late to fake sleeping, Stone wanted to see any danger coming his way firsthand anyway. The man walked with a purpose toward the bed, but didn't reach for the firearm bulging from the right side of his sport coat. Stone eyed him cautiously, prepared to defend himself with the limited means surrounding him at a moment's notice. Though he was new to accidentally siding with purely evil entities, Stone knew from his investigations concerning organized crime and old covert government dealings how such things went down.

Without a word, the man reached into his sport coat and produced a needle already filled with a clear fluid and removed the tip. The bag of saline beside his bed that sent an IV drip and pain medication to the needles stemming from his arm suddenly became his worst enemy. Stone's body tensed as he realized the mortal danger placed before him in the form of an undetectable chemical that would likely mask his untimely death as a complication following surgery. Often such deaths were ruled as heart attacks, strokes, or some form of blood clot. Stone didn't want his wife thinking he died as a result of shady activities, passing away in his sleep like some nursing home patient to boot.

He was about to use the last ounce of his strength to defend his life against the silent assassin when two arms emerged from behind the assassin, finding pressure points along the sides of his neck. With the blood flow temporarily cut off through the arteries in his neck, the man in the suit was helpless within two seconds. His eyes rolled back and he dropped to the floor with a thump, revealing his attacker to Stone.

"That was efficient," the agent said to Clay Branson, who had emerged from the closet beside the door.

"I suspect he was scouring every New Mexico hospital until he found you here, *or* the local police put some information out to your agency," Branson replied, pulling a bag with Stone's belongings from inside the closet. "I took the liberty of recovering these a few hours ago."

"Did you whack a security guard to get into their secure lockers?"

"I haven't *whacked* anyone since I saved your life yesterday. We need to get out of here before this guy comes to and calls his boss."

Stone looked to the plastic tubes sticking out of his arms, trying to indicate he wasn't in traveling condition. In response, Branson clasped his arm and yanked the needles from his veins with such precision that virtually no pain accompanied the swift action.

Left with no healing devices and nowhere else to go, Stone painfully scooted his way off the bed, staring at the unconscious man on the floor. He dressed as Branson monitored the door, still uncertain what his immediate or distant future held. Once he put on his shirt and tie, followed by his slacks and cowboy boots, Stone noticed the holster secured to his belt held no sidearm. He cleared his throat, pointing to the empty holster once his recent protector looked his way.

"You're not getting that back," Branson said without falter.

"It'll be hard to defend myself."

"You won't need to. After what you've done, you need to prove your worth, or you're going to have a lot more hospital bills."

Stone swallowed hard, though he put forth a tough front as he followed Branson out of the room, feeling a bit uneasy and lightheaded with each step. A need to right some wrongs plagued his subconscious, but he wanted to make certain this enigma of a man wasn't just another form of evil placed along his path.

He looked around, noticing one particular clothing item wasn't present. His black cowboy hat was nowhere to be found, but he hadn't been wearing it when he was shot by Givens. As a federal agent he didn't wear it during official business anyway, but he couldn't remember if he left it in the backseat of the Bureau's car, or at the New Mexico office. The location of the hat made a world of difference when it came time to explain the events of the past few days and what spin he placed on the story, if any.

When the elevator reached the parking garage a few minutes later, Branson stepped out first, surveying the area cautiously without allowing the injured agent to fall behind. Stone wondered if the hospital was going to accuse him of skipping out on his bills and turn him over to a collection agency. Until he felt safe, financial burdens could wait he decided as the sounds of unseen vehicles echoed through the parking garage. From his vantage point Stone couldn't tell what level they were on, though he remembered seeing a number three beside the elevator doors.

"Where are we going from here?" Stone asked, feeling his wounds flare with searing pain from movement so soon after the surgery.

He grimaced, struggling to keep pace with Branson until the sound of the elevator spun them both around warily to find a woman stepping forward, wearing heels and business attire.

"We're going to pay a visit to whoever told you to follow me," Branson answered once they started walking toward the line of parked vehicles. "Because the guy I killed in the desert was just hired help like you."

"I'm not just hired help," Stone said firmly.

"So you don't just jump at the mention of money or promises of glory? I know how people like you respond to people like that."

"Glad to know your degree in psychology comes in handy," Stone grumbled.

Branson led the way until they reached a gray Ford Mustang that looked like a rental car, particularly with a Virginia license plate above the rear bumper.

"Who was that guy?" Branson inquired.

"I've never seen him before," Stone replied, "but I'm sure my boss sent him."

The elevator made a dinging sound again, and both men saw the incensed face of the assassin emerge before he drew his firearm to take aim at them.

"I guess you *didn't* kill him," Stone commented before ducking for cover behind the rental car.

Apparently understanding that firing bullets would attract attention, the man did not fire, which left Stone uneasy because he wasn't armed and he wasn't sure Branson possessed the means to disable the assassin without the element of surprise. Stone looked to his right to ask the man a question but Branson was nowhere to be found.

"Mother fucker," Stone muttered, not daring to peer over the car for fear the sudden movement might make a nice target.

Hoping Branson was sneaking around to assault the man, rather than leaving Stone for dead, the agent decided to provide a distraction since he wasn't in any condition to flee.

"Hey, is there any chance we can talk this over?" he asked, receiving no reply.

His arm instinctively reached for his side, but the lack of weighty metal quickly dissuaded him from actually touching the holster. Stone fought to remain calm, but as two hands clasping a Glock appeared from over top of the car, his crouched position suddenly felt rather unsafe.

Thoughts of ducking under the car and rolling for cover entered his mind when a virtually identical scenario from the hospital room appeared before his eyes. Two arms appeared around the man's neck again, and though he moved to avoid being forced into unconsciousness again after his initial surprise, the stocky man only gained a second or two before he collapsed to the concrete. Stone stared upward, certain he appeared as dumbfounded as he felt upon seeing Branson take out a trained killer twice within minutes.

In the same exact fashion no less.

"We're bringing him with us since he refuses to leave us alone," Branson said, popping the trunk lid with the key remote.

After recovering the man's Glock and a secondary firearm holstered around his ankle, Branson also plucked a cell phone from the man's sport coat. He picked up the unconscious man's dead weight with relative ease, dumping him into the trunk with a thump a few seconds later.

"Won't he just burst through the backseat eventually?" Stone asked.

"Only if he wants to lose consciousness again. We can bind him later."

"We?" Stone asked, regaining his footing while his wounds continued to plague him. "If you're including me in your evil scheme I guess that makes us partners."

Branson shot him a penetrating stare, which preceded his slamming the truck lid shut.

"What?" Stone asked defensively. "You don't really think I'm stupid enough to go crawling back to my old boss after this, do you?"

"Based on your errors in judgment thus far, I'm not so sure. Get in."

Branson took the driver's seat, which suited Stone just fine because his wounds continued to sting and his energy felt depleted.

"How the hell did you find me anyway?" Stone asked once Branson backed out of the spot and down the parking garage inclines.

"I brought you to the hospital yesterday, trying to keep things under wraps."

"I mean how did you get there yesterday? We were in the middle of nowhere. Literally."

Branson exited the garage and quickly found a busy road that led toward highways and interstates.

"You're not the only one who can follow people, Special Agent Stone. I'd taken notice of your activities as far back as South America, and it wasn't incredibly difficult to learn your identity."

"South America? You have to be kidding. I was in a fucking plane."

"I didn't actually know, but you just confirmed my suspicions. Whoever you're working for really wanted to know my whereabouts."

Stone felt his blood boil at the thought of being duped by Branson, but his thoughts quickly turned to how Stewart used him before trying to dispose of him.

"I don't care what you think of me and what I've done, but I'm not an evil person," Stone said.

"But you're not squeaky clean, either," Branson said without emotion. "Even so, I think you got in over your head. I need to know everything your boss asked you to do these past few months before we pay him a visit."

Stone wouldn't have dared confront Stewart alone, primarily because the man held rank and power, but he somehow felt the man in the driver's seat couldn't be stopped when he put his mind to something.

"You'll want to head west," Stone said. "We'll have plenty of time to get acquainted before we reach Los Angeles."

He thumbed toward the backseat.

"What about the big lug in the trunk?"

"We'll probably keep him around awhile so he can't contact anyone."

Beginning to realize that Branson wasn't a murderous bastard, the agent believed Stewart had spun his web of lies to suit his own purpose. He used his own people and their skill sets to his advantage. The man wanted Stone dead, and probably would have taken out Givens at some point to tie up any loose ends. Either the man in the trunk was a government agent or someone Stewart hired as a mercenary to carry out the dirty work. Some former soldiers lost all traces of a conscience, willing to follow any orders so long as their bank accounts grew.

Stone wasn't looking forward to the long drive, particularly the informal interrogation, but he wanted to see the look on Stewart's face when he showed up unannounced, among the living.

***

By the time Stone and Branson reached Los Angeles the next morning, the two found an understanding of one another after piecing together the fragments of their individual stories. While Branson continued to hold out on some information, Stone knew more than Alan Stewart ever revealed to him. Still, Stone felt nervous about confronting the man who still technically oversaw his activities within the Bureau.

Because of the late start the pair stayed in a motel toward the western border of Arizona, keeping their unwanted visitor subdued with ropes they purchased at a hardware store, along with a gag to keep him quiet. Stone was curious about the man's identity and background, but Branson showed no interest in questioning him. Stone might have given interrogation a shot except that vehicles were parked in the slots adjacent to their room. Any strange noises or cries for help might have jeopardized their plans.

The next morning Branson opted to leave the would-be assassin miles outside of a community along a seldom-traveled road once they entered California. Without transportation or a phone, the man couldn't possibly make a call for hours, particularly since Branson rendered him unconscious a third time far enough from the road that no passersby would ever spot him. They refused to untie him, buying them more time before he freed himself and began walking. Stone wondered if the man dared show his face to Stewart again because no respectable mercenary got bested three times in one day by the same adversary.

Using the navigation device in the rented car, Stone directed Branson toward the Los Angeles FBI headquarters. Even Stone still got lost in the large, unfamiliar city, but he knew the routine in any government building. He waited until Branson pulled the car into a visitor slot before speaking.

"You can't be bringing sharp, metal objects into this place, you know."

"I have a working knowledge of how municipal buildings operate," Branson replied testily. "Just get me in there however you have to so we can pay Mr. Stewart a surprise visit."

"If he's even here," Stone said, reading his watch.

Seeing it was nearly lunchtime, he imagined Stewart dined with bank presidents and people who dabbled in major stocks, drinking fine wine on their charity. Who wouldn't want one of the highest-ranked government officials on their side in case a sticky situation came their way?

"I'll need my Glock," Stone said, receiving a suspicious look regarding his request. "It'll look strange if a field agent enters the building unarmed."

Branson slapped the firearm into Stone's right hand before opening his car door.

"There are two ways we can do this," Stone surmised once he stood beside the rental car. "I can either register you as a guest, or we can act as though you're a suspect or material witness."

"Do you really think they'd let you bring a suspect to your boss? Just register me as a guest."

Stone shrugged.

"I just wanted to see if you could escape handcuffs, to be honest."

"Guess you'll just have to keep wondering."

Sliding his sidearm into its holster, Stone followed Branson toward the multi-story building, expecting nothing less from his agency's headquarters in one of the nation's largest cities. Once they entered the main lobby and cleared security, Stone inquired where Alan Stewart's office was located.

"Top floor," the secretary answered. "Would you like me to make sure he's in?"

"No, thank you," Stone answered. "He's expecting me."

Stone led the way toward the elevators, wondering how events were going to unfold momentarily when Stewart saw him alive.

"You lie very well," Branson noted once they occupied the first available elevator car. "And how do you *not* know where your boss's office is?"

"I've never actually been here. He wooed me in a neutral location."

Stone had already explained the false promises made by Stewart, and how the man never gave him any further orders than shadowing Clay Branson wherever he went. He also elaborated on how he deviated from the orders, and despite his precautions, Stewart discovered he visited the widow of Jack Turpin. Something within Branson stirred at the mention of the deceased FBI agent, but he said nothing. Stone sensed the man wasn't typically so withdrawn and silent, but this edgy, dark side of a man who stood to marry into a major theme park empire worried him.

"Did you know Turpin?" Stone decided to prod as the elevator car ascended.

"I met him once," Branson replied, his voice and expression devoid of emotion as he focused on the moment. "He offered me a job, probably working for your boss I suspect."

The Bureau didn't typically make it a point to recruit people individually, but Stone supposed the rogue agent program wasn't standard protocol.

"I guess I should feel good about being his second choice," he muttered.

"Don't flatter yourself. He's probably used and abused lots of people since he approached me."

"You have a gift with sentiment. If the theme park thing doesn't work out you might get work in the greeting card business."

Saying nothing, Branson simply glared with a minimal turn of his head.

A few seconds later the doors open, revealing the top floor of the building, which looked as spotless as the ground floor with light walls and shiny floor tiles. On this level there were no government logos imprinted into the tiles to exhibit pride and raise employee morale. Several pictures of ranking government officials, including the president, lined the walls behind the receptionist who basically acted as the first level of defense for the directors who wanted their visitors screened.

Stone scanned the names on a sign behind the young woman, finding Alan Stewart's among them.

"Ma'am," he said in his Texas drawl with a nod, not slowing down one second to allow her to offer assistance.

Branson followed the agent, conducting himself as though he belonged in the building. The pair soon approached Stewart's personal receptionist, a lovely woman with strawberry blonde hair who appeared a few years older than either of them. Stone wondered if his supposedly happily married boss and his receptionist conducted any business after work hours that he kept from his wife. He immediately chastised himself for jumping to conclusions simply because Stewart ordered a hit on him.

"Harlan Stone to see Deputy Director Stewart," Stone said, producing his identification since the personal assistant hadn't laid eyes on him before.

She consulted her appointment book, which looked reasonably blank to the agent as his blue eyes peered over the desk.

"I'm from his rogue agent program and I need to report some findings," Stone decided to add, hoping she at least knew the initiative existed.

A bit of intrigue registered in her eyes, as though she hadn't actually met one of the mythical rogue agents until this moment. Perhaps she liked his accent, or the idea of seeing how the scenario before her played out influenced her decision, but she pressed the intercom button to contact Stewart.

"Deputy Director, you have visitors," she stated, patiently waiting for a reply.

Stone wondered whether cameras were monitoring their movements with Stewart now giving them the silent treatment while reinforcements came to whisk them away from the federal building. Almost a minute passed without reply, which brought a look of concern to the receptionist's face. She tried Stewart a second time, met once again with complete silence for almost another minute. Stone eyed the hallway to either side of him, trying to look natural as he guarded against impending trouble.

Growing outwardly concerned, the woman virtually bolted from her chair while snatching a set of keys from the desk. She walked toward Stewart's door, but the doorknob turned without requiring a key, granting all three of them access to the rather spacious office. As soon as Stone peered over her shoulder, finding Stewart slumped over his desk, the pit of his stomach ached with fear that an even higher power than the Deputy Director was eliminating loose ends. Both of the Deputy Director's hands were laid atop the desk with his palms facing downward, while the right side of his face rested against the desk, his eyes still open as though he died suddenly.

"Oh my God!" the woman stammered, retreating from the room, probably to call for assistance.

Branson wasted less than a second before he moved toward the desk, examining Stewart's body without physically touching it, though his eyes came dangerously close when they scrutinized for the smallest of clues.

"What the hell are you doing?" Stone almost demanded, trying to keep his voice from reaching the hallway. "This is a potential crime scene!"

"It *is* a crime scene," Branson retorted. "And it would seem my former *sensei* was here."

Stone followed the man's eyes to a corner directly behind him where a cleaning cart remained, as though a custodian forgot to take it with him. The agent immediately understood that the cart was left on purpose and the assassin simply used it as a prop to gain entry to the office. He wondered if someone else paid the ultimate price to provide the murderer with a false identity.

Taking a closer look at his former boss's body, Stone found no visible wounds from a bullet, blade, or otherwise. A light purple hue encompassed the bottom of the dead man's palms, indicating the blood had pooled there at least the past several hours. He suspected the killer struck Stewart as soon as the man entered the office, possibly waiting until the assistant outside took a bathroom break to sneak out of the building.

Branson stood suddenly, apparently having found the verification he sought regarding Nosagi. He headed for the door, and Stone didn't immediately realize Branson was leaving because he continued to study the corpse.

"Where are you going?" he finally asked, daring to put some authority in his tone.

"I can't get bogged down in this," Branson answered, barely turning his head. "I've got to start tracking him."

Stone knew exactly who Branson referred to, but he didn't see how tracking a man with several hours head start was much help.

"You can't saddle me with this," Stone complained. "How the hell am I supposed to explain the last two days?"

Branson continued walking without so much as looking back this time.

"Just tell the truth and sort it out."

Stone grunted, thinking that telling the truth was either going to land him in jail or a psychiatric ward. He already felt like a pawn, but revealing what he knew combined with the grand total of facts he never discovered only served to make him look guilty or incompetent. Still, his image and DNA covered New Mexico to California and all parts in between. The truth was due to catch up with him, at least in part, regardless of what he decided to do at this very moment.

He caught a glimpse of Branson walking down the hall as Stewart's receptionist frantically called either building security or 911 for an ambulance. Knowing it was too late for Stewart to make amends, Stone hoped his fate proved kinder. He simply wanted to return home and see his wife, hopefully followed by him returning to his job without penalty.

Stone slowly walked toward the door, prepared to accept his fate and leave the crime scene to other professionals.

Chapter 39

A few weeks passed before Greene's buddy Chase Dalton located the van used when three armed men stole the cursed cubes and murdered Mark Teakon in Massachusetts. It turned out the van was stolen from a nearby town and burned soon after the heist, presumably just before the thieves left town. Greene expressed his concerns that one of the criminals knew setting the van ablaze might erase traces of DNA, or worse, keep Liz from locating any contact points that might provide a psychic connection.

Apparently the fire also made the van more difficult to track in general because it bounced between several police lots, the property of an insurance company, and finally a junkyard. Dalton feared it might be crushed or otherwise demolished before anyone from Greene's team could examine it so he contacted the junkyard's manager to put a hold on any destructive processes.

When Liz and Greene met the federal marshal at the junkyard late in the morning, Dalton gave her an appreciative look because he knew she was partially responsible for saving him in Tennessee. Greene and Dalton shook hands before exchanging a quick hug, and Liz understood that the two men maintained a friendship that went beyond their working relationship. She knew Greene struggled with the decision to ask Dalton for assistance on their quests because doing so endangered the marshal. Only Dalton's insistence kept him in the fold, even though it put his life and career at risk sometimes.

"Glad you could meet us in person," Greene commented as the three stood just outside the junkyard gates. "How did you pull it off?"

"I told my boss I wanted to come to Massachusetts for a prisoner transport detail scheduled for tomorrow or I was going to take some time off," Dalton answered with a cagy grin. "He can't afford to lose any more people right now, so he reluctantly let me fly over here."

"He probably thought you were crazy for *volunteering* to do a transport."

"I'm sure of that. I told him I was taking a day off to visit family over here before the transfer. He didn't ask any questions, so I'm in the clear."

Dalton led them through a secondary set of mesh wire fencing that essentially entered the heart of the facility. In one corner, readily visible to Liz, sat the remains of a charred van. Reduced to blackened metal, the vehicle was barely recognizable without tires, glass, or any color on the inside or the exterior. Whoever set the van ablaze made certain it burned hot enough to destroy any trace evidence throughout.

"What do you think?" Greene asked her, looking for any sign of optimism on her part.

Liz didn't want to falsely raise his hopes by saying anything reassuring. Getting a reading from people wasn't difficult, and objects owned and handled by people were typically a fifty-fifty shot, but she had never attempted anything destroyed or burned beyond recognition before. She truly needed to find something the psychic who sat in the van touched, or some part of him, like a hair, to activate her ability. Much of the passenger seat was lost in the fire, which left her little hope of entering his world.

Drawing closer for a more detailed examination, Liz thought everything looked exactly the same. Only morphed shapes inside the vehicle created any sort of variation, and there was absolutely no way to search for fibers or discarded belongings.

There simply weren't any.

Wincing at the smell of charred fiberglass and metal, Liz observed a man watching them from the hut that served as the manager's office within the premises. He probably expected local police detectives wearing guns and badges to casually survey the scene, but instead received two men dressed in business casual without firearms, and Liz who dressed as though fall weather surrounded her, rather than the nearly ninety degree temperatures that accompanied late May.

Almost subconsciously rubbing her hands together, Liz peered inside the vehicle before reaching her right hand toward the seat.

"I've always wanted to see this," Dalton confessed to Greene. "Never thought I'd be working with a psychic in this life."

"It's not much to observe from our end," Greene whispered back, but not quietly enough to evade Liz's hearing. "And it's not a psychic power in the normal sense."

"There's a normal?"

Whatever else the former partners discussed went unheard by Liz as she touched the seat's remains, tapping the hardened surface with her fingers from top to bottom. As expected, nothing happened, even when she reached the front of the seat, and finally underneath. Considering the windows had all blackened and shattered, or been poked through by the fire department, she seriously doubted anything inside the vehicle survived the intense flames. Someone, probably the police, had pried open the remains of the glove box to search it. Liz looked inside, seeing some paperwork, including an owner's manual that looked deformed and darkened, but not directly licked by flames.

"Is there a reason they wouldn't seize these papers as evidence?" she asked Greene, who stood to the side with his arms folded.

He sauntered over for a look, peering through the vacated window area. Standing close enough for Liz to feel the warmth of his body, along with his usual calm, collected breathing, Greene took notice of the papers inside.

"This wasn't considered a major crime by local police, so I'm sure they wouldn't waste resources testing for fingerprints. I'm sure they had a look through every-thing though."

"Not a major crime?" she questioned.

Greene shrugged.

"They probably figured some teenagers went joyriding in the thing and torched it. I'm not sure they ever put it together that this was the van used on the bookstore raid."

Thinking back to the footage of the raid, and Mark Teakon's senseless murder, Liz wanted to conjure a more productive image in her mind, so she reached inside the glove compartment and pulled out the manual and several loose papers. She carefully held them in one hand, rubbing her fingers slowly over each sheet and every corner, trying to evoke a response from the unknown energies that let her see the past.

"What are you so scared of?" Liz questioned under her breath, wondering what deep, dark secrets her fellow psychic harbored.

Nothing under or around the seat brought about a flashback, and the papers provided no spark, indicating the secretive man hadn't touched them, or the damage proved too great to leave whatever physical trace triggered Liz's visions. Basically grasping at straws, she tried to think of any other ideas that might provide a source of psychic energy.

"Where was the van stolen?" she finally asked, looking between Greene and Dalton.

"Not far from here," Dalton answered.

"Did the thieves throw anything out of the van when they stole it by chance?"

Greene's expression showed that he recognized her line of thinking.

Dalton flipped through the report he'd been holding in case they needed information about any of the cases involving the van.

"Not that the owners reported," Dalton answered after a minute or two of scanning the pertinent report.

"It's worth checking with them," Greene suggested as Liz thought the same exact thing.

Nodding in agreement, Dalton motioned them toward the parked cars.

***

Paul Clouse's research took him from every Orange County library available to the county historian and several people who knew the Springs Valley area exceptionally well. Most of them had family connections to the various hotels, knowing intimate details about what happened during the gambling days when people traveled to the area for spirits, games of chance, and occasionally the cleansing mineral water.

He finally discovered and confirmed that the Woxley Hotel, a two-story hotel built in 1898 contained twenty rooms. It shut down suddenly two weeks before the date the cursed cubes were created and the owner sold the property to an unnamed individual. In those days records weren't scrutinized and questions regarding ownership weren't typically asked if no one was affected negatively. He trusted what the local publications printed in the archives he read, but they weren't published daily back then, so he mentally left some latitude on the dates they stated certain events occurred.

While he continued to work on a few additional details, Clouse looked into purchasing the property where a former secondhand store continued to just barely stand. Faded products that never sold remained visible through the dusty display window and parts of the building's exterior showed major deterioration to the point of crumbling. The store once stood a few blocks behind the main thruway, but the rest of town eventually caught up to it as a few residential buildings were built around the store.

Most of them now stood vacant, or close to it, because business gravitated toward the two largest area hotels over time. The apartments and houses built decades earlier still looked the same, only faded paint and typical deterioration marring their outward appearance.

Despite not having everything finalized, Clouse decided to meet with his old high school friend Tim Niemeyer for lunch to discuss a favor he wanted to ask. His friend lost five years of his life, and in turn much more than that, because of the people who wanted to punish Clouse and make his life miserable. And though he helped Niemeyer make his construction business better than ever, Clouse couldn't get the man his marriage back because Niemeyer's wife had remarried, believing her first husband was lying six feet under a tombstone.

A story most soap operas couldn't pull off, the twists and turns Clouse endured with his numerous enemies left him nearly broken. Getting Niemeyer back after the man was held captive for five years came as a blessing to the millionaire, but the two didn't meet up often enough for Clouse's taste. He walked a fine line between keeping in touch with his friend and keeping Niemeyer safe from unseen enemies. History indicated that those close to Clouse often found themselves in peril when someone sought the cubes.

Walking into a local café, Clouse spied his friend sitting in the corner wearing blue jeans and a black t-shirt with the same Harley-Davidson logo as the large touring bike parked outside. An expensive custom leather jacket sat beside him, and Clouse knew Niemeyer was certainly back on his feet. Left with a fringe of brown hair and a matching full goatee dotted with a few gray hairs, Niemeyer stood to give his friend a bear hug that nearly crushed Clouse's ribs.

"Good to see you too," Clouse said between labored breaths.

Still thick around the waist, and barrel chested, Niemeyer took time to lift weights because he ate so well.

They each took a seat before Clouse thumbed toward the motorcycle sitting just outside one of the large windows.

"I see you still love the open road."

Niemeyer scoffed.

"I don't get far enough to really enjoy it. Business has been booming lately."

"I haven't seen you working any sites lately," Clouse chuckled.

"It takes everything I've got just to keep the business in order. I spend my days in a work truck or talking on the phone. Most nights I don't get home 'til dark."

Clouse used to enjoy the way his friend spoke with a slight drawl, acquired from being raised around his grandfather from Tennessee. It seemed his friend spoke a little more conventionally now, having been back in civilization for the better part of two years. Like most things in life, aspects of their friendship had evolved and changed over the years. Things between them felt tense once Niemeyer regained his freedom, as though he blamed Clouse for him losing five years of his life.

"What's going on with the richest friend I have?" Niemeyer asked once they placed drink orders.

"The usual. People threatening my life and the human population as a whole."

"Sorry I asked."

"It's not as bad as it seems," Clouse said with a nonchalant wave of his hand, regretting that he didn't phrase his answer a little more tactfully.

Niemeyer continued to carry the mental scars of imprisonment, though he put forth a concerned, soft-spoken front whenever he met with Clouse. Loyal to a fault, Niemeyer never refused his good friend, so Clouse felt terrible about asking for a favor, but he needed discretion more than ever.

"How are the kids?" he decided to ask first, not wanting to seem as though he only invited his friend to lunch to ask for help.

In truth, he would never have invited Niemeyer at such a dangerous time if not for the fact he required someone with construction and demolition knowledge. He felt like such a heel for asking anything more of his lifelong friend.

"They're good. I get to see them a few times a week when Vicky has to work. Now that school's almost out I'll see them a lot more."

"You can start training them in the family business," Clouse said with a smile. "Won't be long before they'll be old enough to work."

"And drive," Niemeyer grumbled.

Their conversation halted just long enough for them to place their lunch order. Niemeyer then looked to his friend, concern showing in his blue eyes.

"And how is your family holding up?"

"They're away at the moment," Clouse answered hesitantly. "It's safer that way."

"This has to stop, Paul. You need to distance yourself from this place and the curse around that hotel."

"It's a little more complicated than that."

"Bullshit," Niemeyer said evenly. "It ain't your nature to turn tail and run but you've fought the good fight long enough, my friend. It's time to let someone else watch over those things."

Clouse hung his head momentarily before looking to his friend with a face that expressed the desperation he felt inside.

"I don't have them, Tim. Someone raided the place where we were keeping them and got all of them."

"*All* of them?" Niemeyer asked with disbelief. "How many is that?"

"Seven of the thirteen. But I don't know how many others they might already have."

Shaking his head, Niemeyer uncharacteristically remained speechless for almost half a minute.

"I get the impression you want my help with something," he finally admitted. "I'm not sure I have it in me to help you confront these people again."

"What I need from you is much simpler," Clouse confessed. "I need you to knock over a building and see what's underneath it."

Niemeyer looked skeptical.

"You could pay anyone to do that."

"But I need someone to do the job and keep quiet about it."

Grunting and grumbling aloud, Niemeyer weighed over the decision. His loyalty to Clouse was destined to end at some point when he decided his life meant more than helping his friend keep the world safe. Five years of his life were erased because of his loyalty, and no amount of money could ever bring those back.

"Where is this property?"

"Closer than you think."

Clouse pointed to the aging apartment complex that stood out of habit in front of the property he was purchasing.

"Right behind that building."

Niemeyer drew closer so no one around them heard his words.

"And what do you expect to find in there?"

"The center of this entire mess. I think the cubes might have been created there. And if so, that's probably where they have to come together to do their damage."

It took willpower for Niemeyer not to roll his eyes or immediately blow up and chastise his friend's decision, but he collected himself a few seconds before speaking.

"Why in the hell would you dig that thing up then, Paul?"

"Tactical advantage. If I'm going to confront whoever's behind this, it's going to be there. Better I know the layout so I can plan ahead of time."

"And you're sure that's where the things were created?"

"Not one-hundred percent, no."

Now Niemeyer rolled his eyes.

"Do you own the property outright?"

"I sign the papers tomorrow."

Niemeyer took a few additional seconds to contemplate the offer laid before him. It went unsaid that Clouse would compensate him well.

"What's behind that complex?"

"It's an old store. I need it demolished before you can dig into the ground. A small hotel used to stand there back in the day, and I'm sure it had a basement."

"And what do you expect to find inside?"

Clouse shook his head.

"I have no idea."

Niemeyer rubbed the hair on his chin, obviously contemplating the risk versus the reward.

"I can have one of my employees take down the building," he finally decided aloud. "That way it won't look like I'm doing anything for you, especially if your enemies are watching us right now."

No stranger to hazards that came with befriending Clouse, Niemeyer knew how to evade spying eyes. Whether or not it worked this time remained to be seen, but Clouse felt a sense of relief that his friend was willing to assist him once again.

A thoughtful look crossed Niemeyer's face.

"What if we could access the basement without making a scene?" he finally recommended.

"I've got to assume it was filled in soon after the cubes were created," Clouse replied. "If there's anything to be found down there, they wouldn't have taken a chance."

"I can still take a look and see, can't I?"

"Feel free."

Both friends sat silently a moment until their food was delivered. Clouse forked a bite into his mouth before speaking again.

"I can end this once and for all, Tim."

"What makes you so sure?"

"I still have the one cube they need to pull off their plan."

Niemeyer shook his head.

"I worry about you, Paul. One of these times you ain't gonna be so lucky."

Saying nothing, Clouse knew the risk was one he would take repeatedly until the cubes were all safe from evildoers.

"I don't plan on going anywhere," Clouse confessed. "I didn't start this little war, but no one else is going to end it."

"People shouldn't have to go through what you've been through," Niemeyer said.

"Or what you've gone though. I just wish we still had Ken with us."

Clouse spoke of their mutual friend Ken Kaiser, who wound up a casualty in actions against Clouse some years prior.

"To Ken," Niemeyer said, raising his glass.

"To Ken," Clouse mirrored the toast, tapping his glass with Niemeyer's.

Each of them took a sip before Niemeyer spoke again.

"I hear you're in the horse racing business."

"No longer," Clouse said with a grin. "I kept my promise and let the original owners have full stake in their colt after the Kentucky Derby."

"You wouldn't do something like that unless you had a good motive."

"All the right intentions didn't help me in the end, Tim. Those pricks just waited for me to do the dirty work, then swooped in like hawks. That's why I'm asking for your assistance. These people hold all of the important cards except one."

He took a drink from his glass before speaking again to break the tension that always came with talking about the past and the events surrounding his hotel.

"Besides, the horse came in second at Preakness."

Niemeyer gave a smile, but it appeared forced.

Both of them knew Clouse only made business ventures to protect his assets or keep the world safe from cursed objects. He found no reason to cheer against Desert Phantom or the thoroughbred's owner. In truth, Clouse felt thankful that Margaret Stough trusted him enough to sign the pact with him, which gained Clouse another piece of the puzzle. Unfortunately the acquisition proved short-lived, which disappointed him and forced him to take additional precautions going forward.

Eating much of their lunch in silence, the friends had nearly finished when Clouse spied Clay Branson approaching the front door. He wondered how Branson found him, and why the man was visiting the French Lick area unannounced. Another man trailed slightly behind him, wearing dress clothes and cowboy boots, along with eyeglasses and a black cowboy hat. Clouse guessed him to be a police officer, possibly a Texas Ranger based on his shined boots and perfectly pressed clothing. Considering a firearm clung to the right side of his belt he was either a cop or someone who legally carried a gun through other means.

When the two men drew a bit closer, Clouse thought he recognized the man accompanying Branson. The bushy full goatee didn't look like standard regulation for a federal agency, but some outlying areas in states like Texas and New Mexico sometimes allowed their agents some leeway.

Wiping his mouth with a napkin, Clouse outstretched an arm as a pointer before speaking to Niemeyer.

"Tim, let me introduce Clay Branson and his complete stranger of a friend whom I haven't met."

Niemeyer nodded, though openly unsure whether he should feel honored or threatened by the sudden appearance of two strangers.

"Harlan Stone," the agent introduced himself, shaking hands with Clouse. "I've heard quite a bit about you, sir."

"I wish I could say the same," Clouse said before stealing a displeased glance toward Branson.

"This is important," Branson said, not wavering from his usual serious demeanor.

Clouse felt a bit apprehensive about saying anything more in public, so he set down enough cash to cover the cost of both meals before looking to Niemeyer.

"I'll call you later, Tim."

Clouse led the way outside the café, wondering what might be so important that Branson would visit French Lick unannounced and bring anyone outside of Clouse's group with him. Barely comfortable with the idea of a noncommittal Branson in his fold, Clouse didn't want anyone else knowing about the cursed objects or the mission to hunt them down.

"Let's take a short drive to the French Lick Springs Hotel," Clouse suggested, since he also owned that hotel. "I'm sure we can find an open conference room."

Chapter 40

Matt Teakon remained focused, if not obsessed, on a name stuck in his head since the day his uncle was lost to him a second time.

Jacob Savitch.

Considering the man's name appeared in the ledger that accompanied the cubes eleven times now, Teakon considered the man a formidable threat. He felt surprised the men who stole the seven cubes and killed his uncle never asked about the old book, but perhaps they simply did not know of its existence.

Two more cubes, however, and the man would indeed hold a full deck according to the old book.

"Do you want iced-tea or something else?" Julie asked as she stood from her couch to fetch some items from the kitchen.

"Tea is fine."

Julie hadn't visited the bookstore since the incident, and openly contemplated selling the property. In a nice downtown location, the building wouldn't be on the market long before some potential business owner discovered it and fell in love. Teakon didn't particularly like the idea of either one of them returning to Massachusetts, but Julie wanted to gather some of her belongings. Her refusal to be bullied potentially put them in danger, but Teakon used the opportunity to finally view the leather-bound book that clearly identified which people possessed the cubes, leaving the remainder of the mystery for the reader to solve.

What bothered Teakon about the find was that he couldn't find anything out about Jacob Savitch through his usual means. He suspected the man was the mastermind behind the raid on the bookstore, the attack on the fishing boat during the winter, and possibly the assassination of Chase Dalton's imposter at Clouse's grand hotel.

Not feeling entirely trustworthy, even of his own mind at this point, Teakon said nothing to anyone about the find, including Julie. While he felt reasonably safe around Clouse's people, he didn't know what the mysterious psychic working for Savitch knew about the group and their plans. Keeping such a secret felt dangerous for Teakon and everyone around him, but if the book ever fell into the wrong hands, regaining the cubes would prove nearly impossible. The pressure ate at his mind and conscience virtually every waking second, but he wasn't going to see anyone else around him harmed. If anyone knew about the book and wanted to come after it, he planned to sacrifice his own life to save innocent people.

"Liz called me a little bit ago," Julie revealed from the next room. "She and Russ were in the area to check over that van they used to rob the store."

"Oh?"

Julie peeked in, looking apprehensive about talking about the robbery and murder, as though he might fall apart any second. Already committed to telling her story, she continued after ducking into the kitchen.

"They didn't find anything useful in the van, and they spoke with the owners, but that didn't help either."

"Sounds like a wasted trip then," Teakon said, feeling more deflated than before.

"Are you okay?" Julie asked, handing him a full glass of tea when she made her way back from the kitchen.

"I'm fine," he said, putting forth his best reassuring smile.

"When do you want to head back to Indiana?" she asked.

Both felt safer around Clouse, who provided ample living quarters and security in the form of former military personnel and police officers, despite their earlier objections. For some reason Todd Parish was an exception to the normal hiring practice Clouse employed for bodyguards and security, but Teakon wasn't harboring any ill will toward the man. Both said some rather regrettable words the day they exchanged glancing blows in the hallway and Parish made it a point to avoid any conversations since.

Now put back for safekeeping, the book remained in a bank vault that required Teakon to present identification, possess a key, type in a passcode, *and* scan a fingerprint before gaining access to his property. He wanted some assurance that picking his mind or severing his finger weren't simply enough for some imposter to steal the last good tool he possessed for hunting down the cubes.

Teakon looked at the ring on his finger from the Kentucky Derby, suddenly feeling like most of his life was fake. He spent so much time constructing and executing cover stories that hardly any aspect of his existence felt legitimate. Protecting the world as his uncle had provided very little time for a personal life. Up to his uncle's true death, Teakon hadn't thought much of settling down, despite recently entering middle age. Growing up around ranches taught him many life skills, but dating and interacting socially didn't always come naturally to him. Julie taught him quite a few tips, whether she meant to or not, but he always regarded her as a younger sister rather than a love interest.

More so than any other living person on the planet, Teakon was prepared to lay down his life to protect her.

"Are you ready to see what the others have found?" she asked.

Teakon wished they hadn't taken time for lunch, but after the long flight neither was ready for travel again so soon. Still, he wanted to help her pack so they could avoid the danger zone in Amherst and leave before any more hazards came their way.

After visiting the book within the lockbox, he felt especially paranoid, as though someone might already be reading his thoughts or tailing him.

"I have this feeling we're not moving fast enough," Teakon confessed. "As soon as we learn something it's like we're a day late every time."

"Losing the cubes was disheartening," Julie admitted, "but we still have the means to find them again. And if that many are with one person we can get them back all at once."

"But what if he sells them to the highest bidder?" Teakon pondered aloud. "Or worse, decides to put them all together?"

"Matt, there's no one else out there who can stop that from happening besides us."

"But that was a close call at the bookstore, Julie. If my uncle wouldn't have thought ahead with the panic room, we would've been collateral damage."

"I know. But if Mark was willing to lay down his life for his convictions, I'm not backing down."

Julie's words felt somewhat reassuring, but he hated the idea of placing her in further danger. Still, if she was in for the long haul, he planned to stick by her side.

"Do you trust our people in Indiana?" he decided to ask.

"I don't have a reason not to. They've been helpful so far."

Perhaps Teakon still wanted to find fault for the fiasco on the Bering Sea, or the near miss at the Kentucky Derby, but he knew Clouse meant well. And to this point, all of his people seemed legitimately concerned about retrieving the cubes, each of them harboring mental and physical scars from previous dealings with the cursed objects.

Julie took a drink from her own glass of tea before looking him squarely in the eyes with a concerned look. She was reading him, reaching the conclusion that he'd been concealing a secret since stealing a peek at the book.

"You know who took the cubes from the bookstore, don't you?"

Teakon nodded slowly.

"And for the sake of safety I'm not telling you that name, Julie. If anything happens to me, you can always look for yourself. After what happened to my uncle I can barely trust my own thoughts."

Both of them shared the same access to the bank box, and both jumped through the same hoops whenever they wanted to check the book. The days of keeping it at the store, even in the vault, were certainly long gone. Although the bank box was always available to them previously, set up by Mark Teakon a few years prior, they'd used it sparingly before their lives felt threatened by outsiders.

"We have to be proactive, Matt, even if it puts us at risk."

"You're right. Maybe it's time we stop working as individuals and make this hunt a true team effort."

Julie stood.

"I'll get my things. The sooner we get back to Indiana, the sooner we can get everyone together for some answers."

Teakon wasn't sure he believed his own words, but he didn't want to live with regret later when the world came to an end around him, or countless people died to fuel the cubes individually. He just hoped someone in their alliance could find a clue that led them to Savitch before he possessed all of the cubes.

***

When he reached a vacant conference room at the end of a hallway within the French Lick Springs Hotel, Clouse asked to speak with Clay Branson privately inside while Harlan Stone waited in the hallway.

"How much have you told this guy?" Clouse demanded once the doors closed behind the two men.

"He's pieced a lot of it together himself. Some big cheese in the FBI had this agent tailing me for the better part of two months."

"And you thought the best move was bringing him here?"

"There have been some developments. I just wanted you to hear his story in person."

Clouse felt his body temperature continue to rise. He was infuriated with Branson for several reasons, and he decided to air them before speaking with the agent.

"I realize it probably wasn't right of me to ask you to help us retrieve these cursed objects in the first place. Maybe I was hoping you would put aside your personal vendetta long enough to help us with a greater good. That didn't happen, and you just come and go whenever you please around here."

Branson pointed a finger directly at Clouse's chest.

"I have a fucking life! I'm not some dog at your beck and call. You've got your hired goons to do your dirty work, and I've got a regular job and a theme park to oversee."

"I fully realize that, and I've come to learn that the only way I can motivate you is by dangling Nosagi's name in front of you. And as though I didn't have enough trust issues with you, you bring a stranger into the mix and show up on a whim. Hunting down these cursed objects is dangerous enough without you pulling this stunt. And I know you could probably kill me with your pinky finger but I've fought plenty of my own battles."

"I'm aware of that, Mr. Clouse. Part of the reason I've been reluctant to join your cause is because I've spent so much time researching you. Now that I know you're a good person, and your cause is legitimate, I'm onboard. I'll be the first to admit I've been blinded by revenge, and it isn't going to be easy for me to drop everything and run over here whenever you have trouble, but I *will* do my best. And you've got to trust me when I say you'll want to hear what the special agent has to say."

Almost apprehensively the door to the conference room opened before Stone stuck his head inside, still wearing his black hat.

"Well, I just heard everything you two said, so there's no need to repeat. I reckon the entire hotel might have heard it too."

Stone stepped inside, removing his hat to reveal hair cut close to the scalp, probably due to his receding hairline. He shut the door behind him, holding his hat respectfully at his waist while he looked between Clouse and the man who'd saved his life.

"Look, I've made some mistakes," Stone admitted, "and I don't completely understand what the hell is going on with these things you're hunting, but I'll help however I can. Even if that's just telling you what I know."

Clouse waved an arm toward the open seats.

"Let's start with what you know, Agent Stone."

Once the three men chose their seats, both Branson and Stone relayed the tale about Alan Stewart recruiting the agent from his usual duties and the setup that followed Stone visiting the widow of his fellow agent. It took nearly twenty minutes to provide Clouse with all of the details leading up to the most recent turn of events.

Stone had set his hat atop the table, upside-down to avoid bending the brim, but he fingered the black felt as though pondering where to pick up the strange tale. He finally sat back, cleaned his eyeglasses momentarily with his shirt, and looked to Clouse because Branson already knew the latest developments.

"After Clay here left me to the wolves at my job, I explained the past few months and played dumb when it came to certain details. And while I couldn't exactly leave out everything because surveillance video showed us together at the hospital and the Los Angeles branch of the Bureau, I tried to keep out some of the stranger things I'd seen."

"I especially appreciate the way you sent your agents to Mason to question me," Branson commented.

"Yeah, because I call the shots at the FBI," Stone retorted sarcastically. "I thought you ninja types were supposed to be invisible, so you only have yourself to blame."

Clouse noticed the two men were well past any issues they might have shared initially. Being chummy with a virtual outsider to Clouse's inner circle certainly didn't provide adequate qualifications for full disclosure. Still, he wanted to hear the end of the agent's story.

"As a result of my actions I'm on paid leave until my superiors decide whether or not they believe my story. But a coworker leaked a few details to me, including how Alan Stewart's body disappeared from the morgue before it was embalmed."

"Disappeared, eh?" Clouse asked suspiciously.

"That's what I thought," Stone noted. "Luckily the mortuary, located in an affluent Los Angeles suburb, caught some of the incident on video."

Stone produced a small computer flash drive after reaching into his pocket, holding it up for Clouse to see. He then slid it across the table toward Clouse, which allowed the hotel owner to scoop it up and plug it in after retrieving a laptop computer from a nearby cabinet.

"I take it you two have seen this?" he asked once the computer read the device and prepared to play the recorded video clip.

Both men nodded affirmatively.

Clouse started the video, watching as someone entered the mortuary following regular business hours because the person appeared as black as a shadow from head to toe. The low lighting made it impossible to make out details, but the intruder walked through the main hallway and out of view.

"Did the owners just have the one camera?" Clouse asked Stone.

"They had one in each of the visitation areas, but our intruder went straight to the basement. He comes back around the three minute mark."

Indeed the intruder came back around the time Stone stated, but this time someone walked through the hallway with him toward the front door. The second person, also a man based on his stride, walked under his own power just behind the first. Clouse could not determine any features because both of them basically appeared as silhouettes with the dim lighting mainly behind them.

"So what did your organization make of this?" he asked Stone.

"They figured a first accomplice let a second one in through the back and the two stole Stewart's body."

"And your take?"

"If I'm going to waltz in through the front door, I'm certainly not going to make the return trip if I'm letting my buddy in through the back. Based on what I saw Clay battling down in South America, I'm guessing one of those two men at the end of that footage was probably my former boss."

An awkwardly tense moment passed with no one saying a word, and at least on Clouse's end he didn't want to confirm or deny anything regarding the existence of the cubes or their powers. Branson hadn't exactly provided a stellar reference for the agent, and Stone readily admitted to working for the enemy. Exactly how naïve the young agent might have been regarding his apprenticeship with Stewart remained to be seen.

Based on the information provided by Branson and Stone, Clouse assumed Stewart worked for someone else who wanted to eliminate any loose ends. It made little sense, then, to murder the man and bring him back just a day or two later.

Perhaps Stewart set some kind of failsafe in place to make certain his services remained a requirement, whether he harbored information or some kind of benefit. Any number of possibilities existed, but it seemed whoever wanted the Deputy Director dead took a great risk by eliminating him where he worked.

"You're sure Stewart's death was at the hands of your mentor?" he asked Branson.

"Positive. A tiny hole in his neck indicated some kind of poison was used. I think he wanted it to look natural, like a heart attack, but for some reason he left the cart in the room. Maybe he had a narrow window of escape."

"It turns out he murdered a janitor and assumed his identity," Stone added. "He's on the security footage, but dressed with a baseball cap so you can't see his face. He entered during the overnight when the building is practically empty and waited in Stewart's office until morning."

"I take it you didn't volunteer any information," Clouse surmised.

"I'm in enough hot water already," Stone answered somewhat testily. "The last thing I need is my agency thinking I'm a key figure in assassinating my boss."

Clouse contemplated some risky moves, because once again he found himself knee-deep in a mystery and two steps behind his adversaries. He hadn't dared ask Liz to touch any of the cursed cubes now that he knew someone was able to penetrate her thoughts. If Niemeyer demolished the old store in French Lick and found nothing, Clouse foresaw little other option than to ask Liz for help.

In a few days he might find that weighty decision placed before him.

"I appreciate you gentlemen bringing this before me," he said, intending to wrap up their impromptu meeting.

"That's it?" Branson asked with a raised eyebrow. "You don't have some plan of action?"

"I have several ideas, but they aren't something I can hop to right this second. After what happened in Massachusetts my options are a bit limited."

"What happened in Massachusetts?" Stone inquired, his tone and expression indicating he might possess some useful information. "My boss recently took a flight out there."

Both men stared at him as though they doubted his ability to obtain Stewart's schedule.

"What? I sometimes peeked at his schedule when his assistant went to the restroom."

"Damn it!" Branson stammered. "We may have just let a vital piece of the puzzle walk away."

"I'm confused," Stone said, still out of the loop because he didn't know the backstory.

"What do you mean?" Clouse asked, talking around the agent as though he wasn't in the room.

"If Stone's partner was on Stewart's payroll and he helped rob the bookstore, then maybe Stewart did the talking and the other muscle was the guy who tried to kill Stone in the hospital."

"What bookstore?" Stone asked no one in particular. "Who robs a bookstore?"

"Where did you leave that guy?" Clouse asked, still ignoring the agent's inquiries.

"In the middle of nowhere, basically."

Clouse thoughtfully cupped his chin.

"You need to find him and find out everything he knows."

"He's hired muscle," Branson stated. "Stewart wouldn't have told him anything valuable."

"But they'll kill him just the same," Stone said, finally replacing his hat. "Maybe I can track him down."

"I'm glad," Branson stated, "because I have to get back to Ohio before my fiancée wonders where the hell I've been."

Clouse wasn't particularly fond of the agent assisting the group just yet, but he wasn't willing to risk sending his own people to accompany a suspended government employee. On the other hand, he wanted to test Stone's loyalty, which seemed difficult to measure if he didn't send someone to monitor the agent.

"I'd like to know if you find the man," he informed Stone. "Especially if he knows anything useful."

"It might help if I knew what sort of questions to ask."

"I'm pretty sure you're resourceful enough to get him to squeal without asking too many questions."

Stone nodded, getting Clouse's notion. And with that the three men gathered up their minimal belongings and parted ways.

Chapter 41

A few days later Tim Niemeyer entered Clouse's new property alone around dusk, careful to make sure no vehicles followed him down the short street. He exited his truck, closing the door as quietly as possible before taking a look around. Even at the edge of the town limits no crickets chirped and the traffic sounded extremely distant when Niemeyer finally did hear a passing vehicle.

The surrounding abandoned buildings loomed over him from atop their perch on a nearby hill. Their black, unlit windows stared down like evil faces with hollow expressions, providing no indications about what might be hidden along their abandoned floors.

Gripping the entry key in his right hand, and a flashlight in his left, Niemeyer walked purposefully toward the door, opening it to the kind of musty smell that accompanied a building untouched in years. He found a light switch immediately to his right, but when he flipped it nothing happened.

"Perfect," he muttered, illuminating the main foyer with his industrial-grade flashlight.

Dust mushroomed into the air with every step, but Niemeyer aimed the flashlight toward each wall and floorboard with determination. The entire shop took up about a thousand square feet, taking him little time to sift through. Only a few pieces of furniture required moving for Niemeyer to complete a cursory examination of the defunct store. He saw no indications of doors, conventional or secret, that might lead to any kind of basement. Even the cracks along the floor didn't seem to indicate anything lurked beneath them.

Deciding he wanted to check a hunch, Niemeyer stepped outside to examine the building's foundation. He shined the light, verifying that no small windows lined the old bricks to indicate a basement might exist. Strangely, no vents were present to suggest the building sat atop a slab either. Drawing a perplexed face that no one was present to see, Niemeyer tilted his head in confusion, wondering what kind of contractor erected a building with no ventilation for climate changes.

Thinking he needed to examine the subfloor inside before contemplating his next move, Niemeyer let the flashlight's beam guide him through the front door. He tried some of the floorboards with no success, so he grabbed a pry bar from his truck before making a second attempt. He knew demolishing the little store wouldn't prove much of an undertaking, but a concrete floor beneath it might require extra time or equipment. And when the old wood finally gave way, he stared at the concrete slab beneath it, thinking it wasn't simply poured as a minimal slab to support the weight of foot traffic and heavy items.

Niemeyer tested the thickness of the concrete by dropping one end of the pry bar atop it twice, receiving a hardened thud each time in response. He felt certain the foundation wasn't meant to support a heavy load, or house ventilation and water lines, as no vents existed, but rather it was poured thick to conceal something a very long time ago.

Studying the material, Niemeyer found particles in the mix that might escape a less experienced contractor's eyes. He knew from the history of his craft that coal, wood chips, and whatever else builders could find during the early 1900s often went into concrete mixes to accelerate the curing process. This especially held true during the colder months, like December or January for example.

He felt certain the building's later owners likely didn't see a need to alter the foundation, or realized doing so might cost more than the building was actually worth, so it remained untouched for nearly a hundred years. A best-case scenario meant the concrete was crumbling and easy to break apart, but even that required heavy equipment.

Groaning, Niemeyer formulated a plan for the following morning, knowing when he halfheartedly promised his friend to look at the property that it couldn't possibly go smoothly. Helping Clouse with any aspect of his life these days practically put a target on the volunteer's back. While Niemeyer probably didn't have as much to live for as he once did, the man still valued time with his children and the lucrative life owning a profitable construction business provided. And though Clouse never admitted it, the man brought Niemeyer a *lot* of jobs in the surrounding counties.

When he finally stepped outside, the crickets chirped in the distance, providing him with some comfort that nothing ominous scared them. He hoped his near future held an equally promising outlook, because he didn't feel comfortable helping his old friend when the task at hand was related to the cursed objects that caused them both some dear friends.

He returned to his truck, cautiously looking around because the unusually cool evening and quiet surroundings unnerved him. Either his efforts would help Clouse protect the world one last time, or Niemeyer would leave his children without a father once again.

***

Just before noon, Niemeyer received a phone call from the employee he assigned to demolish the old secondhand store. It turned out the building came down easily as expected, and even the concrete beneath it crumbled into smaller chunks that the backhoe lifted and sorted with ease. The employee called to report in and request permission before digging into the remainder of the concrete slab and the dirt beneath it.

Niemeyer gave permission to carefully dig and sift through the dirt, explaining that there might have been a functional basement beneath the slab at one time. Basically he told the young man not to strike any foundation above or below ground level. He wouldn't have assigned that particular employee to carry out the dig if he didn't trust him, but the kid had grown up working with farm and construction equipment. His precision aim and steady hand allowed him to maneuver large equipment without harming important or fragile items around him.

Immediately phoning Clouse with the news, Niemeyer was a bit surprised when his friend declined to come in person for a look at the property. Niemeyer fully expected to lay eyes on the freshly gutted basement within the hour, but Clouse informed him he didn't want to step foot on the property just yet. He asked his friend to meet Todd Parish at a restaurant for a quick lunch, probably to throw off anyone monitoring their activities, before taking him to the site.

When he stepped into the burger joint, he recognized Parish in the booth farthest from the entrance, looking incredibly out of place with the tourists in their khaki shorts, blue jeans, and light summer wear. Wearing a black suit with a blue and white striped tie, Parish even outclassed most of the local bankers who wore golf shirts with logos, or dressed similarly without the benefit of a sport coat.

"Did you just come from a funeral?" Niemeyer asked as he slid into the booth, knowing Parish just well enough to joke with him.

"Just doing my usual thing."

Niemeyer wasn't sure exactly what duties Parish carried out as of late. Once a bodyguard to Clouse's son and stepdaughter, Parish recently spent more time on special assignments and around the two luxury hotels. Niemeyer took notice because the bodyguard occasionally accompanied Clouse to meetings and lunches as well.

"Well you're a little overdressed for what we're about to do," he informed Parish, who simply shrugged indifferently.

"The boss tells me you're doing a little digging for him."

"More than a little. If you've already ordered, you might want to get your food to go."

Parish indeed took a cup of coffee with him when he followed Niemeyer to the site. When the two pulled their trucks into the lot, Niemeyer noticed his employee had cleared most of the old basement. A mound of dirt sat beside the ruins of the building, and remnants of the old store remained only in large chunks of the four walls in a different pile.

"Do you have a permit, or should we expect the police to raid us any second?" Parish asked half seriously.

Niemeyer didn't appear amused.

"Paul was careful not to purchase this place in his name, and I was equally careful when I applied for the permit. I'm hoping to avoid visitation from anyone this far away from the main parts of town."

A young man approached them and Niemeyer didn't bother with introductions as his young employee, Jake Webster, filled them in about his morning dig. He took them around the foundation, pointing out the walls that once comprised a full basement. Despite using large excavation equipment, the young man had managed to remove most of the dirt right to the edge of the walls without damaging one square inch of the foundation.

"There are stairs over there," Webster said, pointing to the remains of an old wooden stairway that had virtually rotted to splinters after years of burial.

"I think I'll pass on trying them," Niemeyer commented, still looking around the small basement, not seeing any huge secrets looming along the dingy walls.

For the most part gritty dirt coated the walls, but one moist spot appeared where a longstanding leak might have allowed rainwater to seep beneath the floorboards and around the solid barrier below them. Niemeyer felt bad that he hadn't found anything concrete for his friend, but Webster indicated he wasn't finished showing the two men his finds quite yet.

"Have a look at that," he said, pointing to the opposite corner.

Niemeyer only saw a dirty wall at first glance, but when he crouched down and squinted a little, he saw the outline of a door. For the life of him he couldn't imagine why the basement, which equaled the former ground floor in square footage, might have a door. Basements seldom exceeded the size of the constructed overhead space.

"Can we get a ladder down there?" he asked, turning to see his employee was already a step ahead of him.

Looking to Parish, he finally cut loose with a smirk.

"Ready to get that suit of yours dirty?"

Parish's reply came in the form of a grunt while he began peeling off his sport coat as though preparing for a fistfight. Instead of setting it aside, however, Parish draped the sport coat over his right forearm to help conceal the gun holstered at his side in case any nosy people suddenly visited the site. He also didn't want Niemeyer's young employee thinking he was a detective, for fear he might tell some of his friends about the site. Parish figured his white shirt wasn't going to fare any better in the environment that awaited him in the bowels of the old demolished store.

Webster maneuvered the ladder into the hollowed basement a few feet from the sealed doorway below. He asked if Niemeyer wanted him to go down first and check the door, but the construction company owner shook off the notion and descended the ladder himself. He waited beside the door until Parish joined him along the solid bottom of the old basement before looking to the door momentarily. A bit apprehensive, Niemeyer brushed an open palm against the old wooden surface, sending some of the old dirt to the ground and revealing an iron clasp handle, rather than a doorknob. It reminded him of some kind of medieval castle door, rather than any décor from the past century.

"Can you cover me a second?" he asked Parish, receiving an affirmative nod.

Trust didn't come easy for Niemeyer, who literally witnessed people backstabbing his good friend Clouse before trying to kill both of them. He at least trusted Parish enough to have the man keep an eye on things while he entered whatever awaited him behind the cryptic, heavy door.

Putting his weight into the door, Niemeyer used his thick arms to begin moving the object inward, finding it heavier than it looked. He strained a bit until the door finally budged a few inches, revealing a small mound of dirt on the other side that likely squeezed through the cracks when the basement was filled in decades prior. It pooled at the bottom of the door, creating a barricade that refused to give way until the contractor put his shoulder into the effort, busting past the gritty obstruction.

The daylight behind him only provided light about three or four feet inside the opening, but the outline of a tunnel appeared before him, and he knew this was no adjacent storage room. Whatever this tunnel led to wasn't close, and he found no form of illumination to light the way if he dared step inside.

"Hello?" he called, verifying his initial thoughts with a deep echo from within, realizing the tunnel spanned a length further than any flashlight beam was going to span.

He returned to the outside, looking up to Webster.

"I need a flashlight."

Within a minute the young man returned, tossing the flashlight down to Niemeyer, who immediately handed it to Parish as though it were a hot potato. Parish looked to the flashlight, then to the contractor, with mild scrutiny.

"You don't want to see what's in there?"

"I don't," Niemeyer answered sincerely. "The less I know, the better. Besides, you're armed."

Parish shook his head, unable to comprehend why anyone wouldn't want to see one of the greatest potential mysteries left in the state of Indiana, if not the world. If the cubes were indeed designed in this labyrinth, the location might provide some long-awaited answers about how to deal with them once and for all.

Setting down the flashlight momentarily, Parish replaced his sport coat, uncertain what awaited him down the dingy tunnel. He tested the flashlight a few seconds later, ready to discover some answers and hopefully make up for the debacle in the Bering Sea. Parish still blamed himself for not performing better on the boat, but outgunned and outmanned, no one aboard the vessel truly had much of a chance. He was lucky to be alive and walking.

"I'm honestly not sure what Mr. Clouse sees in you," he said, turning to Niemeyer at the doorway entrance.

Niemeyer grinned, apparently thinking Parish was kidding.

"I'm going to tell him you said that."

Chapter 42

Not particularly happy with Niemeyer and the man's lack of commitment to his best friend, Parish started down the tunnel, immediately finding parts of the walls reinforced with stone and brick. He wondered if some of the tunnel might have served as additional storage for the old hotel in the beginning, because the wall supports suddenly ended about ten feet inside. Parish believed someone might have added on to the old storage room later on, because the tunnel walls suddenly became hardened dirt instead. Old wooden timbers ran perpendicular overhead, occasionally supported by vertical beams to prevent collapse from the weight above. Based on some of the nearby buildings aboveground, Parish considered the logic for reinforcing the tunnel quite sound.

"See anything?" Niemeyer called from the doorway, refusing to step inside.

"Get your ass in here if you want a play-by-play."

No reply came, though Parish felt certain he heard Niemeyer mumble something.

Parish shined the flashlight around the walls and ahead of him, seeing no immediate end to the tunnel. He did, however, find hangers and some very old lanterns along the walls. Probably built when electricity wasn't a household item, the tunnel certainly wouldn't have been provided with such an amenity, because power lines would have risked giving away the secret.

A closer look indicated the lanterns used some kind of oil for fuel, but all of them were covered with dust and dirt after seeing no visitors for nearly a century. Parish didn't have time, or a need, to light them as he walked. Simply amazed by the craftsmanship of the tunnel, he wondered if the cursed objects that caused Clouse fits were truly born at the end of the mysterious tunnel. If so, that made the destination a true place of evil, one rivaled by some of Hitler's estates, or modern day lairs used by terrorists overseas.

Any landmark where the demise of thousands was planned over the centuries was always considered a heinous place. Parish hurried his pace, wanting to see what awaited him at the end of the tunnel. He also felt somewhat claustrophobic walking through a tunnel barely able to support the width of two people standing side by side and the height of an average guard in the NBA. He kept telling himself the walls and ceiling had held for nearly a hundred years, but that didn't stop thoughts of collapse from creeping into his mind.

Cobwebs appeared occasionally, though nowhere near as often, or as thick, as the movies made them look in caves. An odor that came with age accompanied the creepy sights, mostly from the wood that deteriorated at a snail's pace due to the lack of moisture and air entering the tunnel until this day. No breeze followed him inside, and the tunnel felt like a basement kept at perfect temperature and humidity.

Monitoring the ground ahead before he stepped foot on it, Parish found the dirt packed to nearly the texture of solid rock. He tried to avoid thinking about the depth of the tunnel, or the heavy buildings above him, continuing to stare at the ground until the texture changed from blackened dirt to some form of tile in an instant. He switched off the flashlight, discovering the tile was illuminated by something directly ahead.

"Wow," Parish muttered, looking into a room that no person ever expected to find at the end of a dingy tunnel.

A pulsating fiery glow emanated from the opposite side of the room that didn't appear to come from nature or any power source Parish had ever laid eyes upon. The glow provided a low light, though enough to illuminate the entire room when the pulse reached its full brightness. Parish tried to take in the entire chamber as he stood at the open doorway, finding it the size of a moderate conference room with some kind of large centerpiece that looked like a strange piece of permanent furniture. He couldn't identify the fixture, but it looked a little bit like an oversized decorative birdbath.

Ignoring the room's décor momentarily, Parish looked to the floor directly ahead, wondering if some kind of snare awaited him once he stepped inside. There was a time when he never would have considered the prospect of stepping onto a brick only to have poisoned arrows firing at him in unison. And back then he wouldn't have believed thirteen cubes could provide people with benefits in exchange for a human sacrifice but he now knew better.

Kneeling down, Parish looked for any tripwire, or variations along the floor. He noticed for the first time that the floor consisted of thousands of small tiles about one inch square apiece. Though they lacked any distinctive patterns sometimes created by different color combinations, he thought they looked exactly like the tiles in the West Baden Springs Hotel's lobby and atrium areas. Based on the time when this chamber might have been created compared to the first renovations ever done at the hotel, a sinking feeling hit the bodyguard.

Staying low, he finally stepped into the room, expecting each step to be his last. Married, with two children of his own, Parish didn't particularly want to throw his life away, even for the greater good of the world. Clouse paid him well, but even Parish's employer didn't expect him to recklessly charge into the unknown and risk life and limb.

With his heart pounding in his chest, Parish took a few crouched steps inside, finally satisfied he wasn't going to be instantly struck down. He stood, finally able to examine the room, finding every inch of the floor covered in the same marble tile. The walls, not to be outdone, were finished in some kind of cloudy marble, in swirls of white and some other medium color Parish could not decipher due to the pulsating orange glow from the far wall.

Before crossing the room, Parish cautiously walked toward the center where the large ornament with a bowl-shaped top stood. From its center, a dozen or so, perhaps even thirteen, small arms protruded outward along the floor, reaching toward an outer ring. The centerpiece held the appearance of a water wheel from above, looking as though someone had simply laid it down upon the floor. No more than eight feet in diameter, and a little more than four feet tall, the custom ornament appeared to be made from some sort of stone, which seemed impossible given its curvature and decorative trim. Parish approached it, finding the wheel portion stood just below his waistline, which provided easy access to any adult standing in his or her assigned spoke. He circled the strange fixture until his foot bumped into something lying along the floor.

Dropping to one knee, he found the skull of a skeleton staring back at him, its head resting against the closest stone spoke. A chain remained attached to one bony foot, appearing to be the culprit for the man never leaving the chamber. Based on lore, Parish assumed the poor soul was the jeweler the original thirteen conspirators hired to construct the cubes before Satan himself cursed them. The legend also told that the man, knowing his life was forfeit, constructed the leather-bound book to record the names and kept it hidden. Apparently people with incredibly unwavering morals found the book sometime later, considering Julie Knowles and Mark Teakon eventually took possession of it.

Not knowing the whole truth bothered Parish almost as much as it perturbed the clan that Mark Teakon once headed. Receiving occasional information through letters and personal items helped, but such testimonials couldn't always be verified or believed. Somehow a group of Chicago police officers obtained the time cube, or the world might have been a completely different place numerous times over. As bad as things seemed with everyone making personal sacrifices and losing loved ones, Parish imagined it could have been *much* worse if not for some unsung heroes over the past century.

He gave the skeletal remains one last examination, finding clothes still intact, though tattered, on the deceased jeweler. They looked like the same attire he might see someone donning on a sepia postcard from around World War I. It wasn't bad enough the bastards forced him to create instruments of evil, but they made him a captive audience for the proceedings as well. Being locked in such a strange room and seeing the demonic procession probably gave the poor working man a heart attack.

With no flesh present on the body, Parish couldn't tell if the man truly suffered before his untimely death. Parish's own skin crawled because he'd never laid eyes on a corpse with just bones before. Not particularly experienced around bodies in the first place, he felt uneasy about seeing anyone in this state, and regretted accidentally kicking the bony figure.

Standing at last, Parish walked the perfectly laid tiles to the source of the pulsating, eerie glow along the far wall. What he found was the source of the strange glow took up virtually the entire wall in the shape of a clock. He drew close, examining the clock with Roman numerals larger than his hands, finding a strange, square indentation beside each of the numbers. Based on the consistency of the pulsating glow, and the fact that he could find no obvious power source, Parish guessed the clock to be powered by unnatural means. Strangely, the entire face of the clock created the ebb and flow of light, though the surface appeared hardened. Made of marble or some form of crystalline rock, the face shouldn't have been able to emit light in any fashion.

"Jesus," he muttered, uncertain if the clock possessed actual workings when he tried studying the metal rods holding the clock's hands in place.

The face of the clock looked very similar to old Victorian grandfather clocks he spotted in antique stores when his wife dragged him shopping. Everything about the room indeed pointed toward the notion that the cubes were born in the room and set free to cause death and destruction throughout the world. Parish sensed some larger picture still eluded him, mainly because he didn't know the local history exceptionally well like his boss. For the first time in a long time he felt like this new information might place Clouse's group on even ground with the people determined to possess every last cube.

Five minutes later he returned to the entrance doorway where the daylight stung his eyes momentarily. Blinking feverishly, Parish was greeted by Niemeyer, who seemed anxious to hear his finds. Parish pulled the heavy door shut behind him as best he could, though it refused to move the last few inches for a full seal.

"Replace all of the dirt," Parish told him. "Bury the basement again."

"What did you find in there?"

"You can hear it when I report to Mr. Clouse, but for now we don't want anyone finding their way down there."

Niemeyer nodded, having some understanding of the difficulties facing the group because the enemy knew their plans the moment they conceived them. He climbed the ladder out of the pit and walked purposefully toward his employee to order the basement filled in once more. Parish followed a moment later, stealing a final look toward the excavated area that led to a place of unspeakable evil and terror. Images of the ominous clock plagued Parish, who considered himself a simple man and no expert on the occult. Instinct, however, told him that the clock and that room were the focal points of whatever diabolical plans the people with the cubes had in mind.

Filling in the basement kept spying eyes and evildoers away for the time being, but Parish prayed for the day when the cubes and the glowing clock below were a thing of the past, remembered by no one.

Chapter 43

Summer passed without incident, which worried most everyone affiliated with Clouse. After hearing about the find beneath his new property, Clouse started formulating some plans, but he never laid eyes on the basement as though he knew eventually his hand would be forced. He kept to himself, encouraging his staff to do the same and not share information, as though paranoid that their thoughts might be plucked from the air at any given time.

Craig Jennings conducted some rounds throughout the hotel on a late afternoon toward the end of September. Sticky morning air gave way to thunderstorms and cooler winds in the afternoon as a stark reminder that the fall season awaited the Springs Valley. He made his way past the front desk in the lobby, coming to a stop at the stained glass front doors. A row of stained glass doors left from the Jesuit occupancy of the hotel grounds were locked beside the clear main doors. One of the truly beautiful features left from the priests, only a few of the doors remained intact when the hotel was found in ruins after being caught up in legislature for nearly a decade. The construction firm Clouse went to work for a decade prior received the bid to piece the hotel together, which included creating replicas of the stained glass throughout the lobby.

Jennings knew some of his employer's past, partly because he had always lived in the area, as did Clouse, and also because Jennings visited the hotel when it stood out of habit. Faded, chipped paint covered the walls both inside and out, while portions of the roof and skylights broke apart during that time. Still, that didn't stop Jennings and countless other people from sneaking beyond the mesh wire fence surrounding the grounds for a look at the old building before a preservation group eventually stepped in to begin saving the hotel.

After some private donations and a few partnerships, the restoration was underway and the public wasn't able to visit the grounds for the better part of a year. Only when the atrium, the ground floor, and the hotel's grounds were renewed did the preservation group overseeing the hotel allow daily paid tours on the hour.

Staring out the clear lobby doors, Jennings saw rain pounding the brick drive that reached the hotel from the highway. It also tumbled down the concrete front stairwell, much like a raging river heading for lower ground. Sometimes barely a drop of rain fell from the sky during the summer months in Orange County, and occasionally the spring season brought enough water to produce a small lake in front of the dome that lasted for weeks.

On a Wednesday afternoon barely a soul was found inside the hotel. Employees and fewer than a dozen guests could be found on the grounds because conventions and weddings often took place closer to the weekends. This week it seemed Clouse's other major hotel down the road received most of the convention business. Staying at the West Baden Springs Hotel cost more, so during the peak vacation season companies tended to take the cheaper alternative a mile away.

Thunder grumbled in the distance, and the lights inside the lobby waned momentarily as though the power might go out, but they recovered. Jennings turned to find Dan Duncan walking in from the atrium as the employees behind the reception desk snapped to attention. By no means a tyrant, Duncan seemed to have the respect of his employees as though he held something over them aside from the ability to terminate their employment.

"Shouldn't you be tending to our seven guests and their every need?" Jennings kidded the hotel manager.

"I'm busy preparing for the additional ten guests coming in tonight," Duncan answered with a chuckle. "I think this weather is scaring people away."

"Not exactly a dream vacation with that monsoon out there, is it?"

"No."

Customarily Duncan refused to wear a suit around the hotel. He seldom interacted with guests because the manager on duty handled the daily affairs, and for that matter he barely socialized with the employees. He ran an efficient, clean hotel, despite having no real experience in the hotel service. A little bit of management schooling, combined with his business background, transformed Duncan into a solid, albeit rather unsociable manager.

Although he never pushed the issue, Clouse asked Duncan to interact more with the staff and guests to practice for the occasions when he needed to appear completely professional in front of wealthy or influential guests and investors. The owner didn't push the dress code, because Duncan knew when he needed to dust off his suit for special appearances.

When one of the lobby doors opened, the two women behind the reception desk looked up while both Duncan and Jennings directed their attention to a lone man carrying a small suitcase. The man wore a suit that appeared slightly wrinkled and very much soaked from the downpour.

"This is your chance to practice," Jennings said, nudging the manager in the ribs.

Rolling his eyes, Duncan grunted doubtfully before stepping forward, struggling to put forth a halfway genuine smile.

Jennings watched the hotel manager greet the man as warmly as possible for Duncan, even shaking his hand and offering to take his bag.

"Thank you," the man said, reluctantly returning the handshake, soiled from head to toe by the unforgiving weather.

At first Jennings entertained himself by watching Duncan struggle to bring forth his amicable side, but as he replayed the man's entrance in his mind, something bothered him about the stranger's appearance.

Even as the man walked to the desk to check in, Jennings wondered where the hell he parked. The parking lot was all the way around the back of the hotel, which meant he would have accessed one of the other entrances closer to the rear if he parked there. Parking at the bank near the highway didn't sound prudent, because the walk to the hotel was currently a hundred yards in torrential rain. Perhaps someone else dropped him off and went to the parking lot, or down to the casino, but Jennings continued with his train of thought, walking toward his security office where he could monitor lots of square footage within the building on a computer monitor.

He felt bad for leaving Duncan, but the manager could handle himself, or hand the guest off to the women working the reception desk. The handshake on the stranger's end seemed forced, as though the man really had no desire for human contact. Jennings remembered seeing that same trait in Liz, although her reasoning was slightly different. She didn't want to know absolutely everything about the people around her, whereas this man acted as though he might be compromised.

Thinking of that led Jennings to his last interesting clue.

Most people who walked in drenched from the rain gave the appearance of having black hair. Jennings arrived at his office, closing the door behind him as he watched the stranger check in and wait for the nearby elevator to arrive. Something about this man struck him as familiar, but it wasn't until the man took the elevator up three levels to the fourth floor where he used his keycard to enter a balcony room that Jennings felt a tingle run through his spine.

Although the man looked somewhat thinner, Jennings felt almost certain this was the man Clouse's group viewed in unison a few months back. He rewound the footage, trying to determine the man's hair color, even replaying the footage in slow motion for a better look. Freezing the screen on a frame where the hallway light struck the man's hair just right, Jennings felt certain he saw several strands of red hair where the rain hadn't saturated them, or they managed to somehow dry quickly.

"Son-of-a-bitch," Jennings muttered, scooping up the phone to call Greene, hoping his initial curious thoughts hadn't given him away.

It wasn't exactly like *Ghostbusters*, where thinking of the Stay Puft Marshmallow Man would cause utter disaster, but Jennings hoped the psychic didn't pick up on any doubts in his mind during the moment he lingered in the lobby.

While Clouse and Parish had basically disappeared since the start of August, Greene and Liz made occasional appearances when they weren't out checking leads on the man frozen on a computer monitor before Jennings. The pair had yet to find any concrete link to the mysterious man, and now he apparently had the audacity to walk into their home ground.

Two rings crossed the earpiece before Greene picked up.

"Hello?"

"Russ, it's Craig. You're not going to believe what just happened here at the hotel."

Jennings spent a few minutes quickly explaining the situation to Greene, praying the red-headed man wasn't somehow picking up on their conversation and heading to the security office with a gun to silence his latest nuisance. As a precaution, while he talked, Jennings stretched the phone cord to its limit and locked his office door with outstretched fingers.

"Craig, Liz wants to know if he touched anything when he came in. Anything she can handle to maybe read his mind."

"Well, the door of course. And Duncan shook hands with him."

"Grab Dan and bring him here."

"Where *are* you guys?" Jennings asked as he returned his monitor to a live feed, making certain no one was sneaking around the ground floor to surprise him.

"We're in Bedford grabbing a late lunch."

"Why can't you bring Liz down here?"

"Are you brain-dead? I can't take her anywhere near that guy."

"But he's *right* here. We could end *all* of this right now."

A momentary pause indicated Greene was at least entertaining the suggestion.

"No," he finally said. "If this guy works for someone and doesn't cough up the name, we're back to square one."

"Fine. I'll grab Dan and call you once we're heading your way."

Jennings hung up the phone, not sure he liked Greene's decision this time around. Maybe thinking of a destructive marshmallow man wasn't his worst course of action after all.

***

Jennings quickly found Duncan in his office and took a route through the hotel that kept them away from prying eyes and hopefully psychic minds. Greene requested they meet in the small town of Mitchell, just south of Bedford but a safe distance away from West Baden. The nearly thirty-minute drive gave Jennings plenty of time to explain the situation to the hotel manager. Duncan didn't completely grasp the concept of being a human conductor for psychic power transference, but he didn't ask many questions.

"Did you wash your hands?" Jennings questioned once they finished passing through the town of Orleans, just minutes away from their rendezvous.

"I don't think so," Duncan answered almost blankly, staring at his hands as though mesmerized by them. "I use hand sanitizer a lot though."

"Did you use it after you shook hands with that guy?"

"I don't know," Duncan answered emphatically, more concerned about being useless to the group than annoyed at the questions hurled his way.

His memory proved less reliable as the years went by. Duncan hated most technology with a passion and considered himself a throwback to when men were rugged individuals. He loved riding motorcycles and enjoyed the occasional expensive cigar, keeping his pleasures simple. Never married, and with no children to complicate his life, Duncan threw himself into business, seldom dating or attending social gatherings unless the job required it. Although he remained very sharp and alert in business, some of the simple things often relating to short-term memory eluded him.

Another concern plagued Jennings because Greene wanted to keep Clouse out of the loop until they knew something more. Despite Greene's wishes, Jennings tried calling his boss. Without so much as one ring the man's phone went straight to voicemail, exactly how others reported it doing so for the past few weeks. Jennings believed his employer was on a mission for the greater good, keeping Parish with him for some unstated reason. Clouse informed Greene, Jennings, and a few others that he wasn't going to be in touch for an undetermined amount of time, and Jennings simply believed the man was protecting his family and possibly investigating a lead.

Another five minutes passed before Jennings reached the town limits of Mitchell, continuing onward until he spotted the Arby's restaurant where Greene asked to meet. Jennings pulled to the back of the parking lot, away from any other vehicles and customers, where Greene and Liz stood waiting beside Greene's pickup truck.

Raindrops still peppered the windshield intermittently as the storm clouds refused to move east. Both men reluctantly stepped from the marked resort car Jennings had commandeered for the trip, which suddenly didn't seem like the wisest mode of transportation since everything about the trip was handled so secretly. In the distance the dark gray clouds began parting, but the smell of rain and a sticky humidity lingered in the air.

"I hope I can help," Duncan said, addressing Liz once they approached the pair.

"It all depends on his skin particles, his DNA, being on your hand," Liz answered. "I think. Hell, I don't know how all of this works. I'm just going by past experience."

Duncan held out his right hand as though he expected to lose it. It trembled ever so slightly as Liz stared at it momentarily and gave him a reassuring smile before finally cupping it gently between her palms.

Jennings watched Liz intently, expecting her to stiffen momentarily as though she read something from Duncan's hand. Nothing happened, which disappointed everyone visibly. He wanted to blame Duncan, a creature of habit, for cleaning his hands, but he faulted his own mind for not identifying the mysterious redheaded stranger sooner.

"Maybe the rain kept his DNA from transferring," Jennings suggested aloud, considering the possibility.

Liz picked up on the idea, beginning to rub her palms over Duncan's hand in a massaging motion in search of the slightest skin particle. Her actions only required a few seconds before her facial expression changed and her entire body shivered in the briefest of moments, stuck between stiffening and relaxing as her mind took in something unseen to the three men around her.

The entire ordeal literally lasted only a few seconds, but it took another minute or so before Liz fully recovered while Greene steadied her by gently clasping her elbow. Everyone anxiously waited for a report of what images entered her mind. Shaking off the effects of a psychic transition, Liz took hold of Greene's forearm to steady herself.

"Did you see anything?" Greene asked first.

"I saw part of his childhood," she stammered, "but then he shut me out."

"Shut you out?" Jennings questioned.

"He knew I got inside his mind and forced me out. His powers, they don't work like mine. His ability only works when he's in proximity of his target and he concentrates on reading their thoughts."

"So he can only target people when he's nearby?" Jennings asked, thinking back to the hotel, hoping he didn't give away any crucial information.

"That's why he had to be nearby when they raided the bookstore," Greene stated. "We now know that FBI guy and his two cronies were the ones who raided the bookstore, but they're all dead or missing."

"We do?" Duncan asked. "I don't recall that information being shared with the rest of us during any meetings."

"That's because we aren't even a collective group anymore," Greene argued, raising his voice. "Hell, the guy who pays us disappeared and Stone said the last henchman he was looking for turned up dead back in June. We were running on empty until the psychic for our arch nemesis waltzed into the hotel an hour ago."

Liz stepped in, trying to maintain the peace.

"Guys, take it down a notch. This guy may be fighting to keep me out of his head, but I have a mental connection to him now. He can't keep me out forever, and he's going to be scared."

"And he's going to run," Jennings surmised. "Should we try and stop him?"

Greene rubbed his chin in thought momentarily.

"I don't want Liz anywhere near him. She's the only person who might provide us with information and I don't want this guy compromising us, or getting to her."

"Dan and I can handle this," Jennings said, tapping Duncan on the arm as they marched toward the company car.

He didn't feel especially confident that the man couldn't pick their thoughts, but if he was still inside their hotel, Jennings thought of no reason they couldn't detain him and wait for someone with interrogation experience to question him.

None of his security staff carried firearms, and none of them were experienced enough to carry out an arrest. They were basically there to keep situations from escalating while calling the local police for assistance. Besides, none of them were informed about the secretive nature of the cube hunt, and Jennings refused to place them in jeopardy without providing full disclosure.

Either way, he planned on confronting the man in half an hour, or chasing down any leads in pursuit of the stranger.

Chapter 44

When Jennings and Duncan returned to the hotel, Jennings parked the company car in a lane near the lobby entrance beside a sign that clearly read no parking was allowed. All employees within the hotel listened to either man's orders, so when Jennings inquired about the one man who had checked in within the last hour, they knew exactly which person he meant.

The woman behind the desk typed in the name, still remembering the floor and exact room after Jennings requested any guest information in their system.

"Have you seen him?" Jennings inquired while waiting for a printout of the guest information.

"No," the woman answered.

"What room is he in?" Duncan asked, likely thinking of heading upstairs to pay the man a visit.

Duncan impatiently let himself behind the counter to watch the employee's progress over her shoulder, openly making her a bit nervous.

"Tyler Johnson," Duncan read the guest's name aloud. "Probably an alias."

Jennings thought along the same lines, but neither of them was equipped to handle an abduction and interrogation. While Jennings could deal with the security cameras, he possessed no means of drugging the man, and no firearm to lead him to the basement. Even with a handful of guests and staff milling around, the notion of silently executing such a plan felt nearly impossible.

Any potential setbacks didn't slow Duncan as he drew his master keycard and headed for the elevator after he found the room number on the screen the clerk was using. Jennings sighed internally and followed, not wanting the manager to stir up trouble and expose the fact that they knew the redheaded man's identity.

He also wanted to protect the older man from harm in case their guest harbored any surprises within the room.

Jennings wanted to check the security footage first, but Duncan appeared determined to visit this man in person.

"You going to play this cool?" Jennings asked as the elevator ascended.

"I'll just ask if there's anything he needs," Duncan replied without much emotion in his voice. "It's a slow day, so he should buy it."

"Just remember he can read thoughts, so try to concentrate on anything except what we're doing."

Duncan nodded, but Jennings didn't feel especially comfortable hoping the manager grasped the severity of the situation.

When the elevator opened a few seconds later, the duo was greeted by the same decorative carpeting laid upon every upper floor. A mix of brown, gold, and green, the pattern mirrored the tile on the ground floor except that the image of a compass was placed in the center of the carpet about every quarter turn. The various compasses always pointed in the true direction as one navigated the two rings of rooms surrounding the atrium.

Hoping they didn't point toward danger and imminent death, Jennings followed them, reading the numbers on the doors he already knew by heart until he reached the correct room facing toward the atrium.

"This is it," he said unnecessarily as Duncan stopped simultaneously at the door.

Jennings stepped aside as his colleague knocked on the door. Unable to refrain from displaying his impatience, Duncan stared at the ceiling while tapping his foot atop the carpet. Several seconds passed with absolute silence from the other side, prompting Duncan to draw the master keycard from his pocket a second time. Before inserting it, however, he rapped on the door several more times with his knuckles, receiving no answer.

Saying nothing, he inserted the key and flung open the door, finding no one inside, and not so much as one travel bag on the floor. The king-size bed remained untouched, its comforter perfectly straight as though nothing touched it and no items were ever placed upon it. As both men stepped completely inside, they found nothing disturbed on the sink, and as Jennings lifted the toilet lid, he saw no evidence of it being used.

"What the hell did he even come here for?" Duncan questioned aloud.

"Maybe he figured us out."

"How? I didn't even know who the hell he was until you told me."

Jennings shook his head.

"Maybe he just picked up on us somehow."

Feeling guilty, Jennings suspected *he* was the only one who might have provided the thoughts that scared the psychic away from the hotel. Still, it made no sense that the man walked up to his room only to leave without so much as a trace of evidence.

He decided even before they finished combing the remainder of the room that he wanted to review the security footage. Something didn't add up about the man making the trip into enemy territory only to leave almost immediately. Whether the psychic hoped to find Clouse, or extract information from the employees might never be known, but Jennings intended to search for answers.

Once Duncan felt content there was nothing useful in the room, Jennings asked the manager to accompany him to the security office.

"You sure you saw him walk in there?" Duncan asked on the way down.

"He went inside the room. How long he stayed, I have no idea."

A few minutes later they accessed the security office and Jennings retrieved the fourth floor footage of the man stepping into his room just to verify his sanity for Duncan. They stared at the video in real time, waiting for the moment when the redheaded stranger stepped from his room. Only a minute passed before the man calmly and deliberately exited the room, carrying his bag. He walked purposefully as though he understood the need to leave the grounds quickly, but his expression showed very little about his intentions. During the elevator ride the man opened his cell phone to place a call. Jennings wished the phone had faced the camera long enough to pick up any information on the screen, but he didn't live in some television show where the picture zoomed in on command with enhanced quality.

Jennings called up other camera footage, following the man from his room to the elevator, then through the atrium out the back entrance where a car waited to whisk him away. Unfortunately the cameras outside simply covered the parking lot and the valet area from a wide-angle distance view. If someone monitored the live feed the cameras could easily zoom in for more detail, particularly if a crime was being committed or security needed to identify a particular person. Unfortunately when Jennings left his post any chance of identifying the driver left with him.

He reviewed the footage several times as the redheaded man slid into the passenger's seat of the sedan, but the driver simply wasn't readily visible. The camera, mounted on an awning just above the valet area, provided a decent view of the driver's side of the car, but the driver wore sunglasses and knew better than to look in that particular direction.

"This stinks," Jennings muttered. "We were that close and he slips away."

"What if he didn't?" Duncan asked thoughtfully. "Maybe we should call Mark Daniels and give him a heads up, then take a little drive through French Lick."

Daniels headed up the security force at the casino just a mile down the road, which worked independently from the security personnel at the hotels.

Jennings couldn't argue with the logic. If the mystery man and his driver indeed planned a reconnaissance mission, it seemed one minor setback wasn't going to deter them. Grabbing the keys to the company vehicle from his desk, Jennings motioned toward the door, wanting Duncan to stay with him a bit longer. Based on the unusual circumstances, Jennings felt uncomfortable dealing with a psychic and any other minions by himself. The fact that Clouse proved unreachable also bothered him, because a feeling that they were drawing close to a confrontation with their unknown nemesis gnawed at the back of his mind.

He hoped the disappearance of Clouse and Parish meant the two men were preparing for the inevitable, rather than hiding. Based on Clouse's credo, Jennings couldn't picture the man backing down all of the sudden, when the darkest hour concerning the cursed objects drew nearer with each passing minute.

***

It turned out Clouse's friend Mark Daniels wasn't working, which made any potential search for the redheaded mystery man nearly impossible. Jennings drove around French Lick and West Baden searching for the sedan from his footage without success. Even the short dead-end streets revealed nothing to him, indicating the man might have left town, or at least provided the indication he did so.

Jennings decided to make a stop at the French Lick Springs Hotel because the parking garage beside it could easily harbor a car on its numerous levels. He stepped inside the main lobby while Duncan headed toward the casino and the nearby garage to cut their search time. Keeping his expectations low, Jennings walked through the lobby toward the nearby hallway that traveled the length of the long hotel, passing gift shops and curio cabinets filled with vintage items along the way.

Although keycards were required by guests to use certain elevators, Jennings knew someone could slip into an elevator with another guest, or hide in one of the numerous areas meant to distract tourists. The basement area consisted of a buffet, bowling alley, and several specialty eateries, along with a tavern. He didn't particularly feel like sticking his head inside every door for a look, knowing full well the psychic might have already left town. Besides, if the man happened to be nearby, how would Jennings know his thoughts weren't being read, allowing the red-headed man to remain one step ahead?

Passing some hotel employees, Jennings gave a friendly nod, noticing he was being eyeballed as though they couldn't figure out how they knew him. Jennings often wore slacks and a tie, but sometimes went corporate casual like Duncan. Today was one of those days where he wore an embroidered polo shirt and khaki pants. Since he wasn't certified by the state as a police officer, and saw no reason to work as a reserve police officer, Jennings didn't carry a firearm at work. Only security personnel at the casino were armed, and none of the hotel personnel were allowed to carry firearms, even if they possessed a permit or police training. Clouse wanted people to feel safe when they stayed at his resort, but he didn't want armed security walking around his grand hotels like the buildings were in danger of lockdowns on a whim.

Thanks to a desire to stay true to history by Clouse and his team, the French Lick Springs Hotel was redone with gold leaf paint, murals, and lots of natural wood. By no means inexpensive, the details provided just as much of a beautiful view as its former rival down the road. Jennings walked along the thick carpeting, looking up to the walls where two gigantic graphically designed murals done with models in vintage attire and backgrounds depicting the two grand hotels and early cars basically advertised the resort as a whole. Further along his path, large canvas posters dotted the lengthy wall, using pictures of more models and resort employees to show absolutely every amenity available between the two hotels.

Jennings didn't mind. The resort, and Clouse, saved him from the drab life of a high school shop teacher. Although his new occupation wasn't the safest, both in his everyday duties and the occasional dangerous quest for cursed objects, he couldn't complain. He wholeheartedly believed in Clouse's quest, particularly after making friends of colleagues like Dan Duncan along the way.

Suddenly thinking about his buddy, Jennings pulled out his cell phone, trying to call the hotel manager who should have made his way from the casino into the garage already. Jennings heard four rings on his end before the phone went to voicemail. He wanted to believe Duncan was experiencing his usual technology trouble while trying to answer his phone, but Jennings worried because the man wasn't always as sharp and alert as one needed to be when part of Clouse's inner circle.

Reaching the end of the hallway at last, Jennings decided not to turn right and head down an escalator into the casino. He walked straight ahead into the garage as automatic doors opened to welcome him into the darker setting. Breathing in the muggy air that still lingered from the thunderstorm, Jennings stepped forward along the first row of vehicles, able to hear his footsteps whenever he walked. Amazingly he found no one else along the central level of the garage, so he continued, looking between parked vehicles since he didn't see Duncan. Calling out for the man didn't seem professional in a place of business, so he tried calling the manager once more on the phone, reaching voicemail a second time.

Groaning to himself, Jennings walked to the end of the row and turned back, rather than move to another level. He passed the entrance doors, rounding the corner to explore the other side of the barrier that separated the various rows of vehicles. Instead of calling out for Duncan, he decided to try the phone once more, hoping to hear the ring of the manager's phone from somewhere in the garage. For all he knew, Duncan might have gone looking for him along the ground floor, or the basement inside the hotel.

When he immediately heard a phone ringing in the distance, but saw no one standing on the entire level, Jennings grew concerned. He picked up his pace, continuing to listen for the phone as he looked from right to left between the vehicles, hoping he didn't find his friend injured.

Or worse.

Realizing the sound originated further down the concrete path, Jennings darted straight for the ringing phone, rather than conducting a search at a jogger's pace. He made an effort to reach the source of the ringing before it stopped, trying to avoid any distractions like looking at his own phone to place another call. Toward the end of the row of vehicles he rounded a large SUV, finding Duncan lying on his side with his cell phone atop the concrete a few feet away.

Kneeling beside his fallen comrade, Jennings tried shaking him, finding no visible wounds or indication why Duncan appeared to be unconscious.

"Dan, wake up," he said, nervously looking around to make sure no harmful figures lurked nearby.

Duncan finally groaned a few seconds later, slow to regain his senses as though he'd been struck in the head. Jennings sat him up, still wary of their surroundings, not seeing any security cameras in their area. He suspected the person, or people, responsible for harming his friend knew the same information.

"Dan, what happened?" he asked, testing whether or not Duncan could get to his feet.

Duncan struggled to assist Jennings, who grasped him by the elbow, but slumped to his posterior before getting very far off the ground.

"Someone hit me from behind," he muttered through the pain, rubbing the bald spot toward the back of his head.

"How long have you been out?"

"No idea."

Duncan started reaching for his phone.

"Were you calling someone?" Jennings inquired.

"No. I didn't have my phone out."

Jennings intercepted his colleague's reach, picking up the phone first and looking at the screen. Right there in plain sight, as though Duncan's attacker *wanted* them to know it, sat Paul Clouse's direct cell phone number.

Only the employees who knew about the cubes and assisted in Clouse's search for the evil objects possessed his personal cell phone number.

And now his greatest adversaries knew it as well.

Chapter 45

Russ Greene grew irritated about staying in hiding with Liz while no positive news reached him through the occasional phone call or secretive e-mail. He played it safe, using no credit cards, avoiding the cell phone except during predetermined talk times, and sticking to rural settings whenever possible.

Even more than him, Liz went stir crazy after living in California for so long where activities were plentiful and human contact wasn't so scarce. Although she seldom interacted with other people, she openly enjoyed being around others and picking up on conversations. She felt a sense of normality, hearing mundane chit-chat and seeing how ordinary people acted. Strangely, she gained a similar sense through conversations with Greene, learning about his childhood and career while sharing some of her own past.

All without using her abilities.

Whenever Greene spoke with Craig Jennings or Julie Knowles, he felt as though nothing was putting them closer to recovering the lost cubes. Clouse and Parish were out of contact with everyone, and a sense of disorganization put a stranglehold on the group. Toward the end of October, after months of a frustrating life in hiding, Greene asked Liz if she wanted to try something that might provide answers, but place their lives in jeopardy if they weren't cautious.

"What do you have in mind?" Liz asked in response, a devious smirk crossing her lips.

"Let me make a phone call."

Greene talked with Julie Knowles and Matt Teakon during the next scheduled phone call, finally proposing that they all meet. His suggestion was met with initial hesitation, but when he all but blatantly explained *why* he wanted to meet, it was Julie who won over Teakon. Greene heard most of their discussion over the phone, and credited the courage of both Julie and Liz for taking the necessary steps toward ending their ongoing ordeal.

Now, on the day before Halloween, Greene drove toward a secluded area in central Pennsylvania. Literally a truck stop gas station off the highway, and the only occupied facility for miles, Greene felt the location was perfect. He remembered it from a case he worked several years prior when he needed to stop for fuel and it was the only alternative for miles. A navigation device helped him locate it before he called Teakon and Julie with a specific location. For the time being they were simply driving toward the highway he specified, bringing the leather-bound book with them.

"Did you see anything last night?" Greene asked from the driver's seat as fall foliage blurred past the side of the vehicle.

Occasionally, in her dreams, Liz saw past and present visions of the redheaded stranger, realizing his past consisted of being bullied and ostracized by his peers. Unfortunately he continued to block most of the pertinent information regarding his current plans, but she saw fragments of things he had visited and seen the past few months, including the French Lick area.

"Nothing new," she reported. "It's like he knew enough to put up a mental fence because someone attempted to enter his mind at some point."

Greene understood her frustration, because Liz didn't back down or allow herself to be intimidated by the unknown adversary. If anything, she faulted her own lack of knowledge to grow and expand her ability because she understood that the man psychically linked to her had honed his gift over the years.

When asked why she thought her dreams revealed bits and pieces about his life, Liz replied that she figured when he slept his mental guard was let down somewhat. She admitted no lingering dreams or images had entered her mind previously after touching people or objects, so the open line of sorts likely came from the stranger's end.

Within half an hour the duo met Julie and Teakon at the truck stop, occupying a table near the back of a national pizza chain restaurant. Two other eateries and a convenience store complete with gift shop took up the remainder of the large building. Truckers stopped for fuel, showers, and supplies, and Greene kept a close watch on every stranger who crossed their paths inside the store.

Outside, gray skies changed the atmosphere as the four sat beside a corner window. Julie slowly produced the book from a silk cloth shroud, placing it atop the table as all four looked around, finding no one else in the restaurant, and the crew behind the counter preoccupied with gossip and typical duties. Liz took a deep breath, looking into the anxious eyes of the people she considered comrades, dedicated to the same dangerous endeavor as her. Part of her hoped to see nothing, and perhaps avoid the pressures of being the one person who might provide answers while Clouse and Parish remained missing, their objectives unknown to anyone else. The other half of Liz wanted to know everything, and confront the redheaded stranger now linked to her already active mind.

Liz reluctantly reached for the book, wondering what images, if any, were about to flood her mind.

***

Paul Clouse's disappearance was by design, and not because he felt a need to hide and protect himself. Instead he wanted to allow Parish the opportunity to formulate a plan without any knowledge of the details. Clouse considered his mind a fountain of information for the enemy to drink from at any given time. Because he already knew where the final showdown was destined to occur, Clouse didn't want to devise a plan himself, for fear that it might be for nothing. He could think of no one more important for the enemy psychic to stalk simply because he and he alone knew where the time cube was located.

Once he felt reasonably certain Parish had managed to devise a plan, Clouse returned to his summer chalet located on the edge of Lake Monroe outside of Bloomington. Thanks to a message, he now knew the man who possessed the remainder of the cursed cubes also possessed his phone number. With his wife, son, and stepdaughter safely tucked inside the custom-built house with windows aplenty to view the lake from any level, Clouse stepped onto the second story deck when an unfamiliar phone number called his cell phone.

Already harboring a mild dislike for the next day's holiday, Clouse wondered if the call's time was bad luck or by design. Closing the sliding glass door behind him, he pressed a button to take the call as the cold and wind slapped him in the face from the lake. Not a soul dared take a water vessel on the choppy water this day as the smell of freshly mulched fall leaves reached his nostrils.

"Clouse."

"Hello, Mr. Clouse," an unfamiliar voice said. "I take it you've been expecting my call."

"I suppose I have. Just so I know it's really you, why don't you tell me what you're wanting before we discuss terms."

A light chuckle crossed the line.

"Right to the point. I like that."

"I'm just used to dealing with these situations."

"And so far you've been lucky. That could all change this time though. I'm not Martin Smith. I'm *much* more dangerous."

Clouse had bested Smith, his arch nemesis, twice on previous occasions, killing him both times. Unfortunately with the cubes not everything always stayed dead.

"You know I want the last of those beautiful little cubes."

"And what exactly do you plan on doing with it?"

"I want to finish out my collection, of course. I've got a little room picked out where I can display them all at once."

From the man's tone, Clouse suspected he already knew about the strange room and the clock occupying one wall.

"You know I can't just hand that over to you."

"I don't see why not. I've played nice and kept all of your friends and family alive. They can all stay that way if you just do as I ask."

"You're talking about the end of the world."

"How would you know that? You're relying on what Mark Teakon told you? He was a fool who didn't know what he was dealing with."

Clouse felt nothing but respect for Teakon, and contempt for the individual speaking to him. He tried to control his anger, but his face flushed and his muscles tightened as the cool wind slapped him constantly when he leaned on the balcony railing. Attempting to calm himself, Clouse watched several clouds lazily cover the sun momentarily.

"And I suppose you have all of the answers?" Clouse finally asked. "Why would you want all of the cubes unless they brought you some kind of power?"

"I never said they didn't give power. Your friend was misinformed about exactly how they worked, however."

"Care to enlighten me so we're on an even playing field?"

"You'll never be my equal, but I will let you see firsthand what their power can do. Meet me at your new property so we can put them to the test."

"And if I refuse?"

An eerie silence crossed the line before the unseen voice spoke again.

"I said I'd played nice with your friends and family so far. Cross me, and everyone you know will die, one by one, until you've attended all of their funerals. Thanks to the cube your good friend Martin Smith possessed, I have forever to torture you and look for the last cube. If you defy me, I possess the ability to pick your mind of every last thought and make the remainder of your life miserable."

Feeling certain the man referred to the psychic when hinting about the mental fleecing, Clouse knew his thoughts could betray him, and had taken measures to counteract that as well. He knew how to play the game when he and his family were threatened, and on his home ground he wasn't going to simply hand over every shred of power to this bastard.

"Believe me, I'll be there."

"Nine a.m. Bring the last cube. Don't be late."

The line went dead before Clouse could say anything more. He didn't have a witty comeback, or anything else to say anyway. Whether this man on the other end of the line knew it or not, the last cube was by far the most dangerous of the thirteen, even by itself. Letting it fall into the wrong hands wasn't truly an option, even if his family and friends were placed in perilous situations. He decided the wildcard in all of this meeting was the psychic. If that man could be taken out of play, preferably without ending his life, Clouse would certainly feel better about his chances of walking away from the morning meeting alive.

He mentally digested the prospects of the following day before opening the door to return to the more comfortable indoors. Leaving his life in the hands of friends wasn't a sound plan ordinarily, but his mind was currently his worst enemy. He didn't feel right about dragging Matt Teakon or Julie Knowles into his current predicament. If Clouse didn't survive, someone needed to pick up the pieces if there was still a planet left to protect. For similar reasons he ordered Greene to keep Liz away from Indiana, partly to protect her, but also in the hopes of severing whatever psychic link she shared with the redheaded man.

After facing death so many times before, Clouse truly didn't fear his time when it came. In his previous career as a firefighter he took many medical calls to various residences from all walks of life. Young or old, black or white, it didn't matter, because in the end no dignity truly accompanied death. He'd seen people shot in the streets and slumped over on toilets from cardiac arrest. Short of using a cursed object, everyone experienced death eventually, and even those who profited from using the cubes typically met horrific ends.

"What's wrong?" his wife asked him when he stepped inside.

"Nothing," he answered, giving her a quick kiss on the cheek.

He married Jane almost nine years prior, having lost his first wife to a gruesome murder that strained his relationship with the West Baden Springs Hotel. Now it seemed his tumultuous time in Orange County was coming full circle for better or worse the following day.

"I know when you're lying to me," Jane said, tracing the collar of his dress shirt with her index finger.

He hadn't exactly kept her abreast of the latest events, not because she was in the dark about the cursed objects or his past trouble, because she certainly knew specifics about all of that. She also knew he had sent her and the kids into hiding for their protection, but Clouse never provided detailed reasons. Only a few days ago he had brought them home, somehow knowing the ordeal was reaching a conclusion. Clouse received the unsaid message that Duncan could have easily been slaughtered, so he hoped terms were going to be amicable. And he never left Jane or the kids without some form of protection at home, in this case some familiar bodyguards just outside who knew his friends and family by memory.

"You're about to do something dangerous and stupid, aren't you?" she asked, not raising her voice in the least because the children were playing a videogame nearby.

Even Clouse's son, Zach, and Jane's daughter, Katie, had survived their share of traumatic incidents in the past. All the more reason, Clouse figured, to keep them distanced from the danger coming for him in the morning.

Sometimes surprised she stayed with him, after all of the danger and turbulence, Clouse awoke each morning thankful Jane remained by his side. Money hadn't changed them, partially because it came as a surprise just before they wed. Their relationship seemed almost like a feel-good romantic movie to some, with Clouse the working-class hero firefighter and Jane a young doctor working near her hometown. She remained close to home due to a strong bond with her mother, who also shared a love for the grand hotels in Orange County. That love inevitably brought Jane and Clouse together, on the grounds of the West Baden Springs Hotel where Clouse worked on his days off from the fire department.

Even after a decade of growing older with her, he still considered Jane beautiful with her shoulder-length brown hair. Highlighted with streaks of a coffee creamer brown, her hair always looked good because she took excellent care of her entire body, inside and out. Very much a country girl, she looked as good in a flannel shirt as she did an evening gown.

Clouse didn't immediately answer his wife's inquiry about exactly where his recently strange behavior was leading, which drew a sour look from her.

"It's time you let someone else carry out your work," she said quietly enough that the children didn't hear.

"We've been through this before," he replied. "How can I possibly trust anyone else to find these things, knowing they might abuse the knowledge and keep them for themselves?"

"We aren't going to be around forever, Paul," she said, placing her finger across his lips. "You'll need a successor someday, and these kids need a father."

With Zach's mother deceased, and Katie's father never truly in the picture, Clouse considered both children his own. He missed birthdays and holidays on occasion, but he never felt it was fair to ask others to risk their lives if he wasn't willing to do the same.

"I might be able to end this once and for all," he said, playfully drawing across her lips with his own forefinger, failing to immediately change his wife's expression.

She finally let a smile through, guarded in nature.

"I know nothing I say is going to stop you, but I'm going to remind you that you thought the last time was going to be the end."

"I can't see the future, dear."

"I just want you to be safe," Jane said, wrapping her arms around him. "Just once it would be nice to fall asleep, not worrying about whether someone is coming after us."

Clouse forced a grin.

"Maybe it will be. I've got a little errand to run tomorrow that may change everything."

As though sent from above, Clouse's good friend Mark Daniels appeared at the stairwell landing, greeting the kids briefly to avoid distracting them from their game.

Clouse touched his wife's hand gently before heading toward his friend, wondering if friendship or business prompted the visit. Following their usual routine, the casino security manager led the way downstairs where they could talk in private, away from the children and Jane's open concern.

Wearing a dark gray suit, Daniels hadn't removed the laminated name badge from the breast pocket, indicating he was probably just getting off work. Clouse doubted his friend would schedule himself to work a late afternoon or evening without a solid reason. Though he sometimes grew a seasonal beard, Daniels was still clean shaven, a full head of dirty blond hair grown in for the impending cold weather.

"What brings you out here?" Clouse inquired as they stepped into the downstairs family room.

"Isn't a neighbor welcome in your home?" Daniels asked with a friendly smirk. He seldom smiled openly.

Daniels referred to the adjacent chalet that Clouse ordered built at the same time his own lakefront property was constructed, specifically for Daniels and his family. Daniels and his wife had recently gotten back together after a marital split, so they lived between their city home and the chalet seasonally.

"I guess I figured you were done with the lake property for the season," Clouse answered. "Hadn't seen you around lately."

"I hear you've been rather busy."

Clouse suspected his friend might have conversed with Dan Duncan and Craig Jennings recently. While none of the three men were loose-lipped, they all knew about the cursed cubes and occasionally spoke about the evil objects within their group. Having such a limited focus group tended to make them talk like old women in a knitting circle when they got together. Clouse didn't mind because it relieved their stress levels, but they often voiced concerns over their boss's plans or actions.

He didn't ignore their opinions, but none of his employees had shared in every one of his horrific experiences, meaning they didn't know all of the facts. While Clouse wasn't arrogant enough to call himself an expert, he figured he knew more than the recent additions to his staff.

"I can't imagine who would fill you in about my plans," Clouse said, sauntering toward the front door where two carved jack-o-lanterns stood on the other side of the glass.

Because the kids took to the Halloween holiday, seeking to live halfway normal lives, Clouse catered to their whims. From the ground level the view of the lake remained stellar, though more of the yard took up the view, rather than the boat dock.

"You can't keep doing this," Daniels warned, speaking generally about the quests to retrieve the cubes.

"Now you sound like Jane."

"Just because this shitty ordeal fell in your lap ten years ago doesn't mean you have to take it to your grave."

"You opted out, Mark, and I've respected that. I haven't asked for your help in any of this."

Daniels shook his head, grinning disagreeably.

"That doesn't mean I don't get dragged into it sometimes."

"And I apologize for that."

"There's no need for sorry. I'm just concerned about you and this obsession of yours."

Clouse felt offended, but refused to display his emotions.

"So saving lives is an obsession?"

"If you're writing a résumé for your ticket to Heaven or something, I think you're already in, buddy."

"I haven't told you everything, Mark. If what I've got planned tomorrow works, this may all be over with forever."

Daniels hung his head, shaking it slowly.

"How many times have we thought this was all over before? I'm just afraid one of these times you're not going to walk away."

"This thing tomorrow," Clouse said slowly, "is an all or nothing proposition. Practically everyone left on the planet who knows about the cubes is probably going to be in French Lick. Might be a good day to call in sick."

"I might just do that."

"I've got to meet this guy tomorrow, and I have to go alone. He'll know otherwise."

"Don't worry. I wasn't going to volunteer."

"I know," Clouse said with a weak smile. "Saving my ass cost you your marriage once, and I don't want you risking your marriage or your life again."

"What's the worst that can happen tomorrow?"

"The guy kills me, takes a cube that can transport him back in time, and life as we know it changes forever. Or he just combines all of the cubes into some kind of demonic device that ends the world."

"Maybe you should call the military for backup," Daniels said, half joking because they both knew the secret of the cursed objects could not be allowed to spread.

Clouse read the sullen expression on his friend's face. Helping him in the past had cost Daniels so much, but his friend didn't want to abandon him either. He decided to try lightening the mood.

"Don't worry. If anything happens to me, I'm sure Jane will make sure you keep your job at the casino."

"I wouldn't count on it. She'd probably blame me, so you better come out of this unscathed."

"If I don't come out of it, you'll probably never know the difference."

"I know you. You have a plan."

"You're right, and I pray it works. But it involves me calling a few key people, so if you'll excuse me."

Clouse plucked the cell phone from his side and held it up for Daniels to see.

"Yeah, well just be careful tomorrow."

His friend walked over to give him a hug, which Clouse considered a very rare showing of affection from the former police detective.

"I'll come check on you tomorrow night," Daniels promised. "Do what you have to do and kick some ass."

"You know I'm not going to let some city slickers come to my neck of the woods and push me around."

"Yeah, I know. Be careful just the same."

Clouse nodded as Daniels let himself out the front door. There indeed remained a few important phone calls to make, which served as the first steps in setting his plan in motion. Clouse was relying upon his knowledge of the area to serve him well, but he also needed a little luck to walk away from the meeting alive.

He needed even more if he hoped to obtain the remainder of the cubes once and for all.

Chapter 46

The instant she touched the old book, Liz was transported back in time, at least in the visual sense, while a flood of images came her way. What transpired over a period of months entered her mind in seconds, and the details simply fell into place as though she had the front row seat at a movie.

First, the vision of a man in a derby style hat, well-dressed for the period, conversed with a jeweler about creating thirteen various gemstones in the shapes of cubes, about one inch square. Though he considered it an unusual request, the jeweler agreed for a very fair price as the man looked around his shop, admiring the décor. As they talked about it, the jeweler revealed he built the shop with help from some neighbors, designing the interior himself with a variety of wallpaper, paint schemes, and multi-colored tiles.

"I just purchased a hotel in French Lick," the well-dressed man revealed during their second meeting, soon after the jeweler began ordering the gems necessary to create such cubes. "Could I possibly hire you to design a small room there?"

"In the hotel?" the jeweler inquired, writing some information down in a journal atop his store counter without looking up.

"Actually close to the hotel, rather than inside. My colleagues and I want a place to hold our meetings each month."

"The same friends on the order forms for these cubes?"

The well-dressed man hesitated before answering, crafting his words carefully.

"Yes. The same people."

"A list of which person wants which color would help me complete the invoices more thoroughly."

"I'll get to work on that. About the room?"

The jeweler finally looked up from his ledger.

"I'd like a look at it before I give you an answer. This project here will keep me plenty busy once the raw gems arrive."

"We'll make it worth your while. And you'll have plenty of time because our meetings require some planning."

At the mention of meetings the jeweler perked up, looking for additional information that never came.

Within a week the jeweler saw the already hollowed out path, which led to a room beneath the hotel, reluctantly agreeing to complete the cubes and create a magnificent meeting room, all in secret. Believing they were some kind of secretive group, like the Freemasons, the jeweler could only assume that the cubes provided some sort of symbolic membership.

Already harboring suspicions about the group, the jeweler asked a lawyer friend to check into the identities of the men once he possessed all thirteen names. He carried out his assignment, often working on the room during the daytime with leftover materials he purchased from the Cassini Mosaic Tile Company that put down new flooring in the West Baden Springs Hotel. He placed an order with them for more tiles once he knew the required amount to finish the secretive room beneath the Woxley Hotel. Both exhausting and time consuming, the room took up much of his daytime, leaving only an hour or so each evening for work on the customized gems. With no time for anything except work and sleep, the man used the generous checks he received each week as incentive to continue the arduous labor.

Luckily for him someone had already shored up the walls of the tunnel leading to the underground room. The braces looked like those of a mine shaft based on what the jeweler had seen in book illustrations. Carting tools and materials to the room from the hotel's basement wasn't particularly easy, but he devised a four-wheeled cart that allowed him to push items to and from the room with relative ease. The hard ground provided little resistance to the cart's wheels, and he seldom required more than one trip per day based on the required time to lay the tiles.

When his attorney friend finally got back with him, the jeweler learned that all thirteen of the men were wealthy and influential. Some held political positions, while others owned companies, or received their riches from inheritances. While it wasn't specifically clear how the group met, the lawyer said they were all from the New England area, possibly forming some kind of alliance in a country club. In 1918, many of the rich and famous still traveled to West Baden Springs and

French Lick to gamble and partake in the mineral waters. The idea of creating a gentleman's club so close to the grounds certainly wasn't out of the question.

After the first ever break-in at his shop occurred, the jeweler decided he truly couldn't trust anyone, because he hadn't laid eyes on most of the men paying his salary. With the names now transferred to a leather-bound book, the jeweler suspected the men were looking to keep their names away from everyone in town, particularly the jeweler. He kept the book in several hiding spots outside of his shop, but he finally decided to place it in the one spot where none of the thirteen men would think to look for it.

One morning he placed it beneath several items in the heavy cart and wheeled the last of his supplies toward the secret room. Everything was now finished except for a few pieces of trim, and the jeweler had already set up a meeting for his final payment from the man who contracted him. By this time all thirteen cubes were masterfully crafted and sitting inside his shop, but he suspected the wealthy men already knew this because he often found himself being studied or followed by strangers.

He never let on that he knew the men were keeping tabs on him, and as the jeweler reached the underground room for the last time in a contractor capacity, he reveled in the masterpiece of a room he created. Based on the specifications laid out by the man who contracted him, the jeweler began to suspect the room's purpose wasn't simply for meetings, but rather for some kind of ritual. While the specified centerpiece was eerie in its own right, the wall-sized clock along the far wall disturbed him greatly. He created a functional clock, just as the work order specified, though the man wanted no winding device attached to the mechanism. How was a clock ever supposed to work if it couldn't be wound to keep time?

Even stranger were the thirteen small, square indentions the men wanted placed along the clock's face. Twelve of them were centered in the Roman numerals that represented the hourly digits, but one was centrally located directly beneath the hour and minute hands. If he were mentally challenged the jeweler couldn't possibly have missed the connection between the cubes and the specified indentions in the clock. Considering there were thirteen cubes for as many indentions, and the cubes would fit inside the housings perfectly, he began to worry that something sinister was brewing. Thirteen spokes, equally spaced, emerged from the centerpiece along the strange wheel laid upon the floor, as though each man had an assigned spot to stand. He couldn't tell anyone his suspicions because there wasn't any proof, but he knew the wealthy men meant to collaborate on something evil.

Oil lanterns lit the room, providing light enough for him to work by on a daily basis. Although electricity existed in Orange County in 1918, particularly at the hotels, the jeweler didn't particularly care to take a chance on his health by stringing together lights with his limited experience in the recent technology. He also didn't want to leave any more traces of his presence than necessary to people coming and going from the hotel above him.

Once the room was sufficiently lighted, the jeweler removed the book from beneath his materials, carrying it with him to the clock's face. About a foot to the right of the center he'd built a secret compartment when creating the clock's face, which remained perfectly concealed because thin seams ran horizontally and vertically across the entire wall. Creating a small, secret compartment that fit into the natural scheme was simple for a craftsman of gems and interior rooms.

No handles or hinges showed on the outside of the compartment, and the little door only swung out a few inches. Opening somewhat like a modern day public mailbox, requiring help from a screwdriver or a thin, sturdy device, the secret compartment provided just enough room to conceal a narrow item such as a book. Once the jeweler hid the book, he completed the room's trim, completing the last of his contracted work. He packed his tools and all of the excess materials into the cart before wheeling them back to the hotel basement over a hundred yards away. Wiping the dust from his hands, he exited the basement and went directly to his store where he conducted business as usual. His final meeting with the man who contracted him was to take place the following morning at the Woxley Hotel, which he now believed one of the thirteen men owned.

The jeweler would never make it to the meeting, or see the light of day the following morning in French Lick. He knew the fate awaiting him, but he wasn't going to stick around to see it come to fruition. After cashing the checks regularly at the bank, he saved the latest one for both traveling money and proof of evil deeds if necessary. He hadn't dared clear out his savings, or venture into the bank other than to cash the checks because the men were monitoring his activities. Instead, the jeweler cleared out the cash drawer at his shop and took some of the money he'd received from the cashed checks and left town rather hastily after making certain no one followed him into the evening.

Making no obvious moves, the jeweler didn't buy a train ticket, or even remove his horse from the barn. Henry Ford's production lines had made the automobile a luxury not only owned by the rich, but still not owned by everyone. Considering the jeweler basically found all of his needs met within the county, he saw no reason to purchase a Model T in the near future. He figured some kind soul would find his horse and tend to it because he needed his disappearance to remain a complete mystery until he chose to return.

He chose to return a week later, after catching a train a few towns over and staying in Indianapolis where the population alone kept him safely hidden. Just as he left, the jeweler returned in the dead of night when only lanterns and a full moon illuminated the streets of French Lick. Though he considered it dangerous, he decided to check on his shop first.

Strangely, he found everything intact, right down to the newspapers piled up on the front landing. He peered through the window, seeing everything the same inside, except that the area where he kept the thirteen gems appeared slightly disturbed. He kept them locked inside a cabinet behind his counter just above shoulder level. The small door was left open as though someone hastily took what they came for and vacated the shop.

Turning to the stack of newspapers, he tucked them under his arm, realizing no major local news had reached him in Indianapolis. Briskly walking from the shop, he headed toward the Woxley Hotel, opening one of the newspapers simply to cover his face when he noticed a story about a local attorney still missing. Immediately stiffening from the realization of his departure's consequences, the jeweler went on to read that Benjamin Land, his lawyer, was the missing person in question.

"Oh, no," the jeweler mouthed his words in silence, knowing his lawyer possessed a spare key to his shop because they often shared a drink after their workdays concluded.

Picking up his pace, he headed directly to the hotel, unconcerned with his own well-being, figuring his friend was a pawn in this evil scheme, meant to lure him out of hiding. Immediately feeling regret for leaving town and placing Land in peril, he left the shadows and crossed streets when necessary to reach the hotel quickly.

When he arrived at the front door, however, he found it bolted shut with a sign that stated the hotel was closed for business. Positive that financial issues hadn't shut down the business, the jeweler peered into a few windows, seeing most, if not all of the furniture still inside. Nearly two-dozen hotels existed between the towns of West Baden Springs and French Lick, but competition was never a reason why one shut its doors. Gambling ensured that the hotels were typically overrun with guests, and the West Baden Springs Hotel in particular was being leased to the military, meaning none of its seven-hundred plus rooms were available.

No, something other than financial woes closed the Woxley.

Returning to the street for a better vantage point so he could figure out where to break in, the jeweler was surprised to hear a voice behind him.

"I hear it's scheduled for demolition," a man carrying a newspaper stated.

Recognizing the strolling man as a local, the jeweler immediately relaxed instead of fleeing into the streets, which would certainly draw unwanted attention. He decided to prod for a bit more information before attempting to make his way into the hotel.

"Demolition? This building isn't even ten years old."

"The owner closed for business yesterday morning and left town. I hear he slated Rudy Halstead and his boys to tear it down this week."

Now fully believing something was amiss with this building before him, the jeweler bid the pedestrian a good evening before examining the building more closely. He took notice that all of the doors had their handles wrapped with chains to deter any trespassing before demolition began. Normally a move to keep looters from breaking in, the chains likely harbored a secret in this instance.

It took another five minutes, but the jeweler found a window along the ground level that wasn't secured, leading into the kitchen area. Not far from the doorway to the basement, the kitchen provided him with a lantern which he lit with some nearby matches once he safely moved from the view of any nearby windows.

After working extensively for months on the secret room, the jeweler knew the layout of the hotel, particularly the area near the basement entrance. While he carried out his work the basement was partitioned into an area for him and another for the kitchen employees because they needed access to their stored goods below.

He found the basement entrance wide-open, as though someone had made a hasty retreat from the secret passage. Feeling a bit less daring about seeing the rest of his completed project again, the jeweler pressed onward, knowing whatever plans the thirteen men created were carried out within the small chamber.

He soon reached the halfway point through the tunnel with only the lantern to guide him. A strange odor crossed his nose, but he pressed forward, finding an eerie orange glow ahead of him when he drew closer to the secret room. Freezing in his tracks when he realized the light was slowly pulsating, the jeweler wondered if someone remained inside, creating the ebb and flow of the unusual illumination. Now able to see, he set the lantern down a safe distance from the doorway just ahead of him to keep from giving away his presence. He practically tiptoed during the last leg of his walk to the doorway before cautiously peering around the edge.

"Impossible," he muttered when he spied the clock, in essence the entire wall, on the opposite end creating the rhythmic pulsating glow.

Completely fixated on the clock, the jeweler stepped into the room, wondering what on earth transpired between the time he completed the room and the present. It took nearly a minute before he finally panned the room for any further clues, making a grisly discovery on the floor that took his breath.

"Ben," he said under his breath when he found the body of his friend on the floor, chained to the centerpiece by the ankle.

The smell of death accompanied his friend, indicating whatever evil deed took the attorney's life happened a day or two prior. Not wishing to handle a body, even his friend's, any more than necessary the jeweler conducted a cursory examination rather quickly, finding two red marks near the man's heart that appeared to have been inflicted through some form of piercing. Feeling a tear reach his eye, the jeweler gently set Land's body atop the ground, deciding only one way to avenge his friend remained.

Standing, he walked with a purpose toward the hidden compartment, unsure whether he dared touch the unnatural clock to retrieve his log. He timidly tapped it with a few fingers in the same fashion people might test for a live electrical circuit. When no harm came to him, the jeweler pressed one palm against the clock, finding it warm and dry despite its surroundings. It continued to glow and pulsate without pause, powered by some unseen force that the jeweler could only assume was the devil himself.

He managed to undo the trim holding the compartment in place by hand before opening it to retrieve the book inside. Somehow the book felt different, almost sturdier in some way, but the jeweler didn't have time to study it while bathed in the strange orange light. Taking up the lantern, he headed back to the surface, ready to find the men responsible for his friend's death and seek some measure of revenge.

***

"Oh my God!" Liz stammered when she finally broke free of the complete trance.

Her three concerned colleagues cupped her by the elbows to steady her as her mind raced to process so much information.

"What did you see?" Teakon asked first.

"What *didn't* I see?" she countered. "There's *so* much about all of this that we didn't know."

After all four of them ordered drinks, including coffee and soda pop, Liz recounted the events leading up to the jeweler recovering his personal ledger.

"So the jeweler was never the one who got killed?" Teakon asked, obviously recalling his uncle's research indicating that was the case.

"No, he let people believe he was dead or missing," Liz replied. "He eventually learned that his book was part of the curse and used it to track down the men who possessed the cubes. And after he located the time cube he asked a police friend in Chicago to keep it safe for all time."

"No pressure in that," Greene said sarcastically.

"If he was tracking down the cubes," Julie said thoughtfully, "he didn't get very far."

Liz took a relaxing sip of her latte before continuing.

"I don't know what happened to him," she confessed. "But I would dare say he put things in motion that we're still carrying out today."

"And what happened to that room?" Teakon inquired. "And the hotel?"

"They tore down the hotel," Liz commented. "The basement was filled in and a new building was erected. It was like the hotel never existed."

A concerned look crossed Greene's face as a realization struck him.

"That's the place Clouse has been toying with the last few months," he revealed slowly, struggling to remember the details. "He didn't think I knew, but he asked his construction buddy to do some digging around some old shop."

"He shouldn't go in there," Liz said, shuddering at the thought of her employer meeting his end in such an evil place. "Those thirteen men left in a hurry for a reason in 1918. If this collector of the cubes lures Clouse in there with the time cube it could literally be the end of mankind as we know it."

"Did you see what would happen?" Greene asked.

"No, but it's not good. Those men planned to have untold power and wealth with those cubes and meet like some kind of fraternity, but they left in a hurry once the cubes were created. Something terrible happened in that room."

"Other than a man being silenced," Teakon said. "Or sacrificed."

"We need to get back to Indiana before Clouse does something foolish," Liz insisted, looking to Greene. "He doesn't know what he's messing with."

"He isn't stupid," Greene countered. "He knows to keep any potential pawns out of play."

"You don't understand," Liz said vehemently. "I had a dream last night where I saw Clouse in his hotel, and again inside this secret chamber. It didn't mean anything to me at first, but now I think he means to meet these people there *very* soon. And he's walking into a trap."

"Damn it," Greene muttered. He directed his attention to Teakon and Julie, who both appeared gravely concerned that the inevitable confrontation was occurring so soon. "You two take that book and keep it safe. It's the only valuable asset we have left at this point. Don't make contact with anyone."

Both nodded in understanding.

Fifteen minutes later the two duos parted ways, but Greene apparently wasn't content with Liz's visions.

"If Clouse confronts these people he'll have help," he insisted. "He's got bodyguards, and he can always call Clay Branson."

"You don't understand," Liz stated as Greene drove them west, directly to Indiana. "Yes, he can counteract the goons, but my nemesis will know the truth and Clouse won't be able to protect his family, and the last cube, all by himself."

Liz didn't want to say too much, but it was as though the redheaded man had somehow established a link to Clouse as well, even though Clouse was not an admitted psychic. Of course any dealings with the dead, or their spirits, left one more susceptible to interactions with the unseen world.

Short of a disaster, they would make it back to the West Baden Springs Hotel by nightfall. Liz still worried that they lacked time enough to assist Clouse, or prepare for whatever battle he planned to virtually carry out by himself.

Her body felt like a bundle of nerves because the world was going to change drastically the next day, for much better or far worse.

Chapter 47

After a virtually sleepless night Clouse made his way out of bed just after dawn. Jane, who hadn't slept very well either, took hold of his hand, but he gently pulled it away, assuring her he would return soon. Without waking the children, Clouse dressed and walked out the front door toward his truck with very little daylight to guide him.

He made the hour-long drive from Bloomington to West Baden, finally stopping at a diner for some coffee and a small breakfast. Basically killing time, Clouse barely touched his eggs and pancakes, occasionally sipping on his coffee and looking to his watch, which barely progressed toward the imposed nine o'clock meeting time.

He continually looked behind him, and outside, wondering if anyone was monitoring his every move. Though nothing obvious appeared, Clouse still felt violated, like some unseen force continued to stalk him. Knowing about the psychic, he tried to direct his thoughts toward anything other than the meeting or the last of the cubes. It came rather naturally for his mind to dwell upon his past, considering he was entering a perilous experience. He thought about his former life on the fire department, occasionally fingering the Maltese cross that still hung on a gold chain around his neck.

Some bonds lingered in part, including the brotherhood of firefighters he worked with in Bloomington. He left a job that he considered far more dangerous than being a billionaire, but that notion was soon disproven. Clouse never asked for trouble, but it came looking for him very close to home. Unfortunately a man he trusted and loved like a grandfather ultimately betrayed him, creating all sorts of controversy that surrounded Clouse and created all sorts of urban legends around Orange County.

After leaving the diner, Clouse drove to his hotel, wanting to take one last walk through the atrium. Still dim because the sun was barely rising at this point in the morning, the atrium was filled with comfortable furniture as usual, but not people. For the first five minutes the atrium was all his until an employee who worked the check-in desk walked through to relieve someone at her post.

Most of the shops opened later in the morning, which left the entire hotel eerily quiet. The silence reminded Clouse of the days during the hotel's renovation after it neared complete ruin. He arrived to work, seeing marked improvement inside the building and along the grounds each morning, greeted by a peaceful silence through all six stories.

Deciding not to linger much longer, Clouse visited several other spots around the two adjoining small towns, constantly monitoring his surroundings. Not one time did he catch anyone spying on him, ducking behind buildings, trees, or shrubs the few times he stole a glance. When he finally parked beside the remains of the torn down shop, Clouse stepped from his truck to find a strong breeze passing through the area. Gray clouds created an overcast sky, and he finally felt his ordeal had come full circle, as though a sign from above.

He figured he needed some spiritual assistance if he was going to survive the impending meeting.

Clouse had asked Niemeyer to dig out only the corner where the old basement door led into the tunnel this last time. Instead of leaving a ladder behind, Niemeyer simply created a sloped surface in which visitors could navigate the dirt surface on foot. Considering he was asked to excavate the corner at dawn, Niemeyer did well to complete the job and leave the area with his heavy equipment. In no capacity did Clouse want his friend lingering at the site with such dangerous people coming to town.

Standing over the descent, Clouse felt a knot form in his stomach as he looked at his watch.

8:56 a.m.

He felt alone, but knew in good conscience Todd Parish wasn't going to let him down. He also placed phone calls to Clay Branson and Special Agent Harlan Stone, knowing both of them wanted a measure of revenge against their respective enemies who were sure to make an appearance. He simply told them the location of the meet and asked that they remain in the vicinity without following him inside. Between the four of them, not knowing what each of the others planned to do, Clouse hoped they might stand a chance against an unknown amount of assailants and their plan. Having knowledge of the area only helped Clouse so much because he was about to confine himself in a small chamber with unforeseen circumstances.

Something near the slightly ajar door to the tunnel caught his eye, and Clouse squinted to see an orange jack-o-lantern against the light brown background. Knowing full well his friend didn't place the gutted vegetable there, Clouse felt certain the sinister person he was about to meet knew something of his past. He took notice of the tiny flame dancing between the facial openings on the pumpkin before turning hastily to grab a small box from the backseat of his crew-cab truck.

Clouse carefully descended the sloped dirt, keeping both hands beneath the fairly heavy box. By no means stupid enough to walk into an obvious trap in the first place, he knew from experience to always have a form of insurance that made it necessary to keep him alive. While he hoped Parish and the two less familiar men planned to back him, they couldn't provide guarantees on his safety.

He gave the jack-o-lantern a light kick out of spite before stepping through the door and walking into the tunnel. Already several lanterns were lit, hanging at intervals along the manmade walkway as though someone who knew his way around the supposedly secret area awaited him inside.

His eyes didn't truly adjust to the darkness before he made his way to the chamber entrance, stepping inside to see the décor for the first time, along with the pulsating orange glow that guided him the last part of his journey. He purposefully told Parish to tell him nothing about the tunnel or the room, because he didn't want either of them to gain knowledge that the psychic might detect when the inevitable confrontation occurred.

Taking a look around, Clouse sensed he was alone as the wall continued to bask him in its glow, like a neon light from the seedy end of a big city. He observed a centerpiece in the middle of the room that appeared large enough to store items inside. The light made it difficult to tell for certain, but Clouse thought the dozens of wooden slats that comprised the centerpiece appeared recent. If the wood was original, he felt certain all kinds of wildlife and bugs would have contributed to wear and tear, if not complete destruction, over the past century. And, strangely enough, he felt certain an odor of freshly cut wood penetrated the otherwise stale, musty smells of the chamber.

Setting the box atop the centerpiece that reached his waistline, Clouse heard footsteps approaching from the tunnel behind him. He turned, hoping to lay eyes on the man responsible for endangering the world and making his life a living hell recently.

Instead of finding just one person walking through the doorway into the chamber, however, he found a man wearing business casual with two gunmen in suits on either side. They looked thick, like ex-military types who made a paycheck doing unspeakable things to strangers without asking any questions. Neither displayed a firearm, but Clouse knew each harbored a sidearm beneath their black sport coats.

"Mr. Clouse," the man stated, rather than asked, because he appeared confident that he knew his adversary very well.

"And who might you be?" Clouse asked, trying to size up the man with dark hair, wondering if the psychic lingered nearby.

If so, he might make an easy target for Stone or Branson, who knew exactly what the redheaded man looked like. Taking the man out of play made the situation markedly easier for Clouse, who could in turn lie or stall for time. Of course Clouse possessed no means of communication, which meant he placed a great deal of faith in his unofficial team.

"You should probably concern yourself more with completing my collection, rather than identifying me," the stranger said as the two men stood stiffly by his side, still not reaching for their firearms.

"Where is your collection?" Clouse inquired, seeing no containers, and seriously doubting this man was going to chance carrying any of the cubes loosely, or in pockets.

"Close. Now, can we get down to this, or do I need to start murdering your friends and family one at a time?"

Clouse wasn't positive this man's voice was the one he heard over the phone the previous evening. He stepped forward, prompting the two men to reach into their sport coats for their firearms. Clouse never intended to pose a threat, but he wanted to verify that the two men weren't just present for showmanship.

"Not a wise move," the stranger said, a rather arrogant smirk crossing his lips.

"You're right about that," Clouse retorted, "but not in the way you're thinking."

***

When Harlan Stone received a phone call from Paul Clouse asking for help in what sounded like a final confrontation with the men who turned both of their lives upside-down the past few months, he nearly turned down the offer. Not only was he lucky to have a job, but now the very people he worked for kept him under constant scrutiny and watched him closely whenever he worked in the office. While most of their suspicions began when Stone's partner was found dead in a desert, things only grew worse for the agent when Stewart was found dead in his office and the body mysteriously disappeared from the funeral home shortly thereafter.

Stone ultimately decided to make the journey to Indiana for the sake of clearing his name, and hopefully laying eyes on his former boss again. Even before he was provided with hints and details about what Clouse and his employees did during their down time, Stone knew deep down that Stewart wasn't truly dead. All of the partial truths and carefully crafted fibs he told during interviews with more experienced FBI agents might actually pan out and clear his name if he brought them Stewart.

At this point he didn't particularly care if the man came willingly, or zipped inside a body bag.

Being highly unfamiliar with the town of French Lick, Stone wasn't particularly sure what vantage point best provided a good view of the area Clouse indicated through a text message. While visibility played a major role in the agent's strategy, the ability to act quickly also factored into his plan.

He ultimately chose the old apartment building that loomed over the excavation site, claiming his spot in time to watch Clouse navigate the slope and enter the doorway. Stone wasn't concerned until three rather unfriendly, well-dressed men entered the same way a few minutes later. From his spot on the second story, Stone turned to find the nearest stairs to follow them into the tunnel for a closer look.

Instead, he found a gun trained on his chest, held by the very man he worked under for a short period of time.

"Surprised to see me?" Alan Stewart asked, his appearance a bit less fresh and lively these days.

"Not really. Some nice people brought me up to speed on your recent nefarious activities. What I can't understand is why anyone would bring you back from the dead."

"That's a pretty big word for someone from your parts."

"You're no better than my boss in New Mexico if you think my people are just stupid hicks."

Stewart gave a brief laugh, his expression indicating he dared not ever underestimate the agent from Texas.

"To satisfy your curiosity, I had information they still needed on a loose end that needed cleaned up, which is why they brought me back. Having something people want is good leverage, and a good way to stay alive. Too bad you don't have anything of value to share."

Stone knew he meant the last agent that he and Clay Branson left stranded when they first entered California during the summer. Of course the man was located and killed before he could ever speak of his experiences to anyone. Stone wanted to punch Stewart in the face so badly that his right fist instinctively opened and clenched slowly, but repeatedly. Fear for his life and anger at himself for letting Stewart sneak up on him provided some balance for the hatred he wanted to direct at his former boss.

Apparently the short period the man spent amongst the deceased altered his physical state, because his flesh still favored a light purple hue. Stone couldn't immediately place it, but the man's eyes appeared different as well. The eyeballs in general seemed to have sunk into the facial structure a bit, and the whites of the eyes themselves now carried a permanent yellow hue that made Stewart look something like a zombie.

"Boss, you're not looking so good," Stone stated, his fingers within striking distance of his sidearm if Stewart looked away for even a second.

Stewart replied with a cagy stare, not amused by the sarcasm from his former agent

"It would serve you better to keep your remarks to yourself," he suggested. "You were all too willing to rise through the ranks of the FBI until you needed to get your hands dirty."

"In my defense, you weren't very forthcoming with my job description."

"And now you're going to be buried six feet under because you don't have an ace in the hole like I did."

"Did?"

"My boss got his information, but he kept me around to make sure no one like you interfered with his plan."

A question suddenly occurred to the agent.

"Why would you even do his bidding? You could just leave all of this behind and escape before he tries to kill you again."

"Money, first and foremost. I don't exactly work for the Bureau anymore. Besides, if I tried to leave, he'd know where I went and find me. He knows everything about everyone."

"You mean his psychic does."

"No. *He* does."

Stewart stiffened the gun once more, aiming it deliberately toward the agent's heart. Stone didn't have time to process exactly what his former boss meant by his last statement.

"You've already heard too much, Stone. It's time for you to join your predecessor in the afterworld."

"So that's how it has to end when you discover your employees have a conscience?"

"Afraid so."

Refusing to simply stand there and take a bullet like an animal being put down, Stone started to reach for his sidearm, prepared to die instantly by forcing Stewart's hand. At least his murder would allow his wife to collect on his life insurance and pension from the federal government and be set for life.

Instead of a flash of light that meant the end of him, Stone saw the tip of a blade protrude through the front of Stewart's throat. It took him a second to collect himself and realize that a sword had run through the former Deputy Director's neck, severing his head from his body before the man's head fell to the floor with a thumping sound. As the body followed suit, Stone saw Clay Branson running toward the nearest stairwell to continue his ascent.

He was dressed in the traditional ninja garb, neck to toe in black cloth because he wasn't wearing any mask.

"Thank me later," Branson called without turning.

"I had this under control!"

Branson still didn't bother looking back, as though a man possessed to find something, or someone, inside the building.

"Well, that was kind of anticlimactic," Stone complained in a murmur, looking down to Stewart's decapitated body, regretting only that he didn't gain a full measure of revenge against the man.

Still, Stone would be free and clear of scrutiny from his own employers, hopefully regaining his old position in a Texas setting. He lost himself in positive thought momentarily until he looked out the window and spotted an unmarked van pulling up to the site with several armed men seated inside. They waited inside the vehicle, but Stone's instincts told him they were going to enter the tunnel sooner than later to make certain things went smoothly for their mysterious employer.

"I should just leave and call it a day," Stone muttered, instinctively reaching for his firearm instead.

Chapter 48

Todd Parish hadn't spent the past few months standing by idly, hoping when the right time came that he happened to be in the right place. Benefitted by the knowledge that it was only a matter of time before their adversaries acquired all of the cubes, Parish spent time examining the tunnel and chamber. From there, he built a box tall and wide enough to accommodate him comfortably, standing upright in the tunnel and perfectly camouflaged by the dim lighting and the surrounding dirt.

One simple text message from his employer the previous day set him in motion. Already knowing where the final meeting was destined to take place, Parish simply used a secret, secondary entrance to the tunnel to gain access without anyone noticing, even before Niemeyer carved out the main entrance through the old basement. Utilizing the old apartment building, Parish created his own small passage that literally dropped into the center of the tunnel, allowing him to slip into the virtually invisible box.

He held nothing but respect for his employer. Though Clouse hardly knew him at the time, he gave Parish a job when the best prospect in his future was working at his father's factory, hoping to someday work his fingers to the bone and inherit a company that barely stayed afloat financially much of the time.

The fact that Parish had worked previously as a bodyguard, coupled with his local ties, inevitably led Clouse to seek him out. And though Parish stayed almost exclusively with the family's two children, Clouse didn't feel right about keeping him in the dark regarding the constant danger around all of them. Little by little Parish learned the truth about the cubes and the motivations for various people to possess them.

Because Clouse trusted him, and because he was brought up to respect the people in his life, Parish remained completely loyal to his employer, even when others lacked the courage to stand by him. In turn, Clouse always provided Parish with the truth and the option of backing out if the situation felt wrong, or it taxed his moral convictions.

Not a trained killer by any means, Parish certainly knew his way around guns, and he felt perfectly willing to fire one at a person to protect his boss. Very well protected by the vertical box he constructed, Parish waited until Clouse passed, followed by the three unfamiliar men a few minutes later. He'd crafted the box from wood, but left a thin steel sheet along the exposed areas of the exterior for his own protection. Able to keep bullets from passing through, he also hoped the metal layer might keep the redheaded psychic from plucking his thoughts.

Carrying his AR-15 assault rifle with him when he left the safety of the protective box, Parish took several quiet steps toward the chamber, listening to the conversation between Clouse and the leader of the three men. He quickly detected that any negotiations weren't going Clouse's way, and when the two henchmen reached for their hidden firearms, Parish was already in position to make certain no harm came to his boss.

Hoping the tunnel muffled any gunfire, rather than amplifying it, he sucked in a breath and held it until he took aim at the left bodyguard's head. Exhaling as he pulled the trigger, he watched the man's head spew a red mist as he immediately trained his weapon on the second threat, hitting him squarely in the chest when he turned around, gun only partially drawn from his sport coat. Just to ensure the leader couldn't pull a firearm, or otherwise threaten Clouse, Parish fired a single round into his kneecap, dropping him to the ground where he immediately clutched the wounded appendage.

Parish sensed the man wasn't very hardened in combat based on the way he moaned and groaned, as though a bullet to the knee was his first major wound. He held the assault rifle in a ready position, walking with purpose toward the fallen man while Clouse walked over to the stranger, still looking very uncertain.

"It can't be this simple," he said, finally standing over the man. "Who are you really?"

Refusing to answer, the man simply continued to clutch his knee and rock back and forth in pain. Parish checked the two henchmen to make certain they were no longer a threat as Clouse kicked at the man's wound, drawing a pained cry.

"Tell me who you really are."

Parish noticed the same thing his boss had a few minutes earlier. There were no cursed cubes anywhere to be found, and he felt certain whoever possessed them wasn't going to let them out of sight so close to acquiring his objective.

Kneeling down, Parish checked the man for any firearms, finding nothing on his side or hidden along his belt. Satisfied the man wasn't carrying a weapon, he nodded to Clouse.

"Get yourself hidden, Todd, in case there are more of them," Clouse ordered.

"Yes, sir," Parish replied without hesitation, returning to the hallway as his employer continued to question the injured man.

Based on the way Clouse's voice barely carried through the tunnel, Parish didn't expect any police involvement because his gunfire probably went completely unheard. Anyone whose ears picked up the noise would probably mistake it for construction work anyhow, leaving them in the clear.

Parish hated being forced to take a human life, but he wasn't going to let any harm come to Clouse. Think of the greater good, he told himself, trying to soften the idea of going against some of the morals he was taught by his parents and the church during his youth. He decided to ask for forgiveness later, after his colleagues and millions of people were safe from the lunatic who wanted to bring the thirteen cubes together.

Opening the heavy door to his camouflaged box, Parish wondered what kind of madman risked destroying the world as people knew it for power. When the door swung open, he found his answer staring him in the face.

"Hi there," the redheaded man said, thrusting a stun gun into the bodyguard's chest, rendering him physically helpless.

Parish felt incredible pain shoot through his body as his muscles betrayed him, allowing him to slump to the ground in a heap once the trigger was released. For the next five to ten seconds, the man could do whatever he chose to with Clouse's only current form of protection.

***

Clay Branson reached the roof to find a man sitting Indian style with several familiar, sharp weapons placed beside him. The old Japanese man kept his hands close to his chest, obviously meditating and mentally preparing himself for the impending battle. Nosagi certainly hadn't hidden from him, purposely standing on the edge of the roof for Clay to spot from anywhere on the ground. Assisting Stone delayed him only a few seconds, and Clay felt certain Alan Stewart meant to kill the agent, so he provided assistance on his way to the top of the vacated building.

Atop this high roof, far back from the road, no residents or drivers passing by were going to spot the skirmish about to begin.

"My sole purpose," Nosagi said without opening his eyes in reasonably sound English, "is to keep you preoccupied so my employer can carry out his business below."

"You have my undivided attention," Clay growled, taking one step forward.

Completely flat, the rooftop was slightly less than half the size of a soccer field, providing no obstructions other than the air conditioning unit in the far corner. Clay had done battle on rooftops before, and while many of his confrontations threatened his very life, none of them held the personal meaning of this brewing altercation. The man ultimately responsible for three deaths of people directly related to Clay and countess other people he had never met remained seated half-way across the roof.

"Is that what your life is now?" Clay asked. "Being paid to murder people for money?"

"It's what my life was *always* about, dear boy," Nosagi answered, finally opening his eyes with a neutral countenance that served only to infuriate Clay all the more. "You were just too blind to see it."

"I was a teenager when you took me to Japan," Clay said, battling inwardly to control his emotions, realizing his mentor hadn't even mentioned the blonde as though his people were disposable. "You were the reason I straightened out my life, the reason I got married and had a son. And now I find out you were the one who took that all away from me? How could you?"

"Your uncle should have told you sooner."

"My uncle? He's not exactly where I'm placing the blame these days. If you wanted to train me alongside your assassination squad, fine, but I never knew any better. You didn't need to send your people after me and my family."

The thin smirk Nosagi had worn faded away instantly.

"Yes, I did. It was only a matter of time before you discovered the truth, and I couldn't carry out my work while looking over my shoulder constantly. I never thought you were skilled enough to overcome my best warriors."

"I practiced *every* single day," Clay stammered. "You taught me tradition, and that meant something to me. You were my mentor, my *sensei*, and for what? So you could murder my family in hopes that I would abandon those untruths and work for you?"

"More or less. But your development of a strong ethical code sent you packing instead."

"You left me with *nothing*. That country was nothing but a bad memory to me, so of course I returned home."

"And now we come full circle," Nosagi said, shifting his stance so he was kneeling instead of sitting directly on the rooftop.

Clay placed the few weapons in his hands atop the ground and assumed a kneeling position as well. Both men were about to engage in the tradition of *kuji-in*, which various warrior clans from Japan believed invoked powers, both mental and physical, to aid them in combat. Nine primary hand symbols were used by men and women trained like Clay and Nosagi, and Clay fully expected his mentor to use many of the same signs as some of the students who had already died trying to assassinate the police officer.

Kneeling completely, both men stared across the roof to one another, placing their fisted hands in front of them, leaning forward to respectfully bow, regardless of their personal feelings toward one another.

Clay went first, forming his fingers into a shape quite unusual to anyone else. Nothing like a gang sign, his fingers virtually meshed together, forming a symbol he had memorized years before. He held them to the left side of his chest, near the heart, for his adversary to see.

"*Rin*," he said aloud, his blue eyes boring into his mentor.

Rin is used to bring strength to the mind and body.

"*Retsu*," Nosagi countered, forming his fingers into a sword-like symbol.

He wriggled the symbol like a slithering snake, down from above his head before thrusting the imaginary sword forcefully toward Clay.

Retsu enables telekinetic powers in a ninja, allowing him to stun an opponent with a touch or shout.

"*Toh*," Clay stated, which allowed the warrior to reach a balance between liquid and solid states of the body.

He called upon that particular symbol primarily out of habit, especially since he continued to walk among the living after several of these deadly encounters.

"*Hei*," Nosagi said with the command of a battlefield general in his voice.

Considering the symbol was used to psychically mask one's presence to another, the irony wasn't lost on Clay, who formed a final symbol before him with both hands.

"*Zen*," he finished, hoping to bring enlightenment and understanding to himself about his opponent and their tradition before the battle found opportunity to kill him.

Nosagi plucked his sheathed sword from the ground beside him while Clay reached behind him, drawing his sword from the sheath attached to the small pack he wore like a backpack. Both men locked eyes before darting across the roof to engage in true mortal combat.

Chapter 49

Clouse continued questioning the man Parish shot, but no answers came his way. He struck and kicked at the wound, and the man did not even attempt to answer his questions, or even lie. To Clouse it seemed the man literally did not know the answers, as though he was simply another henchman in a long line of paid thugs.

To this point he had put the two nearby dead men out of his mind. Like Parish, he didn't condone murder, but in his defense he never asked to be the guardian of cursed objects either. He kept his focus on the present, trying to figure out where the cubes might be, and the surviving man's identity.

"Where are the cubes?" he asked for what seemed the hundredth time.

"Perhaps you're asking the wrong questions," a voice said from the chamber's doorway. "Or the wrong person."

Clouse looked up to find the redheaded man from the security footage at the bookstore standing in the doorway, pistol in hand. He suddenly wondered if he overlooked such a simple solution, that the man before him was the mastermind *and* the psychic. A bit of smoke and mirrors created the illusion that this man was simply a paid employee, or a reluctant assistant to some secluded villain.

"Jacob Savitch," he spoke the name aloud.

"You're better than I thought," Savitch replied with a cagy grin. "It's no wonder you protected the cubes so well."

He had lost some weight the past few months, possibly attributed to the grinding search for the cursed objects. Clouse still didn't see any of the cursed objects, which made him wonder where they resided, and exactly what Savitch planned to accomplish.

"This man is just another loose end," the redheaded psychic said, aiming the gun toward the fallen mercenary.

"No, please," the man pleaded, ignoring his injuries to put his hands up defensively.

"Too late for that," Savitch said, pulling the trigger and putting a bullet in the man's head to end his life.

"That wasn't necessary," Clouse stated.

"And you've never gotten blood on your hands?"

"Only in self-defense. I don't kill for pleasure."

"Nor do I. This is business, pure and simple. I'm simply eliminating some loose ends."

Clouse looked over the man's shoulder, hoping Parish might take him from behind.

"You're not looking for your bodyguard, are you?" Savitch asked with masked emotion. "I've already dealt with him."

Clouse started to take a step forward until the gun was pointed in his direction.

"He's subdued," Savitch confessed. "I might need him later. Maybe I'll even put him to work for me."

"Unlikely," Clouse grumbled.

"You're right. He's loyal to a fault, which will make him another loose end once I've gotten everything I need here."

"I get the feeling *everyone* is going to be a loose end. I'm no psychic, but I doubt even you know what the hell is going to happen when you put these things together."

"Do you?"

Savitch paused momentarily, and Clouse knew he was trying to read his thoughts. Clouse didn't know the answer, and he wasn't going to waste time putting up mental barriers.

"No, you don't," Savitch said with satisfaction.

Still training the gun loosely on Clouse, the red-headed man stepped in reverse toward the doorway, scooping up a small satchel from just beyond the threshold. Clouse wondered how Parish was holding up, but he wasn't in a position to check on his employee just yet. Instead, he watched Savitch take the pack to the center-piece and dump all twelve cubes in his possession atop the flat surface. Clouse had never seen so many of the shiny, cursed objects occupy one space before. He never dared bring them together, but he supposed they weren't dangerous when grouped without some kind of ritual.

"I take it you have the last cube," Savitch said casually as he took a handful of the cubes over to the clock embedded in the wall and began inserting them into the slots that were created specifically for them. "We wouldn't want anything to happen to your family."

"Like you care," Clouse replied sharply.

With each cube placed into a slot, something unusual occurred in the center of the room. From the bowl-like middle of the centerpiece a hologram with no specific source appeared, showing a natural disaster of sorts in only the color of the cube. A red cube depicted a ground-shattering earthquake, while a pearl white cube showed pounding rains the likes of which Clouse had experienced only a handful of times in his life. The display all occurred within a neutral gray outline of Earth, like some kind of futuristic sci-fi hologram aboard a starship. Strangely, it even provided authentic sounds that chilled Clouse to the bone because the destructive weather being displayed sounded equally fierce.

He doubted the world was literally falling apart around him, so the cubes were simply showing their hand, indicating what their part in the end of the world would be once they all came together.

"Why would you do this?" Clouse stammered, unwilling to believe anyone could willingly choose to wipe out mankind.

"You really don't remember me, do you?" Savitch asked quite seriously, turning around from his work momentarily to address Clouse personally. "It was *you* who put me in this position and gave me every bit of information I needed."

"No," Clouse muttered, unwilling to believe such a lie. "I would never."

"But you did," Savitch insisted. "You and I go way back, to the time when you first began work on the hotel."

Clouse's head began spinning as he tried to imagine how he and this young man shared any kind of bond. He wasn't sure he particularly cared, because if he didn't find a way out of this situation, the end of the world as he knew it was inevitable.

***

Stone felt like a man with no master and no particular loyalty to either side in this skirmish. Yes, he still worked for the FBI, but his colleagues hadn't exactly been endearing themselves to him lately. Stewart tried to kill him, not once, but twice, and nearly succeeded on both occasions. He didn't really owe Paul Clouse anything, because the man refused to trust him enough to reveal any details about his quest to the agent, even though Stone felt he had proven his worth sufficiently. Perhaps, Stone decided, his own actions hadn't exactly put him in a good light after all, but at this moment he might be able to change some opinions.

Or die trying.

Besides, no world meant no human race, and Stone cared truly and deeply for his family. He wasn't about to let petty squabbles with his agency or the people around him sway him into taking the worst action possible.

Based on the fact that Clay Branson rescued him from almost certain death twice, and Branson allied himself with Clouse, the agent decided to follow suit. As he darted along the windows toward a secondary stairwell, he noticed the sky graying severely outside. He didn't recall any severe weather forecasted, or even thunderstorms for that matter, and he'd made the effort to look when choosing his vantage point.

Even as he descended the stairs, barely hearing his boots hit the carpeted wood because he moved so quickly, Stone's mind raced for an idea to stop four or five armed men. It occurred to him that conventional methods would surely spell the end of him, so he considered ways to keep them from entering the tunnel instead.

Stone didn't consider himself on the level of a double agent or government spy when it came to survival and crafty ideas, but he was brought up to think resourcefully. Splitting time between a rural farm and the urban setting of Houston, Stone found a number of things that fascinated him as a boy. He dabbled in everything from electronics and computers to repairing farm equipment.

Despite his array of knowledge and developed skills, a rather simple solution occurred to him as he reached the bottom step on the ground floor. He headed to the back of the building, finding his own leased van from the rental company still parked behind the old apartment complex. He wanted a van specifically for potential surveillance purposes, but now he considered a different use for the vehicle that might stall the armed men and buy Clouse and anyone with him some time inside the tunnel.

Scurrying along the parking lot, Stone unlocked the van with the remote control and immediately opened the side door so he could open the middle window on the passenger's side. What he planned required a little bit of luck, and even if he succeeded there wasn't a guarantee he wouldn't be riddled with bullets before escaping the vehicle.

"Hope Clouse will cover the damage deposit," he muttered once the window ajar before jumping into the driver's seat.

He wasn't certain why the henchmen in the other van waited before entering the tunnel, but he suspected some kind of signal was arranged. Stone needed to get into place before that message was received, so he started the van and stomped on the gas. The tires spit up rocks and dirt before engaging the deteriorated parking lot surface, sending the vehicle lurching forward. Stone narrowly missed the apartment building's nearby corner in an effort to steer directly toward the tunnel, which stood about ten feet down a sharp decline in elevation.

Considering the entrance was just barely past the elevation drop, Stone slowed the van at the last possible second, hoping to drop the van down the ten foot drop without destroying it, landing the lengthy passenger side squarely in front of the tunnel. If he landed correctly, the van would block the entrance and provide him with a means of escape. Engaging several individuals with automatic weapons in a gunfight wasn't wise, but he prepared for such an event if his egress was blocked.

He barely shifted his eyes to see the shocked looks of the henchmen as the van flew over the embankment, landing hard, and awkwardly, atop the dirt mound beside the doorway. Stone felt his back jar from the impact, but adrenaline kicked in once he realized he had overshot the intended target.

"Shit," he muttered, throwing the van in reverse so he could better block the doorway.

As it stood, the van was merely an inconvenience to walk around, parked at an incline due to the sloped dirt mound. It immediately shifted, but the wheels didn't respond when he pressed on the gas pedal. They simply spun, unable to grip the dirt in the rear.

Stone yelled out several obscenities as he tried to rock the van from his seat, already feeling several pairs of irritated eyes locking on his position. In a matter of seconds they would draw their weapons and mow him down in a hail of gunfire. He couldn't imagine they possessed any fear of being heard or seen so far from the heart of downtown French Lick.

"Damn it!" he said under his breath as he tried putting the vehicle in forward and reverse.

Although his home state never saw snow accumulation, experience working in the eastern states provided him with knowledge of how to escape a snowdrift. Loose dirt, it seemed, wasn't a far cry from such extreme weather.

He rocked back and forth in his seat, hearing one wheeling spinning in the soil while the other made no sound at all, indicating it might be touching nothing except air. The embankment left by Niemeyer wasn't at all smooth or steady, making it difficult to get all four tires touching solid ground.

Two of the men, dressed in black military style pants and light jackets, stepped from the van with their weapons trained on Stone. Refusing to yield, he threw his weight against the back of the seat one last time while stepping on the gas, finally catching some dirt beneath the back tire that had been spinning in the air. Now the van literally flew backwards toward the entrance, forcing Stone to cut the wheel sharply before the vehicle hit the solid dirt wall in yet another useless position.

He couldn't afford another mistake because now four men were ready to yank him from the van and end his life without fanfare. The van responded to his hard turn of the steering wheel, and he barely applied the brakes in a timely manner, but the passenger side of the vehicle pressed directly against the tunnel entrance, creating a barrier. Though hardly impenetrable, the new wall would make it difficult to enter the tunnel without severe risk of being hit by gunfire from the four mercenaries.

Stone put the van in park, yanked out the keys, and used the remote to lock the entire van within one second. Already expecting bullets to hit the van like rainfall, he couldn't afford to dawdle a split-second in his escape attempt. Realizing the extent of his plan, the four men raised their weapons to fire before one of them spoke up and ordered them to hold their positions. Open gunfire was a greater risk after the commotion with the van, so he ordered them to gain an entry point to the van. Stone heard all of this as he was crawling out the already open side window, scrambling for his life in case the vocal henchman changed his mind.

In too much of a hurry to be concerned with style, Stone fell out of the side window, hitting the ground hard on his right shoulder. He groaned in pain but quickly regained his footing, doggedly running into the tunnel as he clutched his shoulder. Stone decided to see if any assistance awaited him inside, because raising his primary shooting arm wasn't going to be easy with the new injury. He was trained to shoot with his left hand, but against four heavily armed, military-trained men Stone didn't like his chances.

About a minute later he came across a prone body lying face down on the dirt path. Fearing he'd found his second casualty within the last ten minutes, Stone knelt down, reaching to check for signs of life when the person suddenly stirred, startling him. Parish turned to one side to get a look at the agent, unable to move too far because his hands and feet were bound with zip ties. A rag of some sort was stuffed into his mouth to keep him from speaking or calling for help. Stone fished his trusty pocket knife from a pocket and cut the bodyguard loose before pulling the rag loose.

"We need to help Mr. Clouse," Parish insisted immediately, though very quietly so Savitch didn't hear.

"Your boss is on his own," Stone said, immediately glancing toward the chamber easily within walking distance. "We have four armed men about to enter this tunnel and I can't hold them off by myself."

"That son-of-a-bitch used a Taser on me," Parish muttered angrily, looking toward the chamber, obviously wanting some measure of revenge.

"Those pissed off mercenaries up front are going to use live rounds on us if we let them get in this tunnel. I'm thinking that's our priority."

Parish nodded before he stood, looking along the ground for something. With his eyes already adjusted to the light, he found both his Glock and his AR-15 lying nearby where Savitch had discarded them. Scooping up the weapons, he motioned for Stone to lead the way toward the entrance. Though the agent still didn't feel great about his chances against the four men, he felt a little better having some backup with him. He suspected in a few minutes he was going to be pleasantly surprised or dead.

Chapter 50

Knowing he needed to overcome Nosagi's experience, Clay exchanged offensive and defensive attacks with his former teacher, realizing that being several decades younger didn't offer him much of a physical advantage. Perhaps it was an illusion, or Clay recalling the days of arduous training in Japan, but Nosagi hadn't appeared to lose a step.

Both men took turns swiping and slashing with their blades, but each countered the other without much issue, leaving their swordplay on equal footing. Clay leapt over a blade aimed at his feet, deciding to distance himself from Nosagi by carrying out a backflip, all while grasping his sword in his left hand.

Instead of giving chase, Nosagi threw a smoke bomb close to where he anticipated Clay landing, trying to disorient his former student. Already wise to the trick, Clay did not land squarely on his feet, choosing to tuck and roll instead, dodging a fatally aimed blow from his adversary's sword that would have pierced his heart. Immediately regaining his footing from the tuck and roll, Clay went for Nosagi's head, feet, and waistline in succession, each of his quick strikes strategically blocked.

Without warning Nosagi began sprinting toward the large air conditioning unit seated along the far corner. Clay gave chase, wondering if the man meant to lead him further away from the action, or simply escape to fight another day. Either way, Clay wasn't having any of it, because his feud with the man ended on this morning one way or another.

He gave chase, expecting his former mentor to cleverly leap over the side of the building with some plan to break his fall, or simply take the higher ground for an advantage. Instead, Nosagi ran to the edge of the unit and jumped to the closest edge of it, springing from the higher surface into a backflip as Clay drew dangerously close. Clay barely reacted to the sudden move in time when Nosagi sailed over him, thrusting his blade toward Clay's heart. Deflecting the potentially fatal blow, Clay turned to confront Nosagi, putting his back to the air conditioning unit as the wind picked up and the clouds turned ominously gray overhead. He sensed the new weather pattern was unnatural, but he was in no position to help Clouse inside the tunnel.

He chastised himself for distracting his mind, because any momentarily lapse in concentration gave Nosagi an advantage. Clay watched his adversary pull off the end of the sword, revealing a small chain from within the handle. Nosagi twirled the chain briefly before tossing the end at Clay's feet in an attempt to wrap his ankle and trip him. Narrowly avoiding the metal, Clay lifted his foot as though skipping rope before lunging at Nosagi with his blade pointed toward the man's chest. Nosagi deflected the blow with his own blade, all the while retrieving the chain with his free hand.

Instead of backing off, or trying a completely different offensive tactic, Nosagi flipped the chain toward Clay, who ducked to one side, realizing too late that the chain was aimed at his sword, and not his body. Like a frog's tongue catching a fly in midair, the chain removed Clay's sword from his grip, sending it well beyond his reach and behind Nosagi.

Clay immediately reached for the two *kama* located in the pack strapped to his back. With the appearance of small sickles, about a foot long with wooden handles, the weapons held short, slightly curved blades that tore into flesh or delivered a killing blow just as easily. Clay twirled both weapons in his hands with the dexterity of a cheerleader using a baton. Showmanship was wasted on a seasoned killer like Nosagi, but he needed the feel of the weapons in his hands to loosen up his fingers.

In the meantime Nosagi wrapped the chain in his left hand while holding the sword in the other. He swung the chain first, which Clay blocked with one *kama* while the other locked against the sword, placing them at a stalemate. Improvising, Clay freed one weapon from the chain, smacking his former *sensei* in the face with the wooden end before kicking him solidly in the gut. As Nosagi reeled, finally proving a tad slower, or more susceptible to fatigue, Clay landed the pointy end of the same *kama* in his forearm.

The weapon struck bone, but Nosagi immediately swung his sword toward Clay's forearm, forcing him to release the weapon altogether. In the closest thing to rage that Clay had ever seen from the man, he stiffly yanked the blade from his arm and threw it on the ground. Still holding the sword, he went on the attack as the winds swirled around them from the unforeseen, impending storm.

Parrying, slashing, and stabbing at one another for close to thirty seconds, neither man landed another blow until Nosagi gained a glancing slice of his sword along the outside of Clay's left leg.

Unlike his last battle, Clay experienced no taunting, because both men held to tradition, letting their actions speak for them. Neither of them had left anything unsaid and each knew the other's position. Their conflict spoke volumes as each went for numerous killing blows.

Left with only one weapon, Clay deflected several strikes, but found himself on the defensive, being backed toward the edge of the roof. When Nosagi used both hands to thrust his sword toward Clay, attempting to push him back even further, Clay caught the blade inside his *kama*, and spun his arm twice in a clockwise motion, dislodging the sword from Nosagi's grip as a commercial pipe behind him tripped him.

As Clay fell to his back, losing the other *kama* in the process, Nosagi found time to assemble two pieces of a wooden rod with a simple snap and stab the dangerous, bladed end toward his former pupil's face. Clay batted the wooden staff away once with an open palm before it could inflict damage. He struck it away a second time with the opposite hand as Nosagi thrust it downward, but his mentor guessed correctly the third time, and Clay found no time to safely bat the weapon aside without risking severe injury. Instead, he caught the blade itself between his palms as it neared the bridge of his nose, threatening to penetrate his brain if he let it go while under Nosagi's full force.

Using his power advantage, Clay pushed the staff back, in turn preventing an eventual tumble off the roof as he regained his footing. Both he and Nosagi grasped part of the staff, vying for control as they twisted and turned it. When they struck simultaneous punches to the face, the staff flew into the air between them. When it came down each of them caught an end and pulled it into its two original components. Much to Clay's dismay, he received a hollow wooden portion that served as a sheath for the short sword that Nosagi pulled, possibly by design.

Nosagi immediately went on the attack, but Clay's sheath deflected the blade until he found an opening to kick his former mentor in the chest without risk of losing a foot. As Nosagi stumbled back a few feet, Clay pulled his own smoke bomb, tossing it to the ground before retrieving his sword and hopping atop the air conditioning unit.

Thunder grumbled in the distance, followed by a lightning strike that returned the illumination stolen by the dark clouds, if only for a split-second. Completely focused on the task at hand, Clay fended off another attack with the short sword from Nosagi when it came. He leaped over the blade at one point, having to side-step several jabs in between. Unable to accomplish anything, even with the high ground, he dodged another sword jab by flipping to the ground behind Nosagi.

Neither immediately rushed into an attack, so Nosagi, pulled on the handle of his short sword, revealing that a stubby knife occupied the center. Only about three inches in total length, the knife was half blade, and half handle wrapped in black silk. Meant for throwing, rather than close proximity combat, the blade could be potentially deadly in either scenario, but Clay wondered if Nosagi created all of his weapons in the form of nesting barrels. In rather brazen fashion, Nosagi displayed the knife along the flat of his palm before throwing it at his former student.

Knowing the weapon was aimed at his heart, Clay turned sharply to his left to reduce his profile, hoping the blade might sail completely past him. Instead, the sharpened end plunged into his shoulder as an immediate indication of his failure to prevent the injury. He pulled it out, followed by a thin trickle of blood, and used his left hand to return the favor with a sudden throw. Nosagi caught the blade in midair with one hand, turning his hand to display the feat to Clay, who was truly impressed at the man's quickness and instincts. Perhaps a bit too awed by the reaction, Clay reacted too slowly to prevent Nosagi from throwing down another smoke bomb and disappearing from his sight.

Clay looked all around the rooftop, realizing he was completely alone. With the stairwell access behind him, Clay knew Nosagi couldn't have escaped his sight unless he went over the side of the roof. Sucking in a deep breath, he headed toward the air conditioning unit to begin searching for the man who both saved him and murdered his loved ones.

***

"I don't remember you," Clouse said, deciding to stall for time while Savitch continued to savor the moment, slowly placing the cubes in the clock's indentations.

"Of course you wouldn't," Savitch replied, sliding a cube into place. "You were a big shot, walking around the dome like you owned the place."

"Really?" Clouse contested the statement. "I was doing a job, trying to make a living."

"Funny how you actually came to own the place. Isn't it weird how life sometimes throws those little curveballs? They aren't always a bad thing."

Clouse stood and observed while Savitch walked over to retrieve another cube. He seemed rather nonchalant, as though exponentially confident nothing could foil his plan. Clouse didn't know what kind of backup the man brought along, or what knowledge led him to his confidence, but Clouse needed one of his allies to come through for him.

He struggled to remember this young man's identity because ten years had passed since renovation took place at the hotel. Obviously numerous events, many tragic, occupied his mind and put aside many of the older, better memories. His time working at the hotel ended on a particularly sour note after several attempts on his life and a man he thought of as family turned on him.

"I sense that you're struggling to remember me," Savitch said. "For the life of me, I don't understand how you and I are linked, but we are."

"What usually links you to someone?"

"If they have psychic powers of some sort, it's rather easy. But you certainly aren't a psychic, which leads me to think maybe you've had some sort of spiritual experience. Maybe you died at one time? Or someone close to you communicated with you after they passed?"

Clouse thought back to his first wife, who died under violent circumstances, presenting herself to him twice in his bathroom mirror in spectral form. He always thought her appearance was simply a figment of his imagination, but now he questioned its authenticity. Temporary insanity occurred to him as a possibility for Angie's appearance, but the timing on both occasions felt appropriate, and not like something his mind conjured up for reassurance.

"Your wife?" Savitch asked, turning from his work at the giant clock, the gun still clutched in his left hand. "You saw her?"

"Get out of my head," Clouse growled.

"No, not until you remember," Savitch said, walking over to the centerpiece with a deliberately slow pace to retrieve another cube.

Clouse believed six were already in place, and that left another six, plus the dark blue cube he had yet to produce. He quickly turned his thoughts to the past, concentrating on his first wife accidentally, before trying to remember his days working at the hotel. He guessed the man before him to be in his middle twenties, but it made no sense that he would have associated with a teenager while advising a construction crew ten years prior.

Also, the last name failed to register with him.

"You're thinking about this all wrong," Savitch said, retrieving the next cube from atop the centerpiece. "I wasn't on the grounds that often, but you should remember a conversation you had with my stepfather."

"I had lots of conversations back then," Clouse spoke before truly thinking.

It then occurred to him that the stepfather probably had a different last name and hadn't adopted this young man.

"Coming to you yet?" Savitch asked, narrowing his eyes like a hawk.

Suddenly an image of the past *did* come to Clouse, and he remembered a red-headed teenage boy who came to work with his father occasionally. Bob Lowery often spoke of how uninterested his stepson seemed about almost everything. He voiced his concerns that the boy was lazy, but also that he acted strangely around certain people as though he needed to learn people skills.

"I think you have it," Savitch said with a satisfied smile that virtually glowed red in the chamber's tinted lighting. "But I wasn't lazy. While most teenagers were busy playing sports, or worrying about getting a driver's license, I picked up on a way to get rich and powerful. I couldn't act on it until later, but you and Martin Smith provided me with all of the information I needed."

Clouse did battle over two of the cursed cubes with the benefactor who provided his millions on several occasions, considering the matter a local affair that he mostly hid from the press. Only after he ridded the world of Smith and his brand of evil did Clouse learn about all of the cubes and embark upon a worldly conquest to remove them all from evil hands.

"My stepfather dragged me to the hotel grounds occasionally, saying he was going to make a man out of me. I played his game and pretended to observe his work, but I was really spending my time observing you and your problems."

"Me and my problems, huh?" Clouse asked as Savitch inserted yet another cube into the wall, bringing about catastrophic ocean tides in the hologram. "I do remember you now, and how strangely you acted. I just thought you had troubles at home, or maybe you were special needs. I remember Bob Lowery as a gruff worker, and if he was like that at home I'm sure your childhood wasn't the best."

"Don't even play that card," Savitch said bitterly. "You can imply that I was lazy or stupid and I'll let that slide, but bringing up my childhood isn't the opening you're looking for. The only thing that can save you is producing that last cube I need to make all of this happen."

"Why?"

"What do you mean, 'why'?"

"Why do all of this? Even if you basically destroy the planet and you're the only person left to rule over the ruins, then what?"

Savitch lowered the gun slightly, but not from compassion or understanding. He wanted Clouse to see his face and hear his tone, even in the strange confines of the chamber.

"You can't possibly understand what it was like being me as a child," he said with a sneer. "All of the taunting and teasing simply because I could *see* things, visualize things that they could not."

"So you were picked on and now you want millions of people to pay for the sins of a few? That sounds a bit selfish if you ask me."

"This world as a whole needs to be taught a lesson, but that's not why I'm doing this. It's inevitable that someone is going to put these cubes together one day, and you never had the balls to go through with it, so I will."

"Your power is a gift and you've done nothing but abuse it," Clouse said, shaking his head, feeling he'd experienced a nearly identical confrontation once with Martin Smith.

Appealing to the man's faith was an obvious waste of time, and Savitch didn't appear to have much of a conscience if the lives of millions meant so little to him. Running out of time and options, Clouse felt sickened over the worldly visual display centered in the room. If the cubes truly held the ability to tear apart the planet when combined, it was only a matter of time before Savitch succeeded in wiping out a majority of the human race. Perhaps the prediction of a global event in or around 2012 wasn't so far out of touch after all, but even ancient civilizations could never have anticipated the greed of men creating their own doom.

Clouse's attention remained divided between his new adversary and the strange hologram, but he felt certain the pulsating orange light brightened and subsided at a faster rate with each cube added to the wall.

"You're a man with religion," Savitch stated as though Clouse had wasted his entire life believing in something that didn't exist. "Your good book says not to associate with my kind, yet you went out and hired your own medium."

"The same book also says not to wear clothing of different threads, but I'm pretty sure I've broken that rule a few times. What's your point?"

Savitch walked over to retrieve yet another cube, eyeing the box Clouse had brought with him and set atop the wooden centerpiece. He had yet to inquire about the box, probably having too much fun trying to pluck Clouse's thoughts in the meantime.

"My point is we have one life and one only, so why not make the most of it? You stand atop your pedestal and preach your moral garbage. Your money and influence may have convinced the people who work for you that they're doing right, but you're all just spinning your wheels and wasting your lives away."

"So I should have used my money and power to put these cubes together and kill millions instead?"

"Exactly. But now it's too late for you and everyone you love."

"I don't believe that. Just like I don't believe I surround myself with people who care only about the checks they cash from me. Every one of them is told the entire truth, and every one of them has the right to step away whenever they choose. How can someone like you, who sees the unseen, not have religion?"

"Because I'm above all of that. I choose to live for the moment and make the most of my life after people like you did nothing but shit on my childhood. You're lucky enough to be the one person who witnesses my triumph."

"Funny, I don't feel very lucky."

Savitch took another cube, this one yellow, from the pack atop the wooden centerpiece. He shot Clouse an almost mischievous look as he walked over to place it in yet another empty slot, bringing forth another hologram. Clouse felt tense, and sickened, as only three cubes remained before the strange glowing clock felt sated and began hypothetically tearing apart the world. He wondered if any chance remained for one of his people to save the day, or he needed to take a major risk on his own.

Chapter 51

Still not entirely familiar with the FBI agent who freed him from his bonds, Parish found little choice except to trust the man, but exercised caution nonetheless. He rounded each bend of the tunnel with his AR-15 held in a ready position, wondering if someone waited for them in similar fashion.

When the two finally saw daylight near the entrance, Parish carefully positioned himself against the wall, trying to safely assess the situation ahead.

A van blocked the entrance, and he looked questioningly at Stone, who gave a playful shrug. One of the men the agent had mentioned was partway through the vehicle, about to reach the side door with the open window and breach the tunnel. They had apparently broken the front windshield to gain access to the vehicle before unlocking the doors and sliding the side door open.

"Warning shots or wait for them to start coming in?" he asked Stone.

"They didn't seem like the types to be scared of a little gunplay. I say we hit 'em directly."

Parish felt torn between defending his boss against this invading horde and taking his side directly inside the chamber. He had left Clouse an advantage, if only it presented itself in a timely manner and his boss knew how to use it.

Returning his attention to the task at hand, Parish waited until the man presented his full body mass at the van's open door before firing, virtually ensuring his assault rifle wouldn't miss the mark. The man never stood a chance of defending himself, much less pulling his own weapon into position, before the three-round burst peppered his chin, neck, and chest in under a second.

If the bullets didn't stop his heart from beating, the awkward fall where the butt of his chin made contact with the hard soil and contorted his neck certainly finished the job. Parish dared take a step closer, hearing hushed concern among the three remaining mercenaries. By no means panicking, they were instead planning a strategy to enter the tunnel without drawing public attention while wiping out any remaining defenders.

"My kingdom for a grenade," Stone muttered with a sour look.

"I hope that's not what they're thinking," Parish replied, wondering what kinds of toys ex-military types might have at their disposal.

Each of them exchanged concerned looks, realizing they had just put the mercenaries on the defensive, which might have proven a terrible idea. Parish couldn't fathom the three remaining henchmen throwing an explosive device or a gas canister into the tunnel until they were reasonably certain of gaining entry. He could think of nothing outside the entrance that might provide them the means to move the disabled van, and crawling beneath the van with their packs and equipment would slow them down too much and make them easy targets.

Finding his options extremely limited, Parish found his arsenal rather useless unless the mercenaries started trying to break inside. The option of calling local authorities was really no option at all if he wanted to keep Clouse's secrets intact. He considered using the secondary entrance from the old apartment complex, but doing so would require a boost from Stone. Heading back to the area would also leave the front door exposed, and while he doubted the henchmen were going to make their way past the van and try shooting their way inside, he wasn't sure he dared take the risk.

"What are you thinking over there?" Stone asked, obviously seeing his mental wheels churning.

"There *is* another way out of here," Parish admitted, "but I'm not even sure it's a good option."

"Why's that?"

"It leads to the apartment building that overlooks the entrance," Parish said, pointing toward the blocked opening. "Even if one of us got up there, we don't have a sniper rifle, and we'd get mowed down after firing a single shot."

"At least the cops would show up."

"We don't want that either."

Stone rolled his eyes in frustration.

"I know you're trying to keep all of this a big secret, but is it worth dying for?"

Parish nodded slowly and thoughtfully in the affirmative.

"You bet it is."

Stone seemed to accept the situation and Parish's stand.

"Let me have a look at this other entrance."

Parish glanced worriedly toward the tunnel opening, where only a few beams of light pushed past the van.

"They aren't coming, at least not until they regroup. Besides, they can't risk killing the guy who's paying them if he's inside."

Agreeing with the FBI agent's logic, Parish walked him back to the secondary entrance, not far from his protective box. Stone looked up at the hatch which automatically sprung to a closed position after someone dropped down through it.

"There's no way I can lift you up there," Stone chuckled. "You're going to have to let me try it."

"There's no need for fat jokes, you know."

Parish felt reluctant, partly because he didn't fully trust the agent, and also because the man wasn't armed well enough to make much of a difference.

"I can at least make a distraction out there and buy you some time," Stone insisted.

Groaning, Parish set down his rifle and cupped his hands together to try boosting Stone upward toward the hatch. As the agent stepped into the makeshift step, Parish lifted his hands, allowing Stone access to the hatch. It opened with ease, and after a few seconds of struggling to pull himself up with elbow strength, Stone disappeared through the opening. Taking up the AR-15, Parish debated whether to assist Clouse or return to the tunnel entrance. He ultimately decided the three men needed to be stopped or there would be no hope for anyone on his team, so he returned to the blocked opening.

***

Clay exercised caution when descending the stairs to the level just below the rooftop, knowing many of the apartment doors remained wide-open. Nosagi could be lurking around any corner, just waiting for the right moment to ambush him. Keeping his sword before him wherever he walked, Clay stepped from the last stair, finding a hallway full of open doors ahead of him. Any of them might be concealing danger, so he stepped forward, his senses attuned to his surroundings.

Even his sense of smell seemed heightened as various musty smells of mildew and mold entered his nostrils, along with animal urine that felt overwhelmingly toxic to his nose. Unsure of why the building was open to humans or animals in any sense, Clay doubted the old complex housed squatters like vacant houses often did in the larger cities.

He concentrated on other, more useful senses instead, listening for any movement on either side of the hallway. Part of his training with Nosagi was to develop a sixth sense of impending danger that came from an almost spiritual intertwining with the physical body and the elements around it. Whether an unseen sword came at him, or an arrow whistled through the air, Clay often detected such dangers before they struck home.

If not for the sense instilled within him from hours of meditation, practice, and focus, he knew he would long since be rotting away beneath a tombstone. Too many times during his young life death had sought him out, and somehow Clay beat the odds.

After passing the first four doors with the utmost caution, Clay barely found time to react when Nosagi jumped out from the next one, prepared to run a sword through his torso. Clay blocked the stabbing action and slashed his own sword toward his former mentor, lodging it in the wall when it missed the mark. Left with no time to free the weapon, Clay dodged another stab toward his chest with a sidestepping motion, ducked a sweeping blade aimed at his head, and a slice toward his arm as he raised the appendage just in time. Clay kicked Nosagi's hand as the blade sailed upward, helping lodge the tip of it in the deteriorated ceiling.

Both men were temporarily weaponless, leaving them on even ground for the time being as they exchanged kicks and punches, trying to gain an upper hand. If one landed a solid blow, it easily meant broken bones, torn cartilage, or crushed organs for the other. Of course delivering such a forceful strike required more than the split-second each gave the other between offensive moves.

Nosagi went for a punch that Clay blocked with his left hand before throwing a solid fist of his own, striking the older man in the bridge of the nose, stunning him momentarily. For the first time Clay sensed the longer the battle went, the greater his chances for success in spite of Nosagi's excellent conditioning, age took a toll on his body and endurance.

Clay watched the man recover from the blow rather quickly, backpedaling a few feet before throwing down another smoke bomb. Already accustomed, and weary, of the man's tricks, Clay drew a *shuriken* star from a padded pocket within his garb, throwing it directly down the hallway where he felt positive Nosagi would retreat, simply trying to hide and recover before his next round of attacks.

If the four-pointed star struck home, Clay would have a blood trail to follow so Nosagi couldn't keep hiding from him. He didn't particularly relish the idea of stalking the man like a wounded animal, but Nosagi had sent nearly half a dozen assassins to murder him *before* the incident at the island, so Clay's sympathy only traveled so far.

Brushing the artificial smoke aside with his hands, Clay found his weapon had indeed caught Nosagi in the right shoulder blade before the man ducked into a room three doors ahead of him. Not allowing his mind to trick him into thinking he was close to securing a kill, Clay dislodged his blade from the wall before darting to the side of the open door. He exercised caution by holding the sword before him, knowing Nosagi still possessed several weapons hidden within his gear.

A glance toward the ground revealed blood droplets, so Clay backed up to the opposite wall for a better look inside. Seeing nothing except an open window, he wondered if Nosagi might have tried escape once again, but left his mind open to the possibility of a trap. Instead of rushing headfirst into the room, he shot forward, but ducked and slid into the room like a baseball player stealing a base. Like a slow-motion movie shot, Clay's view of the ceiling above him as his back slid along the linoleum floor revealed Nosagi bracing his entire body with his arms and legs like a spider just waiting for his prey to appear beneath him.

He clutched a *sai* in his right hand, which surely would have forcefully entered Clay's skull had the former apprentice entered the room conventionally. The weapon, barely over a foot in length, looked a bit like a pitchfork with three prongs, the two exterior of which were almost twice as short as the sharpened center blade.

Holding out his hand, Clay stopped his own momentum near the center of the old apartment, quickly regaining his feet as Nosagi dropped from the ceiling, using the *sai* with precision skill. Clay deflected the attacks from the single weapon, backing off slightly, which allowed Nosagi to pull another *sai* from inside his black clothing. Seldom did one use the weapons in singular form, and two of them used by a master were absolutely deadly.

During the next few seconds it was every bit of focus and skill Clay could muster to fend off the furious assault from the pair of weapons using just his sword. Forced to go on the defensive, he backed up toward the only window in the room, quickly running out of room in the process. He received cuts in the left shoulder and the right side of his abdomen from the weapons, though both were grazing wounds and he ignored the pain. It wasn't until Nosagi lunged with one of the *sai* and Clay deflected it with his sword that the other *sai* came down in a stabbing motion from above. Turning his attention to the second weapon, Clay made certain his sword kept the first *sai* at bay while he grabbed Nosagi's wrist, turning both of their bodies toward the window like two dancers in an awkward stride.

His momentum carried him into the structurally weakened glass and he wasn't about to fall three stories without taking Nosagi along for the ride. Using his sword arm he locked Nosagi's arm with the inside of his elbow, continuing to clasp the man's wrist with his other hand while their momentum took them tumbling out of the window.

Falling three stories took only a few seconds, but Clay couldn't let his guard down one instant. Not enough time existed for either of them to jockey for a safer landing position because they were too busy keeping the other's weapons at bay. Both men knew better than to land with tense, stiffened muscles that came with fear of impact because their bones and tendons would certainly snap, possibly leading to serious injury or death. They had overcome any fear of death and injury years ago because of their training, but they still had to wait until the last possible fraction of a second to relax their bodies.

To Clay, the impact still felt like getting struck by a bus as his chest and neck hit first, followed by the whiplash of his legs and feet bouncing off the unforgiving ground. It took him a second to figure out if he was going to lose consciousness or not, and once his body refused to pass out, he tried to assess the physical damage.

His mind contemplated the immediate danger before getting too analytical and he scrambled to separate his body from Nosagi's. Only once he backed away from his former mentor's injured form did he realize how fortunate he was to land atop the older man. Clay discovered several aches and pains throughout his muscles, figuring the adrenaline kept his body from feeling the full extent of his injuries. On his knees, still grasping his sword about two feet removed from Nosagi, he took a moment to assess the damage his former mentor endured.

Nosagi's arms extended to his sides, and one appeared broken based on the hump only a few inches from his right elbow. His weapons lay beyond fingertip reach, but the fact that he was visibly and audibly coughing up blood informed Clay that their skirmish was indeed over. Glass had rained down upon the ground with the two men, and based on the pool of blood emerging from beneath Nosagi's back, the man had landed on something sharp enough to penetrate his flesh and internal organs.

Clay's ribs ached from landing so hard atop another human being. Extremely fortunate he hadn't suffered any serious injuries, he realized Nosagi was mortally wounded without immediate medical assistance or the use of one of the techniques used by their clan to self-heal over a period of time. Both men knew Clay wasn't going to allow any benefit to come Nosagi's way, so they simply stared at one another, breathing rather heavily even by their own standards.

Despite his injuries, Nosagi remained a dangerous individual, but Clay recognized something from the few precious seconds it required to recover from the fall.

"You could have killed me," he stated thoughtfully, realizing his mentor wasn't evil through and through.

"I have nothing left to offer in this life except yours."

"You were like a father to me, Ryo," Clay said, calling his *sensei* by his first name for the first time in a long time. "But everything you and my real father taught me was built on lies."

"Not everything," Nosagi said, his breaths becoming a bit more labored. "You must let go of the past and be the man you were meant to be."

"But you both robbed me of everything," Clay said, shaking his head.

"You'll be married again," Nosagi said before coughing up some blood. "Make peace with your father, and be a better father than he was for you."

Realizing for the first time that his enemies were no more, Clay saw a figurative light at the end of the tunnel. He *could* wed Casey, he *could* work and retire as a police officer, and he *could* make his fiancée's family business stronger. Clay loved his career, and for the first time since the untimely death of his first wife, Casey made him happy. Only one task remained before he returned to Ohio to finally enjoy his new life.

As he watched Nosagi's body shudder while the man gasped his last few breaths, Clay gripped his sword and stood to see if he might be of assistance to Clouse and his colleagues.

Chapter 52

"I realize you followed me and my people around to steal all of the cubes, but I have to know how you retrieved one from the ocean," Clouse said, drawing a rather sly smile from his latest nemesis.

"Over the years I've learned to use my talents for financial gain," Savitch answered. "Sometimes I use blackmail, sometimes I gather sensitive information for cash. Let's just say I had someone who owed me a big favor and got me the use of a Russian boat and its research team. We already had the location where your lackey dumped the cube, so it was easy to find once we found it lodged in an old crab trap."

"How fortunate," Clouse said, adding a layer of sarcasm.

"You really shouldn't be upset. After you put your faith in regular people, you should expect no less. I work with predators."

"And you throw them away like common trash once they've done your bidding."

Clouse had taken notice of the orange light from the wall pulsating at a faster rate with each added cube, as though the wall grew excited with anticipation. He didn't know how architecture could possibly comprehend such things, but it likely synced with the cubes since they were created together. On a primal level, the cursed objects likely sensed one another and the destruction they were about to cause. Clouse still didn't know exactly how the wall emitted light in the first place, considering it was covered completely in small tiles.

"You've got some blood on your hands as well," Savitch said. "Your best friend was murdered in a hospital where your beloved Jane worked, you basically let your brother-in-law fall to his death, and twice you killed the man who bestowed you with your millions. Being friends with you, Paul, is a death sentence."

Though the facts were wickedly twisted, the words still stung Clouse because not a day passed that guilt didn't eat away at him. He never asked for any of the terrible things that happened to him, and he certainly never sought riches, but it seemed one cataclysmic event started a chain that carried through the past ten years. Clouse felt his face flush with anger, beginning to lose his cool with the evil stranger before him for the first time.

"Good," Savitch said with eerie satisfaction. "I can *feel* your anger."

Unconcerned with his own health, Clouse began taking a step forward, but Savitch aimed the gun toward his heart.

"I don't want to kill you. I want you to be a part of what you created."

"What I created?" Clouse asked incredulously. "You either haven't been paying attention, or your powers aren't getting the gist of what I'm thinking at all."

With the gun trained on Clouse the entire time, Savitch finished placing the last of the twelve cubes he already possessed within open slots, exciting the wall even further. He then turned his attention to the box Clouse had brought with him, openly disgruntled when he looked inside and saw the box stacked from top to bottom and end to end with cubes of the same navy blue color.

"You knew I wouldn't just hand it over," Clouse said, standing his ground.

"But I've read your thoughts and it's just a matter of time before I find the correct one. My only hope is we'll be able to watch your friends and family die together until you're left with nothing."

Clouse felt his blood boil. He wasn't going to stand around much longer and simply watch this man incidentally murder those he loved while tearing the world to shreds.

"So much for your charitable side," Clouse grumbled.

"My charity ran out when you decided to make things tougher than they needed to be. You're simply stalling, hoping your friends will come through for you one last time. Well not this time. Nosagi will take care of any threats, including his former student, before joining me in here."

Savitch took the box of cubes and unceremoniously dumped every last bit of the contents on the tile floor. Clouse watched with a feeling of dread, knowing the real cube wouldn't simply sit there and let its purpose, its destiny, simply pass it by. He wondered if the cube might have regrets or second thoughts like its creators apparently did, not wanting to join its siblings.

Any such thought was fleeting because the cube barely waited a second before shimmering, making its presence felt even in the dark amongst so many pretenders.

"See?" Savitch asked with a smirk and a raised eyebrow. "A little cooperation goes a long way."

"I hate those things," Clouse muttered.

"I don't. Now kindly take a few steps back so we can witness the end of the world together."

Clouse complied, knowing that getting himself shot and killed wasn't helpful in any sense. He also harbored a suspicion that Savitch was about to be unpleasantly surprised. He put his hands in the air to imply compliance, stepping back from the centerpiece and his latest adversary.

Taking up the cube as though it were a fragile egg instead of an indestructible cursed object, Savitch carried it slowly toward the wall, ready to fulfill the destiny he'd imagined for himself since childhood. He stopped suddenly, just short of the wall, turning to give Clouse a look as though Clouse had just insulted his mother, or whatever Savitch held most dear.

"How do you know about that?" Savitch asked with anger and surprise in his voice.

Clouse's mind scrambled to find the answer, certain he hadn't truly let any thoughts enter his head that might provoke such a reaction.

"How do I know about what?" he finally asked, exasperated.

"You couldn't possibly have known about that," Savitch said slowly, unable to process whatever statement he thought he plucked from the air.

He pointed the gun at Clouse's heart, visibly shaken about whatever he thought someone knew about his past. Taking a step back, Clouse didn't particularly care to be shot for something he didn't initiate. He began to question whether Savitch possessed all of his mental faculties because his powers had read Clouse like a book until the past thirty seconds. Perhaps the man was clinically insane, hearing voices inside his head, or maybe his powers picked up someone else's thoughts. Clouse couldn't imagine what other person the psychic might tune into, considering he was the only person near Savitch. The only good thing about the mysterious distraction was that it kept the man from placing the final cube in the wall.

"No," Savitch finally said, shaking his head. "You aren't going to stop me from fulfilling my destiny."

As though anticipating the insertion of the last cube, the hologram began providing sound effects that accompanied the natural disasters the various colors projected. Clouse fully understood how men in 1918 were shocked and frightened by the prospect of what they'd accidentally created. They should have known that making a deal with the devil didn't mean they were the only ones gaining something from the pact.

Clouse began taking a step forward when the large wooden centerpiece in the room shifted slightly. He stopped as Savitch continued toward the wall, unaware of the movement behind him that soon revealed Greene and Liz once several pieces of the structure came apart. They had remained hidden inside the recently constructed addition to the room the entire time. Greene appeared especially sweaty, already clutching a firearm in his right hand as Liz escaped the confining wood to make her way toward Clouse. Savitch seemed too preoccupied with the voices inside his mind to even notice.

"You had me worried," Clouse confessed in a whisper.

"Me too. We need to leave."

"Why?" Clouse questioned. "Savitch won't get what he wants."

"I know, but your bodyguard gave Russ something rather destructive."

"Oh."

Clouse wanted to stick around to see the look of disappointment on his enemy's face, but getting Liz to safety took precedence above all else. He hoped Greene knew what he was doing as he watched Savitch carefully place the last cube into a slot that was perfectly centered within the mammoth clock face. Backing toward the doorway, Clouse looked to Greene, who gave a reassuring nod that he knew what needed to be done.

"Did you put those thoughts in his head?" Clouse asked Liz quietly.

"Yes. I brought up some rather bad childhood memories for him."

Once he and Liz were safely on the other side of the doorway, looking in, Clouse observed Savitch turned from the clock, expecting to see some grand miracle awaiting him in the centerpiece. Instead, a look of disbelief crossed his face when he saw the wooden part of the centerpiece lying in chunks, and the thirteenth element and color floating within the hologram. Complete with sound and lights, the entire hologram hovering above the centerpiece looked like a laser light show, but nothing more. Clouse wasn't sure if the man expected fireworks, or some sort of sign from above, but the hologram simply continued to circle a pattern within itself.

"Nothing?" Savitch questioned aloud, obviously expecting the ground to tremble, the skies to open, and the seas to part. "This *can't be*."

"Hold it right there," Greene warned, his firearm already trained on Savitch, who had no chance of outgunning the former marshal after allowing his gun hand to fall limply to his side.

Savitch directed his attention to Liz next.

"Bitch. You were the one inside my head. How did I not detect you?"

Clouse had shielded Liz behind him, but she emerged from the doorway with the danger averted.

"You were too focused on Mr. Clouse to notice anything else," she answered. "And I've learned a few things after dealing with the likes of you, like how to quiet my mind."

Savitch scoffed at the words, unable to believe he was bested by a fellow psychic. A scowl crossed his face when he stared at the hologram as though it and the cubes somehow failed him.

"Why didn't it work?" he finally asked Clouse, certain the hotel owner already knew why his plan fell apart.

"You're missing a key component."

Savitch concentrated on picking up thoughts a moment, and despite his best efforts, Clouse couldn't help but let the answer come to mind.

"Ledger," Savitch said thoughtfully. "Your failure will come full circle after I kill your friends and complete the clock."

"You're not going anywhere," Greene said with a tone of authority obtained from his government days.

Savitch grinned sadistically.

"This isn't over by a longshot."

***

Clay found Harlan Stone standing near the edge of the excavated basement, looking down upon the three mercenaries who were about to execute a hasty plan to yank the van from the entrance with their own vehicle after shifting the van into neutral. With its hind end against a hardened wall of dirt, the van could only move forward or toward the driver's side, the latter of which wasn't a realistic option in this case.

He silently took the agent's side, startling the man who never heard him approach.

"I wish you wouldn't do that," Stone said after collecting himself.

"Just pointing out your weaknesses for you."

Stone sighed as they observed one of the men jumping into the large SUV the mercenaries drove to French Lick, parking it on the opposite bank.

"We going to attack them or just let them spot us?" Stone inquired as the driver got out of the SUV, tossing a thick chain to his colleagues as he wrapped his end around the vehicle's hitch.

"You're okay at hand-to-hand, right?"

Stone shrugged casually, indicating he could take care of himself.

"Follow my lead," Clay said, jumping into the pit before the agent found time to answer the inquiry.

Doubting Stone possessed confidence enough to confront men and their automatic weapons with just fists and feet, Clay made quick work of disarming the two men beside the van. The first, standing beside the van, turned when he heard Clay land behind him, but a quick upward kick knocked the firearm upward with his arms. Following the kick with a punch to the nose, Clay knocked the man off-balance enough that he twisted the automatic weapon, giving the henchman the option of releasing the gun or breaking some bones in his hands. Clay discarded the firearm quite a distance behind him, leaving the henchman for Stone, who had finally joined him in the excavated pit.

By this time the man hooking the chain to the front of the van came around the side to check on the commotion, carrying his weapon in a ready position. Clay smacked the barrel down with an open palm, discovering the henchman didn't have his finger on the trigger because no shot was fired. Knowing the man above them on ground level was going to take aim or jump down, Clay took hold of the automatic weapon with one hand to keep it from being used. He forcefully yanked the man toward him, swiftly drawing the large knife sheathed at the man's side and striking him between the eyes with the handle. Stunning him momentarily, Clay turned the knife around and stabbed him in the shoulder, away from any vital organs, drawing a brief scream before he pinpointed a punch into the carotid artery. The man went limp instantly, collapsing to the ground and allowing Clay to focus on the third hired gun.

Without turning around, Clay heard Stone doing battle with the first merce-nary, apparently holding his own. He figured the agent was still armed if things turned sour in unarmed combat.

Deciding not to shoot, the third henchman showed an expression that indi-cated he wished he could, because he wanted no part of jumping into the pit and being rendered unconscious. Because of his previous orders, he knew not to shoot and compromise whatever plans were occurring inside, so he pulled two large knives from straps along his legs, displaying them for intimidation purposes before jumping down into the excavated basement.

"Uh huh," Clay said under his breath, not impressed.

He immediately discovered the man was well-trained with blades, but Clay managed to dodge several stabs and slashes that came his way with the deadly knives. He figured his adversary was likely trained in the Special Forces based on his quickness and dexterity with handheld weapons. Taking a few steps back, Clay waited until the man used the same attack a second time, catching his wrist when the knife flashed past him as he ducked. Predicting the man would come from the side with the second knife, Clay needed to block the blade before he was able to look.

Guessing a fraction of a second too late, with his arm just slightly off-course, Clay blocked the blade, but at the expense of a laceration. He swung a kick over his arm that still held the man's forearm steadily, landing the blow upside the mercenary's skull. As his adversary staggered, Clay drew a short sword from his pack, better equipped to deal with multiple blades as blood dripped from the fresh cut along his forearm.

Holding the blade in his right hand in reverse, the mercenary took a swing at Clay, trying to catch his neck along the backside. Clay ducked the knife, kicking the man in the knee, which gave way with a snapping sound before he chopped the man in the side of the neck using the flat side of his hand. With the man's other hand out of range, Clay grasped his armed wrist and forced it upward, behind the mercenary's back as he twisted the wrist, finally seeing the knife drop to the ground.

A fighter to the last, the man swung with the other knife once Clay released his compromised arm. Clay blocked the attack easily this time, catching the knife with his sword's blade. The man appeared perplexed by the sight of the sword, which bought Clay enough time to punch him in the gut and elbow him in the nose before thrusting the back of his head against the van, rendering him unconscious.

Hearing nothing behind him, Clay's sense of danger flickered within his mind, so he turned to see how Stone had fared.

Standing erect, with the first thug laid out a few feet behind him, Stone aimed his sidearm where the last thug had been positioned. Clay realized quickly, however, that the agent meant him no harm, particularly once he holstered the Glock.

He provided a country grin before speaking to the man who twice saved him from certain peril.

"What took ya so long?"

Clay frowned outwardly, though he felt relieved the agent had suffered no harm.

"Remind me why I keep saving your ass again?"

"It's because I'm so damn charming."

"Definitely *not* that," Clay retorted, looking to the van. "We need to get in there."

Parish poked his head through the open window of the van on the opposite side.

"Have your best buddy there unlock the doors," the bodyguard suggested.

"Oh, yeah," Stone said, indicating he should have thought of doing so much sooner.

He held up the keyless remote, unlocking the entire van with the press of a button, which provided access to the rear hatch. It opened automatically, providing Clay and Stone the opportunity to head inside and assist Parish and Clouse with whatever final stand was unfolding at the end of the tunnel.

Chapter 53

Liz couldn't believe the bizarre setting before her might be the end of the hunt for the thirteen cubes, or the beginning of a redefined planet. Parish provided them with the means to hide within the chamber if they so desired, and ultimately handed Greene a device that served as a game changer. After removing the original metal spokes and outer rim that surrounded the centerpiece, Parish constructed the new wooden portions specifically with the idea of someone hiding inside. Up until the moment she and Greene ducked inside the new addition, Liz questioned whether she endangered their plans.

She succeeded beyond her wildest expectations, quieting her mind and keeping Savitch from violating her thoughts as he had in Illinois and later in Indiana. Granted, he spent a lot of time focused on Clouse for the past decade, and that fact distracted him from searching for her thoughts in this case.

Now, standing in a room that pulsated orange at a greater rate than ever before, Liz took Clouse's side, wondering what Savitch meant with his ominous last statement.

"This isn't over by a longshot."

From left to right, Liz saw Greene standing with his gun drawn, a corpse lying atop the tile floor, chunks of the wooden centerpiece, the original centerpiece with the multicolored hologram floating above it, and Savitch refusing to back down. In fact, the man still held a firearm loosely at his side, despite Greene's orders to drop it.

Liz fought to silence her mind and shield it from Savitch, but he already appeared to be concentrating deeply on something as he assessed the room around him. Clouse tensed, apparently noticing their adversary was up to no good, but unwilling to ask Greene to execute him. At this point, with the floating holo-gram circling itself ominously, and millions of lives at stake, Liz found no moral dilemmas restraining her. She was about to yell for Greene to pull the trigger when something appeared to materialize from nowhere behind the former federal marshal.

She couldn't imagine where they came from, or how they managed to get behind Greene, but two men wearing suits went unseen by his eyes. They both immediately reached for firearms hidden inside their sport coats.

"Russ!" Liz screamed. "Look out!"

Greene followed her eyes, but looked absolutely befuddled when he looked behind him as though he saw no threat. He turned his attention to her with a con-fused expression for an explanation as the two men fizzled from Liz's line of sight. She immediately knew Savitch had used her as a distraction, implanting images within her mind, but her guilt only compounded when she saw Savitch raise his firearm against the only threat remaining within the room.

The split-second Greene turned to Liz was enough for Savitch to carry out the second part of his plan and raise his firearm against the former marshal. Greene somehow sensed the danger, turning and firing at the same time as Savitch. Both men reeled from bullets striking their bodies, but Savitch got off a second shot before collapsing to the floor, striking Greene again as his body jolted from the impact. Greene fell to the floor first with a thud that echoed through the small chamber, losing his firearm in the process. Savitch swayed momentarily, shaking his head as though mentally spent after creating the elaborate mental hoax. He collapsed behind the centerpiece and the wooden components a moment later, leaving no evidence about his true injuries.

"No!" Liz screamed, dashing across the floor to take Greene's side and assess the potentially fatal damage she unwittingly helped Savitch cause.

Although she heard scuffling noises from behind the centerpiece, Liz focused her attention on Greene, who immediately displayed signs of labored breathing. One bullet entered in the lower part of his abdomen, but the other was more cen-tralized in his torso, quite possibly striking a lung. Sweat already poured from his forehead as he reached up to touch her face, gently rubbing a few fingers along her hair and her cheeks.

"Go," he insisted.

"No, I can't leave you. I'm so sorry."

"It wasn't your fault," Greene spoke each word between labored breaths.

The entire time the pair had worked together Greene had presented himself as a gentleman, opening car doors and never letting their relationship escalate above business, even though they both showed subtle signs that they wanted it to. All those times in close proximity, sharing personal stories and their past, coming close to physical contact, never materialized beyond a bond they shared through work.

Greene was too old-fashioned and professional to let their relationship become physical, while Liz dared not touch him for fear of seeing his past. Knowing a person's past, she discovered early in life, tended to distance people from her, rather than create some form of a lasting bond.

"But it was my fault," Liz reiterated. "I'm sorry, Russ."

"It was Savitch. I forgave you the second it happened."

Liz felt a tear come to her eye as her chest heaved and she fought to hold back the river of emotions ready to burst through the floodgate. The tear slowly rolled down her cheek, landing atop Greene's shirt that was already soaked with sweat and blood.

"Go," Greene insisted again. "I've got this."

His words sounded reassuring, and she knew what he meant to do. Liz no longer harbored fears about knowing this man, or his past, because he was genuinely good through and through. She gently placed her lips on upon his, and he reciprocated the kiss at length, with enough emotion that Liz regretted never following through with her earlier instincts. She felt no jolt, followed by a vision of the past, when they finally touched. Liz harbored deep disappointment and sadness, knowing this man might have been the one. For some reason he was immune to her ability, or perhaps his clean slate of a life required no explanation, but either way she was destined to never see him again.

Clouse knelt beside Liz, looking over Greene's wounds with a solemn expression. As a former EMT on the fire department, Clouse knew how to treat wounds, and the chances of survival from a variety of injuries.

"Are you sure about this?" he asked Greene. "We can call an ambulance."

Greene shook his head weakly.

"There isn't time, and I just winged him," Greene answered painstakingly. "Let me end this before that bastard gets up."

Clouse briefly considered grabbing the gun beside Greene and ending the situation himself, but he wasn't certain about the extent of Savitch's injuries. Someone needed to get Liz to safety before the other psychic regained his footing and mowed them all down with gunfire. A quick glance around him didn't reveal the firearm's location because he at least wanted to give Greene ample opportunity to defend himself.

"Don't worry about it," Greene said, sensing his thoughts. "I won't need it."

Clouse hung his head, hating to lose yet another person in his camp to the evil cubes. A noise across the room quickly reminded him of the danger, and he took Liz by the arm.

"We have to go."

Liz already felt the tears streaming down her cheeks as Clouse lifted her away from Greene. She followed his lead toward the door, stealing one look back at Greene who was already focused on his final task.

They ran down the hall for cover, because only certain doom awaited them if they stayed inside the chamber. A few seconds later they encountered Parish, Stone, and Clay Branson. The three men looked like hell, but none of them appeared gravely injured.

"We need to get out of here," Clouse informed them immediately.

"Why?" Stone questioned. "Where's the guy behind all of this?"

"Back there," Liz answered.

Parish understood the urgency, since he was the one who installed the failsafe device and provided Greene and Liz with the trigger mechanism. He motioned for everyone to head the opposite way in a hurry, just in case the explosive devices he planted inside the chamber went off without warning.

Continuing to look behind her, Liz felt warm moisture atop her cheeks and forming below her eyes. She couldn't believe after everything she and Greene had endured that their story was ending like this. Unfortunately theirs was a tale that could never be told to the public, which meant Greene's sacrifice would go without spoils.

But not without virtue.

***

Greene placed his palm flat against his upper bullet wound, trying to keep it from sucking in oxygen, which made conventional breathing more difficult and painful. He knew he didn't have very long without true medical assistance, because the pain grew more intense by the second when the lung began to collapse. Still, he felt determined to wait until the arrogant Savitch stood up to confront him once again.

He didn't have to wait long once Clouse ushered Liz from the chamber for the psychic to slowly regain his footing and painfully saunter his way. Greene dared not move too far from his spot because of potential blood loss, so he simply remained reasonably still, even as Savitch loomed over him.

Examining the damage his bullet did to the man's side, near the waistline, Greene felt a little satisfaction. Had Greene been permitted a split-second longer to aim before firing, the bullet surely would have struck Savitch in the heart, ending the affair much sooner. A year prior, the man working for the federal government wouldn't have believed in fate, but after experiencing a year around cursed objects and psychics, Greene knew he was lying on the tiled floor of this chamber for a reason.

"So, your friends abandoned you?" Savitch taunted.

"Not exactly," Greene answered, feeling the intense burning inside his body from the bullet and the damaged lung.

It was like someone had heated pokers in a fireplace, stuck them inside of him, and left them there.

"I'm going to enjoy killing you and using one of these cubes to heal myself," Savitch said with his usual smugness, as though nothing in the world could touch him.

A bullet wound in his guts said otherwise, but he wasn't about to acknowledge any weakness.

Once Liz left with Clouse, Greene managed to locate the firearm, which one of them had been obscuring in their attempts to assist him.

Greene attempted to reach for the gun just over an arm's length away, but Savitch kicked it toward the opposite side of the chamber. With only one play left, Greene simply tapped the little remote switch located in his pants pocket, finding it still in place. His breathing felt labored, partly because of the lung injury, but also due to what he figured was internal bleeding. The lower bullet passed through his intestines and out the back, but the first bullet struck more susceptible organs and remained inside so far as he could tell.

Giving a malicious smile, Savitch slowly walked toward the mammoth clock embedded within the far wall.

"Nothing is going to stop me now that I've picked your mind clean," Savitch taunted as he walked with what seemed a little jovial skip in his step. "I know about the leather-bound journal, and soon I'll possess it and complete this wall."

Greene said nothing, beginning to wriggle his body toward the main entrance to avoid being shot before he activated the present Parish left for him. He snagged a nearby piece of the dismantled wooden centerpiece that was part of the rounded exterior. It had a handle on the inside, so he was able to hold it like a shield, still inching his way toward the main entrance as Savitch busied himself with trying to figure out which cube was most beneficial to him in the present scenario. None of them were of any assistance unless he killed someone, and Greene didn't plan on being a sacrificial lamb.

Still agonized whenever he took a breath, Greene watched Savitch continue to look over the cubes. Greene tried remaining silent, but dragging his own weight, along with the protective piece of wood, slowed him immensely. The sounds from the hologram centerpiece provided some audible cover, but Greene still needed to move quickly and quietly. He couldn't possibly tell which cube the man was bent on retrieving, because they all looked the same, illuminated by the haunting orange light emitted by the cursed clock.

With no position of comfort, and his body growing weaker by the second from internal bleeding, Greene fought not to scrape the curved wood against the floor. The moment Savitch noticed him moving, the man was certainly going to begin firing at him, because it didn't matter how the victim died to satisfy the cubes.

Although Savitch's activities were mostly blocked by the centerpiece and the scattered wooden pieces, Greene saw him finally pluck a cube from the wall. Deciding he needed to hide from the man's view at any cost, Greene struggled to his knees, still holding the makeshift shield between his body and Savitch. Not hearing any steps along the floor as of yet, Greene fought the burning within his body, trying to regain his footing for a final push toward the tunnel opening. Greene figured he was a goner either way, but he wanted the final word, just to let Savitch know he wasn't as all-powerful as he portrayed himself.

Greene stumbled toward the opening once he stood, clutching the wooden handle with his left hand to cover his exposed side while reaching into his left pants pocket awkwardly with his right hand. He retrieved the detonation device, placing it into his left hand as he slipped the hand through the wooden handle, allowing his wrist to carry the weight of the imperfect shield.

Barely having time, even during his hours inside the newly-created center-piece with Liz, to study the little black detonator, Greene knew how to operate it. A black and a red trigger, both small in size, needed to be flipped after the protective cover was removed from the front side. Greene reached the doorway, supporting his weight against the side of the opening with his free arm, reaching over just long enough to pluck the small cover from the detonator. He was about to steady himself once more when a push from behind knocked him to the ground.

Greene fell hard atop the solid dirt of the tunnel, turning to find Savitch standing above him, ominously pointing a gun at his chest.

"Did you really think you could escape?"

"No," Greene answered, finding it difficult to utter even a few words.

His wrist kept the wooden makeshift shield in place, but when he struck the ground, Greene accidentally dropped the detonator from his palm onto his lower body. Unsure of exactly where, he searched with his concealed left hand while Savitch basked in his glory momentarily, likely feeling empowered having to carry out his own dirty work.

"You couldn't have made it more simple for me," the possessor of thirteen evil objects bragged. "You've given me the means to heal myself, then I'll take a little trip back in time."

"You can't," Greene muttered weakly, his fingers touching the detonator, trying to gauge its position.

"And why not?" Savitch asked testily, aiming the gun at Greene's upper body to finish the job he started.

"Because you can't time travel when you're dead."

It took a split-second for Savitch to comprehend the words before he grew enraged, pulling the trigger as Greene pulled the wood over his torso and head to protect the most vital areas of his body. A thin metal lining inside the wood, meant to provide protection from being given away inside the chamber, now saved Greene in a different way. The bullets dented the thin metal, one after another, but none of them passed through completely.

While shielding his torso, Greene reared his legs back, taking a chance that they might take damage from some bullets. The sound of repeated gunfire from close range hurt his ears, but it also let him know Savitch wasn't moving from his spot, hoping the bullets passed through the wood and into Greene's already compromised flesh. Pulling his legs back to buck like a mule, he let his feet fly during a moment when the shooting ceased, striking Savitch somewhere along the waistline. His offensive action sent the man flailing backwards into the chamber. Savitch let a few more bullets fly, even as he tumbled awkwardly, his back striking the authentic centerpiece heavily as Greene dared removed the wooden shield for a look. Savitch hit the remainder of the wood surrounding the centerpiece rather hard, which cost him his footing. Without any balance, his back slid downward along the wood while his feet kicked out before him.

Savitch tried to shake the mental cobwebs after landing so hard. After a few seconds he scooped up a nearby firearm, full of ammunition, before looking to Greene with a disgusted look. He looked determined to finish the job, regardless of whatever effort he needed to put forth.

Greene took just a second to glance at the detonation switch in his left hand, flipping it over to see Parish's brief instructions on a tiny sheet of paper taped to the back side.

BOOM!

Greene couldn't help but grin, despite the agony inside his body. He looked over to Savitch, whose eyes seared with anger, staring holes through the former federal marshal. Savitch struggled to regain his footing, striking his head against the curved top of the centerpiece. The blow barely slowed him as he angrily held the gun outward before moving again. Savitch was more careful and deliberate the second time he tried to regain his footing. When he finally stood, Savitch stretched his neck to one side, giving an evil grin that indicated he wasn't going to fail a second time and Greene was going to be just another one of his forgettable victims.

"Goodbye, Jacob," Greene said, flipping the black switch, followed by the red switch, bringing forth an incredible explosion that consumed the chamber before heading for fresher air down the tunnel.

Chapter 54

Even before he and Liz were halfway down the tunnel, attempting to reach safety, Clouse pulled his cell phone from his side, calling 911. He hated the risk of police swarming the premises, but he wasn't going to let Russ Greene die if hope remained. Clouse knew most shots to the torso below the heart were typically survivable with prompt medical attention.

He owed Russ Greene a chance at life, even if calling 911 put his entire secret operation at risk. Years of work might be deemed worthless if the authorities asked too many questions and the chamber filled with cubes was discovered. Considering the nearest ambulance service was at least ten minutes away in Paoli, he figured the group had a little bit of time to clean up the mess. He attempted to make the call from inside the tunnel, discovering the phone didn't have a strong enough signal when it beeped repeatedly in his ear.

"Damn," he muttered, continuing to prod Liz toward the entrance.

She continued to look back, worried with good reason about Greene. Both of them knew he intended to blow up the chamber with Savitch, and possibly himself, still inside. Knowing he did no one any good while still inside the tunnel, Clouse hurried along, getting Liz to keep stride. She knew he intended to call for help, so when they saw daylight ahead, she practically tugged Clouse to the opening.

When he finally stepped into the excavated basement, Clouse discovered a complete mess with Stone, Parish, and Clay Branson standing beside a damaged van. The body of a henchman dressed in black lay nearby, his fatal bullet wounds very much visible to Clouse. Three other mercenaries dressed in black were already subdued with plastic zip ties binding their wrists. One had already regained consciousness and began struggling against his restraints, but Clouse didn't have time to deal with everything at once.

"You got a phone?" he asked Liz, his mind already formulating a plan.

"Yes."

"Wait about one minute and call 911, and request an ambulance only because you found someone on the ground," Clouse told her with strong reassurance before turning to Parish. "I need this mess out of here five minutes ago, Todd. The vehicles, these assholes, and the three of you."

"Understood, sir."

Parish turned to begin his task but stopped in his tracks, turning abruptly.

"Oh," he said, as though suddenly remembering something.

He carried a shotgun, which Clouse figured he lifted from one of the subdued mercenaries or brought from his personal arsenal. Parish walked as though on a personal mission toward the rear of the van, so Clouse followed, discovering the lit jack-o-lantern remained on the ground, not far from the tunnel entrance. Its toothy grin continued to flicker visibly in the restrained daylight, the gutted vegetable appearing unscathed by all of the recent violent activity.

Without warning, Parish approached the pumpkin, took aim with the shotgun, and fired downward. The vegetable exploded into dozens of sinewy strands that landed on the old basement wall, the van, and practically everything nearby.

"Was that necessary?" Clouse asked when his hired hand brushed past him.

"Yes," Parish replied without breaking stride, prepared to carry out his employer's orders with his usual rugged demeanor.

Both of them knew the symbolism of the jack-o-lantern in Clouse's life, serving as an omen of impending danger. Clouse really couldn't blame his employee for taking out some frustration on the lingering vegetable, and at least the shotgun blast hadn't carried very far. He doubted the noise even escaped the old basement area with so much surrounding dirt dampening the sound.

"Todd," he called, regaining the man's attention. "Get those three out of here and make them bury their buddy. And make sure they don't have the means or any desire to come back here."

Parish nodded, indicating he understood perfectly. He turned to confer with Stone and Branson, pondering the most efficient method to move two vehicles and three underlings quickly. Clouse was about to make a suggestion when the ground trembled and a muffled boom came from within the tunnel. Everyone turned to look, knowing the explosion had rocked the chamber within, possibly compromising it, but Clouse found Liz already calling 911 for an ambulance. He doubted any residents heard the boom, since the abandoned area wasn't very close to existing homes and businesses.

"Go," he insisted to Parish, who wore a look of concern.

"But—"

"*Go*, Todd," Clouse said with more emphasis. "I'll deal with whatever happened in there."

Parish followed his employer's wishes, openly unhappy about not sticking around to protect Clouse and examine the remains of the chamber with him. He turned from his employer without a word, asking the FBI agent and the Ohio cop for assistance, since they weren't paid by Clouse or obligated to provide any help beyond their personal vendettas.

Clouse wasted little time returning his attention to Liz, who was already speaking with a local dispatcher. He heard enough to know she was requesting an ambulance and he motioned for her to remain outside as he stepped toward the tunnel entrance. Feeling both pressure to hurry and apprehension about what awaited his arrival, Clouse darted toward the tunnel, which remained barely illuminated by the dwindling lanterns hanging along the sides.

When he drew closer to the chamber, however, Clouse found several of the lanterns shattered atop the ground, some of their handles still swaying along the nails where they once hung. He felt somewhat shocked when the eerie orange glow of the chamber remained, guiding him during the last portion of his journey when the lanterns failed to withstand the concussion provided by the explosion.

Clouse expected the room to look like the remains of a town bombed heavily during wartime. His eyes widened when he found several charred lumps across the room's floor. Standing along the right side of the doorway, Clouse knew not to touch anything around him because the residual heat felt intense on his skin. It reminded him of raging fires from his days on the fire department when he didn't have part of his gear fully donned. Fearing the bottom of his boots might melt and merge with the superheated tile floor, Clouse remained at the doorway, observing the carnage.

He fully expected the room to be compromised, possibly on the verge of total collapse from above, but every tile remained in place without the least little bit of damage. The wall with the clock built into it continued to produce orange light, pulsating rhythmically as a dozen of the cubes remained in place. The thirteenth cube glistened, attempting to gain his attention, beside a charred pile that continued to smolder. Clouse quickly assessed the mass as that of a human body, possibly Savitch or Greene because the shot henchman's body remained where the man was murdered in a charred heap. He still couldn't believe the room remained unscathed, figuring the curse placed on the cubes and the leather-bound book applied to the chamber where they were created. His heart sunk, knowing none of the curse would ever be put to rest, and because Russ Greene apparently sacrificed his life for a cause he believed in wholeheartedly.

Clouse stood on tiptoes, trying to find Greene, determined to give the man proper treatment for his heroic actions, including an appropriate burial. The rest of the organic material burned within the room appeared to be the separated centerpiece components. Their wooden exteriors were charred and black, with tiny splinters sticking up like hair follicles along several edges.

He failed to locate any additional masses that looked anything like charred human remains within the chamber. Growing frustrated, Clouse took half a step inside, hearing a hiss when the bottom of his right foot touched the floor. He retreated immediately, thinking he might have to create an excuse for Liz to tell the medics when they arrived so they didn't enter the tunnel.

"Where the hell are you, Russ?" he questioned under his breath, still looking at the eerie scene before him.

"Down here," a weak voice said from the ground, a few feet to Clouse's left.

What Clouse initially regarded as a chunk of wood thrown to the doorway from the blast proved accurate, but it camouflaged the man lying beneath it. He immediately dropped to one knee, lifting the large rounded piece of charred wood from Greene before checking the man for additional injuries.

The dim lighting made a cursory examination rather difficult, but Greene appeared intact and healthy along his upper body, other than the bullet wounds. Clouse's eyes followed his employee's body below the waistline, finding every part of Greene's legs below the knees suffered burn damage from the explosion.

"Were you thrown?" he asked, suspecting a possible head or neck injury.

"No," Greene answered quietly. "I covered up when I pushed the button."

Clouse took a closer look at the burn damage, finding most of it superficial in nature. Luckily Greene chose to wear blue jeans instead of slacks for hiding inside the new centerpiece, which likely saved him additional damage.

"How do your lower legs feel?" Clouse inquired.

"They're burned, but I think the doorway shielded them pretty well."

Daring to take a closer look, Clouse lifted the cuff along one leg, finding the flesh reddish, and mostly free of blisters. Knowing Greene wasn't plagued by third degree burns made his next request significantly easier.

"Medics are on their way, Russ. I need to carry you to the entrance so no one steps foot near the cubes."

"I understand."

Greene tried to help remove some of the burden from Clouse, but he proved to be practically dead weight. Clouse sat him up before turning him slightly and placing him over his shoulder. Greene groaned, though not from protest, when his injured torso came in direct contact with his boss's back. Clouse took hold of his legs to ensure he didn't drop him before heading into the tunnel. He hurried along, feeling absolute respect for Greene, who was being a complete trooper despite his life-threatening injuries.

It took a little over a minute for Clouse to reach the entrance, but his ears immediately detected sirens in the distance.

The daylight stung his eyes momentarily, but he spotted Liz standing on ground level above him. Both vehicles were gone, along with his colleagues, the three living henchmen, and the body of the last thug. He watched Liz cup her face worriedly with both hands, looking anxiously toward him for answers as he labored to carry Greene up the hill.

"Is he?" she asked, unable to finish her question when Clouse drew closer.

Instead of answering, Clouse gently laid Greene down on the ground, reassessing him after having to carry his already compromised body through the tunnel. Greene's breathing grew more labored as the sirens grew closer, and Clouse worried it might be too late. He watched helplessly as the man's body convulsed when he coughed, as though the internal bleeding had taken a major toll.

Clouse applied pressure to the wounds with his bare hands, even though they weren't really leaking much blood at this point. Liz took Greene's other side, holding his hand as she looked into his eyes.

"Don't quit on me," she insisted.

Greene's face lit up when his eyes finally focused on Liz, but Clouse knew the former federal marshal was fading fast. He heard the ambulance drawing extremely close, so he looked to Liz.

"Go with him to the hospital, Liz. Act like you're too distraught to talk to the police and I'll handle them from here."

Liz nodded before Clouse turned to Greene, also clasping his hand.

"Hang in there, Russ. I can't have our hero leaving us after saving the day."

"I'll try," Greene replied.

He grimaced when he tried providing a weak smile as the ambulance pulled beside them in the otherwise abandoned lot.

Unfortunately for Clouse the local police showed up almost immediately, either because Liz told the dispatcher Greene was shot, or the medics called in additional information when they arrived. It mattered little because Clouse was forced to conjure up a story almost immediately to police officers who always took whatever he reported with a grain of salt. After hearing so many fantastical stories over the years, authorities seemed to always know they weren't getting the full truth from Clouse or his people, but his very charitable donations to the community bought him a lot of leeway.

He put a tight spin on the truth, stating that he and Liz were working on the property when they heard gunshots ring out. They ran from the basement area to level ground, finding Greene lying on the ground from bullet wounds. Clouse did not deny that Greene worked for him, though he reported that he didn't know why Greene was on the grounds or how he traveled to arrive there.

Fortunately the medics surrounded Greene while they worked on him, which prevented the police from getting a close look at his injuries. When they asked about the odd coloration of his blue jeans below the knees, Clouse simply said he didn't know what caused the damage and that they would have to ask Greene when he was able to talk. The last thing Clouse wanted was for the police to ask for permission to search inside the tunnel, so he kept everything about his fabricated story outside of the old basement and the visible doorway.

More concerned about talking to Greene, the police took a brief statement from him before leaving for the hospital. Clouse promised a more thorough statement later, which also provided him an opportunity to strengthen his story. Parish returned to the site near the end of the entire ordeal, waiting until the authorities left before informing his employer that everything else was under control.

"We shouldn't have any more problems from those goons."

"Good," Clouse thought aloud. "It's been one hell of a day already."

"Everything okay, sir?" Parish inquired, a look of concern etched across his face.

"I think so," Clouse answered, realizing he probably appeared numb, because he certainly felt that way. "We still have some cleanup to do."

He started toward the excavated basement, wishing he could check on Greene at the hospital instead of worrying about the thirteen cubes awaiting human contact inside the chamber. Even with Savitch dead nothing about his mission, or his life in general, felt any different. Danger from unknown people was always going to be a threat, because if someone like Savitch could wait ten years to strike, Clouse knew other enemies likely existed.

Parish followed him down the slope, into the partially excavated area after Clouse took a few staggered steps. His knees still felt rubbery after barely surviving the latest attempt on his life. Even worse, more of his own people were hurt because he put them in harm's way. He felt his eyes well with tears, the emotion of the incident, in fact the entire past ten years, catching up with him.

"Sir?" Parish asked hesitantly.

"I'm okay, Todd," Clouse answered, trying to brush back the moisture along his eyes while he inhaled stiffly through his nose to keep the snot at bay.

"I can take care of this, sir."

Clouse dropped to the sloped dirt short of the doorway, patting the ground for Parish to join him.

"This is my burden," he said. "I'll take care of it."

Parish said nothing momentarily, as though wondering exactly how to console his boss. Always respectful and loyal, Parish seldom spoke out of turn, and certainly never interjected his opinion unless Clouse asked for it.

"Sir, you're not alone in this," he finally said, looking straight ahead to avoid viewing his employer in a moment of weakness.

Always loyal, Clouse thought, feeling even worse that he put such good people directly in the path of evil.

"It's my fault Russ Greene might not make it," Clouse said slowly. "Back when all of this started and I lost some friends, that wasn't any of my doing and I knew that, Todd. I *knew* it. But now, with everything I've learned, and the things I feel compelled to do, it *is* me putting all of you in harm's way."

Parish finally looked his way now that Clouse had dried his eyes and composed himself a bit.

"Sir, you laid this out for me early on. You recruited Greene and Liz after you researched them thoroughly and they knew the score. They didn't have to say yes, and I seem to recall you giving me plenty of opportunities to back out. We do this because we *choose* to, sir. You can't do this alone, nor should you have to. Most people in your position would just let the chips fall where they may, but you still personally risk your life."

"How could I not with everything I ask of all of you?"

"And that's why I've gone through hell with you, sir. There's no other job in the world I want after all of this, especially since we might finally be free and clear."

Clouse shook his head negatively, certain he could never live comfortably because he was the key to locating the cursed cubes for those rare few who knew about them.

"These things will never go away," Clouse bemoaned. "We're going to be forever defending the world from them."

"Not *forever*," Parish said with a chuckle, drawing a thin smile from his employer.

"No, not forever. I'm sure we'll find suitable replacements down the road. History won't remember our deeds, Todd, and they can never be allowed to."

"I'm pretty sure they'll remember *you*, sir."

Feeling reasonably certain his life would be little more than a footnote, Clouse didn't mind. He needed the spotlight away from him to make the job of protecting the cubes much easier. Looking upward, he noticed the previously ominous gray clouds drifting away while growing lighter in color. He couldn't recall a single drop of rain falling from the sky, which made the strange sight that much more unusual.

Clouse finally set his arms out, using the ground to help him regain his footing when he stood. Taking a deep breath, he decided to clear out the mess inside the chamber before the police returned with more questions or a warrant.

"I can take care of this," Parish offered.

"Thanks, Todd, but I've got to get those things out of there and formulate a new plan for them."

"And Savitch?"

"I think I have a final resting spot for him that's just perfect. It'll give me a chance to make sure my other nemesis is still at rest."

Parish nodded with an understanding smirk. Clouse never revealed exactly where he buried Martin Smith to anyone, with good reason, and so far no one had discovered the man's remains. Logic told him that Savitch wouldn't be highly missed, and even if he became a reported missing person, decades would likely pass before anyone dug up his charred remains.

He turned to Parish at the old basement doorway.

"If you don't mind, just keep an eye on the door while I go fetch what I need from inside."

"You got it, sir."

Clouse wasn't sure how he wanted to secure the cubes in the short or long term, but he knew they needed to be hidden from all human beings and kept far, far away from the chamber at the end of the tunnel. He slowly made his way down the dark tunnel, plucking one of the functioning lanterns from the wall to carry with him. Once he neared the chamber the eerie glow would illuminate the area for him, but he didn't want to bump into any walls in between. Clouse planned to gather the remains of Savitch, grab the cubes, and never lay eyes on the evil sanctum again.

Chapter 55

It took some time for the two adjacent towns in Orange County to return to normal after local news stations reported that a man was shot in the streets of French Lick. Even in a casino town violence was rare, and speculation ran amuck that Paul Clouse was a key figure in the investigation since his employee was shot. Locals considered him both savior and pariah, but what they thought they knew amounted to a fraction of the truth.

A tiny fraction.

Clouse closed the West Baden Springs Hotel for two consecutive weekdays in early December for a private outing with his family and some of his most valued employees. It wasn't uncommon for the hotel to be booked on a weekend, at a hefty price, for a wedding and reception, but a few guests weren't happy their reservations were changed to the French Lick Springs Hotel down the road. Clouse made amends, giving them resort perks, including credit at the casino and a free night's stay at a later date of their choosing at the dome.

Despite the looming shadow the cubes permanently cast over him, Clouse found reason for celebration. Russ Greene survived six hours of surgery, making a speedy recovery over the following weeks with Liz a constant at his side.

Though he harbored reservations about their blossoming relationship, Clouse refused to say anything. He knew all too well that loved ones were sometimes used as pawns by villains who cared little for human life. Clouse also hoped if they were truly in love that nothing came between them because the work environment would surely be poisoned at that point.

He spotted them sitting in one of the oversized plush chairs within the atrium and walked over to them. The chairs were large enough to accommodate couples, lengthy and curved so that people could sit in them with their feet off the floor. Liz and Greene shared the chair, side by side, Greene with his arm comfortably around the psychic until Clouse approached them. He stiffened a bit, even starting to retract his arm, not wanting his boss to think he was being lazy or cohabitating with a coworker. On this day, Clouse didn't mind one bit.

"At ease," Clouse said to Greene, drawing up a smaller chair of his own. "You're still recuperating, remember?"

Greene gave an uneasy smile, still uncertain what Clouse thought of his relationship with Liz. It wasn't as though anyone, even Greene himself, expected his feelings for Liz to escalate beyond a workplace friendship.

"How are you feeling?" Clouse asked.

"Doing well," Greene answered. "The feet are feeling good, and my insides don't feel like churned butter."

Clouse smiled.

"Glad to hear it. I do have one question for Liz that I've been meaning to ask these past few weeks."

"Oh?" Liz asked curiously.

"How did you ever get inside Savitch's head? I thought that was his specialty."

Liz looked to the floor momentarily, as though Clouse had brought up a bad memory for her. Clouse knew it wasn't easy for her to deal with her fellow psychic when the time came, but she overcame a great deal of adversity to better him.

"When he started reading my mind, he created a two-way portal of sorts," Liz explained. "I started seeing every aspect of his life in my dreams, so I finally wondered if I could return the favor and start sending messages his way. It took a little practice, and a ton of concentration to pull it off. I felt like my head was splitting for two days after that, so I just focused on staying with Russ and making sure he got better."

Clouse nodded in understanding.

"I appreciate everything you've both done, and I'm glad you came."

"Truth be told, we didn't really have anywhere else to go," Greene said, only half kidding, since they were still living in the hotel's sixth floor until more permanent residential plans were formed.

"We'll remedy that soon enough," Clouse said, providing a reassuring smile. "You'll just have to let me know what arrangements you have in mind."

By his last statement, he meant to imply they needed to choose one residence, or two, and they both blushed a bit as he stood to give them some privacy. He couldn't help but wonder if their bond was real, or just a reaction from Liz over Greene's recent heroics. Because Jane stood by him unconditionally, Clouse would never dream of interfering in whatever love they thought they shared.

Clouse bid them a temporary farewell before crossing the atrium, finally settling at an open table near the bar that extended from the hotel into the atrium that provided a great view of the vast atrium.

From there, Clouse watched his son and stepdaughter run carefree through the vast space for the first time in months. Decked out with tables, chairs, and lots of activities, the atrium served as a hub for the two days and all of the events Clouse's wife planned for the group. It felt good to see the employees he held dear and their families all around the atrium. Parish, Jennings, and Duncan were all present with their families. Clouse had also invited Niemeyer and Mark Daniels, even though Niemeyer didn't technically work for him. With Thanksgiving still fresh in his mind and Christmas just around the corner, Clouse longed for time with family and friends, glad so many of them accepted a vacation on short notice.

When he looked up to some of the glass from some of the interior rooms, he thought he spied a dark shape darting across one of the hallway lounge doors along the third floor. Clouse didn't give it a second thought, figuring a member of the staff or one of the guests was simply walking by. His days of living in fear of mysterious strangers stalking him or his family were definitely over.

He no longer viewed the hotel as the place where terrible things happened to him and his loved ones. A change in perspective accompanied the notion that the only people left who knew about the cubes he considered allies. He knew a slim chance remained that someone outside of his circle knew about them, but after a few weeks of separation from the events inside the chamber Clouse felt more at ease.

Harlan Stone had left without a word to anyone except Clay Branson, returning to his job at the Bureau. Clouse learned the agent finally received a transfer back to Texas once he was cleared of any wrongdoing, particularly after he helped his agency wrap up the mystery surrounding his former boss. It seemed the FBI tidied up their case without much fanfare, deciding Stewart went rogue like the small band of agents he was supposed to supervise. Clouse felt certain they put some sort of real world spin on the situation instead of opting for a supernatural explanation. Fortunately Stone was able to truthfully say he wasn't there for Stewart's death, or his disappearance from the mortuary, which left the Bureau with little to hold against the agent.

Clouse never told the agent that he was one of his top picks for Russ Greene's current position. The only thing that held the federal agent back was his questionable ethics in some cases, along with the fact that he was married. For all of his flaws, Stone was truly a devoted husband, and because of that, Clouse didn't want to take a chance on the man's wife becoming a pawn in someone's scheme down the road.

Clay Branson had thanked Clouse for helping him settle his vendetta before graciously declining the offer to stay on the payroll. Thanks to Savitch, no cubes remained on the loose, and Branson wanted a normal life in Ohio with the woman he loved. He seemed content to work as a police officer and learn the security director job at his new family's theme park. Branson did not leave on bad terms by any means, considering he left Clouse his contact information and said he might be available if a sticky situation arose in the future.

Clouse also felt relieved because he wasn't alone in his situation. Julie Knowles and Matt Teakon continued to work with him to ensure the cubes were permanently safe from evildoers, and far apart from one another.

Jane finally approached him, far less worried about allowing the children to run unattended than she had in years past. She bent over, planting a kiss on Clouse's lips before taking the seat beside him. He felt blessed because he was surrounded by people with unimaginable devotion to his cause. After misjudging people earlier in life, Clouse knew to weed out the bad apples when looking for people to aid him. The local police may not have trusted him, but his feelings toward them ran parallel. Trust never came easy when wealth and power were easily available to the morally damaged.

"You look happy," his wife commented, taking hold of his hand.

They sat, watching their friends and employees mingle momentarily across the atrium.

"Do you forgive me?" he asked for what seemed the twelfth time since the day everything went down inside the chamber.

"You know I do," Jane answered, "but promise me you'll never keep that kind of secret from me again."

Like Mark Daniels, Jane wanted nothing more to do with the cursed objects, but Clouse believed she shared his optimism that the group finally had a handle on the situation. He loved his wife and children, but Clouse felt like a soldier when it came to their family life. During the figurative peacetime, when he wasn't tracking the cubes, he seldom left his family except for regular hotel and casino business.

During wartime, however, he tried to separate himself from them for their own safety, though it tore him apart doing so.

"There are a couple of things you never fully explained to me," Jane said thoughtfully as a hotel waiter delivered a beer for Clouse and a glass of chardonnay for his wife.

"Like what?" Clouse asked before taking a long swig.

"Why did the original thirteen conspirators take off so fast once the curse was completed?"

Liz had experienced further dreams after her encounter with the leatherbound book, which she explained to Clouse. Glad to have an expanded knowledge of the curse, and how it came about, Clouse made certain Julie and Matt Teakon were also informed.

"I guess the thirteen men picked out the colors for their cubes and what benefit they wanted to receive, but they didn't anticipate the devil himself making an appearance. Liz said the whole thing looked surreal, like a movie, with the multicolored hologram in the middle and Satan in some kind of reddish spectral form looming in front of the clock. She said he spoke in tongues with a deep voice and let out some kind of maniacal laugh afterwards. I guess the thirteen each grabbed their cubes from the wall and scattered."

"What about the skeletal remains Todd found in the chamber?"

"Liz said when the devil manifested inside the chamber the man fell dead to the floor. She thinks the wounds his friend discovered on him were telekinetically inflicted, killing him instantly. He was the sacrificial lamb for their little soiree."

"Poor man," Jane said with genuine sorrow.

"Poor *us*," Clouse added emphatically. "We've been the ones cleaning up this mess for years now."

Clouse didn't want to reveal to his wife exactly what Liz put inside Savitch's mind that almost caused the psychic to shoot him in the chest. It turned out that Savitch's stepfather did more than demean him verbally. Often psychological torment escalated to physical strikes from the construction worker, which made young Jacob's life a living hell. His fear turned to aggression with age, and when he became an adult Savitch took the scattered footnotes of a plan and put them together. He watched Clouse's torment at the hands of numerous enemies over the years, never once intervening, but rather waiting like a patient serpent for the right time to strike.

From what Clouse recalled, Savitch's stepfather died in a mysterious accident where he operated a piece of heavy machinery in his backyard alone and ended up beneath several tons of metal in the form of the excavator. Everyone wondered how such an experienced construction worker was careless enough to operate a machine with no one else present, but what seemed even worse was the fact that Bob Lowery got beneath the machine to inspect something along a hill. The excavator somehow rolled over part of his body, pinning him and eventually suffocating him over a period of hours. What seemed like a tragic accident Clouse now firmly believed was the work of a devious stepson.

"I'm going to mingle for a bit, if you don't mind, dear?" he said as he turned to his wife.

"Go ahead. I'll catch up with you."

Clouse made the rounds, surprised at how many of his friends and employees knew one another. Of course the people invited to his abbreviated vacation were part of an elite group. No, not a specialized military faction, or the wealthy elite, but rather people who risked their lives in a most unusual way to save others and asked for nothing in return. Of course Clouse took care of these people like they were all family, including Russ Greene when his hospital bills began arriving in the mail.

He held brief conversations with a few people until he spied Tim Niemeyer leaving the atrium, presumably toward the lobby area. Clouse excused himself from Craig Jennings and his wife, quickening his pace to follow Niemeyer through the lobby. Clouse hadn't grabbed any outdoor gear, but Niemeyer brought a leather motorcycle jacket that he threw on before stepping outside to the brisk early December temperatures.

Niemeyer walked straight to the railing, leaning down upon the green metal as though fighting off a headache.

"You okay?" Clouse asked, startling his buddy who hadn't seen him trailing behind.

"Not bad. Just not used to drinkin' more than a beer every now and then. Wow, I'm startin' to feel kinda old."

Clouse noticed his friend had taken advantage of the open bar, ordering some spirits stronger than the typical draft beer. He remembered the times when Niemeyer and Ken Kaiser drank beers with him in the fields by the old farmhouse his parents owned, or down by Lake Monroe when they went camping. He didn't feel they were old just yet, but having marriage, children, and responsibilities matured them over the past twenty years.

The odor of wood burning in the distance reached Clouse's nostrils, briefly taking him back to the days when he battled blazes for a living. An unusually still air kept the smell lingering, allowing him to determine that someone was simply burning wood in a stove down the road. Even years removed from his old job Clouse knew the various smoky smells by heart and what caused them.

"I wanted to thank you," Clouse said as he turned around, basically sitting on the rail while he looked to his friend.

"For what?"

"Taking care of things at that site for me."

"You paid me, Paul. It was a job, and I appreciate it. Hell, if it wasn't for you, I would never have gotten back on my feet."

Clouse exhaled through his nose, letting some of his pent up emotion escape as he looked upward toward the veranda's ceiling with its Victorian light fixtures. He appreciated his friend's modesty a great deal, still feeling guilty because Niemeyer essentially lost years of his life while being used as a pawn against Clouse.

"If it wasn't for me, you wouldn't have gone through all of the hell you did for five years."

"You're forgetting the time I got thrown from the second floor inside your hotel," Niemeyer kidded, though the event was quite real and etched inside Clouse's mind.

Finally smiling, Clouse gave his friend a playful punch to the shoulder.

"I haven't forgotten anything you've done for me, Tim. I'm just glad you took care of things over there for me so I didn't have to call an outsider."

Niemeyer had filled in the chamber and the entire tunnel with dirt once Clouse completed the removal of the cubes and Jacob Savitch's body. It wasn't an easy task, requiring several days, even after the dirt was delivered in bulk. Clouse never strayed far from the area until the task was complete, allowing him some level of comfort that no one was going to find the evil altar again for quite some time.

He still owned the property, and planned to take steps for the near and distant future to ensure no one ever found a reason to dig into the ground again.

As for Savitch, Clouse buried him in the same plot where Martin Smith, his other major nemesis, remained six feet deep. Interred within a concrete mix that made certain his body couldn't simply rise again, Smith was visibly decayed when

Clouse dug the hole for a look. He unceremoniously dumped Savitch's remains in with those of Smith, hoping they both burned in hell where they belonged.

"That place was creepy," Niemeyer admitted. "I always knew the stuff you were dealing with was evil, but that was downright satanic."

Clouse nodded, positive his friend didn't know the half of it. He patted his old high school chum on the back, thinking at their roots they were still the same country boys who rode tractors and put up hay during the summer. Maybe the values and beliefs instilled within them as kids created the men capable of confronting evil several times over and never wavering. Clouse hoped so, because he needed to draw from the strength of his friends and family going forward. Though he felt confident about the plan he and Julie Knowles were still in the process of finalizing, Clouse needed a little support and a lot of luck.

He leaned against the railing, much like his friend, staring out to the sunken garden on the hotel property that lacked color with winter fast approaching. In the spring it would bounce back as always, displaying colorful blooms from one end to the other, with the centralized fountain spraying water against sunny backdrops. Taking a deep breath, Clouse planned to see plenty more springs at his luxury hotel, hopefully with his friends at his side and lots of fond memories that didn't include cursed objects and unfriendly faces.

"You feeling good enough to head inside?" he asked Niemeyer, who no longer required the railing to steady himself.

"I reckon."

Putting an arm around his friend's shoulder, Clouse led him toward the lobby doors where just inside a skeleton crew waited to serve the private party during the few days.

"Maybe you should stick to pop," Clouse joked as he stepped inside, finally at peace with his grand resort after so much bloodshed occurred on the grounds.

"Maybe I should," Niemeyer grumbled heavily, as though his skull was already hurting from the alcohol.

Assured Niemeyer wasn't going to collapse, Clouse left him in the lobby when he saw Jane in the atrium looking for him. The kids were by her side, and Clouse finally felt at peace in the domed hotel. It wasn't the building's fault that so many terrible things had occurred over the past ten years. Every ounce of trouble was caused by greedy individuals who wanted money and power, but each of them was now dead and buried while Clouse carried on, fighting the good fight.

Although his son thought he was getting too old for affection, Clouse knelt down and gave Zach a tight hug that the boy halfheartedly resisted to no avail. When he stood, he put his arm around Jane, thankful for the gifts in his life and the opportunity to enjoy them a bit longer. He saw the people he cared about talking, eating, and in a few cases, dancing with spouses inside the atrium. Glad they were having fun, Clouse decided to join them, hoping to get some photos with many of them, and a group picture toward the end of the festivities. Soon he would return to his self-appointed job of saving the world, confident no immediate threats awaited him.

After that, he planned to take a well-deserved and long overdue vacation with the family.

Continue reading for character biographies and an exclusive alternate ending

Craig Jennings — The man in charge of Paul Clouse's security at the two grand hotels, Jennings gave up his old life for better pay, though his current position isn't routine by any means.

Chase Dalton — A United States Federal Marshal who assists the group after a narrow brush with death, Dalton is a close friend and former colleague of Russ Greene.

Matt Teakon — Nephew of Mark Teakon who begrudgingly takes over the daunting task of hunting down the cubes and keeping the world safe from the evildoers who would use them.

Dan Duncan — An already wealthy businessman entrusted to run the daily affairs at the West Baden Springs Hotel. Duncan's great-grandfather helped develop the Springs Valley where the hotel was built by helping bring the railroad to the area in the late 1800s.

Harlan Stone — An FBI agent who is fueled by a desire to do something more thrilling than solve white-collar crimes. Tempted by one of his superiors to carry out questionable deeds, he must choose to grasp the power within his reach or assist a group of seemingly good people he's never met.

Todd Parish — One of Paul Clouse's most loyal employees, Parish is entrusted with watching over the man's family when not assisting on dangerous missions to retrieve or dispose of cursed objects. There is probably no other employee Clouse trusts more than Parish, and because Parish is always highly respectful of his boss, Clouse occasionally seeks his advice in significant matters.

Russ Greene — A former United States Federal Marshal, Greene is recruited by Paul Clouse to take charge of the retrieval and disposal of the cursed cubes that have haunted the man. In essence, Greene is asked to protect the world, a challenge for any one person, but he discovers some useful resources around him.

Paul Clouse — Once a firefighter by trade, Clouse inherited millions from a benefactor and uses his wealth to keep the world safe from cursed objects and the people who would use them. After losing so many close friends, he's determined to see no one else harmed by standing idly by. His gravest challenge stands before him when an unknown entity begins collecting the very cubes he's worked so hard to conceal worldwide.

Jane Clouse — As the wife of Paul, she has stood by his side for years, constantly worried that he puts the family in peril by dealing with cursed objects. She understands, however, why he takes such risks and hopes for a day when she won't have to look over her shoulder. After giving up her medical practice, Jane realizes that even their riches cannot protect them from truly evil individuals.

Tim Niemeyer — The one remaining childhood friend of Paul Clouse, Niemeyer owns his own construction business and has literally lost years of his personal life due to standing up for his friend. When called upon one last time, Niemeyer assists Clouse, understanding the stakes from personal experience.

Alternate Ending

By the time Clouse finished retrieving the cubes from the chamber he had already phoned Tim Niemeyer and requested his friend order plenty of dirt to fill in the entire tunnel and chamber area. Niemeyer owned some smaller equipment that could basically push the dirt almost as easily as snow. Though the job would require several days to a week, Clouse felt confident his friend would pack the dirt tightly to ensure the chamber wasn't found any time soon. For his part, Clouse planned to tear down the buildings above and create a community center or playground that was basically funded forever through one of his foundations. He didn't want anyone to ever have a reason for unearthing the terrain and discovering the bizarre sights below.

Ever loyal, Parish remained at the doorway and watched for any potential troublemakers or police. The bodyguard informed his employer that Clay Branson had returned for the body of his former mentor, located behind the abandoned apartment building. Clouse supposed that despite their differences, Branson planned some sort of ritualistic burial or cremation for Nosagi, rather than allowing the man's remains to become an unsolved John Doe in the morgue.

While he gathered the cubes, a dark thought entered his mind, and it wasn't the first time he thought about drastic measures when he plucked the time cube from the wall. Turning the dark blue cursed gem between his fingers and thumb, he contemplated what could have been as it glistened in the low light.

Had he never met Martin Smith or known about the cursed objects, Clouse knew his life would now be completely different. His first wife wouldn't be dead, he would be close to drawing a pension from the fire department in Bloomington, and he certainly wouldn't be estimated in the low billions by several financial magazines. While he could have lived with any of that, Clouse wondered about a life without Jane, or the chance to spend more time with his high school friends. He had done a lot of good since coming into millions of dollars, but the notion of changing things in the past didn't stem from his life alone.

Still holding the cube, he pondered how many hundreds, perhaps thousands of people died during the past century because of the cursed objects. He personally knew dozens of people who died because of the cubes, and plenty more who suffered after losing family members. Those people, along with the police, constantly questioned if he orchestrated some kind of evil scheme when their thoughts couldn't be further from the truth.

When he reached the doorway to the old basement after his last trip inside the chamber, Clouse barely noticed Parish because his mind continued to dwell upon an alternative.

"Sir, are you okay?" the bodyguard inquired, a puzzled look crossing his face.

"Just doing some thinking, Todd."

A strange odor crossed his nose, and Clouse remembered that he had set the remains of Jacob Savitch just inside the doorway until he was prepared to leave the site for the last time. A strange mix of charred flesh and the onset of decay, the smell emanated from a large canvas sack that Clouse retrieved from the hotel grounds. A sturdy, stable method of transporting heavy items for the grounds crew, he was able to procure the bag from a maintenance man who knew him by sight.

Clouse turned around to grab the bag before Parish could offer, simply throwing the strap around his shoulder and hoisting the bag out of the tunnel. He felt relieved that the entire thing was cleared and ready for Tim Niemeyer to seal off forever.

"Wish I could say I've never done this before," Clouse commented, looking toward the bag.

Parish forced a knowing grin, since Clouse had personally buried two men, and dealt with any number of dead patients during his fire department days.

Clouse loaded the bag into the back of his truck after trudging up the hill with its weight. He carried a leather satchel with him to transport the cubes. While they were grouped together in this instance, they weren't anywhere near the wall. They could shimmer all they wanted, but no one was going to spot them inside the bag, or after they reached their final destinations.

"Sir, do you need help with any of that?" Parish offered.

"Thanks, Todd, but no. I'll get it handled once I borrow a shovel from our grounds crew at the casino."

Parish nodded, standing by until his employer slid into the driver's seat and drove away from the scene after a brief wave.

***

By the time he finished digging six feet of dirt and replacing it, Clouse found his shirt drenched in sweat. He had borrowed a ladder and a shovel from the grounds, finding the tools adequate to dig the hole and climb out when necessary.

Even in the late morning hours he didn't expect anyone to discover his activities because the small cemetery where he laid Smith to rest was filled with corpses from the Civil War era and a few decades beyond. While it remained mowed and tended, the cemetery only received a handful of visitors each year. The grave markers were old and rigid mixtures of gray and black coloration, some crumbling along their edges to openly indicate their age. Off the beaten path, Clouse didn't expect company, and during the few hours he spent digging and refilling the already marked grave, he received none.

While the grave was indeed marked at the edge of the cemetery, it wasn't Martin Smith's official resting place. Clouse simply benefitted from a cruel trick Smith played on him the last time they met, filling in the plot with Smith's body burned and entombed beneath a concrete slab. Finding the slab in place, and one of Smith's partially deteriorated arms jutting partway above the top of the concrete, Clouse felt relieved when he dumped the bag containing Jacob Savitch's remains atop his other adversary.

"You two were made for one another," he commented before throwing the first scoop of dirt atop their corpses, anxious to finish his task in case someone did happen past the cemetery.

Replacing the dirt went much faster than the loosening and digging had, and when he finished, Clouse wiped his brow, instantly soaking his shirtsleeve with perspiration. Considering he didn't have professional tools with him, the sod didn't look half bad after he laid it over the overturned dirt. Clouse wasted little time placing the shovel and stepladder in the back of his truck, prepared to leave when his cell phone rang.

He looked at the phone's face, realizing Parish was calling. Considering the bodyguard volunteered to travel to the hospital in Bloomington to provide updates on Greene's surgery, Clouse decided his departure from the cemetery could wait.

"Hello, Todd," he answered.

"Hello, sir," Parish replied, the tone in his voice indicating he wasn't bearing good news.

"What's wrong?"

"They had Russ on the table for almost two hours," Parish said slowly. "He didn't survive the surgery."

Clouse felt his heart sink and his legs rubberize beneath him. He couldn't find any appropriate words to reply, or any questions to ask as his back bumped against the bed of his truck and he slid down to the ground. In the back of his mind he knew Greene's death was a possibility, and a very likely possibility at that. He just couldn't believe after a day of such good fortune that his only casualty was the man who saved the entire world from destruction without one ounce of acknowledgement.

Taking in a few somber, deep breaths, Clouse felt the tremble within his chest each time he breathed.

"Sir?" Parish called across the phone. "Are you okay?"

Clouse numbly raised the phone to his ear while the wheels churned in the back of his mind. Instinctively, his thoughts returned to that dark place they traveled to earlier, contemplating how things might have been without Savitch, without Smith, and without any cursed cubes.

Ever.

He rubbed his head in frustration, on the verge of breaking down, whether he cried out loud or shouted something at the top of his lungs.

"Todd," he said, collecting himself long enough to speak a few words to his employee.

"Yes, sir?"

"I want you to make sure Liz gets home safely. Hail her a cab, or drive her yourself if there isn't anyone there for her."

"Yes, sir."

Looking to the blue sky, Clouse closed his eyes tightly, wishing he didn't always have to make the tough decisions. He had already reached an answer on the most important debate of his life, and though it affected numerous lives, he wanted to make a significant change.

"When you're done, please give me a call, Todd."

"Yes, sir."

***

Parish hadn't been allowed to see Greene after the unsuccessful operation, but the hospital staff bent their rules slightly for Liz, even though she wasn't family. Greene was survived by his parents and a sister who lived in Georgia, but none of them were able to make it to Indiana in time. After going through Greene's phone contact list, Liz made the painful calls to each of them, relaying the news that Greene was entering surgery, followed by what minimal updates she received until the end.

Basically inconsolable after hearing the news, followed by visitation with Greene's body, Liz had no one left to take her side. Her mother was on the other side of the country, having no idea what kind of dangerous work her daughter did on a daily basis. Aside from Greene, no one else in Clouse's stable spent much time with her, so Parish offered his shoulder and a few hugs when she emerged from the room where they placed Greene's body temporarily before transporting it to the morgue.

Considering she was heading back to the dome, not far from where Parish expected to meet his employer, Parish offered to drive her. The thirty minutes it took to drive from Bloomington to West Baden felt torturous to Parish because comforting words simply didn't exist and the silence filling his truck made him feel awkward. Liz seemed okay with no sound except the low volume of the FM radio station. Perhaps she was numbed by the death of her close colleague, because she said nothing except a weak thank you when she exited the truck beside the hotel.

Parish hung his head momentarily, feeling emotionally drained because he had lost a colleague in Greene, but also because he didn't realize the bond the former marshal shared with Liz. He watched her slowly make her way into the back entrance where the valet station was located, hoping Clouse checked on her later.

Realizing he was holding up business at the hotel, Parish drove to the parking lot further up the drive, behind the grand building. Only when he was safely parked did he pull his cell phone from the center console to call his employer.

"Clouse," his employer answered after one ring.

"Sir, I brought Liz back to the hotel."

"Are you still there?"

"Yes, sir."

Silence crossed the line momentarily as though something weighty preoccupied Clouse before he made his next statement.

"I'll be there in ten minutes. Meet me in our usual conference room.

"Yes, sir."

Parish decided to kill some time by walking to the coffee shop along the ground floor to purchase an overpriced latte, figuring he deserved to spoil himself after helping save the day. He didn't really feel like he had contributed as much as he wanted to, but he did save Clouse from legal ramifications once again. Sipping from the large brown cup, Parish walked along the ground floor of the hotel until he reached the steel door leading down to the basement that held nothing except conference rooms.

He walked to the door of the room where Clouse often held meetings for their group, startled to find his boss already seated in a chair, rather despondent with his elbows atop his knees and his hands cupping his face.

"Sir?" Parish asked, closing the door behind him, sensing the meeting was intended to be private between the two of them.

When Clouse finally looked up, his face was puffy and red, as though he might have been overcome by emotions once again. He didn't seem strong or self-assured, which worried Parish that something drastic plagued his employer.

"Have a seat, Todd," Clouse said, his voice full of defeat and deflation despite the overall success the morning brought him.

Parish said nothing, simply sliding into a nearby chair before setting his coffee atop the conference table.

"I've given a lot of thought to how much different the world could be if the cubes never existed."

Immediately, Parish knew which direction the conversation was taking, forcing him to contemplate his own morals versus his loyalty to Clouse. He still said nothing, wanting to hear his boss's take on the situation, knowing the boss had endured a great deal of stress the past year since the Bering Sea incident.

"So many people have died as a result of these cursed objects," Clouse said slowly, almost with a dark, distant tone in his voice. "People I know, people you know. I lost my best friend almost nine years ago when a scythe pierced his chest. I've seen a man doused in gasoline and set on fire, I've lost Mark Teakon twice, and my first wife was butchered in my own house, Todd. And that's just the beginning. So many senseless deaths, all because these *things* were created in my backyard."

Parish said nothing, because he instinctively knew Clouse hadn't made his point quite yet. He already felt certain the man was broken beyond repair, as though Greene's death was the decisive loss that pushed Clouse over the edge.

"It's not fair, Todd."

Parish nodded his head in agreement, still saying nothing.

"I mean what I want to do isn't fair. To you."

Parish stiffened, beginning to wonder if his employer might have lost his mind, intending to bring harm to his most faithful employee.

"Sir?"

Clouse sat momentarily without saying a word, simply breathing in and out through his nostrils with an eerie calm.

"I want to set things right," he finally said without looking at Parish. "And by that I mean I want to change events in the past. Doing so is unfair to you because everything you've done for me would be erased, including the life you've made for yourself."

Parish considered his life one of stability, nobility, and occasionally honor. Ultimately he felt no regret for his actions, even when he found it necessary to take a life. If money had been his primary motivation, Parish wouldn't have been the kind of person Clouse sought to protect his family.

"Sir, *that* I could live with, but I'm worried about you. My life would be pretty dull if you hadn't hired me."

"What I'm talking about is a rather radical plan, Todd, and it's also the other reason I feel like I'm being unfair to you."

Parish swallowed hard, unsure of where the discussion was leading.

"I want you to go back in time and prevent the cubes from ever being cursed in that chamber."

Unsure of how to process such an extreme plan, Parish wasn't prepared for the more unthinkable half of Clouse's master plan.

"Sir, that goes against everything you've ever believed in," he decided to argue, finding Clouse shaking his head because his mind was made up.

"That's not all of it, Todd. Because I don't want anyone else hurt in all of this, I want you to kill me and use the time cube. If you're willing, that is."

Parish couldn't believe the words entering his ears, feeling a slight tremble throughout his body as his mind and muscles betrayed him. Like his employer, Parish maintained religious convictions that included not killing people and certainly not using cursed objects. He sat momentarily, unsure of how to answer the request, hoping deep down his boss was testing him, but already knowing that wasn't the case. Paul Clouse never kidded when talking about business related to the cursed objects.

Abhorred by the thought of harming his boss, much less murdering him, Parish knew he couldn't possibly say yes to this absurd proposition.

"Sir, I couldn't."

"It has to be you, Todd," Clouse said, finally coming out of his mental haze. "I can't trust anyone else."

"I'd even be willing to let you take my life and set it right, sir," Parish volunteered, still not certain he meant the words.

He counted on Clouse to refuse his counterproposal either way.

"I'm not that good with guns, Todd," Clouse replied slowly and truthfully. "And you know how to work with explosives."

"Only because I worked demolition with my uncle for six months, sir. What you're proposing is just immoral on so many levels."

"I've considered that," Clouse said, rubbing the sides of his face a few times with his palms. "And though I'm not sure two wrongs make a right, I feel that carrying out this plan will erase any wrongdoings we commit in the end."

"And what if your opinion isn't shared by a higher power?" Parish asked, finally taking a stand because he vehemently opposed the plan. "What if we've reached the end and all of this is really over? I have to believe we as human beings are meant to play the cards we're dealt."

Clouse gave him an unmoving stare that stated he believed otherwise.

"And what if that deck is stacked against mankind?"

Parish knew what he stood to lose and gain if his life reverted back to the path his destiny was originally meant to follow. So many questions ran through his mind, but he didn't see a way he could be swayed to his employer's line of thinking. He understood how much more the man had lost over his lifetime, but Parish couldn't fathom why Clouse suddenly wanted to carry out such an extreme plan.

"Is this because of Russ?" he dared ask.

"This is because of everything," Clouse replied bitterly.

"If we did this, neither of us would be around to see the results, if anything really did change. For all we know, going back in time could create some alternate universe and none of this would ever change."

Clouse buried his head in his hands momentarily, and Parish hoped he might be reconsidering his logic.

"Todd, take an hour or two to think about it while you get what weaponry and explosives you think you would need to successfully eliminate the problem in

1918. I want you to meet me inside the chamber when you're ready. I'll bring the appropriate cube."

Parish started to say something in protest, but Clouse held up a foreboding finger.

"I can't make you do this, Todd. I'm just asking you to meet me once you've gathered those items."

Feeling as though his hands were tied, Parish felt caught between a rock and a hard place. He didn't want to shoot the man who signed his checks because so many things could go wrong with the promised gift from the time cube. Parish knew about the story of a cop going back in time to see his father's death and how simple the process sounded, but he wasn't sure he believed the journal entry. On the other hand, if he didn't carry out his boss's wishes, Clouse might dismiss him from the payroll and carry out his plan some other way. If that happened, and the man Clouse asked to execute him, and his plan, didn't have a straight moral compass, time could forever be altered for the worse.

"I'll see you in about an hour," Parish decided aloud, grabbing his lukewarm cup of coffee before heading for the door.

***

While gathering some of his firearms at the house, Parish's emotions ranged from mental detachment to anger toward his employer. The most difficult part of his brief trip home was basically ignoring his wife and two children. Still uncertain about whether or not he could carry out Clouse's request, he didn't want to say any final goodbye to them. He remained incredibly skeptical about the cube even working, so killing his employer didn't seem like a wise move from that aspect.

Even on the drive to the property where the chamber still remained blocked off, but not yet filled in by Niemeyer, Parish nearly hit a vehicle from behind. The driver ahead of him suddenly applied his brakes for construction, and Parish, still in a mental fog, barely noticed the brake lights in time to stop.

Parish felt as though his life was flashing before him and he was powerless to stop what came next. He wanted to believe he had a choice in the matter, but the circumstances surrounding him said differently.

He pulled into the parking lot of the old apartment building, still undecided as he removed two large duffel bags from the back of his truck. Clouse's truck was parked closer to the entrance, so Parish decided not to waste time. He made his way down the sloped dirt, hoping to talk his employer out of such a risky move.

On the other hand, Parish had spent a little time contemplating what he would do if he traveled back in time. If that happened, he needed to ensure none of the thirteen men survived, and he questioned whether the lawyer could be allowed to live. He supposed the jeweler knew the men were up to no good, but he never knew the extent of their sinister plan until he saw the aftermath. If that was the case, his lawyer friend surely didn't know what kind of ritual he was about to witness until his untimely death.

Making his way through the dark tunnel, which Clouse didn't bother to light in any way, Parish took a small flashlight from one of the bags to guide him until the orange pulse became visible. Parish stopped short of the chamber entrance, taking a deep breath because he still didn't know if Clouse was using better judgment at this point.

When he finally stepped inside, he found Clouse pacing the floor, staring at the pulsating light along the opposite wall. The irony that a giant clock took up most of the glowing wall wasn't lost on Parish, who didn't particularly want to step back in time.

Upon seeing the bodyguard of his children, Clouse tossed him the navy blue cube, which Parish snatched from the air.

"Guess this means you haven't changed your mind, sir?"

"No. Maybe we should get this over with."

Clouse seemed impatient about the process, especially since he was usually very analytical about such important decisions.

Still, Parish wasn't going to simply execute his own boss without speaking his peace first.

"Sir, I think you're playing God. We aren't meant to alter events in the past or future."

"Then why did God allow these thirteen abominations to be created?"

Parish simply shook his head negatively, seeing that Clouse wasn't going to be swayed easily. He had obviously thought out both sides to his own argument more so than Parish originally believed.

Unzipping the first of the duffel bags, Parish pulled out a few semiautomatic pistols, along with a fully automatic MP5. He still wanted Clouse to change his mind, almost robotically going through the motions of carrying out the plan.

"Sir, you're going off one document," he argued. "*One* document that supposedly says what this cube does."

"We verified it three ways until Sunday, Todd."

Parish unzipped the second bag, pulling out a bomb vest he crudely constructed from leftover explosives and an armored vest. If Parish truly went back in time, he didn't want any trace of anything left in the chamber. He certainly didn't want a second version of himself running around for decades, possibly changing the timeline immeasurably.

"If this doesn't work, sir, you'd be leaving behind a lot of unfinished business," Parish added, continuing to unpack the bags just the same.

Now Clouse gave him a cagy smile, understanding that his employee really didn't want to carry through with the plan.

"It's going to work, Todd. And there's nothing here that couldn't be accomplished if I were to suddenly disappear or die. My wife, son, and stepdaughter would mourn me and live fairly good lives after that."

"You'd leave Zach without a mother or a father?"

Now his employer's expression turned much more serious.

"That's not fair, Todd."

"And neither is putting the fate of the world on my shoulders, sir," Parish said, absolutely exasperated. "I don't want my life to change, and I certainly don't want to hurt you."

"You have to, Todd. This, this bullshit we go through on a daily basis won't stop for us. And the best we can hope for is to leave our successors a better scenario. But eventually they'd let their guard down and some asshole would bring all thirteen of those things here again. I want a life where I can kick back and enjoy myself once in a while, Todd. Even if I have to work for a living again, and even if my first marriage ends in divorce, the way it was heading, I don't give a shit. *Anything* is better than looking over my shoulder every day of my life."

Parish worried that he might carry out the deed and be stuck as a casual observer in 1918, unable to make any difference at all. Still, if he did as Clouse asked, and succeeded, all of his sins would be hypothetically erased. Parish had only killed men in self-defense or the defense of others, but even that blood would never spill in the new reality.

Looking at his hands, he realized everything he needed was already out of the duffel bags and ready for action. He slipped on the vest, still unsure of whether he really wanted to give up on his present life.

"If you don't do this, Todd, I'll get someone else I don't trust as much," Clouse admitted.

"No pressure there, sir."

Clouse tried to force a grin, but it just didn't come. Parish looked to the pistol in his right hand, feeling the weight of the world on his shoulders. For the first time since meeting his employer, he wasn't sure he truly liked the man as he ran short of reasons not to pull the trigger.

"Do it, Todd," Clouse said with an even tone, still refusing to be forceful under such dire circumstances.

"Goddamn you, sir," Parish muttered as he raised the gun and pulled the trigger in a flash, seeing blood spatter from his employer's forehead as he turned away immediately.

Fighting back his emotions, Parish holstered the sidearm, pulling the blue cube from a small pouch inside the vest as he tried to avoid looking at the man he just killed. Had it been justified, or some kind of mercy killing, Parish might have felt far less regret, but ordered to or not, he had just murdered the man who signed his paychecks. If he failed in any way, or did nothing at all with the cube, he couldn't possibly face Clouse's widow and two children again.

He approached the body, still unwilling to look at the damage he caused until he had to locate some blood to satisfy the cube. Feeling convulsed after simply seeing a glimpse from the corner of his eye, Parish found his boss's eyes wide-open, blood ebbing slowly from his forehead. He clutched his stomach to keep from vomiting, taking the cube and rubbing it against the fresh pool of blood atop the man's body, knowing what to do as though internally directed.

Knowing the cube wanted him to use it, he doubted it maintained anything above primal instinct, certainly unaware that he meant to end its existence.

Daring not take even an extra second to collect his thoughts and emotions, Parish focused on where he wanted to be and exactly when while clutching the cube.

And suddenly he was there.

Though the cube didn't travel back with him, Parish found himself at the entrance of the chamber, immediately after the last of the thirteen conspirators filed inside. Everything from the lights to the dirt walls appeared fresh, and no musty smell accompanied the tunnel this time. Still armed with everything he carried when he shot his employer, Parish stepped forward, finding all eyes turn his way when he entered the chamber. Thirteen wealthy men and one individual chained to the metal spokes Parish removed when he modified the chamber in the future all looked to him with shock and awe.

Based on the way he was dressed, Parish imagined he looked almost alien to them.

Deciding not to waste any time in case the wealthy men brought backup with them, Parish fired off some shots from the MP5, startling the conspirators who had certainly never seen the likes of such a sleek weapon. Feeling determined to see Clouse's plan through, Parish hoped all of the wrongs he carried out within a five-minute span made one impactful right.

"Everyone get back!" he shouted, drawing an immediate response from the openly nervous men.

As they backed toward the wall, which did not glow an eerie orange with a functional clock, Parish approached the man chained to the metal spoke. One of the men stepped forward with his palms open, as though he wanted to speak and negotiate with the gunman who dared interrupt their ceremony. Parish pointed the MP5 deliberately at the man's chest and fired, drawing a stunned look from the man as numerous bullets entered his chest within a second's time. He slumped to the ground, prompting his fellow conspirators to take a defensive step backwards with panicked utterances.

Redirecting his attention to the man helplessly tethered to the metal center-piece's extension, Parish aimed the MP5 at the chain, firing the weapon to snap one of the links. He helped the lawyer to his feet, grasping the man's forearm before allowing him to leave.

"Tell no one what you've seen here, or what happened," Parish ordered him sternly. "Even your friend the jeweler."

Saying nothing, the man nodded nervously, sweat already dripping profusely from his forehead. He darted toward the tunnel, taking his leave before the man with all of the unusual weapons changed his mind.

Parish returned his gaze to the dozen surviving conspirators, knowing they wished they'd never entered into such a sinister plan. He wanted to tell them how much pain they were destined to cause, how many lives they ruined, and how their selfishness nearly destroyed mankind. If he were so inclined, Parish might have told them about the man who fought to undo all of the chaos these conspirators caused, and how his spirit was ultimately crushed.

In the end, Parish wasn't a man of many words, so he reached into his vest and pulled out the small detonator that activated the explosives lining the black vest. Knowing what amount worked the first time around, Parish had matched the weight of the plastic explosives, hoping to obliterate everything inside the chamber.

He removed the safety cap from the small device, looked to the twelve trembling men before him, and flipped the first of the two switches. Knowing his life in the future was going to take a different course, it was too late now for anything except setting things right and carrying out Clouse's plan.

"Goodbye, gentlemen," he said before hitting the second switch with his thumb.